THE ORIGIN

# Books by Irving Stone

## BIOGRAPHICAL NOVELS

LUST FOR LIFE
(Vincent Van Gogh)
IMMORTAL WIFE
(Jessie Benton Fremont)
ADVERSARY IN THE HOUSE
(Eugene V. Debs)
THE PASSIONATE JOURNEY
(John Noble)
THE PRESIDENT'S LADY
(Rachel Jackson)

LOVE IS ETERNAL
(Mary Todd Lincoln)
THE AGONY AND THE ECSTASY
(Michelangelo)
THOSE WHO LOVE
(Abigail Adams)
THE PASSIONS OF THE MIND
(Sigmund Freud)
THE GREEK TREASURE
(Henry and Sophia Schliemann)

THE ORIGIN (Charles Darwin)

## BIOGRAPHIES

SAILOR ON HORSEBACK
(Jack London)
THEY ALSO RAN
(Defeated Presidential Candidates)

CLARENCE DARROW FOR THE
DEFENSE
EARL WARREN

## HISTORY

MEN TO MATCH MY MOUNTAINS

## NOVELS

PAGEANT OF YOUTH

FALSE WITNESS

## BELLES-LETTRES

WE SPEAK FOR OURSELVES
(A Self-Portrait of America)

THE STORY OF MICHELANGELO'S
PIETÀ

## WITH JEAN STONE

DEAR THEO
(Vincent Van Gogh)

I, MICHELANGELO, SCULPTOR
(Autobiographies through letters)

## COLLECTED

THE IRVING STONE READER

IRVING STONE'S JACK LONDON

## EDITOR

THERE WAS LIGHT
Autobiography of a University
Berkeley: 1888–1968

LINCOLN: A CONTEMPORARY
PORTRAIT
(with Allan Nevins)

## BOOKS FOR YOUNG READERS

THE GREAT ADVENTURE OF MICHELANGELO

# The Origin

## A BIOGRAPHICAL NOVEL OF
## Charles Darwin

by Irving Stone

EDITED BY Jean Stone

DOUBLEDAY & COMPANY, INC., GARDEN CITY, NEW YORK, 1980

ISBN: 0-385-12064-8
Library of Congress Catalog Card Number 79-6655
Copyright © 1980 by Irving Stone

Dedicated to:

my long-time wife, editor,
companion and friend

JEAN STONE

# ACKNOWLEDGMENTS

It is with intense pleasure that I thank the descendants of Charles Darwin for their warmhearted welcome, cooperation, and friendship during the five years it took to research and write this book. Lady Nora Barlow of Cambridge, Charles Darwin's last remaining grandchild, has been particularly generous, as she has been to all Darwin scholars for the past half century, in the permission to quote from her published works, and the use of unpublished personal family materials. My thanks also to her son, Professor Bernard Barlow of the University of California at Berkeley and of Cambridge University. Mr. George Darwin of London, Charles Darwin's great-grandson, and his wife, Angela, have been wholly supportive in our use of Charles Darwin's vast correspondence, both published and unpublished.

In Cambridge the Keynes family: Sir Geoffrey, eminent surgeon and author, Professor Richard D. Keynes, working on *The Beagle Record*, Dr. Milo Keynes, editor of *Essays on John Maynard Keynes*, and Quentin Keynes, all but Sir Geoffrey great-grandchildren of Charles Darwin who have provided insights and precious unpublished material, some of it in preparation for their own books.

Sir Hedley and Lady Judy Atkins, who were responsible for the refurbishing of Down House for the Royal Society of Surgeons, as it was during the forty years that the Darwins lived there, after our first two yearly visits, invited us to live and work in Down House for several weeks the following year as their guests.

Lastly, my deepest appreciation to Cambridge University Library, where most of Charles Darwin's manuscripts and correspondence are housed and catalogued in a special Darwin wing ably presided over by Peter Gautrey, M.A., who was indispensable over the entire five years of work. And to the late Cambridge University librarian, Eric B. Caedel, who showed how best to use the services of the Library. Dr. Sydney Smith of St. Catharine's College acquainted us with the Darwin's stacks and imparted some of the invaluable knowledge he keeps in his head.

All of the Darwin Scholars of Great Britain and the United States, with one exception, were generous with their own research and helped to authenticate this biographical novel. Their contribution will be set forth at the back of this book.

Irving Stone

London, Cambridge, Shrewsbury, Maer, Down,
Plymouth, the Galapagos Islands, Beverly Hills
1975–1980

# IRVING STONE

## By Allan Nevins

The central fact upon which all of us who know Irving Stone and his work well would insist is his professional integrity as a biographer and literary artist. As Marguerite Yourcenar says in a note appended to her *Hadrian's Memoirs*, history has its laws, and poetry or imaginative reconstruction also has its laws; "the two are not necessarily irreconcilable": Irving Stone believes that in the hands of a conscientious writer they are perfectly reconcilable.

He has written both conventional biography and—like Miss Yourcenar, Robert Graves, Catherine Drinker Bowen—biography which admits imaginative detail. In books like those on Jack London (*Sailor on Horseback*) and Clarence Darrow (*For the Defense*) he scrupulously restricts himself to proved fact and direct inference. In his earlier books such as *Lust for Life* (Vincent Van Gogh), *Immortal Wife* (Jessie Benton Fremont), *The President's Lady* (Rachel Jackson); as with his later books *Those Who Love* (Abigail Adams) and *The Passions of the Mind* (Sigmund Freud); he lets a controlled imagination fill some gaps, but is careful not to go beyond the reasonably conjectural or to alter the spirit of historic truth.

These rules exact from Irving Stone a research more laborious, and a composition more scrupulous, than any but his close friends are likely to realize. He spares no pains, and like Macaulay will travel hundreds of miles for a single precise fact. He believes some use of the imagination will make his characters more human, but he talked with fifty men to get an exact measure of Debs's pacifism when Debs was sentenced to ten years in federal prison (*Adversary in the House*). He knows how to write description with color, but he goes through shelves of old newspapers to find how a street in Lexington, Kentucky, looked when Mary Todd walked along it in girlhood (*Love Is Eternal*).

Thus he meets the historical canons which he learned under Herbert Eugene Bolton at the University of California, where he graduated in 1923. I have heard from Anna Strunsky, whom Jack London valued for her "flashing soul," of the pertinacity with which he drew from her all she could tell about London. I have heard elsewhere how when he prepared to write of the Lincolns in the White House he insisted on knowing the precise plans of their second-floor domestic menage. Nobody knew, not even William Adams Delano, expert on White House architecture. Partitions had been shifted, dimensions altered, new facilities installed. Yet Irving Stone felt he had to know the size and aspect of the guest room in which Willie Lincoln had died, and of the hallway which Lincoln paced when bent under the burdens of the war. In the end, levying on memoirs, letters, newspapers and other sources, he drew a plan of the mansion which he could trust as accurate, and could therefore visualize without fear of error.

Irving Stone prides himself on being a man of letters, depending on his pen alone. As a man of letters, he puts system, assiduity and vigilant care into his occupation. He is at work before 9 A.M. Whether inspiration comes or falters, he remains at his desk, for he knows that patient effort will bring it, and then, as he says, "I am *there*." A light lunch, a walk or a swim, and he is back in his workroom until six.

Success came gradually; the Stones have reared their two children under as many difficulties as most families meet; and it was not until he settled himself to write his Western history, *Men to Match My Mountains*, that he was able to hire his first full-time research helper. In Italy, dealing with the mountainous accumulations of data on Michelangelo for *The Agony and the Ecstasy* in Italian, French, German and Latin, he had to employ expert assistance on a larger scale.

Irving Stone has been especially happy in seeing final success come in two forms. His *Lust for Life* (translated into three score of tongues) probably did more than any other single book to break down the barriers to appreciation of impressionist and postimpressionist painting. Artists and amateurs of art alike have offered many tokens of gratitude.

Meanwhile, he has seen abundant evidence that his books on historic figures have given a lively impression of the past to hundreds of thousands of readers who could have been reached by no method less vivid and vigorous than his.

> Allan Nevins, long Professor of American
> History at Columbia University

Book-of-the-Month Club *News*

# THE BOOKS

"The mind is its own place, and in itself
Can make a Heav'n of Hell, a Hell of Heav'n."

Milton, *Paradise Lost*, 1667

"Books are the legacies that a great genius
leaves to mankind, which are delivered down
from generation to generation, as presents
to the posterity of those who are yet unborn."

Joseph Addison, *The Spectator*,
September 10, 1711

"If I lived twenty more years and was
able to work, how I should have to
modify the *Origin*, and how much the
views on all points will have to be
modified! Well it is a beginning, and
that is something. . . ."

Charles Darwin to Joseph Hooker, 1869

"Novels which are works of the imagination,
though not of a very high order, have been
for years a wonderful relief to me, and I
often bless all novelists. A surprising number have been read aloud to me, and I like
all if moderately good, and if they do not
end unhappily—against which a law ought to
be passed. A novel, according to my taste,
does not come into the first class unless it
contains some person whom one can thoroughly
love, and if a pretty woman all the better."

Charles Darwin, *Autobiography*, 1876

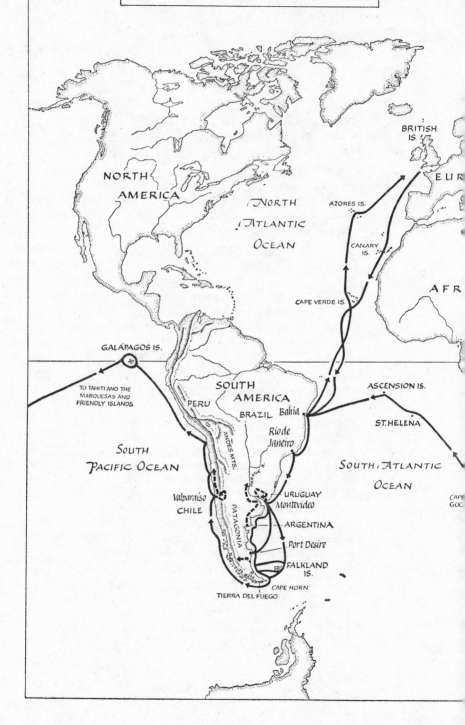

THE BEAGLE VOYAGE

BRITISH
IS.

NORTH
AMERICA

EUR

NORTH
ATLANTIC
OCEAN

AZORES IS.

CANARY
IS.

AFR

CAPE VERDE IS.

GALÁPAGOS IS.

ASCENSION IS.

TO TAHITI AND THE
MARQUESAS AND
FRIENDLY ISLANDS

SOUTH
AMERICA

PERU

BRAZIL   Bahia

ST. HELENA

SOUTH
PACIFIC OCEAN

Rio de
Janeiro

ANDES MTS.

SOUTH ATLANTIC
OCEAN

Valparaíso
CHILE

PARANA R.

PATAGONIA

URUGUAY
Montevideo

CAPE
GOO

ARGENTINA

Port Desire

FALKLAND
IS.

CAPE HORN
TIERRA DEL FUEGO

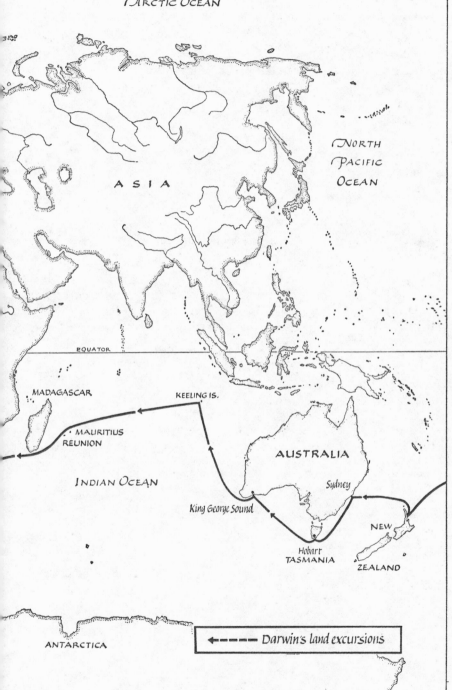

ARCTIC OCEAN

ASIA

NORTH PACIFIC OCEAN

EQUATOR

MADAGASCAR

KEELING IS.

MAURITIUS
REUNION

AUSTRALIA

Sydney

INDIAN OCEAN

King George Sound

NEW

Hobart
TASMANIA

ZEALAND

ANTARCTICA

←----- Darwin's land excursions

# PART ONE

## LANDSMAN

# BOOK ONE

*"Find Me One Man of Common Sense!"*

1.

HE stood before his mahogany shaving stand, stirred his brush in the white shaving bowl with blue flowers which sat on a circular shelf, added hot water from a copper jug, lathered his light-complected face and then opened his finely honed steel razor with its ebony handle.

For twenty-two-year-old Charles Darwin shaving was a pleasant, hardly arduous task since he wore his reddish-brown sideburns full to the angle of his jawbone. All he had to clear was his ruddy cheeks and fully rounded chin. His red lips were a bit small compared to the remarkable stretch of his brown and purple-specked eyes which observed and recorded everything.

He washed his face clean of suds, picked up a pair of silver-backed brushes and parted his longish orange-red hair abruptly on the right side to cover most of his ear, then brushed the thick swath of it straight across his largish head until it fell in a graceful curve over his left ear. He took a fresh white shirt from the walnut chest of drawers, buttoned the high starched white collar whose points circled under the sideburns, then wrapped a dark tan cravat around the high collar, tying a thick bow in front. Ordinarily he shaved when he rose in the morning but he had wanted to spend the day on the river in the family skiff fishing and collecting along the Severn, and had put off dressing until time to receive Professor Adam Sedgwick.

Up the broad staircase there drifted the delicious aroma of Annie's goose pie, Shrewsbury's favorite dish, which Annie baked when they had a distinguished guest coming for dinner. As a boy Charles had often watched her prepare the delicacy until it rested in the oven of her eight-burner wood and coal stove. Though half a house away from the spacious kitchen, he could still in his mind's eye see her bone the large goose, then bone a large chicken which was stuffed inside the goose, then stuff a pickled tongue inside the hen, and place the ensemble in a high-standing piecrust which was sprinkled with beaten mace, pepper and a half pound of butter.

Marianne, Charles's oldest sister, had found a doctor and married out early, at twenty-six. She had not wanted to take over the management of The Mount when her mother died, though at nineteen she was capable of doing so. Instead, she let the burden fall on the willing shoulders of seventeen-year-old Caroline, next oldest girl. After her marriage Marianne moved with her husband to Overton where she bore two sons and rarely returned to The Mount; she and her sisters exchanged letters periodically. Caroline had tried her best to oblige Annie to keep her kitchen doors closed while she cooked. Annie, a robust Shropshire farm daughter, refused.

"Family's got a right to know what's for dinner. Kitchen's most important room in The Mount. . . ."

Dr. Robert Darwin calmed his daughter.

"That's why Annie's a great cook. She worships everything that goes inside her piecrust and every delicious odor. I can tell before I leave on my rounds whether she is turning out a giblet or duck pie, a pigeon pie or herring and potato pie. Keeps me content during the long drive between patients."

When it came to food it took a lot to keep Dr. Darwin content. He was a prodigious-sized man, weighing three hundred and twenty pounds, albeit twenty pounds less than his gargantuan father, Dr. Erasmus Darwin, famous throughout England for his published books of poetry, natural philosophy, medicine and the laws of organic life . . . and for the girth which had forced him to cut a semicircle into his end of the dining table in order to fit himself in.

From the wardrobe Charles extracted a blue velvet waistcoat with wide lapels, then a tan suit, the long-tailed coat high in the collar with even wider lapels. From the bottom of the wardrobe he chose a pair of short boots, placed them on the Axminster rug, laid out the clothing on the brass bedstead with its large-knobbed posts. His gold watch he carried on a slim chain around his neck, the watch resting low in the pocket of his waistcoat.

Fully dressed, he surveyed himself in the tall looking glass, not without some modicum of pleasure, for he had achieved the six feet in height he had so much wanted. His nose, however, was a bit on the longish side. He was no more conceited than was usual for a tall, lean, tireless and well-proportioned young male who had graduated in theology only four months before with a Bachelor of Arts degree from Christ's College in Cambridge, Class of 1831. He had finished tenth in the list of successful candidates who did not seek honors, and would be ordained in the cathedral at Hereford, not far from where the Darwins and his relatives, the Wedgwoods, had their homes.

There was no hurry about the ordination; his father was not pressing him, nor did the Church of England set any specific time after graduation when young theologians were obliged to be ordained. There would be a wait of a year or two in any event before a deaconship or curate's office would become available. The position of deacon or curate was at the bottom of the ecclesiastical ladder; assistant to the vicar or, if in a wealthier church, apprentice priest to a rector. The bishop of his diocese would make the appointment. If the duties of a curate were modest, and the pay equally so, Charles did not mind. The light job of work would leave him free for his collecting and pursuing of the natural histories, along with hunting, which he adored, the great enjoyment of his life.

Perhaps after his three-week geologizing trip in the mountains of northwest Wales with Professor Sedgwick, and then his month of shooting at Maer, he would think about a date to be ordained; or better yet, the following year, in the summer, after he and Professor John Henslow of Cambridge, along with two young friends, took a merchant vessel to Teneriffe in the Canary Islands for their first visit to the tropics and to see the dragon tree made famous in Humboldt's *Travels*. His father had agreed to the Teneriffe trip for the following June. Charles was entitled to his wander-year just like his older, and only, brother Erasmus, who had been traveling the world before entering the practice of medicine. Time enough for a young man to settle down!

Having done with the Church for the moment, he made a final survey of himself in the mirror.

"The way I have put on my best apparel," he mused, "one would think I had an engagement with the beauteous Fanny Owen."

No one had declared him handsome, but he was attractive in a mild, easygoing fashion, with large expressive eyes; a pleasant, fun-loving young man with an inbred charm and good manners. He liked people and took no pains to conceal his pleasure in their company. People liked him: his relatives, his comrades and professors at Cambridge. In particular older men enjoyed him because he had the rare talent of not recognizing differences in age or generation. He was a favorite of Josiah Wedgwood, his mother's brother, with whom since childhood he had spent his Septembers at Maer Hall shooting partridge and other game; of William Owen, on his visits to Woodhouse where he was expected at the first hard frost to "slay some of Owen's pheasants"; of John Stevens Henslow, his mentor and guide through the marvelous mysteries of nature. Henslow, former professor of mineralogy at Cambridge University, had for the past four years held the chair of botany and was the curate of the exquisite Little St. Mary's just off Trumpington Street, a few steps from the river Cam. It was Professor Henslow who had persuaded his friend Adam Sedgwick to take Charles along on an exploring expedition. Charles was wearing his best because Sedgwick, ruggedly built, still a bachelor at forty-six, was a dandy even while on his celebrated geological journeys into the Alps or the mountains of Wales, wearing a tall white hat and stylishly cut long coat. In Cambridge the students said:

"He wears his tall white hat so that hunters won't mistake him for a buck and shoot him between the eyes."

Ready to receive his visitor, Charles picked a copy of *The Antiquary* by Sir Walter Scott from the bookshelves of the room in which he had been born, and settled into an upholstered armchair by the window. The velvet draperies were looped back. Through the inner lace curtains he had a good view of the Darwin spacious front lawn with its old oak, fir and sycamore trees and, beyond The Mount, which was the name of this high hill outside Shrewsbury and of their home as well, the meadows and the ruins of the fortress castle constructed by the early Britons.

Charles had spent his three and a half years at Cambridge quite pleasantly. He read considerably; both the Darwin and Wedgwood families had good libraries and were inveterate readers, but for enjoyment rather than education. His favorite spot in good weather was under the mulberry tree in the Fellows' Garden at Christ's College where John Milton had lolled and read omnivorously some two hundred years before him. He was an attentive listener, was good enough in the subjects he had been obliged to digest and then regurgitate, Paley's *Natural Theology* and Euclid's *Elements of Geometry*, to pass his "little go" examination after he had been at Cambridge for two years, and a perceptive learner in subjects which interested him.

There had been an abundance of outdoor activity and comradery. Before joining his friends for hunting he frequently held a rehearsal in front of the mirror above the chest of drawers in his rooms at Christ's College, throwing his gun to his shoulder to see that he threw it up straight. When he could get a friend to wave a lighted candle he would fire at it with a cap on the nipple, and if he aimed accurately the little gust of air would blow out the candle. The explosion of the cap caused such a sharp retort that a tutor remarked:

"What an extraordinary thing it is! Mr. Darwin seems to spend hours cracking a horsewhip in his room, for I often hear the crack when I pass under his windows in the court."

Professor Henslow frequently took his botany students into Cambridgeshire. Charles never missed an opportunity to go along, sometimes for weekend expeditions into distant woods and marshes. On a collecting trip to Gamlingay he caught so many natterjack toads crawling through the long grasses that Professor Henslow said proudly:

"Darwin, you've got a good eye!"

Later, when Charles had caught more of them than all the other students combined, Henslow asked amusedly:

"What are you going to do with all those, Darwin? Make a toad pie?"

Charles hesitated for only a moment.

"Now, Professor Henslow, you know I can't cook!"

Henslow was an inveterate collector in entomology, the area of the earth's myriad insects, of which Charles and his coterie at Cambridge were beetle aficionados. Charles maintained that no pursuit at the university gave him so much pleasure as collecting beetles. One day, on tearing off some old bark, he saw two rare beetles and seized one in each hand. Then he saw a third, a new kind which he could not bear to lose, so he popped the one he held in his right hand into his mouth.

"Alas," he told Professor Henslow that evening, "it ejected some intensely acrid fluid which burnt my tongue so that I was forced to spit the beetle out, which was lost. I lost the third one as well!"

"So much for greed," Henslow said with a chuckle. "Be continent, my boy, in collecting beetles and money, both."

When John Stevens Henslow had reached Cambridge thirteen years before Charles Darwin, science was considered anti-religious. Because the subject was not tolerated in a university which had been founded in the twelfth century for the purpose of training theologians, no courses were given that would lead to a university degree. A botanic garden in the center of town was a deserted wilderness.

Professors Henslow and Sedgwick changed all that. Together, in 1819, they formed the Cambridge Philosophical Society, where interested professors and graduate students met frequently to read papers and discuss the problems of the off-limits but budding fields of natural studies. Now botany and geology courses could be taken as part of a gentleman's education. Professor Henslow invited to Friday evening "at homes" during the school year a number of his bright undergraduates as well as the university tutors and professors interested in the possibilities of science. Charles was treated as a member of the Henslow family. After dinner they would take long walks in the countryside and often on weekends to the fertile Fens, collecting herbs, meadow rue, milk parsley, iris, thick brush, as well as grasshoppers, glowworms, snipe, spiders, moths. From this companionship Charles became known as:

"The man who walks with Henslow."

Henslow was dearly beloved. The university had no higher degree to confer.

Charles absorbed Henslow's wisdom, for Henslow possessed a good deal more than information, as though through the pores of his skin. It was a relationship similar to the one he had enjoyed with his brother Erasmus during his years at Shrewsbury's Royal Free Grammar School. Ras, as he was called, was five years older and a chemistry enthusiast who had set up a laboratory in the tool shed of their garden on The Mount. He had made Charles his assistant in mixing formulas of gases and compounds. Erasmus taught him how to dilute sulphuric acid in five times its weight in water, to pour the mixture over small iron nails and to collect the escaping gas in a flask. The experiment which made the two boys *persona non grata* in the neighborhood was the dissolving of one part of quicksilver in two parts of sulphuric acid, which boiled to dryness in the bottom of a flask. A suffocating smell permeated the hill. Dr. Robert Darwin, never altogether comfortable with his two sons, remarked dryly:

"Couldn't you boys practice some rather less obnoxious form of chemistry?"

Erasmus, who was far less concerned about Dr. Darwin's good opinion than Charles, answered:

"Father, how are we going to know what kind of a stench our acids will make until we produce them? You wouldn't want to crush our adventurous young spirits, would you?"

Dr. Darwin knew when he was being needled about his size. He turned to his gangling sons and with mock irony, in a voice which seemed to come from the bottom of the Shrewsbury gravel pit, replied:

"Heavens, no! I've spent my entire adult life in a concerted effort not to crush anything."

For an instant Charles felt sorry for his father. Why did all six of the Darwin children favor the Wedgwood side: lean and sinewy? Why had not at least one of the sons been as astonishingly large?

Though Charles was only fourteen, he and Erasmus often worked late into the night. Word of this, and the smell of the burning sulphur which had engulfed The Mount, caused Charles's fellow students to nickname him "Gas."

It also earned him a public rebuke from the renowned educator, Dr. Samuel Butler, headmaster of the Royal Free Grammar School of Shrewsbury, founded by Edward VI in 1552, and considerably expanded by Queen Elizabeth. The school was far from free; in fact it was expensive, but it did have a splendid classroom building, chapel and library. Dr. Butler exclaimed before the student body:

"Darwin, you are wasting your time on useless subjects. Stick to your Greek grammar and Latin literature. They are the unfailing marks of an English gentleman."

There was the sound of crunching gravel on the curving driveway which led up to the front door of The Mount. Charles put his Waverly novel alongside a vase of flowers, rose and pushed back the lace curtain of the window. There, in his gig, which he had driven from Cambridge by the circuitous route of the coal fields of Wolverhampton and the fine conglomerate of Alberbury which was burnt for lime, was the redoubtable Professor Adam Sedgwick, the reins in one hand, whoaing his horse to stop, the other hand tamping down his tall white hat.

2.

Charles descended the broad staircase two steps at a time. He found Adam Sedgwick standing back from the high oak door and portico with its four supporting marble pillars, arms thrown out, an admiring smile on his face.

"This is the way I like a house to be built. Solid! It would take a Vesuvius or Etna to blow it off its base."

"That's what my father intended when he bought the twelve acres of this hill. It was known as The Mount, and so the house is called The Mount. So, parenthetically, is my father."

He called a stableboy to take care of Sedgwick's horse and gig. Edward, their long-time house steward, had already picked up Sedgwick's bags and carried them upstairs to a guest room overlooking the river Severn. Charles asked that a pot of hot water be brought up so that Sedgwick might refresh himself after his one-hundred-and-seventy-five-mile meandering geological tour from Cambridge.

"Had a good summer, have you?" Sedgwick asked.

"I spent July working like a tiger at geology. Professor Henslow suggested that I make a topographical map of Shropshire as a beginning exercise. It was not as easy as I expected. I made a colored sketch of several sections which I think is accurate, but I'm not sure about my dips and strikes."

"I'll have a look after I wash. If you will take a hammer in hand and pound enough rocks in the mountains you can become a fairly qualified geologist in two years."

Charles took a side glance at the square-built northern Yorkshireman, a handsome man with a long, bony face, thick black eyebrows over enormous eyes, curling black hair and a sizable nose which nonetheless failed to overshadow his generous lips and jagged chin. He was a brilliant lecturer at Cambridge, radiating energy even while complaining about his rheumatism. He had bad vision from his early days of geologizing when a rock chip flew into his eye. Like his friend and ally, John Henslow, Sedgwick had been ordained and was a deacon of the Church as well as a Cambridge professor. He preached frequently in his home area, Dent in Yorkshire. He was an intensely moral and religious man. As far as Charles could gather he had never known love or a woman. His stricture about marriage was also well known to the students:

"Marriage may be all well enough when a man is on his last legs, but you may depend on it that to be linked to a wife is to be linked to misery."

In spite of this jaundiced view he was considered "an eligible bachelor who was engaged out to dinner every day." Charles had never attended one of Sedgwick's popular lectures on geology, having been anesthetized at the University of Edinburgh, whose medical school he had attended between his sixteenth and eighteenth years, by the incredible dullness of Professor Robert Jameson's lectures on geology. Professor Sedgwick had colossal vanities but no petty ones. He made it clear to Charles that he did not hold this aberration against him.

Adam Sedgwick called his hammer "Old Thor" after the Norse god of thunder, and handled it fondly as if it were a personal friend. Henslow commented:

"If Sedgwick ever finds a young lady he can handle as lovingly as Old Thor, he'll marry her."

"It's going to take quite a woman to compete with the Alps," Charles replied.

Dr. Darwin had not yet returned from his calls; Charles's three sisters were dressing for dinner.

"That gives me a chance to show you our gardens," Charles said when Sedgwick returned downstairs. "They are our pride and joy."

"Flowers to an Englishman," Sedgwick pontificated, "are like blubber to an Eskimo. The beauty of them keeps our insides warm all winter long."

They walked past the gardener's cottage beyond the stables to the formal gardens Dr. Darwin and his wife Susannah had laid out thirty years before. There were herbaceous borders and climbing vines against the walls, dark rust, yellow and crimson, with deep summer fragrance. Pansies were the main bedding flower. There were patches of blue lobelia, of snapdragons, multicolored pinks. Farther on the blue larkspur had grown four feet high and, behind them, standing like sentinels, were five-foot-high hollyhocks. The rose garden was separate: ramblers on supports, bush and tree roses in abundance.

"You have found yourself a fine gardener," Sedgwick murmured.

"Joseph found us, matter of fact, while Father was building The Mount. His son now takes care of our kitchen garden. We buy very little in the market: condiments, beef, dairy products. My mother wouldn't allow my father to keep cows because their sad lowing during the night before birthing distressed her so much she couldn't sleep."

The kitchen garden was walled for protection. Against the brick were espaliered peach, plum and pear trees. The two men walked past beds of potatoes, carrots, string beans, leeks, strawberry patches covered over with straw, and over all a net to keep the birds off. Beyond were rows of cabbage, cauliflower and brussels sprouts, which were always ready at Christmas and, like the little new potatoes, had only a short season in the spring. They admired the beds of mint, parsley and rhubarb.

"We put up our fruit for winter, also greengage and lots of other jams."

A deep sigh arose from Sedgwick's expansive chest.

"Makes our bachelor days at Cambridge look flinty."

Charles turned them back toward the house. "My sisters will be down now, and Father's yellow chaise should come rumbling up the drive any moment."

As they went through the double-winged library, with marble columns sustaining its high ceilings, Sedgwick ran his fingers along the shelves containing his favorite authors, the classical writers of Greek and Latin. In another alcove he murmured aloud the names he saw on the spines: Chaucer, Milton, Pope, Dryden, Goldsmith, Walter Scott, Shakespeare.

"This is where we keep our modern novels," Charles said, indicating the last alcove before entering the solarium.

Sedgwick pulled down a copy of *The Mysteries of Udolpho*, enormously popular for years.

"Are these novels any good?" he asked, a perplexed frown on his handsome dark face. "I've never managed to read one."

"They come in all qualities, good, bad and indifferent. We never know in advance. When someone in the family goes to London we invariably ask them to bring us back a good read. Sometimes the bad ones are the best fun. We read them aloud, each taking a turn. It's great sport before a crackling fire in the cold months of Shropshire. My mother's people, the Wedgwoods, have always read aloud to each other. We sometimes use what we call 'skipibus,' skipping over the dull parts."

They entered the open doorway of the solarium with its greenery and the warm, humid, damp smell of moss; the glassed-in roof let in the sun and light. Charles's sisters had done themselves proud for the evening with the famous Professor Adam Sedgwick, having curled their hair by the hearth of an upstairs bedroom.

The men walked through the solarium to the far end where Caroline, thirty-one, was holding court at a tea table. On either side were maidenhair ferns, calla lilies, pink and red geraniums, potted plants on wooden shelves and terra cotta pots containing chrysanthemums, dahlias, white violets in little wooden boxes.

"Professor Sedgwick, may I present my sisters. This is Caroline, in the middle is Susan, and my younger sister Catherine, known fondly as Katty."

Sedgwick took the hand of each of the girls, bowed low, murmured formal pleasantries.

Susan, twenty-eight, was tall, high-spirited, the golden beauty of the family, adored by her father, the only Darwin child who was. It was a rule of thumb in the Darwin and Wedgwood families that their girls would marry around the age of thirty, the men a good deal later. No one had expected Susan to survive the age of twenty unmarried. Half the young men of Shropshire were in love with her; she encouraged them all . . . equally. She was also Charles's favorite, despite the fact that he said of her:

"Anything in coat and trousers from eight years to eighty is fair game to Susan."

She brought Sedgwick a glass of Madeira and smiled enchantingly into his eyes.

Katty watched Susan, amused. Katty was twenty and very like Charles. When Leonard Jenyns, Professor Henslow's brother-in-law, visited The Mount and first saw Katty, he had exclaimed involuntarily:

"Why, there's Charles Darwin in petticoats!"

She had a pert face, wore white dresses with puffed shoulders and white stockings, brushed her hair forward with a slight part above the eyebrows. She had poise and an outgoing calm. Katty was good company, with affectionate sympathies, yet was somehow lost between the high character and vitality of Caroline and the effusive beauty of Susan.

Caroline was as tall as the Wedgwoods, but not good-looking, though she had brilliant eyes and coloring and glossy black hair. One of the Wedgwood cousins had observed:

"She looks like a duchess."

Everyone loved her . . . except Charles. In being a surrogate mother to him after their mother's death when Charles was eight, Caroline had become a stern disciplinarian. Even now at twenty-two, whenever Caroline came into a room, Charles thought:

"Oh dear, what will she blame me for?"

He admired her sterling though zealous character. She had founded an infant Sunday school for poor children under four in Frankland, the poor part of Shrewsbury below The Mount, where they were taught the multiplication tables and the Lord's Prayer. The children were pale, sickly, inadequately clothed. Caroline spent most of her spare time trying to raise funds not only for books and equipment but for food, medicines and warm apparel. Nobody outside the Darwin family supported her but she persevered.

Susan poured Professor Sedgwick another glass of Madeira. He toasted the young ladies' health, then turned to Charles:

"To our weeks of rock hunting. Are you sure you would not like to stay out with me for a longer trip?"

Charles grinned sheepishly.

"At this time I should think myself mad to give up the first days of shooting at Maer Hall for geology or any other science."

Sedgwick nodded agreement.

"I must say in early life I counted as much on my shooting days at Dent. I was a keen sportsman until I became a qualified geologist. So soon as I was seated in the Woodwardian Chair at Trinity College, I gave away my dogs and gun."

"Tell me, Professor Sedgwick," asked Susan, "what is the excitement about geology that attracts a man of your superior talents?"

Adam Sedgwick studied the long, golden curls, the flashing sea-green eyes, the complexion as creamy white and shell pink as the most delicate of the vases Susannah Wedgwood had brought to Dr. Robert Darwin as part of her dowry. His voice, when he responded, was deep, mellifluous, but no more exciting than the intricate and closely knit skein of his thoughts. Charles knew from the Friday evening soirees at the Henslows' that Professor Sedgwick was marshaling his considerable assets to make a captivating impression.

"Miss Susan, my good friend, the poet Wordsworth, disliked men of science who looked upon nature with other eyes than his. Yet he made an exception in my case and wrote a love poem to geology."

Adam Sedgwick was a habitual quoter in half a dozen languages:

"He who with pocket-hammer smites the edge
Of luckless rock or prominent stone, disguised
In weather-stains or crusted o'er by Nature . . ."

The admiring silence was broken by a slamming of the front door.

"The tide has come in," commented Caroline, a touch caustically.

Charles went quickly to the hall to greet his father. There was no special show of cordiality on either man's part, though each believed he loved the other; and indeed they enjoyed a genuine affection which neither knew how to manifest. Dr. Robert Darwin, who had celebrated his sixty-fifth birthday the previous May 30, had been almost unfailingly kind to Charles, even if sometimes abrupt after a twelve-hour day in Shrewsbury and on the bumpy, muddy roads of Shropshire, visiting patients. Charles could remember only one painful scene with his father, when he was withdrawn, at sixteen, from the school in Shrewsbury, a year before the completion of his courses there; neither high nor low in his class, considered by his masters and his father as a very ordinary boy, below the common standard of intellect. To his deep mortification his father had said to him:

"You care for nothing but shooting, dogs and ratcatching, and you will be a disgrace to yourself and all your family."

Charles had felt the rebuke to be unwarranted. He had memorized his forty or fifty lines of Virgil or Homer each morning in chapel, worked conscientiously at his classics and never used a crib. He had greatly admired Horace, taking pleasure from the odes. He was simply not a scholar and had no desire to be.

"Father, that's unjust."

The incident was never referred to again. Instead, Dr. Robert Darwin announced that Charles must join his brother Erasmus in the study of medicine at the University of Edinburgh so that both boys could become doctors, as he had followed his own father, the celebrated Dr. Erasmus Darwin, before him.

"You will make a successful physician, Charles. The chief element of success in the practice of medicine is exciting confidence. You created confidence last summer when you took care of some of my poorer people in Shrewsbury, particularly the children and women. . . ."

Charles had written a full account of the dozen cases his father had sent him to attend, with all the symptoms, and surprised his father at the thoroughness of the accounts which he read aloud to him each evening.

"You also did a good job of mixing the powders I prescribed."

Charles was buoyed by his father's approval. Dr. Darwin was obliging him to go to medical school; but then, he had no objections to speak of. Perhaps his father was right.

But it had not turned out so. He had matriculated that autumn, in October 1825, sharing rooms with his brother Erasmus on Lothian Street, one of nine hundred medical students, and registered for classes in materia medica, chemistry and anatomy; but from the beginning his nature had rebelled. He attended surgery in the operating hospital where he saw two operations performed without anesthesia, one on a child, and in both instances had rushed away before the operation was completed. Nothing could induce him to return.

Nor did he have any better luck with his lecture classes. Dr. Duncan's lectures on materia medica at eight o'clock of cold and dark winter mornings he found fearful to remember; he hated every remorseless moment of them. Dr. Monro's lectures on human anatomy seemed incredibly dull.

"So is the good professor himself," he commented to Erasmus. "The subject simply disgusts me."

"Then you'll have to become a 'listening doctor' like Father. I don't think he cares any more than you or I do for anatomy. He lets his patients pour out their troubles to him. The women weep, divulge their anguish at the bitterness of life, take Father's placebos and feel a lot better. Except of course those who die."

Charles studied his brother's face. Erasmus was the only swarthy Darwin. He enjoyed good facial bone structure but his nose, like his mother's, appeared to buckle in the middle before sprouting into assertive nostrils. He combed whatever strands of hair he had on top of his head in a sweep from left to right to cover the nearly naked skull. His best feature was his mouth: slender lips expressing an almost tremulous sensitivity. He had his father's rounded Shropshire chin, which led one to think he had a resolute character; this was categorically denied by his semiwithdrawn brown eyes which did not look out to visualize the life of his times but turned inward to discover what kind of perplexed person lived within his own cranium and rib cage.

"Ras, it doesn't seem to me that you're terribly enthusiastic about the practice of medicine either."

"I'm not! Oh, I'll go to Christ's College after another year here, and get my degree. After that . . . ?"

Charles had known long before his second year was finished that he himself could not become a practicing physician. He granted that it was a noble profession but he simply did not feel fitted for it despite the fact that his grandfather and father had practiced widely and well for seventy years. He had been writing to his sisters of his disaffection and anticipated a rough time with his father when he broke the news that he would not return to Edinburgh after his second year.

His father had greeted him coolly when he returned to The Mount at the end of the spring of 1827. It was late in the afternoon when they met in the library.

"You are leaving the study of medicine. Why?"

"I was never really committed, Father. I went to medical school because you wanted me to."

"I still want you to." Dr. Darwin's voice was heavy with disappointment. "Doesn't that carry any importance with you? Are you revolting against your family tradition?" He had become angry. "And what is your decision now, pray tell?"

"I want to go to Christ's College in Cambridge, where Ras is."

"Are you following him or picking the most jolly college in Cambridge?"

"No, Father. I'm past eighteen and quite independent of Ras. I've met several men from Christ's College and I like what they tell me about it. I'd like to work for my Bachelor of Arts degree there."

"To what end, Charles?"

Charles flinched. His light-complected face became mottled. Dr. Darwin was seeking medication for his son's educational ills.

"To become a clergyman."

". . . The Church of England? We've never been a religious family, there isn't a preacher among the Darwins or Wedgwoods, except for John Allen Wedgwood, who has just become vicar of Maer. But it is at least a highly respected profession."

Susannah Wedgwood had joined the Unitarians, a good deal less fervent than the Church of England. Robert Darwin had taken his children to church on Christmas and Easter only. There were no prayers said at The Mount, and only an occasional grace, when an ecclesiastic came to dinner. Nobody questioned religion in the household, or argued about it. It was simply part of the landscape, taken for granted. One was not impassioned, neither was one a backslider.

"I think it is a calling I can honor," proffered Charles. "I like people of all ages. We get along. Perhaps I could be of some value to a congregation. But there are other professions to follow once the Bachelor's degree has been earned. Law, the diplomatic service, the civil service, teaching. . . ."

"No, Charles, the clergy is best."

Charles pulled himself up to his full six feet; even so his eyes would have been two inches lower than his father's.

"If that's what you prefer, the clergy it will be. You have my word of honor. I am not one to give up, I am a stayer. You must believe that."

A smile stretched across Dr. Darwin's face like a warm wave. He stood up, embraced his son.

"Charles, I know you'll keep your word. And now that the painful idea of your not succeeding me has dulled a little, I like the idea of having a clergyman in our family. We are in agreement. Christ's College it is!"

3.

Erasmus had done his father considerably less than justice by designating him a "listening" doctor. While it was true that he was known throughout Shropshire as such, his talent lay in his diagnostic powers, for he judged correctly symptoms which other doctors missed. A physician could only postulate his best guess based on experience and intuitive reasoning. There was no way for him to peer beneath the skin of the human body, or into the head or torso. Dr. Darwin was twice the size of most of the men he treated and three times the size of the women. His imperial bulk engendered confidence in the patient. How could a man of such enormous stature, who had himself rarely been ill, not understand a patient's problem?

To his family he was the "talking" doctor. When he reached home at dark he washed, settled himself in a large-framed settee, made certain that all of his children and guests, and there were always guests, usually relatives, were present, then started a two-hour monologue. He had little chance to talk during his rounds. Politics, human nature, the intricacies of business and homespun philosophy were his safety valve. It was by no means a rambling or disconnected two-hour speech. The doctor organized his materials well on the drive home in his sleek yellow chaise. Everything he said made sense and was related to the main body of his thesis.

His children and guests were used to the ordeal, though Charles's favorite Wedgwood cousin, Emma, had once commented wryly, "One becomes fatigued with two whole hours of the doctor's talk just before dinner." They were frequently restless yet no one dared interrupt. His children, at least, knew that their father needed this bravura performance in order to relax, enjoy his dinner and fall into a fast sleep. He listened "patiently" all day, they declared, a pun with which they reconciled themselves to his monologues.

"Small enough price to pay," Charles thought, "to keep him happy. For he must be a lonely man."

It was fourteen years since his wife had died. Dr. Darwin had never been known to show interest in another woman. Apparently he was never going to marry again or even love. Unlike his own father, the gargantuan Dr. Erasmus Darwin. Dr. Erasmus Darwin, eleven years after the death of his first wife, Dr. Robert's mother, and several intermittent love affairs, had gone courting the most ravishing widow in Derbyshire. Elizabeth Pole was being wooed by far younger and more attractive men. But it was Dr. Erasmus Darwin who won, sired seven children by her and lived joyously with his second wife for the twenty-one years until his death. Charles sometimes wondered what it would have been like to have a stepmother governing The Mount. Caroline might be pleased to have the rucksack of chores unbuckled from her back but he himself was happier that his father had not married again.

Nor was it out of loyalty to his mother, whom he simply could not remember except for the lingering image of her deathbed, her black velvet gown, her curiously constructed worktable and one or two walks he had taken with her. There was something strange about this vacuum; it disturbed him. A son likes to think about his mother, in particular one so comely and genteel as Susannah Wedgwood. Although his mother had been bedridden for some time, there were the earlier years when they must have been together a great deal. He remembered nothing except her one remark:

"If I ask you to do something, it is solely for your own good."

On the day of his mother's death, when he was eight and a half years old, he could recollect only being sent for, going into her room, meeting his father, who was crying. A giant sponge seemed to have expunged every other detail, robbed him of every memory. He ascribed this strange phenomenon to the fact that his sisters never spoke about their mother or mentioned her name, and his father followed their example. It was as though Susannah Wedgwood, who had been married to Robert Darwin for twenty-one years and borne him six children, had never existed. Adding to Charles's sense of loss was his vivid memory of the burial of a dragoon soldier when he had been sent to Mr. Case's daily school shortly after his mother's death. He could still see the horse with the man's empty boots hanging from the saddle and hear the firing of his comrades over the grave.

Professor Sedgwick rose as Dr. Darwin walked the length of the solarium, sank into his chair and stretched his legs in front of him. He welcomed Professor Sedgwick and, out of courtesy and respect for the Cambridge professor, confined the day's résumé to one hour.

Sedgwick found Dr. Robert Darwin to be a mountain of a man, yet not gross. He walked his three hundred and twenty pounds with a surprisingly light step. His children regretted that his voice was not as soft and gentle as his feet. His huge head, with wide sloping scalp in front and back, had just enough hair at each side to make his ears look adorned. In earlier years Charles remembered his curiously delicate eyebrows as being very dark; now they were faintly shadowed arches over heavy eyelids and small albeit wide-spaced eyes, a fair distance from the bridge of a nose which seemed to extend endlessly. Earlier too Charles remembered his father as having a chin so widespread that one could not distinguish where it joined his cheeks; now it had become one with the opulent jowl resting on his clean white cravat. It was a powerful face, a big clock face high above the throng, hammering out bell-like the hour of his family control.

It was not that he bullied his children or threw his considerable weight and bulk around, but rather, as Katty commented:

"He occupies so much space in a room that the walls seem to lean inward and sometimes crush me."

"Is that what happened to my mother," Charles wondered, "after twenty-one years of marriage?" He had been told that she was slender, fragile. No one had ever known of what she died. Had it been a slowly debilitating disease, or had she, at the age of fifty-two, taken to her bed and withdrawn from the world?

The Mount was also monumental, yet not out of proportion to Dr. Robert Darwin's large earnings, or his capital investments of both his own money and his wife's. Josiah Wedgwood, his father-in-law, whose staggering genius had brought the moldering pottery business of England, mainly a cottage industry making rude cups and milk jars, into the realm of an internationally acclaimed art, had willed his daughter Susannah twenty-five thousand pounds plus other securities. Josiah had been a lifetime friend of that other outsized genius, Dr. Erasmus Darwin, and was delighted to have his daughter courted by Dr. Darwin's son. Robert Darwin had proved to be an acute businessman, investing his wife's money in secure ten per cent interest bonds, and keeping meticulous records of every pound and penny taken in and expended by the Darwin family. By the time of Susannah's death this amounted to a sizable fortune.

The Darwins, with their first child, Marianne, had moved from The Crescent in Shrewsbury to The Mount, in early 1800. Charles was born there nine years later. In creating The Mount, Dr. Robert Darwin had blocked out in the landscape the equivalent of his own Falstaffian figure. Both his frame and his home served him well, instilling confidence in patients who had to be cured by this ingredient because there was little else the medical doctor could offer aside from bleeding and physicking.

Edward, their long-time manservant, appeared at the opening of the solarium dressed in his aging black long-tailed coat, white starched dickey, "weskit" and pointed collar extending over black stock, black breeches and white stockings. He tipped an almost imperceptible wink to Charles, whom he had helped to raise, as he announced dinner.

The dining room, with its ceiling-high broad windows each separated into twelve panes, overlooked the Darwin woods, the river Severn and the lush green meadows beyond. Charles had enjoyed this airy, spacious room, some thirty feet long and eighteen feet wide, ever since he and Katty had completed their apprenticeship in the children's quarters across the hall and been admitted to the company of the adults at table. The room was permeated with the pleasant smell of the beeswax used to polish the long reddish-brown mahogany table with its massive claw legs. This transition from childhood to maturity had been made by Charles as soon as his feet had been able to reach the parquet floor with its Turkish rug now mellowing with age.

Dr. Robert Darwin presided at the head of the table in an oversized armchair upholstered in damask. Caroline seated Professor Sedgwick on Dr. Darwin's right, with Susan next to him and Katty opposite. She and Charles took the next two ladder-back Chippendale chairs. It was one of those rare occasions on which there were no other guests: relatives, friends, neighbors who drove twenty to thirty miles in their family carriages to spend a fortnight or a month visiting.

"The table seems a bit underpopulated," Charles murmured.

"But not the room itself," Caroline replied. "I've long felt we were surrounded by too much furniture. You remember that Dr. Johnson said: 'Nature abhors a vacuum.' That's Father's philosophy."

The long sideboards, also of mahogany, were serpentine, with bow fronts and mirrored backs. Decanters of red and white wine stood ready to be served. The family's Wedgwood china was displayed on the open shelves of a Welsh dresser. Cupboards on either side held the silver serving bowls and trays. The table was laid with a white damask cloth, serviettes folded into an elaborate fan shape on the imposing service plates.

Since Charles's bedroom was on the south side of The Mount, overlooking the front lawn with the road to North Wales buried deep beneath its bank, he had earned the right to a dining chair facing north so that he could watch the wandering river Severn and the green meadows beyond, with Herefords resting under the shade trees after a day of grazing.

Adam Sedgwick enjoyed singing for his supper:

"Once, when I was working in the countryside, I went into the cottage of a peasant who was digging for me. He had several rocks on his mantelpiece. 'Surely you don't think they're valuable?' I asked. 'No,' replied the peasant, 'I just keep them there to show what a Cambridge professor will load his horse's saddlebags with!' "

"My father wished me into the medical profession," Dr. Robert Darwin said; "who propelled you into geology?"

"Me. I really wanted to read for the law but I had a father and two younger brothers to support, so I managed a fellowship in mathematics at Trinity. I had no originality in maths, I was a drone. So were my students; none of them wanted the course. As a result my health failed. I realized I was unfit for sedentary labor; I sought a profession which would keep me out of doors several months every year. I became a candidate for the professorship of geology. Geology has paid me nobly."

Sedgwick's eyes sparkled.

"Can you imagine the excitement of finding a complete fossil fish, the *Palaeothrissum macrocephalum*, embedded in marl slate? Of investigating rock formations to discover in descending order red marl and gypsum, red sandstone, thin-bedded limestone, lower red marl and gypsum, yellow magnesian limestone. . . . How did each layer come to be laid there? How old is each stratum? What chemical combinations did God use to create all these different minerals? A man who works in geology lives in a perpetual state of awe and reverence. I consider myself a knight of the hammer!"

Charles caught glimpses of Nancy, his old nurse, who had been with the family since he and most of the other children were born, watching in the wide pantry as the two young serving girls in their smart white caps and crisp white aprons, took from Annie in the kitchen the wide-lipped plates of creamed mushroom soup, then the aromatic goose pie, followed by divided platters of fresh vegetables and three kinds of potatoes: baked, boiled and fried. There were pickles, cooked fruits and savories. There was no procrastinating at Dr. Darwin's dinner table; food was not to be treated cavalierly.

"Darwin, tell me what you found in your geological explorations of Shrewsbury," Sedgwick demanded.

Charles indicated a shell on the sideboard.

"I was studying an old gravel pit near here when a laborer brought me that worn tropical volute shell which he had found in the pit. When I first tried to buy it from him he refused to sell, which convinced me that he had really found it in the pit. Professor Sedgwick, what is a spiral-curved tropical shell doing in our pit?"

"Someone threw it there," Sedgwick replied offhandedly.

Charles was taken aback.

"Professor, I'm utterly astonished at your not being delighted at so wonderful a fact as a tropical shell being found near the surface in the middle of England."

Sedgwick's dark brow became furrowed with frown lines.

"If that shell were really embedded in the pit it would be the greatest misfortune to geology. It would overthrow all that we know about the superficial deposits of the Midland counties. Science, my dear Darwin, consists in grouping facts so that valid laws or conclusions may be drawn from them."

Charles rarely disputed his elders but he was mildly hurt at being put down in front of his family.

"I'm sure you're right, Professor. Yet in my mind's eye I see the chimney pieces in a number of the cottages of the neighborhood where I have gone with my father to attend patients. Many of them have similar shells which they use as ornamentation. We cannot assume that someone dropped all of them in front of the cottage doors. Even in the remote possibility that they had been brought by ship from the tropics, these peasants would never have spared a ha'penny to buy one."

Sedgwick smiled wanly.

"Don't be out of humor, all students make mistakes. In particular, me! I stayed stultified the whole of my professional life by believing in a single great flood, Noah's deluge, as the cause of the changes we see in the earth's surface. I even published an article back in 1825 maintaining the reality of a single great diluvian catastrophe during a comparatively recent period in the natural history of the earth. . . ."

Charles's father and sisters nodded their assent. Did not the Bible say, Genesis 6, "And God saw that the wickedness of man was great in the earth. . . . And the Lord said, I will destroy man whom I have created from the face of the earth; both man, and beast, and the creeping thing, and the fowls of the air; for it repenteth me that I have made them. . . ."

Only Charles was not nodding agreement, for he had learned from Professor Henslow of the more recent, almost revolutionary step Adam Sedgwick had taken before a body of his peers.

"Last February," Sedgwick continued, "when I stepped down from the presidency of the Geological Society, I confessed the error of my ways. I had founded my judgments not on the organic remains I had discovered but upon a set of preconceived conclusions on the authority of the Bible. I acknowledge now that there was no single deluge but a whole series of catastrophes, of changes in the earth's surface which have given us our rock strata and their chemical structures."

Susan, whose mind was sharper than she cared to let her admirers perceive, asked:

"What force caused these catastrophic changes, Professor Sedgwick?"

Having asserted before the world that he had been wrong for a period of years, Sedgwick felt he had earned the right to wear the hair shirt of honesty.

"Miss Susan, I just don't know."

Annie's dessert was served: little thin cakes made of eggs, cream, rose water and loaf sugar beaten to a powder and baked in a quick oven. Adam Sedgwick ate a dozen, for each was little more than an indulgence in the mouth.

"Darwin, this is the only delectable food we shall taste in the next three weeks."

The following morning the men rose at first light. Charles's father had to have his hour's constitutional down through the trees on the steep hill of The Mount, on what had become known in Shrewsbury as "The Doctor's Walk," to the bank of the Severn, and then along the river for a mile or two. Charles and Professor Sedgwick had the gig packed, ready to leave. When Dr. Darwin returned the three men ate a prodigious breakfast, for none of them would eat again until nightfall. Dr. Darwin said au revoir to his son, adding:

"Charles, for heaven's sake take care of yourself. You've told me of Sedgwick's reputation: he climbs mountains from dawn to dark like a goat. Don't take any violent fatigues and do your health great harm."

Charles did not know whether he was more touched or astonished by his father's solicitude. Ever since his early youth he had taken all-day, solitary walks. Aloud he replied:

"Father, I climb and collect as naturally as I breathe."

4.

It was by no means Charles's first trip to neighboring North Wales, where his family liked to spend their holidays. When he was four he had spent three weeks sea bathing near Abergele, of which his chief memory was fear of the white foaming waters while their carriage crossed a broad fjord. When he was ten he had gone again for three weeks to Towyn, south of Barmouth. As Sedgwick's gig moved across the countryside he recalled the evening of a blowy day when he had walked across the beach by himself watching the gulls and cormorants wending their way home on a wild and irregular course. The following year he had taken a tour on horseback with Erasmus to Pistyll Rhaiadr, the most remarkable waterfall in North Wales. He remembered his astonishment that fish could jump up the falls. At seventeen he had gone on a walking tour into North Wales with two friends, one of them Nathan Hubbersty, newly appointed assistant master of the Shrewsbury Royal Free Grammar School. Even carrying heavy rucksacks, the young men had covered thirty miles a day. At the end of that summer he had made another horseback tour with his sister Caroline, stopping at Bala. Dr. Darwin had sent a servant along with saddlebags carrying their fresh clothing.

It was something over twenty miles to the border of North Wales. The summer sun rose over the lush green fields separated by hedges of intertwined shrubs. The road was bordered by wooden rail fences covered with hawthorn. The trees had rarely been uprooted from the meadows; they afforded shade for the Hereford cattle with a big white mask for a face. There was only four to five inches of topsoil sitting on the land's rock base but it was sufficient for the market gardening of carrots, brussels sprouts, peas and cabbage. The houses were of native brick stained a rust color by the chemicals of the earth. The paths to the front doors sported rhododendron bushes with single pink blossoms. Strip grazing allowed frequent changes of the cattle's fields.

Everywhere was nature's bountiful gift of grass, never reseeded, growing of its own free will. Sedgwick commented:

"There is something in the graceful, undulating roll of mild hills that eases the pain of the heart."

Charles gazed about him at the magnificent sweep of the English landscape.

"Green is the most restful and satisfying of all colors. How many different shades do you think we can see?"

"I once counted to a hundred and stopped," Sedgwick replied. "You're right, green is the color to unravel the knots in life's rope. Blue is colder, red more explosive, yellow turbulent. . . ." Then, without changing tone, "I spend all my free time trudging up the world's mountains. Can you see a woman trudging up granite peaks with me?"

Sedgwick's dapple-gray mare liked the fresh, early morning air and jogged the twenty miles effortlessly. Beyond the border the country changed, became hilly, the grass and foliage sparser, the houses smaller and more huddled in stony isolation. Sedgwick sighted his first interesting outcropping. He jumped out of the gig, tied the horse to a tree trunk and shouldered his heavy leather bag.

"Take your specimen bag, Darwin. It's simple enough to walk through a small area identifying rocks. Our job is to identify a whole region, to ascend the mountains and pursue each stratum as far as our eye can see. The ability to understand the overall features of a geological setting is what makes a skilled geological observer."

His enthusiasm literally poured from him.

". . . Get out your notebook. We'll need accurate observations and figures. Remember to note the vegetation on the rock, it will reveal to you the nature of the strata which lie below. Be sure to number your specimens and key them into your notes. You must give yourself explicit clues so that tonight you will be able to write a full account of your findings and draw accurate maps. Leave nothing to memory."

It was another seven miles to Llangollen, their first stop in North Wales, but the geological layers were so fascinating that they spent until nightfall collecting rock samples for their leather pouches. Each man used the sharp steel point of his hammer to split away the specimen. Charles exulted boyishly:

"I like the feel of my hammer. The wood handle nestles firmly in my hand, particularly when I stretch my thumb along the steel shaft for a total grip. I can see how a man's hammer would become his closest ally; it's like a natural extension of one's arm."

The Welsh hills rolled back like waves of the sea. North Wales had a harsh, frequently explosive climate; in a single day one could experience sleet, snow, be whipped by freezing winds and then suddenly warmed by brilliantly gold-yellow sunshine. There were level fields with abundant hay packed solidly in oblong bundles and stored under a protective roof against the omnipresent rains. By midafternoon they had ridden into a dome of angry ash-dark overcast sky.

By dusk they were at the Hand, the horse washed down, walked dry and fed her supper of oats and hay. Charles and Professor Sedgwick were set up for their dinner on an open porch facing the mountains on the horizon. The innkeeper's wife served them a steak and kidney pie, the vegetables of the neighborhood, a rice and raisin pudding, all downed with pewter mugs of ale.

Charles was fascinated by Sedgwick's fine art of eating and talking at the same time, without losing a single bit of beef or blurring a syllable. Charles had been trained to keep up with his father at table. His favorite meal had always been breakfast; and during his years at Christ's College he had breakfasted in his rooms with his cousin and friend, William Darwin Fox. Charles sent his gyp to the college kitchen to bring back chops and steaks, beer, coffee or chocolate with sweet rolls. Midday dinner and supper in Hall were rather silent, solemn affairs, even for their convivial group. Charles liked his food spiced with laughter and high spirits; it was good for the digestion. Mutton served in Hall after evensong and the *Nunc Dimittis* in the chapel sat a little longer in the stomach.

At coffee he and Sedgwick were joined by Robert Dawson, the ordnance draftsman for the area, who provided them with surface maps and information about neighboring escarpments, quarries and what was known in the vicinity as "wild rock." They retired early. Sedgwick grumbled as they climbed the ancient groaning stairs.

"One last admonition: fill out the day's notes before you go to sleep."

Inside his tiny bedroom with its minuscule turret window Charles lit the candle on the battered chest of drawers, undressed, sponged standing up in the tub of cold water the innkeeper had brought. Dried and in a nightshirt, he mused:

"As the curate of a small country parsonage I will have no use for this training except to interest myself on holiday trips."

They had a hearty breakfast by candlelight and at dawn the mare was brought out, sniffing the cool air as though anticipating adventure. They were no sooner on the road than a storm engulfed them. Sedgwick complained:

"As the Prince of the Air will have it, we are going to be drowned in this thunderstorm. The greywacke hills are enveloped in clouds so we might as well cross to the Vale of the Clwyd and hope at least to do some work among the secondaries."

At different parts of the road they observed beds of diluvium from the moving gig. When the rock strata changed color or formation they climbed out of the carriage and, with hammer and leather bag, climbed up the sides of the hills, sometimes to the top of the range.

Despite the fact that Charles had detested Professor Jameson's lectures on geology at the University of Edinburgh, some of Jameson's knowledge had managed to penetrate the cranium of the sixteen-year-old lad. Professor Henslow had also given Charles some rudimentary training in mineralogy and geology. But now he was in the hands of a master, for along with Charles Lyell, whose innovative volume called *Principles of Geology* had recently been published, Adam Sedgwick was one of England's most respected and knowledgeable geologists and teachers.

"Your rock samples should be about as large as your fist. Always assault the outcrop itself, don't pick a rock off the ground. You never know how it got there; it may be weathered and its minerals altered."

Charles found the most important lesson was how to use the two indispensable tools of the geologist: the "strike," or the direction along which a rock formation was exposed; and the "dip," the angle at which the rock dipped into the ground. These two critical pieces of information were essential for the making of a map which would show the extent of the rock formations on the surface, and the visible faults. From these observations he could draw a cross section which would indicate the formations beneath the earth on which they were standing.

At the top of each hill Sedgwick showed Charles how to trace the rock beds disappearing into the distance, and the compass relationship of each formation to the adjacent rock masses or mountain thrusts.

"Standing above the ground, testing our rock sample, the geologist can tell which minerals the stone is composed of: hard sandstone that has been cemented together by silica; soft limestone, close-packed crystals which look like teeth coming down from an upper gum. We face the amazing fact that huge rock formations, hills and mountains have no unity of structure but are composed of sometimes hundreds of thin strata of varying kinds and thicknesses laid flatly, one upon the other, over the millennia. Cause? Perhaps flood or earthquake, perhaps volcanic eruption, a catastrophe caused by God in which He visibly and deliberately altered the earth's crust.

"If God can create the earth in the beginning, He can re-create it in any form He chooses at any moment. That is what He has done. Our task is to get down to the primary or oldest rock, the one God first created, study its chemical content and structure: the angle at which it dips into the ground and the direction along which the formations strike. There is plenty of primary rock to be wrestled in North Wales . . . yes, wrestled. Geology in the field is intensely physical. That's why

I have swollen knees and ankles every night, combating the mountain ranges."

"Who wins in this contest, Professor?"

Sedgwick grimaced.

"The mountain! We can scale its lofty heights and say we have conquered it. We can take pieces of it back to the laboratory, use a blowpipe and spirit lamp to determine its content. In that way we add minutely to the sum of human knowledge. But how God managed to create a mountain chain, that we will never know. We have to be content to use our hammers to pound out a simulacrum of information; even knowledge, if the word flatters you."

On the road to Ruthin they got drenched from the intermittent showers. They passed the Valle Crucis Abbey but only the church was in any state of preservation and even that was choked with the crumbling remains of the abbey itself. The two men dug around for a while, for the abbey was known to be the finest ruin in North Wales. When they left, Charles crossed to the bank where he took a set of measurements for the dip and strike. Continuing on where they passed beds of diluvium, Charles said:

"These are very like the ones I examined in Shropshire, but they have no sand in them."

"They're mixed with boulders of trap, probably volcanic rock."

Beyond the grand limestone escarpment they found gentle slopes of much softer clay slate. The greywacke, dark-colored sandstone, was covered by dark green gorse, heath and fern; the limestone was either bare or carpeted by much brighter green plants. Down the road they stopped at a clay-slate quarry which contained organic remains in the form of scallop shells and collected good specimens. Beyond Dafarn Dywyrch they came upon black bituminous limestone and discovered organic remains in it as well as a veined quartz. Sedgwick commented:

"It is the organic residue that makes these rocks so dark in color. Limestone is normally a light cream-colored rock."

That evening in the Cross Keys Inn at Ruthin Charles excused himself immediately after dinner, went to his room and sat down at a little table to write:

> Saturday 6th *Valle of Crucis.* The bank facing the abbey consists of Clay slate, which breaks out at regular intervals, striking NW by N, dipping 25° to the NE by N. At different parts of the road observed beds of diluvium. Very like Shropshire, only no sand. . . .

On Sunday morning they went to church together. Sedgwick was an intensely religious man, as was Professor Henslow; he participated in the hymn singing and prayers with gusto.

"He's going to make sure that God hears him," Charles thought.

They took a leisurely ride from Ruthin twelve miles into Denbigh where they passed through an area of new red sandstone. Charles was interested to observe that Sedgwick did not take notes or collect specimens. He teased him good-naturedly:

"'And on the seventh day God ended His work which He had made; and He rested on the seventh day from all His work which He had made. And God blessed the seventh day, and sanctified it.'"

Sedgwick chuckled.

"God is good for my rheumatism. My joints never swell on the Sabbath."

On the fourth day out, after spending the night at the Crown in Denbigh, they came upon two caverns, the upper of which had been excavated for about thirty yards. They found some bones and a perfectly preserved tooth.

"Rhinoceros, I would guess," commented Sedgwick.

"What is a rhinoceros tooth doing so far north, sir?"

"I could say that someone dropped it here, the way they did the volute shell in your gravel pit in Shrewsbury, but I'll take it back to Cambridge and let the fossil specialists work it out."

Charles found great pleasure in his geological hammer. When he wanted a very precise and thin layer of rock he slid his hand up along the steel with his thumb entrenched under the curling pick end, obtaining specimens from the softest sandstone to the extreme granites. One could play the hammer on rock with all the delicacy and precision of his cousin Emma Wedgwood striking the keyboard for Mozart's *Resta o Cara*.

Later that day Professor Sedgwick astonished Charles by instructing him to go out by himself on a line distant but parallel to his own.

"Bring back specimens and mark the stratifications on the map."

"Am I sufficiently trained, Professor? It's only been . . ."

Sedgwick ignored the remonstration.

"I want straight-line traverses across meaningful sections, at right angles to the direction along which the rock bed crops out of the surface of the ground. In short, go at a right angle to the strike, *across* the outcroppings. Climb the mountains on either side of your traverse all the way up on one side, all the way down on the other, for a survey. Rock formations are three-dimensional; our studies can tell us which are the oldest and how they have become deformed or broken up in the process of mountain building."

It would have been a totally heady experience for Charles to be so entrusted had he not a gnawing feeling that Sedgwick had wanted to be alone for a while.

They separated at St. Asaph, Sedgwick taking the direct road into Conway, Charles going by an indirect road, hardly more than a track, which cut across the top of North Wales past Bettws-yn-Rhos, Colwyn Bay, Little Ormes Head. He slept in an inn along the way, eating only a light supper. They met the following day at the Bull and Harp in Conway, on the bay. After dinner Sedgwick read Charles's notebook.

The next morning when they had walked a mile or two searching for mysteriously missing turf pits, Sedgwick, who had been walking in gloomy silence, burst out:

"Darwin, I have to return to the inn. I'm certain that damned scoundrel, the waiter, has not given the chambermaid the sixpence I entrusted to him for that purpose!"

"My dear Professor, there is no reason for suspecting the waiter of perfidy."

Sedgwick's eyes cleared.

"You think not? Very well, I'll accept your judgment in the matter. Let us press on."

Charles shook his head in disbelief.

"Poor man, he gets the vapors. He's a kindly, cheerful human being with a great mind, and as expert in music and literature as he is in Dutch landscape painting. Who would have suspected that greatness is a veritable mixed bag?"

He made sketches of everything he saw: the view from St. Asaph, where the rock strata had been disturbed by natural forces; the red color of an escarpment which he attributed in his notebook to the ferruginous clay seams in the rock itself. He regretted that he was untrained in making truly scientific drawings.

They crossed the river Conway and ascended to Llansantffraid, a name which Charles had trouble pronouncing, as he did Penmaenmawr and Llanerchymedd.

"Do you suppose this language was invented by a practical joker?" he quipped.

Sedgwick gazed at him reprovingly for a moment, then acceded to the light tone.

As the days passed Charles filled his leather shoulder pouch with specimens but their search for rock strata did not blind them to the dramatic beauty of the countryside. There were no vast horizon-seeking fields making for loneliness, rather there were many intimate fields bordered, boundaried, giving a sense of neighborly security and warmth. The roads were more winding than those in England, the mountains stained a bright red by the iron veins lying below the earth. In some of the valleys two rivers flowed, one higher than the other with tiny villages perched stiltlike on the slopes. Wild golden gorse climbed upward like shafts of lightning. It was inedible for man and animal alike, having a great mass of prickles and thorns.

The Welsh people seemed more hospitable than the English. When they stopped for fresh water to drink, or a meal and bed if there was no inn handy, they found a ready acceptance.

The air grew warmer as they approached the sea. They stayed at the Bull Hotel in a wayside village. Black and white speckled cattle grazed on a strip field in the clear afternoon sun. Hazy smoke rose from chimneys, telling that though few people were on the roads the area was inhabited and families inside the stone walls were boiling water for tea. It was prosperous country, with the stone milking parlors newly whitewashed; the Welsh sheep individually marked with a red dye to distinguish their owners. At a swift-running brook with sweet fresh water they drank their fill and bathed their faces and heads. Just beyond were the fields where tens of thousands of potatoes had just been harvested, for potatoes were as substantive in England and North Wales as bread.

The sun had been shining warmly; now a sudden gray dome of rain closed them in.

On August 12 Professor Sedgwick took the gig into Anglesey to check out some geological maps that had been drawn by John Henslow in 1821. Charles, left to his own devices, found the situation most pleasurable. As a young boy he had developed the habit of going for all-day walks through the countryside collecting beetles and other odd specimens which he attempted to classify from his small reference library. Now he walked some twenty to thirty miles a day over the mountainous area, enjoying the scenery and filling his pouch with rock samples, staying in the evenings at inns with names like the Ugly House, the White Swan or the Black Lion. He no longer kept the complete notes Sedgwick had obliged him to write out every night before he was allowed to go to sleep.

Eight days later, on the twentieth of August, Professor Sedgwick joined him at Caernarvon. He was in a jubilant mood. All of his dear friend Henslow's maps had proved to be correct. Charles studied Sedgwick's hour-by-hour account of his findings. After a pleasant dinner in a small inn, he said:

"With your permission, Professor. I'd like to strike on down to Barmouth. I have some friends from Cambridge who are being tutored there. We promised each other a few days together."

Adam Sedgwick was amenable. He smiled gently.

"It's been nice to have you along as a companion. Not to mention as a sounding board. I must say you have been most patient. However in return I hope I've taught you a good deal about both theoretical and practical geology. It may come in handy when you get bored with collecting beetles . . . or preaching sermons."

The next morning he struck out on foot for Capel Curig, making his way in a straight line by compass and map across the mountains. He came on strange wild places and occasionally diverted his path when he saw a distant hill or valley that looked especially interesting.

The first night he stayed at Maentwrog and after a full breakfast at dawn tramped miles through the Harlech Dome with its staggering mountains of slate quarries.

"It lies on the sides of the hills like dark gray tumbleweed," Charles exclaimed.

His friends were staying at a modest hotel in Barmouth overlooking the sea. He joined them for several days of companionship, swimming in the warm water of Cardigan Bay and attending sessions of the Glutton Club which they had formed in Cambridge in order to get away from the institutional food in Hall. Robert Lowe, the younger brother of Henry Lowe, a Cambridge friend, was fascinated by Darwin's collecting enthusiasms, by his leather pouch full of rocks, his fourteen-ounce geological hammer and fastidious notebooks. On the day Charles was to leave for The Mount, Robert asked if he might walk along the road with him for a short way.

They set out along the coast in the direction of Shrewsbury shortly before dawn and were amazed when they stopped at a village inn for a bite to eat to find that their sturdy long legs and Robert's rudimentary but penetrating questions about the structure of the earth's crust had already carried them twenty-two miles.

Robert exclaimed over their mugs of ale:

"I must say this walk has been somewhat canine in nature. I have literally followed you for twenty-two miles of your walk home. I assure you that I never did that with anyone before, nor shall I ever do it with anyone after you."

"You mustn't go any further," Charles admonished. "I can't make it into Shrewsbury before dark so I shall stop along the way wherever I can find an unoccupied bed. That will still give me a couple of days at home with my father and sisters, and to visit a special . . . friend . . . before I ride up to Maer Hall for a month of shooting. I want to be out at the crack of dawn on September 1, and be the first to bring down a partridge."

5.

He circled the southern end of Shrewsbury at dusk, still fresh after his twenty-five-mile walk through the fertile greenery, and made his way through the eastern gate past the school where he had been a reluctant student and boarder. The building was an imposing yet pleasing structure of gray freestone with a high turreted clock tower and next to it an almost equally tall, narrow chapel with stained-glass windows, beautiful when the sun penetrated; cold, damp and dismal in winter. He had not minded the compulsory early morning and evening chapel, for that was where he did his homework: memorizing Cicero and Virgil on Monday, Pindar and Theocritus on Tuesday, Tacitus and Demosthenes on Wednesday. . . .

He put down his knapsack for a moment while he stood on the lawn in front of the high authoritative double doors, memories of the early years washing across his mind like the sudden Welsh rains. He could still see vividly the week's implacable schedule nailed to the main hallway board: *Thursday, chapel. Repeat Horace. Show up Latin verses. Homer. Lecture in algebra. Friday, chapel. Repeat Homer. Juvenal or Horace, the Satires and Epistles. Tacitus, Plautus. Saturday, chapel. Repeat Juvenal or Horace. Lecture in Euclid . . .*

He permitted himself a sigh as he remembered the seven years he had spent here, with little in them for the development of a young boy's mind . . . except a grudging bit of ancient geography and history. Gazing up at the decorative stone trellis on the roof, he was hard pressed to see the relationship between the memorizing of fifty lines of Homer or Virgil in morning chapel which he would regurgitate to one of the assistant masters an hour or two later, and education, or even the establishing of the innate good manners and balanced values of a gentleman.

That was not all. Though the tuition was expensive, the food had been not only inadequate but sometimes inedible; there were only foot pans of cold water in which to bathe; and both he and Erasmus had had to sleep in a dormitory room with thirty other boys and only one window. Riots on the part of the boys against the barbaric conditions were ruthlessly put down by the headmaster, Dr. Samuel Butler. When Charles was recovering from a bout of scarlet fever one December, Erasmus had caused his own revolution by complaining to their father.

"Charles's bed is as damp as muck! He must have another blanket to keep him warm."

Dr. Darwin wrote to Dr. Butler asking if Charles, so recently recovered, might have another blanket.

Dr. Butler denied that Charles's bed was damp, insisted that all bed linens were warmed before the kitchen fire, that complaints arose from the boys returning to school after enjoying "domestic indulgences," and that he could not favor one student over the others. However if Dr. Darwin, being a respected physician, believed that Charles should have another blanket, he would undertake the expense of providing another blanket for every boy in the school.

Charles picked up his knapsack, strode through the central hallway that split the school in half and admitted to the outside dormitories and the headmaster's house. From here he descended a pair of rough stone steps to the playing field and ran across it diagonally, then walked through a meadow to the river Severn which he followed for a short distance to the Welsh Bridge.

He had frequently run this identical route while in school, between the callings-over and locking-up time at night. It was only a mile each way and took him but ten minutes, since he was a fast runner. A short way up The Mount he entered the bottom of the Darwin gardens with their long rows of roses and azaleas. He had not liked being cut off from home; he was a family boy who had a deep-seated love for his kin. He could spend only forty minutes with his sisters and father but it was important to him to maintain their close affection and interest . . . including playing with his two dogs, Nina and Pincher, to whom he was ardently attached, and feeding the horses a little sugar off his palm before making the run back through the garden, down the hill, across the bridge, along the riverbank, the open field and playing ground, and taking the steep steps two at a time. His younger, look-alike sister Katty asked:

"How do you keep from getting caught?"

"When I reach the river, if I think I'm late, I pray earnestly to God to help me."

"Apparently God favors you over Dr. Butler."

"That must be."

It was after dark by the time he opened the front door to The Mount. He found his sisters in the library, reading. Each in turn kissed him on the cheek. Caroline offered him high tea. Susan said:

"There's a rather bulky letter for you from London. It arrived two days ago. On Saturday. I'll fetch it."

Caroline brought him a kipper, browned in butter and steamed, a boiled egg, bread and butter and tea. He drank thirstily but before he could attack the food Susan returned with the letter. The handwriting on the envelope was unfamiliar. He used a finger as a letter opener. Inside he found two separate letters, one from Professor Henslow at Cambridge, the other from George Peacock, a fellow of Trinity College and aspirant for the Lowndean professorship in astronomy, whom Charles had met at Henslow's Friday evenings.

He read Henslow's letter first. His hand began to tremble.

Cambridge 24 Aug. 1831

My dear Darwin,

I shall hope to see you shortly fully expecting that you will eagerly catch at the offer which is likely to be made you of a trip to Tierra del Fuego & home by the East Indies. I have been asked by Peacock, who will read & forward this to you from London, to recommend him a naturalist as companion to Capt FitzRoy employed by Government to survey the S. extremity of America. I have stated that I consider you to be the best qualified person I know of who is likely to undertake such a situation. I state this not on the supposition of yr. being a *finished* naturalist, but as amply qualified for collecting, observing, & noting anything new to be noted in natural history. Peacock has the appointment at his disposal. . . . Capt. F. wants a man (I understand) more as a companion than a mere collector & would not take anyone however good a naturalist who was not recommended to him likewise as a *gentleman*. The Voyage is to last 2 yrs & if you take plenty of Books with you, anything you please may be done. In short I suppose there never was a finer chance for a man of zeal and spirit. Don't put any modest doubts or fears about your disqualifications for I assure you I think you are the very man they are in search of. Do conceive yourself to be tapped on the Shoulder by your Bum-Bailiff & affect$^e$ friend

J. S. Henslow

The expedn. is to sail on 25 Sept: (at earliest) so there is no time to be lost.

When he finished his skin was pale, there was a glaze over his eyes. Susan took his long slim face in her hands.

"Charley, what is it? I've never seen you so shaken."

His voice came as from a hollow barrel.

". . . an offer . . . not really possible . . . bolt from the blue. . . . Here, read the letter from Professor Henslow. I will read the one from Peacock."

My dear Sir,

I received Henslow's letter last night too late to forward it

to you by the post, a circumstance which I do not regret, as it
has given me an opportunity of seeing Captain Beaufort at the
Admiralty & of stating to him the offer which I have to make
to you: he entirely approves of it & you may consider the situation as at your absolute disposal. I trust that you will accept it
as it is an opportunity which should not be lost & I look forward with great interest to the benefit which our collections of
natural history may receive from your labours.

Captain FitzRoy (a nephew of the Duke of Grafton) sails
at the end of September in a ship to survey in the first instance the S. Coast of Tierra del Fuego, afterwards to visit the
S. Seas Islands & to return by the Indian Archipelago to England. The expedition is entirely for scientific purposes & the
ship will generally wait your leisure for researches in natural
history etc. Captain FitzRoy is a public spirited & zealous
officer, of delightful manners & greatly beloved by all his
brother officers. He engages at his own expense an artist at
£200 a year to go with him. You may be sure therefore of
having a very pleasant companion, who will enter heartily into
all your views.

The ship sails about the end of September & you must lose
no time in making known your acceptance to Captain Beaufort & Admiralty Lords.

The Admiralty are not disposed to give a salary, though
they will furnish you with an official appointment & every accommodation. If a salary should be required however I am inclined to think that it would be granted.

> Believe me
> My dear Sir
> very truly yours
> Geo. Peacock

He was completely stunned. There had never been the faintest suggestion, yet here he was being *offered a voyage around the world . . . as
a naturalist!* An incredible offer! Instead of sitting idly for several years
waiting for a parish, he could see South America, the Andes, so thrill-
ingly described by Humboldt, Tierra del Fuego, at the outermost
reaches of the globe; the Indian Ocean. . . . He felt faint with astonishment and shock.

By now his three sisters had read both letters. They were staring at
him wide-eyed, and with a variety of emotions from incredulity to terror. Charles began pacing the solarium, locomotion being his most

effective form of emotional expression. Caroline, the taskmistress, said, not unkindly:

"You can't accept the offer, you know. Two years. Tierra del Fuego, sailing in dangerous waters . . . !"

"Why should I not?" Charles interrupted. His expression was more startled than angry. "It's a chance of a lifetime. How else would I ever have the opportunity of traveling around the world?"

Katty asked:

"But are you qualified to handle such an important assignment, Charles? Because you have collected a few beetles?"

"Henslow says I am. And Peacock has obviously agreed with him." The intensity left his face and he added with a laugh, "I am an *unfinished* naturalist."

He sank into a wicker armchair, his long legs sprawled out in front of him. His voice was only a little strained as he said:

"First let us have a definition of what constitutes a naturalist. No one really knows, of course. A naturalist is someone who observes, studies, collects, describes and catalogues all living things, plant as well as animal life."

"Then a geologist, like Professor Sedgwick, is not a naturalist?" Caroline demanded. "Mountain ranges are not alive, are they?"

". . . no . . . not as a tree is, or a fish, or a reptile or a beetle. But they are subject to change by natural forces: wind, storm, flood, eruption. . . . I'll have a better answer after I get back from the voyage."

He rose from the chair, his eyes bright, voice trembling.

"By the time I went to the Rev. Mr. Case's day school, at nine, my taste for natural history was well developed. I tried to make out the names of plants, and collected all sorts of things, shells, coins, minerals . . ."

". . . and a number of slimy creatures you brought to my room," added Katty with a grim laugh.

". . . passion for collecting was very strong in me, and is clearly innate, since none of you girls or Ras has a single touch of it."

"We thought one zany in the family was quite enough," quipped Susan.

"Quite so! Then there are my two years at the university in Edinburgh. Granted I didn't do well in surgery or my lecture courses. My best hours were spent in extracurricular activities but my professors were not interested in what I did outside their classrooms. I met new people, young men and old. We came together because we had interests in common. The Natural History Museum was in the western section of the university, a matter of a few minutes' walk. . . . Ah, that museum! It was created by Professor Robert Jameson and was noted for its large collection of birds and its scientific arrangement. . . ."

He wound in and out among the white wicker chairs, every nerve in his body tense, the physical movement helping him control his inner turmoil.

The university Natural History Museum in Edinburgh was presided over by two young but experienced naturalists, Dr. Robert Edmund Grant, thirty-three, an authority on comparative anatomy and zoology; and William Macgillivray, only thirty-one.

"The *museum* became my university," Charles exhorted. "The authorities believed in my enthusiasm and ability to learn about things I cared for; they became my friends and teachers. They allowed me to learn by helping them with their cataloguing and dissecting. Dr. Grant often took me with him to collect animals in the tidal pools. One day we found a lumpfish on the black rocks at Leith.

" 'How did it get stranded?' I asked.

" 'Must have come to the rocks to spawn and was left there when the tide went out,' Dr. Grant answered.

" 'Wouldn't that be unusual?' I said. 'If the lumpfish had trouble spawning, wouldn't it be extinct by now?' "

Grant had given him a glance of approval.

" 'Let's dissect her and find out. But first get her measurements down in our record book.' "

Charles also added the note that it had extraordinarily small eyes. When Grant slit the fish with his knife they found that "its ovaria contained a great mass of spawn of a rose color." Charles jotted in the notebook, "It appears very free from disease and has no intestinal worms."

"With Macgillivray I took long walks and learned to haunt the decks of Newhaven fishermen. They sometimes allowed me to accompany them when they dredged for oysters. Dredged up was all sorts of marine life. I collected and recorded it all in my notebook."

Almost every day he had found specimens the oystermen had no use for: a small green aeolid, a type of mollusc with an elongated, sluglike body; a *Purpura lapillus*, a kind of marine snail, making sketches to show how they looked out of their capsules.

He had been invited to meetings of the Wernerian Natural History Society where he heard John James Audubon read papers on new bird discoveries. He became acquainted with students and teachers who belonged to the Plinian Society, which met every Tuesday evening to hear a paper on a new discovery in natural science, and had himself written two papers which he read before the twenty-five members, the first on his discovery of the power of independent movement on the part of the eggs or ova of the *Flustra*, a mosslike marine animal; and a second in which he showed that little globular bodies which had been supposed to be the young state of *Fucus loreus*, a brown algae, were the egg cases of the wormlike *Pontobdella muricata*.

He had been so highly regarded by the Plinian members that he was elected a member of the ruling council of the society. During his second year, when Erasmus had moved on to Cambridge, Charles had kept the rooms on Lothian Street, less than two hundred yards from the entrance to the university, and made more friends among the biologists and botanists. He had learned taxidermy for an hourly fee from John, a former slave who had traveled with Charles Waterton, whose *Wanderings in South America* Charles had read, at the same time that he was copying a hundred genera of birds from Brisson's *Ornithologie*. . . .

"Then came my years at Cambridge, Professor Henslow and a hundred trips to the Fens on collecting sprees." His voice was so serious it became stern. "I worry that I haven't convinced you yet because I certainly will have to convince Father. . . ."

There was the sound of the front door being slammed. Caroline jumped up.

"I'd better go and see about Father's mood. If he is tired, as he is more often these days; or depressed because he has had a death on his hands, I would recommend that you save your letters and virtuoso performance for the morning. When he has returned from his walk he will be more amenable to what you must confess, my dear Charles, is a rather shocking development."

Dr. Darwin went to bed immediately after dessert. Charles sat in his own room trying to read. The print blurred. He went out to the stable, whistled up Nina and Pincher and took them for a walk up the dark and deserted North Wales road. It was an hour before his legs finally tired after the day's long excursion, and he returned home exhausted. Still sleep escaped him. He tossed and turned, writhed the light summer blanket into knots, got up, doused his face with cold water. Before his bloodshot eyes there passed a long procession of tropical and exotic lands, some pictures out of his childhood book *Wonders of the World*, others from travel books he had read, Humboldt, Captain Cook, Admiral Beechey's *Narrative of a Voyage to the Pacific and Bering Strait*, William J. Burchell's *Travels in the Interior of South America*.

His mind was staggered by the opportunity. Naturalists had sailed on exploring expeditions before; most often the surgeons on board had done the collecting. For a young man, just out of the university, to be offered such a prestigious position on a two-year voyage was unbelievable; it was unbelievable also that such a stroke of fortune should have befallen him. Then, thoroughly worn out, at the lowest ebb of night, just before the suggestion of first light, came the reaction to facing two years away from home, family and friends, pretty Fanny Owen, all the activities he so thoroughly enjoyed. All his comforts and conveniences and pleasures would be gone.

He dressed, accompanied his father on his "Doctor's Walk" down through the woods below the house and along the river to the end of their property and back, briskly. Breakfast was set out the moment the doctor entered the dining room.

Charles patiently bided his time, ate sparingly, waited until his father had finished his steamed haddock, four boiled eggs which he guillotined with his knife, lamb kidneys and bacon, a rack of toast cut into triangles, coffee with hot milk poured simultaneously into the doctor's oversized mug by Edward in his morning cutaway. The doctor took a moment of leisure over a second cup of coffee. This was the most fortuitous time to break the news.

"Father, I've had the most extraordinary offer."

"Oh! What is that?"

"To travel around the world for two years as a naturalist."

"Naturalist? Since when have you become a naturalist?"

Charles had the good grace to blush.

"Well, not a *finished* naturalist. But one with some background in the field, and the ability to learn."

"From whom does this offer come?"

"Our Royal Navy."

Dr. Robert Darwin stared at his son in astonishment.

"You've been offered a commission in the Royal Navy?"

". . . no. I would travel as a civilian, but as part of a naval surveying voyage."

Dr. Darwin was big-eyed.

"Charles, suppose you start at the beginning. When did you receive this outlandish offer?"

"Yesterday evening. When I returned from North Wales."

"Why didn't you tell me last night?"

"You were upset over the death of your patient . . . even though he died of old age."

He took the two letters out of his coat pocket, handed them across a corner of the mahogany table.

"I suggest you read Professor Henslow's letter first. The second is from George Peacock, a fellow of Trinity College. He is a long-time friend of Captain Beaufort of the Hydrographic Office at the Admiralty."

Dr. Darwin read the letters slowly. Charles was disappointed to see not the slightest sign of pleasure on his father's face at the compliment being paid his youngest son. Dr. Darwin finished Henslow's letter with his brow plowed into deep furrows. He said nothing; nor did he look up, but shifted to the sheets of George Peacock's letter. Charles watched his father's pink and white skin flush, then redden. When he had finished he tossed the letters across the table to his son. His voice was flat.

"It's a wild scheme!"

"Wild? How so? An official British Royal Navy expedition?"

"It would be disreputable to your character as a clergyman thereafter."

". . . disrep . . ." Charles was shocked by this judgment. He rose, walked agitatedly to the big bow window overlooking the tool shed, then thought better of it and returned to the table.

"Professor Henslow would not recommend an expedition that was not well regarded, manned by good navy men."

"The necessity for haste sounds as if this place of naturalist must have been offered to others before you. From its not being accepted there must be some serious objection to the vessel or expedition."

"I can't answer that. I don't know. But it doesn't necessarily follow."

"Your accommodations would be most uncomfortable for a two-year journey."

Charles waved a dismissing hand.

Dr. Darwin looked his son squarely in the face.

"I would consider it as again changing your profession. You would never settle down to a serious life thereafter."

Charles rubbed both eyes as though the motion would clarify his thinking.

"I am committed to becoming a clergyman. I have no plans other than to enter the priesthood. You yourself said it would be at least two years before I could find a parish. You approved of my travel plans to Teneriffe next summer. I even went so far, with your encouragement, as to secure an introduction to a shipping merchant in London and obtain a sailing date for next June."

All color had drained from Dr. Darwin's face. He looked pale and distraught, his eyes hooded. He sat slumped in his big chair.

"It would be a useless undertaking."

Crushed, feeling that he had shrunk inwardly to half his size, Charles said in a hollow tone:

"Father, I would not go with you disliking the idea. It would take away all my energy, and I shall want a good stock of that."

"I do not decidedly refuse you. I am only giving you my strong advice against it."

"I should not be comfortable if I did not follow it. You have always been kind and generous to me, and I will observe your wishes."

Dr. Darwin rose. He seemed fatigued by the contretemps.

"Charles, I don't mean to be harsh. If you can find any man of common sense who advises you to go, I will give my consent."

Bitterly disappointed, Charles said, his voice off-key:

"I'll write to Professor Henslow and George Peacock this morning declining their offer."

He mounted the stairs to the desk in his bedroom and wrote to Henslow, repeating his father's objections:

> As far as my own mind is concerned, I should I think *certainly* most gladly have accepted the opportunity which you so kindly have offered me. But my father, although he does not decidedly refuse me, gives me such strong advice against going that I should not be comfortable if I did not follow it. If it had not been so, I would have taken all risks.

## 6.

He slung his well-oiled and -cleaned guns across the saddle, mounted Dobbin, and rode the gray across the English Bridge past the Abbey Foregate and the bustling cattle market, heading northeast to Maer Hall. There were cherry trees and elms along the road, but only an occasional farmhouse in this rich agricultural country on the main route to Newcastle-under-Lyme, with Frisian cattle grazing in flat fertile fields divided by wooden fences. The gently rolling hills on the horizon had thick stands of pine and golden gorse.

Charles knew this twenty-mile ride intimately, for he had been traveling it since he was a babe in arms. His mother was a Wedgwood, and her brother, Josiah, whom Charles fondly called Uncle Jos, had been close to Susannah right up to her death, and counted Dr. Robert Darwin as his closest friend. For Charles, Maer Hall had always been a second and beloved home. "Uncle Jos," was the son of the first Josiah Wedgwood and managed the Wedgwood potteries since the death of his father. He was a complex man: tall, lean, handsome, elegant and silent. The family stood in awe of him.

. . . but not Charles. Josiah's own children, his nieces and nephews had always been astounded by the sight and sound of Josiah talking animatedly to this nephew, as though the forty years' difference in age did not exist, and he actually enjoyed the repartee.

Charles thought of Uncle Jos as his one forlorn chance to find "a man of common sense who would advise him to go." But why should Josiah commit himself to a possible quarrel with Dr. Darwin? Their fathers too had been lifetime companions; that was how Dr. Robert Darwin had met Susannah Wedgwood. Why should Uncle Jos take the responsibility for committing Charles to several years of dangerous voyaging? Suppose the ship went down, was wrecked, and Charles lost his life?

"No," he thought as Dobbin rode him easily past a herd of Jerseys, a handsome stand of poplars and a group harvesting a late potato crop, "it's too much to expect of any man."

Though he was riding through tranquil country, with a dozen shades of green rising in depth from the grassy fields to the deep stand of trees, his mind and bosom were in considerable turmoil: fear of leaving the known and familiar for several years colliding with the fear of losing the fabulous opportunity; fear of ruining his future banging up against his fear of having no future at all. But mostly his apprehension that Josiah would find this an occasion for one of his silences.

He stopped at the Squirrel to give Dobbin a drink and damp down his own emotions with a tankard of cool ale.

"Uncle Jos is an upright man with clear judgment," he told himself. "I don't believe any power on earth could make him swerve an inch from what he considers the right course. I will accept his decision . . . without regrets or a harrowing sense of lost opportunity. . . ."

He passed the cutoff road to Market Drayton. There were many small pleasure boats on its canal-like river, after which he rode into Staffordshire. The woods grew thicker as he climbed into the foothills. He descended into a pleasant valley with freshly plowed fields to his left, and then he was at the entrance to Maer Hall, with its well-clipped lawns, high flowering rhododendron bushes with double pink flowers and, farther along, gracious multilimbed Spanish chestnuts, limes, elms, oaks, copperbeech. The intimate landscaping on the private road to the house had been done by one of England's most illustrious landscape gardeners, "Capability" Brown.

Now Charles came in view of the lake, fed by fresh-water springs, which ended in what the Wedgwood children described as a fishtail beyond the rolling lawns, flower gardens, stone balustrade with large carved balls mounted on its stone columns. There were wild ducks and diving birds in the lake, and great crested grebe. On the opposite side was a pleasantly uprolling hill dotted with green beech, scarlet oak and sweet chestnuts, grazing cattle.

Charles turned his horse over to a stableboy, took his traveling case, hunting boots and guns from the saddlebags and walked toward the front portico of Maer Hall. There had been a manor house on this land since 1282. Josiah Wedgwood had bought it in 1805, considerably renovated it so that it stood in simple three-story elegance, with leaded pane windows, an arched double door and semicircular stone steps leading down to the lake. From the wood-paneled drawing room came the sound of Emma Wedgwood playing the piano, and her two-year-older sister Fanny singing an accompaniment. The two girls had such agreeable natures that the family had dubbed them "The Doveleys."

For Charles this had always been an enchanted spot.

"The Mount is rooted in rock. Maer Hall lies deep in the verdant countryside. The Mount sits heavily on its base. Maer floats. The Mount is walled in by narrow road and river and massive trees. Maer is open to the skies, the gently rolling hills, the crystal-clear lake. The Mount is a solid professional residence. Maer is lighthearted fantasy. The Mount is duty. Maer is joy. The Mount is rigid. Maer is fancy-free. The Mount is reality. Maer is a work of art. The Mount is filial friendship. Maer is love. The Mount is bourgeois. Maer is bohemian. The Mount is demanding. Maer gives. The Mount is pledged. Maer is free. The Mount is comfort. Maer is happiness. The Mount is containment. Maer is release."

He opened the front door, dropped his possessions in the front hall and turned left to the drawing room. He could see his cousins playing and singing though they had not yet caught sight of him. Fanny was short and plain. Charles saw the spots of color high on each cheek, but she was pale-faced otherwise, like a French rag doll. Her mother called her "Miss Pedigree" because of her penchant for keeping records: household bills, temperatures, garden tools, sacks of seed and feed, the number of animals on the two-hundred-acre farm. Her security lay in knowing "how many and how much." Her brothers said teasingly:

"Fanny has a mind for figures, but no figure to mind."

"Emma is another story," Charles thought.

Emma, just a few months older than himself, had long been his favorite among the Wedgwood cousins. She had large, luminous brown eyes which observed everything about her but made no judgments. She parted her finely textured brown hair in the center and wore short curls down the side of her cheeks. Her nose was pleasantly unobtrusive, her mouth, her most attractive feature, was wide, the lower lip full and deeply red. Her chin was strongly molded, yet neither assertive nor aggressive. No one had ever thought to call her beautiful but everyone agreed that she had an open, friendly . . .

"In plain truth," Charles thought, "lovable face."

Even as youngsters they had been confidants, free to discuss any subject, no matter how controversial or delicate, knowing that no word would be repeated. Over the years they had covered for each other if either was in danger of parental discipline. Emma and Fanny had spent month-long holidays at The Mount. At Maer Emma sometimes went shooting with him, or rowing and fishing on their lake; at The Mount she was his companion on the river Severn and for long walks to the distant hills. They enjoyed each other's company and cared about each other's interests.

In particular he liked her voice; quiet-pitched, there was neither tension nor anxiety in it. Her figure too was lovely: plump, rounded shoulders with a clear rose-tinted skin; an ample, shapely bosom; not quite flat-stomached, but with slender hips, slim legs, feet large enough to grip the earth. Fastidious about her person, she preferred to hang her clothes on the bed, chairs and sometimes the floor rather than in her cupboard. For this idiosyncrasy her mother had nicknamed her "Little Miss Slip-Slop."

She finished the sonata, then, sensing his presence, turned toward the door and ran to him with a hearty kiss on the cheek. They had not seen each other for several months. Emma stepped back, her hands on his shoulders, saw an unusual tightness in his eyes and posture.

"Charles, something important has happened."

"It was on its way to happening when it met with an accident. Is your father here? I'll tell you both at the same time."

"He's in the library. Join him there. I'll have tea brought in."

Charles walked through the drawing room into Josiah Wedgwood's library. It was an oak-lined room with a large fireplace and two tall windows admitting light. Josiah was sitting in a leather chair placed under one of the windows reading Pindar's *Odes*. He had been educated at the University of Edinburgh, loved literature and the arts, and retained a lifetime interest in scientific invention and mechanical advancement. Though he rode several days a week to the potteries in Etruria, he was more interested in ceramic colorings and the aesthetic quality of the Wedgwood *objets d'art*. The potteries created by his father had prospered except for the period of the Napoleonic Wars when the demand for Wedgwood dishware fell off so sharply in both England and Europe that Josiah had been obliged to close Maer Hall for several years because of the heavy cost of upkeep and move back to an earlier and more modest house in Etruria.

Josiah Wedgwood was a many-sided man. He loved hunting and at the same time was a founder of the Royal Horticultural Society with gardens near Kew. He was a member of the Bath and West England Society for the Encouragement of Agriculture, Arts, Manufactures and Commerce. He was vigorously liberal in politics, having pamphleteered for the Reform Bill which would have extended the English suffrage and made a beginning effort toward the abolition of slavery, the slave trade itself having been ended in 1807. Josiah had been defeated that spring in his attempt to represent Newcastle in Parliament; little daunted, he was planning to be elected from Stoke-on-Trent for the first Reform Parliament meeting in 1832. Maer Hall served as a gathering place for Staffordshire Liberals and intellectuals.

Young Emma Caldwell, from a neighboring family, exclaimed:

"I never saw anything pleasanter than the ways of going on of this family, and one reason is the freedom of speech upon every subject; there is no difference in politics or principles of any kind that makes it treason to speak one's mind openly, and they all do it. . . ."

But the great love of Josiah's life was books. He had so many that they had to be stacked two deep on the shelves. This would have meant chaos and confusion to any less well-organized reader; Uncle Jos evolved a card index system which told him precisely behind which volume of Plato he would find Sir Walter Scott's Ivanhoe.

Charles and Josiah greeted each other warmly, enthused over the hunting that would start at dawn. One of the bonds tying them together—was it not true that boys got along better with their uncles than their fathers?—was that Josiah, like his father before him, had from childhood been interested in natural history and a collector in botany, entomology and ornithology, so much so that the father, despite the fact that he had two other sons, had written in his will:

I give and bequeath all my books, prints, books of prints, pictures and cabinets of experiments, of fossils and of natural history, unto my said son Josiah Wedgwood.

Charles heard the tea bell clang in the outer hall. In came the Wedgwood children: Elizabeth, the eldest of nine, was thirty-eight, fifteen years older than Emma, twenty-three, the youngest. Elizabeth had been born with a curvature of the spine which kept her in constant pain; the only prescribed remedy, whipping her back with nettles. She never allowed the pain to be visible, and served as a doctor to the poor children of the neighborhood, physicking them, giving them calomel, bleeding or blistering them, and achieving many a cure. As had Caroline Darwin in Frankland, Elizabeth had set up a school at Maer Hall for poor children, teaching classes herself for a couple of hours each morning. She planted the flower beds at Maer, worked with her hands in the earth, separating bulbs, weeding, cutting enormous bouquets for the house. Charles admired Elizabeth but he had never been close to her. Nor had he been to the youngest Josiah, called Joe, who was now thirty-six and wore the mantle of the prestigious Wedgwood plant rather heavily around his shoulders. Everyone knew that Joe and Caroline Darwin were in love and would one day marry. Charles was closer to Charlotte, thirty-four, who had her special room at the back of Maer Hall where she took art lessons from Copley Fielding and did her water colors. She was one of the favorites of the Darwin sisters at The Mount.

There were three other Wedgwood brothers: Harry, a barrister and graduate of Cambridge, who wrote poetry and was married to his cousin Jessie Wedgwood; Frank, thirty-one, also employed in the potteries, and planning to be married the following year. Hensleigh, twenty-eight, had come down from his bedroom for tea. He had received his Master of Arts at Christ's College the year Charles got there and was now awaiting his appointment as a police magistrate. He had a beginning reputation as a philologist, was planning to write books on the science of language, and was engaged to his cousin, Fanny Mackintosh.

There was another visitor at Maer Hall, Dr. Henry Holland, forty-two, of medium height and spare, whom Charles admired and envied. He was not only well known as a travel writer, having published several chapters in *Travels in Iceland*, and later his own books, *Travels in the Ionian Isles, Albania, Thessaly, Macedonia*, but was already a medical attendant for the Princess of Wales, and a fellow of the Royal Society. His maternal grandmother had been a sister of the first Josiah Wedgwood.

Dr. Robert Darwin was not enthusiastic about Dr. Holland, remarking to Charles, "His medical work is more fashionable than scientific."

Charles excused himself to pay his respects to his Aunt Bessy; he bounded up the steps two at a time, knocked gently on the door of her bedroom and heard her quiet "Come in." She was buried deep in the cushions of a chaise longue reading Shelley's *Prometheus Unbound.* Bessy Allen Wedgwood was sixty-seven now and had married Josiah Wedgwood when she was twenty-eight and Josiah only twenty-three, an unusual marriage because she was the older, but a genuine love match. Bessy had been an absolute beauty, as Charles saw in the portrait of her by Romney, a wedding gift which she kept in her bedroom. A year and a half ago she had suffered a seizure, mysterious in origin. Dr. Darwin thought it might have been caused by an overdose of poppy syrup which she took to quiet her nerves.

"Welcome, Charles, I've been waiting for you and the first of September to arrive simultaneously. You'll stay the month?"

Charles suppressed a sigh.

"You're looking well, Aunt Bessy."

"I have a new cap on. I always put it on when I mean to be charming."

Charles agreed that she had charm, and a singular sweetness of voice and manner. Sir James Mackintosh, an uncle by marriage to the Wedgwood children, who had told Professor Henslow after a Friday evening soiree in Cambridge, "There is something in that young man Darwin that interests me," said of Bessy, his sister-in-law:

"I never saw any other person whose acts of civility or friendship depended so little on rule or habit. I used to rally her on the gentlest mistress in England having the noisiest household."

"How is your sister Caroline?" Aunt Bessy asked.

"She is faring well, as usual, waiting patiently for your Joe to marry her."

"I don't know what to do about that lackluster son of mine. They love each other. Why don't they marry and give me grandchildren?"

"Joe is in love with the potteries."

"The potteries be damned. Joe can make terra cottas and babies at the same time! Why, Charles, I believe you are blushing."

Charles re-entered the library. The family was seated around the long leather-embossed library table with its neat pile of magazines, monographs, newspapers, political pamphlets. He made sure he had the seat next to his uncle.

A serving girl in a blue pinafore and cap brought in pots of China and India tea. Another girl came behind with a three-tiered stand stacked with sandwiches made of wafer-thin white bread, hot buttered scones, currant buns and tea biscuits. There were whole cakes on Wedgwood platters. The hot water jug to refill the teapot was placed on a stand with a spirit lamp; alongside was a china slop basin for the cooling remains of first cups. Emma cut a caraway seed cake into generous portions while everyone attacked the sandwiches.

Everyone except Charles. He downed cups of tea with milk and sugar in a spasm of anxiety and felt as if ants were swarming inside his arms and legs. He could not intrude his problem into this leisurely tea, with everyone talking, laughing, joking in comradery. He wished he knew an appropriate prayer to mumble to himself but could remember nothing fitting from the Book of Common Prayer. If anyone noticed the intensity of his silence, he or she was too busy drinking the ritualistic three cups to comment. To add to his discomfort, Dr. Henry Holland, bald on top of his pate, with eyes not quite level and an outthrust underlip, was holding forth about his experiences during his last trip to Europe. However there was a sadness in his voice. He had lost his young wife after only eight years of marriage, the same Emma Caldwell who had so vividly characterized the boisterous, good-natured life of Maer Hall.

Charles glanced at his uncle, as always with admiration. Uncle Jos at sixty-two wore his thin crop of dark hair curled across his head. He had huge discerning dark eyes, a strongly molded Roman nose, compressed mouth and obdurate chin. He was fastidiously dressed, a white cravat knotted around his neck, the ends tucked into a white waistcoat and over all a handsome coat with flaring velvet collar and row of cloth-covered buttons down either side.

Emma caught the earnestness of the glance, put down her cup.

"Charles, now that we've staved off hunger, won't you tell us your news."

He took the two letters from his coat and passed them to Josiah.

"Uncle Jos, would you be so kind as to read them aloud? The one from Professor Henslow first. Then everyone will know what's going on."

Josiah passed the sheets of handwriting to his youngest daughter. Emma's voice was articulate and well modulated. As she moved deeper into the message and its intent became clear, a profound silence fell upon the room. Charles sank deeper into his leather chair, legs stretched out under the table. The group listened with rapt concentration until she had completed the reading of George Peacock's letter.

Then a great hubbub broke out. Emma threw her arms about Charles's shoulders. Hensleigh came over to shake his hand. Elizabeth and Charlotte called their congratulations. Josiah's fingers were interlaced tightly across his chest. The first one to voice an opinion was Dr. Henry Holland.

"I would be hesitant if I were you, Charles. No details are given. You'll be in servitude to the ship's beck and call. When a naturalist travels he must be free and independent, as I've always been."

Charles protested. "They offer me every opportunity . . . even to leaving me in port while they survey the coast. . . ."

He looked over to his uncle.

"Uncle Jos, my father asked me to give you this note."

Josiah took in the message, said, "Why don't we go into my study? This wants discussion."

7.

The two men went through the library door. Charles was not surprised to find Emma slipping an arm through his and accompanying them. She was the only one who did, murmuring:

"This is simply a glorious chance. What other young man will be given such a golden voyage? You've always been a naturalist at heart. You must go. . . ."

Charles shook his head.

"It's up to your father now. He has the power to send me on a world journey or keep me at home."

Josiah's study, which he sometimes called his office, was bare and small. There was a desk, writing materials, two pens in an inkstand and three hard chairs. He sat at his desk, gazed up at Charles.

"I gather your father has objections to this expedition. Sit down here and list them in sequence."

Concentrating on a piece of Uncle Jos's stationery, Charles picked a quill pen out of its bed of pebbles, dipped it in the inkwell and began writing, quickly. He handed the sheet to Josiah, who read its contents attentively, a brooding intensity in his dark eyes. He articulated his sentences clearly:

"I feel the responsibility of your father's application to me on the offer that has been made to you. You have put down what you conceive to be your father's objections. I think the best course I can take would be to state what occurs to me upon each of them."

He paused, then began:

"I should not think it would be in any degree disreputable to your character as a clergyman. I should on the contrary think the offer honorable to you. The pursuit of natural history, though certainly not professional, is very suitable to a clergyman."

"I tried to persuade Father of that."

"A 'wild scheme'? I hardly know how to meet this objection. You would have definite objects upon which to employ yourself. That should enable you to acquire and strengthen habits of application. . . . That many others must have been offered the place? The notion did not occur to me, I see no ground for it. . . . There must be some serious objections to the vessel or expedition? I cannot conceive that the Admiralty would send out a bad vessel on such a service. In any case, nothing would, I think, be inferred if it were known that others had objected.

"If, in comparing this mode of spending the next two years with the way in which you will probably spend them if you do not accept this offer, your father thinks you more likely to be rendered unsteady and unable to settle, is it not the case that sailors are prone to settle in domestic and quiet habits?"

"Uncle Jos, I know little about sailors, or the sea, for that matter."

Ruefully Charles rose, moved around the desk as he indulged a rare bout of self-examination.

"It's true that I have lived a carefree life; there was a delightful set of chaps at Christ's College. We hunted, rode horseback, stayed up late at night drinking, laughing, chaffing each other. I read widely . . ."

". . . you always have," observed Josiah. "I've seldom seen you without a book in your hand. If one cannot be carefree and joyous in his youth, there is really no other season. If I saw you now absorbed in professional studies I should probably think it not advisable to interrupt them. But this is not, and I think will not be, the case with you. Your present pursuit of knowledge is in the same track as you would have to follow in the expedition."

Charles could not put down his tremor of exultation.

"Yes, natural history. I really have been working hard at that since I was a small boy. Dear God, if only it were a profession so that I could earn my livelihood. . . ."

Uncle Jos smiled indulgently; he had always had confidence in this lanky reed of a nephew.

"Let's take up your father's last objection, that the undertaking would be useless as regards your profession. Looking upon you as a man of enlarged curiosity, it will afford you such an opportunity of seeing men and things as happens to few."

There was a moment of quiet. Emma, ever practical, asked quietly: "What do we do next, Papa?"

"I shall write a letter to Dr. Darwin setting down the views I have expressed here. Why don't you go into the garden? We'll have twilight for another hour yet."

Charles and Emma walked down the central path to the lake and started around it, swinging along, hand in hand, Charles's face aglow. So, he observed, was Emma's.

"We are, you know, transported," Charles said, "on board the ship taking us around the world."

"You are being transported. I must stay here at home. You'll write as often as possible, won't you, Charles? Your sisters will send the letters to us as soon as they have consumed them."

"At every port. I'll also keep a journal. Your father is a remarkable man. He pitched in to save me as though I were his most beloved son."

"You are the spitting image of his youngest brother, Tom, and apparently have the same mind and manner. Father doted on Tom. He was brilliant; the first man to develop the process of taking photographs. Brilliant, but terribly ill. Father sent him halfway round the world to recoup his health. Nothing helped. He died before he had time to develop a fixative so that his images could be preserved. Daguerre came behind him and gets all the credit for inventing photography."

The sun was beginning to tip the green western hills.

"Have you never studied the portrait of Tom in the drawing room?" she asked. "That's why you are Father's favorite."

Her unguarded expression said:

"You are mine, as well."

Before going to sleep that night he put his hunting boots in position by his bedside so that he could cascade his feet and part of his long legs into them as he sprang from between the sheets.

He was up at first light, had a cup of freshly brewed coffee, and made his way to a distant part of the Maer estate where Dr. Holland and several of Josiah's neighbors would join him shortly. With the gamekeeper they would trudge the whole day through thick heath and young Scotch firs.

He had been out in the fields only a little time when a groom came running toward him.

"Mr. Darwin, you are wanted at the Hall."

Charles ran back to the house. When he burst into the door on the lake side, he found Josiah Wedgwood in the breakfast room dressed in traveling clothes.

"Charles, I decided during the night not to send the letter to your father. . . ."

Charles was staggered.

"A letter might reach him when he was in the wrong mood. I want to take it myself. I think you should come along in case your father has further questions. You can hitch Dobbin to the back of my carriage."

Dr. Robert Darwin put up no further contest. He read Josiah's letter; listened to his brother-in-law's assurances of the rightness of the journey. He thanked Josiah for undertaking the long trip on his son's behalf, then turned to Charles:

"I told you yesterday that if you could find any man of common sense who would advise you to go I would give my consent. There is no man I admire more than your Uncle Jos. You have my permission."

Charles threw his arms about his father, but there was just too much of Dr. Darwin to embrace. However Dr. Darwin shook his son's hand warmly. Uncle Jos had conquered the field, as he had fully intended to do.

# BOOK TWO

*"My Feelings Are Swinging Like a Pendulum"*

1.

HE dressed hurriedly by candlelight and was at the Shrewsbury Town Hall by three in the morning to catch the *Wonder* coach at the start of its sixteen-hour trip to London. The passengers from the nearby inns had pre-empted the more comfortable inside seats so that he found himself sitting on top of the coach amidst the bags of mail. They stopped for breakfast at Birmingham while the horses were being changed, then continued southeast through Coventry. At Brick-hill he left the coach and hired a horse and two-seater carriage which he drove for the remaining forty miles on rutted country roads to Cam-bridge, and arrived at the Red Lion Inn just down the street from Christ's College late in the evening, disjointed of bone. Before throwing himself onto the lumpy bed he wrote a note to Professor Henslow:

How soon should I come to see you in the morning?

and gave it to one of the Red Lion's boys to deliver.

If his sleep was short, it was also deep. When he opened his eyes at daylight he saw an envelope under his door. Henslow, who rose with the birds, had placed it there himself.

Come as soon as you waken. We'll hold breakfast for you.

As Charles left the Red Lion to walk to Henslow's house a wave of nostalgia swept over him, though it was only four months since he had departed with a diploma safely stowed in his bag. After Shrewsbury, Cambridge was his favorite town, for he had spent the three happiest years of his life here. Though his base was Christ's College, he had known students from many of the other colleges: the beetle collectors represented half a dozen colleges; those who loved music met in King's Chapel of a Sunday morning; others went out on weekend expeditions with Professor Henslow; there were the members of his Glutton Club. . . . A university town is unlike any other; there was a special quality to the air: students rushing in their black caps and gowns from one college to the other to attend lectures or to meet friends, their arms loaded with books. There was a sense of excitement, of young vigorous minds on the prowl. The knowledge that so many of England's great men had studied here before venturing into the world of action and reality—Milton, Newton, Dryden, Francis Bacon, Wordsworth, hundreds of others—gave the town a historical impact.

Cambridge was a medieval magnificence with its seventeen separate stone colleges; imposing stained-glass chapels, greenswards, ancient trees, the glorious gardens of the masters' houses and of the fellows; the picturesque stone bridges over the Backs spanning the river Cam where the students delighted in punting or swam naked off Sheep's Green while the ladies going by this narrow passage unfurled their parasols and buried their blushing faces deep in their silken protection. The long, white stone, many-windowed building of the Senate where he and his fellow undergraduates from Christ's as well as the other colleges had been called up, one college after the other, to have their degrees bestowed upon them was a beauty of classical serenity.

He traversed the few steps up Petty Cury to the massive entrance of Christ's College, entered through a cool stone hallway with the porter's lodge on his left, walked around the quad to the south side of the first court, and stood gazing up at his rooms on the second floor. During his first year he had lived over a tobacconist's shop on Sidney Street. He admired the geraniums in his former flower boxes. If he had not learned much of an academic nature here, Christ's College had certainly cured him of his dislike of education.

He retraced his steps through the stone arch. St. Andrew's Street merged into Regent Street with its row of houses, their small front gardens and narrow paths leading to brightly painted doors. The slate roofs were outlined with gutters which disposed of the rain water into the gardens.

Professor Henslow's house was somewhat larger than the others, with a basement, the top half of whose windows showed above the garden level. It was a three-story dwelling of tan brick, each floor having its windowed bow. There was a stone arch over the blue-painted door and, enclosing it all, a four-foot wall of cut stone. It was a pleasant and comfortable house, albeit rather narrow, having few pretensions to indicate a full professor at prestigious St. John's College, where most of Shrewsbury's graduates went, but which both Erasmus and Charles had rejected as being too rigidly disciplined. Unlike so many of his colleagues, Professor Henslow had no family money, a profound fact of life he and Adam Sedgwick shared. Despite his holding two offices, university professor of botany and curate of the Church of England, he had to tutor privately for pay, sometimes as many as six hours a day, in order to support his wife and three children, his constant purchase of books and rare plants for the botanic gardens, and his open house for faculty and student alike for which his wife Harriet always managed to come up with a bottle of Madeira and a platter of parkins, oatmeal cookies with ginger in them.

Charles gave the bronze door knocker seven sharp claps, for which he was known in the Henslow family: five fast and two slow ones. Professor John Henslow threw open the door with a welcoming smile and warm handshake. His was, Charles always thought, the most handsome, pleasure-giving face in all Cambridge. He had a big head, a mop of soft, richly textured black hair, long and full sideburns down to the jawbone. The heroic forehead was high, broad, strong, the bold features toned down by the personal modesty of the man: wide-spaced, gentle but all-consuming eyes, arching eyebrows, ample but non-assertive mouth and mildly dimpled chin with the clean, finely textured sun-bronzed skin of the outdoors man. His strong, huskily built figure was indefatigable. He was a man who loved work because it contained the germinal creation of life, renewed as each day passed.

He wore the usual under-the-chin highly starched pointed collar, black stock, long coat and lapeled waistcoat with large decorative buttons. He had good hands, helpful to his work in botany, with slender sensitive fingers. He also wore the expression of a man who had a tremendous amount to give and who asked only that people come to an understanding of the natural world around them.

John Henslow had become the most important man in Charles's life. He was one of those disciplined teachers who were at the same time infinitely patient, conveying not merely information but scholarly attitudes, a love of learning, techniques of research and methods with which to assimilate the fields of human endeavor. He was never dull, didactic or dictatorial; he taught with wit, a sense of excitement and involvement. From his five years at Edinburgh and Cambridge universities, Charles knew this kind of teacher to be rare, and a blessing for the scholars and students around them.

Harriet Jenyns Henslow came down the stairs carrying her two-month-old son bundled in her arms. She kissed Charles, murmured:

"Welcome home. You now have a godson."

"So I see. Congratulations! And to you too, my dear Henslow, with your male heir to carry on your name."

Harriet was not much over thirty, beautiful of manner though not of face: gentle, affectionate, a lovely homemaker. She parted her soft brown hair in the middle and pulled it down over both ears. Her eyes too were a soft brown. She came from a good family; her father, the Rev. George Jenyns, a canon of Ely and a magistrate for Cambridgeshire, was sufficiently prosperous to own a house in Connaught Place, London, and put his son Leonard, Harriet's brother, through Eton and St. John's at Cambridge. Although Harriet's father inherited

Bottisham Hall in Cambridgeshire from a second cousin, there remained only a modest amount of cash for Harriet's dowry. Even without this, Harriet might have married to better advantage; but hers had been a love match and still remained so after nearly eight years of marriage and three children. Since her husband had adopted Charles Darwin as a companion, Harriet too accepted him as a member of the family . . . but not without an original modicum of doubt.

"I like young Darwin; he's a charming youth," she remarked to her husband. "But why do you favor him above the others? He doesn't seem to me quite as brilliant as some of your honors students."

"Perhaps he isn't, at least not yet; but he has a brain in that large skull of his, not only for sopping up knowledge like litmus paper, but for speculative theory. He goes from the particular to the universal by second nature. He'll make his way, I don't know when or how, and neither does he, but the potential is there. That's all teachers have to work on. What life does to that potential is something we can neither predict nor control."

"Yes, Professor," she replied demurely; "I shall drop that pearl of wisdom into my jewel box."

Charles and Henslow settled in the combined living room-library where the Friday evening get-togethers were held. The furniture had been purchased with Harriet's dowry and was beginning to show signs of the Henslows' popularity. There were deep rust sofas and armchairs, ladder-back chairs with velour cushions, tables holding books, plants, boxes of recently acquired beetles, a marble fireplace with a black grate, shelves of books. On the walls were a series of Rembrandt etchings, a wedding gift, and other important engravings the Henslows had added over the years. Henslow had been Charles's first guide to the Fitzwilliam art collection which was housed in a large lecture and gathering room in the Perse Grammar School on Free School Lane, close to Christ's College.

Charles lost no time in conveying the news of Josiah Wedgwood's intervention and that he now had his father's consent for the voyage. Henslow was elated.

"Capital! We were so disappointed to learn from your letter that your father had objected. I felt as badly as I did when I had to turn down the appointment myself."

Charles stared at his mentor in astonishment.

"You had the offer? You never told me."

"There seemed no reason to. Actually, I had accepted. Harriet gave her consent without being asked. But she looked so miserable, I at once settled the point. Leonard Jenyns had the first offer and was so near accepting that he packed up his clothes. He's had years of training as a naturalist in the Fens near his home at Bottisham Hall; but having two congregations, he did not think it correct to leave them. We must write to Peacock immediately."

"My father was shrewd in assuming earlier offers had been made. I suppose the position calls for someone like myself who has neither family nor responsibilities."

"Yes. It has finally fallen into the right hands."

After breakfast Charles and Henslow went into the back garden, redolent with early September chrysanthemums. Henslow was exultant, his voice deep and melodious, originating in his chest and gaining momentum as it reached his lips.

"For six years I've been trying to do something with that five-acre neglected botanic garden in town. The university governors would not give me the funds to remodel it. Last week they bought thirty acres on the outskirts of town, part of it Fen country. The land is rich and untouched, and can be beautifully landscaped. I'm to have the funds to create a miniature Kew Gardens. We'll have space for the vastly increased number of trees and shrubs that have been introduced within the last half century."

He ran his fingers through the mass of thick curling hair.

"Let us walk out there."

As they rose from the battered cane chairs under a giant dogwood, Harriet brought out a caller, a Mr. Wood, nephew of Lord Londonderry. Charles had met him at Henslow's Friday evenings. He had never heard Wood's first name, nor did he know what Wood did, or why he bothered coming to the soirees he called "Friday-night science," since all he talked about was politics, slavery, suffrage, and why the Reform Bill was misguided idealism which would never work in a practical world.

Wood was short and stocky, with hair like coiled wire and a voice that started immediately behind his teeth. He was dressed in the height of London fashion from his pointed-toe shoes and black fitted trousers, strapped under the instep, to the double-breasted frock coat and glossy silk top hat. He carried himself with the proud knowledge of having come from nobility. His pleasure in seeing Charles was genuine.

"My dear Darwin, what a charming surprise. I had imagined you already buried in a Shropshire parsonage, pursuing souls on Sundays and beetles on weekdays."

"Not yet, Wood. I appear to have a two-year reprieve."

"How splendid. Do tell me."

Charles had barely begun when Wood broke in:

"How extraordinary! Captain FitzRoy and I are related! Some kind of cousin through Lord Londonderry, who is a half brother to FitzRoy's mother. Rumor has it that it was Lord Londonderry who obtained the command of H.M.S. *Beagle* for Captain FitzRoy."

"The *Beagle*," echoed Charles softly. "It's the first time I've heard the name of the ship."

"I am a great friend of Captain FitzRoy," Wood exclaimed. "I shall go back to my rooms immediately and write a commendatory letter about you. Do you believe in fate, Darwin? I do. The very fact that we met this morning, on Saturday, when you are journeying into London on Monday to make your final arrangements!"

"It's very kind of you, Wood."

"It's nothing. Nothing!" He turned to Henslow. "I dropped by to say hello but you must excuse me if I am to get the letter onto the one o'clock coach for London. I want it in FitzRoy's hands this evening."

The two long-legged men strode down Trumpington Street past the entrances and quads of four or five of Cambridge's sculptured colleges, beyond Henslow's Little St. Mary's on St. Mary's Lane which led to the river Granta, the small but gracious church where the Rev. Mr. Henslow preached to his congregation every Sunday morning. As they passed the church with its ancient cemetery at the rear, Henslow studied Charles's face.

"Charles, do you really want to become a clergyman? Do you think you will be good at the task?"

Charles was taken aback; no one had bothered to ask him this question.

". . . I think so. I did rather well in my theology courses, and know Paley's book quite thoroughly. I have every reason to believe that I can write and deliver a meaningful sermon . . ."

"But you're not . . ."

"Passionate about the Church? No one in my family ever has been. But we're faithful. I think mine will be a simple approach to caring for a flock."

They walked quietly for a few minutes, then Charles said:

"My dear Henslow, perhaps you'd better give me a crash course in preserving specimens. My friends in Edinburgh gave me a start on marine biology and you've shown me how to dry flowers and preserve my beetles. That's the sum total of my knowledge. During the long stretches between ports I'm going to have to preserve everything I collect on shore."

Henslow laughed. It was a pleasant sound.

"Let's start with geological specimens and fossils. Wrap them in paper first and then in unrefined hemp fibers known as tow, which is plentiful and cheap. You can find it in any port. Label each find with

indelible ink directly on the specimen, including shells and bones. . . .
You must also go to William Yarrell's bookshop in London and buy a
copy of Charles Lyell's *Principles of Geology*. It is of the utmost value,
but by no account accept the views therein advocated. He has some
outlandish theories. . . .

"Now as to soft-bodied invertebrates, amphibians, reptiles and fish.
All have to be preserved in spirits of wine or grain alcohol. Get the purple domestic form, it's cheaper. Your solution should run seventy per
cent alcohol, thirty per cent water. Nine out of ten specimens which are
spoiled are owing to the spirit being too weak! With larger specimens it
is necessary to slit the belly and to preserve the internal organs separately. Trust nothing to memory. Keep a list with the name and date of
the ships by which every box of specimens is sent home. Be sure the
receiver keeps equally accurate dates."

Charles took a quick look at his friend.

"But who is that to be?" he asked. "If I'm out two years I hope there
will be a very large number of boxes with thousands of specimens. . . .
I can't send them to The Mount. They wouldn't know what to do with
them."

"No, they must be sent to someone knowledgeable so that he can examine the state they are in and check your duplicate catalogue to see
that everything fits."

"Forgive me, my dear Henslow, but I think you've just painted a self-
portrait. I don't know another soul who would be able or willing to undertake such a task."

Henslow's smile was both pleased and touched with resignation.

"Try the societies in London first. They may help. . . . Use glass jars
whenever available. Earthenware and wooden casks tend to leak or
allow evaporation. Close your jars with a bung covered by a bladder,
twice by common tin foil and by bladder again. Keep three or four bottles open at the same time so that one may serve for crustacea, another
for animals for dissection, another for minute specimens . . . always
put the fish into the strongest spirits. Use arsenical soap for all skins but
do not neglect to brush the legs and beak with a solution of corrosive
sublimate. Pack insects of all orders, except butterflies, between layers
of rag in pillboxes. Put a bit of camphor at the bottom of the box."

They had walked the several miles to Henslow's newly acquired acres.
He drew out from his coat pocket a folded landscape map, crouched in
the shade of an ancient tree and spread the map on the ground. He had
already designed the thirty acres.

"My dear friend, never start after the fact. As soon as you have an
idea, do all of the beginning work. Then when you get your 'thirty
acres,' you've already started. I want some rolling mounds, waterfalls

and fish and a rock garden. We'll leave several acres of the Fens *in situ* so that our students can continue to observe and collect. We'll have greenhouses and hothouses for the care of tropical plants. There will be many wide paths; it is to be as much a public park as a botanic garden so that parents will bring their children here and teach them the names of the plants and herbs and trees. . . .

"You never know, Darwin, we may convert botany, yes, and entomology and marine biology as well, into studies almost as important as mathematics, Latin, Greek and classical literature. The fault of our English universities is that our educators look down their noses at the natural sciences as worthless branches of knowledge. It's our job to turn that around in our lifetime."

2.

On Sunday morning Charles and the Henslow family dressed for church. The intimate Little St. Mary's had a vaulted ceiling of quarter-circle, hand-axed timbers, and an excellently trained choir. The Rev. Mr. Henslow, looking majestic in his rich black robe, preached his eleven o'clock sermon from Luke 8:16–17 specially for Charles: "And he said unto them, No man, when he hath lighted a candle, covereth it with a vessel, or putteth it under a bed; but setteth it on a candlestick, that they which enter in may see the light. For nothing is secret that shall not be made manifest; neither anything hid, that shall not be known and come abroad."

After the services, while the Henslows visited with their congregation, Charles took the two little girls, Frances and Louisa, in their white Sunday dresses, down to the river. Many Cambridge families were already out in their punts, picnic baskets piled high in the bows. When they returned home they found Mr. Wood pacing the library, his skin ashen.

"Mr. Wood, what has happened?" demanded Henslow. "You look upset."

". . . I am. . . ." His voice was almost inaudible.

A silence hung in the library. A piece of vellum stationery was trembling in Wood's hand.

". . . an answer to my letter to Captain FitzRoy. . . ." He forced himself to face Charles.

". . . sorry . . . so terribly sorry. . . . Captain FitzRoy is against your going. Darwin, I am miserable at having ruined your chance."

"But how could you have?"

Wood gritted his teeth, then got out the few hoarse words of self-recrimination:

". . . only praise . . . but it was my obligation to tell him . . . my relative . . . that you are a Whig . . . a liberal . . . you favor the Reform Bill . . . extending the franchise. . . ."

"That's true," Charles heard himself reply. "It would extend the vote to property owners worth ten pounds a year or more."

Wood did not mean for the two men to hear him groan.

"We Tories see the Reform Bill as 'chaos come again.'"

"While we Whigs," said Henslow in a flat, calm voice, "see it as the harbinger of a new age. But what in the world has politics to do with natural history?"

". . . nothing. But H.M.S. *Beagle* is such a small ship. Captain FitzRoy wants a naturalist who can be a friend. No one else on the ship is permitted to become a friend of the captain. . . . A congenial person to share his meals . . . no one else is allowed to eat with the captain or enter his cabin. . . ."

From Charles's bile rose the bitter disappointment that had swept over him when his father had rejected the journey. The opportunity was again lost.

"Wood, have I ever intruded my political opinions upon you?"

"No! Of course not! You're a gentleman. I wrote only to tell FitzRoy what an agreeable person you are. . . . But if you fought with FitzRoy over the Reform Bill . . . he would never forgive me. And you would find the *Beagle* untenable. Captain FitzRoy has given the position to a long-time friend, a Mr. Chester. He's in office somewhere in the government, I suppose. . . ."

With Wood gone, Charles circled the room blindly.

"After all the trouble I caused my father and Uncle Jos. I am crushed."

Only one emotion had been left out of Henslow's nature: anger. But now crimson burned high on his cheeks.

"Peacock has acted very wrong in misrepresenting things so much. He assured me that the appointment of a naturalist was in his power and his alone."

Charles snorted, an equally uncommon mode of expression for him. He said satirically:

"How can a captain be forced to eat three meals a day with a Whig liberal? He'd run aground at the first shoal. When you think that the Reform Bill, if it can ever be got past Parliament, enfranchises only seventeen per cent of Englishmen at most . . ."

All light had gone out of Henslow's expression.

"People go to war over politics. They go to war over religion. They go to war over boundary disputes. The human brain rarely fails to find an opportunity to kill off half its species. . . ."

The men became silent. At one o'clock Harriet entered the room to announce that dinner was ready. They toyed with the food. When the young serving girl passed the silver sauceboat with its onion, clove and nutmeg sauce, neither Charles nor Henslow had the will to spoon it over his bread pudding. Then Charles quietly laid down his utensils. Henslow looked up from his plate, his eyebrow cocked quizzically.

"Any second thought? Or is it too soon?"

"No, not too soon. Not by a moment. I'm catching the *Star* at dawn for London. The position of naturalist was officially offered to me. Captain FitzRoy is going to have to look me square in the eye tomorrow and tell me that he has refused me the job. I'll settle for nothing less!"

The *Star* deposited him and his portmanteau in London at midday at the Old Bell Inn on Holborn. He had visited the city a number of times with family and friends but the big, noisy, sooty metropolis had seemed confused and alien to him. He proceeded down Fleet Street, past the church of St. Clement Danes standing nearly in the middle of the roadway, and onto the Strand in front of St. Mary-le-Strand, across from Somerset House. He continued past the Adelphi Theatre and eventually came to the newly named Trafalgar Square, a vast cleared space which had been created by tearing down the Royal Mews and the flanking "vile houses" in Lower St. Martin's Lane. The new National Gallery, just beginning construction, was on a rise above the vacated space of the square.

He was fortunate to find lodgings at 17 Spring Gardens, a two-block street across from the Admiralty. He had a spacious corner room, in which he washed and changed into fresh linens. As he moved to a window facing the Admiralty a vagrant thought hit him.

"Suppose Captain FitzRoy is not in London! Have I come on a fool's errand?"

But when he walked through the ornate arch of the Admiralty entrance on Whitehall, proud griffins perched on top of its columns, and the guard had sent up his name with a messenger boy, the response came back quickly:

"Captain FitzRoy's respects, sir. He requests that you repair to his office at once."

Charles ascended a flight of steps and followed the boy down a long hall. The messenger knocked, opened the door.

His first impression was of the room's bareness. When naval officers returned from long voyages they were given home leave and spent only a few days at the Admiralty to complete and submit reports of their missions. Presumably they did not need permanent offices.

There was nothing bare or austere, however, about Captain Robert

FitzRoy. As he rose from his desk, Charles saw that he was tall, slim, patrician from the top of his curly, forward-brushed dark hair and long dark sideburns through his elegantly shod feet. His ears were molded close to his head, his eyes were luminous and dark under black slashing brows. He wore a distinguished mustache. It was a sensitively formed face with perfect features . . . except the nose, which drooped. He was dressed in the height of fashion, not as a Beau Brummell, but as a man of experience and authority.

Robert FitzRoy was illegitimately descended from King Charles II and Barbara Villiers, the Duchess of Cleveland. There was no element of disgrace in this illegitimacy; Charles II had had no legitimate descendants. Captain FitzRoy himself was a grandson of the Duke of Grafton and the son of Lord Charles FitzRoy. If he had superb poise with a bit of arrogance and authoritarianism, he had earned the pretension, though his large personal fortune had been inherited. He had entered the Royal Naval College at Portsmouth at the age of twelve, graduated at nineteen with the First Medal, and been recognized as having a superb knowledge of mathematics, meteorology and the handling of a sailing ship in some of the worst weather the world could provide.

In October of 1828, while stationed at the British Royal Naval Base in Rio de Janeiro, at the age of twenty-three, he was ordered, upon the suicide of the captain of H.M.S. *Beagle,* to take command. For some fourteen or fifteen months he had captained the surveying vessel to the admiration of the Admiralty, and brought it back to England with "most perfect charts." Great Britain, intending to dominate the world through its fleet, wished to chart the coasts of the various continents to find the proper landfalls and the best possible ports, and to survey and map the rivers which flowed to the sea.

FitzRoy's dark, luminous eyes sparkled as he welcomed Charles.

"Your timing is perfection, Mr. Darwin!"

"How so, Captain?"

"Had you come ten minutes earlier, I would have had bad news for you."

"And five minutes earlier?"

"Good news. This note arrived from my friend, Mr. Chester, regretting that he cannot sail with me because he cannot absent himself from his office. Had I been able to take my friend it would have meant that there would be no room for you on our small and crowded vessel."

Charles's senses flipflopped over the abrupt change in fortune.

"Then I am accepted!"

"I am most pleased you came to London so promptly. I apologize for my hasty response to Mr. Wood's letter. On sober reflection I realized that two young men, if they were compatible, could never quarrel about

English politics whilst mapping a South American coast, or the Pacific Ocean, thousands of miles away from home."

"Sir, I don't have a quarrelsome nature."

"Good! I offer to share my meals with you in my cabin; you'll have to live on water and the plainest of dinners; I drink no wine or rum while in command of a ship. You will also have the use of my divan for quiet hours of reading or rest. Shall you bear being told that I want the cabin to myself when I want to be alone?"

"Everyone has a need for privacy. It's sometimes more of a craving than food or sleep."

"If we treat each other this way, I hope we shall suit. If not, probably we should wish each other at the Devil. Won't you sit down? We can talk across the corner of this desk. I must warn you, though I will afford you every accommodation I can, they will not be numerous. I think it my duty to state everything from the worst point of view. Nothing would be so miserable as to have you with me if you were uncomfortable. The *Beagle* is a small vessel, and we must all be thrown together."

"May I ask where I bunk?"

"In the poop cabin. We'll sling your hammock in one corner. We keep our library in there. It's a bit larger than my cabin, and with an equal-sized skylight. The chart table will be convenient for your working purposes. John Lort Stokes will have his hammock in the corner opposite. He's nineteen and will serve as mate and assistant surveyor. He was a midshipman on the *Beagle* during its first voyage. It's a very young crew, Mr. Darwin, though most have sailed under my command before. I think that you would fit in well. However if you do not choose to remain with us you can at any time get home to England. Many vessels sail that way."

"Thank you. The only thing that might bother me is seasickness."

"The stormy sea is exaggerated. During bad weather, probably two months of the year, we can leave you in some healthy, safe country. We have many books, all instruments, guns, at your service. We anchor the ship, then remain a fortnight to conduct our surveys and draw our maps. You can remain ashore during that time doing the work of a naturalist. At times I will join you. I also am interested in natural history and collecting."

Charles's face was aglow with anticipation of stays in exotic tropical ports.

"But you should see H.M.S. *Beagle* before you decide. I'm going to Plymouth by steamer next Sunday. Why not accompany me?"

"I should like that."

"Then we're agreed. I imagine you want to meet Captain Beaufort now to discuss terms. Do be so good as to plague him about the South Seas, stir him up with a long pole. And if you are not spoken for, please have dinner with me at my club this evening. We could have a bottle and a bird."

"That would be my pleasure."

"Your friends will tell you that a sea captain is the greatest brute on the face of creation. I do not know how to help you in this case, except by hoping you will give me a trial. We sail from Plymouth on October 10."

Captain Francis Beaufort had been appointed the Royal Navy hydrographer only twenty-seven months before Charles knocked on the door of his seven-room domain on an upper floor of the Admiralty. The walls and worktables of the Hydrographic Office were filled with maps, charts, drawings and yellowed Old World globes. The man behind the huge mahogany desk, Francis Beaufort, had been born in Ireland, son of Dr. Daniel Beaufort, an erratic Irish divine who had trained himself to become an expert surveyor and topographer, and drawn the first authentic map of Ireland. The father was a tiny man, under five feet, brilliant of mind. His son, who adored him in spite of his faults, spent most of his adult life trying to rescue his father from debt.

The boy wanted nothing but to go to sea and did so at fifteen, signing on an East India Company ship. Young Francis studied celestial navigation and map making and, probably through his father's example, developed a flair for infinite detail. He joined the Royal Navy in 1790, making the first surveys of the south coast of Turkey in 1811; twenty years later they were still honored as being the most reliable. He later made an excellent survey of the coast of Syria. Unlike his father, he was ambitious, wanting to fight in Britain's wars so that he could capture enemy ships, win money prizes, earn promotion.

He did none of them. Mostly he got himself shot at, wounded and, disgruntled, retired in 1801 on a half pension. He came back into the Royal Navy in 1805 when they needed him to command a ship to India. Though he had only five months of academic science education at the Dunsink Observatory, he was elected a fellow of the Royal Society and made, without compensation, a series of one hundred and seventy maps for the Society for the Diffusion of Useful Knowledge, which won him high repute.

When he took over the Hydrographic Office in 1829 it was a position of neither honor nor envy. The department had been ignored, sometimes despised, always underbudgeted, trampled underfoot by the Admiralty's First Secretary Croker, and neglected by the great Arctic explorer, Edward Parry, who held the post but spent most of his time on his own explorations. The office had perhaps a thousand maps. They were using the charts of whoever went exploring: French, German, Italian, Spanish, many so woefully inaccurate as to be dangerous. Francis Beaufort turned these decades of sloth into a whirlwind of disciplined activity, a "surveyor's harvest." By the time Charles walked into his offices, Beaufort had two young naval lieutenants working with him as indexers and curators, four trained draftsmen and a secretary to draw up sailing instructions; and the best engraver-printers, lithographers and bookbinders to be found in London. Even as H.M.S. *Beagle* was being outfitted, he had eleven other naval ships at sea or being prepared for surveying tasks. He had logbooks and notebooks rolling in from the seven seas, maps and charts which would make the British Royal Navy, now in command of the oceans, safe and secure wherever it might venture for profit or conquest.

Francis Beaufort had suffered for years from what he called his "blue devils," feelings of anxiety, inferiority, depression, arising out of the years of being passed over for promotion in favor of men not half so qualified but immeasurably above him in social position. His arrival as the head of his own department in the Royal Navy at the age of fifty-five had finally brought him a measure of internal peace. The man at whom Charles found himself gazing looked short as he sat in his desk chair, with shining bald pate, eyes sunk deep in their sockets, a nose and chin molded sloppily of putty. In the instant before Beaufort looked up at him Charles sensed the years of self-torture and humiliation on the weather-beaten face.

"Mr. Darwin, your name is not unknown to me. I had the pleasure of meeting your father in 1803, before you were born. My sister Louisa and I took our mother across the Irish Sea to consult with him. We had learned even in Ireland of his reputation for helping women patients. My mother had not been in good health for years; in particular she suffered from a skin eruption on her legs. Your father said at once that he was more interested in Mother's health than in the scaling on her legs. He visited her several days in succession, then sent us home. Her health, if not her rash, improved immeasurably. She lived to the age of ninety-four."

"I hope I can maintain the family reputation."

Beaufort's smile involved a minimum movement of his lips or expression in his eyes.

"You've seen Captain FitzRoy? A splendid cartographer. What has he told you?"

Charles repeated the essence of his conversation with Captain FitzRoy, particularly the admonition to stir Beaufort up with a long pole about the South Seas.

"Darwin, if you start and do not go around the world, you shall have good reason to think yourself deceived. You will stop a week at the Madeira Islands, and the Canaries as well. . . ."

"Excellent!" Charles exclaimed. "We'll see Teneriffe and Humboldt's marvelous dragon tree."

Beaufort frowned, then decided not to be angry with this brash young man who imagined H.M.S. *Beagle* to be going out on a naturalist's voyage.

". . . I am even now drawing up the track through the South Seas. It is probable that you will return home by the Indian archipelago. That will take three years at a minimum."

Charles blanched. Three years instead of the two agreed upon! It was not that he feared the extension of a year as a hardship on himself; he would adjust to the new life as it was required of him. But his father and sisters! They had had a difficult time accepting the two-year separation! What would his father say to this new turn of events? He was certain to be upset. He might even think himself to be deceived, threaten to withdraw his permission! He dreaded the moment he must inform them. For a fleeting instant he considered withholding the information.

He swallowed hard.

"The longer the voyage the greater will be my experience and knowledge."

"Well said. I shall put you upon the boards and then it will cost you only thirty pounds a year for your victuals, like the other officers. As I informed Peacock, the Admiralty is not disposed to give a salary, though they will furnish you with an official appointment. If a salary should be required, however, I am inclined to think that it would be granted."

"On that latter point, Captain Beaufort, I would like to consult with my father. He has given me a generous allowance at Cambridge, and I gather he intends to continue it."

Beaufort unconsciously ground his teeth as he thought of his own years spent in paying off his father's debts. Charles sensed the changed mood.

"I believe no salary is indicated, sir," he said diffidently. "I have no way of knowing whether I can be of any real service on the *Beagle*. Of course I intend to collect in all the branches of natural history. . . ."

Beaufort saw that he had challenged the young man's sense of security. The muscles of his jawbone unknotted. He spoke gently.

"There should be no problem about your collections during the voyage. Ship them home each time you have a boxful. Here is a list of supplies you will be needing. Check them off, one by one, as they are loaded on the *Beagle*."

Charles ran his eyes over the list. He was astonished at its thoroughness and expressed his gratification.

"Actually I drew this up before you were appointed. It was my hope that Dr. Robert McCormick, the ship's doctor, would put them to good use. He has done some collecting on earlier voyages."

"Is he going to be unhappy about my taking the place?"

"He shouldn't be. He is a navy surgeon and his first job is to take care of the health of the *Beagle*'s seventy-plus crew. In tropical countries that's a full-time job. He was never permitted to stay in port while the ship went surveying."

"I'm relieved to hear that, Captain Beaufort. I would not want to feel that I have an enemy on board."

"It will work the other way round; everyone on board will be glad to have someone *not* in the Royal Navy to grouse to. Be ready for an October 10 sailing."

Charles rose, thanked the captain for his kindness. Beaufort's head was already bowed, studying the maps before him with an almost frightening intensity.

Charles stepped out into the streets of London, his head spinning after his two interviews, walked along Whitehall as far as the Treasury, then cut down to the riverbank, strolled along the Thames past the majestic Houses of Parliament, doubled back to the Westminster Bridge and stood watching the green river water swirl beneath him on its way to the English Channel. His hands had broken out in a rash. This had happened once or twice before when he had been under nervous pressure, a condition his easygoing nature deplored.

"Shakespeare was right. There is indeed 'a tide in the affairs of men,' and I have experienced it. At one o'clock today I had given up the voyage. At two-thirty I have been offered not only an official position but the possibility of a salary as a naturalist to boot!"

He returned to his rooms, bathed, changed his clothes in preparation for a congenial dinner with Captain FitzRoy at his club.

3.

When he entered Yarrell and Jones's Bookshop on the corner of Bury and Little Ryder streets the next morning his nostrils were assailed by the most delicious of all commercial smells, that of fresh ink still in the process of drying on good stock paper. William Yarrell came forward to greet him, merely glancing at the letter of introduction from Henslow. He was about fifty, had a good face, long and lean, with high color in the ascetic cheeks from his frequent expeditions. His soft brown eyes were sympathetic. The scant hair left on his brow was curly; the slender nose set off an abstemious mouth. His face's lone idiosyncrasy was the triangle formed above his eyes by the thick dark eyebrows.

Charles knew of his background from both Professor Henslow and Leonard Jenyns; he was the only naturalist in England who made his living from a bookstore and newspaper agency, and had been publishing erudite monographs in the *Zoological Journal* since 1825 en route to two books he meant to publish about British fishes and British birds. He had already authored eighteen zoological articles.

"Yes, yes, I know about your appointment. Word spreads fast among our little fraternity."

"I know little about London prices and there are things I need: a good-sized telescope, compass, dissecting equipment . . ."

"I'm your man!" exclaimed Yarrell. "I'll tell my cousin that I'm leaving."

Yarrell enabled Charles to buy at a reasonable price a telescope, a geological compass to attach to it, several dissecting instruments. He would write to Susan to ask her to send his microscope to London. As they left the last shop, Charles asked:

"Do I get the impression that you can bully these merchants?"

"In London, that is called bargaining. You must learn the art if you are ever to live here."

In addition to helping Charles buy scalpels and dissecting knives, Yarrell gave him a one-day course in the care and preparation of birds and fish for shipping home. What impressed him most about Yarrell was the close bond felt by what he described as "our little fraternity" in natural philosophy.

"Since no one else respects our work," Yarrell explained, "we succor each other. As we gather more and more knowledge, we will conquer the last areas of prejudice."

For the first time Charles found London pleasant. His other stays had been short holidays; he had seen some plays and exhibitions at the Society of British Artists and been showered by coal soot. Now the hurry, bustle and noise were in unison with his inner feelings.

When he was awakened at five in the morning by the discharge of artillery in nearby St. James's Park, the cannonading reminded him that this was coronation day for the sixty-six-year-old King William IV and his Queen Adelaide. Leaving his room at six o'clock, he found men graveling the road to Westminster Abbey. Scaffoldings for seating were erected in front of most of the houses along the line of march. He felt guilty at being child enough to pay a guinea for a seat from which to view the procession.

Twenty thousand spectators were jammed along the way as far down as Charing Cross where another three thousand persons were crowded onto wooden stands and platforms. The Scotch Greys and the 7th Light Dragoons were stationed in the park, the Life Guards and Royal Horse Guards, in blue uniforms, lined the streets. The Abbey was protected by foot guards stationed within and without. The weather was "lowering," with an occasional light shower, but at ten o'clock the sun came out.

As the red and gold carriage of the King and Queen started out from St. James's Palace, cheers burst from the people lining the route, bands struck up "God Save the King." Charles could see hats, handkerchiefs and flags being waved in the air. He was happy to hear the cry "Reform! Reform!" mingled with the shouts of approval. King William IV was dressed in his admiral's uniform and Her Majesty in white with a bejeweled headdress. He appeared to look well, and seemed popular, yet there was no overwhelming adoration.

When, during the ceremony in the Abbey, it finally began to pour, a wit seated beside Charles cried:

"Thus begins the 'rain' of King William IV!"

On Friday morning he walked back to Yarrell's to buy a book on astronomy.

"After all, I suppose I would astonish a sailor if I did not know how to find the latitude and longitude."

He worked on the text until Captain FitzRoy picked him up in his gig to go shopping for his personal guns.

"I'm all for economy," FitzRoy said, "except on one point: firearms. I strongly recommend you get a case of pistols like mine, and never go on shore without loaded ones."

"Are they expensive?"

"About sixty pounds."

Charles whistled.

"I'll help you to find a less expensive pair," volunteered FitzRoy. "I'll use the art of bargaining on your behalf. You must bring a good rifle as well; you'll appreciate the luxury of fresh meat while on a long journey."

Captain FitzRoy was as good as his word, spending the rest of the day going from gunsmith to gunsmith until Charles was able to buy a case of strong pistols and a newly designed rifle for fifty pounds. He saw with astonishment that the captain was spending up to four hundred pounds for his own firearms, and choosing, one by one, six of the twenty-two chronometers the ship would carry to secure precise readings on longitude while his ship went around the world.

Late that afternoon, back in his rooms at 17 Spring Gardens, drawing up lists of necessities, and then striking out half of them, he felt certain that despite its hardships the expedition would suit him. FitzRoy was his "beau ideal" of a captain. He looked forward to his first visit to the ship.

4.

He had been six days in London. On September 11 he left with Captain FitzRoy for the three-day trip on the steam packet which sailed out of the mouth of the Thames, past Ramsgate and Dover into the English Channel and then due west past the Isle of Wight to Plymouth. At the last moment Captain FitzRoy had asked:

"Are you certain you want to travel by water? The *Defiance* coach will take you into Plymouth in twenty-six hours. I'm afraid if the Channel kicks up it may frighten you off the *Beagle*."

"Nothing is going to frighten me off the *Beagle*."

"Did you mention whether you had been on a ship before?"

"Only once, four years ago, when my Uncle Josiah Wedgwood invited me to accompany him to Geneva to bring home his daughters. I did not feel quite well but made a very hearty dinner on roast beef."

The family of thirteen-year-old Charles Musters, who had signed on H.M.S. *Beagle* as a first-class volunteer, had asked Captain FitzRoy to take the lad under his wing since it was the boy's first time away from home. Charles took his turn caring for the boy.

They sailed into Plymouth Sound in the gloaming of a brilliant mid-September day, the skies and sea a flawless turquoise. Inside the enormous breakwater the packet made its way through the narrow opening into Sutton Pool, where it was secured at a wharf off the Barbican quay. Sutton Pool was surrounded by three-story, massive stone warehouses with pulleys suspended from their roofs to haul up and store arriving freight. As Charles descended the gangplank Captain FitzRoy pointed out a crowd gathered close by.

"Sutton Pool is where the Plymouth Corporation has its ducking stool," he explained. "They're ducking some wrongdoing or unruly woman of the town. By the by, those steps on the other side are the ones the Pilgrims descended to board the *Mayflower* in 1620 and set off for North America."

FitzRoy summoned a hackney carriage. Young Musters and their baggage were installed on top. The captain instructed the driver to take them to the top of the Hoe, the High Place, a great green promenade and esplanade overlooking almost the whole of Plymouth Sound. Dozens of sailing ships were moored in a cove of nearby Mount Batten and in the safe pockets of the Catwater. On their right was the impregnable citadel, mounted with tremendous brass cannons to drive off any aggressor imprudent enough to think it could invade England by ship. On the other side was Mill Bay where ships from the Baltic brought in Scandinavian timber. On the far point was the Royal William Victualing Yard and straight ahead the tiny island on which Sir Francis Drake had planted his compass in 1582, two years after circumnavigating the globe.

"It's breathtaking!" Charles cried.

The carriage then took them down Union Street to the Stonehouse Bridge. On the way through the center of Plymouth, Charles gained the impression of a prosperous, bustling city, with many splendid buildings of Greek and Gothic architecture. The residential areas were lined with Elizabethan and Jacobean homes, numbers of the highly decorated upper stories projecting over the narrow cobbled streets.

Once in Devonport, FitzRoy directed the driver through a maze to a slight elevation over the Royal Naval Dockyard.

"There she lies!" he exclaimed. "Isn't she a beauty?"

Charles felt his insides plummet; for H.M.S. *Beagle*, without masts or bulkheads, was little more than a skeleton of skewered timbers.

"She looks more like a wreck," he exclaimed, involuntarily.

Captain FitzRoy was not perturbed.

"That's because you don't know how she will appear when completely refitted. Today is September 13. The *Beagle* was only commissioned for this second expedition on July 4. As she required a new deck and a good deal of repair about the upper works, I obtained permission to have the upper deck raised. This will be of the greatest advantage to her as a sea boat and will add materially to the comfort of all on board, giving us an extra eight inches aft and twelve forward for eating, sleeping and working. You see, Darwin . . ." FitzRoy's dark, handsome face was aglow with pride, ". . . I resolved to spare neither expense nor trouble in making our little expedition as complete as my means and exertion would allow."

Charles thought of the eighteen-foot ceiling height in the downstairs rooms of The Mount, the ten- to twelve-foot bedroom ceilings:

"We plan in feet, FitzRoy deals in inches!"

FitzRoy continued:

"Her bottom was pretty well rotted out. We are putting on a sheathing of two-inch fir planking. Over the fir planks there will be a coating of felt, and then new copper."

"But surely you can't complete all this by October 10?"

"We've postponed the date to October 20."

Charles involuntarily breathed a sigh of relief. It would take time getting used to the size of that skeleton below him.

Night had seeped down as though with a fine rain of charcoal powder, obliterating the docks and ships. FitzRoy turned away.

"I suggest we find our supper and rooms in the Royal Hotel in nearby Fore Street. The manager, Mr. Loving, is a friend and will take care of us. They serve a hearty breakfast at dawn. Then I'll take you directly to the *Beagle,* introduce you to our officers, and show you where you will live. You are a landsman but the *Beagle* will change all that. A full-rigged ship, sailing before the wind, is the most beautiful sight in the world!"

The sun rose warm and lemon yellow in a sky full of drifting tufts of clouds. At the dockyard they found workmen, tools and materials in hand, moving over the hull of H.M.S. *Beagle* like streams of purposeful ants. Captain FitzRoy took Charles over the ship, affording him a nautical lecture of which he understood only the barest portion. The young captain's voice was filled with pulsing excitement.

"This new sheathing will add about fifteen tons to her displacement, and nearly seven to her actual measurement. Our new rudder is being fitted according to the plan of Captain Lihou. Here in the galley we're installing one of Frazer's stoves, with an oven attached, instead of a common fireplace. Lightning conductors invented by Thunder-and-Lightning Harris—he'll be here to help us install—will be fixed in all the masts, the bowsprit and even in the flying jib boom. Our ropes, sails and spars are the best that can be procured. All the cabins will be finished in mahogany. Six superior boats are being built expressly for us. Two of them are my private property; I felt we needed two more than the Admiralty approved. All will be so contrived and stowed that they can be carried in the heaviest weather. . . ."

Charles's head spun as he was dashed up and down the fore and aft hatchways, in and out of unfinished cabins, the gun room, midshipmen's berth, sick bay, sail room and coal hole.

"I was an idiot, sir, last night, to say that the *Beagle* looked like a wreck."

"I'll tell you one thing, Darwin, no surveying expedition will ever leave England better equipped to circumnavigate and map the world! Now I want you to meet my fellow officers."

Charles was gregarious by nature and made friends easily, yet he felt considerable tension now that he was about to meet the men with whom he would live for the next three years in confined space. Would they like him? Would these men of the sea resent his Cambridge education, his modest but private income, his non-usefulness aboard ship?

Would they consider him a burden, an appendage? Would they take umbrage at his privilege of dining with the captain? To the best of his knowledge no naturalist had accompanied a British ship on so long a voyage. Would he, as a naturalist, be considered, as his father had origi-nally suspected, merely an idler who pursued beetles? It was harrowing, actually his first such bout of introspection. He had had no such fears or doubts at nine when he entered the Shrewsbury Royal Free Grammar School, or at sixteen the University of Edinburgh, or at nineteen Christ's College in Cambridge. Yet he knew that he would not go out of his way aboard the *Beagle* to please, mollify, truckle; take pains to show that he was really a likable fellow! The answers must fall on his head as naturally as the warm sunshine or the cold rain.

The officers of H.M.S. *Beagle* were in their undress uniforms, with gold lace binders on their shoulders for epaulets and white summer trousers. Captain FitzRoy chronicled:

"John Wickham, a first lieutenant, is the executive officer who sails the ship. Master Edward Chaffers controls our navigation. Everyone has a superior to whom he reports. I run the scientific surveys; I deter-mine where we go next, and how long we stay in any one place to com-plete our surveying."

Charles studied his future shipmates. John Wickham was middle-sized, lean and lithe, suffering a red summer sunburn. He did not exert authority; he exuded it. John Wickham had had no formal education, but he was well read and had taught himself Spanish so that he could, when necessary, represent Captain FitzRoy to the officials of South America. The captain was God, upon whom mere mortal dared not cast an eye. Wickham was next in line; his orders were carried out quickly and effectively, because he knew more about the ship and how to sail it than anyone else on board. His agate-blue eyes held intense powers of penetration.

"Mr. Wickham, this is Charles Darwin. He's coming along as our naturalist."

"Welcome aboard, Mr. Darwin. We'll try to give you a smooth ride."

"Thank you, Mr. Wickham. Is Tierra del Fuego as bad as I've heard?"

"Worse. But we'll get you through with a whole skin."

As they moved aft, FitzRoy commented:

"He signed on as mate of the *Adventure* during its first expedition, but made lieutenant within a year."

Captain FitzRoy next introduced Bartholomew James Sulivan, a sec-ond lieutenant, two years younger than Charles, who had graduated with full marks from the Royal Naval College. His first year at the college had been FitzRoy's last but the two had become friends. Sulivan had served on H.M.S. *Beagle* for a while during its first expedition, and FitzRoy had specifically asked for him as his second lieutenant for this journey.

Sulivan was a good-looking man with rich dark hair, a high forehead, dark eyes, a broad prominently boned face and a tight-set mouth which belied his loquacious nature. He had been born on the banks of Falmouth Harbor, the son of a Royal Navy commander, and so was destined for the sea. Even at the age of twenty he wore his epaulet easily, a good-natured, openhearted chap who loved his life in the Navy and fully intended to become an admiral. Everyone agreed that Sulivan "takes the palm for talk." In addition to his extraordinary talents as a sailor, he had the capacity to give and receive friendship. He greeted Charles with a booming heartiness. His first quip was:

"Never thought I'd get to meet the grandson of Dr. Erasmus Darwin. Remarkable man, and a great medical writer. I've read the *Botanic Garden* twice over! My father used to read me your grandfather's doggerel when I was a boy:

> "Oh mortal man that liv'st by bread!
> What makes thy nose to look so red?
> 'Tis Burton Ale, so strong and stale,
> That keeps my nose from growing pale.

"But my favorite, more serious verse, is the one where he writes about fire and earth and 'the vast concave of exterior sky.' "

It was in the sick bay that he met the man who was to become one of his most loyal friends during the voyage: twenty-eight-year-old Benjamin Bynoe, six years older than Charles though he hardly looked it. He had been born in Barbados of English parents and been sent back to England for his education. He obtained his medical diploma in March of 1825, joined the Medical Reserve Corps and had the good fortune to be assigned to H.M.S. *Beagle* as assistant surgeon. When Captain FitzRoy was appointed commander of H.M.S. *Beagle* in 1828, the two men became friends. Simultaneously with H.M.S. *Beagle*'s being commissioned for its second voyage in July 1831, Benjamin Bynoe passed his final examinations and was expected to be named chief surgeon for the voyage.

He was light-complected, with friendly smoke-gray eyes and a gentle nature. He underwent, however, a complete metamorphosis when attending to an ill or injured officer or crew member in sick bay. He was famous for having shouted at a sick seaman:

"You may want to die, you idiot, but I won't let you. Think how bad it would look on my record! So, dammit, I'm going to keep you alive whether you like it or not!"

He was a "no-relapse" man; before he released a sailor he had to be sure he could climb to the top of the mainmast.

The Admiralty for some inexplicable reason appointed Dr. Robert J. McCormick as chief surgeon for this second voyage. Benjamin Bynoe became McCormick's assistant. He took the matter philosophically.

"It's only a question of time," he observed. "I respect McCormick. He handles the crew with care and knowledge. The only patient he can't do anything for is himself. He loathes the tropics and the heat. They make him ill, whether physically or mentally, I don't know. The Admiralty knew he was invalided home twice before from the West Indies. Why would they deliberately send him out again into personal adversity?"

Captain FitzRoy next took Charles to the top deck where the yawl would be fastened, as well as two twenty-eight-foot whaleboats on skids toward the stern. Then he led him to the poop cabin, behind the wheel, which read ENGLAND EXPECTS THAT EVERY MAN WILL DO HIS DUTY.

"The advantage of the poop cabin for you," FitzRoy explained, "is that you enter it directly from this top deck and you have three large skywells for light, the same as I have, except that I'm on the lower deck and on the water line. The only disadvantage of your quarters is that you're at the very stern where you will feel more motion. You'll get used to that."

"Do all sailors?"

"No, frankly. Even our redoubtable Wickham gets seasick in smaller boats."

When Charles walked through the door of the poop cabin he fairly gasped in astonishment, then paced the room's length and breadth. It was a little over eleven feet wide, part of it used up by bookcases, now empty, instrument shelves and banks of drawers. In the center were markings for the map table, which was to be six and a half feet wide and four and a half feet long.

"That leaves two feet on either side of the table," Charles exclaimed.

"Three feet at its widest point, two at its narrowest," FitzRoy replied. "You can count on two feet of walking space around the map table. We'll sling your hammock in this corner, near your drawers. Stokes, who will be working at the map table most of the day, will sling his hammock catercorner from you. You'll both be sleeping over the chart table, but with a full two feet between your head and the top deck. A midshipman by the name of Philip King will also share the use of the table. I can imagine the poop cabin seems small to a landsman."

Charles managed to murmur:

"I'll make the best of it."

"I felt you would. I was offered a larger vessel but took this one because of its proven excellence in handling and safety in the most treacherous of storms. Size is not the ultimate desideratum. A ship's safety depends first on the soundness of its structure, then on the knowledge of its officers and the skill of the crew. Do you still want to sign on?"

"Yes, Captain. My spirits about the voyage are like a tide running in favor of it; but it does so by a number of little waves which represent all the doubts and hopes that are continually changing in my mind. Please forgive such a highly wrought simile."

Captain FitzRoy smiled, his lean dark face sympathetic.

"Let's find our other officers. They would not do for the Court of St. James's, but they're a fine group. . . ."


5.


Settled back at 17 Spring Gardens four days later, on September 17, he wrote to Susan:

> What wonderful quick traveling the coach is. I came from
> Plymouth, 250 miles in 24 hours.

There was a letter from Professor Henslow inviting him to stop in Cambridge on his way home from London. Charles replied:

> . . . I will most gratefully accept it in every point but one,
> viz sleeping at your house. I shall arrive in the middle of the
> night by the *Mail*, & after 2 or 3 days shall start *very* early in
> the morning to Birmingham. Will you be kind enough to
> order a bed for me at the Hoops'. . . .

The two men walked into town to buy Charles a reliable rain gauge. When a search of the shops failed to turn up a proper iron net for shells, Henslow offered to have one made and send it down to Plymouth. He also sketched the dimensions and shapes of bottles needed for fish and marine life, which Charles could find in London.

Charles reported that Captain Beaufort had suggested that his collection be sent to the Admiralty.

"Send them to Falmouth," advised Henslow. "Most of our ships coming in from long voyages stop there first. I will ask my scientist friends in London if they will store the boxes of materials."

"My father has offered to send checks to those who pay the freight."

The following afternoon Henslow walked with him to the stable of the Hoop Hotel. Charles had arranged to rent a post chaise which he would drive to St. Albans, where he would stay the night on his way to Shrewsbury.

"My dear Darwin," Henslow declared, "I'm going to saddle you with one piece of avuncular advice. I exhort you sincerely and affectionately never to feel offended at any of the coarse or vulgar behavior you will infallibly be subjected to among your comrades. Take St. James's advice and bridle your tongue."

When they had to say good-by, Charles reached down from the carriage seat, took the professor's hand firmly in his own.

"I cannot say farewell without telling you how cordially I feel grateful for the kindness you have shown me during my Cambridge life. Much of the pleasure and utility which I may have derived from it is owing to you."

The next morning he caught the *Wonder* coach for Shrewsbury, crossed the Welsh Bridge and one uphill climb later entered the bottom of The Mount's gardens. His sisters were waiting for him. They had been raised in amateur dramatics, played not only for family and friends around Shropshire but sometimes for holidays in Shrewsbury. They fell into a light comedy called "Nobody's Going Away."

His aging nanny, Nancy, had sewn him a dozen white shirts.

"What else can I do for you, Mr. Charles?" she asked.

"Could you embroider the name DARWIN on the cuffs so they won't be lost in the laundry?"

Edward had been bargaining with Clemson, the local gunsmith, to secure the extra parts Charles needed for his old guns: two spare hammers, two main springs, four nipples or plugs for each barrel.

When Dr. Darwin came home from his rounds he embraced his son and, refraining from his monologue, wanted to hear about Captain FitzRoy and the ship.

"I take satisfaction from all you've told me, Charles. The officers sound like a good set."

"They've all sailed with Captain FitzRoy before."

Then he broke the news that the voyage of H.M.S. *Beagle* was extended from two years to three. Dr. Darwin's face paled for an instant, but he said nothing. Could he be thinking that he was sixty-five and might not live to see his son again? He managed a wan smile. The Darwin sisters swallowed hard but were silent.

After dinner a letter from Professor Sedgwick was delivered. Charles had written to him asking what books to take along.

Sedgwick replied:

. . . I cannot but be glad at your appointment & I truly hope it will be a source of happiness & honor to you. I really don't know what to say about books. No. 1 is Daubeny's A *Description of Active and Extinct Volcanoes*. I don't think Blakewell's *Introduction to Geology* a bad book for a beginner. For fossil shells, what is to be dône? Go to the Geological Society and introduce yourself to W. Lonsdale as my friend & fellow traveller & he will counsel you. Humboldt's personal narrative you will of course get. He will at least show the right spirit with which a man should set to work. Study the Geological Socys. collection as well as you can & pay them back with specimens. I am to propose you for membership when the meetings begin. . . .

Dr. Darwin took a hard look at his son, asked:

"How old are the members of the Geological Society?"

"They would start at about forty, I should imagine."

"And Dr. Sedgwick is proposing that they take you in at twenty-two?"

Later that evening he invited his son to accompany him into the library. The room was alight with several oil lamps under green glass shades. Robert Darwin made port in another of the huge armchairs he had had constructed to his dimensions in Shrewsbury. Charles pulled up a footstool in front of him.

"Charles, I wouldn't want you to go away feeling that I reacted too harshly that first morning to your opportunity to sail round the world. My feelings had more to do with Erasmus than with you."

"Ras? How does he come into it?"

"It's more than three years now since Erasmus graduated from Christ's. He hasn't done a spittle of work since, certainly not in the medicine he was trained to practice. I approved of his grand tour of Europe before settling down but he doesn't come home any more, or write to us. I think he's afraid of facing me with his future because I doubt that he has any! I think he means to drift, idle would be the more proper term, and never work at all. The Darwins have been hardworking yeomen with some few wealthy landowners mixed in since 1500. To the best of my knowledge we have never had a man who spent his life pouring water into a sieve or whistling jigs to a millstone. The thought that Erasmus will do nothing with his life galls me. When I thought I saw you drifting away to lotus land in the tropics . . ."

Charles was deeply moved by his father's distress.

"Please don't worry about me, Father. I shall never be an idler. I know I have been rather extravagant at Cambridge, but I should be deuced clever to spend more than my allowance whilst on board the ship."

"But they tell me you are very clever." Dr. Darwin's face broke into a wide grin. Then, seeing his youngest son flinch, he added, "I want to talk to you seriously about money. Charles, I'm sure you gathered from allusions I have made that I will leave you property enough to live on in some comfort. What I want you to know is that your inheritance will not come from me alone. Half of it will come from your mother's estate."

"How is that, Father?"

"Josiah Wedgwood willed his daughter twenty-five thousand pounds to serve as her dowry, in addition to twenty shares in the Monmouthshire Canal which he had built to bring in bargeloads of his clays, and on which to ship out his finished bone china and porcelains. I invested your mother's money carefully, I might even say shrewdly, in railroads, canals and Consols. But more particularly in mortgages on landed property. In the thirty-five years since our marriage, your mother's *dot* has more than trebled. I've kept her accounts separate all these years, first because I never needed the money and, secondly, because I felt that I held it in trust for her children. My father left me twenty-five thousand pounds and, combining that with the income from my practice, all of it invested in a steady ten per cent return, I needed nothing more."

Charles did not know how he was expected to respond.

"Until I earn my own competence, I shall hold down my expenditures as best I can. I would like to thank you . . ."

". . . no . . . no. If you wish to express gratitude go to church and pray for your dear mother's immortal soul."

He rose early and had the stableboy saddle his horse for the twenty-mile ride northwest to Woodhouse, the Owen family estate. The Owen family, which ran sheep and cattle most profitably, was one of the oldest in Shropshire. The estate was composed of nine separate farms bought over a century with a fortune made from their wool exchange in Market Square in Shrewsbury, and one very large area of hilly forest with some of the best shooting in Shropshire. The Darwins and Owens had been close friends ever since Charles could remember. William Owen rarely failed to visit with several of his nine children, to stay at what they called the Darwin Hotel for Hunt Week. Dr. Darwin not only took care of the Owens' medical problems, but the Darwin children visited Woodhouse for weeks at a time.

There were two attractions at Woodhouse for Charles. One was the shooting each autumn in the Forest, as the Owen children called the estate. The second was the equally irresistible, adorable Fanny Owen, of whom Charles was enamored. Fanny hunted with him and when he brought down his quarry exclaimed:

"Charles, you have become an undeniable shot."

Charles kept an exact record of every bird he shot throughout the season. His companions found this meticulousness odd and amusing. Two years before, when shooting with several of the Owens and their cousin, Major Hill, he had found that every time he fired and thought he had killed a bird one of the group cried out:

"You must not count that bird, for I fired at the same time."

The gamekeeper backed them up. After some hours they revealed their joke. Charles had not been amused. He had shot at a large number of birds but did not know how many he had hit and could not add them to the account, which he kept by making a knot in a piece of string tied to a buttonhole of his jacket.

Charles's sister Katty had earlier remarked to him:

"I never saw such a charming girl altogether as Fanny is."

Charles had written to Fanny frequently while at Cambridge, wanting her to know about his activities and to keep himself vividly alive in her mind. She was a negligent correspondent. Yet she always begged his forgiveness, saying that she trembled at having the boldness to begin a letter to him after having left his last "effusion" so long unanswered.

Much later, after she had received a newsy letter from him, at Cambridge, she confessed that she was reproaching herself bitterly for having delayed so long in sending him an effusion.

In a return confidence to Katty, he said:

"Fanny, as all the world knows, is the prettiest, plumpest, most charming personage that Shropshire possesses."

Riding the twenty miles through some of the finest farmland in England, he thought:

"Fanny is a lot more than that. She is fun-loving, affectionate, and always the belle of the ball. She lives her life the way children play with jam around their mouths after wolfing bread with strawberry spread."

He knew by all the signs that Fanny was fond of him. When he had failed to visit Woodhouse during the Christmas season of 1829, she had been hurt, demanding to know why he had not come home for Christmas. She confessed that she had fully expected to see him; then pulled his leg by supposing that some "dear little beetles" in Cambridge had kept him away.

Was there a touch of jealousy in that reference? He hoped so!

There were other, more important signs. Each year when the strawberries came ripe he would go to Woodhouse for a week. He and Fanny would lie full length upon the strawberry beds, grazing by the hour, exchanging kisses with their mouths stained red.

She was a great sport and companion, riding hard and fast with him through the countryside; a wild one in her fox hunting.

"Riding with the hounds is my idea of bliss on earth," she exclaimed. "It is such exquisite fun galloping on the Downs as hard as one can go."

Only the year before, she had used his rifle just for the change. When she fired he saw the gun recoil and the butt hit her shoulder. Fanny laughed it off, but at that night's party, for every night was a party night at Woodhouse, they were standing in a window bow between waltzes, when her blue and yellow muslin slipped off her shoulder exposing a large black and blue bruise.

All three Darwin girls visited Woodhouse and had wonderfully bright times at the dinners and balls. However when they began to sense that the growing relationship could turn serious, there developed a subtle opposition. Fanny felt it strongly. At the end of a long letter she suggested that she had better put the pages into a well-sealed envelope, for she knew that sisters had a tendency to peep; and she hoped to keep their relationship a mystery.

If her wording was a little florid, Charles appreciated her tact. At the bottom of each letter she wrote: "Burn this." She did not want the proprieties challenged if anyone should learn that she was corresponding with Mr. Charles Darwin. When Charles protested that family friends could correspond, and that there was nothing in any of their letters that was intimate, she replied that she hoped their messages to each other would not reach other ears.

From a distance he could see Woodhouse sitting majestically on a knoll, looking rather like a French château, a two-story earth-yellow brick house with high Gothic pillars to create an imposing vestibule for the massive front door. There were tall banks of windows in the front and the back, with espaliered trees covering the brick like a dark green carpeting. No one had ever counted the number of rooms in Woodhouse; but with nine children and gregarious parents, there was rarely an unused bed. To Charles it was a third home, along with The Mount and Maer Hall.

A stableboy took his horse, a butler ushered Charles into the lavishly furnished Regency drawing room with striped wallpaper in varying shades of green, bow windows with gold satin draperies held back with green cords and tassels; glass chandelier, circular mahogany table, writing cabinet, rosewood teapoy and portraits on the walls.

Fanny Owen was stretched out on a sofa reading a light romance from a Shrewsbury reading club. Charles gazed at her appreciatively. She had honey-colored hair which was turned to spun gold by the sunshine coming in from one of the bows, and was worn long and loose, counter to the current fashion of curled hair piled on top of the head. She had marvelously rounded shoulders, a flat stomach, modest hips and long slim legs outlined under her poplin dress of yellow-gold to match her hair and trimmed in blue to accentuate her eyes. It was her eyes, large, widely spaced and sea blue, and the flawless skin framing her features that had the men of Shropshire pursuing her.

Fanny glanced up, ran to Charles, kissed him.

"My dear Postillion. Welcome to the Forest. Life is so exile here with nothing to do but read novels! I'm quite ashamed of being so troublesome to you, but good-natured people do get imposed upon. Did you bring my bottle of asphaltum? I can't finish my dairymaid painting unless I have that color. Father keeps me hard at work on that odious picture. And I'm so happy that you came, despite all the sisterhood could say or do to prevent you. Tomorrow night we shall have a party in your honor."

Charles squirmed, but he had not much room with Fanny's arms about him. He did not like his sisters being accused of anything.

"Yes, my dear Housemaid, I have the oil color. Also the half dozen small brushes you asked for."

"And did you bring me a juicy book of some kind, anything you could purloin?"

"Nothing quite as juicy as you like. A copy of Walter Scott's *Antiquary* off my bedroom shelves."

"Now, pray tell me some Shrewsbury scandal," she demanded.

Charles's news was simple: he was leaving for a three-year voyage around the world! He had come to say good-by. But he found that he could not bring himself to talk about it. He would tell them tomorrow, after the party. He racked his memory for stories, for he was not a collector of gossip. There had been a quarrel between Dr. Dugard and Mr. Hill, Dr. Dugard declaring Mr. Hill promised him a certain sum, a thousand pounds a year, if he brought the marriage to bear between Sir Rowland and Miss Clegg. John Price, one of Susan's numerous suitors, had reproached her for writing on only one side of the note paper when obliged to send him a message for her father. Susan was furious at his impertinence. . . .

William Owen came into the room. He was known as a "peppery and despotic squire of the old school." He wore gray metal spectacles which matched the gray in his thick tousled hair. Though he had five grown sons of his own, he felt somewhat as Josiah Wedgwood did toward Charles: a bright, pleasant, amiable young "nephew" who gave him much pleasure and no pain. It was a genuine friendship.

"The game is running, Charles. The shooting is best in the early hours."

"May I come too, Governor?" Fanny asked.

"No. I'm going to have a male morning for a change," Owen replied. "With all five of you girls underfoot all day I feel as though I live in a convent."

Fanny said to Charles:

"The Governor's nose is out of joint because of what happened to him last night. Papa, may I tell the story on you?"

She had preserved a certain childlike affectation of mispronouncing words for comic effect: leetle for little, hagitation for agitation, horreed for horrid. How she had evolved her nicknames for the two of them, Postillion, or courier, for him, and Housemaid for herself, Charles had never known . . . unless it was satire, for he never led in anything except in collecting toads in the Fens outside Cambridge, while Fanny was very little of a housemaid.

"Papa imagines he hears people walking around at night. He decided to trap them by piling a mass of crockery at the head of the stairs. Hearing a noise late last night, he went out to catch the offender. Only he forgot about his trap and sent himself and the crockery flying downstairs!"

Charles laughed. It was a typical roistering Owen story.

"There's a new carriage in the stable, Charles, and a couple of matched grays. Take Fanny for a drive."

Fanny sat with her arm linked through his while he held the reins on the horses.

"How are you getting on with your countless beaux, Fanny?"

"Mostly frightful, as so few of them dance. They also drink too much and get elevated. I suppose the fault is mine. I can never see an empty glass but that I fill it. At tomorrow's party I must be a leetle careful, as I have happrehensions. Oh, not about you, my dearest Postillion. You give us more joyful effusions sober than those other shootables drunk."

"I'm the best waltzer you know, as well."

She squeezed his arm in affirmation, snuggled closer.

"It's a puzzle how to dine twenty-nine. But I want you next to me, so I'll perform a leetle trickery when I hand you your ticket out of the basket."

He leaned over, kissed her cheek, smooth to his lips and freshened by a slight scent of cologne.

"Fanny, you're irrepressible!"

She gave him a shrewd, sideward look.

"I don't ever intend to be repressed!"

The next morning he came down to the dining room, its table

brightly laid with a bowl of red and yellow dahlias, to find the entire Owen family assembled. He joined them at the sideboard laden with porridge, haddock baked in milk, boiled eggs and masses of warm golden toast. While the housemaids poured the coffee, he proceeded to relate the letters from Peacock and Henslow, his interviews with Captains FitzRoy and Beaufort, his trip to Plymouth and view of H.M.S. *Beagle*, and concluded with the news that he would be absent for three years.

There was a silence, then the men cheered; Mrs. Owen was patently frightened, Fanny gazed at him in consternation.

6.

He had been home only a couple of days when he became uneasy, then anxious. He admitted that there was an element of worry about the long separation from his family and friends, but there was something more . . . Fanny Owen.

"I've never fully admitted it before, but what I feel for Fanny is love. I'm convinced she feels the same about me. . . . But what am I thinking? There's no way Fanny could be contained in a quiet country parsonage. If she didn't have five 'blowouts' a week . . . if she had not high society to fit into, she'd be miserable."

He had had a wonderful time at the Owens' party; he and Fanny had made each other happy all evening. But when he left in the morning he had not had the courage to ask for a commitment, even an indication that she would wait for him.

"Now I'm nowhere," he murmured to himself, "up in a balloon, drifting out to sea. For a deuced long time!"

He simply had to go back to Woodhouse, if only for an hour or two.

His father had just bought a stupendous horse from Mr. Wynne, the trader, the largest Shropshire animal offered, standing over eighteen hands high. Charles secured permission to ride him to Woodhouse; he was a strong, fast brute who would cut old Dobbin's time in half. His father was not concerned that he was returning to the Forest so soon, but what Fanny called the sisterhood pursed their lips in disapproval.

He rode at a brisk pace through the quiet of the Sunday morning. Charles found William Owen in his office at the back of Woodhouse toting up the wool shorn from his lambs. He looked over the metal rims of his spectacles, saw who it was and sprang up.

"Charles, how good of you to make another visit before you sail. Sarah has good news. That eternal never-to-be-ended Edward Williams affair has finally culminated. He asked her to marry him and she accepted."

"And where is our effervescent Fanny?"

"Gone traveling with friends for a few weeks. Offer came up suddenly. I couldn't deny her."

Charles was crushed. He had counted on seeing her. He stood staring sightlessly over the dying flower beds, tears smarting behind his eyes. He had been a fool not to have spoken to her when he was here.

The older man crossed to him, put an arm on his shoulder.

"Charles, I've never made a secret of the fact that I've been very happy watching you and Fanny together."

"It's a bad omen, missing her this way." He rubbed an index finger under each eye. "I will be gone a very long time."

"You'll be exchanging letters. I know she is more fond of you than of any other man. If you choose, you can leave a message with me."

Sarah Owen came into the room. Charles gave her a bear hug of congratulations. Plain-looking, plain-speaking Sarah had been his friend over the years.

"Father, could I borrow Charles for a walk?"

"Be back in time for a sherry. I have a favor to ask of him."

The sun was warm on their faces. Several rambunctious bulls who did not appreciate the intrusion tried to charge them through the fence.

"Tell me about your betrothal, Sarah."

"I've known for a long time that Edward loved me," she said. "He's trembled on the edge of proposing. What was he afraid of?"

"Marriage. Most men are. How did Fanny take it?"

"She's glad to have me out of the way. You know the tradition, younger sisters shouldn't marry before older ones. . . ."

He was stung.

"Is Fanny in so much of a hurry?"

Sarah stopped in the cool grove of elms.

"Now, Charles, you are not to worry about that. Fanny adores you. She said she wanted to make some pincushions for your cabin. She thought you might find them useful."

"So I would. Did she make them?"

"You know Fanny. The chance for this trip came along. . . . Now, what can I give you to take on the voyage so you won't forget us here at Woodhouse?"

"A lock of your hair," he grinned.

"Are you serious?"

"Always."

"Do you have a knife in your pocket?"

"Always."

"Then cut it off, right now. I'll have Mr. Baker, the silversmith, put it in a locket for you." She folded the lock into her handkerchief. "I don't know what Woodhouse will do without you for so long but I hope and trust we may both meet with success in our respective new careers. God bless you, my dear Charles."

"My dear Sarah, that sounds like an obituary. Do you know what favor your father wants to ask?"

"Yes. He wants you to recommend my brother Francis to go along on the *Beagle* as a midshipman."

"I'll write to Captain FitzRoy immediately."

Riding home, Charles reasoned:

"With Francis aboard, the Owen family will be tied closely into the voyage; there will be mail from Woodhouse. The youngster, in turn, will write about the voyage, and probably about me as well."

His contact with Fanny would remain unbroken, as it had been during his years at Cambridge.

He received a cheery but disappointing letter from Captain FitzRoy.

> Devonport
> Sept. 23, 1831
>
> Dear Darwin,
>
> . . . I am sorry it is out of my power to take young Owen because the number of Mids allowed has been complete since the Vessel was commissioned. There is no chance of a vacancy. I would not have refused had I been able to oblige you.
>
> I have Beechey's *Voyage* but not Head's *Rapid Journeys Across the Pampas and Among the Andes*. You are of course welcome to take your Humboldt, as well as any other books you like, but I cannot consent to leaving mine behind; all my goods go with me. There will be plenty of room for books.

The dockyards were making such slow progress on the *Beagle* that Charles could remain away another week, if he wished. Since he was allowed to carry on board only one portmanteau, Caroline packed and repacked his case a dozen times in an effort to get in the most of his clothing: his best suit, along with waistcoat and cravat for social calls, and the polished boots to go with it; thick socks and a wool cap which she had knitted for cold weather; as well as woolen underwear that fitted from neck to ankle; several pairs of loose-fitting, wide-at-the-bottom trousers made of kerseymere and nankeen for the tropical waters; cotton and worsted stockings, several pairs of duck trousers and jean trousers, twenty-four handkerchiefs, Nancy's dozen shirts with DAR-WIN on the cuffs, twenty-four towels, four pillowcases, washing materials. His work boots and straw hat for warm weather he could buy in Plymouth.

At the end of a week she declared triumphantly:

"It's nothing short of a miracle! I'm getting twice as much into the compartments now than I did when I started."

Katty went walking with him while he collected and tried out the formulas from Henslow for preserving plants, flowers, insects. Her concern was not how much clothing could be packed into his traveling case but how much confidence could be stowed in his heart for a three-year journey around the world.

"Father is more proud of you than he likes to admit."

"I haven't done anything yet."

Her smile was a mirror image of Charles's.

"But you have, Charley. You've earned the friendship of Professors Henslow, Sedgwick, Peacock; and men in London such as FitzRoy and Beaufort, all of them older than you."

There remained only his good-bys at Maer.

As always, all complexities seemed to resolve themselves as he entered the grounds.

He found Josiah in the library delicately rubbing oil into some of his more precious leather-bound books.

"Ah, Charles! All goes well, I can see by your smiling countenance."

"Uncle Jos, you are my First Lord of the Admiralty."

"I always did want to go out on a naval expedition as a naturalist. I would have liked to go with Captain Philip King, in 1817, when he surveyed the coast of Australia and laid down a new route from Sydney to Torres Strait, inside the Barrier Reef. So you see Charles, I was not totally philanthropic when I rode to The Mount and persuaded your father to let you go."

Emma heard Charles's voice and came into the library, embraced him, then accompanied him upstairs to her mother's room.

"Can you have a picture painted of yourself as a sailor?" Aunt Bessy asked.

"Captain FitzRoy has engaged an experienced travel painter, Augustus Earle, nephew of a famous American painter. Perhaps I can get him to do a sketch of me."

"Will you be wearing a sword or a dirk?"

Charles was amused. "Now, Aunt Bessy, you've been reading too many romantic novels. The only weapon I'll carry is a scalpel."

Before dinner the Doveleys, Emma and Fanny, played and sang Goethe's "Veilchen," which the Wedgwoods considered to be a Mozart masterpiece. At the dinner table several of the Wedgwood sons and daughters collected to say good-by. Charlotte took him to her workroom where she had been making water-color sketches and pencil drawings of Maer.

"They're good, Charlotte! I wish I could draw. It would be such a help on the trip."

"For paying me that compliment, my dear Charles, I shall write to you often and give you all the news of Maer Hall."

Emma had the backgammon board set up in the living room. They had been playing animatedly for a number of years. She kept a small notebook in which she recorded their wins and losses. Half a dozen games later they stood on the front steps.

"Remember, Charles, write home as often as possible so we'll be able to follow your travels."

"I'll catch every packet carrying mail to England. I'm bound to be homesick sometimes. When I am, my mind will come back to Maer with love and gratitude."

"It's good to know we'll be in your mind. For you'll never be out of ours."

"Emma, have you heard from Ras?"

"No."

"He hasn't written to any of us."

"Then why should he write to Maer Hall?"

"Because we thought he had tender feelings toward you."

Emma was silent. It was a deep silence. She did not avoid Charles's eyes but her expression revealed nothing. Charles realized that, close as he and Emma had been as cousins and friends, he had no way to divine her thinking. It was equally apparent that Emma wanted no more of the discussion.

The first two days of October were his last two days at The Mount. His father and sisters tried to be casual as the hour for his departure approached but with no marked success. He himself had taken a two-hour walk along the familiar Severn in a depressed mood of farewell, as if to assure himself it would all be here on his return.

Katty observed:

"Charley, we all seem to be in the moods."

Charles nodded his head in agreement.

"My feelings are swinging like the pendulum on our grandfather clock. I keep repeating to myself that it is a grand and fortunate opportunity; there will be so many things to interest me: fine scenery and an endless occupation, joined to the grand requisite of there being a pleasant set of officers. Then again I must learn about navigation and meteorology, and get accustomed to the movement of the sea. I have moments of glorious enthusiasm, when I think of the date and cocoa trees, the palms and ferns, so lofty and beautiful, everything new, everything sublime."

"Everything cannot be sublime, my dear Tacitus," said practical-minded Caroline, calling him by an early nickname. "There will surely be some rough going."

"Of course," he conceded. "No man can live for any length of time without ups and downs. I've learned that about myself. For the first time actually. It is most painful when I think of leaving for so long a time so many people whom I love."

The hardest moment was that of his predawn departure. His father's driver had the yellow chaise ready and had already taken up his possessions. The family were in their long night robes. He embraced his three sisters, his father embraced him. Their eyes were proud and shining. But Edward closed the front door an instant too late, and Charles saw the misery of parting flood over their concerned faces.

The chaise went out of the circular drive, then downhill and across the Welsh Bridge to the Town Hall to meet the *Wonder* coach for London.

7.

The Romans, when they invaded England under Caesar in 54 B.C. and again during the reign of Claudius in A.D. 43 to conquer the Celtic tribes, had made the brilliant decision to create their capital and defense fort on this particular right-angle flow of the river Thames. Some of their brick defense walls and watchtowers were still standing. Yarrell loaned him a copy of a just-published *Topographical Dictionary of London*. This book in conjunction with a newly published map of the city gave Charles a reliable guide through the maze of heavily traveled streets, mews and squares to take care of his shopping and visiting needs.

He went directly to 17 Spring Gardens where he had stayed before. It was convenient . . . and lucky . . . for him. In his traveling bag was an inexpensive edition of Boswell. While eating breakfast the first morning he picked up the journal and read aloud to himself as an appreciative audience of one:

"I have often amused myself with thinking how different a place London is to different people. They, whose narrow minds are contracted to the consideration of some one particular pursuit, view it only through that medium. A politician thinks of it merely as the seat of government in its different departments; a grazier, as a vast market for cattle; a mercantile man as a place where a prodigious deal of business is done upon 'Change; a dramatick enthusiast as the grand scene of theatrical entertainments; a man of pleasure as an assemblage of taverns, and the great emporium for ladies of easy virtue. But the intellectual man is struck with it as comprehending the whole of human life in all its variety, the contemplation of which is inexhaustible."

To balance Boswell he turned to an observation William Cobbett had made only ten years before after a trip from his house near Kensington to ride the fifty miles to a town in Sussex. His journey had taken him through the southern outskirts of London, across Kennington Common, past the clusters of new houses at Stockwell and the stucco villas which lined one side of the long slope up Brixton Hill. For him the district between "London and Croydon is as ugly a bit of country as any in England." London itself was nothing but a great festering sore, an "infernal Wen," a "smoking and stinking WEN."

He would have twenty days to complete his purchases and preparations before he was obliged to leave for Plymouth on October 23. Using his map, he went first to the Apothecaries Hall on Water Lane. In the retail shop he bought the talcum powder Captain FitzRoy had requested, a can of Jewsbury and Brown's Oriental toothpaste, some arsenic to put on his lips and fingers if they should break out in blisters; Kayes Wordsdell's Pills, which claimed to cure indigestion, headache, dyspepsia, constipation, bile and nervousness. One of the crew members had asked him to find an unguent for his hair, so Charles bought some of Rowlands' Macassar oil.

He made no attempt to plot the quickest route through the city as he found himself enjoying the tumultuous life of the largest capital in the Western world. Going past him in the streets were brewers' drays with runners in place of wheels; sedan chairs carrying decorative ladies; omnibuses, stagecoaches; covered wagons in from the country with their products and produce; the traffic an undirected, shouting, sprawling, interlocked procession.

He could not help but observe that the young men affected dandyism. They walked delicately, wore high stocks set with jeweled pins, velvet collars, strapped trousers, white thread gloves and canes. They wore their hair long, flowing over their ears and coat collars, and shining in the sunlight. He could smell the bear grease from across the street. The thoroughfares were filled with itinerant merchants, the "criers" of London, selling the small things that were beneath the dignity of shopkeepers to sell: bootlaces, stays, needles, thread, pins, lavender, fresh water, cherries, slippers, matches, salt. Then there were the craftsmen: chair menders, knife grinders, carpenters.

Mixed in with the medley of the criers were the ballad singers and musicians, grating organs, Panpipes, vocalists singing operatic arias for coppers, since the theaters and inns were unappreciative of their talents.

His next two needs were a stout pair of hiking boots, which the bootmaker Howell cut precisely to his measure; as did Hamilton and Kimpton, tailors on the Strand, who recommended for his warm winter sea coat a dark blue woolen cloth, measured to fit his shoulders and six-foot frame.

Walking through the city, he found himself torn between the reactions of Boswell and Cobbett. He loved the theater. At the Royal, in the Haymarket, he saw two excellent performances: on Wednesday, *Macbeth*, and on Friday, in almost the same seat, he heard *The Barber of Seville*. What bothered him most was the flow of funeral processions on foot through the streets; the churchyards where skeletons, skulls and bones had been washed up by heavy rains and left to lie about caked in the mud.

He called on his distant relative, the highly favored society doctor, Henry Holland, on Brook Street near Grosvenor Square, who asked what had transpired since their tea together at Maer Hall, then seemed thoroughly disinterested, preferring to talk of himself.

"Charles, the family doesn't know this yet, but I'm courting the daughter of Sydney Smith, our witty and brilliant divine. She seems to like me."

"I'm impelled to ask: do you love her?" Charles responded.

"I don't know . . . yet. . . . Love at thirty-four, when I married my first wife, is different from love at forty-two, when I have four children and a wife only one year dead."

"I understand."

"Did you also understand, when you saw me at Maer Hall, that I had fallen completely in love with Charlotte Wedgwood? I told her my intentions were serious. She replied: 'I esteem you and like you, Dr. Holland, and I think you would really be an affectionate husband. But I will not have you.' Isn't that sad?"

Late one afternoon there was a knock on the door to his chambers.

"Mr. Charles Darwin?"

"The same."

"I have a message for you from Captain FitzRoy. H.M.S. *Beagle's* departure has been delayed again, until November 4."

Charles groaned.

"I too dislike the waiting. By the by, I'm Augustus Earle, engaged by Captain FitzRoy to paint us around the world."

"I suspected as much. You somehow look like a painter. Come in. My landlady is about to serve tea."

"I accept with pleasure. As a calling card I've brought you a printer's proof of my new book."

Charles read the title, A Narrative of a Nine Months' Residence in New Zealand, skittered through several pages. Earle wrote well. Over the top of the book he made a quick study of the painter's face and presence. Though he was already thirty-eight, he had a boyish, almost naïve, clean-shaven, unmarked skin and thick black eyebrows. He wore the wide loose trousers of the sailor, no waistcoat, an ample expanse of rumpled white shirt, scrubby shoes, a straggling black stock and a sailor's round hat with a wide brim.

Earle's father and brother were both professional painters, trained at the Royal Academy. Augustus was literally born into a studio. He had never wanted to work at anything else and had exhibited his first painting at the Royal Academy at the astonishing age of thirteen. When the Napoleonic Wars ended, he became an itinerant, sailing for such distant lands as Australia, Carthage, the Barbary States, Chile, India, painting not only the exotic landscapes but the life, economy and war preparations of the primitive people who took him in and found amusement in a grown man daubing colors on a piece of wood or canvas.

A housemaid brought in the robust tea which Earle set about consuming with a sharply honed appetite.

He had picked up a good education by osmosis and reading. His stories were related with the exuberance of a child, in particular his battle with the British missionaries among the Maoris. He had lived and painted with them, which shocked the missionaries so deeply they charged him with demoralizing the aborigines and organized a plan to drive him out.

"They accused me of being irreligious. Sheer rot! All the while I lived in Tristan da Cunha I read the Church of England service to that little community every Sunday morning. I believe in things divine, don't you?"

"Yes, I do. My invitation to join the Beagle took divine intervention."

Shortly after Earle left, an errand boy from Rodwell's Bookstore delivered a package. Upon opening it Charles was delighted to find a copy of Charles Lyell's Principles of Geology, a gift from Captain FitzRoy.

Henslow had written letters of recommendation for Charles to Robert Brown, the botanist; William Burchell, writer-traveler; to the presidents of the Geological and Zoological societies, as well as to the director of the British Museum; but he had failed to include a letter to Lyell. Charles knew that Henslow and Lyell had met when Lyell spent a week in Cambridge in 1826. Was it because he believed Lyell's excellent descriptions of the changes in the earth's crust but considered him staggeringly wrong in ascribing their causes?

Above all Charles wanted to meet Lyell, who at the age of thirty-three, after years of incorporating newly found facts from all over the world, had published what some few scientists, rising above the heat of battle over Lyell's conclusions, called "The authoritative text on geology." Back in 1795 a Scottish geologist, James Hutton, had published *Theory of the Earth*, in which he wrote: "The Scriptures are not to be taken as a textbook on geology or any other science," but Hutton's writing had been obscure and unreadable. Charles Lyell wrote magnificently.

Charles read voraciously until well past midnight. It was not difficult to perceive the basic reason for the rejection of Lyell by Henslow. Henslow measured geological time in a few thousand years, as the Bible did. Henslow's school believed that after God created the world and populated it, as so movingly portrayed in Genesis, He had grown dissatisfied with His creatures and had sent a catastrophe to destroy the earth and begin all over again. Charles Lyell attributed the geological processes and phenomena to forces operating continuously and uniformly over millions of years.

It was a revolutionary concept. While Adam Sedgwick had come part of the way to believe in a *succession* of sharp catastrophes, he would not accept the concept of a slow process controlled by natural forces rather than the hand of God.

It was past one in the morning when he blew out the lamp and lay motionless in the darkness of the room, attempting to assimilate the new theory he had gulped down. He recalled one of his Christ's College tutors telling him:

"Books are the final repositories. Of all that is good and all that is evil. All that is true and all that is false. All that is wisdom and all that is ignorance."

With a start he bounded up in bed. Why had Captain FitzRoy sent him that particular book? It was an unlikely gift, for Charles had heard rumors around London that FitzRoy was a religious zealot; that the main reason he had agreed to take Charles Darwin as naturalist was because Darwin had a planned career in the Church. He went to the windows overlooking the Admiralty and pushed back the curtains. Captain FitzRoy must know the nature of Lyell's book. There'd been enough controversy over it in the press. If he sent it to him, the rumors must not be true! He had not known FitzRoy long, but he had never heard him say, as Professor Henslow had, "I should be grieved if a single word of the Thirty-nine Articles were altered." In fact, he had never once heard him mention religion or the Church of England!

He climbed back into the bed, relieved.

"I am certainly not going out on the *Beagle* for three years with any preconceived notions, or to prove the validity or non-validity of the Scriptures. I'm going to observe and collect. The sea, the earth, the mountains, will reveal their truth to me. Captain FitzRoy and I will never quarrel about theology."

8.

He felt intense joy when he returned to his rooms from buying a medical kit, unrefined hemp fabric and indelible inks to find a letter from Fanny Owen. His fingers were unsteady as he opened the envelope.

> Exeter
> Oct. 6, 1831
>
> My dear Charles,
>     Our letters must have crossed in the mails. Yours I received a few days ago. It was written indeed in a *Blue* Devilish humor. I cannot bear to think, my dear Charles, that we are not to meet again for so long, three years you say. . . . But that you will enjoy yourself, I have not a doubt. To remind you of the time you are to be absent is nonsense & selfish. One last farewell I cannot resist sending you. . . .

She went on to say that she did not doubt he would find her in *status quo* at the Forest when he returned, and that there would never be a change in her opinion of him, or a forgetting of "the many happy hours we have had together. . . ."

He folded the letter and slipped it between the pages of the Lyell book.

With most of his shopping completed, he started using his letters of introduction to the prominent men in the natural philosophies. Robert Brown, the famous British botanist, now an august fifty-eight, educated at the University of Edinburgh, in 1801 had been offered the post of naturalist to the expedition fitted out under Captain Matthew Flinders for the survey of the coasts of Australia. He had returned to England with nearly four thousand species of plants and was almost immediately appointed librarian of the Linnean Society, began publishing volumes on plant classification, and became famous in England for their accuracy.

He had an almost rectangular head, with a squared-out jaw as broad as his skull, and an outthrust underlip like that of a bulldog. It was a face with features scarcely designed to fit each other. Scant neck, broad shoulders and heavy chest; a heavy man with a deep voice and manner.

Robert Brown had turned the rear portion of his residence at the Linnean Society in Soho Square into a laboratory, tearing down two inside walls so that he had space for his long tables, thousands of specimens, microscope and other technical equipment, rather like a laboratory of the new London University that had recently opened on Gower Street near the British Museum.

Brown led Charles to one of the instrument-laden worktables and said:

"Have a look through this microscope and tell me what you see."

Charles looked carefully; he had been trained in the use of the microscope in Edinburgh, and by Henslow in Cambridge.

"It's a beautiful sight, Mr. Brown, but I can hardly name the elements I'm looking at."

"Try."

"I would say a viscous semi-fluid contained in a vegetable cell."

"Fairly good guess."

"Do tell me what I have seen."

"That is my secret."

"Why, Mr. Brown, I'm hardly more than a boy and I'm on the point of leaving England for three years. Are you afraid that I might steal your discovery?"

"Young Darwin, have you not heard that I am a miser? It happens to be true."

That shook Charles. He was silent for a moment.

"You do not like to spend money?"

"Money is of no great relevance. It's plants. In particular my dried plants and my discoveries. I am not planning to use them all, neither am I going to squander them."

On his frequent visits Robert Brown talked to Charles for hours, pouring out a magnificent knowledge of botany. Charles asked:

"Mr. Brown, why have you not published since your work in Latin on the flora of Australia in 1810?"

"I live in mortal dread of making a mistake. I can make a mistake here, with you, today, and I can correct it tomorrow or next week. But once in print, I am condemned to live with it. Print is a gallows; never get yourself into its noose, or you will regret it all the days of your life."

"Don't we have to print our observations and discoveries so others can learn through them? Cannot errors be corrected along the way? Full understanding is not vouchsafed to any one mortal. Each of us is allowed to discover a small part of the universe, and the human mind will ultimately put it all together."

"Romantic nonsense. I will die with all my information crammed inside my head. That's a very good place for it."

Charles went back to the bookshop to see his friend William Yarrell. The front of the shop was always busy at this early hour, for although Yarrell did not stock all eighty newspapers published in London, there were head-high stacks of the *Times, Morning Herald, Morning Advertiser, Morning Chronicle, Sun, Standard*; and just a few feet deeper into the shop, formidable piles of the weekly and monthly reviews and magazines: *Edinburgh*, the *Quarterly*, the *Westminster, Fraser*, the *Literary*, the *Athenaeum*, dozens more. Men on their way to work streamed in, buying several papers at sevenpence each, an expensive price. England was newspaper mad, now that the type face had been improved, and bought twenty-five million copies each year.

William Yarrell came forward, his eerily angled eyebrows stretched high with pleasure.

"A good day to you, sir," said Charles. "I'm wanting some books for the *Beagle*."

"Any title I fail to have in the shop I shall order and send to the *Beagle* as a gift as penance for my negligence."

Charles grinned.

"First I need *A Description of Active and Extinct Volcanoes* by Charles Daubeny. Adam Sedgwick recommends it. I'll need *A New General Atlas* by A. Arrowsmith; *An Introduction to Entomology; or Elements of the Natural History of Insects* by William Kirby in four volumes; *Travels in Chile and La Plata* by J. Miers in two volumes . . ."

One by one the books he wanted were placed in his hands.

"What else are you about to need?"

"A good lightweight mountain barometer to carry with me inland to ascertain the height of my ascent."

"Let's walk over to Covent Garden; either Garrick or Newgate Street is what we want. I know a shop where they make accurate barometers you can carry over the Andes. You *are* to cross the Andes . . . ?"

His next problem was how to get all his belongings to Plymouth, since he could carry only one traveling case on the stagecoach. He finally decided to ship his heavy possessions by steamer: the new boots, warm sea coat, microscope, mountain barometer, cans of medication, books.

Having delivered his boxes to the Puddle Dock, he made one last circuit of the scientific societies asking if they would take in his crates of specimens as he shipped them home, and store them in their copious cellars.

He followed Professor Sedgwick's stricture to visit William Lonsdale, curator and librarian of the Geological Society in Somerset House.

"Can we house your geological collection?" Lonsdale echoed. "How can one tell, my dear fellow, when we have no idea what you will send back? Come to see us when you get back."

At the British Museum on Great Russell Street in Bloomsbury, Charles Konig, the keeper of natural history, showed him around the former Montague House, a vast old converted palace.

"You can see the state we're in, Darwin. It'll take us at least another ten years to complete the renovations, let alone segregate the collections we already have."

The Marquis of Lansdowne, president of the Zoological Society at 33 Bruton Street, not far from Grosvenor Square, was also apologetic. However, when William Yarrell, who had helped found the organization five years earlier, proposed Charles as a corresponding member, he was accepted.

Charles was thrilled.

Even Captain Beaufort knew no way to help.

"We have no such storage space here in the Admiralty, Darwin. Nor do I know who would accept the responsibility. Have you nowhere else to turn?"

Yes. One! It was bound to come out at that. He should have known and not embarrassed the overburdened people in London.

He crossed the street, mounted the steps to his rooms, took out his writing folder.

> 17 Spring Gardens
> Tuesday 18 Oct. 1831

My dear Henslow,

I seize the opportunity of writing to you on the subject of consignment. I have talked to everybody: & you are my only recourse. If you will take charge, it will be doing me the greatest kindness. The land carriage to Cambridge will be as nothing compared to having some safe place to stow them; & what is more, having somebody to see that they are safe. I suppose plants and Bird skins are the only things that give trouble: but I know you will do what is proper for them. Will you give me as minute instructions about the directing as if you were writing to an Otaheite savage. About paying for them, I should think the best plan will be, after the arrival of one or two cases, to write to my Father, & he will place the sum to your account at any bank in Cambridge you may choose. I will write to him on the subject. . . .

> Believe me, my dear Henslow
> Your ever sincerely obliged
> Chas. Darwin

It was his last chore in London. He could now leave for Plymouth, and prepare to sail around the world.

# BOOK THREE

*"There Are No Mountains to Climb at Sea"*

1.

WHEN he stood on the same rise in Devonport where Captain FitzRoy had first shown him H.M.S. *Beagle*, he gasped in astonishment. The ugly duckling had become, in the thirty-eight days since he had last seen her, a beautiful swan. The structural work had been completed. He observed the stoutly planked hull, the raised upper deck, the bulkheads and towering masts, the higher chart room at the stern. The ship was small compared with the other ships moored in the dockyard but she had the elegance of symmetry. H.M.S. *Beagle* carried a small decorative figurehead of a beagle. There were three skylights, two of them had three windows each: one skylight was over the chart room; the second was over the captain's cabin; the third skylight over the larger gun room where the officers ate, had four windows on each side.

As he made his way down to her mooring dock he could make out the crew in a state of bustle, painting the fore part of the ship. When he went on board he found the carpenters fitting up drawers in the poop cabin and installing handsome mahogany panels in the officers' cabins and, wherever possible, in the officers' mess.

"How do you like our wreck now?"

It was Captain FitzRoy standing behind him, his lean, handsome face expressing amusement and gratification. Charles blushed.

"A most beautiful brig. Even a landsman such as myself must admire her."

"A brig has only two masts. However a third sail has been added in order to assist with steering. We think her the most perfect vessel turned out of the dockyard. She is structurally sound, my dear Darwin. Without that imperative, these rich mahogany panels might never make it back to England."

On his earlier trip Charles had visited the Clarence Baths on Richmond Walk, close to the waterfront, named after His Royal Highness the Duke of Clarence, who had officially dedicated the luxurious establishment the year before. Captain FitzRoy had moved into the officers' quarters just inside the protective wall of the dockyard. Charles elected to move his possessions into one of the six elegantly furnished lodging houses just above the area of the two large swimming baths, hot and cold showers, vapor room, private plunging and shampooing baths. Fresh sea water was pumped into the pools from the Atlantic through cast-iron pipes. Charles's house was advertised in the newspapers as "replete with conveniences" and so he found it, with a spacious, immaculately clean bedroom, sitting room and dining room overlooking a channel of the Hamoaze and, beyond it, the green opulence of rising Mount Edgcumbe. It was a cold, wet day, but after settling his books on the tables and shelves and placing his belongings in the drawers and cabinets, it was a reasonably comfortable place in which to await the sailing. Only a few steps away were the Baths' coffee and newsroom as well as a confectionery room. Close by were the taverns: the Course, the Hunt, the Regatta, as well as the Fountain Tavern and Thomas's Hotel, patronized largely by naval officers.

A few days later he was invited to join the "gun-room" officers in their commissary in the dockyard: Lieutenants Wickham and Sulivan; the master, Chaffers; Dr. Robert McCormick; Assistant Surgeon Benjamin Bynoe; George Rowlett, the purser. Augustus Earle had also been invited. The officers amused themselves by giving Charles a terrifying and boisterous account of what Neptune would do to him on crossing the equator for the first time. Though it was near the end of October, the day had turned up clear, with a freshening sea breeze. The men were in high spirits, for they were certain that once the ship's orders were received they would be ready to sail when the wind came out of the north to carry them south.

Charles enjoyed the comradery, mused:

"They are a fine set of fellows, if they are rather rough."

He was more concerned that their conversation was so full of slang and sea phrases that most of it was as unintelligible to him as Hebrew.

The time went by pleasantly though the weather was inconstant, not unlike North Wales: cold, intermittent rains, billows of fog, then bright sunlight. He spent almost every day on board the *Beagle*; his main task was to keep out of the way of the crew which, under the direction of the sailmaker, were threading through the sails the robust sheets by which they would be drawn aloft, held securely in place, and brought swiftly back to the deck in a moment of crisis. He roamed the ship, becoming familiar with its decks and quarter-decks. On the forecastle was a six-pound carronade. Close to the bulwark on each side of the waist were the "booms." Abaft were four brass guns, two nine-pound and two six-pound. Twenty-five-foot whaleboats hung from the *Beagle*'s quarter davits, while two twenty-eight-foot whaleboats were carried upon skids over the quarter-deck. Her largest boat, the yawl, was carried amidships, the cutter nesting in it, to save space. Astern was a dinghy.

He completed his shopping in Plymouth; bought nightcaps to keep his head warm while sleeping and a cape of India-rubber cloth with a pouch in one corner for carrying water.

His evenings too were occupied, for Plymouth, which prided itself on the beauty and defense security of its harbor, had also turned itself into one of the richer cultural centers of England. He attended the seven o'clock scientific lectures given at the Athenaeum, with its Doric four-columned portico overlooking Plymouth Sound, its excellent library and colorful lecture hall. He borrowed recently published books from the imposing Greek temple known as the Proprietary Library in Cornwall Street, went to services at St. Catherine's Church with its beautiful wood paneling, and took long walks through the city. Plymouth was booming with its vast fish trade and shipping, its iron foundries and manufactories of soap, cement, sailcloth, rope.

He found himself fortunate in his partner at the chart table and sharer of the poop cabin, nineteen-year-old John Lort Stokes from southwest Wales. Captain Philip King had watched the lad, who was only thirteen when appointed to the *Adventure-Beagle* expedition in 1825, and described him as a steady, plodding, old-fashioned fellow.

Charles and Stokes struck up a friendship, which was just as well, Charles told Captain FitzRoy, since they were going to share that poop cabin for a matter of years.

"You'll get along," FitzRoy replied calmly. "Stokes is my most constant ally on the *Beagle*. When we were commissioned for this second voyage I got him promoted to mate. I wrote to the Admiralty that 'his work appears to me to support my request that he be promoted to the post of assistant surveyor, particularly since it will involve no increase in pay.'" He shrugged his left shoulder, a gesture he used for lost causes. "Denied. Too young. But I made him my *unofficial* assistant surveyor. He's talented. You'll see. So will the Admiralty in time."

John Stokes had a bland, open face, good to look at because he had a pleasant nature. He was clean-shaven, with clear smoke-gray eyes, and a fine growth of rich black hair which he parted so precisely it might have been accomplished with a surveying instrument. He was of medium height, not yet filled out; had an unhurried voice, never intrusive or harsh, but with a soft Pembroke accent, and the steady hands of the born draftsman. When Charles asked if he had been badly disappointed when the Admiralty declined his promotion, saying: "You have the name, you should have the game," Stokes replied nonchalantly:

"My father used to say about good fortune: 'Never expected, never got it.' There's time. I expect to spend my whole life in the Navy and to be captain of the *Beagle* on one of her expeditions."

Charles laughed softly. "With that attitude, Stokes, you'll end up an admiral."

"Likely. Shall we go for a sail? I can requisition a small boat."

Thirteen-year-old Charles Musters was showing the first symptoms of homesickness so they took the boy along.

They landed at Millbrook, tied up the boat and set out down the west coast of Mount Edgcumbe, with its farmhouses and stone barns which looked as though they had been built at the time of the Crusades. The village squatted in a depression at the base of tall hills, with Mount Edgcumbe gazing imperiously down upon it. There was one narrow road, wide enough for a donkey and cart, with the plaster-over-ancient-stone houses hugging it, and only an occasional garden separating the inhabitants from the mountainous world. They passed a small parish church and cemetery as they left the town and began the twisting turns upward.

"I'm most alive when walking!" Charles cried with joy. "When my legs are devouring mountains, uphill or down, I feel a whole man."

Stokes grinned.

"There are no mountains to climb at sea. But wait until the *Beagle* starts climbing storm waves!"

They were now on a long steep drop down to Cawsand, a lovely village on Plymouth Sound, with high trees and prosperous houses. There were stone fortifications below them, and on either side fertile fields with grazing sheep. They ended in a little stone square just above the water and went into the Smugglers for a glass of ale.

"You're wrong, Johnny Stokes," Charles said; "there are mountains behind every port where the *Beagle* will dock. I intend to climb them all."

The next morning Stokes invited him to go along to the gardens of the Athenaeum.

"I'm going to prepare the astronomical house belonging to the *Beagle* for observations on the dip needle."

"What is a dip needle?"

"You have used a compass? Well, it's a compass too, very important to navigation. It has been known since the time of Gilbert, about 1600, that the earth acted like a large dipole magnet whose force has two components: a horizontal one, which is detected by the regular compass, and a vertical one, which is responded to by the dipping needle. At the magnetic equator the vertically suspended dip needle lies horizontally, and at the poles it stands vertically. It's the way the needle dips east or west that gives the navigator declination. Formerly the ship's captain had only his compass and the stars to steer by; now the dipole needle gives him his longitude and latitude. He can plot his location north and south, east and west in relation to the two poles and the equator.

"It's generally agreed that Plymouth is the geographic center of the world," Stokes added. "Once we establish a central time here, all ships at sea, by charting their location, can roughly approximate their time, and what time it is in this Athenaeum garden."

"When I am going through the Strait of Magellan, I'll be able to tell precisely when the 7:00 P.M. lecture starts here in the Athenaeum!"

"*Reductio ad absurdum*," cried Stokes. "I only had four years of school and I'm better trained than you are!"

"Different disciplines, me lad, different disciplines!"

His education was expanding daily.

On his frequent junkets to the commissioner's dinners with Captain FitzRoy, Charles had met and talked with Captain Philip Parker King, whose two-volume *Narrative of the Survey of the Intertropical and Western Coasts of Australia* Josiah Wedgwood had recommended at Maer Hall. Captain King took him aside and said:

"My fourteen-year-old son Philip is going out as a midshipman on the *Beagle*. This is not his first voyage. He was with the *Adventure*, serving as a volunteer for the whole five years. He was only nine when we started out but I was there to watch over him. I cannot ask any officer to keep an eye on him, that would be seeking special privilege. But since you are not a navy man, I can ask that favor of you. I would feel more secure if he had a friend on board."

"I will be pleased to do everything I can," Charles assured him. "I already have young Musters entrusted to my care. I'll take them out naturalizing."

Captain King's weather-beaten face relaxed into a paternally grateful smile.

"Thank you, my dear Darwin. In return, while the *Beagle* is in port let me teach you some of my hard-earned meteorology, how to use instruments to anticipate williwaws or whirlwinds, hurricane squalls, waterspouts; how to record the barometric pressure, dew point, strength of the wind, nature of precipitation. . . ."

Up to this point the great achievers in his life had been the scholars, Professors Henslow, Sedgwick . . . whose contributions to botany and geology were establishing them as exact sciences. Now he was meeting a different kind of man: the practical inventor and engineer. The first was Thunder-and-Lightning Harris, a forty-year-old native of Plymouth who had graduated from the medical school of the University of Edin-

128 "THERE ARE NO MOUNTAINS TO CLIMB AT SEA"

burgh, served as a militia surgeon, then returned home to enter general practice. Upon his marriage at the age of thirty-three, he had abandoned medicine to devote the rest of his life to harnessing electricity to man's manifold uses and had already published several articles on electricity in the learned journals. Charles met him at a dinner party at the Fountain Tavern and was immediately taken by the man's effervescent enthusiasm.

William Harris was in process of installing a lightning protection system on H.M.S. *Beagle*.

"Mr. Harris, would you be good enough to explain the techniques of controlling lightning?" Charles asked.

Harris's eyes and white teeth flashed brilliantly.

"We do not 'control' it, Mr. Darwin. More properly, we *ground* it."

"I understand how you do that on shore. But at sea?"

"Similarly. I am going to demonstrate at the Athenaeum on November 21 using an electric machine as a thundercloud, a tub of water as the sea, and toys for a line of battleships. My plan consists of plates of copper folding over each other, let into the masts and yards and connected to the water beneath. The advantage derives from the principle that the electric fluid is weakened by being transmitted over a large surface to such an extent that no effect is perceived even when the mast is struck by the lightning. The *Beagle* will be fitted with conductors on this plan. I am confident that over your three years you will hear plenty of thunder and see blinding flashes of lightning but will never lose a mast or a shipmate."

A second "doer" he met at the Athenaeum during a lecture. Sir John Rennie was the thirty-seven-year-old engineer who had just completed building the new London Bridge from plans drawn up by his father. Sir John was in process of rebuilding the huge breakwater which was to stretch across the entrance to Plymouth Sound, breaking the force of the storm waves roaring in from the English Channel and the North Atlantic. His father had begun dumping masses of limestone in 1812, and brought the breakwater above the water surface in one year. But the storm of 1817 and the hurricane of 1824 damaged the structure so severely that it had to be rebuilt . . . again the son completing his father's work, understanding better, perhaps, one generation later, that nature is more skilled in tearing down than man is in building up.

He was most friendly.

"I'll be working on the breakwater tomorrow morning, Mr. Darwin. If you can catch a ride, come on down and I'll show you what structural changes we are making."

Captain FitzRoy was going out in the commissioner's yacht and invited Charles to "tag along." When FitzRoy returned in the commissioner's boat from measuring the angles of the breakwater, Charles remained behind with Rennie on the wind-swept rocks watching work crews drop huge blocks of limestone from the Oreston quarries.

"Our first error," Sir John explained, "was to build a perpendicular embankment. We soon learned never to let the sea get at a perpendicular surface! In an angry mood it could toss the one-ton blocks around as though they were pebbles. The new breakwater will outwit the most violent sea. We are building it like the slanting roof of a house! The water will cascade off it."

Charles looked about him at the turbulence of the water and the jutting limestone arms of the embankment.

"You are very like Thunder-and-Lightning Harris," he exclaimed. "You're both out to prove that the brain of man can outwit the forces of nature."

"One word of warning, Mr. Darwin. It is unhappily not true that the brain of man can control all the forces of nature. There is one which the human brain cannot outwit or control."

"Which one is that, Sir John?"

"The human brain!"

### 2.

November 4, the sailing date Earle had brought to Charles in London, had come and gone. Aside from being restless, Charles found the officers and crew to be a congenial lot who got along quite well together, many of them having been shipmates on the Beagle's earlier voyage. The one exception, he was told, was Dr. Robert McCormick, a tactless curmudgeon except to the men who came to the sick bay for treatment. His patients were treated with good medicine and good humor. It was clear that his nose was out of joint. Charles Darwin he shrugged off as non-existent. Sulivan exclaimed:

"Worry not. The doctor is rarely happy unless he is quarreling. He must stay on the ship except for a few hours of leave now and then. He could do only a little collecting and make no inland explorations. You will get the whole job done."

A few days later Dr. McCormick invited Charles to join him for a walk on Mount Edgcumbe. From the doctor's comments on the flora and fauna as they climbed to the peak through the harvested fields, Charles saw that the man was well trained in natural philosophy. He was also obviously disturbed about something. At last he wheeled on Charles and demanded:

"Darwin, tell me honestly! You know my cabin. Do you think it should be painted a French gray or a dead white? There are advantages to each."

Charles was relieved.

"Have both," he answered lightly. "One wall gray, the other white."

"No, no! That would make me appear indecisive, and I'm anything but that! For example, I'm the lone soul who will say publicly that months have been dawdled away in fitting a small, ten-gun brig for sea."

"My dear Doctor," Charles exclaimed in alarm, "I hope you won't let that get back to Captain FitzRoy or Lieutenant Wickham. They would be hurt . . ."

". . . the truth never hurt anybody," McCormick interrupted. "Only a congestive state of the internal organs hurts. And I know how to cure that: a glass of quinine water, with the same quantity of citric acid in the port or sherry bottle. Our captain doesn't approve of wine drinking at sea. The more fool he! . . ."

Charles changed the subject.

"Tell me how you started as a boy to collect nests and eggs in the meadows around Yarmouth. . . ."

A few days later Charles came upon Captain FitzRoy scowling mightily, his face flushed.

"That impossible doctor of ours! I never wanted him in the first place. Ben Bynoe was acting surgeon on our first voyage, and a good one."

Charles grimaced; no need to ask what McCormick had done.

"McCormick has criticized me at the Athenaeum for wasting months in refitting. What am I to do with that infernal ass?"

It was a rhetorical question. FitzRoy expected no answer.

Sometimes it happens, not often, that two men meeting for the first time can see into each other's depth of mind, personality, character, and know that they can become friends. When they met, Charles and Benjamin Bynoe had hit it off at once. Bynoe was an easygoing man, as much interested in shooting, collecting and natural philosophy as Charles. He was six years older but hardly looked it, his face as smooth and unlined as a child's. Charles soon learned why; he did not know the meaning of such words as envy, spite, aggression.

Bynoe flashed him a white-toothed grin.

"Are you a betting man, Charles?"

"We played van john all through Christ's College."

"Vingt-et-un, eh? I'll bet you five bottles of Madeira against three that I'll be chief surgeon on this estimable tub before six months have passed."

One evening toward mid-November Captain FitzRoy asked Charles if he would like to drive over to the docks at the Barbican to gather up the three Fuegians whom FitzRoy had brought back to England on the prior voyage, and Mr. Matthews, the missionary who was going to accompany them and remain in Tierra del Fuego to set up a Christian settlement.

"Three Fuegians!" Charles exclaimed. "However did you come into possession of them?"

FitzRoy threw up his arms in a gesture which said, "I don't make anything happen; things happen to me. By the will of God, no doubt."

In March of 1830 he had sent a small group of men in their whaleboat to survey the inlet around Cape Desolation. When they left the whaleboat unprotected, it was stolen. FitzRoy had been so infuriated that he took a large armed group on shore with him to demand that the whaleboat be returned. All they could find was some of the boat's gear, part of a sail, an oar, an ax and the boat's tool bag. A violent fight ensued during which one Fuegian was killed, and a group of Fuegians, who had in their possession small parts of the whaleboat, were captured, including three children whose mothers had abandoned them. When they went out again the next day to search for the whaleboat all of the male prisoners escaped by swimming ashore. They left behind the children. Captain FitzRoy sent them back to their tribe, all except a plump nine-year-old girl who made it clear that she wished to remain. She was a smiling, attractive youngster and was kept as a hostage for the stolen boat. Very soon FitzRoy was teaching her English. He named her Fuegia Basket after the makeshift canoe which the stranded H.M.S. *Beagle* men had fashioned out of wickerwork covered with pieces of canvas and lined with clay to get them back to their ship.

Charles asked what they did about the whaleboat.

FitzRoy had on his proud smile.

"We found a quiet cove, Christmas Sound, where we built a new one."

Before leaving Cape Desolation they took as hostage a stout, sullen man whom they needed as an interpreter and guide. They named him York Minster after the promontory where they took him; it had been named York Minster by Captain Cook. Finding traces of the whaleboat in some of the wigwams of Christmas Sound, FitzRoy took another young man: Boat Memory, about twenty years old; and a few days later, while exploring the Beagle Channel, FitzRoy persuaded the resident tribe to put on board a stout boy whom they named Jemmy Button because they paid beads, buttons and other trifles for him.

When the expedition was ready to leave the Fuegian coast the four natives seemed so contented with their life on board ship that Captain

FitzRoy thought it might be a valuable idea to take them to live for a short time in England. One of the four, Boat Memory, died from a series of inoculations at the Royal Hospital in Plymouth. The other three were placed in a school affiliated with the Church Missionary Society in Walthamstow, just northeast of London. They had been taught well and were popular. The Queen had asked that Captain FitzRoy bring the girl, Fuegia Basket, to the Court of St. James's. Fuegia had had a fine haircut and wore an English dress. The Queen gave her one of her own bonnets to wear and also took a ring from her finger and put it on Fuegia's, in addition to a sum of money with which to buy clothing when she should leave England and return to her own country.

Now they were being returned to Tierra del Fuego to start farming and to build a missionary house. The Church Missionary Society hoped to convert the Fuegian tribes, one by one, to Christianity.

When the three Fuegians came down the gangplank Charles was amused that the men were dressed as proper English gentlemen with white collars up under their chins, wide black stocks around the collars, long English coats with wide lapels, creased strap trousers and shined shoes. The girl had her dark hair cut short and brushed forward to cover half her ears and brow. Though her nose and mouth were fleshy, she had large and expressive dark eyes. The minister's wife at the school had dressed her well in a simple wool frock buttoned down the front. She and Jemmy were attractive, with their smooth copper-colored skin. York seemed formidable: he had strong animal passions, was self-willed and determined, and at the same time reserved and suspicious. All three shared normal speaking voices three times the power of an English voice. It had taken months of patient coaching to bring them down to a polite murmur.

The purser of the steamboat which had brought them to Plymouth came down the gangplank.

"Captain FitzRoy, we have simply dozens of boxes and crates of paraphernalia for the Fuegians and for Mr. Matthews. I would say enough to build and furnish several houses."

"That's the generosity of the members of the Church Missionary Society," FitzRoy responded. "They want to be represented in Tierra del Fuego, and help to civilize the savages. I'll send some navy wagons over in the morning."

Where to sleep the Fuegians was a serious problem. Captain FitzRoy ordered that the storeroom next to Benjamin Bynoe's cabin be cleared for Fuegia Basket. The two males were outfitted in sailor's clothes at FitzRoy's expense and given hammocks to sling in the men's mess, well forward on the ship.

Captain FitzRoy had ordered his twenty-two chronometers installed in the small room immediately in front of his own cabin. Many days were spent by George J. Stebbing, son of a highly respected mathematical instrument maker from Portsmouth, in preparing the room, for each chronometer had to be suspended in gimbals, within a wooden box, and each box placed in sawdust and divided by partitions upon wide shelves. The bottom sawdust was three inches thick as was the sawdust at the side of each box, which caused the chronometer to rise above the gravity of the box itself. They were labeled for each letter of the alphabet and a chart kept of their daily record. Only I and J, Q and U were omitted.

"We've got them between decks," FitzRoy explained, "which is imperative, but not precisely at the vessel's center of motion, which would have been desirable. However, placed in this manner, neither the activity of men on deck nor the firing of guns nor the running out of chain cables can cause the slightest variation."

Of the twenty-two chronometers six were owned by FitzRoy, eleven had been provided him by the Navy, four came from their makers, Arnold and Dent, Molyneux, Murray, for testing purposes; and one had been loaned by Lord Ashburnham. Stebbing was a meticulous worker, more interested in machinery than people, and completely happy as long as he had precise mechanical objects to care for. He had been hired by Captain FitzRoy to supervise all the navigational instruments aboard, his wages being paid by the captain, since he was not a navy man and the Navy would not provide a man whose sole purpose it was to watch the chronometers.

"How can I tell when they're not vibrating?" Stebbing replied to Charles's question. "We scatter powder on the glass each day and watch it with a magnifying glass while the vessel is responding to some jar or shock."

The chronometer was an instrument for measuring time with great accuracy in determining longitude at sea. Once at sea, no one would be allowed to enter the chronometer cabin except Stebbing, the captain and Stokes, and these only for the purpose of winding, comparing time and checking against vibration. After watching the meticulous placing of the instruments in their sawdust wombs, Charles, who felt himself to be, during the long days of waiting, an alien entity, and useless, said to Captain FitzRoy:

"The paint isn't dry in the poop cabin so I can't set up our library. Could you assign me some regular employment?"

"If you wish. Each morning at nine when we wind our one- and two-day chronometers, you can read the barometers and set down in the logbook the differences in the atmospheric pressure."

"Thank you, Captain. You have just taken the first step in converting a landsman into a sailor."

On November 15 a long and thoroughly detailed memorandum arrived from the Admiralty for Captain FitzRoy. It was the official release of the ship: H.M.S. *Beagle* could set out for sea as soon as the last of its equipment was installed, tested and made secure. Captain FitzRoy was jubilant.

> You are hereby required and directed to put to sea, in the vessel you command, so soon as she shall be in every respect ready, and to proceed in her, with all convenient expedition, successively to Madeira or Teneriffe; the Cape Verde Islands; Fernando Noronha; and the South American station; to perform the operations, and execute the surveys pointed out in the accompanying memorandum. . . .

He scanned Captain Francis Beaufort's memorandum:

> A considerable difference still exists in the longitude of Rio de Janeiro, as determined by Captains King, Beechey and Foster, on the one hand, and Captain W. F. Owen, Baron Roussin and the Portuguese astronomers, on the other; and as all our meridian distances in South America are measured from thence, it becomes a matter of importance. . . .

Captain Beaufort went on to remind FitzRoy that since no vessel would ever have left the country with a better set of chronometers, he should be able to reduce that difference.

Captain FitzRoy next glanced at the areas to be surveyed:

> . . . as far south as the Strait of Magellan and the northeast coast of Tierra del Fuego. . . .

There followed instructions for charting the west coast of South America and the permission to traverse the Pacific.

> If you should reach Guayaquil it would be desirable to run for the Galápagos . . . and other spots, which have crept into the charts on doubtful authority. . . .

He was also to do a nautical survey and get the perpendicular heights of all hills and headlands and some views of the land to accompany the charts and plans; and to set up constant observations of the tides, the distance to which they carry salt water up the rivers and hundreds of other specifics.

When he had finished his cursory reading, FitzRoy announced a bit wryly:

"These instructions are for the historic record rather than for me. I know all the chores we have to perform, and they will be done thoroughly. What makes them welcome is that we are now free to circumnavigate the globe. After we cross the Pacific to Tahiti we can survey the other southern islands and put in at New Zealand and Australia coming home via the Cape of Good Hope at the foot of Africa. . . . It is now official!"

He placed the papers on his desk.

"However . . . to fulfill all of Captain Beaufort's instructions, it will take us four years, I should think."

Charles felt his breathing stop. *Four* years! God in heaven! What had started out as a two-year jaunt, quite easily handled by himself and his family, had now doubled in length. He quailed with doubt. What would he do for an interminable four years? Would there be half enough work for a naturalist to keep him interested and of even modest value?

How could he break this new development to his father? Although he had been writing home fairly regularly, reporting not only his own activities but the ongoing progress of H.M.S. *Beagle*, his sisters would find it shattering. He could not tell them!

Something tumbled inside his chest; anxiety fastened on his throat. Four years! Away from family, friends, relatives . . . Maer Hall, Woodhouse, Cambridge . . .

Four years at sea!

### 3.

The Royal William Victualing Yard's wagons brought the last of the H.M.S. *Beagle*'s provisions. It was a great day, almost a religious rite for the crew, all of whom pitched in to get the stores into the proper places in the hold.

Charles assisted George Rowlett, the purser, in checking off the various foodstuffs as they were taken from the wagons and handed up the moving chain of crewmen. Everything was stored below the water line. Beneath the captain's cabin were stacked the bags of thick-crusted biscuit. Under the main hatchway and gun room were the tightly sealed iron tanks of fresh water; the rum and spirits were stored in kegs beneath the midshipmen's berths. There were cases of anti-scorbutics: pickles, dried apples and lemon juice. Of these Captain FitzRoy said:

"Scurvy has been the curse of every ship that sailed the seas until

Captain Cook. That's why these supplies are in as great abundance as we can stow away."

There were five to six thousand cans of Kilner and Moorsom's preserved meat, vegetables and soup, all of them passed along the line into the hold with loving hands. Barrels of salt pork and salt beef were also stored beneath the crew's mess. It was customary to carry an eight months' supply of provisions.

From the Medical Department H.M.S. *Beagle* received Captain Beaufort's medications, antiseptics, as well as articles needed for preserving specimens of natural history. The calomel, morphine, carbolic acid, iodine, tartar emetic were stacked in the pharmacy, a special storeroom next to Dr. McCormick's cabin, along with the bandages, splints, unguents, salves and liniments. Charles, preparing to check off his own list, asked FitzRoy where his equipment for preserving specimens would be stored.

FitzRoy replied wryly, "I can spare a little space in the storeroom behind my cabin but I think that much of them are going to have to go into sick bay. I'll have to tell McCormick that all naturalist supplies will be under your supervision, that no one may take anything without your permission."

After several hours, Charles remarked to Lieutenant Wickham:

"You don't lose an inch of room, do you?"

"When we get through, the hold will be able to contain scarcely a lizard. Captain FitzRoy means us to eat well. All these stores, along with the fresh meat we'll shoot, and fish we'll catch, not to mention birds, should keep us in good health."

The boxes and crates sent with Mr. Matthews for the Fuegians were now opened. There was boisterous laughter as one by one the men brought out wineglasses, butter-bolts, tea trays, soup tureens, a mahogany dressing case, fine white linens, beaver hats, a large quantity of clothes, tools, books and a full set of crockery, including hand-painted chamber pots. One of the marines cried:

"Can't you just see a whole set of those naked savages sitting in a row in a Fuegian hurricane, taking a shite in these little pots!"

Captain FitzRoy, Charles and Bynoe had been standing by.

"God in heaven," exclaimed the captain, "what could those good people have been thinking about? Tools they can't use, books they can't read, dishes for butter, tea and soup that they never heard of, and mahogany dressing cases which will be used for firewood. Waste, all waste. Beaver hats and white linens in the wilds of Tierra del Fuego!"

That afternoon, with the last of the stores securely tamped down, Captain FitzRoy ordered enough sail to carry them one mile across the narrow stretch of the Hamoaze to the Mount Edgcumbe amphitheater where H.M.S. *Beagle* entered the beautiful and safe Barnpool, which was surrounded on all sides by an irregular coast of inlets and promontories. Barnpool gave the appearance of a large lake, the many vessels coming and going, adding life to the picture.

Charles was enchanted by his first passage, the coxswain's piping, the manning of the yards, the men working at the hawsers to the sound of a fife, the foretopmen climbing aloft on rope ladders with the grace and speed of up-swooping birds.

The day also arrived when the paint in the poop cabin was dry. Charles and Stokes brought the books over from the mainland. The shelves were four and a half feet long by seven feet high and would accommodate the two hundred volumes, a very representative library for one small ship. The major reference works were the seventeen volumes of *Dictionnaire classique d'histoire naturelle* and the *Dictionnaire des sciences naturelles*. Many of the titles were in multinumbers such as Charles's eleven volumes of Euclid and the several volumes of von Humboldt. He contributed his Spanish books, one on taxidermy, and the *Wonders of the World*, which he had owned since childhood, and the books he had secured at Yarrell's, as well as volumes on algebra, trigonometry, *Nomenclature of Colors*, and a French dictionary. They put the travel books on the top shelf, on the one just below, the mathematics, astronomy and electricity texts. On the next shelf lower, the natural history, most of which belonged to Captain FitzRoy, who had been collecting for a number of years, but to which Charles made a substantial contribution.

Captain FitzRoy promptly put George Stebbing in charge of the library. FitzRoy's rules were strict but generous. The books were available to all officers, including the midshipmen, but they had to make the request of Stebbing, who would bring the volume to their cabin. At the end of a stipulated number of days Stebbing would retrieve the book and leave a receipt. Every book had to be temporarily covered by the officer who had it in use. No volume could be removed from the vessel.

The proper arranging of the volumes took Charles and Stokes the better part of two days. When the job was done they both catalogued the library's content.

Now it was time for Charles to attend to the stowing of his clothing and personal possessions, and to have his hammock attached. Until this moment he had put out of his mind his concern over the lack of space.

The poop cabin, lined with the bookcases and chests of drawers, ended up with a little less than ten feet of free space, of which the chart table, bolted to the deck, occupied four and a half feet in length and six and a half feet in width. Captain FitzRoy had been accurate when he said that Charles would have two feet of walking space around

the chart table, and that was all! There were a bare four inches on either side of him in which to move his arms and legs while dressing and
undressing; if he extended his elbows more than these four inches he
would hit either the bulkhead or his chest of drawers. He would have to
develop the technique of dressing vertically, with his arms rigidly in
front of him; put on his undershirt, shirt, waistcoat or coat with his
arms crossed as though he were wrestling with himself. Thanks to Captain FitzRoy's redoing of the interior, the poop cabin was six and a half
feet high, six inches higher than on the earlier voyage. He would have a
few inches between his flatly combed, sandy-red hair and the wooden
ceiling.

Trying to get his clothing, including his suits and personal possessions, into the chest of drawers in the corner angle of the cabin in
which his hammock would be slung and into the small cabinet along
the bulkhead was an ordeal. He was on the verge of despair when John
Stokes reassured him.

"The cabinets hold more than you suspect, Charley. It's a matter of
organizing the space. Let me show you. Don't stuff anything. Slide your
socks flat inside your underwear. Fold your port clothes the way tailors
do so that they are totally flat."

The most trying moment came when Stokes strung Charles's hammock between its wall hooks. The hammock extended only a little over
five feet.

"What am I to do, Johnny, hang my feet over the netting?"

"You'll get used to it. There are a lot of us over five feet on board
this ship. You just have to sleep rolled up like a cocoon."

"I've spent too many years totally stretched out like a plank of
lumber."

Captain FitzRoy heard Stokes's loud laughter and poked his head
into the poop cabin.

"What's the problem, Darwin?"

"The hammock is too short."

"The hammock isn't too short. The space is too short."

"Either way, Captain, I'm not going to have enough length."

FitzRoy studied the corner and said to Stokes:

"Fetch the carpenter. Tell him to bring some foot clews."

Mr. May, the carpenter, came quickly. Captain FitzRoy removed the
top drawer of Charles's chest. He said to the carpenter:

"Affix your foot clews at the back of the chest. In that way we can
reroute the hammock a little."

When the hammock had been strung on the slightly different angle,
with an extra foot of space, and the top drawer of toilet articles was sitting under the chart table, it was time for Charles to practice getting in.

He sat down in the center of the hammock, putting all his weight on it. The hammock promptly rumpled out from under him, dumping him on the deck. Sulivan had come in by this time; the three witnesses laughed heartily. Charles did not see anything funny about it. He was holding his bruised behind. Nobody proffered any advice. He straightened out the twisted hammock and once again sat down in the middle, this time very gently. He no sooner put his legs up onto the canvas than once again it reared like an untamed colt and threw him out.

FitzRoy shook his head from side to side, amused.

"The trouble is, Captain, I'm being rejected."

"No, no," boomed Sulivan, "you're being *ejected*."

FitzRoy murmured, "Be so kind as to fetch the sailmaker."

James Malcolm, a man from Devonport with reddish hair and hazel eyes, recut the canvas and sewed new rope holes. He flattened the canvas sufficiently for Charles to feel comfortable. This completed, the trio cried:

"Now let's try again."

"The great fault of your jockeyship," Sulivan said, "is that you're trying to put your legs in too soon. Since the hammock is suspended, you're only succeeding in pushing it away from you."

"What do I put in first, my head? It's feeling empty enough at the moment, and shouldn't weigh much."

Stokes chuckled, shook his black hair a vigorous "No."

"The correct method is to sit accurately in the very center of the hammock." He demonstrated the act. "Then give yourself a dextrous twist so that your head and feet come into their respective places at the same moment. It's really no more difficult than getting on a rearing horse."

It took Charles a number of tries with Stokes and Sulivan at either end of the hammock guiding his head and feet, but he finally managed it. However FitzRoy still thought the hammock the wrong size and shape. James Malcolm redid the canvas twice more before it fit Darwin's gangling frame.

Since no one was sleeping on board yet, he kept his comfortable rooms and excellent bed at Clarence Baths, leaving the dockyard late in the afternoon, walking along Richmond Walk under Mount Wise and passing the Admiral's Stairs just before reaching his own haven. He had breakfast in his rooms at the Baths, and only if specifically invited did he eat dinner in the officers' mess. He did not wish to take anything for granted. If no officer happened to mention it, he went to the Hunt or the Regatta, where he ate alone. Occasionally, when the waters of Plymouth Sound were not too turbulent, he went aboard and slept in his hammock, wanting to get used to it before putting out to sea. It swung back and forth over the chart table and kept him nauseously awake.

He was living in a vacuum. He did not enjoy the unbordered feel of it.

Because H.M.S. *Beagle* was about to sail, all shore activity was stepped up. The Royal Navy was highly social, everyone wanted to entertain the officers of a ship about to depart on a long voyage. Charles attended a series of luncheons, dinners and dancing parties. Though he frequently was the only non-naval man present, he was received cordially by the commander-in-chief, Admiral Sir Manley Dixon, at his official home at the end of the Mount Wise Parade; by the officers of H.M.S. *Caledonia*, a large warship carrying one hundred and twenty guns, to which he was carried for a visit on the commissioner's yacht; at dinner with the Plymouth friends of Thunder-and-Lightning Harris, at dinner with Captain Philip King and Captain Alexander Vidal, who had spent eight years surveying the coast of Africa; and at a leisurely breakfast with Colonel Hamilton Smith, who was writing a book with Cuvier, the famous French naturalist, on the wide spectrum of the sea's fishes.

To some of these parties he was invited because he was a friend of Captain FitzRoy. But to his surprise, since he had never really thought about it, he was also accepted because he bore a proud family name. His grandfather, Dr. Erasmus Darwin, was famous throughout literate England as a nature writer and poet. His father, Dr. Robert Darwin, as Charles had learned from Captain Beaufort, had a reputation for excellence in medicine not only in Shropshire but in London and Ireland as well.

"I could go a long way on my name," he decided. "In fact, I already have. But what am I to do in the years ahead to justify my carrying that name?"

Could he become an outstanding clergyman? A famous lecturer and wit like Sydney Smith?

At a farewell party to celebrate their imminent departure and to repay his many hosts, Captain FitzRoy gave a luncheon on board the festooned H.M.S. *Beagle*. Charles joined FitzRoy and Lieutenants Wickham and Sulivan as a reception committee to welcome the naval officers, their wives and daughters, to a seven-course meal which the dockyard commissary provided. That evening the captain continued the festivities with a waltzing party in the ballroom of the comparatively new Royal Hotel on George Street. The officers were handsome in their blue coats with scarlet stand-up collars, wide cuffs and rows of highly embossed gold buttons, ten in each downward march. The three top officers boasted a single gold epaulet, with gold lace on the coat and around the cuffs. The imperative waistcoats were single-breasted, with buttons carrying the same insignia as the full-cut coat. The trousers were of matching blue cloth, with gold lace down the outside seams, and around them, belts of blue morocco leather. By now Charles had learned to distinguish rank by the width of the gold braid and the number of stars on the epaulets. He was impressed by this grandiloquent full dress, though by conservative Cambridge tastes it appeared a trifle ostentatious. He found himself wondering whether the gaudy uniforms enlarged the man within them. Or, like a coat of mail, protected little men hiding behind the rows of gold buttons. He surmised that an answer would be vouchsafed to him during the four-year cruise.

Charles found the women attractive in their elegant ball gowns of muslin, silken gauze and organdies of white, yellow, soft pinks and blues. The wide skirts were puffed out by layers of petticoats with wide-ranging ribbon and floral decorations above the hem of the skirt. He became the victim of a bout of nostalgia as he pictured his sisters, the Wedgwood girls and, lingeringly, Fanny Owen. He was aware that Captain FitzRoy had a glowing excitement in his eyes while he danced with Mary O'Brien, a cousin, daughter of a country gentleman and major general, and as frequently as possible escorted her to the champagne table. Lieutenant Sulivan was having an equally good time with the charming daughter of Admiral Young.

"Poor chaps, us," Charles mused, "we won't see our beautiful girls again for four years. I wonder which of them will wait?"

The next time he boarded the *Beagle* he found Sulivan in a towering rage.

"Frigged myself, that's what I done!"

The story was funny to everyone but Sulivan. He had been working since dawn; when he went to his cabin for a nap he instructed the steward to rouse him in time for tea so he could dress for that night's ball. At teatime Sulivan appeared in his nightshirt and nightcap, shouldering a big duck gun he kept hanging on the wall of his cabin. He put the gun in a corner, drank the tea put before him, rose, shouldered the gun and went back to bed. His brother officers decided he was sleepwalking and should not be awakened. Sulivan slept straight through the night, missing the ball and his engagement with Miss Young.

"Now I won't be able to give her our post stops."

"Her father will know our ports. I'm sure she will inquire," comforted Charles.

"Thank you for the kind words, Philosopher. I'll write to the young lady right now and tell her an outrageous lie about being forced to defend the *Beagle* all night! With a duck gun, no less!"

The humor was welcome. The ship's barometers indicated bad weather.

4.

The barometers were right. Within an hour the sun had disappeared and a fierce southwest wind came off the Atlantic, nailing the ship to its mooring haven. Soon there came rain off the sea, a heavy pelting rain. When the temperature dropped, the rain turned to sleet and then hail. H.M.S. *Beagle* bobbed around like a cork in a rain-filled barrel. Charles had never felt such penetrating cold. The storm went on for several days. He was alternately seasick, homesick and despairing of ever getting out of the harbor.

Late on the afternoon of December 2 he was sprawled in the big chair in the living room of his apartment at Clarence Baths, where he had returned to get a respite from the ship's movement. He was reading *Essay on the Theory of the Earth* by Cuvier, which he had borrowed from the Proprietary Library, when there was a tattooing on his door. He opened it to find his brother Erasmus standing there, traveling bag in hand.

"Hello, Charley. Susan wrote to me telling me where you were. Came to pay a visit."

Charles's jaw dropped, his eyes bulged with surprise. Erasmus looked well, was dressed expensively, though by no means foppishly, in a wide-lapeled wool coat and waistcoat riding high on a tight white collar, and a beautiful silk shirt and black stock. He had a deep tan over his already swarthy complexion. His hair was thin at the center of his head, compensatory tufts sprouting from either side like bird's wings. His eyes, dark and attractive, were withdrawn.

He hugged his brother to him, then took Erasmus's coat and bag, pushed his books off the table and called for tea. It was three and a half years since Erasmus had graduated from Christ's College. After a brief visit at The Mount he had gone off to London, then for a long tour of France and Austria. When he complained about the hotels or the difficulties of travel, Charles wondered why he did not return and be comfortable.

"Exactly what I intend to do," Erasmus replied. "I'll divide my time between my quarters in Regent Street and the Windham Club on St. James's. My wandering years are over. I'm going to settle down in London and languorously watch the years go by."

"No practice of medicine?"

"Only what I take internally. Actually, it's not my health that fails, but my vital spirits. Half the time I don't feel up to very much."

Charles was shocked. After all those years at Edinburgh and Christ's College, and Erasmus had been a good student, not to carry on the highly respected profession for which he had been so well trained! He remembered his own resolution not to spend his life with the ill and afflicted, but he had quit early, had shifted to theology. Where would Erasmus turn for another profession?

"Nowhere, my dear Gas. Those years at Edinburgh and Christ's appear to have exhausted me. Or my ambition, at least."

For the first time Charles understood his father's rage when he had shown him the offering letter from Henslow: it was a wild scheme . . . useless . . . he would never settle down to a steady life thereafter. . . . It would be severely traumatic for Dr. Robert Darwin to have reared two dilettantes, remittance men, really, living off the hard and devoted decades of work of the Darwin and Wedgwood families . . . "parasites," they would be in the moral values of Dr. Darwin, who had devoted forty-four years of selfless service to his fellow humans.

"I have no intention of being an idler merely because I don't have a steady occupation."

"Then you do have a plan? Ras, I'm glad."

"Everybody in London is so preoccupied they have no time to give to friendship. I mean to have that time, as much as my precarious health will allow."

Charles had not known his brother to have "precarious" health. He had always seemed well and strong.

"Just how do you intend to give that friendship?"

There was pain etched down the lines of Erasmus's face. It was an emotional trial to have to justify himself to his younger brother.

"I've thought about that a lot. I'd like to establish a comfortable, modest home in London where people could come for food and drink, for companionship and stimulating conversation. I've met a number of writers. They are among the loneliest people I know. Confused, too, many of them; rootless. I would like to help them know that they have friends with whom they can meet and discuss their problems." Then, plaintively, "That's not being an idler, is it, Charles?"

Charles's affection for his older brother asserted itself.

"No . . . Ras. I shouldn't be surprised if you cured as many ills that way as you would by bleeding and prescribing nostrums."

"I'm twenty-seven and quite worn down to the nub." He opened his arms wide, pleadingly, trying to actuate for his younger brother what he had arrived at so desperately. "It's simple, Charley. We pour out our substance into preparation for adult life. Now that I've reached adult life I find it wasn't worth preparing for. Somebody, maybe I myself gilded the myth of maturity. I don't intend to be juggled again. Life is but a passing dream? Let it pass."

It was not energy that Erasmus lacked. Charles took him on long walks up Mount Edgcumbe, from the top of which they could see Devonport, Stonehouse and Plymouth, each situated on its own arm of the sea; H.M.S. *Beagle* in the harbor of Barnpool waiting for the winds to change. He secured permission to show Erasmus through the Royal Navy Dockyard, probably the busiest and most colorful in the world, seventy-one acres protected by a wall of slate and limestone in some places thirty feet high. They entered the foot gate on Fore Street, immediately passed a small neat chapel, thirteen officers' dwelling houses and the basin for the smaller boats belonging to the dockyard. Then, in succession, the rigging house, a slip for hauling up and cleaning the bottoms of small vessels; the boathouse where boats were built and repaired; the blacksmith's shop, hammering anchors in and out of the fires with the aid of cranes, and forging chains in immense fires which threw a smoke and yellow glare over the spacious building.

They passed the boiling house, in which the planks to be curved were boiled in water, the mast house where masts and yardarms were constructed; after that the pond in which an immense number of masts and yards were floating to keep them from cracking in the sun. There were the dwellings of the master ropemakers, storehouses for hemp, the burning place for old copper; plumbers, braziers and armorers' shops; the gun wharf, storehouse for muskets, pistols, grapeshot. . . .

Erasmus was wide-eyed.

"I can see why you are fascinated, Charley. Does it all tempt you? When you return, do you think you might like to join the Royal Navy? Perhaps as a career naturalist? I'm sure there'd be no difficulty in your getting a commission."

"No, Ras, I'm going to become a clergyman. I promised Father I would. He paid for my training; I have an unshakable obligation to him."

Erasmus flushed; looked away.

Charles took Erasmus with him to the *Beagle* each day; Erasmus followed him on his round of recording the barometers' readings, helped with whatever chores he had to do, marveled at Charles's acceptance of them. He became excited about the voyage and rejoiced with Charles when the date of December 5 was announced as H.M.S. *Beagle*'s new sailing date.

Charles thought:

"Poor Ras, he is the one who is lonely. That's why he wants his salon, for people to bring him their warmth and friendship."

Once, he asked quietly:

"Ras, what about marriage? Does that fit into your plans?"

"I don't think so. I don't want that kind of responsibility."

"Not even if you fell in love?"

"You're the romantic male in the family, Gas, chasing over the landscape with that coquettish Fanny Owen. Truth to tell, I've never known love. It's foreign to my nature."

"Not all that foreign, I can remember when you were a mite infatuated with Cousin Emma Wedgwood. Time was, when the family tongues were clacking about you two marrying."

A warm smile bathed Erasmus's face.

"Ah, Emma! Our delightful Miss Slip-Slop! Emma and I never even held hands. If anyone spoke of marrying it is because the Darwin and Wedgwood cousins are supposed to marry each other. Actually our good sisters would prefer me to marry Fanny, the other half of the Doveleys."

"I've always thought you were closer to Cousin Charlotte, myself. She has beauty and charm and is an accomplished water colorist."

"Now, now, Charles, you don't fit the role of a marriage broker."

Erasmus's departure brought on a bout of genuine unhappiness for the first time since he had reached Plymouth. It was an emotion he had rarely felt.

On Monday morning, December 5, the skies were clear. After the sights had been taken, Captain FitzRoy gave the order:

"Clear the ship for sailing!"

The crew was relieved. Charles was exuberant . . . until a heavy gale came out of the south, again locking H.M.S. *Beagle* into its harbor. He muttered to Stokes across the chart table:

"I'm going back to Clarence Baths. I mean to treat myself with sleeping on a firm, flat, steady bed."

"Don't overdo it," Stokes warned. "If the wind comes down from the north it can take us out of Plymouth before you get out of your nightshirt."

He stayed in his rooms in Clarence Baths as one gale succeeded another. It was daily becoming more wearisome. When he went on board to cheer himself up, the *Beagle* rolled so badly he was forced to beat a hasty retreat. Day by day the officers kept close watch on the barometers.

It took five days for the wind to change. At nine o'clock they weighed anchor. As soon as they doubled the breakwater the sea ran high. Once again the barometers gave notice. They were in a heavy gale coming from the southwest. The vessel pitched bows under. Charles became seasick and suffered the most miserable night of his life. The whistling of the wind, the roar of the sea, the hoarse screams of the officers and the shouts of the crewmen made a concert he would not soon forget. In the morning Captain FitzRoy ordered the ship back into Plymouth to wait for a more favorable wind.

Charles returned to Clarence Baths.

The following two weeks were horrendous, with unrelenting bitter cold, snow and ice. Charles made a daily round of the barometers, ate little and slept less. He lost weight, grew melancholy. His shipmates became grumblers and growlers. Mate Peter Stewart, Charles's age, who had entered the Navy at the age of fourteen, and with whom Charles visited on his night watch, said:

"There is somebody on shore keeping a black cat under a tub. Stands to reason that's what is keeping us in harbor. Give us a gentle breeze from the north! Our sailing'll be hailed with joy. Gawd, how I yearn for the tropics."

When the gales abated even a little he put on his heavy boots, big black rain hat and raincape and crossed to Mount Edgcumbe, walking for hours in the dreary cold, unaware of the dramatic fury of the waves pounding the sand and rock beneath him. He held his face up to the wind and rain which washed under the deep hat. Then, looking downward to the turmoil of the sea, murmured:

"I'm aghast! Is this the dreadful sea I am going to spend years of my life enduring? However shall I withstand it?"

On Sunday he went with Charles Musters to the chapel in the dockyard. It rained torrents all evening.

He first became conscious of pain, then palpitations of the heart. This could mean serious trouble, but "my troubles are my own," he groused. "I shall confide in no one."

The palpitations increased. Unmistakably. He had had enough training during his two years at the University of Edinburgh medical school and experience with his father's patients to know when a heart was beating irregularly. He took his pulse; kept his left hand under his breast and on his heart.

What to do about it? Despite H.M.S. *Beagle*'s tribulations, he was not so much frightened of dying as he was of missing the voyage. He could not tell Dr. McCormick; he would have him recalled to London instantly. Nor could he rely on Benjamin Bynoe's confidence. He was a stickler for health.

He would have to take his chances. If his heart gave out, and the palpitations did seem to grow stronger each day, they could bury him at sea. From this decision he developed an intense pain; a full acre of pain, he observed.

His spirits suffered an eclipse. He no longer went to the lectures at the Athenaeum or borrowed books from the Proprietary Library. He turned down all invitations to tea and dinner, took no more walks up Mount Edgcumbe or along the fiercely battering sea. He remained on board the *Beagle* caught in a siege of depression while thunder, lightning and torrential rains beat and crackled all around him and his heart pounded against the rocks of his ribs until he thought they would crack like boulders and tumble into the sea. They were the worst days of his life.

But when the rain stopped and it seemed that the weather would remain good, he found himself shopping for a flycatcher and a silver pencil; walking with Sulivan and young King near the Ramshead, another day dining in the midshipmen's mess, a hearty group of seven between the ages of fourteen and twenty-three who looked up to him with respect because he had had a prestigious university education which would never be afforded them. The palpitations ceased.

He went with Benjamin Bynoe and Stokes for a wind-swept walk to Whitson Bay, murmured to his friends:

"The sea here has a glorious and divine appearance." And, after an instant cried: "Heavens above me, I've just preached my first sermon!"

For nearly a quarter of an hour they gazed out on a confused mass of breakers. The white covering of foam looked like so much snow. The waves, as they dashed against the rocks, threw their salty spray high on the hill, wetting their faces. Bynoe observed:

"The ocean exerts the most powerful force on earth."

Stokes replied, "Bad pun, Ben, even if unintended! Charles and I like the water better when it's calm and reasonable. Don't we, Charley?"

Charles responded with an "Amen."

It was mid-December when Charles dined for the first time in Captain FitzRoy's cabin. FitzRoy had furnished it with superb good taste, converting it into a room resembling his family home. The mahogany bulkheads set off the French writing desk and two comfortable chairs which he had brought with him; a small hand-carved chest held a few of his favorite books, on top, some of his prized possessions: medals and cups won in the Navy, a pair of silver-backed hairbrushes and, to Charles's delight, a small but exquisite Wedgwood vase. Above hung a portrait of his mother.

The round dining table, set by the captain's personal steward, Fuller, whose salary he paid, was covered with crisp linen, sparkling glassware and highly polished silver. The ship's cook had shopped at the Plymouth market that morning for fresh meat, vegetables and fruit, but only after having bought a basketful of fish off the fishing boats as they were rolled up the sandy beach. Fuller served each course silently.

Captain FitzRoy was in a relaxed mood, dining in a soft civilian coat and ruffled shirt.

"Do I mind the delays?" he answered to Charles's question. "Yes, but not emotionally the way the others do. I don't hold to the black cat theory. The important point is that the *Beagle* is shipshape. I can control what goes into the building of a ship but not the southwest wind or a storm. Only God can control the forces of nature. Today we will drink a glass of wine to a happy and constructive four years. I've also chosen a fine bottle of red for our roast beef. Drink up, my dear Darwin, for once the north wind blows us out of Plymouth, this cabin will be as dry as a stale sea biscuit."

"Of all the luxuries and kindnesses you have given me, sir, none will be so essential as that of having my meals with you."

"Ah, yes, the gun-room mess. Gets a mite noisy in there. The officers try hard to amuse themselves." He turned serious. "I must tell you the rest of the meal discipline. My meals are served promptly: breakfast at eight o'clock, dinner at one, tea at five, supper at eight. We must try to be on time; but if one of us is delayed, the other should start eating at once. Nor do we have to finish together; first one through goes back to work."

"I understand."

"There is one other thing you must understand. We have enjoyed a great deal of convivial society here in Devonport and Plymouth. I'm sure I've spilled as many words to the admirals and their lovely daughters as you have. But at sea, particularly in difficult weather, or when I fail to get the maps and charts I want, I become intensely preoccupied. I don't talk to anybody about anything but the technical details of the job; and no one is permitted to speak to me. So we will sometimes eat our meals in absolute silence, and it could be several days in a row. I want you to know that it is nothing personal. I have no small talk at sea."

"Captain FitzRoy, I have already promised not to enter this delightful cabin when you want to be alone. I add the further pledge of silence when you want it. I will have Stebbing make me a barometer which will record your desire for silence or loquaciousness within a hairsbreadth."

FitzRoy was delighted.

"You'll do, Darwin, you'll do." An impish smile lighted his usually solemn eyes. "I almost rejected you the first time you walked into my office in the Admiralty. Do you know why? Because I am an ardent disciple of Lavater, the German physiognomist. I am convinced that I can judge a man's character by the outline of his features. For a split second there, as you sat across the Admiralty desk from me, I doubted whether anyone with your longish nose could possess sufficient energy and determination for the voyage."

Charles was unable to take this seriously.

"Oh, come, my good Captain, you must know that Lavater was a poet and mystic. He wouldn't have welcomed a scintilla of scientific evidence in his theory."

Captain FitzRoy was not offended.

"I had Mr. John Wilson, surgeon on the earlier *Beagle*, do a character study of the Fuegians: their self-will, honesty, cunning, passions, memory. . . . Then we did a phrenological study of their skulls. It's all recorded in my logbook."

Charles's brows raised in astonishment.

"You studied the bumps in their heads to determine their mental qualities?"

"Yes. Quite fascinating."

Charles studied the soft inner pads of his fingertips for a moment.

"Captain, would you run your hand over the hull and prow of the *Beagle* to determine her sailing qualities?"

FitzRoy greeted this with a self-deprecatory grin; but there was a slight stiffening of his backbone.

On his way back to his quarters, Charles ruminated:

"I wonder if besting him is a luxury I can afford."

5.

When the ship was not rocking too badly in its mooring in Barnpool, Charles spent his free time arranging and rearranging what he called his "nick-nackeries," sentimental mementos brought from The Mount; and reading Basil Hall's *Fragments of Voyages and Travels*. On top of his chest of drawers he put out the silversmith's locket containing Sarah Owen's lock of hair. Each time he passed the locket it evoked a picture of her lovely sister Fanny. The lock of hair took the place of the pincushion Fanny had resolved to make for him but had not got around to.

The weather continued to attract bad news: a brig which had left Plymouth three weeks earlier was driven back into Plymouth by the southwest winds, its crew both seasick and disgusted. When, after another four stormy days, the sun shone red through the mist, Captain FitzRoy ordered their own ship to prepare for departure. They started at eleven in the morning with a light northwest wind, and while tacking around Drake's Island, the master steered them upon a rock that lay off the corner of the island. There being no wind or swell on the sea, the vessel stuck fast for half an hour. Without reproving the crestfallen master, Captain FitzRoy took charge, tried a number of maneuvers, which failed, then pursued a new tack.

"I want every man on board in motion. Move as fast as you can from port to starboard and back, then stern to bow and back. We need a strong rocking motion."

It worked. H.M.S. *Beagle* came free of the rock. On inspection it was found that the copper keel had not been injured. They no sooner cleared the breakwater than Charles felt uneasy. At four o'clock he went to the captain's cabin and fell asleep on the divan in the cubicle opposite the one that held FitzRoy's bed. At eight he awoke, went up the aft hatchway and vaulted himself safely into his hammock.

At first light he and Stokes both awakened. Stokes shook his head, puzzled.

"Something's wrong. We're moving backward. Let's see that pocket compass of yours."

At that moment Mr. Wickham stuck his head in the door.

"We should be back in Plymouth Sound in an hour. The wind started to change during the middle watch. By the time we were eleven miles out a gale blew in from the southwest. Captain 'wared' ship, and we're returning to our old home at eleven knots."

The following day, while dropping anchor, it got enmeshed in the chain. It took officers and crew eight solid hours to get it untangled. Charles stayed on board, keeping out of the way, but wondering how such an excellent ship and experienced crew could get themselves into trouble twice in two days.

Captain FitzRoy ordered a double portion of rum issued to solace the exhausted men.

"There's one compensation," he said over their tea; "several vessels which sailed when we did have had to put back into port as well." His voice took on a happier note. "In a couple of days we'll celebrate Christmas here in Plymouth, and if the day after is fine, we'll set out again for Teneriffe."

Charles rose early on Christmas Morning and walked to the beautiful chapel at the foot of Fore Street, with its double aisles and tower, stained-glass windows and carved wooden balconies. To his surprise the visiting preacher was William Hoare, a man he had known in Cambridge. Hoare had received his degree from St. John's in the Senate building on the same day Charles had been handed his parchment from Christ's College. Hoare had been a brilliant student and received a first in the classical tripos. He was also a good Hebrew scholar, and preached a scholarly sermon on ecclesiastical history, which Charles found interesting but not particularly apropos. When the congregation had departed for its Christmas dinner, Charles and William Hoare had a comradely chat on the front steps. Hoare was a delicate man, in dubious health.

"It's good to see you, Charles. I heard you were going out as a naturalist. That means you won't be preaching for several years."

"After the voyage I must still find a parish. How about you, William? Do you have a congregation of your own?"

"Oh no, no. I'm going back to St. John's to take my M.A. I would like to become a fellow of the college, teach . . . write books."

By the time he got back to the ship he found it almost abandoned. Captain FitzRoy had locked his cabin door. Charles went into the gun room to have Christmas dinner with the officers. He could see from their flushed faces and puffy eyes that they had been drinking for quite a while. Wickham and Sulivan moved over to make a place for him.

"What's become of the crew?" Charles asked.

"Most of them are ashore," replied Sulivan, "getting roaring drunk. That's their privilege. They've always felt that Christmas Day was their own."

"You fellows are not doing too badly yourselves," Charles observed.

"Ah," said Wickham, "you have to understand the difference. We drink like gentlemen, in our own quarters, disturbing no one. Half the crew will be in the Plymouth jail by morning."

"Don't sit there in judgment, *Reverend* Mr. Darwin," cracked Bynoe. "Join us. Here's a glass. Bend your elbow. It's the best possible exercise on Christmas Day."

He did.

But it ceased to be enjoyable as night fell. Crew members stumbled up the gangplank, spewing Lieutenant Wickham's holystoned decks with vomit. The situation, as Charles watched it, having slept off his wine in his hammock, grew increasingly worse. The men broke their leave, came aboard late and quarreling among themselves. Captain FitzRoy emerged in full-dress uniform, and the sobered officers tried to establish control, but the drunken ones were beyond reason or assistance. The last sentinel at the gangplank staggered below declaring he could no longer stand on duty. Charles found fourteen-year-old Philip King standing duty with a pistol in his belt and a shotgun in his arms.

"My God, Philip, that gun's bigger than you are. Have you ever shot a gun?"

"Why, Mr. Darwin, I was bringing down pheasant and duck from the time I could hold a gun."

The night got worse, crew members stumbling blindly aboard. They could not recognize Captain FitzRoy, Lieutenants Wickham or Sulivan; were destructive, insolent, disobedient; in short, gone. Captain FitzRoy ordered several of the more incorrigible ones put in irons in the hold. It was a shocking experience to Charles; he had never seen drunkenness at this chaotic and abandoned level.

Boxing Day dawned clear and sunny, with the ideal northeast wind for which they had been praying these many weeks. But now they could not sail because of the drunkenness or continued absence of a large part of the crew. The officers were sober and distressed; Captain FitzRoy was furious. He spent the day grim-faced and tight-lipped.

By nightfall all the crew members had returned. Several more were put in irons. It was a heavy penalty to endure the repressive chains for eight to nine hours. They burst into crying spells, cursed everybody and everything on board.

H.M.S. *Beagle* weighed anchor at eleven o'clock on December 27, with Lieutenant Wickham in command; the commissioner brought his yacht alongside and sent word that he would like to tender Captain FitzRoy, Lieutenant Sulivan and Mr. Darwin a farewell feast. The *Beagle* tacked out with difficulty. The commissioner treated them to a luncheon of mutton chops and champagne, then at two o'clock sailed them back to their ship. Once on deck, Charles said, in an aside to Sulivan:

"Mutton chops and champagne! I hope that excuses my total absence of sentiment on leaving England."

"You'll think back to that meal with pleasure many a time before we return home," exclaimed Sulivan.

Every sail was filled with a light breeze. They scudded away at a speed of seven to eight knots. The sea was calm. Charles went to bed early, feeling fine. Not so the next day; the ship was pitching. . . .

At midafternoon he heard the call:

"All hands aft to witness punishment."

The officers stood in a single file in full-dress uniform on the quarterdeck. Lieutenant Wickham signaled Charles to join them. Below, the full crew was lined up at attention. Captain FitzRoy called out:

"Bring up the first prisoners."

Five men were brought up. The first was William Bruce, twenty-three, able seaman from Devonport. A short man, only five feet seven inches, with a sallow complexion, he was demoted one rank. Thomas Henderson, a boatswain's mate, married and also from Devonport, was dark-complected and older than most of the crew; he also was demoted. So were Stephen Chamberlaine and John Wasterham, both able seamen; and lastly, James Lester, the *Beagle*'s cooper, married and from Devonport and thirty-seven years old. He was demoted from able seaman to landsman. The five disciplined men were led to one side. Captain FitzRoy called:

"Bring up the rest of the prisoners."

John Bruce, an able seaman from Devonport, was brought up. Bruce was ordered to strip to the waist, then a leather apron was strapped around him to protect his kidneys. He was then roped by his wrists and knees to the grating. The cat-o'-nine-tails that the boatswain's mate had in his right hand was an inch thick, two feet long. Captain FitzRoy ordered:

"Twenty-five lashes for drunkenness, quarreling and insolence."

Bruce bent and swayed, cried out as the blows brought blood upon his back.

"David Russel, carpenter's mate, thirty-four lashes for breaking leave and disobedience of orders."

Russel was lashed until he fell unconscious.

"James Phipps, maintopman, forty-four lashes for breaking leave, drunkenness and insolence."

The blows were delivered.

"Elias Davis, cook and captain's steward, thirty-one lashes for repeated neglect of duty. . . ."

Charles was sick at heart and stomach, responding to the brutality. It was the first time he had witnessed such violence, and expended upon what he had decided the day before were "naughty children." He dreaded having to face FitzRoy after the floggings but considered it better to join the captain for tea so that he might not take offense. However when he entered the cabin and took his seat at the table, he found himself unable to look into his friend's eyes. FitzRoy said quietly:

"You disapprove, Charles?"

Charles gulped, knowing he had no right to intrude into Royal Navy matters.

"I was . . . not prepared . . . I hadn't known . . . seems brutal. . . ."

"Every naval officer knows the absolute necessity of a certain degree of what inexperienced persons might think unnecessary coercion, when a ship is recently commissioned. Abhorring corporal punishment, my dear Darwin, I am nevertheless well aware that there are too many coarse natures which cannot be restrained without it, not to have a thorough conviction that it could only be dispensed with by sacrificing a great deal of discipline and consequent efficiency. The conduct of affairs on board a ship depends upon immediate decision, upon instant and implicit obedience."

Captain FitzRoy's back was ramrod stiff; he had looked Charles full in the face while he talked. In the silence that followed Charles knew he would have to accept the challenge. He would be four years at sea under this man's command . . . and the rule of the Royal Navy. How to indicate to the captain that he was "on board"?

"I am a little fearsome about the flogging of the cook, sir," he ventured quietly. "Won't he avenge himself on the officers?" A smile touched his lips as he spoke.

"How could he do that?"

"By putting too much salt in the soup."

FitzRoy also smiled, tenuously. The tension relaxed in his shoulders. The knots in Charles's throat untied. The constrictions around his heart vanished as though someone had lifted a hundred-pound sack of potatoes off his back.

"Now it's open sea, with a fine wind in our sails all the way down to Teneriffe and South America," FitzRoy said quietly. "You will soon be going to work as a naturalist."

"What a glorious day that will be for me! It shall be as a birthday for the rest of my life."

# BOOK FOUR

*A Capacity for Wonder*

1.

T HEY were almost four hundred miles from Plymouth, in the Bay of Biscay, with a good deal of swell on the sea. The wind had increased, driving them onward into the Atlantic as fast as a heavily laden small vessel with her scuppers in the water could be forced. The master steered as southerly a course as was safe in hopes of keeping the east wind longer. They scudded away at seven knots but when Charles waked in the morning to an eight-knot wind he became seasick. He could keep down nothing except a few raisins and dry biscuit, a diet his father had recommended. Since the W.C. was immediately outside the poop cabin he managed to make it in time, a towel held tightly against his mouth. He was able to stretch out flat in his hammock and read for a few minutes . . . until the next frantic dash for the W.C.

"I went through the same ordeal during our first voyage," said his cabin mate, John Stokes, sympathetically; "it took me quite a while to get my sea legs."

"What I need is a sea stomach," muttered Charles. "The misery is excessive. It far exceeds what a person would suppose who had not been at sea."

Mr. Bynoe poked his head in the door.

"You're going to lose strength on that biscuit and raisin diet. I'll show Officers' Steward Ash how to mix sago with wine and spice, very hot. You'll enjoy it."

"Permit me to doubt."

Bynoe returned with a full soup dish of the mixture, put a pillow under Charles's head and fed him spoonfuls.

"How does the sago taste?"

"Like chewing balls of rubber. But the hot wine is wonderful."

Captain FitzRoy had named eighteen-year-old Syms Covington, the ship's fiddler and a second-class boy, to be the poop cabin boy. Syms was a former shoemaker from Devonport, with dark hair, blue eyes and a fair complexion. His oval face had well-modeled features but with a down-nose, put-offish manner, perhaps because he was a bit deaf. Neither Charles nor Stokes particularly liked him but he kept the poop cabin in good shape.

The next day Stokes and Covington helped him to dress. His legs were weak but he made it to the captain's cabin.

"Still alive, Darwin? How do you feel?"

"Retch-edly. Bad pun, but the best I can conjure up."

"Make yourself comfortable on the divan."

It was the last day of 1831. He stretched out on the sofa, spent a pleasant afternoon chatting with FitzRoy and reading Humboldt's glowing accounts of tropical scenery. He was able to have tea with the captain, then went on deck where he watched a shoal of porpoises crisscross gracefully in front of the *Beagle*'s bow. The ship flew a common commissioning pennant from the top of her mainmast, which bore St. George's Cross and a tail of red, white, and blue, almost thirty feet in length. He murmured to Sulivan:

"First life I've seen at sea."

"First life I've seen in you. Welcome aboard."

This was the hour when the crew took its leisure on deck, smoking, playing cards, some of the men dancing to Covington's fiddle, others singing sea chanteys, telling ribald jokes and swapping tales about their adventures in exotic ports. The crew was issued its rum allowance, a gill a day, half rum and half water. Most of them saved up their noon ration to go with their end-of-work ration. It was the first time Charles had seen the crew high in spirits. They were happy at play, somewhat like the enchanting dolphins.

The sea, he learned, was a capricious mistress. One day she took him into her calm loving arms; the next she spat choppy spray in his eye and he was so sick he could not get up, even to see Madeira when within twelve miles of it.

Then the weather turned steadily beautiful, the air mild and warm. It was like a spring day in England. Charles moved about the ship easily. He had lost a few pounds but his strength returned. At one o'clock he had dinner in the captain's cabin, FitzRoy encouraging him as he put away a hearty meal of soup, Kilner and Moorsom's preserved beef with pickles, fresh vegetables, dried apples and a sweet pudding.

"Now I know we won't have to bury you at sea," the captain commented.

"I assure you, you won't bury me anywhere, at sea or on dry land. The Darwins have always been tough old buzzards."

After ten days at sea they approached the sun-burned town of Santa Cruz on the island of Teneriffe with its great peak which FitzRoy called "the monarch of the Atlantic." In the calm of the sheltered bay Charles studied the town and the mountain through his spyglass. This was the island he had planned to visit with Professor Henslow and two of his Cambridge friends the following June. Alongside him stood Dr.

Robert McCormick, who entertained a congenital hatred for all tropical centers.

"It's an ugly and uninteresting town."

Charles could not contain his surprise at such a remark.

"Dr. McCormick, it strikes me as much the contrary. Those gaudy houses of white, yellow and red; the oriental-looking churches; the low batteries with the bright Spanish flag waving over them are all most picturesque."

There came the cry, "Heave to!" At that moment a small boat came into view with four rowers at the oars. Standing in the prow was a man in an official navy coat with a bright sash of authority across it, but wearing a cheap straw hat and rumpled pair of trousers. Behind him stood a Spanish officer.

"It's the British consul," said Wickham. "We generally report to him on shore."

"State your name, captain, port of debarkation," the consul called up.

"His Britannic Majesty's Surveying Sloop *Beagle*, Captain Robert FitzRoy commanding. Request permission for crew to land."

The officer behind the consul shook his head a vigorous "No!" The British consul called upward:

"Permission to land any member of the officers or crew is denied."

Lieutenant Sulivan, who could outshout Wickham, called down to the bobbing boat:

"Why? What's wrong?"

"There's cholera in England. Spreading from Newcastle on Tyne to London. They're afraid it will infect the island."

"We have no cholera on board!" cried Dr. McCormick.

The health official made a frightened speech.

"You must observe a strict quarantine of twelve days' duration."

Captain FitzRoy was fluent in Spanish. He replied:

"Invite them aboard to see our doctor's logbook and inspect our crew. They will find no cholera."

The health official was vehement in his rejection of the offer. They would not touch foot on an English deck.

Gloom spread over the ship like a tightly roped tarpaulin. Swearwords echoed through the crew. The men had not been longing, as Charles had, for Humboldt's dragon tree but for Teneriffe's girls.

The island rowers made for shore. FitzRoy held a railside conference.

"What would compensate for our delay?" he asked.

"Nothing, Captain," replied Sulivan, "except that it would be a great disappointment to Mr. Darwin."

There was a moment of silence while the officers studied Charles's

face. He tried to put down his bitter frustration. Not to see Teneriffe
. . . His first island and he could not land! Captain FitzRoy spoke
quietly:

"There are hundreds of other islands and other peaks he will scale in
the next four years. Up jib! Set sail for the Cape Verde Islands and a
landfall at St. Jago."

At ten o'clock that night they were still becalmed. Charles went on
deck in his shirt sleeves to chat with the man on watch. After a few moments he murmured:

"The warm night is doing its best to soothe our sorrow. The only
sounds I can hear are the waves rippling on our stern and the sails idly
flapping around the mast."

They beat about the rest of the night in a light baffling wind. When
Charles next went on deck the sun was rising behind the Grand Canary, its rugged form defined in the clearest outline. Everybody on
board, officer and crew alike, was smiling and active, some fishing, all of
them lighthearted because they could not withstand the delightful
weather.

"Me either," Charles declared to himself. "I'm going to work."

He went into the poop cabin, rescued from under the chart table the
strip of woolen bunting he had bought in Plymouth, as well as the
semicircular wooden hoop he had had steam-bent in the boiling house
at Devonport. He then sought out Harper, the sailmaker, asking him if
he would cut and stitch the woolen bunting to fit around the bent
hoop.

"Glad'a, Mr. Darwin. Get me outer the becalm."

With his woolen bunting forming a bag, Charles found Mr. May, the
carpenter, and asked him to cut a piece of wood to fit the curving top
half of the bag. Charles now had a bag four feet deep, with a wide-open
mouth. His next stop was at Borsworthick's, the ropemaker. Charles
asked him how long his drag lines should be.

"About twenty-five feet."

"Will you make me three twenty-five-foot lines, one end to be attached to the stern, the others to the wood support of this bag?"

"Take only a mo'."

The carpenter, sailmaker and ropemaker stood with him on the stern
when Charles made his first castoff. The twenty-five-foot ropes kept the
bag upright, its open mouth a couple of feet below the surface as it was
hauled at eight knots southward through the Atlantic Ocean. Charles
ran three trials of the bag, dumping his catch on an old piece of canvas
to protect Wickham's polished quarter-deck. He found a minuscular
amount of vegetation, which he combed out, then took his haul of marine life into the poop cabin. There were not yet any survey maps for

Stokes to draw and Charles had the chart table to himself. Wickham and Sulivan came to watch the show, as did Bynoe and the two youngsters, Musters and King.

Charles divided his spoils. The largest number of sea animals were jellyfish from the group of invertebrates known as Radiata. He also had some small dark blue creatures allied to the Portuguese man-of-war. There were minute crustacea, tiny relatives of the shrimp and crab. He sorted the normal sea plankton; then another variety of jellyfish known as medusae. There was a shout of laughter when he picked up his first sea squirt, which resembled a small bag with two holes, and got himself squirted squarely in the eye.

There was little use for his scalpel with this catch. He placed each category, including the Atlanta, small transparent molluscs, and the velella, a still different species of jellyfish, into small glass bottles with preserving spirits as he had been instructed by Henslow and Yarrell, marked each with a tin label, specified that they were found at 22° North, and then entered the number, content and date of each bottle in his "Catalogue of Animals in Spirits of Wine."

He looked up at the ring of fascinated faces surrounding the map table. Wiping his hands on the apron he had tied around his waist, he exclaimed:

"I'm taking the bag out for another haul, but I already feel triumphant."

There was some motion of the ship but his squeamishness vanished in the absorption of gathering more bags of sea animals and getting them accurately described, preserved and entered into his catalogue. He had taken in copepods, with an outer shell and feathery antennae; branchiopods, which looked like small yellowish shrimp which swam upside down and had many legs; the Portuguese man-of-war with tentacles which hung down two feet. Before he packed his fresh catch of medusae he decided to use his smallest scalpel for a dissection. He found there was not enough substance to these jellyfish to cut up.

He got out his marine biology notebook and wrote:

Its body is umbrella-shaped and fringed with tentacles. Around the mouth are four grooved oral arms. It also has four pouches containing the gonads or reproductive organs.

Stokes asked, "What do you suppose they live on?"

"Small invertebrates, I imagine. But I know what eats on them: the bigger fish. They explain why larger fish can live so far from land. These creatures are so low in the scale of nature, and yet so exquisite in their forms and rich colors. It creates a feeling of wonder in me that so much beauty should be apparently created for such little purpose."

Stokes studied a Cleodora under Charles's microscope.

"Why do you say their beauty serves no purpose? I was taught that beauty was sufficient unto itself."

"Because no one except fish ever sees them! The fish would swallow them just as avidly if they were formless and colorless globs."

All the way to St. Jago, a ten-day sail almost entirely south, he worked on the continuing produce of his net. He was now so busy that he found life at sea quite pleasant. He commented to Captain FitzRoy:

"I am become indifferent whether we arrive a week sooner or later at any port."

Charles and Captain FitzRoy settled into an amiable relationship. They had an ample breakfast at eight, dinner at one, which included rice, chick-peas, cheese, well-baked bread, fruit. There was only water on the table. Tea was served at five, after which the crew took its leisure hour on deck, making music on their flutes and whistles. There was a light supper in the evening. Meat was served from their supply of tins, along with such anti-scorbutics as pickles and oranges. All hands were served the same foods and portions. The midshipmen had all their meals an hour before, and the gun room an hour afterward. On land eating one's meals together was a social function; not so at sea. Whoever arrived first started eating. When through he returned to the job at hand.

Charles found Captain FitzRoy to be not so much moody as preoccupied. He obviously enjoyed having Charles around, and Charles liked to read on the captain's comfortable couch. But he was careful not to be in the cabin too often or for too long. FitzRoy was aware that Charles was leaning over backward in consideration, and appreciated his tact. Lieutenant Wickham, who admired Charles's classical education, had already dubbed Charles "Philosopher." When the crew watched him with a neat movement of his fly nippers collect a large gray-colored cricket resting after a nearly four-hundred-mile flight from Africa, he was promptly labeled "Flycatcher." But the name that stuck and brought him the most respect from the crew was "The man who eats with the captain."

"It's odd," Charles commented to Sulivan; "in Cambridge I was known as 'The man who walks with Henslow.' Now, only a few months later, my chief claim to fame is that I'm the man who eats with the captain!"

Sulivan could not resist even the feeblest of jokes. "The crew considers the captain God. Think of what it means—no sacrilege intended —to break bread with God! It makes you one of the disciples. . . ."

2.

It was three in the afternoon of a mid-January day when H.M.S. *Beagle* anchored in the bay of Porto Praya, near the western coast of St. Jago. To Charles the view seemed desolate. Volcanic fire of past ages and the scorching heat of a tropical sun had in most places rendered the soil sterile and unfit for vegetation. In between the massive strata of black lava he noticed a horizontal white band in the face of the sea cliff and could think of no explanation for it.

When he went ashore with FitzRoy and Wickham to call on the Portuguese governor, and on the American consul who also acted for the British, he was exultant. He was at last setting foot on tropical ground! He strolled about the town absorbing impressions the way a thirsty man laps river water.

Porto Praya seemed a miserable place, with a square and one broad street. In the middle of the *ruas* were lying goats, pigs, black and brown children, some without shirts. They were watched by black soldiers armed with wooden staffs. Rowlett, the purser, had come ashore to buy whatever fresh food he could. Charles feasted on oranges, which cost Rowlett one shilling a hundred. Rowlett also bought ripe bananas, urged Charles to try one.

"Good food for men at sea. Come along and help me make a contract with the most influential man here, an American married to a Spanish woman."

The American gave them coffee in his large and airy front room. Rowlett, a bookkeeper by nature, pulled some papers from his coat pocket.

"Each day we are in port we will require seventy-four pounds of fresh beef, thirty-seven pounds of vegetables, and one hundred fifty oranges."

"Delivered to your ship?"

"Quayside. Noon each day."

Charles found Stokes wandering around the main square.

"Take a walk with me, Johnny? From the bow I saw what looked like a deep valley."

In front of them the country rose in successive steps of tableland, interspersed by truncated, conical hills, the horizon bounded by an irregular chain of lofty summits. When they reached the valley, Charles got his first sight of tropical vegetation. His body quivered with a sense of fulfillment.

"Look, tamarinds, bananas and palms flourishing at our feet. See the gracefulness of their forms and the novel richness of their color.

Here's a grove of coconut trees. What happiness to come fresh from the sea and find yourself in the tropics that Humboldt described."

They returned to the shore, Charles treading on volcanic rock for the first time, hearing the notes of unknown birds and seeing new insects fluttering about still newer flowers.

Before returning to the ship he began a study of the horizontal band of white rock at a height of forty-five feet, which continued for miles along the coast. It consisted of calcareous matter with numerous shells embedded and rested on ancient volcanic stone. It was covered by a stream of basalt which must have entered the sea when the white, shelly bed was raised by volcanic action from the bottom of the ocean. He took his geological hammer from his pouch. For a thickness of several inches he found that the white matter had been converted into pure limestone. He brought out his notebook and silver pencil, recorded what he had seen. Walking back to the quay where one of H.M.S. *Beagle's* boats, filled with surveying equipment, was tied up, he observed to Stokes:

"It has been a glorious day, like giving eyes to a blind man. He is overwhelmed with what he sees and cannot justly comprehend. Such are my feelings, and such may they remain."

"They will, Charley. You have a capacity for wonder."

After breakfast the next morning he accompanied Captain FitzRoy and Lieutenant Sulivan to Quail Island, a desolate spot less than a mile in circumference. Here they set up an observatory and tents to serve as headquarters for checking instruments. Charles broke off pieces of volcanic rock, the first he had ever handled, studying the black porous material which had been spilled out from the bowels of the earth. He returned to the observation hut, showed Sulivan the peculiar honeycomb structure of the long-quiet lava:

"The first examining of volcanic rock," he exclaimed, "must be to a geologist a memorable epoch; and little less so to the naturalist at seeing live coral."

He collected numerous sea animals at the shore, many of them unknown to him. Then he went to have a lunch of tamarinds and oranges, resting below a low cliff of lava with living sponges and corallines in the tidal pools at his feet.

H.M.S. *Beagle* remained in St. Jago for three weeks. The days were hot. Although Charles returned to the ship at sundown, thirsty and covered with dust, he felt little fatigue. He returned with what he called his "rich harvest" of specimens and spent the evenings examining the rocks, plants, marine life. On his walks he invited along those friends who were free that day. He went to particular pains to have the two young ones with him, Charles Musters and Philip King. Both Bynoe and McCormick would have liked to go ashore each day but one of the doctors was obliged to remain on board. Only Lieutenant Wickham remained on board always; he was uncomfortable with the feel of earth under his feet.

"You landsmen love it. I was born in a watery womb and I'll die in a watery tomb. That's my epitaph."

One day while following a broad watercourse which served as a road for the country people, the path led Charles and Dr. McCormick to a baobab tree rumored to be six thousand years old. Charles no longer needed to feel deprived at missing Teneriffe. They measured its height and circumference. Charles was the only man on the *Beagle* with whom Dr. McCormick deigned to be friendly, yet he could not resist saying:

"I'm sure you know by now, Darwin, that you are on board as the captain's companion."

Charles decided not to take offense.

"When I see the rigid caste structure aboard a ship I'm certain the captain could use a little companionship. However I was recommended by Professors Henslow and Peacock as a naturalist, and hired on by Captain Beaufort as such."

Charles found life good while anchored in the bay. For dinner there was fresh fish which the cook called "barrow cooter," along with sweet potatoes bought from the natives. One day, crossing Red Hill, composed of recent volcanic rock, he, Rowlett and Bynoe met two black men from whom they bought all the goat's milk they could drink for a penny. A circle of bright-eyed black children surrounded them, chattering, drawing from Charles's copious pockets silver pencil, gun, compass and mountain barometer, all of which brought shouts of astonishment and laughter. When Charles caught a stinging ichneumon the children shouted warnings, pinched themselves to show the insect could pain him.

He walked with Musters along the coast and returned by an inland path. The island gave full scope to his enjoyment of geology. Nothing met the eye but plains strewn over with black and burnt rocks rising one above the other.

"There is grandeur in such scenery, and to me the unspeakable pleasure of walking under a tropical sun on a wild and desert island."

Musters' face was peaked.

"All I see is desolation, Mr. Darwin. I wish I was home in our greenhouse, with the damp smell of moss and hanging baskets of flowers."

Charles put a comforting arm about the boy's shoulders.

"Musters, you are this minute walking over one of the most explosive stories this world has ever known. Do you know what is happening inside our earth? It's a constantly boiling, erupting mass! If we walk in new and strange places, perhaps we can learn why."

Every day was a learning experience.

On board Charles used his time preserving and capping his marine organisms. He exclaimed to Bynoe:

"Have you noticed how all animated nature becomes more gaudy as it approaches the hotter climates? The colors in these marine animals will rival in brilliancy those of the higher classes."

Augustus Earle roamed the island, sketching with a keen eye and a strong fist.

John Stokes had begun drawing his maps, charts, tables of St. Jago and Quail Island. He was tolerant of his cabin mate's activities as each day Charles returned with a full pouch of rocks, birds, fish, insects, plants, shells, which he dumped onto his own half of the table.

"Glad to see you earning your vast salary, Charley," he said with a grin, "but do you mind getting some of those fresh-water creatures into your bottles with the triple covers? Else they're going to stink up this cabin."

"Right away, me boy. But seriously, geology is my chief pursuit. Look at this lava. Like spun glass. There is something in the comparative nearness of time which is very satisfactory while viewing volcanic rocks."

"Nearness of time? How near?"

"Perhaps ten million years . . . ?"

One Sunday a month they held divine service on board. The entire ship had been scrubbed clean on Saturday night. Charles exclaimed:

"Wickham, your lower decks would put to shame many gentlemen's houses."

Most sailors were religious because the sea was an unnatural place for man to live. God could plunge the ship to the bottom whenever He wished. It made sense to stand in well with Him. Though sailors read little else, most had been taught to read sections of the Bible and to memorize others. It was a solemn hour. The crew was dressed in clean clothes, the officers in full uniform. Charles wore the same long-tailed topcoat, double-lapeled velvet waistcoat, white shirt, high collar and tan stock with highly polished boots which he wore every evening to dine with the captain. The men assembled according to rank, in front and on either side of a table supporting a large ceremonial Bible from which Captain FitzRoy and Sulivan read in turn. Wickham sat considerably behind them, his crossed legs clad in white linen trousers, reading his own Bible but putting some distance between himself and the fervent ones. Charles suspected that the first lieutenant believed that, if he kept H.M.S. *Beagle* shipshape, God would temper the wind to the shorn-of-sails lamb. Augustus Earle set up his easel and canvas at the rear of the mess and painted an oil of the assemblage, with faithful portraits of every man and uniform, as he had done on another ship.

Charles spent his last morning in St. Jago studying the geological structure of the island, at one in the afternoon returning to the spot below the lava cliff where he had first grasped the origin of the white streak. Drinking a little water from his canvas-covered canteen, eating biscuit and tamarinds, it dawned on him that he might write a book on the geology of the various countries he visited. He reacted with delight to the concept, for there was the possibility that he might further document Lyell's *Principles*. It was a memorable hour. Then his sense of humor burst forth.

"Write a book on geology! Me? A cabin boy on his first journey, only six weeks out of Plymouth. Geologist . . . author . . . indeed!"

Though they set sail on a calm and beautiful day, the very fact of being at sea again made him uneasy. He plunged into cataloguing as the best antidote. On deck the crew was handling the sails so adroitly that H.M.S. *Beagle* overhauled the packet *Lyre* bound for Rio de Janeiro. When Charles and Stokes heard the triumphant cheers, they rushed out on deck to watch the *Beagle* close the gap. Mr. Chaffers, the master, who controlled navigation and course, was beaming with pride.

Stokes confided to Charles, "Another ship in a harbor is pleasant to have for company. 'Speaking' to another ship in blue water gives every man in the crew the assurance that he is living on an inhabited globe."

The afternoon ritual of "the day after port" was not pleasant. Charles was once again called up to the quarter-deck to watch the punishments. John Bruce, whom Charles had seen flogged after sailing from Plymouth, was given thirteen lashes by the boatswain's mate for excessive drunkenness in St. Jago.

"He'll desert in Rio," Sulivan whispered in Charles's ear. "As the expedition moves on we get rid of the drunks, by either desertion or discharge."

Captain FitzRoy ran a taut ship. He was a perfectionist. His early morning inspection of the tiniest detail of deck, mast, rigging was a ritual, though he never criticized his officers in front of the men. He had hand-picked Wickham, Sulivan, Chaffers. It was the midshipmen who caught the blast of his temper if a single spot of the deck had not been holystoned to a high gloss, or metal showed a beginning speck of rust. His tongue-lashings were so severe that at midmorning when the relieving midshipmen came on deck they would ask:

"How much hot coffee has been served out this morning?"

Yet when Charles met the captain in his cabin for breakfast, Fitz-

Roy was his usual genial self. Charles soon found out why: FitzRoy did not leave the deck until the caulking, chipping, painting, sail, rope or mast repairs had been completed.

He also learned that a ship is very much like a human being. Not everything appeared on the surface or could be seen by the naked eye. H.M.S. *Beagle* was a maze of complexities, contradictions and subtle nuances; in short, a microcosm, a floating world. He got along amiably with the officers as he had with his friends at Cambridge. Among the seamen he came to know the craftsmen who helped him with his work: the carpenter's crew, the sailmaker, the ropemaker, the armorer, the officers' cook, the two boatswain's mates.

It took considerably longer to become acquainted with the crew, for they were polyglot, speaking in half a dozen tongues, most with light hair and blue eyes. Though they all wore the same seaman's rough clothes and cap and were well tanned, there was usually an idiosyncrasy which marked one off from the other. John Macurdy from Aberdeen, Scotland, had a strong Scotch burr. John Davis, from Ireland, still had an Irish lilt in his voice. George Phillips was, like Charles's cabin boy Covington, a shoemaker, with gnarled and scarred fingers. Joshua Smith, a maintopman from Plymouth, had a pox-marked face. Ben Chadwick, from London, had a cockney accent. James Tanner, from Bristol, was as bowlegged as an American cowboy. Charles called the crewmen by name. It made it easier for them to accept him.

He enjoyed listening to the argot of the sailors, gradually coming to understand the meaning of such terms as yar, swabber, wind-bound in a port, "Ho, there!" and "Ha, boy?," a very snug frigate, well rigged (an attractive girl), sea calf, stinking tar barrel, "May I be keelhauled if . . . ," a taut gale, "ach-me of a sailor's hopes," clew line, sheets let fly, "All's a-taunto," "he goes to leeward," "half seas over," "spin up a rope like a spider," "longing for some flip. . . ." However he absorbed none of it into his own vocabulary. Nor did he attempt to master the techniques of sailing; he had work enough of his own as a naturalist.

He dined often with the gun-room officers. Here the clothing was less formal and more comfortable, as were the table manners and conversation. It was a good time to relax. The officers were allowed wine, and enjoyed a number of good vintages. What they were not allowed was to get drunk. That privilege was reserved for the crew when the ship was in port. He enjoyed the wine and the conviviality it sometimes occasioned; yet he felt a want of intimacy among them, owing perhaps to the gradation of rank.

He asked Lieutenant Wickham, who controlled the sailing, and ruling officer over the gun-room table, why none of the officers appeared to be good friends.

"The generally accepted maxim aboard a ship, Philosopher," he responded thoughtfully, "is that best friends may turn out to be worst enemies. That's why each of us maintains his independence. Blame it on the fact that we have to work together, week in, month out, in such a confined space. Also the fact that orders have to be handed down, and friendship gets in the way of their being carried out properly."

He wrote home on February 10:

2 DAYS' SAIL S.W. OF ST. JAGO<br>Lat. 11N.

My dear Father,

We have had a most prosperous, quick and pleasant voyage. At first—indeed till the Canary Islands—I was unspeakably miserable from sea-sickness, and even now little motion makes me squeamish.

There is only one sorrowful drawback; the enormous period of time before I shall be back in England. I am quite frightened when I look forward. As yet everything has answered brilliantly. I like everybody about the ship, and many of them very much. The Captain is as kind as he can be. Wickham is a glorious fine fellow. And what may appear quite paradoxical to you, is that I *literally* find a ship (when I am not sick) nearly as comfortable as a house. . . .

Give my very best love to everybody and believe me, my dearest Father,

Your most affectionate son,<br>Charles Darwin

Though he had written that he found the ship a comfortable home, he had as yet two unconquered difficulties: shaving and dressing in the cramped space. Though he had taken along his steel razor in its ebony case, as well as the strap on which to hone it, and Syms Covington brought him hot water from the galley each morning, the movement of the ship made him the servant rather than the master of the shave, emerging with cuts on his upper lip and chin. The tropical sun was turning his reddish hair several tones lighter; he let his sideburns grow almost to his chin so he would have less skin to scrape.

"Why not raise a beard?" Mr. Wickham twitted; "then you won't look as though you've come out of a duel every morning."

Dressing was irksome if less dangerous. He could wiggle into his loose-fitting seaman's trousers, with their broad bottoms, his socks and short boots by sitting on his chair. But when he had to stand up to get into his ankle-length underwear, shirt, loose stock tie and short seaman's jacket, most of which he had bought in Plymouth, he felt like a contortionist. When he was seasick he did not bother to dress or undress; even feeling well, it had taken him more than a month to don his simple seaman's clothes without scraping his elbows on the dresser or the bulkhead, and dressing formally for dinner with the captain was a monumental undertaking.

He turned twenty-three on February 12. The officers gave him a rousing party in the gun room.

3.

It was a week's sail to St. Paul's Rocks, their next stop. During several of the days a swell of the sea made him uncomfortable. He could not even read. From his hammock he lamented to Stokes:

"I have spent the last three days in painful indolence, whilst animals are staring me in the face without labels or scientific epitaphs."

The next morning he was awakened early by caulkers pounding away on the deck above him. He growled:

"A ship is a true pandemonium."

Stokes volunteered:

"A ship has to be repaired every day of her life at sea."

A strong trade wind drove them along. For Charles H.M.S. *Beagle* became a thing of beauty, with the wind billowing her sails like a series of pregnant women in starched white aprons. He was standing next to the captain on the quarter-deck above the wheel when FitzRoy caught St. Paul's Rocks in his spyglass.

"The rocks appear extremely small. Had we not been looking out for them I doubt whether they would have attracted attention. There's no record of any human ever having landed there."

Two of the whaleboats, with a half dozen oarsmen, were lowered three miles from the submarine mountain, one with Stokes and an assistant for surveying, the other with FitzRoy, Wickham and Charles for geologizing and shooting. Charles had become adept at lowering himself by means of the rope ladder over the side of the ship. He enjoyed watching these long rowboats pointed at each end, designed to move and turn swiftly.

The island was about forty feet above the water and a half mile in circumference. The sea broke with violence on the rocky coast. They found a somewhat quiet cove and affected a landing through the surf, trouser legs rolled up and shoes tied together around their necks. Once ashore they were staggered by the sight in front of them: multitudes, tens of thousands of close-packed birds, boobies and noddies. The birds did not budge. They had never seen humans before and were not aware they were dangerous.

Charles cried in astonishment:

"There's not even a way to walk among them without moving them aside."

FitzRoy and Wickham found sticks and beat the birds over the head, killing them for fresh food. The undisturbed birds made no move to fly away. It was an amazing sight, including the cliffs completely white with bird droppings. Wickham cried:

"Darwin, lend me your geological hammer."

"No, you'll break the handle."

Then, overcome by the exertions of his two friends, he too started banging away.

A determined struggle was also going on where the crew members had fishing lines over the side. When Charles walked back to the landing place with his quota of boobies and noddies, he saw that the sailors had hooked numbers of fine fish, which bit eagerly at every baited hook. But as soon as a fish was caught there was a rush of voracious sharks to share the spoil. In spite of the crewmen beating the water with oars and boat hooks, the sharks were getting at least half the catch.

Before he left St. Paul's Rocks, Charles dug out a specimen of the white dung of the multitude of sea fowl, plus some samples of the rock below, which he described, placed and dated, and then packed for shipment to England for a chemical analysis.

Next, H.M.S. *Beagle* crossed the equator. Captain FitzRoy received Father Neptune and his wife, Amphitrite, aboard. Charles and the thirty other initiates were gathered at 9:00 A.M. on the lower deck, the hatches battened down. It was hot and dark. Charles was prepared for any extravagance. He remembered the admonitions given him by Sulivan during his first dinner with the officers in their commissary in the dockyards.

Presently four of Neptune's constables came after him, blindfolded him and led him up on deck. As he stumbled forward buckets of water were sluiced over him from all sides. He was made to walk the plank. His face was lathered with pitch and paint. He was then shaved by two seamen using iron hoops. This ablution completed, he found himself tipped into a sail filled with sea water. His blindfold was removed.

One look at the open deck convinced him he was among madmen. One of the quartermasters, dressed as Neptune with a long white beard, was seated on a throne. Captain FitzRoy was surrounded by a set of the most demoniacal beings that could be imagined, stripped to the waist, their arms and legs daubed with color, broad circles of red and yellow pigment circling their eyes and streaked down their faces. He watched the demons dance a nautical war dance, exulting on the fate of the victims below.

Charles was applauded for his good sportsmanship. Captain FitzRoy, in white shirt and trousers but without his white uniform jacket, asked: "Are you thoroughly baptized?"

"I'm thoroughly wet down, if that's what you mean."

He watched the other novitiates get the same treatment. Then, as though by accident, he and FitzRoy were drenched by buckets of water by the cavorting constables.

Over dinner that night, bathed and dressed in a fresh white uniform, FitzRoy was in good humor.

"It's the crew's one chance during the voyage to get even with us," he said.

It was two more days' westward sailing before they reached the small island of Fernando de Noronha. Charles went ashore to explore the woods, returning with delicate flowers from magnolia and laurel trees, with crystals of glassy feldspar and a few needles of hornblende.

They sailed that night but ran into a dead calm, the ship's head standing the wrong way. The weather continued hot and moist. He felt as though he were sleeping in a warm bath, and stretched out on the chart table, finding its hardness pleasant after the round soft hammock. At midnight he went up on deck to gaze at the star-infested sky: the Southern Cross, the Magellanic Cloud. In the morning Sulivan harpooned a five-foot-long porpoise. The crewmen's knives started skinning at once.

Bahia, the first good-sized town on the eastern bulge of Brazil, was the nearest port to refresh their water and food staples. A steady trade wind drove them the two hundred and thirty miles toward the coast of South America. They were doing between twenty and thirty miles a day. The best so far.

Shortly after eleven in the morning at the end of February, they sailed into Bahia's Bay of All Saints, passing close along the steep but luxuriantly wooded north shore. The calm bay was alive with ships at anchor and under sail, as well as innumerable canoes with brightly colored sails. Charles had a view of the town which, embosomed in a luxuriant wood, rose like an amphitheater from the waterside to the crest of its hill. The houses glistening white in the sun seemed lofty.

"It's the windows," said Ben Bynoe. "See how long and narrow they are. The wide porticos, the public buildings and the convents, they all make a wonderful contrast."

He started out alone on his first penetration of a Brazilian forest. Every step set his brain awhirl; he was talking to himself, the tumult of his thinking and feeling would not have permitted him to hear or answer another human being. He beat his way into the jungle with its multicolored orchids growing as thick as weeds on the interlaced bushes and trees; the elegance of the grasses, the novelty of the parasitical plants, the glossy green foliage, all bewildered him.

"If my eye attempts to follow the flight of a gaudy butterfly, it is arrested by some strange tree or fruit. If I am watching an insect, I forget it in the flower it is crawling over. . . ."

He saw hundreds of strange flowers, plants, insects but he collected only a few specimens: butterflies, snapping beetles, ants, centipedes, spiders, land crabs. Caught in a sudden tropical rainstorm before he could reach the landing place, he took shelter under a thick tree. In a matter of moments a torrent began flowing down the trunk and he was wet to the skin.

Covington set out dry clothing. It was dark when he went up on deck and joined Lieutenant Wickham on the break of the poop. He heard a strange, loud noise coming from the woods.

"Wickham, what in the world is that? I swear to you that within the recesses of the forest a universal stillness reigns."

Wickham smiled indulgently.

"That is so, during the day. At night the insects sing their songs. Why not? They're safe in the dark."

"I want a sample of every insect in that cacophonous symphony."

The next day King and Musters joined him. Augustus Earle was barely able to contain his excitement at being able to paint in the jungle again. All four carried baskets and pouches to collect the brilliantly colored flowers that would delight Professor Henslow back in Cambridge.

They walked miles over small hills into the interior, each valley more beautiful than the last. Charles confided:

"These woods are so full of enjoyment that one could fervently desire to live in retirement in this grander world."

"Not me!" exclaimed King. "I want to sail the seas and become a captain like my father."

At the crest of a hill Charles flung out his arms.

"Brazilian scenery is nothing more nor less than a view in the Arabian nights, with the advantage of reality."

They did well, finding bats, lizards, winged ants, bedbugs, one of which drove its proboscis deep into Charles's finger; frogs, exotic grasses and strange parasitical plants. Then, returning to the shore, sea urchins, crustacean and fish shells, marine gastropods. When they dumped their collections on the chart table Stokes cried out:

"Get those slimy bugs and fish off my part of the table!"

Again Rowlett went into town to buy supplies: sugar, flour, raisins, cocoa, tea, tobacco, rum. The town looked better than it smelled, for waste materials were thrown out of the windows into the street below, not only rubbish and pots of used water but night soil as well. All labor was done by black men, who stood in great numbers around the merchants' warehouses. When dogtrotting under heavy burdens they beat time and kept themselves cheered by chanting.

"These are all slaves," Rowlett explained to Charles. "When the plantation owners don't need them, they come to town to earn a few coins."

"It's the first time I've seen *actual slaves*. It hits me in the viscera. How do they stand it?"

"They have no choice."

"How do the Brazilians stand it, living off slave labor?"

"Quite well. It frees them for more important pursuits, like making money . . . or love."

The next day he persuaded Lieutenant Wickham, who hated all cities, to accompany him and Sulivan for a walk through Bahia. They were undaunted by the fact that it was Carnival Day. The moment they entered the mobbed and celebrating town they were unmercifully pelted by wax balls full of water and were wetted through by large squirts out of tin cans. It took them an hour to reach the safety of the countryside; they decided to wait until dark before returning through the carnival crowds. To complete what Charles called their "ludicrous miseries" a heavy shower again drenched them to the skin.

Charles wrote in his notebook:

> One of the great superiorities that tropical scenery has over European is the wildness even of the cultivated ground. Coconuts, bananas, plantain, oranges, papaws are mingled as if by Nature, & between them are patches of the herbaceous plants such as Indian corn, yams and cassada.

The next day the sky was cloudless and the sun hot. Charles and Philip King stayed in the forest for eight hours. Charles commented:

"This heat could bring on indolence if we were not motivated. I've got some rocks in addition to numberless small beetles and that beautiful large lizard. It's a pleasant thing to be conscious that naturalizing is doing my duty."

"It's a happy thing you enjoy doing your job," said young King.

"No, Philip. Naturalizing isn't my job, except for this *Beagle* journey. When I return I must find a parish."

Before dawn he was awakened by a throbbing pain in his knee. He knew that he had pricked it on a thorny bush while capturing his large lizard; now the knee was badly swollen. He waited for dawn, then asked Stokes to summon Mr. Bynoe. Bynoe came at once, in his nightshirt, skillfully extracted the buried end of the thorn, went to the galley to get a pot of boiled water with which he bathed and then put a poultice on the inflammation.

"The problem is not the thorn," he said. "The area is feverish. It could be poison from the bush. You'll have to stay in your hammock until the swelling goes down, or on deck where it's cooler. I'll go into Bahia as soon as the shops open and buy whatever medication the locals use."

It was six days before he could walk around. His friends came by to visit, officers, the crew and craftsmen as well. Covington kept him well fed, sponged and cool. On deck he watched the sailors scrub their hammocks and clothes, loose the sails to dry, send the boats for kegs of fresh water, repair the ropes, paint the outside of the ship, get their mail, and take the captain's reports to the Admiralty over to the *Robert Quail*, a merchant brig leaving for Liverpool. In the warm evenings he listened while Covington played his fiddle and the crew members gathered around his deck pallet and sang:

"A sailor's life's a pleasant life,
He freely roams from shore to shore;
In ev'ry port he finds a wife;
What can a sailor wish for more?"

Or:

"I'm here or there a jolly dog,
At land or sea I'm all a-gog,
To fight, or kiss, or touch the grog."

In spite of the pain and the loss of collecting days he was not unhappy. For he knew that he had been accepted.

He dressed for a dinner which Captain FitzRoy was giving on the quarter-deck for Captain Charles Henry Paget of H.M.S. *Samarang*, anchored in the Bahia harbor. The conversation at the officers' table turned serious as Captain Paget spoke about the revolting condition of slavery in Brazil, tales of horror about the treatment of the blacks that made one's gorge rise.

"It is utterly false," Captain Paget proclaimed, "that even the best-treated slaves do not wish to return to their families in their own countries."

"They appear happy to me," said Captain FitzRoy. "It is for the greatest good of the greatest number. The slaves are infinitely better off under benign masters here than they were in the wild jungles of Africa.

They are cared for, given homes, assured food, medical help if they need it. How can anyone pretend that these savages are not better off in a white man's civilization?"

There was a silence on the quarter-deck.

Charles remembered that Mr. Wood in Cambridge had said that Captain FitzRoy was a conservative. He held his tongue. Then he thought of his father's lifetime work against slavery, his Uncle Jos's fiery pamphlets attacking the slave trade. To remain quiet would be cowardly. He kept his voice low and calm.

"If, to what nature has granted Brazil, man added his just and proper efforts, of what a country might the inhabitants boast! But where the greater parts are in a state of slavery, and where this system is maintained by an entire stop to education, the mainspring of human actions, what can be expected but that the whole would be polluted by its part?"

After Paget's departure, Charles spent an uncomfortable hour in the poop cabin regretting the altercation. Then the captain's steward summoned him. FitzRoy was standing by his desk in his cabin, his face pale.

"Darwin, you are very prejudiced. While you were laid up I visited a great slaveowner. He called up many of his slaves and asked them whether they were happy, and whether they wished to be free. They all answered, 'No.'"

"Do you believe the answer of slaves in the presence of their master is worth considering?"

He had not meant to be critical but he heard it in his voice. He was shocked at his own bad manners. Captain FitzRoy was furious. His face became a brick red, his spine stiffened.

"Since you doubt my word, we can no longer dine together!"

Charles walked blindly to his own cabin.

"Now I shall be compelled to leave the ship! When we have only just started. I've thrown away my great opportunity. What a fool am I. . . ."

He was standing by his bookshelf berating himself when Sulivan, Bynoe and Rowlett appeared. All three talked at once.

"The news has spread. . . . From now on you mess in the gun room. . . . Our food's as good. . . . The company is better!"

Charles was deeply touched.

"Gentlemen, I thank you most heartily. But I can't do it. It would make the captain angry with you."

Bynoe said, "Come along."

The gun-room officers were quietly jubilant. On a Royal Navy ship no one dared talk back to the captain. The underlying restraint due to their difference in rank was gone. But Charles had a gnawing anxiety. What was his own status on board now? True, the captain had not suggested that his services were no longer needed. . . .

At that moment Lieutenant Wickham walked in, a diabolic smile twitching one corner of his mouth. When he saw Charles, he exclaimed:

"Confound you, Philosopher, I wish you would not quarrel with the skipper. He has kept me in his cabin for several hours berating you."

Lieutenant Sulivan said:

"We felt you'd want Darwin here with us, now that he has no place to eat."

"Welcome to the gun room. But I think we're underestimating our captain."

Wickham proved to be right. It was only a short time later that the captain's steward appeared.

"Mr. Darwin, the captain asks that you please repair to his cabin."

There was silence in the gun room. Above all, Charles did not want another encounter with FitzRoy. He was unaccustomed to quarreling, to losing friends. He seemed unable to get up from his seat.

"Go along now," Wickham commanded. "Nobody disobeys the captain's orders."

Charles found Captain FitzRoy relaxed and amiable.

"Darwin, I offer my sincere apologies. I should not have spoken to you as I did. Of course you will continue to share my cabin. It's that outrageous temper of mine."

Charles felt as though the ship's surgeon had removed a stone from his heart.

"Sir, I apologize for my miserable tone of voice."

"We'll say no more about it. The slave trade has already entailed some of its lamentable consequences upon the Brazilians in demoralizing them by extreme indolence."

Captain FitzRoy was proud of himself.

"In the morning we are sailing to make soundings on the bank which runs on down for miles. There may be some ugly weather ahead and there's little sense in your getting seasick if you don't have to. Why not sleep ashore for a night or two? You'll find the Hotel Universe comfortable."

"Thank you. A flat bed in an unmoving room would have some charm for me."

At the Hotel Universe he found that he got along very well with the host by using the three words he had picked up: comer, to eat; cama, a bed; and pagar, pay. The flat motionless bed was such a joy that he wanted to stay awake and savor it but he was asleep by the time he sank one side of his nose into the high bolster.

The next morning he found an Irish boy to serve as an interpreter. He collected a great number of rocks, plants and insects. He caught a diodon, a porcupine fish, swimming near the shore. It was about an inch long, blackish-brown with yellow spots underneath. He found four soft projections on its head. A close study showed it had several means of defense; it could bite hard, squirt water from its mouth and at the same time make a curious noise with its jaws. He entered his observations in his ichthyology notes.

Warm from the heat of the sun, they entered a *venda*, a public resthouse, and drank sangaree.

The coast of Brazil belonged to a granite formation. Geologists believed the huge area, some two thousand miles long, had been crystallized by the action of heat under pressure. He asked himself:

"Was this effect produced beneath the depths of a profound ocean? Or has a covering stratum since been removed? Good question for my geology book."

4.

Only a few men were sufficiently qualified to handle H.M.S. *Beagle's* surveying instruments, to get and to chart results that checked out a dozen times and more, so that the information was completely authentic and reliable: the outline of the coast, the position of rocks, sandbanks, channels, anchorages, depths. The men who had been trained at the Royal Naval College at Portsmouth were the experts: Captain FitzRoy, Lieutenant James Sulivan; but there were others who had come up through the ranks who were equally reliable: Lieutenant John Wickham, Mr. Chaffers, the master, Stokes.

They in turn trained the young midshipmen who were preparing for a life in the Royal Navy. Those officers who were engaged particularly with the survey did not take part in the routine duties of the vessel; any more than the foretopmen, the maintopmen, or the sailmakers, carpenters or ropemakers were expected to handle the chronometers, sextant, transit, compass, telescope or theodolite, a heavy but portable surveying instrument used for measuring horizontal angles, which needed a level, unmoving base and so could not be used on shipboard but had to be based on shore.

Captain FitzRoy had a particularly good sextant which he had had made expressly for him by Worthington and Allan in London. This sextant was hand-held and could be used on board; despite the ship's motion it was accurate in measuring the angular distance between objects. FitzRoy had taught young Stokes how to hold it vertically to look through the built-in telescope and take sights of the sun, moon or a star. Its index error never varied. Each day Stokes watched eagerly for the sun's meridian altitude, with the sextant to his eye.

Sulivan, Stebbing and Stokes tried to teach Charles to take rounds of angles, measure base lines, determine precise longitude and latitude so that he could know exactly where he was; but he was invariably more interested in the flora and fauna of the various coast lines seen through his telescope than he was in learning from Stokes who, in the chart room, was using his plotting instruments, the proportional compass, dividers to make arcs of circles, the T square for perpendicular and parallel lines.

He did learn how to use his telescope to observe the passage of a celestial body across the meridian; and how to use the very good Gilbert's compass which was placed on a stanchion above the poop. On his land trips his own compass was always in his bag. When the weather was clear and fine he would stay up on deck watching the officers and midshipmen taking the bearings and angles necessary to map the coast properly. On shore he sometimes saw as many as six observers seated on the ground, each with his own instrument, taking the sun's circum-meridian altitudes or observing the stars at night. They made observations for latitude, time and true bearing, on the tides and magnetism. Nor was the time spent in port an idle one; a detailed plan of the harbor had to be made, its environs and triangulations, including the sounding for depth, all visible heights, the more remarkable features. H.M.S. *Beagle* carried six Massey's sounding leads which came with three hundred fathoms of line. FitzRoy kept leadsmen on the small platforms on the sides of the ship; one of whom, at least, had to sound constantly when the ship was close in. When the sea permitted the work was done from small boats.

For two months Captain FitzRoy had been testing his ship and checking his instruments for accuracy.

"Now," he told Charles over dinner on March 18, 1832, "we are ready to begin the serious business of our voyage, and the work will not stop until we have returned to Plymouth. We'll cruise the harbor until the charts are finished, then we'll draw the rocks and dangerous shallows southward of the port. All ships must guard against them when approaching Bahia as we did. The current generally sets toward the south; ships have gone ashore on the shoals as a consequence."

Heading toward the Abrolhos Islands, they reached the parallel of the islands and, being eastward of soundings laid down in any known chart, FitzRoy ordered three hundred fathoms of line let out. He could find no ground. Chaffers ordered the helmsman to steer westward; leads were dropped every two hours.

At two in the afternoon they still had no bottom. One hour later the lead hit bottom at thirty fathoms.

"How can this be," FitzRoy asked, "without there being the slightest change in the color of the water or in its temperature?"

They hauled to the wind, working eastward to ascertain the precise limit of the bank. Wickham swore as they lost their sounding as suddenly as they had struck it.

"I think we ought to put a grapnel over," he suggested.

"Give it two hundred fathoms of line," the captain added. "We'll steer westward again until we hit."

Charles watched the sounding operation with fascination, saw a heavy pull on the line and a sudden jerk. The grapnel, an anchor with three iron claws, was hauled up. The claws had been straightened out.

Stokes bent over his sketching paper.

They turned and headed for Rio de Janeiro, which would be their base for some time to come. Charles spent the long hours describing his collections in his separate notebooks. He did not know whether he was writing too much or too little. He did not know, since there was so little published material, whether what he found was known or unknown, important or even urgent.

He was often in the captain's storeroom at nine o'clock in the morning reading the barometers and recording the day-by-day differences in atmospheric pressure. It was one of his anchor points and gave him a sense of usefulness on board.

He found the ocean to be endlessly exciting; always alive, moving, changing, inhabited. He saw his first waterspout. From a black bank of clouds a small dark cylinder, shaped like a cow's tail, joined itself to a funnel-shaped mass which rested on the sea. The marines fired their biggest gun to break it up and the spout vanished in a heavy rainstorm. The sailors harpooned a big shark and the entire ship joined in the excitement of trying to bring it aboard. It got away. One day when fishing alone and using salt pork on a hook as big as his hand, Charles caught a young shark and became a momentary hero. The meat proved tough and distasteful.

There were frequent rain spells; quantities of Mother Carey's chickens, a sea bird of the petrel kind, hovered over the stern.

On April Fools' Day the whole ship was involved in mischief. At midnight the watch below was awakened by a series of tragic cries:

"Carpenters, we've sprung a leak!"

"Quartermasters, a mast is sprung!"

"Midshipmen, reef your topsails!"

The men ran out in their nightshirts. Charles swore he was not going to be fooled, but when Sulivan came into the poop cabin crying, "Darwin, did you ever see a grampus spouting and blowing?" he rushed out onto the deck only to be received by the watch with a roar of laughter.

Warm tropical nights, waterspouts, sharks, April Fools' jokes; these were what made life bearable, as Kotzebue had said in A New Voyage Round the World, "for crews when they are several months together, wandering on an element not destined by nature for the residence of man."

He was slowly becoming acquainted with the three Fuegians aboard. FitzRoy did not require the two males to work. They did so because they needed the respect of the crew with whom they took their meals and slept in the men's mess, their hammocks slung alongside.

Charles visited with sixteen-year-old Jemmy Button as often as possible but was thwarted by the fact that "no person exists with such a small stock of language, his own tongue forgotten, with only a modest amount of English having been acquired." Though Jemmy was the more amiable of the two he did not like taking orders from the officers, and had flare-ups of anger. He enjoyed the role of lookout, high in the crow's nest. When he quarreled he would retort:

"Me see ship, me no tell!"

One day Jemmy came looking for Charles.

"Me have dream in head. Me tell? Big animal chase me. Eat me. Me eat bad fish. Die. Me catch snowstorm. Freeze. Me die. What fashion you call that?"

"Where do these things happen in your dreams? In Tierra del Fuego?"

"Ya."

"Sounds as though you're frightened to go back. Are you?"

"Me no know. Me like warm bed, good clothes, good eat. What fashion you call that?"

"I would say that you like your comforts, Jemmy. I hope England hasn't spoiled you for life with your tribe."

"No speak tribe. All forget."

Jemmy liked the English. He would have liked to return to England with the Beagle.

Not so York Minster, who at twenty-eight catered to no one. He was frequently sullen. For him the Beagle was a prison.

It was plain that York bullied Jemmy, but he was protective of the eleven-year-old Fuegia Basket. He did not allow any of the crew near her. Fuegia's tiny cabin was guarded by Mr. Bynoe. A carpenter had attached to the wall of the cabin a table which could be lowered by the captain's steward when he brought Fuegia her meals. When the weather was good she spent her days on deck sewing her own clothing as she had been taught at the society, at other times crocheting, as Charles had so often seen his sisters crochet. She would explain to whoever stopped by:

"No idle hands."

Her attitude toward returning to Tierra del Fuego appeared to be halfway between Jemmy's and York's. Charles asked:

"Fuegia, will you be happy to get home to your family?"

"Me no make thing happen. Thing happen me. Captain take me England, me go England. Captain take me home, me go home." She smiled shyly, shrugged a shoulder. "Me live."

At sea there were few temptations to get in the way of his academic work. There were ferns and leaves to be stitched onto herbarium paper, specimens to be dissected, described, bottled or put in protective coverings. To make his records complete he wrote at considerable length in his day-by-day diary, describing not only the tropical sights but the character, condition and mores of the native peoples.

"I think you enjoy the writing," Stokes observed from his catbird seat on Darwin's right.

"You're quite right, Johnny. I'm completely at ease with a pen in my hand."

H.M.S. *Beagle* was a beehive of activity. The gunner was busy cleaning the small arms. The men on watch were "pointing," attaching short pieces of flat braided cord at regular intervals on the hawsers, the large ropes used in warping and mooring. The sail room was cleared and the sails aired; cables and chains cleaned; the lower deck washed, the maintopmast shifted, the rigging examined and repaired. All hammocks and clothing were washed twice a week.

Charles commented:

"The sailor's life is not a lazy one on board this ship."

"It would be dangerous for morale," said Wickham. "We keep every man jack hopping. It's not 'made work' but rather that every iota of our gear must be kept in a first-class state of repair. At sea that can be the difference between a wreck and a safe passage."

There were other dangers, unforeseen.

H.M.S. *Beagle* was heading south, not far off shore, when the greater part of the crew began to line her railing. She was coming into Cape Frio, site of the tragic wreck of the *Thetis* on which Captain FitzRoy had been a lieutenant for four years before its fatal end. Charles learned that the sailor does not openly fear the sea, not even in the worst of storms; yet there was an anxiousness in the back of his mind that one day his ship might become a *Thetis*, destroying herself and her crew against a rocky cliff. Using his telescope, FitzRoy stood on the quarter-deck and exclaimed:

"If any seaman were asked on what frequented shore there was least probability of a wreck, I almost think he would answer on that of Cape Frio. Yet against these high cliffs the Thetis crashed 'stem on,' going nine knots."

The Thetis had sailed from Rio de Janeiro on the fourth of December 1830 and worked against a southerly wind and thick foggy weather. From four o'clock to six she ran, by log, twenty-one miles; after six the weather became thick and rainy. At eight o'clock it was so dark and raining so hard that nothing could be distinguished half a ship's length distant.

William Robinson, now a foretopman on the Beagle, a veteran of long voyages yet only twenty years old, said:

"I called to Borsworthick here, who was on the forecastle, 'Look how fast that squall is coming.' "

Borsworthick, now the Beagle's ropemaker, put in:

" 'Twasn't more'n a minute when I see this cliff looming through the rain and darkness. I yelled, 'Land ahead!' and right then an officer shouted, 'Hard aport!' Then our bowsprit crashed into solid rock, and down come our three masts with a fall of thunder."

The deck was strewn with killed and wounded men. H.M.S. Thetis gave a tremendous yawn and sank.

The boatswain had succeeded in throwing the end of a rope to the rocks. On this rope men were slung, in turn, and hauled through the surf to a rough craggy cliff. Twenty-five perished. The accident was called a disgrace.

"But," exclaimed FitzRoy, "an English man-of-war may incur risk in consequence of a praiseworthy zeal to avoid delaying in port, which a merchant ship would be obliged to do."

"In short," volunteered Charles, "the Thetis was under orders to get somewhere fast?"

"It would certainly appear so, though I doubt it will save the captain from court-martial. Does the fate of the Thetis frighten you?"

"Frankly, yes."

"Only a fool would not be."

H.M.S. Thetis became the vivid symbol of destruction which would underlie every fearsome storm.

At dusk in early April they came into the harbor of Rio de Janeiro, the most beautiful the world and geology could present, with the mass of Sugar Loaf silhouetted against the clear night sky. As it was too late to secure a good anchorage, Captain FitzRoy put the ship's head to the wind and they cruised amidst great quantities of shipping, a flotilla of the British Royal Navy, and even larger squadrons of porpoises, sharks and turtles. Rio de Janeiro was the base for the British Royal Navy in South America.

Charles retired late to his hammock and dozed fitfully until dawn. He had been out of Plymouth four months. There should be letters from home; a sign that he had a place in England.

Because of the light winds it was not until late in the afternoon that Captain FitzRoy, in the full panoply of his uniform, went off by small boat to report to his commanding officer, Admiral Thomas Baker, on the flagship H.M.S. *Warspite*. H.M.S. *Beagle* had been dressed with its full quota of colorful flags. Lieutenant Wickham and Chaffers tacked gracefully about the harbor, taking in every inch of sail, then immediately setting it again, until they received a message from the flagship congratulating them on their beautiful order and discipline, adding that it was an event hitherto unknown for a "sounding ship" to make such perfect maneuvers. It was only then that Charles learned of Captain FitzRoy's order before he left:

"Show off the *Beagle* to her greatest advantage!"

While waiting for the mail to be delivered, Charles tried to dissolve his homesickness in the magnificence of the view: mountains as rugged as those of Wales, clothed in green vegetation, a row of palms outlining their crest. At the bottom of the nearest hills, commanding a vast bay studded with men-of-war carrying the flags of every nation, was the gaudy-appearing "Capital of South America," the city of Rio de Janeiro, with its mole, palace, cathedral and towers. H.M.S. *Beagle* would be using this harbor as its base for a month, sounding and charting up and down the coast. Captain FitzRoy had told Charles that he could live ashore the entire time. Augustus Earle, who knew the city well, suggested they rent a house on Botafogo Bay, four miles from the center of town, from which spot Charles would find himself in a collector's paradise.

At last the mail boat came alongside. All discipline vanished as the crew members deserted their posts and scrambled to find letters to them. Lieutenant Wickham thundered:

"Send the letters below! Every fool is looking at them and neglecting his duty."

Hellyer, the captain's clerk, reluctantly gathered the thick envelopes and took them below, distributing them to the men who were not on watch. It took a full hour before Charles could get his letters to his cabin. There were two from his sisters: one from Caroline and one from Katty; a third letter from Charlotte Wedgwood at Maer Hall; and a letter from Henslow forwarded from Plymouth. He devoured the

news like a starving man, for the letters were filled not only with the
current happenings but with affection and loving concern.

Caroline wrote:

> I have been able to think of little besides you and though I
> hope and believe all you see will be great enjoyment, the
> selfish feeling of the great separation from you and the *long,
> long* time it must be before I can hope to see you again is
> painful enough. In short, dear Charles, you will be properly
> valued when we do see you again. I find that Eras. has hopes
> that you will return at the end of two years & how we shall
> rejoice if his prophecy proves true.
>
> Papa is very well. . . . Our days pass much as usual, cards
> in the evening & after Papa is gone to bed, Ras, Charlotte &
> me draw round the fire and have an hour's cosy talk together
> generally about you. . . .

The Wedgwoods had come for a visit at The Mount; the Darwins
had enjoyed a long visit at Maer Hall. Erasmus went with them. For a
time it appeared that he was romantically interested in Charlotte
Wedgwood.

Charlotte had started her letter to Charles in mid-January. When she
completed it two weeks later, she announced her engagement to Mr.
Charles Langton, a young clergyman without a pulpit, and was about
to marry him.

To Charles it seemed that his leaving England had caused a hurricane of marriages. His cousin Hensleigh Wedgwood had married *his*
cousin, Fanny Mackintosh.

He continued headlong through the letters looking for word from
Fanny Owen; and came upon a shocking paragraph: Fanny Owen had
announced her engagement to Robert Biddulph of Chirk Castle, a
man with a none too good reputation. Fanny was to be married in
March. . . .

This was April 4. Good God! She was already married!

"And I've been letting her lovely image rest on my eyelids every
night to put me to sleep," he cried aloud. "I'd been gone from Shrewsbury only three months when she announced her engagement to Biddulph. And I thought she cared for me!"

There were tears in his eyes. For a long time he lay still in his hammock, aching.

"I've been a fool," he mourned. "Blind to all the facts that surrounded me. Mr. Owen wanted me as a son-in-law, but that was the
end of it. Fanny was every man's favorite. Her first need was for admiration and attention. There was no more chance of her waiting three or

four years for me than porpoises in the sea could wait on top of a mast
three years for water to swim in."

He picked up Katty's letter:

> I believe Fanny and Biddulph go first to Chirk Castle for a
> week and then to London for the Spring. . . . You will find
> her a *motherly old married* woman when you come back. I
> hope it won't be a great grief to you, dearest Charley. You
> may be perfectly sure that Fanny will always continue as
> friendly and affectionate to you as ever, and as rejoiced to see
> you again, though I fear that will be but poor comfort to you,
> dear Charles.

He sat down immediately at his corner of the map table and wrote
to his sister:

> If Fanny was not at this time Mrs. Biddulph, I would say poor
> dear Fanny till I fell to sleep. I am at a loss what to think or
> say; whilst really melting with tenderness, I cry "my dearest
> Fanny."

Then a strange thing happened to him. The picture of Woodhouse
and the Forest which he had loved was blocked out of his mind. In its
place came a distinct picture of the sunny flower garden at Maer Hall.
Of Uncle Jos and Emma fighting for his opportunity to sail round the
world.

He rose, went to his chest with its memorabilia from home, closed
the silver locket containing Sarah Owen's lock of hair, went on deck and
dropped it into the sea.

5.

He landed with Earle at the palace steps and wandered through the
crowded streets. From the bright colors of the houses, ornamented by
balconies, from the numerous churches and convents and the numbers
of people hurrying along, the city had an appearance which bespoke the
commercial capital of South America, and seemed in a perennial state
of fiesta.

Earle made an excellent guide.

"This town could drive a painter mad. The splash, the color, the
greenery. . . . I painted it before and I shall do so again, but we're
competing against God, who painted His masterpiece here in Brazil."

"I also want to get into the interior from which no one has reported," Charles said.

The captain had asked if they would take Philip King in with them. It was an enchanting four-mile walk on a dirt road along the coast, with the mountains at their back to Botafogo. Botafogo Bay was a natural amphitheater of beach and sparkling sea. They found a pleasant clapboard house painted pearl gray, with screened porches on three sides; a modest sitting room and three bedrooms, each with a small cot, rough wood table and chair. The rear porch, just behind the kitchen, was an eating area overlooking the mountains. The house and garden were overwhelmed by flowers and situated close to a loch.

Mr. and Mrs. Bolga, the owners, gave them a good rate, twenty-two shillings a week per person. They lived in a small cottage at the back of the grounds from which Mrs. Bolga, with a face like the waxed mahogany dining table at The Mount, would emerge to cook their breakfast and dinner.

Back in town, Earle introduced Charles to his friends as they sauntered into the Table d'Hôte restaurant, whose rum drinks were the tallest and coldest. There were British and American businessmen, consuls of several countries, naval officers, habitual travelers. Shortly after they were seated at the round "English speaking" table, a red-haired Irishman named Patrick Lennon came in and greeted Earle.

"Couple days later, I'd have missed you. Going upcountry to the Rio Macae. Eight years ago I purchased forest country up there and sent an English agent to develop it. Never received a single pound in remittance. I leave to investigate."

Charles asked, an excited gleam in his eye:

"How long a journey is it? Through what kind of country? I'd like nothing better than a chance to come along."

"About a week each way," answered Lennon. "I could use a companion; and another gun. Won't have anybody to talk to except my young nephew and a Scotsman named Laurie. Got calluses on your arse so you can sit a saddle twelve hours at a crack?"

"I ride and I shoot. When do we leave?"

"In three days. Be at Praia Grande, a village across the bay, by nine in the morning. Bring a blanket. We'll eat off the land. I'll rent a horse for you."

It took Charles an entire day to get his passport for the interior; the Brazilian officials saw no reason why a hasty young English stranger should importune them in the heat of an April day. The next evening he, Earle and Philip King moved some of their possessions from the *Beagle* to Botafogo. When Charles set up his table with his microscope, bottles and containers for specimens, the room took on the appearance of a laboratory.

On the third day he had himself ferried to the village of Praia

Grande. Lennon was waiting for him. The party included a young
friend of the Scotsman named Gosling, a Brazilian guide from the interior; a black boy to serve as general factotum. Charles had his flycatcher
in hand.

They passed through an intensely quiet woods abounding in large
elaborately colored butterflies, some cultivated fields, and then were
again in jungle, with gleams of sunshine penetrating the entangled mass
of foliage, the trees loaded with parasitical orchids. At noon they rode
through the small village of Ithacaia, with good Brazilian houses surrounded by the huts of the slaves. They slept that night at a *venda*,
which provided them only with straw mats, and left before sunrise,
passing through a narrow sandy plain between the sea and the interior
salt lagoons. Charles was tantalized by the number of fishing birds in
the air: egrets and cranes. The light and heat from the white sand
distressed his eyes. His thermometer stood at 96°. But the view made
up for it, the wooded hills reflected in the water of the lagoon.

"I hate scenery," said Laurie. "I brush it out of my eyes the way I do
flies."

That night they stayed at a larger *venda*, built of thick upright posts
with interwoven tree branches. There was a roof and an earthen floor.
After they had unsaddled their horses and fed them Indian corn, they
were led to the front veranda set with tables and benches. Lennon
bowed low to the host:

"Would you do us the favor to give us something to eat?"

"Anything you choose, sir."

"Any fish?"

"Oh no, sir."

"Any dried meat?"

"Oh no, sir."

"Any bread?"

"Oh no, sir."

Two hours later there was still no food on the table. To Charles's
question, Lennon answered:

"It will be ready when it is ready. If we remonstrate we shall be told
to proceed on our journey as being too impertinent."

Finally they were served a bowl of fowl, rice and farina. The guide
said:

"We're lucky. Often the guest is obliged to kill his own poultry."

Charles looked about for knife and fork; Lennon's nephew indicated
his ten fingers.

Charles went to sleep on the wooden platform covered by a thin
straw mat; but not before observing that the room was filthy.

"If all I wanted was clean sheets," he declared, "I should have remained at The Mount."

Yet the next evening, at Campos Novos, they fared sumptuously in a clean and agreeable *venda*: biscuits, wine and spirits with dinner, fresh fish for breakfast, all for a little over two shillings a person.

"Luck of the road," observed Lennon. "Digest the bad with the good and you survive."

The following two days Charles collected plants, insects, shells from the fresh- and salt-water lakes they passed. They entered still another forest with lofty trees. He wrote in his notebook:

*"Wonderful, beautiful, flowering parasites."*

They came upon conical ants' nests measuring twelve feet high. Charles stopped to cut out a piece for chemical analysis back in London. They arrived at Ingetado after ten hours in the saddle. They rode together, ate together and kept their rifles at the ready, but few words were spoken . . . except when Laurie, the Scotsman, insisted on having an itemized bill for everything he was served. He never got one.

One morning Charles awoke feeling unwell. Waves of shivering swept through his body like wind over sails. He told no one. He crossed the Barra de St. João in a canoe, his horse swimming alongside. When the party stopped for food he was able to swallow nothing. He traveled on until dark, digging his knees hard into the horse's flanks to remain in the saddle.

That night they stayed at the Venda da Matto. He dropped off into short nightmares; he was ill, in a foreign country where he did not speak the language, where there was no doctor or medication. He awoke in a fevered sweat but the moment his head cleared he put away his terror.

"I ate or drank something that poisoned me. I'll fight it off."

He did. He got through the day's travel to Socego, the comfortable home of Senhor Manuel Figuireda. From a distance they heard a bell clanging and then a cannon shot. Laurie cried: "That's our welcome!"

The house, constructed like an English barn, was built on top of a hill with a brook running beneath it. The pasturage had cattle, goats, sheep, horses; around the house were orange and banana trees. Close by was a shed for cooking and a large storehouse. There were stables and workshops for the blacks. The house was floored, thatched with reeds, the windows covered with shutters. The sitting room was furnished with gilded chairs against whitewashed walls.

Charles considered he had done himself proud through the first half dozen courses when there appeared from the kitchen a roasted turkey and a roasted pig. Senhor Figuireda was an intelligent patriarch and a good executive who was building roads to the nearby towns on which to transport his goods. His hundred and ten black slaves were well treated, reasonably well dressed and well fed, trained in a craft. The way the children kept coming into the dining room and having to be shooed away through the entire meal indicated they were certainly not living in fear.

He recouped so completely that he went out with Senhor Figuireda to tour the fazenda, a large cleared ground cut out of an almost boundless forest. He made notes about the coffee harvest, mandioca or cassada, the roots of which were ground into a pulp, pressed dry and then baked into farina.

The next day they traveled through a forest where Charles saw toucans and bee eaters. They were well received by Mr. Cowper, Mr. Lennon's agent, but it was obvious that the fazenda was poorly run. The slaves were overworked and underfed. Lennon and his agent fell into a violent disagreement. Lennon became so angry that he threatened to sell at public auction an illegitimate mulatto child Cowper was so attached to, it was believed to be his.

Back at Socego, Senhor Figuireda finally arbitrated the differences; no slaves would be sold; Lennon would begin to get some money out of his investment.

After wonderful days as a guest at Socego collecting reptiles, flowers, ferns and plants that Charles believed had not been seen in England, as well as an assortment of strange insects, Charles, Lennon and his nephew, started the journey back to Rio de Janeiro. It turned intensely cold; there was a downpour of rain, the wooden roads became quagmires; several wooden bridges were down, obliging them to make wide detours; the *vendas* were so poor they were reduced to sleeping on Indian corn. Having lost their passports en route, they were detained by guards at Rio de Janeiro until they could prove that the horses they were riding were not stolen.

Charles exulted over his adventure into the Brazilian interior, and his two saddlebags full of specimens.

Paying a visit to the *Beagle*, he was surprised to see how many changes had taken place during the two weeks of his absence. Riding out from the wharf in the tender, he found himself surrounded by new faces. Three of the able-bodied seamen who had been flogged had deserted. Two others were invalided home. Seven crewmen were discharged or transferred to H.M.S. *Lightning*, two others to H.M.S. *Warspite*. They were replaced by men from other Royal Navy ships. Wickham said:

"We anticipate this sort of thing when we reach our first Royal Navy

Base. We weed out a few, a few more weed themselves out. Note that the officers don't change. By the way, drop in on the skipper."

Dr. Robert McCormick, by common consent, was in process of being invalided home. He made it clear to Charles that he bore him no animosity.

"Darwin, I've found myself in a false position on board this small and very uncomfortable vessel. I've been disappointed in my expectation of carrying out my natural history pursuits. Every obstacle has been placed in my way. I am to be allowed passage home on H.M.S. *Tyne*. I board at midnight. . . . But first I must purchase a gray parrot in the market place."

Captain FitzRoy was in his cabin comparing his Bahia charts with those published by the French expedition under Baron Roussin. He glanced up, his face a study in concentration, as Charles entered.

"I'm invaliding the *Beagle* back to Bahia in a few weeks for more charting. Our results accord completely with the recent high-level findings of Captain Beechey. Unfortunately there is a difference exceeding four miles of longitude between his charts and those of the Baron Roussin. I'm resolved to return to Bahia and ascertain whether the *Beagle*'s measurements are correct. . . . That will give you landfellows another two months on shore. Does that make you euphoric, Philos?"

Charles was warmed by the foreshortening of his nickname.

"It does, sir. Rapturous."

"Fuegia Basket has not been well. Mr. Bynoe can't determine what it is. Can you find room for her in your Botafogo house?"

"I'm sure Mrs. Bolga will take the girl under her wing like a mother hen."

He moved more of his possessions into Botafogo the following morning. Two seamen unlashed the jolly boat behind his own poop cabin. They loaded it with his books, writing supplies, boxes, corking materials. He directed the seamen to head at an angle for the white sand beach of Botafogo. Just before landing two waves broke over and swamped the boat. Charles, drenched, cried out when he saw his books and supplies floating about.

"Oh, good God, no! Everything that's most valuable to me . . ."

"No offense, Mr. Darwin, but let's move fast instead of teeth-chattering."

He moved at his swiftest, the two seamen securing the boat, then helping him drip water out of his supplies. The three of them carried armfuls to his nearby house, where he spread everything on the porches, out of the direct sun. His writing materials were in a water-resistant bag, but the books and cases showed sea stain. It took all that day and the next to get the repair job done.

He now had until July 5, when H.M.S. *Beagle* was scheduled to sail for Montevideo, almost ten weeks of freedom, to collect. He worked at the host of sea animals with which every ditch abounded. One hour's catch kept him in full employment preserving and capping for the rest of the day. He wrote up his diary for the two-hundred-mile Rio Macae trip, commented to Earle, who was ailing and not able to paint:

"When the naturalist takes his walks in England he enjoys a great advantage in frequently meeting with something worthy of attention. Here he suffers a pleasant nuisance in not being able to walk a hundred yards without being fairly tied to the spot by some new and wondrous creature . . . a howler monkey, a click beetle or a stinkhorn mushroom."

"Look out for this jungle," Earle said with a pale smile. "It will render you unfit to live in any moderate clime. England in particular!"

During the first days in May, Stokes brought Charles two letters which had been delivered to the *Beagle*. One from his sister Susan, the other from Fanny Owen, dated March 1, 1832.

Susan's letter, dated February 12, congratulated him on his birthday. Each sister was taking one month to write in turn, not a letter started at the last moment before the packet sailed, but a continuing day-by-day diary so that Charles would know everything that was happening:

> Harry and Jessie Wedgwood are spending a fortnight with us. They fall into our ways so nicely, and take to the rubber of whist as kindly as possible. Harry Wedgwood reads aloud to us from *Joseph Andrews*, which, with plenty of skipibus, we found very amusing. I have just been reading the *Mutiny on the Bounty*. It is a very old story but very interesting from Beechey's account of the happy state he found the mutineers in at Pitcairn Island. Your friend, Professor Adam Sedgwick, stayed over on his way to North Wales. He put me to the blush. I have played a good deal of music this winter for your sake.

She also wrote that Charlotte Wedgwood and her husband Charles Langton had a chance of a parsonage at Wistanstow. It set his mind to wondering about his own future chances for a parsonage. Would the post carry a living? How soon after he returned could he hope for a congregation? Would it be in an area where a naturalist could take delight in his collecting?

The letter from Fanny Owen told him of her engagement to Biddulph and of her coming marriage. The wound of the first news had healed. The letter sounded shallow, flighty. Rereading it, he concluded that Fanny had indeed cared for him as an amusing playmate. That her

feelings of "sincere regard and affection" were little more than what she
described as "a merry chat" or a playful romp, all done in the high spirits
of youth. She had had no love for him.

He came to the conclusion also that he had been fortunate . . . nevertheless he continued to feel a vacuum where his love had been.

He kept up a running letter to The Mount to be dispatched every
time a packet or man-of-war departed for England, addressing his letters
to Caroline or Katty or Susan, though they were primarily written to
keep his sixty-six-year-old father involved in the *Beagle* journey and free
from anxiety. Knowing how troubled his father was about his youngest
son becoming a wanderer and dilettante, he added:

> Although I like this knocking about, I find I steadily have a
> distant prospect of a very quiet parsonage, and I can see it
> even through a grove of palms.

After his letters had been read aloud several times, without skipibus, by
his Mount family, they would be sent to Maer Hall for the Wedgwoods.

6.

The days glided quietly away. There were torrents of rain when, clad
in his oilcloth hat and cape, he was able to go out for only an hour or
two between showers. Mrs. Bolga fussed over Fuegia Basket and
Augustus Earle, dosing them with her own herbal medicine. When he
took young King to the *Beagle* to report for duty for the trip back to
Bahia, he found that of the twelve men who had made an excursion in
the cutter to the Rio Macacu, which he had missed because he was drying out his drenched supplies, three had come down with a malignant
fever: Charles Musters, John Jones, a promising young boy who had a
promotion coming the day he went down, and John Morgan. Charles
asked Mr. Bynoe:

"Why these three out of twelve?"

"Because they disobeyed orders. They were told not to go bathing in
the Rio Macacu. All the rivers flowing into the Macacu are pestilen-
tial."

"They'll be all right?"

"I can't tell. I brought out the two most highly regarded doctors in
Rio de Janeiro. They agreed it would be better to leave them on board
with me where I can watch them."

Among his plants he had a wide variety of orchidae, creepers, rope-
like liana, mimosae, tropical herbs and shrubs of the bean family;

camphor, breadfruit, jaca, hymenophyllum; agave, with its numerous flowers on a spike; Spanish moss; samples from the coffee bean tree, cinnamon, cabbage palms.

The earth and air proliferated with insects: fresh-water scavenging beetles; fireflies, cicadae, a type of locust; vampire bats; shining elaters; leaf-cutting ants, swallowtail butterflies; rapacious Hymenoptera, wasps, walking sticks, praying mantises, cockroaches, palm weevil, snout beetles . . . many of which he had never heard of. It was a giant task to describe, classify, catalogue, dissect, pin, preserve them all. He loved every moment of the work, both sides of the exhilarating adventure: outside, collecting; inside, preserving. It was, admittedly, a job of work. His specimens, boxes, jars, rocks, fish, marine life and insect collection outgrew his bedroom and spread onto the verandas where he did his dissecting and pickling in strong spirits of the fish and marine life.

With all this plethora of nature's live resources, he did not neglect his cardinal interest, geology. He found that the district was formed almost exclusively of gneiss, composed, like granite, of quartz, feldspar and mica, but with a foliated structure whose composition had been changed by heat and pressure. The gneiss abounded with garnets. He observed boulders of greenstone; and on the islet of Villegagnon, two large dikes, long, narrow crosscutting masses of igneous rock, and at the base of the Corcovado, iron-bearing quartz.

On May 18 he wrote to Professor John Henslow, telling about what he had seen and done so far on the voyage, the geology of St. Jago, the expedition to the Rio Macae . . . that he was "now collecting fresh-water & land animals, and am at present red-hot with spiders. They are very interesting, & if I am not mistaken I have already taken some new genera. . . ." He had determined not to send a box till they arrived at Montevideo, and he asked Henslow please to "tell Prof. Sedgwick that he does not know how much I am indebted to him for the Welch expedition," which had given him an interest in geology which he would not give up for any consideration.

He climbed the Corcovado, about two thousand feet high, with Augustus Earle, following the aqueduct, ascending the steep sides to the very summit, which was clothed by thick forest. Gaining the peak, he beheld the view which was one of the most celebrated in the world. He exclaimed:

"If we rank scenery according to the astonishment it produces, this most assuredly occupies the highest place."

He spent agreeable evenings at home with Fuegia Basket and Earle, reading Anson's book of travels. At the same time he found that an eligible young bachelor, a few months out of England, was a prize in the English-speaking set of the city. Mr. Aston, the British minister, invited him to his home for dinner. Captain FitzRoy had apparently spoken well of him to his commander-in-chief, for he was invited several times to dine at Admiral Thomas Baker's. Admiral Baker invited him to an inspection of the H.M.S. *Warspite* and to dinner on board, where he met convivial young Royal Navy officers. The British attaché invited him to hear a celebrated pianoforte player. Earle teased him:

"Flycatcher, you're the most popular young man in Rio. I'm confident that someone is going to offer you a handsome job and a handsome daughter in marriage."

He found Philip King at the Botafogo house the evening the *Beagle* returned. He could tell by the expression on the young boy's face that something was wrong.

"What's happened, Philip? Were our charts inaccurate?"

"On the contrary. The skipper was gratified to find that our measurements from Rio de Janeiro to Bahia confirmed those we previously made, to a second in time. Our maps will be the accepted ones now."

"Good show."

There was silence before King went on.

"John Morgan died of his fever. We buried him at sea. Five days later John Jones died . . . and Charles Musters. We buried them both in the English cemetery in Bahia."

Charles slumped into a chair. Young King was crying.

"I know how you feel, Mr. Darwin. You took care of Musters like a brother."

"Poor little fellow," mourned Charles. "Only fourteen; he hadn't begun to live yet. He was so homesick. Now he'll never see home again. My heart breaks for him."

During his last two weeks in Rio de Janeiro Charles went constantly into the forest, a "gold mine to a naturalist." At this point he was forced to admit that "it is wearisome to be in a fresh rapture at every turn of the road; but you must be that or nothing."

While the *Beagle* was being provisioned with fresh food he spent his last days working on his corallines and taking a climactic walk through a Brazilian jungle. High above him Charles saw a huge bearded monkey hanging stiffly by its prehensile tail. A mulatto boy accompanying a young Brazilian had an ax with him. They started cutting down the enormous tree.

"You cut down a whole tree to get to a dead monkey?" Charles asked, round-eyed.

"Why not? Too many trees; too much forest."

The tree fell with a tremendous crash, tearing up the earth and breaking other trees on its way down.

It was symbolic of Brazil's prodigal abundance.

That evening the quiet neighborhood of Botafogo celebrated the eve of St. Juan. There were huge bonfires and a continual firing of rockets, guns, fireworks throughout the night. Toward dawn, still wandering around quite sleepless, Charles encountered Earle looking wan.

"Does this seem to you a curious way to honor a saint?" he asked Charles. "Sounds to me like they're trying to blast him clear out of heaven."

On July 1 Charles attended divine service aboard H.M.S. *Warspite*. He found it an impressive ceremony, particularly when the six-hundred-and-fifty-man crew took off their hats at the playing of "God Save the King."

Later that day he moved his possessions back onto the *Beagle*. It felt strange to sit once again in his confined corner of the poop cabin. The eleven weeks had passed delightfully. His feelings on leaving Botafogo were full of regret and gratitude.

As H.M.S. *Beagle* sailed past H.M.S. *Warspite* and H.M.S. *Samarang* the crews of the two warships manned the rigging and gave them a true farewell, with three gusty cheers. The band on H.M.S. *Warspite* struck up "To Glory You Steer." Charles exclaimed to Captain FitzRoy:

"There is a fraternity of the sea."

"Doubly so because each ship sails alone so much of the time."

H.M.S. *Beagle*'s masts were strongly supported by larger crosstrees and tops and by larger rigging than usual in vessels of her tonnage. In no place was a block or a sheave allowed which did not admit the proper rope or chain freely. There were large trysails between the masts, made of stout canvas, with several reefing points.

For the first three days sailing southward to Montevideo and Buenos Aires, Charles found the weather provoking; light variable breezes and a long swell. He was not seasick, merely miserable. On the fourth day a stiff breeze came up; to his eyes it seemed a gale. Mr. Chaffers thought so too, for he lowered the topgallant yards and struck the masts. H.M.S. *Beagle* now glided gracefully over the waves, "appearing as if by her own choice," Charles said to Stokes, "to avoid the heavy shocks."

The *Beagle* had become a living, breathing creature, with a character all her own: strong, forceful, resilient. There was no longer any way for him to think of her as an inanimate object hammered together of wood, copper, caulking, ropes, canvas and masts. The ship itself was the most important individual on board, more so even than her captain, for on her steadfast performance and reliability the fate of the entire crew depended. Including its unfinished naturalist.

In mid-July he awakened to a bright sky and smooth water. The sea and air were alive with whales, petrels and Cape pigeons. There was a new feeling aboard. When he breakfasted in the gun room the officers were excited about seeing and exploring the as yet undescribed coast of Patagonia. Sulivan said:

"Now that we're going into the wilds of Patagonia, why don't we raise beards so we too can look like wild men?"

They did. At first Charles's growth was itchy but soon he sported a scraggly red beard and was overjoyed not to be nicking himself with his razor. Going on deck after breakfast, he breathed in jubilant lungfuls of cool fresh air as the ship moved gracefully ahead at nine knots.

It was time to have the carpenters build the first crate in which his specimens would be sent home. There were four carpenters on board, but Jonathan May, their chief, who had helped Charles put together his marine-life net, insisted that he wanted to do the job himself.

First Charles laid out his geological specimens, two hundred and fifty-four separate ones, taken from St. Jago through Rio de Janeiro. Next came his plant collection, properly dried and stitched and pressed between sheets of paper, the labels being placed between the sheets. Once back in Cambridge, Henslow would mount them on heavier herbarium paper. There were four large bottles with animals in spirits, an enormous collection of spiders, a good many small beetles in pillboxes, two species of elegantly colored planariae which bore a false relation to snails; and then the infinite variety of marine life also in a strong solution; the birds on which he had worked as taxidermist; the fish in the strongest solution; a number of invertebrate animals, many of which he had dissected; then the containers of lizards, snakes; the mounted butterflies and other flying objects; the wide range of insects. . . .

Carpenter May rubbed the stubble of his beard.

"Give me a day or three, Mr. Darwin, and I'll build you a wood fortress: rocks on bottom, butterflies on top."

They were running a record one hundred sixty miles in twenty-four hours and congratulating each other, "We'll soon have a landfall," but by evening they had a gale blowing right in their teeth. Once again the topgallant masts were sent on deck; they beat up against the heavy sea with close-reefed main-topsail, trysail and foresails. Charles stretched out on the captain's divan reading Captain Philip King's two volumes on the survey of Australia. The next morning there was a good show at sea. He studied a herd of grampuses, blackfish and killer whales, following the ship, estimating them to be about fifteen feet long. They rose together, showing now their blunt rounded heads, then their high dorsal fins, splashing and cutting the water with great violence. In the distance black whales were blowing close by a shoal of porpoises, next came the flying fish, penguins, seals, a bird like a yellow hammer. The day felt like an autumn day in England.

"It won't last," Sulivan warned. "We're only sixty miles from the mouth of the Plata. There's bound to be a thick fog."

By evening the wind freshened. The night was dirty and squally. In the middle watch, between midnight and 4:00 A.M., Chaffers, who was in command, awakened Lieutenant Wickham.

"Mr. Wickham, I believe I can hear cattle lowing on shore."

"On shore! We would be way off course. That's what happened to the *Thetis*. Let's get up on deck!"

Wickham checked the instruments, then went to the bow. He could see nothing through the fog, but listened intently and turned to Chaffers with a wisp of a smile.

"Penguins and seals! They make an ungodly racket! Keep her on course."

After twenty-one days of voyaging, they reached the mouth of the Río de la Plata. Though the river water was muddy it floated on top of the sea water where the two intermingled. Charles, watching with Mr. Bynoe as they moved toward an anchorage at Montevideo, exclaimed:

"It baffles me, Ben. Isn't the mud of the river heavy enough to sink below the sea water?"

"No, the sea has greater specific gravity."

They anchored close by H.M.S. *Druid*. A boat put off from the frigate. Captain Hamilton informed Captain FitzRoy that there had been a military coup and the new government would not allow any British seamen on shore.

"We need provisions. Will they allow my purser to land?"

"With money to spend? You can lay your last shilling on it!"

While Rowlett went ashore on the cutter with a pouch full of cash to find fresh meat and vegetables, Charles and FitzRoy were rowed in one of the small boats to nearby Rat Island. The captain took sightings. Charles went hunting and found some strange-looking animals. One particularly curious creature he showed to FitzRoy.

"At first sight everyone would pronounce this to be a snake, but these two small hind legs, or rather fins, could mark the passage by which nature joins the lizards to the snakes."

FitzRoy looked startled.

"You sound like your grandfather in *Zoonomia*, trying to project a transition from one species to another. I remember him writing about the great changes we see naturally produced in animals after their nativity."

"I didn't believe him when I read *Zoonomia* at fifteen. He had not amassed a sufficient body of evidence to prove his thesis."

"He was wrong. So are you. Lizards and snakes are exactly the same now as when they were formed at the Creation."

The next morning Captain FitzRoy broke out warm clothing to offset the sharp, biting cold. Charles's prize was a bulky, badly made and ill-fitting coat which covered him like a woolen blanket. He went ashore with King and a few of the midshipmen for some shooting, heading for the mound, well outside the troubled town, which had given Montevideo its name. He got a brace of partridges, some wild ducks and a variety of lizards, one of them, an iguana, three feet long. When they returned to the ship the cook was pleased.

"Guano, this time year, supposed to be good eating."

At dinner FitzRoy said, "I've just learned that there are some old Spanish charts of Patagonia in Buenos Aires. It's only a hundred miles upriver. I've decided to have a look at them."

"I hate to leave Montevideo without getting an impression of the town," said Charles. "If we wear our good street clothes, we wouldn't look too dangerous."

"Just two English gentlemen out for a stroll!"

They went alone into the city, the capital of the newly constituted republic of Uruguay. There was no appearance of revolution or civil war but the town did not have much in its favor. The streets were dirty, the architecture a hodgepodge of unrelated buildings; the roads leading out of the town in an incredibly bad state. Even so, Charles's quick eye saw that it would be rich country for the natural histories.

Back on H.M.S. *Beagle* there was a young man waiting alongside the guard.

"It's Robert Hamond," exclaimed FitzRoy, "an old shipmate and much-esteemed friend. I asked for him."

It did not take the personable Hamond long to explain. He had been transferred from the *Druid* to take Charles Musters's place on the *Beagle*.

Charles reflected:

"No one is irreplaceable. Now poor Musters is officially gone and replaced. How little any one mortal means!"

On entering the outer roadstead of the Buenos Aires harbor, a hundred miles up the Río de la Plata on the opposite bank from Montevideo, H.M.S. *Beagle* passed a guardship which fired on them. A moment later another shot was fired. When they arrived at their anchorage, three miles from the landing place, FitzRoy ordered two boats lowered. The boats were stopped by a quarantine ship.

Once again they were refused entry because of cholera in England, and ordered to pull back to their vessel at once.

There was a strong tide running and the wind was dead on-end against them. The sailors cursed in rhythm as they rowed.

H.M.S. *Beagle* returned to Montevideo, where the town's chief of police and the captain of the port came out in small boats to ask for assistance in preserving order against a mutinous uprising in the town.

"We do not have the authority," Captain FitzRoy replied.

"We grant you that authority."

Ashore, the British consul general declared:

"Captain, you must afford the British citizens living here any protection in your power."

Fifty-two well-armed men left the *Beagle*, Charles among them, carrying his pistols and a cutlass. They garrisoned the principal fort, holding the mutineers in check until government troops could be brought in. Sulivan's eyes were snapping with excitement at the prospect of a battle. Charles exclaimed:

"Never imagined I'd be in a war."

"If you shoot any mutineers send them home as specimens," Sulivan quipped. "*Homo sapiens.*"

He was not obliged to shoot. Neither was anyone else. In the afternoon the men amused themselves by cooking beefsteaks in the courtyard. At sunset a boat returned to the *Beagle* to fetch warm clothing. Charles had developed a headache from the unwonted excitement; he returned with the boat to find the remaining crew working hurriedly to trice up the boarding netting, loading and pointing the guns at shore, clearing the deck for action. When darkness settled in, Chaffers said:

"We can now make the best possible defense if the *Beagle* should be attacked."

"Why would the mutineers attack our ship?" asked Charles.

"To obtain ammunition."

Charles's headache vanished as he spent the night on deck with the watch. Reinforcements for the government arrived at dawn. The uprising was ended. FitzRoy announced:

"Now we can begin the slow and monotonous examination of the shore."

Charles collected scorpions under stones, leeches, crabs, samples of the Diptera order of insects: gnats, mosquitoes, flies, fleas; fresh-water shells from running brooks; birds he had never seen before: a specimen of the Fringilla or finch family, a curlew, with habits like a jacksnipe, a type of lark; and a wide variety of snakes, lizards and beetles . . . all of which found their way to a third of the chart table, with Stokes and Philip King avidly drawing survey maps of the Río de la Plata on the opposite side.

The next day a number of the men went out shooting, hoping to chance upon a flock of ostriches. Charles was so astonished by its appearance when he did see one that he did not get a shot. By midafternoon Wickham and Sulivan found themselves so tired they sat down under a tree and declared they could move no farther. Charles offered to find a horse to carry them.

He hired two horses, who carried the others by turn so that they reached the town before the city gates were locked.

"Good thing we didn't get an ostrich," bragged Charles; "we would have had to find a third horse to carry him."

"How does it happen you're such a prodigious walker?" Sulivan demanded. "I'm twice as strong and thick as you. I could snap you in half like a promethean."

"Perhaps you could, seagoing fellow, but you'll never outwalk me because I've been rehearsing these all-day excursions since I was a boy."

The next time he went out alone; coming across a large capybara, which looked like an enormous guinea pig, he chased it and shot it through the head. When he tried to lift it he found that it weighed just under a hundred pounds. He was going to have to find a horse to get the game on board!

His roundup of live species completed, Charles turned his attention to the geology of Montevideo. The area afforded fascinating complexities. The rocks consisted of varieties of gneiss, with the feldspar often yellowish, granular and imperfectly crystallized, alternating with beds of fine or coarse-grained dark green slate. North Wales certainly had trained him for this *Beagle* voyage.

Jonathan May had completed the box for his specimens, an ingeniously devised system of small and larger compartments held securely to and away from the outer lumber by a series of nailed-in wooden supports.

"Should arrive shipshape in England," May decreed.

On August 19, 1832, Charles, with the help of friends, got the big box lowered into the whaleboat and transferred to the packet H.M.S. *Emulous* en route to Falmouth. Charles asked how long it would take to get the box to Cambridge.

"Couldn't say, sir. We got a couple of stops up coast. By Christmas, I expect. Christmas present for somebody at the university?"

Charles chuckled, envisaging Professor Henslow receiving the crate.

"I sincerely hope he thinks so!"

7.

H.M.S. *Beagle*'s next task was to survey the coast of Patagonia to the south. They weighed anchor and made sail under treble-reefed topsail, continually sounding. There was a fresh breeze from the northwest which began emptying the river. At night they had eighteen feet under their stern, in the morning only thirteen. The ship shifted its anchorage. The instant they tripped their anchor the wind drifted the ship within a few yards of a buoy which marked an old wreck. One false rope and they would have grounded. But Mr. Chaffers's trained crew set sail and got away.

"I'd as soon not have any more such close calls," he declared.

He did not get his wish. The captain announced his intention of verifying the leading points of the coast. For miles the shore was a line of sandy hillocks without break or change; the country within uninhabited.

"It's the most desolate place I've ever seen," Charles groused to Stokes. He had a sudden nostalgia for the fragrant and colorful gardens of The Mount, for the roses, the patches of blue lobelia, the stands of trees along the Severn.

"Ships never visit this coast. But we do need point-by-point maps in the Hydrographic Office in London."

They enjoyed several fine days under a cloudless sky, then came torrents of rain, with the atmosphere so thick it was impossible to continue the survey. Soon the seamen had lines overboard. Everybody caught, with shouts of glee. The catch was large enough to provide fish for dinner.

Only Captain FitzRoy showed signs of uneasiness.

"I feel it in my bones that the barometers are going to rise and we're in for a wind from the opposite quarter. A gale to accompany it. I am to be called, as always, the moment the barometers turn."

At one in the morning Charles heard all hands being piped on deck. The barometers had turned. While he and Stokes rapidly dressed, Charles said:

"The captain's bones work several hours ahead of the barometers."

"All good captains have instincts about the weather at sea."

They had a bad start. The anchor became stuck in soft clay which had hardened over the iron claws. They broke off. In the process of hauling up the remains they lost their buoy and buoy ropes. By morning they were well out but the sea was heavy; the carriage holding the four-pound howitzer broke, the cannon fell overboard. FitzRoy was icy with anger over the double loss.

"Who catches hell?" Charles asked Sulivan.

"Wickham and I are in charge of inspection. The cannon was not well anchored."

Again an anchor, one of the best and largest on board, broke off as the former one had, its fluke having worked itself into a clay as hard as rock.

"So early in the voyage," Sulivan mourned, "it is a great loss."

During the gale Charles was seasick for two days. He found a curious thing had happened; physically he was just as distressed but emotionally he was no longer afraid of the attacks.

On September 2 he wrote in his diary:

> This day will always be to me a memorable anniversary inasmuch as it was the first in which the prospect of my joining the voyage wore a prosperous appearance.

They made a temporary anchorage outside of Blanca Bay. It was impossible to land in the furious surf. Again the fishing lines went over the sides. Charles would not let the fish be cut up until he had set down a description of each in his ichthyology notebook. The crew indulged him.

Captain FitzRoy was vexed; the charts they had of the area left them at as much of a loss as if they had none.

To his further vexation, they found themselves anchored at the head of an inlet which blocked further progress. A small schooner flying a Buenos Airean flag came toward them. FitzRoy ordered a whaleboat under Lieutenant Wickham to approach the schooner and seek information. At noon the whaleboat returned with an Englishman aboard:

"James Harris, at your service, sir. I own the schooner; I sail on the Río Negro and trade along the coast."

"We could use a pilot. We're looking for a safe entrance into the harbor of Port Belgrano."

"Then you'll have to weigh anchor and stand across the great north bank in very little more water than you will draw until we get into the channel, where there is enough water for any ship."

At dusk, with Harris, a middle-aged man with deep, salt-incrusted lines semicircling each side of his ruddy cheeks, at the wheel, the Beagle sailed rapidly into the excellent but little-known harbor of Port Belgrano and anchored near the wells under Anchorstock Hill. They were some six hundred miles south of Montevideo.

"There is a succession of similar inlets indenting this half-drowned coast," Harris remarked.

"It is absolutely necessary we examine them," FitzRoy replied. "Could you take a small party of us up to the Buenos Aires settlement?"

Charles ran to his cabin, took his leather pouch off its hook and his hammer from his chest of drawers. They set out in the captain's fast gig with four sailors doing the rowing. Harris took the first creek he could find. After some miles it grew so narrow the oars touched on each side. All Charles could see was mud. By waiting for two hours for the tide to rise they were able to row over the mudbanks in the midst of the rushes. After more hours they reached a guardhouse, four miles from the settlement. Looking upward, Charles saw a group of men watching them. FitzRoy exclaimed:

"What an assemblage of grotesque figures! Earle should have been along to paint them."

The men were *gauchos*, all wearing the poncho, a large shawl with a hole in the middle to go over the head. Round their waists were bright-colored shawls forming a petticoat beneath which were fringed drawers. Their boots were made from the hide of the hock joint of a horse's hind legs, a tube with a bend in it. These they put on fresh and, drying on their legs, they were never removed. The spurs were enormous. They were mounted on powerful horses and equipped with sabers and short muskets, but the men themselves were far more remarkable than their dress; the greater number were half Spaniard, half Indian; some were pure blood and some black.

James Harris explained who the *Beagle* men were, and arranged for them to mount behind the cowboys to the fort, a mud-walled polygon structure surrounded by a narrow ditch. Captain FitzRoy and his party were not received cordially; the fort's commandant was civil but his second-in-command was uneasy. He pointed to Charles, in civilian clothes, asked Harris:

"Who is he?"

"An Englishman, Mr. Charles Darwin."

"What does he do?"

"He is a *naturalista*."

"What is a *naturalista*?"

"A man who knows everything."

The major was now frightened. He demanded of Charles, with Harris translating:

"What is this everything you know? About what?"

"Rocks. Fish. Insects. Birds. Plants. Shells."

The man turned to FitzRoy.

"Are you spies sent in to reconnoiter before an attack?"

"Major, we are here on a surveying mission."

"But you like our harbor for ships?"

"It is splendid. We could anchor the entire British fleet in there."

The major screamed in anger, "So that's the truth! You will bring in the British fleet to conquer us! I conquer you! Get out of my fort! Take this *naturalista* with you. He is a witch doctor."

Harris intervened.

"I have a Spanish friend close by. He will take us in."

The friend's house was only one room, but comfortable. The men ate a light meal, having been without food for twelve hours, and fell asleep on the floor. Charles was sandwiched between Rowlett and Harris. In the morning the Buenos Aires officers closely watched their every move. Excuses were put in the way of their leaving the settlement. Finally an escort was provided. When they reached the *Beagle* at noon they found a troop of soldiers bivouacked on a high point to watch the movement of the ship.

Charles retreated to his hammock. Stokes had a grin spread over his open, pleasant face.

"So you are a man who knows everything! Just imagine, I've been sharing this cabin with you for months and I never suspected."

After lunch, FitzRoy summoned Stokes, Wickham and Sulivan to his cabin. His cheeks were flushed, his dark eyes sparkled. Charles listened as he said:

"Gentlemen, I have come to a conclusion. After what we saw yesterday of the neighboring waters and shores, I am convinced that the *Beagle* alone cannot explore them so far as to make our surveys of any real use unless we were to sacrifice a good deal more time than would be permissible. Harris and his partner own two small vessels, decked boats, schooner-rigged. The larger is fifteen tons, the smaller one, nine. Harris has agreed to rent them to us. Mr. Harris will serve as pilot on the larger boat, his friend, Mr. Roberts, will be pilot of the smaller. Both men have spent years frequenting this complication of banks, harbors and tides. They seem capable of fulfilling the desired object under the command of steady and able officers."

"Which officers?" demanded Wickham and Sulivan simultaneously.

"Wickham, I'd like you to take the larger boat. Stokes, you take the smaller. This will give us a great advantage: while you two are mapping this area, the *Beagle* can return north to Montevideo, then sail south to Tierra del Fuego and return our three Fuegians and Mr. Matthews."

"Assuredly two extra boats can get a lot more accomplished for us," Wickham commented, a bit pale around the lips. "May I ask an Admiralty question?"

"About the cost? It's a serious difficulty. I am not authorized to hire or purchase assistance. But I don't dwell on it, for I am sanguine about the result. I have made an agreement on my own responsibility for such payment as seems fair compensation. Wages, rent of the boats, food for the two owners. The boats will have to be reconditioned, but we have the materials and the craftsmen on board."

Going up the rear hatchway to the open deck, Sulivan murmured to Charles:

"I'm glad the captain left me out. I get seasick on small boats. But then, so does Wickham."

Divine service was on this Sunday morning, after which Charles accompanied a group of officers ashore to study the succession of sand hillocks thickly covered with coarse herbage; then came the pampas, which extended for many miles. On Monday morning the crew went ashore, one contingent employed in wooding, another dug wells and filled the ship's water kegs. Captain FitzRoy dictated a contract to Hellyer, his clerk: the owners were committed to provide their services and boats for eight lunar months. In return FitzRoy agreed to pay one hundred forty-eight pounds sterling per lunar month. FitzRoy could cancel at the end of any month after December 1832.

Harris left to get the two boats. Rowlett went with him to scout for supplies at the settlement. Charles went hunting with Wickham. The captain's servant, Harry Fuller, asked permission to accompany them. Charles got a fine buck and a doe, but Fuller put him to shame by getting three bucks.

"We need a wagon to get them back to the ship," Charles said.

"No wagon," replied Wickham. "Sailors. Fuller, go back and get help."

When the two men were alone, Charles commented:

"I look forward to our separation with much regret."

"I'll miss you too, Flycatcher," replied Wickham. "You know I'm not a sentimental man but it has been good to have a friend on board I neither have to command nor obey."

They had not been gone much over an hour but when they returned they found that the vultures and hawks had picked one carcass clean.

"The price of negligence," said Wickham with a hearty curse as he gazed upward at the circling birds.

"I've learned a lesson," grimaced Charles. "There's always something around that's hungrier than we are."

Captain FitzRoy moved the *Beagle* a few miles up the harbor to be closer to a good watering place.

"We will be here several weeks," he explained. "Until the small boats are refitted. We'll sail out of here together."

The crew had learned to cast their nets at the right movement of the tide, and each day came up with a ton of fish. Earle sketched the sea and landscape, while Charles separated the new species and described them in his ichthyology notebook. It was mid-September, a year since he had arrived in Plymouth. By the eighteenth, three days after the equinox, there was a beginning of spring. The plains were covered with flowers of pink wood sorrel, wild peas; the birds began to lay their eggs.

Each passing day was harvest time for Charles. Among the plants he gathered clover, a sweet-smelling flower he found by the sea but could not identify, succulents. Among his reptile catches were toads, a nonpoisonous snake of the Coluber genus, a snake with broad jaws and a nose which terminated in a triangular projection. When he dumped the snake on the chart table, Stokes cried:

"One thing about being out on the schooner is that I won't have to work with your ugly snakes crawling all over my beautiful maps." His plaintive voice belied the words.

Charles went hunting with the gauchos whom Rowlett had hired to get fresh meat for the *Beagle*, wearing rough sailor trousers and a jacket. He was surprised when they offered to lend him a horse for one of the excursions. The gauchos slept on the bare ground, killed their food as they traveled, a puma or a lion, ostriches, and searched for ostrich eggs. Charles was the only one with a gun. He was warned: "Do not shoot." The gauchos caught everything with the *bola*, two or three iron balls fastened to leather thongs.

One gaucho went ahead, endeavoring to drive the animal toward the others; the gauchos pursued it at a reckless pace, each man whirling the balls around his head. The foremost threw them. In an instant the animal rolled over, its legs lashed together by the thongs. Charles admired their riding, the quickness and precision.

They found sixty-four ostrich eggs. They also caught numbers of armadillos. In the middle of the day they made a fire, roasted some of the eggs and the armadillos in their hard cases. Charles relished the meal.

Seated round the fire, he saw for the first time that one of the gauchos was a woman. She pretended to be frightened at his gun:

"*No es cargado?*"

He lied gallantly, "No, it is not loaded."

In his animal catch Charles had an agouti, the hare of the pampas, three species of armadillo, zorrillo, the South American guinea pig. In the stomach of an ostrich he found an intestinal worm.

His collection of birds and their eggs was growing rapidly. He acquired the egg of a *Struthio rhea*, the South American ostrich, cliff-dwelling plovers, terns which lived amidst the salt marshes, parrots, short-billed snipe. He worked at night under candlelight preserving, describing, cataloguing. The captain, who looked into the poop cabin occasionally to see what Charles had acquired that day, commented:

"If you do this well for four whole years, Professors Henslow and Peacock are going to prove to be good prophets."

He cruised the bay with Captain FitzRoy and Sulivan. When they reached Punta Alta, about ten miles from the ship, his attention was attracted to low cliffs about a mile in length. At the striking of his geological hammer on the lowest bed he discovered stratified gravel.

"Captain, look what's showing through! Bones! Fossils! The first I've ever seen *in situ*. Come and help me dig them out."

The conglomerate gave easily. Soon Charles had in his hands the bones of gigantic, ancient mammifers. He was trembling so hard Sulivan had to help carry them down to the boat.

"I've got a lower jaw," he cried. "Tarsi and metatarsi, quite perfect."

"Of what?"

"Professor Sedgwick said not to guess about fossils but wait for Cambridge to study them."

He slept fitfully, awoke at first light, roused Syms Covington, told him to get a pickax from supplies, had a cup of tea at the cook's stove, and left in a whaleboat. Scrambling up to the Punta Alta cliffs, he and Covington attacked the third stratum from the bottom and found shells. Where the gravel and red mud from the level beneath passed into each other, he found more bones and a near perfect head of a huge, long-extinct animal. It took them three hours of hard digging to get it out.

"What did we get?" Covington asked, perspiring from the heavy work.

"My first thought is that it is allied to the rhinoceros."

When they returned to the ship Charles dumped the contents of his makeshift canvas bag onto the deck. Lieutenant Wickham, who had grown irritable over the long delay in getting the two schooners down to the bay, shouted:

"Confound you, Darwin, get your damned beastly devilment off my beautiful clean deck. Look at the filthy mess you've made! If I were the skipper I would soon have you and your damned mess out of the place!"

"Now, now, John, you know you like me and my beastly devilments," Charles protested.

"I'll like you, all right, when I see you at the other end of a slop bucket and a thick holystone."

After dinner Wickham came into the poop cabin, a sheepish grin on his face.

"I apologize, Flycatcher. I shouldn't have been so hard on you."

The two schooners arrived the next morning. Wickham took on shore a sizable crew including the sailmaker, cooper, armorer, carpenters. A tent camp was set up on the bank of a small creek, the schooners beached for examination and refitting. The *Paz*, even to a landsman's eye, was ugly and ill built. It was filthy and smelled rancid. The *Liebre* looked even worse. Both boats had been carrying seal oil and sea elephant oil. Charles said to Philip King, who had volunteered to join Wickham on the *Liebre:*

"Your act has become heroic."

"It will be good experience for me, Mr. Darwin. My father will be pleased."

The cabin in Stokes's craft was seven feet long, seven wide and thirty inches high. In this three men would have to stow their hammocks. In a small space forward, five more men were to live. The larger boat carried the instruments, sextant, transit, theodolite, plumb line, azimuth altitude mechanism . . . her cabin was the same size but was four feet high and had a table and seats.

"Wickham's Royal Navy," Charles said laughingly. "I always knew you'd become an admiral."

"Give us three weeks to clean them, refit the cabins, spread some fresh paint, new masts, sails, rudder, wheel . . . they'll be beauties."

Punta Alta was a gold mine of ancient bones. He found the lower jaw of a large animal with a quantity of its teeth; the bones of two or three gnawing animals, bones of the extremities of some great megatherioid quadruped.

"How did these animals get trapped up here in a cliff?" Covington asked.

"They didn't. From the presence of the marine shells and the fact that there are barnacles attached to some of the bones, we can feel certain that these remains were embedded in the bottom of a shallow sea."

"And something pushed that sea bottom up in the air to become cliffs?"

"Yes. Not a volcano, there's no lava here. Probably not an earthquake, either, or they might have been sucked down and disappeared. What then? I don't know. Some mysterious boiling force. I wish I had Professor Sedgwick or Charles Lyell here to tell us."

When he dumped his catch gently on the deck of the *Beagle*, Sulivan, as officer in charge, looked down at the pile of bones, chuckled, and mimicking Wickham, shouted:

"Ah, Darwin, some more of your rubbish! GET THAT DAMNED BEASTLY DEVILMENT OFF MY POLISHED DECK BEFORE I THROW IT AND YOU OVERBOARD!"

Bynoe wanted to know how old the head and teeth and rib bones were.

"Your guess is as good as mine, Ben. But surely they're antediluvian."

"What's the date of the Flood?"

"Who can answer that?"

"The Church of England," replied Bynoe. "They gave us the date of the original Creation: 4004 B.C. It must have taken God at least a thousand years to get so angry with man and every other creature on earth that He decided to wipe them out."

"Are you suggesting that these animals died in the mud of our shallow sea about five thousand years ago? I'd like to read you a section I found in Lyell's *Principles of Geology* last night."

He had left a marker in the book. Bynoe took the seat opposite him at the chart table.

"Lyell believes that the geologists have been thinking in terms of thousands of years whereas the language of nature signifies millions . . . a pre-Creation world. I know it's a shocking concept, Ben. Professor Henslow warned me against accepting Lyell's conclusions. Yet from what I've seen so far on this journey, Lyell could be right and Henslow wrong."

Captain FitzRoy moved H.M.S. *Beagle* to a cliff near the entrance of the harbor to erect a landmark for future ships coming into the area. They anchored under Mount Hermoso. A large crew got into the four whaleboats loaded with tools and timber. While FitzRoy searched for the most visible site, Charles and Philip King went geologizing. By early afternoon the wind had freshened and altered its direction. When Charles and King returned to the beach they found two of the boats hauled up on the shore. White breakers pounded the beach. The others had gone back to the *Beagle* two hours before. They had had difficulty getting off.

"We spend the night here, obviously," said Stokes. "It's an unpleasant prospect, sleeping in thin clothes on the bare ground. With very little food."

They made a screen from the sails of one of the boats. It was already bitterly cold.

"No supper tonight," Stokes ordered. "If this sea remains high we could be stranded here for several days."

Eighteen men had been left on shore. By huddling behind the screen they managed to sleep fitfully. Until the rain came.

At daybreak the sky looked dirty; it blew a gale of wind, a heavy surf pounded the shore.

"This weather is going to last," muttered Stokes.

Out at sea the *Beagle* was pitching badly.

Dinner that night consisted of fish washed up by the tide and the little that had been left from the day before. By evening the wind eased off enough for Captain FitzRoy to get within a hundred yards in his whaleboat and throw over a cask of provisions.

"I need two strong swimmers to volunteer to get that casket," said Stokes.

Two young fellows stripped and swam out to the keg, pushing it back to the beach. There was plenty of food and rum to warm their blood, but the wind and cold became even more intense. Charles's body shivered in successive waves.

"I never knew how painful cold could be," he muttered hoarsely to Stokes, lying next to him.

By the middle of the third day they were rescued. Bynoe checked out each of the men, prescribing rum and tea and their hammocks with plenty of blankets. Charles watched Stokes swinging contentedly in his hammock catercornered from him.

"After that adventure," he said, "I can thoroughly enjoy the *Beagle*'s luxuries."

The sea settled down. Charles spent long hours ashore, hammer, notebook and silver pencil in hand. Digging deep into the cliffs of Punta Alta, he came upon a jawbone containing a tooth and parts of a curious osseous bony protective coat, which convinced him that the fossil was the remains of the great antediluvian animal the Megatherium. He had heard in Cambridge that the only Megatherium specimens in Europe were locked up in the King's collection in Madrid.

"Land's end!" he cried. "Could I have the only Megatherium that can be shown and written about in England?"

8.

The *Beagle*, the *Paz* and the *Liebre* started south on October 17, the *Paz* and the *Liebre* sparkling under their new coats of paint and sails. The three-ship fleet anchored at the entrance to Bahía Blanca, and the next noon the two schooners sailed for the south. The men on H.M.S. *Beagle* gave them three hearty cheers to speed them on their way, then sailed north for Montevideo and Buenos Aires to replace the lost anchors and provision the ship for the journey south to Tierra del Fuego. They were eating salt pork and salt beef.

Entering the poop cabin, Charles suddenly realized that he would have the whole chart table to himself. He spread his finds before him and knew that no collection in England, even at the British Museum, could remotely touch his.

En route to Montevideo he asked chief carpenter May to begin to build the stout box needed to send home his second collection. He again segregated his marine life and fish, mounted his insects, skinned his birds, leaving the wing bones, leg bones and skull but removing all fleshy parts except the brain, then stuffing them with fiber and treating them with poison to keep away insects. He dried his plant specimens, stuffed his variety of shells, labeled his fossils. He thought gratefully of the training he had received from Dr. Robert Grant and

William Macgillivray in Edinburgh; of the lessons from John, the black man who had been on Charles Waterton's expedition to South America.

"One cask won't do it, Mr. Darwin," said Mr. May. "You'll need two large casks for your fossil bones alone."

Tired after a sixteen-hour working day, Charles went up on the deck to visit with the watch, enjoying the star-strewn sky. When he returned to his cabin and undressed, he took up his pen. For his confidential diary, the wellsprings of the poet who lived deep within him flowed freely:

> The night was pitch dark, with a fresh breeze. The sea from its extreme luminousness presented a wonderful & most beautiful appearance; every part of the water which by day is seen as foam, glowed with a pale light. The vessel drove before her bows two billows of liquid phosphorus, & in her wake was a milky train. As far as the eye reached the crest of every wave was bright; & from the reflected light, the sky just above the horizon was not so utterly dark as the rest of the Heavens.

The great excitement of mooring at Montevideo was that there was mail for most of the men on board. Charles received two letters, the daily journal from his sister Susan, which she had ended and posted on May 12, and the one from Caroline, which was finished on June 28. Susan's news would be more than five months old, Caroline's four. He closed the door of the poop cabin behind him and flung himself into Susan's several neatly written pages.

The family at The Mount had received his first letters on two successive days:

> We were all joy stricken at your good health and seeing fabulous sights.

His father was proud that his prescription of raisins and biscuit had helped during the seasickness. Dr. Darwin had also given up his comparison between a ship and a jail now that he learned that Charles considered the *Beagle* a comfortable home. After his three sisters had read the letters to their father, and then aloud to their servants, Nancy and Edward, to the old gardener Joseph, discussing all of Charles's trials and triumphs, one sister made a copy for Uncle Jos and the Wedgwood family at Maer Hall. A second made a copy for William Owen at Woodhouse; the third copied out passages for his friends at Cambridge. The originals were sent to Erasmus in London with instructions to show them to Charles's faithful friend among the Wedgwoods, Charlotte, and the Rev. Mr. Langton.

One paragraph from Susan's letter gave him considerable pleasure:

> Professor Sedgwick dropped in here last week on his way into Wales. He talked much about you and sends his kind regards, and begged you might be told to examine the gravel banks of small rivers for animal remains.

Another was upsetting: Robert Biddulph had delayed his marriage to Fanny Owen for months over the dowry.

"Now there's a love match for you!" he cried.

He thought he was prepared for Fanny Owen's marriage but when he read Caroline's description of the wedding ceremony he had palpitations around the heart for the first time since that bleak period in Plymouth:

> Fanny was beautifully dressed in white, of course, with her bonnet and veil on. Mr. Biddulph looked very handsome and gentlemanlike and extremely nervous during the ceremony. He looked quite white and his hands were blue. Fanny looked very handsome and happy. They went to London for a month.

In the rash of romantic gossip revealed by the letters not one word was said about Emma Wedgwood. Emma, now twenty-four, was an attractive young woman with a delightfully quiet, sympathetic personality; she was intelligent and talented. He had imagined that she would be among the first to marry. He saw her face before him, the luminous brown eyes, the fine brown hair, the full, live mouth; and felt a wave of longing for beautiful Maer Hall with its fishtail lake, rolling green hills. . . .

To assuage the ache of nostalgia for home in the wake of the various "effusions," he turned to the batch of newspapers and read for several hours.

On October 30 they sailed upriver to Buenos Aires with a fresh breeze in their teeth the whole day. Captain FitzRoy had communicated with the Buenos Airean government, informing them that he wished to use his chronometers to measure the meridian distance between Montevideo and Buenos Aires, and the guardship let them by.

With his crates readied for England, Buenos Aires provided the first holiday Charles had had since Plymouth. He went on horseback along the shore; Sulivan and Ben Bynoe joined him when he went shopping in the English shops for goods from home, replenishing their clothing, toilet articles, buying several scientific instruments and a good supply of containers for Charles's specimens. They visited the churches, admired the brilliance of the decorations for which the city was celebrated, enjoyed its museum, rode six leagues out in the countryside to an *estancia* where the willows and poplars planted along the ditches reminded Charles of Cambridgeshire; went to the theater, where they could understand not one word; had dinner with Mr. Gore, the English chargé d'affaires. Rowlett was buying everything he could lay his hands on: ascorbics, vinegar, pickles, lemons; fresh beef, vegetables, fruit; tobacco, rum, soap, cocoa, tea and coffee, potatoes; hundreds of staples, iron and coal for the forge. They were in high spirits as they roamed the city; it was months since they had been in a metropolis.

"No wonder all foreigners believe English sailors are more or less mad!" proclaimed Sulivan.

Charles admired the Spanish ladies, their hair beautifully coifed with an enormous comb, a large silk shawl folded around the upper part of their bodies; their walk graceful. For a short while he saw Fanny Owen's face on every Spanish girl he passed.

Charles had heard about General Rosas, commander-in-chief of the state of Buenos Aires, who was killing and driving out the native Indian tribes so that the pampas could be made safe for the cattle ranches; and knew that he would have to procure a passport for any travel into the interior of the country he might have an opportunity to do. He approached the local officials and got a letter of introduction to the commandant at Patagones and passports as the "Naturalist of H.M.S. *Beagle*."

They returned to Montevideo in mid-November after having conquered "as foul a wind as ever blew." A few days later the *Duke of York* packet came into port. Charles supervised the careful transfer of his four boxes and casks into the hold of the ship, to be delivered to Falmouth.

He received two more letters from home, one from Erasmus.

Susan, in her mid-August letter, thought Erasmus was becoming fond of Fanny Wedgwood and might marry her. His father had lumbago so his sisters were trying to persuade him to give up his yellow chaise and see patients only at The Mount. The family hoped Charles would not allow any false shame to prevent his returning home whenever he felt inclined. She wrote:

> I am very much pleased to find the quiet parsonage has still such charms in your eyes. It is delightful to look forward and fancy you settled there, and in spite of this marrying year I am sure you will find some nice little wife left for you.

Erasmus's letter was another kettle of fish. He had no intention of marrying Fanny Wedgwood or any other woman. . . .

> I have written to you all the politics, though I suppose you are too far from England to care much about it. Politics won't travel.

"He is wrong!" Charles cried as the letter announced that the Reform Bill had, at long last, passed; however a vast proportion of the electors, either through neglect or ignorance, were unwilling to get themselves registered so they could vote. In the same vein, Erasmus concluded:

> I am sorry to see in your last letter that you are still looking forward to the horrid little parsonage in the desert. I was beginning to hope I should have you set up in lodgings somewhere near the British Museum or some other learned place. My one chance is the Established Church being abolished!

Almost as welcome as the letters from his family was the package containing the second volume of Lyell's *Principles of Geology*, in which Lyell turned his attention to the changes in progress in the animate creations. Lying in his hammock in the stillness of the chart room, he read Lyell's germinal question:

> . . . whether there be proofs of the successive extermination of species in the ordinary course of nature, and whether there be any reason for conjecturing that new animals and plants are created from time to time, to supply their place?

He lay quietly thinking forward to the day when he could show Charles Lyell the fossil bones he had discovered in Punta Alta. Then, in a burst of energy, he wrote to his brother with a flock of commissions, including a good set of mirrors, lace, needles and pins, pillboxes, Cuvier's *Molluscs*, von Humboldt's *Fragments*, a book on botany by Linnaeus, Scoresby's *Arctic Regions*. . . .

It could be as many as nine months before he would see another letter.

H.M.S. *Beagle*, refitted and replenished, sailed out of Montevideo on November 27 bound for Tierra del Fuego, the two-hundred-and-fifty-mile extreme tip of South America which lay below the Strait of Magellan. Cape Horn sat in about the middle of the tip, where the awesome forces of the Atlantic and Pacific oceans lashed each other. Magellan had named it "Land of Fire," but he could as well have named it "Land of Lashing Storms." The Spanish had tried to acquire the area by sending in a settlement of over two hundred men in 1585, but most had died in the first winter. No nation wanted it now, not even the insatiable English. Those who knew its terrors used the children's phrase, *al diablo*, created by or belonging to the Devil.

Augustus Earle decided to remain behind in Montevideo. Suffering agony from rheumatism though he still had not reached his fortieth birthday, he wanted to recoup his health. Charles advised fondly:

"Look out for those tall rum drinks at the Table d'Hôte, Gus."

"Charley, my stomach won't hold rum or any other spirituous liquid. Makes a man wonder whether it's worth while staying alive. But maybe I'll find a pretty girl. That's always compensation."

Charles laughed.

"If your appetites aren't all they used to be, your imagination will make up for it. See you on the way back."

The three Fuegians knew they were heading for home and nothing but a disaster could prevent it. In Jemmy there was a nervousness. He began to act aggrieved, as though he were about to be victimized. He would no longer look Charles in the eye.

"Me no want go home."

"But that was Captain FitzRoy's agreement with you. He would take you to England for a year or two, to see the country and be educated. Then he would return you to your home."

"Captain say. No me say. What fashion you call that?"

York on the other hand seemed to puff out with a sense of pride, even victory. His superior attitude toward the sailors appeared to say: I have defeated you. You tried to make me an Englishman. But I have prevailed!

"Me go shore rich man," he said. "Much presents. Me be chief Alikhoolip."

"Where are these riches coming from, York?"

"Captain. Me take for pay. For make captain fame. Him name in paper. Fuegian take him court. Him see Queen."

Charles laughed heartily.

"York, I think you will become a chief. You have the mind of a politician."

As for Fuegia Basket, with so many early memories replaced by the comforts and kindliness of the Society, she had no way of knowing what to expect. Uncertainty created a touch of fear; she would have no say about her future. She had stopped crocheting and making clothes for herself.

"No need. Tear quick. Me wear guanaco skin. No more sew."

By four in the afternoon the ship was surrounded by multitudes of white wings. The sailors cried:

"It's snowing butterflies!"

It was an incredible sight.

"Where do they come from?" cried Charles.

"They're being driven down by a gust from the northwest," explained FitzRoy.

"I'll bring up my sea net and sweep them in."

By the time he raced from the poop cabin there was a double-reefed topsail breeze. He was panting.

"They're as numerous as flakes of snow in the thickest shower," said Bynoe. "See the space they occupy: it can't be less than two hundred yards in height, a mile in width and several miles long."

Charles held his face up, letting the butterflies fall gently on his hair, his brow, nose, mouth and chin. He murmured:

"Now I know how the Israelites felt when God sent them manna from heaven."

"One crucial difference," Sulivan responded with his boyish laugh; "don't swallow the butterflies. They're inedible."

It took only a week under fine sailing to reach San Blas. Soon after daylight on December 3 they saw some low islands and stood directly for the shore. Suddenly they struck a wide breadth of discolored water; the depth shoaled from ten to three fathoms. They hauled off southward with the ebb tide. Jemmy at the masthead was the first to sight them:

"Cockboats! Cockboats!"

Soon the two little schooners from which they had parted seven weeks before pulled alongside. Wickham was the first on board. He had been so scorched and blistered by the sun he could barely speak through his cracked lips. Stokes and King came on board. They too were sun-blistered. Everyone gathered around to greet them and to laugh at their parboiled appearance from the hot sun and fresh wind which kept them constantly wet with spray.

Their maps and sounding charts were so well executed that Captain FitzRoy persuaded them to survey the coast from Port Desire. Charles was glum when after two days they again parted. He would not see them until a reunion at the Río Negro, more than five hundred miles south of Montevideo, a little less than halfway down the coast of Patagonia, the following March, three months off.

He spent the next days collecting crustaceans in his net behind the stern, crabs, oysters, shrimp, studying the mechanism by which they shed their shells. Then on December 11, exactly a year since H.M.S. Beagle made its first attempt to sail out of Plymouth Sound, a heavy breeze hit from the southwest. Charles knew he would get seasick. It would be raisins and biscuit again.

"I'll tell you how to conquer the heavy squall that's coming," Sulivan offered. "Capture it in prose. Make it your prisoner. That way, the squall belongs to you and not you to it."

"I'll clean my quill and get my notebook ready." Shortly after he began writing:

It is always interesting to watch the progress of a squall; the black cloud with its rising arch, which gives passage to the wind; then the line of white breakers, which steadily approaches till the ship heels over and the squall is heard whistling through the rigging.

9.

In mid-December they sighted through the fog the land south of the Strait of Magellan, the intricate inland passage connecting the Atlantic Ocean with the Pacific which the great Portuguese navigator had daringly forced in 1520. Charles joined the officers on the quarter-deck, fascinated by the sight.

They made Tierra del Fuego the following day. FitzRoy altered their course to sail along the coast. Very quickly there came a smoke signal. Through his glasses Charles could see a group of Indians watching the ship. The breeze was fresh and the *Beagle* ran fifty miles down the coast, anchoring off low country of horizontal rock with abrupt cliffs facing the sea.

The ship rolled so heavily during the night because of the exposed anchorage that Charles could find neither comfort nor sleep. He rose at daylight, about 3:00 A.M., watched H.M.S. *Beagle* get under way. A little after noon they entered the Strait Le Maire, a strong wind at their backs. Over dinner, FitzRoy said:

"Imagine how great a sea will rise when the wind and the tide are at each other's jugular. The motion from such a sea is called 'potboiling.' It breaks irregularly over the sides."

"I doubt I want to imagine it, Captain. More likely sooner or later I'll have to live through it."

They anchored that afternoon at Good Success Bay, just over one hundred miles north of the tip of South America and Cape Horn, where Captain FitzRoy announced his intention of surveying for some days. A group of Fuegians was perched on a peak overhanging the sea. They were waving their skin cloaks and shouting to the men lining the deck as they followed the ship moving up the harbor. Just before dark they saw the fire in front of the wigwam that had been improvised for the night.

The harbor of Good Success was a fine piece of water surrounded on all sides by low mountains of slate. It was memorable for being the first place Captain Cook anchored on that coast, back in January of 1769. That night there blew a gale of wind and rain. Heavy squalls swept down from the mountains. It would have been a bad night at sea, but here in the harbor the *Beagle* indulged in very little motion. In the morning FitzRoy sent in a whaleboat with Charles, Jemmy and a group of officers, with Lieutenant Sulivan in charge, to look for a watering place. As the boat neared the shore Charles examined the crowd of Fuegians. Their skin was a dirty copper color. A broad red band of paint reached from ear to ear across the upper lip. Above and parallel to it was a white band, so that the eyebrows and eyelids were completely covered. Their hair was black, dank and down to their shoulders. Charles wondered what symbolic meanings the bands of paint had and for how many aeons they had been handed down from father to son.

Four Fuegians ran toward them shouting vehemently. Their leader was an old man wearing a cap of white feathers and a tattered guanaco skin over one shoulder. The other three were six feet tall, looking to be young and powerful. One man's face was painted black with a white band over the eyes.

He had never seen such a spectacle.

When Sulivan landed the whaleboat the Fuegians were wary but continued shouting and making forceful gestures. As they jumped onto the beach Sulivan murmured:

"Notice there are no women or children in sight. Won't be until they decide whether we are friends or enemies."

Charles exclaimed, "I would not have believed how entire the difference is between savage and civilized man! How do we go about making friends with them?"

"Give them gifts. Greatest known medium of exchange."

Each of the Fuegians was given a piece of red cloth, which they immediately wrapped around their necks, shouting with joy. They were now friends. The old man came close to Charles, gave him three hard slaps on the chest and back at the same time, spoke in a language that resembled the peculiar noise of people feeding chickens, then threw back his guanaco skin, baring his chest.

"It's their equivalent of a handshake," Benjamin Bynoe explained.

The Fuegians cried, "*Cuchillas* give us knives," making a gesture of cutting blubber out of their mouths.

"They're dangerous enough without knives," Sulivan muttered. "Jemmy, ask how far it is to your home place."

Jemmy did not have much of his native tongue, but even that little the Fuegians could not understand. All five of them started shouting at him at the same instant.

"Me no understand," Jemmy said plaintively. "What fashion call that?"

The Fuegians knew that Jemmy was different from the other *Beagle* men. They examined his well-cut hair and his skin, obliged him to take off his shirt. They also examined two of the officers, fairer and shorter than the others, albeit with beards.

"Squaw!" exclaimed Jemmy. "Me know word. Think you squaw!"

If an officer coughed or yawned, the Fuegians coughed or yawned. Hamond made faces like a monkey; one of the young Fuegians mimicked him. The sailors sang songs and danced; a Fuegian insisted on waltzing with Hamond. They seemed healthy and strong, yet their manner of living appeared miserable; the wigwam being a few bushes by a ledge of rock which could in no way keep out the wind, rain or sleet. They lived off seals, birds, mussels, whatever was washed up on the shore, and occasionally guanaco. Their clothes were skins and rags, their only property their bows, arrows and spears.

Returning to the whaleboat, Charles commented:

"I believe if the world was searched no lower grade of man could be found."

"True, Charley," said Mr. Bynoe, "but purely out of geography and circumstance. Look at the incredible progress the captain made with our three. They were just as primitive, yet they adapted themselves to English life, proved that they had malleable brains in those squared-off, oblong heads."

Charles was determined to penetrate some way into the country. Captain FitzRoy insisted that Covington accompany him, armed.

"I haven't issued you many orders, Darwin, but this one is urgent. In primitive countries you may never go on shore unaccompanied, or unarmed. It's dangerous both from the natives and from the wildness of nature itself."

There was no level ground. The woods were thick, the tree branches so close to the ground they had trouble pushing their way through. He found the course of a mountain torrent; although it was choked with dead trees, he managed to crawl along, Covington close behind. Then he left the gloomy depth of the ravine and emerged on the crest of a hill. There was grandeur in the scene but all around were evidences of universal violence: irregular masses of rock and upturned trees. The wood below him was composed of antarctic beech.

He took his hammer out of his leather pouch and began pounding rocks. The results were disappointing. He did secure a fine crop of lichens, moss, ferns, algae, beetles, hairy spiders. His real delight was his knowledge that this part of the forest had never before been traversed by a white man.

The *Beagle* got under way southward at 4:00 A.M. the third night, with a light wind. In a region where wind and water never cease fighting, the ship doubled Cape Good Success in a calm sea. The next morning's watch saw the breeze freshen into a fine easterly wind which took them past Cape Deceit. Charles felt so well he was exultant.

"This weather is as rare an event as getting a prize ticket in a lottery," FitzRoy exclaimed.

They were to double weather-beaten Cape Horn and make the robustious sail almost across to the Pacific waters to resettle Fuegia Basket and York Minster with his tribe; then double back through the Beagle Channel, discovered by Captain FitzRoy on the first *Beagle* voyage, to return Jemmy Button to the Tekeenica on the tip of Navarin Island. At three in the afternoon they were at the southernmost end of the world, with nothing between H.M.S. *Beagle* and Antarctica except Drake's Passage. The evening was calm and bright; by nightfall they ran into a gale.

"Cape Horn demanding its tribute," growled FitzRoy, pushing aside his supper to go on deck and watch the crew trim the sails so she would not fall away from the wind.

By morning Cape Horn was on their weather bow and they could see what the sailors called "the notorious point" veiled in mist, its outline surrounded by a storm of wind and water. Black clouds rolled across the sky, squalls of rain and hail swept by with great violence.

"Run for Wigwam Cove," commanded Captain FitzRoy.

It was good to be in the quiet cove, for the next day was Christmas, a year since they had finally set sail from Plymouth. Charles thought with satisfaction of the two shipments he had sent home; wondered if Professor Henslow was at this very moment receiving the first one; and relived the most exciting moments of his life. All duty was suspended in favor of divine service and a gala day with feats of strength, singing and dancing to Covington's fiddle. Several of the sailors went ashore with guns to hunt, the younger ones just to shoot. Charles, Sulivan and Hamond decided to climb Kater's Peak, a steep conical mountain overlooking the bay, thick with antarctic birch.

They were fatigued when they reached the 1,700-foot summit. Hamond asked:

"Darwin, what do you make of the geology of this series of islands?"

"They appear to be the termination of the Andes chain. The mountaintops have been barely raised above the ocean. I can scarcely credit that man lives on them."

"Ah, but men do, Charley," said Sulivan seriously. "I could feel the Fuegians following us up the mountain."

They reconnoitered among Fuegian wigwams, four feet high and round, hastily put together of random branches, rushes and grass, the result of about an hour's work and made to last only as long as the available shellfish remained to feed them. From the accumulation of waste outside the wigwams Charles collected wild celery and scurvy grass.

In the middle of the night they were awakened by the order, "All hands on deck!" It was the beginning of a long and tortured stretch of harsh weather. Though it was the middle of summer in Tierra del Fuego, the temperature dropped as low as 38°. Charles, who had withstood the heat of the tropics better than most of the men on board, suffered from the cold. No amount of warm clothing, the woolen cap, the coat made in London, could ward off the prickles that stung his nerve ends. Only his astonishment at the curious birds inhabiting the sea drove him to his diary:

> The sea is here tenanted by many curious birds, amongst which the Steamer is remarkable; a large sort of goose which is quite unable to fly, but uses its wings to flapper along the water. . . . Here also are many Penguins, which in their habits are like fish, so much of their time do they spend under water. . . . So that there are three sorts of birds which use their wings for more purposes than flying: The Steamer as paddles, the penguin as fins, & the Ostrich its plumes for sails to the breeze.

By the opening days of January 1833 he came to the conclusion that one never grew accustomed to seasickness. He could not hold down even the biscuit and raisins, and made for the air of the deck wrapped in his heavy sea coat held tightly around his neck. He clung to the wood railings; the salt-laden spray stung his eyes. He learned the meaning of the proverb: "Those who would go to sea for pleasure would go to hell for pastime." Some ships took months to beat around the Horn; some were forever driven back and never made it into the Pacific.

"Sulivan, how long can this last?" he anguished. "I doubt my spirits and stomach will hold out much longer."

"Till doomsday," the officer replied. "But you'll hold out. What else can you do, jump overboard and swim past Cape Horn?"

After four days of trying to make their way west around the Cape in the gale and heavy seas, H.M.S. *Beagle* had gained less than three miles!

"A lesser gale has dismasted and foundered many a good ship," said FitzRoy.

By carrying a press of sail they got within a mile of Christmas Sound, the country of York Minster. The crew could hear the officer in charge telling the lookout man to look to leeward; the captain did not know their exact position, his horizon limited to one small compass because of the thick spray being carried by the wind. In Charles's mind was the picture of H.M.S. *Thetis* smashing against the rocks of Cape Frio. It was the first time he had stared death in the face.

By noon of the following day the storm struck its height. A great sea came on board. The sound was deafening, the spray a fury. The tackle of the quarter-boat gave way. Captain FitzRoy ordered an ax to cut away the whaleboat. In a moment it was sucked under and completely disappeared. H.M.S. *Beagle* was now on her beam-ends, having been hit by three tremendous waves in succession; the sailors were working in water up to their waists. Captain FitzRoy, standing on the quarter-deck, shouted:

"Open the ports."

The carpenters drove handspikes against the ports. When they burst open the water poured off the deck before the next sea could hit. The ship righted herself. The hatches had been thoroughly battened down; little water got below deck . . . except into Charles's collections, and, as they later discovered by the horrendous stench in the hold, into some of the tins of preserved meat.

When Benjamin Bynoe came into the poop cabin he saw the desolation on Charles's face.

"In a storm like that it's impossible to keep water from seeping into the forecastle lockers," he explained.

"I know I should be glad we're all still alive. But look! My drying paper and plants are wet with salt water. It's an irreparable loss."

Bynoe put a consoling arm around Charles's shoulder.

"Nothing is irreparable, Charley, except death."

The storm abated. Captain FitzRoy exulted:

"That is the worst gale I've ever been in. The roller that hove us on our beam-ends was the most hollow I've ever seen, yet our losses were minimal: one whaleboat, some netting washed away. But we've made only *twenty miles* in *twenty-four days!*"

"What do we do now?" asked Charles plaintively.

"Put back into Goree Sound where we can moor the ship safe from wind and sea. That's Jemmy's country. York Minster has decided to settle there with Jemmy and Fuegia since we can't get him home."

The next day they took two boats, landed and walked miles searching for a piece of flat land. They found only a dreary morass occupied by wild geese and a few guanaco. Charles reported:

"This section shows turf or peat about six feet thick. It won't do for agriculture. I'm afraid the whole area is a swamp."

"Then we'll have to take the Fuegians farther upcountry. If we find nothing fit for cultivation we'll take them back to Ponsonby Sound."

10.

Three whaleboats and a yawl left H.M.S. *Beagle* with twenty-eight people and the farewell presents given to Matthews and the Fuegians by the Missionary Society. When the articles were loaded in the Devonport Dockyard they had appeared hilariously funny. Now, in the incredible wilds of primitive Tierra del Fuego, the wineglasses, tea trays, soup tureens, mahogany dressing cases, fine white linen and beaver hats became a culpable folly.

The captain steered the whaleboats toward the entrance of Beagle Channel. By evening, gliding through a land indented with coves and inlets, the little fleet found a snug corner concealed by small islands. Here they pitched their tents, supported by the boat oars, and lighted their fires to cook supper. After nearly "a month of hell on water!" Charles found it a romantic scene. "Tonight I shall sleep on hard, unmovable land," he cried joyously.

The following morning they explored the channel. They were in thickly inhabited country. The Fuegians were surprised by the sudden appearance of the four boats. Some lighted fires to attract attention, many ran for miles along the shore to keep up with them. On a cliff towering over the yawl five naked men with long streaming hair waved their arms around their heads and sent forth hideous yells.

The boats pulled to shore in midafternoon. The Fuegians kept their slingshots in readiness. The men kept shouting one word:

"*Yammerschooner. Yammerschooner.*"

"What does that mean?" asked Charles.

" 'Give me.' You'll hear it for quite a while."

They found an uninhabited cove for a well-guarded night's sleep. The next morning a fresh party of Fuegians arrived, picking up stones and banishing their women and children to the woods. FitzRoy ordered all guns at the ready. Charles cried:

"Captain, you wouldn't order us to fire on such naked, miserable creatures?"

"It's to frighten them off."

The Fuegians did not frighten. The captain fired double-barreled pistols over their heads; they only rubbed their ears at the noise. When he flourished his cutlass, they laughed. Chagrined, FitzRoy said:

"We'd better find neutral ground between this tribe and Jemmy's family."

"Why don't we appease them with a few more gifts?" asked Charles.

"They want knives and boats."

That night they took up their quarters with a family of the Tekee-nica people, relatives of Jemmy. They were quiet and friendly, joining the *Beagle* crew around a blazing fire. Charles, barely warm enough in his heavy clothes, saw that the naked Tekeenicas were streaming with perspiration.

A large group of Fuegian men arrived. They had run so fast during the night that their noses were bleeding. They walked so fast that their mouths frothed. Studying them one by one, Charles saw that each had a quite different design of red, white and black paint on his face.

The *Beagle* party started out to find Jemmy Button's parents, brothers and sisters. Though Jemmy said he could not understand the native language he very well knew the way up the Beagle Channel and guided them to a cove where his family had lived. He found a brother and, later, his mother, other brothers, two sisters and an uncle arrived.

"The reunion is not so interesting as two horses meeting in a field," Charles commented to himself, disappointed.

Jemmy heard that his father was dead.

"Are you sad about that?" Charles asked quietly.

"Me no help it."

They arrived at a place called Woollya. Here there was clear and rich ground. Captain FitzRoy was triumphant.

"European vegetables will flourish here," he said. "Now we have to get their colony established."

The Fuegian men sat all day and watched while the women worked. However they were not completely idle; they spent their time stealing everything the sailors took their eyes off.

Charles and Hamond went walking and collecting in the hills. Matthews, the carpenters, Jemmy and York set up tents and built a couple of single one-room houses. The sailors used their shovels and hoes to show the Fuegians how to cultivate the land and then sow, a to-tally inexplicable activity to them.

Bynoe commented:

"You live on land near the sea. You eat off what you find on the land and in the sea. If there is plenty, your belly gets all swollen; if there is scarcity, your belly shrinks. That's the natural way for these people since the beginning of time."

"We'll change that," said Richard Matthews shyly, for he was a scarce-spoken young man. "We'll teach them how to live a balanced life on their own produce."

When the men from the *Beagle* awakened in the morning they found all the women and children gone, except Jemmy's immediate family. The Fuegian men were massed on a hill above them watching hostilely.

"Jemmy, York, what happened?" FitzRoy demanded.

"You clean gun," answered Jemmy.

"No. Fight," said York. "Old man told not come close. Do. Sailor spit in eye. Old man make sign, skin, cut him up."

"Then we don't sleep here another night," announced FitzRoy. "Transfer all goods to Jemmy's family houses," he ordered.

Missionary Matthews, Jemmy, York and Fuegia Basket were left behind.

"Will they be safe?" asked Charles.

"They have to learn how to live with their own people," FitzRoy answered.

One of the whaleboats and the yawl were sent back to the ship. The other two whaleboats set out up the Beagle Channel to map the islands around its western entrance. The day became overpoweringly hot. Charles joined the others in stripping to the waist, adding a red sunburn to his white skin. They were reminded that the hundred-and-twenty-mile channel, which made its way in a straight though narrow line to the Pacific Ocean, was an arm of the sea by the number of whales spouting within a stone's throw of the shore. That night they stopped at a pebbled beach which Charles found dry and comfortable under his blanket bag.

It was his turn to take the watch until one in the morning. He recorded carefully in his mind for his notebook:

> There is something very solemn in such scenes; the consciousness rushes on the mind how remote a corner of the globe you are then in. All tends to this end; the quiet of the night is only interrupted by the heavy breathing of the men & the cry of the night birds; the occasional distant bark of a dog reminds one that the Fuegians may be prowling close to the tents ready for a fatal rush.

The days passed brilliantly as they entered the northern arm of the channel, so full of icebergs it looked like the Arctic, sounding, charting, drawing maps which grew daily more detailed even as Charles's leather pouch filled. Toward the end of January they pulled into a small bay to have their midday meal around a fire on a sandy beach. The two whaleboats were made secure. Charles was calling attention to the beautiful beryl blue of a sheerly vertical glacier half a mile from them when, without an instant's warning, a huge mass of the overhanging glacier face fell with a clap of thunder into the channel. A great wave came rushing at them.

"The boats!" cried Captain FitzRoy. "They will be dashed to pieces!"

Charles and three seamen were the fastest on their feet as all started to run. Charles's long legs reached a whaleboat first. He seized the ropes and put all his strength into hauling it up onto the beach, one of the seamen pushing from the rear. A second seaman secured a hold on the whaleboat ropes when the breaker knocked him over. The speed of the four men in reaching the two boats saved them. When the second and third waves had receded they returned to their meal.

"Gentlemen, you saved the day," declared FitzRoy. "Had you not seized those boats they would have been tossed along the beach like empty calabashes and been swept away from us irrevocably. I have no medals to pin on your panting, ocean-drenched chests, so I urge you to accept these words as your commendation."

Charles felt a pulsing inside what the captain had accurately described as his "panting chest." Sulivan added:

"Philosopher, you ran like a gazelle with a tiger on its tail."

"Pure dumb instinct."

The next day the whaleboats were sailing parallel to the granite ridge which appeared to be the backbone of Tierra del Fuego. They came into a large expanse of water. Captain FitzRoy raised his arm to get attention.

"Gentlemen, I herewith name this expanse of water Darwin Sound, and it shall be so recorded in our survey."

The color rushed to Charles's face. He was taken wholly by surprise, and felt as proud as a student at the Shrewsbury School who had won the prize for reciting Virgil.

That night, lacking a beach, they slept on boulders. The water came up to the edge of their tent, washing up a putrefying seaweed. Charles was oblivious to the discomfort.

Returning to Woollya, they encountered a party of natives in ceremonial dress. With them was a woman dressed in a loose linen garment which had belonged to Fuegia Basket. Others were wearing pieces of white linen as well as ribbons and bits of tartan cloth which had been left with Matthews.

"We'd better get back to our people as soon as possible," said FitzRoy.

By noon their boats touched shore. To their relief Matthews came to greet them. York and Jemmy were dressed in their English clothes; Fuegia, when she emerged from a wigwam, seemed unchanged. York and Fuegia reported that they had fared well but Jemmy had had everything stolen except the suit on his back. The new garden had been trampled over and obliterated.

Mr. Matthews had suffered the most. They had held his head down by force and stolen all his possessions except for the larger tools, which he had hidden in the rafters of his hut and in a cave he had dug. He had had no peace by day or night; the men demanding everything they saw; several of them holding large stones and threatening to kill him if he refused them, others forming a circle around him and if he had nothing to give pulling the hair of his face and pushing him about. He was convinced they were going to kill him if only to seize all his possessions.

The women had been kind. While Jemmy guarded the hut they had made a place for the minister by their fire and shared their food.

Captain FitzRoy weighed the missionary's chances.

"Matthews, I don't think you ought to remain, however willing you may be to try to help them. There'll be no missionary work accomplished here, and you ought not again to be exposed to these savages." He glanced at the hundred Fuegians squatting on their heels watching. "How do we get your chest and the remainder of your property safely into the boat in the face of these men, who would be more than a match for us?"

"By giving them little chance to realize what we are about," Charles ventured.

It was done almost in a flash of action; the hut and cave were emptied, the contents put aboard the two boats. When the last man was embarked, FitzRoy showed his acumen by distributing a few axes, saws, nails. The Fuegians put down their stones and allowed the two boats to be pushed off the beach.

As Charles watched the beach and its people grow smaller he felt melancholy about leaving their Fuegians among their countrymen. They had lived among civilized people; how would they adjust to the return to primitive life? How simple it had been for Captain FitzRoy's kind gesture to turn cruel.

They slept that night at the entrance to Ponsonby Sound. They reached H.M.S. *Beagle* next evening after their two whaleboats had sailed some three hundred miles.

"I feel like a seasoned explorer!" Charles said, laughing at himself as he entered the familiarity of the poop cabin.

He dumped onto the chart table the treasures of his big leather pouch: a lark, a sandpiper, a finch; winged insects, sea urchins, freshwater snails, samples of excellent slate.

The rest of the table was piled equally high with the hundred-odd maps and charts drawn during their three weeks of exploration of the Beagle Channel.

Somewhere on one of those charts was a large expanse of sea-blue water called Darwin Sound.

# BOOK FIVE

*"It's the Best Preparation for Marriage"*

1.

I<small>T</small> was a three-day run to Berkeley Sound in the Falkland Islands almost directly east of the Strait of Magellan. The Falkland Islands
had recently been colonized by a group of Buenos Aireans who were
reported to be prospering. To everyone's surprise a British flag was
flying over the settlement. There was a single whaling vessel in the harbor. Charles, standing by the break of the poop overlooking the drop to
the lower deck, saw a small boat put out from shore. A chief mate came
aboard, saluted Captain FitzRoy and explained that his ship, *Le Magellan*, had foundered in the storm and was lying wrecked on shore, her
men impatient to get back to a civilized port.

"We saved our stores, which might be helpful to you."

When the men from the *Beagle* stepped ashore they found a forlorn
little town, a few half-ruined stone cottages; some straggling turf huts.
While there were plenty of sheep, goats, pigs, cows, Charles saw only a
few desolate-looking humans. Mr. Dixon, the English representative, a
middle-aged man with rheumy eyes, the teeth on the left side of his
mouth ground down by an ever present pipe, explained that it had been
a prosperous town . . . until it became a victim of clashing nations. . . .

"These islands had been uninhabited for thousands of years until the
Buenos Aires government claimed them and sent in colonists. They
prospered. Last month H.M.S. *Clio* arrived to take possession for the
British and found that the U.S. corvette *Lexington*, a year ago, had surprised, assaulted and unwarrantably destroyed both the property and
buildings. The gauchos fled to the interior, frightened by the violence.
This is good anchorage, plenty of fresh water and game. Should be a
thriving colony supplying ships round the Horn. But no more."

Clerk Hellyer brought on board the new rope, bread, salt meat and
small stores which the Frenchmen had saved. Captain FitzRoy also
agreed to take twenty-two crewmen and officers with him to Montevideo. They would sleep on deck. Then Edward Hellyer returned
ashore to hunt. Some time later his gun, watch and clothes were found
on shore. He had apparently shot a duck which fell into the water, shed
his clothes and swum out to retrieve his hit. He was found by Mr.

Bynoe, entangled by kelp; the seaweed had to be cut away to get at him. He had been dead for some time.

He was buried the next day on rising ground in sight of H.M.S. *Beagle*. A British ensign was thrown over the coffin made by Mr. May; Captain FitzRoy read the funeral service. It was a melancholy moment. When Charles joined the captain in his cabin, he found him slumped into his chair. He said softly:

"This is as severe a blow to me as it is to his messmates. Mr. Hellyer was a gentlemanly, sensible young man. Now all I can do for him is write a sympathetic letter to his family in England. It's most difficult for me since I feel the motive which urged him to strip and swim after the bird was probably a desire to get it for my collection at home."

Charles unwrapped a canvas package he had placed on the floor.

"Mr. Bynoe cut the duck from the kelp. It's a variety I've never seen before. And here is Hellyer's bullet that felled it."

FitzRoy shook his head. "I'll keep the bullet. You take the duck for your collection. Mighty costly duck."

While the *Beagle*'s surveyors went about their chores off the ship and on shore, Charles spent three days of cold weather riding about the countryside, a covering of brown wiry grass growing on a peat soil. Though he complained that there was little material for his journal, over the next weeks he managed to garner snipe, wild geese, a wolflike fox, owls, a jackass penguin, starfish; a variety of fish caught in the rocks and kelp, and sea slugs which laid their eggs in ribbon adhering to the edge of the rocks.

Other sailing vessels arrived in the harbor. Captain FitzRoy considered the *Unicorn* the most important; William Low, its part owner and sealing master, sometimes doubled as pirate and slave trader. He met with FitzRoy and the officers in the gun room.

"The weather has been so much against me that I return from my six-month cruise a ruined man with an empty ship. It has been the worst season I've known in my twenty years' experience. Haven't taken a seal. I've got to sell. Fast. Captain, do you know anyone who could use a mighty good schooner at a cheap price?"

FitzRoy's eyes lighted.

"How cheap?"

"Six thousand dollars for immediate possession, payment to be made into my partner's hands at Montevideo."

FitzRoy's thoughts went scudding before the wind. When Low had left he sat at the head of the mess table, spiked open the portholes of his mind and let his thoughts flood off the deck into the turbulent sea of his words.

"On our first voyage we had a second ship, the *Adventure*, always with us to serve as tender and double our surveying work. I have become fully convinced that the *Beagle* cannot execute her allotted task without losing the most interesting part of her journey, carrying a chain of meridian distances around the globe. The Pacific journey and return home through Australia and the Cape of Good Hope might eventually be sacrificed to the tedious although not less useful details of coast surveying."

There was a deep silence in the gun room.

"Our working ground will lie so far from ports at which supplies can be obtained that we will be obliged to occupy whole months in making passages merely to get provisions. I have often anxiously longed for a consort adapted for carrying cargo, rigged so as to be easily worked with a few hands, and able to keep company with the *Beagle*."

FitzRoy and Chaffers went to inspect the *Unicorn*. Mr. May examined the interior structure. FitzRoy reported to the officers, "A fitter vessel I could hardly have met with, one hundred and seventy tons burthen, oak built, copper fastened throughout, very roomy . . . a good sea boat. I have reason to believe it cost at least six thousand pounds in building and first outfit. At thirteen hundred pounds she's a bargain."

"What will she cost to outfit, Captain?" The question came from Rowlett, the purser, who would have to pay the bills.

"We can get what we need from the wrecked *Le Magellan*, anchors, cables, small spars, for a little over four hundred pounds, less than a third of the market prices in frequented ports."

The officers assured each other that it was a burglar's bargain. Charles, brought up in a household where every pound was held accountable, was disturbed. The Admiralty had not yet approved Captain FitzRoy's one hundred and forty pounds a month rental for Mr. Harris's two schooners. They had been out for six months now, at a cost of eight hundred and forty pounds.

When the two men faced each other over FitzRoy's small dining table, Charles asked:

"Captain, may I have your permission to voice a question which is outside my position and privilege?"

"Why not? You are a discreet man."

"Would it not be wise to have Admiralty approval on your schooner rentals before purchasing the *Unicorn*?"

"Under ordinary circumstances, yes. But these are not ordinary circumstances. Approval is undoubtedly in the mail. Besides, the opportunity to buy such an excellent sailer at so low a price could never happen again. My wish to purchase her is unconquerable."

The bargain was struck. A week later, after minimal repairs to the newly christened H.M.S. *Adventure*, Chaffers and a crew of volunteers from the Beagle left for the Río Negro, some eight hundred miles north of the Falklands, to find Wickham and Stokes. Meanwhile the Beagle's carpenters repaired their yawl, the sails were loosed to dry, ropemaker and armorer worked on shore where a small party went each day to wash its clothes and scrub the hammocks. A coil of hemp cable was brought up to air, the yardarms braced; while Charles dissected, classified, stuffed his birds.

They took on board almost seven hundred pounds of fresh beef, filled their water kegs, and on April 6, 1833, unmoored the ship, weighed anchor and hoisted sail. Charles was happy to be moving north again. He was yearning for the heat and luxuriant foliage of the tropics.

They stood out to sea on their way to the Río Negro off the coast of Patagonia, a gale of wind in the right direction keeping them scudding before it. They ran a long distance for two days but it was rough going. Every part of the ship seemed dark, wet, the picture of discomfort. Charles spent much of the time doubled over the side, retching. Then the weather turned beautiful . . . "celestial," Charles called it. The sky was a cloudless blue, the water smooth. Lieutenant Sulivan, since becoming second in command of H.M.S. Beagle, had grown less funloving.

"That's the sailor's life, Charley; from a cold storm to warm quiet, and back again to storm all within twenty-four hours. It's the best preparation for marriage."

They were only a few hundred miles from the fury of Tierra del Fuego. It took five days to reach the mouth of the Río Negro. Captain FitzRoy was upset at not finding their two little schooners anchored there, though neither he nor any of the officers would admit they were worried. The following day the watch sighted a sail to the southwest. The Beagle gave chase. It was the Adventure. Mr. Chaffers reported that it had made good weather despite heavy gales. FitzRoy was pleased.

"Then, Mr. Chaffers, would you be so good as to proceed to Maldonado in the Río de la Plata and await our arrival. We will continue our search for Wickham and Stokes."

A small trading schooner brought news: the captain had seen and spoken with both Wickham and Stokes; they had been sailing south to the Bay of St. Joseph off the Gulf of San Matías. All had been well, except that a marine named Williams had fallen overboard and drowned. FitzRoy was distressed at the death of his marine but enormously relieved that the schooners were safe. They were all his responsibility.

They set sail for the Bay of St. Joseph to join the schooners. They were nowhere to be found. So strong a tide was setting into the bay that they were obliged to let go a stream anchor, used in calm water for mooring the vessel. Charles was able to get a glimpse of the nearby cliffs, which appeared to abound with fossil shells, but there was no way to get ashore.

That evening he wrote to Henslow:

> . . . As I consider myself your pupil, nothing gives me more pleasure than telling you my good luck. I am very impatient to hear from you. When I am seasick & miserable, it is one of my highest consolations to picture the future when we again shall be pacing together the roads around Cambridge.
>
> I am convinced that the Megatherium sent to the Geological Society belongs to the same formation which those bones I sent home do, & that it was washed into the River from the cliffs which compose the banks.

When in the morning a fresh breeze sprang up, Captain FitzRoy decided to make sail for Montevideo. He told Charles:

"Since we have to make the *Adventure* shipshape and we have considerable surveying to do in that area, there should be a good two months for you to be ashore. Where would you prefer, at the close-by small settlement of Maldonado, Montevideo or Buenos Aires across the river?"

Charles's eyes shone at the prospect of two months of uninterrupted naturalizing and surcease from the discomfort of a pulsing sea. He had learned to dress and undress fairly quickly in his cramped corner between his chest of drawers and cabinet for his specimens without skinning his elbows, barking his shins, getting a crick in his neck, or pulling a muscle in his back, and had earlier told his cabin mate Stokes, "I've become a contortionist," but there was nothing like having a home on the land.

"Maldonado, I think. It has two great advantages: retirement and novelty."

"You should seek lodgings at a well known old lady's, Doña Francisca. I won't go so far as to say that she'll make you comfortable but at least the roof doesn't leak."

At Montevideo Charles went ashore to visit Augustus Earle. To his practiced eye Earle did not look any better for the four months of rest.

"We missed you," he told Earle. "Have you been able to paint at all?"

Earle smiled his crooked smile.

"Bet your last tuppence on that, chum. I tied a brush firmly between my swollen fingers and went out every dry day."

Charles saw the stack of canvases against the wall, took them one by one and studied them. There were delicate landscapes, portraits of harbors, small trading boats and intensely lifelike portraits of blacks on the quay carrying bundles on their heads.

"Beautiful, Gus. Your hand hasn't lost its skill in getting down what your eye sees."

"Thank you, Philos. I've been waiting for a knowledgeable word. When I get back to London I intend to show these at the Royal Academy."

He too had been waiting for a "knowledgeable word," and was badly disappointed not to hear from Professor Henslow. He had hoped that his first box, shipped on the packet *Emulous* eight months before, had reached Cambridge. He felt desperately in need of criticism and advice. He was an amateur, inadequately trained, facing the whole myriad flow of nature; he had no way of assessing whether he was handling himself and his copious materials in a professional manner. Most urgently, he needed to know whether his variety of specimens was reaching Henslow properly preserved, treated, boxed, identified.

His sisters Caroline, Susan and Katty had continued their day-by-day diaries. Caroline's letter had been posted on September 12, Katty's October 14, Susan's November 12. The news was from five to seven months old, but ah! how wonderfully life-giving to receive. Yet there was crushingly bad news from Maer Hall. Fanny Wedgwood, the older half of the happy Doveleys, had died suddenly of a bilious fever. Emma was inconsolable. Aunt Bessy was so badly stricken that she could no longer manage Maer Hall. Uncle Jos had been wonderful, "keeping the family securely at anchor while riding out the storm of grief." Charles felt particular compassion for the sensitive and loving Emma. Only she and pain-ridden Elizabeth were at home now. Young Joe came and went.

The report from The Mount was comforting. His father often sat under the banana tree he had planted in the greenhouse at Charles's suggestion, in high spirits because he was sharing the tropics with his son. He still visited some old patients but let it be known that he would no longer drive any distance. A new doctor, who had come from York, was taking over most of the practice.

"What a shame," Charles thought. "Between my grandfather and father, the Darwins have been practicing medicine for nearly a century. Erasmus should have taken over Father's practice. . . . Perhaps . . . even I."

Letters from The Mount, like a kaleidoscope, clicked colorful pictures into his mind: the family gathered around the dark mahogany dining table with its sweet smell of beeswax; the warm afternoons in the greenhouse with its damp smell of moss; the pillared library, dipping into the classics and alternating with the recent books of Scott and Thackeray.

The view from his bedroom of the road to North Wales and the castle towering above Shrewsbury beyond. . . .

He sighed deeply against his will and started to pack the belongings he would take on shore. The mere handling of his leather pouch, net and hammer sent his spirits soaring again.

Maldonado!

2.

He readily found Doña Francisca's house in the small village with its mostly Spanish, but some mixed Spanish and Indian population. Doña Francisca was an ancient one, behaving as though she were merely old; dressed in fastidiously cared-for clothing that looked as though it had been part of her dowry. She welcomed Charles, informed him of the meal hours, then escorted him to a large room with a high ceiling and very small windows. All rooms were on the ground floor and opened into one another, precluding any privacy. What made him gasp was the furniture: a narrow bed on rough wooden legs, a half-unraveled cane chair and several wooden boxes off ships of the past placed on top of each other to form a chest. He spent the day in a vain effort to make the room comfortable; he did at least manage to buy a rickety, unpainted table for his instruments and bottles. His half dozen books he strung face out along the floor on either side of the bed. Leafing through Milton's *Paradise Lost*, he came across the lines:

> Have ye chos'n this place
> After the toil of Battle to repose
> Your wearied virtue, for the ease you find
> To slumber here, as in the Vales of Heav'n?

He stretched out on the bed, his feet dangling over the end, hands locked behind his head, no more secure than in his hammock!

"Not to worry! I'll soon be out in the countryside, sleeping on the earth with a myriad of stars above my head, the saddle for my pillow."

It was not to be that soon. Torrents of rain fell. The rivers rose. The Maldonados had not yet invented the bridge. Between outbursts he walked the village, finding his Spanish inadequate, the town almost deserted. As in all Spanish towns, the streets ran in parallel lines. He walked the streets, down and across, which more than satisfied him. He then spent the days in his room studying patience and Spanish, reading when he could close his ears to the noise of the rain. Had he always had this much patience, or was he becoming more deliberate because he was being fulfilled?

The rain stopped. The sun came out. The pools turned to mud, then dry clay. In the interval he had made a single friend, Don Francisco Gonzales who, with his servant, Morante, offered to serve as his guide and companion on a trip through the interior.

On a morning of fine weather the three men left the town, driving before them a troop of fresh horses, a luxury since it insured against having a tired or lame horse under one. Horses were plentiful and cheap, three of them going for the price of a mediocre saddle. Nobody walked, not even beggars. The young boys rode the colts bareback, chasing each other over hill and dale. Charles thought they were the most graceful young riders he had ever seen. He agreed to pay two dollars a day for all expenses on the journey. Don Francisco and Morante were armed with pistols and sabers, which Charles considered excessive; he was carrying only one gun. The first news they had on the road was that a traveler from Montevideo had just been found with his throat cut.

The country was hilly and uneven, the surface covered with a short green turf. Since they had no set destination, Charles used his hammer to examine several beds of marble, banging away to Don Francisco's vast amusement. The plains abounded with quiet cattle; they passed large bands of ostriches. Charles found them wonderfully graceful in flight. He was now sufficiently a sailor to describe the scene as "up with their helm, and making all sail by expanding their wings right down the wind."

They rode through low wild mountains which he ascertained to be slate. He took samples; also from an abandoned gold-mining shaft. They arose early to ascend the Sierra de las Animas, which afforded an extensive view of Montevideo to the west and the plains of Maldonado to the east. They tethered their horses so Charles could collect. Don Francisco admired him for being able to distinguish between venomous and non-venomous snakes, but he was flabbergasted watching Charles put scorpions, spiders, lice, planarians or flatworms, on beds of cotton in little pillboxes. When he saw Charles open up the cavy, or guinea pig, he had shot, take an intestinal worm from its stomach and wrap it almost tenderly in cotton, he exclaimed:

"Señor Darwin, you no *fatuo*, stupid. You plenty smart. Why you take cavy worm?"

Charles was still skittish over trying to define a naturalist. It was more digestible to be called *fatuo* than "the man who knows everything." He explained briefly and, to spare his guide any further perplexity, turned to collecting plants: cacti, agave, dwarf flowers, a fleshy-leafed plant, fresh-water grasses when they came upon a lake. He also collected frogs, lizards, toads, which brought back vividly Professor

Henslow's query in the Fens near Cambridge: "What are you planning to do, Darwin, make a toad pie?" He collected almost furtively nine different kinds of snakes and eight varieties of mice. Don Francisco generously pretended not to see what his unfortunately demented friend was doing.

His small pocket compass created unbounded astonishment. His first host asked:

"Señor Darwin, what is that strange instrument for?"

"Señor, it can tell me in which direction each road in your country runs."

"Can you show me in what direction the road runs through my *estancia?*"

"Assuredly." He stepped out onto the open veranda, adjusted the compass to the track ahead. "It runs northeast."

The host said with admiration:

"You, a perfect stranger, can know the road to places where you have never been!"

News travels fast in simple remote country. Late the next afternoon when they asked hospitality of a friend of Don Francisco, they were told that a young daughter was ill. The mother begged:

"Señor, would you be so kind as to come to my daughter's room? She has heard of your magic. I think it would cure her."

In the home of a large Spanish family with grandparents and many grown children gathered around the supper table, the grandfather asked:

"Señor Darwin, is it the earth or the sun that moves?"

"The earth, señor."

One of the sons asked, "Do you have any more magic, Señor Darwin?"

Charles took out a promethean and ignited the long wooden match by biting the end between his teeth. The natives used an opaque cream-colored flint to strike fire. The family was awed.

The father asked, "Señor Darwin, would you let me have one of those? I will pay you a whole dollar for it."

His hosts were so delighted with Don Francisco Gonzales's stories of how Señor Darwin broke stones with a hammer and collected insects that few of the families would accept any pay for their hospitality.

At one *estancia* a son of the family who could understand nothing of what Charles was saying, queried:

"Señor Darwin, you were born unable to speak Spanish?"

"*Sí, señor.*"

The young man shook his head with pity.

Several times they came across a group of gauchos hunting for fresh meat with their *bolas*. One of the men undertook to teach Charles how to gallop and whirl the balls. Charles, adroit at snaring a fast-running insect or bird with his flycatcher, was slow in learning to handle the *bola*. The free ball he was whirling struck a bush, fell to the ground and caught the hind leg of his horse. The second was jerked out of his hand and further entrapped the horse's legs. The gauchos roared with laughter. The young instructor cried:

"I see how to catch all animals, but I never see a man catch himself."

One night they stopped at a *pulpería*, or drinking shop. There was scarcely a place to sit down. Darwin found the young, cigar-smoking gauchos a striking-looking set of men, tall, handsome, with proud dissolute expressions. They had drooping mustaches and long black hair curling down their necks, spurs clanking on their heels, and always a knife stuck like a dagger at the waist.

They were excessively polite to Charles. Each in turn refused to drink the spirits without Charles taking the first swallow. Charles knew he would become thoroughly drunk. Nor could he get away for a few hours' sleep; it would have been considered a grave infraction of manners.

They rode the countryside for twelve days. Charles relished the strong horses under him, the superb clarity of the warm air, the solidity of the pampas earth. He made notes on the geology of the crystalline rocks that protruded from the crest of every hill. In several places he found remains of great extinct animals, indicating that these immense plains had been covered by brackish water from the Río de la Plata and had undergone gradual elevation. He tried to explain this to Don Francisco, holding his arm straight ahead of him:

"Look, *amigo*, my left arm is water, my right arm is land. When water falls, land rises. When waters rise, land disappears."

"How you know?"

"From the rocks, what they are made of. The mountains are the history books of the past. That's why I collect the fossils and shells that were once under water."

Don Francisco bowed gravely. Charles never knew whether the courtly man either understood or believed him.

Some fifty to sixty miles north, in the valley of the Tapas, Charles's hammer beat out a good-sized piece of igneous rock which had its cavities lined with quartz crystals, indicating their volcanic origin, its constituent parts having been rearranged during the metamorphosis of the entire region.

"How we all bumble into thinking of mountains and rocks as solid and immutable," he declared, "when at some distant time they were gaseous and fluid."

He returned to Doña Francisca's and laid out his twelve-day collection of life forms from the pampas. It never occurred to him that his rocks were not as alive as the cacti, snakes or scorpions he had gathered.

Existence in Maldonado was monastic. Unlike the good-sized port city of Buenos Aires only a hundred and thirty miles up the Río de la Plata, there were no restaurants, theaters, concerts, graceful young Spanish ladies with big combs in their hair. He made no friends; ate his meals alone, obliged to keep his own company. The food the cook served was as blameless of flavor as his bedroom was naked of furniture. His beard, which he had grown for the wilds of Patagonia, had come in several shades darker than his hair. It had grown rapidly, perhaps because he brushed it several times a day, thinking, "This beard does not make me look any handsomer a sea dog, but at least I can keep it neat." He became nostalgic about the Beagle and began to look forward to its visit.

If Maldonado was lacking in people, it was rich in bird life. He had been neglecting his ornithology and prepared a campaign embracing all kinds of traps and contrivances; within a few days he had collected eighty different species. He caught an ovenbird, which built its nest on a most exposed situation; one resembling the butcher bird but which hunted like a hawk; parrots which fed in large flocks in the open plains; condors, turkey buzzards, mockingbirds, woodpeckers, carrion-feeding hawks. It was an enormous task to stuff them all. He had to work fast too to preserve his reptiles, insects, the fresh-water crustaceans, fish he found along the beach.

Overworked, he grudgingly came to the conclusion that he needed an assistant. He would be willing to pay his full wage and the cost of his victuals. According to quick calculations, that would amount to some sixty pounds a year. It was a year and a half since he had left England, and his expenses had not risen above two hundred pounds per annum. He was sure his father would allow the expense. His mind went to Syms Covington. He did not like the twenty-year-old as a person, but Covington took training well and had helped with some of the preserving. He shot and stuffed birds quite usefully. He would ask the captain if he could transfer him from seaman to his assistant if the boy were willing.

H.M.S. Beagle arrived late in May. Charles thirsted for a sight of his mates after nearly a month of solitude. Only three days later John Wickham and Philip King arrived in a small vessel which FitzRoy had rented in order to bring them back from the Río Negro. Lieutenant Wickham was to supervise the conversion of the Adventure for its journey as the Beagle's sister ship and tender. Stokes had been left in command of the two schooners and was continuing the surveying. The arrival of Wickham and King was cause for celebration in the gun room.

Charles exclaimed to King, "Philip, you've grown a full foot since I saw you five months ago."

"I don't know how," the boy replied with a rueful grin. "I've been sleeping in a cabin two and a half feet high and just long enough to curl up like a snake."

Charles repaired to the captain's cabin for tea. It was a joy to be back in the mahogany-paneled room with its elegant appointments, the crisp linen on the table, the sparkling water glasses, fine bone china and polished silver.

"Captain, it feels like coming home. I haven't spoken a word of English in weeks, in fact not a word in any language. I might have been in that monastery in Fiesole where the monks are pledged to silence."

FitzRoy chuckled. "I missed you too, Philos. Eighty separate species of birds! That has to be a record."

"I'd like to discuss that with you, Captain."

"Clear for action."

Charles told Captain FitzRoy how many hours of sheer labor were needed not only to preserve, stuff, dry out, pickle in spirits, but also to transcribe from the little three-by-four pocket notebooks scribbled in rough shorthand the clues for complete descriptions later. He then asked if it would be possible for the captain to transfer Syms Covington to his employ at his expense. Covington had frequently accompanied him ashore fulfilling FitzRoy's orders that no one could wander alone. FitzRoy considered for a moment.

"Yes, that's possible. As boy to your poop cabin he has no urgent duties on deck except to play his fiddle, and 'Nancy Dawson' at eight bells to signal the crew that grog is ready to be served. He'll want to continue that. I'll keep him on the books for victuals, and write to the Admiralty for permission. Consider it done."

Syms was more than willing. He moved into Doña Francisca's house, building a worktable on the outside veranda. When the weather was boisterous Charles remained in the house working on his specimens; the weather good, Syms carried his big gun while he tramped the country-side accumulating deer, water hogs weighing close to a hundred pounds, rodents with the habits of moles, opossum-like animals, cavies.

One of the more important changes that took place with the acquiring of Syms Covington as his personal helper was that Charles Darwin, whose greatest excitement and pleasure had been the months of partridge shooting at Maer Hall and in William Owen's Forest, who hunted each spring with his friend Tom Eyton; who had spent hours before the mirror of his rooms at Christ's College practicing the throwing of his gun to his shoulder, had now worn out the pleasures of shooting. Charles did not know exactly why this early love had slowly evaporated until he recalled Adam Sedgwick saying in the solarium at The Mount:

"I was a keen sportsman until I became a professed geologist. So soon as I was seated in the Woodwardian chair I gave away my dogs and gun. My hammer broke my trigger."

"I suppose the same thing has happened to me," Charles reflected.

H.M.S. *Beagle* had become his Woodwardian chair.

3.

July brought trouble. Captain FitzRoy, highly pleased with his maps and charts, received a serious rebuff from the Admiralty. The letter came from Captain Beaufort; it reflected other thinking in the Admiralty than Beaufort's but was nonetheless a severe blow. Charles found him in his cabin, sunk in gloom.

"The Admiralty has disapproved my rental and refurbishing of Harris's two schooners. They say I outstepped my authority. They refuse to pay a farthing of the cost. Worse, I have made Captain Beaufort uneasy. Apparently I have injured myself at the Admiralty."

Charles said tentatively:

"But they have not seen the fine results from the schooners, the soundings and charts they have brought in."

Captain FitzRoy shook his elegant head sadly.

"How could we have sent maps and charts from the wilds of Patagonia? Besides, there's considerable work to be done before the Admiralty sees them. I want Captain Beaufort to have our completed survey of this coast. It will be the most comprehensive on record. But that may not be ready before the end of the year."

Charles reflected the captain's distress.

"As soon as the month is up I shall have to return both schooners. I've been toting figures for their eleven-month rental. It comes to seventeen hundred pounds, plus whatever materials I bought to refurbish them."

He dispiritedly glanced about the cabin as though in search of a decanter. Since he found none, he returned his gaze to Charles's sympathetic face.

"Very well, I will discharge the schooners. I do have the *Adventure*. But the Admiralty may not approve my purchase of the *Adventure* either; although it was bought for a far more valuable purpose, and can help us chart around the entire globe."

He rose from his chair, paced the cabin, his spine rigid.

"I must write to Captain Beaufort and ask forgiveness for the additional plague I have caused him. I shall redo the *Adventure* and complete our surveying of both coasts of South America. The costs are on my own head! After that, *quién sabe?* My dear Darwin, would you forgive me now, I need to be alone."

Charles went up on deck, sat with blind eyes in the sun. Having lived with the equally monumental authority of Dr. Robert Darwin, he had been uneasy about Captain FitzRoy's rental of the *Paz* and the *Liebre* without Admiralty permission. But he bitterly resented his beau ideal of a captain being brought down by desk sailors in London who had never been pounded by the Atlantic seas.

It was late July when H.M.S. *Beagle* got under way for the return five-hundred-mile cruise south to pick up John Stokes and his crew aboard the schooner *Liebre*, and to survey the outer banks near the Río Negro and Bahía Blanca. Captain FitzRoy chose a wild-looking night for their departure, the sky brilliant with lightning, but after the three-month pause at Maldonado and Montevideo, the breath of the Admiralty on the back of his neck, he was impatient to be sailing and to complete the east coast survey. Lieutenant Wickham would remain behind to supervise the re-outfitting of the *Adventure*.

Charles glanced up at the sky, said softly, "Let us all sing the praises of Thunder-and-Lightning Harris."

A nasty headswell hindered their progress for several days. A succession of gales kept him queasy for the full nine-day sail. In the roughest of the gale and wind and rain his skin grew red and blotched, only to resume its smoothness of texture when the weather quieted and the sun came out. At the mouth of the Río Negro the ship's signal guns were fired. Soon the *Liebre* came bobbing out to join them. Charles quickly lowered himself down the rope ladder into the tender to transfer to the tiny schooner and give Stokes, his former cabin mate, an enormous embrace. He could not believe it had been eight months since they had enjoyed their couple of days of reunion in early December. Stokes, now twenty-one, was bronzed and filled out to the proportions of an adult, his eyes were resolute, his face had taken on an expression of authority.

"John, how have you managed to survive these coastal gales? We lost a whaleboat and many other ships went down."

"Our smallness was our protection. The sea, instead of striking us, sent us before it."

Stokes delivered his maps of the hitherto uncharted coast, which brought him high praise. As a reward for his accomplishments Captain FitzRoy gave him a tiny cabin immediately off the chart room, which had become available. Both men would now have more privacy. After the joyous hilarity of dinner in the gun room, Charles went back with Stokes to the schooner. They made their way into the mouth of the Río

Negro to a quiet mooring. The wind died down; Charles and Stokes sat on deck most of the night exchanging tales.

The following day Charles walked several miles along the coast searching for a pass that would enable him to ascend to the plateau above the cliffs. When he reached the top, quite out of breath, he faced as sterile a landscape as he had seen: a sandstone base with natural salt pans, dry grass and a variety of bushes with formidable thorns. He wrote in his notebook:

> Those inhospitable plains will forever remain useless to mankind.

John Stokes was free the following day. The two men rented horses and rode ten miles upriver to Patagones, located on a cliff overlooking the river. It was a small town inhabited by Spaniards and Indians who appeared to get along well even though the rest of the country was involved in a chronic Indian-Spanish war. Many of the houses were built deep into the native sandstone; the river was wide, deep and rapid. There was no agriculture, no cattle, no trade. No one appeared to be working, yet the young Indians were wearing clean, bright clothing.

Everyone was friendly. A crowd gathered. From Stokes, who had picked up considerable Spanish during the past ten months, Charles learned that the government in Buenos Aires supported them, sending in old horses for meat. The women earned a few coins by making horse rugs and boots for the gauchos from the horses' hind legs. But the key word was *sal*, salt, repeated over and over again. They rode out to the *salinas*, large shallow lakes of brine which dried in the summer, leaving a field of snow-white salt for harvesting. The men of Patagones drove bullock wagons out to the lakes and dug up the salt which, in some places, was several feet thick.

"They have enough salt here to supply the entire world," Stokes said.

"And in Montevideo they import English salt. I saw the packages!" Charles retorted.

They rested while Charles got his notes written: there were large crystals of gypsum embedded in the mud; in some places the mud was thrown up by numbers of worms.

"Johnny, how can such creatures exist in a fluid saturated with brine? Why would those flamingos inhabit this salt lake except to live off the worms? What do the worms live off? Primitive, single-cell animals!"

"Charley, you do ask a lot of questions," Stokes declared.

"I'm interested," Charles shot back. "I think what we are seeing is a small world within itself, adapted to these inland seas of brine."

"When you return to Christ's College you should go for honors."

"I am not returning to Cambridge. Not unless a parish there is desperate for a young deacon."

The *Liebre* had been returned to Harris. Charles and Stokes returned to H.M.S. *Beagle* where they learned that the ship would remain in the area for another few days to complete its soundings, then return, after a stop at Bahía Blanca, the five hundred miles to Montevideo and Buenos Aires to prepare the complete set of charts, all they had drawn up since they had left Plymouth, to be shipped back to the Admiralty in London. That accomplished, they would staff the *Adventure,* provision both ships for the eight-month voyage back to Tierra del Fuego and via the Strait of Magellan enter the Pacific Ocean.

Charles sought out Captain FitzRoy.

"Captain, this would be a fine opportunity for me to take an overland trip to Bahía Blanca. It's something more than a hundred miles."

"Splendid idea, Philos. But be sure to find a reliable guide and plenty of fresh horses. I think James Harris might accompany you. I've paid him off for the two schooners. He's on his way to Buenos Aires."

Charles found a willing James Harris in his home in Patagones, a trained guide, plenty of horses and a group of five more gauchos in white boots, broad drawers, scarlet *chilipas,* who, with their horses and dogs, were going on business to General Juan Rosas's encampment on the Río Colorado, eighty-five miles distant. General Rosas and a small army had been sent out by the Buenos Aires government to exterminate rebellious tribes of horse Indians.

"Those gauchos are as glad of companions as we are," Harris exclaimed. "This whole area is in an uproar."

Though they rode through miles of brown withered grass and spiny bushes, the early morning air was fresh in their nostrils. Charles was carrying his heavy metal water can which he was able to refill from the puddles of each day's rain. Since some of their horses had been stolen from the corral during the night, they had to ride slowly behind the horses loaded with supplies for General Rosas. Ostriches, guanaco, a humpless camel which resembled a deer, and hares crossed their track but there were few other living things. They also came upon a tree which the Indians worshiped as a god. Charles dismounted to find himself surrounded by the bleached bones of horses slaughtered as sacrifices. Hanging from the branches were portions of bread, meat, cloth; the poor pulled a thread from their ponchos to leave there.

"Why go to the trouble of building a church when nature has already grown one for you?" Charles commented.

A small group of Indians approached. The men dismounted, reverentially poured maté, a green tea, into a hole leading to the tree, then squatted and blew the smoke of their cigars upward through the branches.

Charles shook his head in amazement. "The ancient Greek warriors in Homer's *Iliad* roasted the thigh of a bullock so that the smoke would reach heaven and please their gods. Has that form of worship come straight down through three thousand years? Or does each people invent it for themselves?"

Two leagues later the gauchos decided to stop for the night. They spotted a cow, rode for her at breakneck speed, dragged the animal back by a lasso, slaughtered it and roasted the meat for supper. After dark they banked the fire, hobbled the horses and drew their saddles around the fire in a close circle.

Charles stretched out on the ground, nestled his head on his saddle, covered himself with his saddle blanket. He was happy and comfortable. Harris was already asleep. There was a deathlike stillness on the plain; the gauchos' dogs were keeping watch. He thought, "This scene will live in my mind a strongly marked picture which I will not soon forget." He too thrived on the totally independent outdoor life.

The party took a week to reach the Río Colorado. Three leagues later they left the sandstone plain and came to fertile country of turf, clover and little owls, all a relief to the eyes and the horses' hoofs. General Rosas's encampment was close to the river. Along with the Buenos Airean cavalry were some six hundred Indian allies. The camp was set up as a square of some four hundred yards closed in by supply wagons, mud and straw huts. The greater part of the cavalry was of mixed Spanish, Negro and Indian blood. No one smiled or looked pleasant.

"Ferocious, rather," Charles thought.

The gauchos delivered their goods. Charles and Harris found the only rancho, a hovel, really, where an ancient Spaniard offered them hospitality and a long story of how he had served under Napoleon on his march to Russia. Charles was directed to General Rosas's secretary, to whom he showed the letter of recommendation he had received five months before. He did not know what to expect. He had heard that General Juan Manuel Rosas was a cruel man, exterminating whole tribes of Indians who did not want to be driven off their land, massacring the men and women, selling the children into slavery. Rosas was also known to have enormous areas of land on which he ran three hundred thousand cattle and grew quantities of corn. He was without formal education but had cultivated himself along the years, was very much the gentleman and spoke English. He wore gaucho dress and was a despot who enjoyed unbounded popularity with his troops, equaling their feats of horsemanship.

An armed guard admitted Charles to General Rosas's tent, a comfortable one with tables and writing supplies. Charles had not been prepared to find so handsome a face, more European than South American, with wavy black hair, penetrating dark eyes set widely apart and a powerful chin. He waved Charles into a canvas folding chair.

"You are a naturalist on H.M.S. *Beagle?*"

"Yes, General, and I have been for almost two years now."

"What brings you to my encampment?"

"I wanted to see your country. I hope to write a book about the geology of South America."

Rosas remained sober.

"What can the Buenos Aires army do for an English naturalist?"

"I wanted to go overland from Patagones to Buenos Aires but I was told that the country beyond Bahía Blanca is not safe because of marauding Indians. . . ."

"It is safe now. I have established *postas* through the five hundred miles, all with armed men and extra horses."

"Then I have a favor to ask. Since I can pay for everything I need, would you permit me to stay overnight in your *postas*, and secure fresh horses?"

Juan Rosas studied Charles's lean, sunburned face intently. When he answered his tone was both enthusiastic and grave.

"My secretary will write you the permit. You will be safe because you will pick up my soldiers carrying my messages to Buenos Aires. There will be no charges because you will be delivering my horses to the next *posta.*"

Charles's face was wreathed in appreciation.

"General, I don't know how to thank you."

"Thank me by writing your book about South America. My father helped drive the British out of Buenos Aires in 1807. But I have respect for your country. Someday I shall visit there. Your letter will be ready before dark. Learn much."

Charles returned to the mud rancho. He found Harris stretched out on the rough cot.

"Rosas is tremendous!" he cried. "He is providing us with fresh horses and hospitality in his *postas* all the way to Buenos Aires."

Harris shook his head sadly:

"I'm too sick to go with you, Darwin. Got to stay here until this fever passes. Take the guide, it's too dangerous to travel alone."

Charles left early in the morning for what he called an "exhilarating gallop," up the Río Colorado through saltpeter marshes and swamps. Unfortunately his horse stumbled and Charles went flying over his head into the black mire. When he picked himself up, he exclaimed:

"I'm well soused!"

They arrived at Bahía Blanca late in the evening, wet and filthy. H.M.S. *Beagle* was nowhere to be seen. He slept at the home of Don Pablo, a friend of Harris's. The following morning he persuaded the commandant of Bahía Blanca to lend him a soldier and a pair of horses. They rode for two hours without a sight of the ship; when they tried to return, the exhausted horses gave out. Charles and his soldier companion caught an armadillo which they roasted for dinner. He fell asleep with his head on a saddle, protected from the night air only by his mud-caked clothing, and without water to drink.

"You must buy yourself a young horse," Don Pablo declared.

He found a young mare for four pounds, after bargaining hard, bought himself a strong pair of trousers, shirt and coat and rode with the guide out to Punta Alta where he had found the Megatherium fossil the year before. It started to rain. His new clothes got thoroughly drenched. They slept that night under the saddle blankets. When he returned to Bahía Blanca he found James Harris at Don Pablo's, his fever not quite cured.

"I must tell you," he said to Charles. "One of General Rosas's *postas* was wiped out by Indians two nights ago. The soldiers were killed. If you insist on going overland, mind you sleep with both eyes open."

It was six days before the *Beagle* was sighted. There followed two tedious days with so high a wind that the ship could not send a boat ashore. Finally Chaffers put out a whaleboat. Charles helped him buy meat for the ship, then the two men returned to the vessel. It was fifteen days since Charles had seen his shipmates. He had supper in the gun room; each of the men offering a bottle. Back in the chart room he was welcomed by Syms Covington with a warmth of feeling Charles had not known he possessed.

When Charles told Captain FitzRoy that he wanted to continue the inland crossing from Bahía Blanca to Buenos Aires, FitzRoy hesitated, a concerned expression on his face.

"No Englishman has ever made that journey." He studied General Rosas's letter, the anxiety lifting from his eyes.

"You must have made a good impression on the general. He's not known for his cordiality. A Jesuit by the name of Falkner mapped the country some years ago. I found a copy; I'll have my clerk locate it for you in my papers."

FitzRoy had determined to sound again along the dangerous banks of Anegada Bay, eager to do his utmost to prevent vessels from foundering there in the future. They would anchor when they could to preserve their station and connect triangles but would often be obliged to weigh again at short notice, always keeping a careful lookout on the deep-sea lead.

Charles grinned as he bade FitzRoy *au revoir*.

"My dear Captain FitzRoy, you're going to be honored by the Royal Naval College . . . and the Admiralty!"

4.

Once again he was free to emulate the gauchos he admired; able to pull up his horse and say, "Here we shall pass the night."

He found a guide who had made the passage to Buenos Aires, secured a renewed passport from the commandant of the fort, carefully placed his permit to ride with General Rosas's horses, and the map of the region drawn by the Jesuit explorer, in his saddlebag and started north. They passed the first *posta* with only a brief visit and continued to the Río Sauce, crossing it in water up to the horses' bellies. The mile-wide valley of the Sauce was fertile, with tracts of wild turnips which proved to be good eating, though a little acrid. When there was nothing to observe he locked the oblong notebook and returned it to his capacious coat pocket.

They reached the second *posta* in mid-afternoon. Charles asked the lieutenant in charge:

"How far are we from the Sierra de la Ventana?"

"About six leagues. I'll send a second guide with you."

The Sierra de la Ventana, of whitish-gray quartz, proved a disappointment: treeless, solitary and desolate-looking. It was dark before they found fresh water. The three men bivouacked by the streamlet at the base of the mountain. When they could find no sticks on which to stretch their meat over the fire they used thistles. The night was clear and cold. The dew which covered the saddles turned to ice by morning, and the water in their kettle froze solid. He wondered how he had slept so comfortably on the ground, under only one blanket, then boasted, pleased with himself, "I am becoming a gaucho."

His first guide, who had been informed that he was accumulating material for a book on geology, said, "Climb to ridge. Walk along edge to summit. Caves, coal, gold, silver there. We stay here by fire."

It was a rough, tiring climb. He carried his supply of water in the corner of a cape of India-rubber cloth tied at the top with a thong. When he got to the summit he found that his eyes had deceived him; he was separated from the four peaks he had wanted to reach by a precipitous valley. He saw two horses grazing, took out his telescope and studied them, at the same time working out a cramp in his thigh before tackling the first peak. He found no caves, coal, gold or silver.

It was two in the afternoon before he reached the summit of the second peak. "No need to climb the other two," he decided. "These first ones have answered every purpose." With a start he realized that he should be frightened; any band of hostile Indians would bury a dozen spears in him. Instead he chuckled:

"A little danger, like salt to meat, gives it a relish."

He found an easier road out, joined his companions at sunset, drank much maté while writing up his notes with his silver pencil, smoked several little *cigaritos*, made up his bed and went to sleep with a furious wind blowing over his head.

They reached the Sauce *posta* in the middle of the day. It was well manned, for his guide told him:

"I here when Indians kill many men. Women run to saddleback, roll down big stones on Indians, save themselves."

Supper consisted of what the soldiers had caught: deer, ostrich, armadillo. They slept on thistle stalks. This was where General Rosas had informed Charles that an officer with a party of soldiers would meet him and accompany him on his journey. They were joined by two men carrying a parcel for the commandant. That night the soldiers gathered around a fire, playing cards: a fine young black man, another half Indian and Negro, an old Chilean miner, other mixed-breeds. Charles climbed a low cliff to observe the scene: around the men were sleeping dogs, guns, remnants of deer and ostrich, long spears upright in the ground, the horses tied up for any sudden danger. A dog barked. One of the soldiers left the fire, placed his ear to the ground.

The passing days were rich in experience. The plains abounded with three kinds of partridge and their destroyer, a small fox. He participated in chases, using a *bola*, but without success. Two of the soldiers killed a lion, of which they ate only the tongue, and found sixteen ostrich eggs which made an excellent supper. Charles and his guide joined the men belonging to the next *posta*, galloping through low, swampy country to the Sierra Tapalquen: first fine damp grass, then soft black peaty plains, then shallow beds of reeds.

The fifth *posta* was a rancho built on the edge of a large lake teeming with wild fowl including black-necked swans. That evening the soldiers brought in seven deer, partridges and armadillos and three ostriches. The ride to the sixth *posta* was on soft black soil, making for laborious traveling, but the neat rancho was built of posts, rafters and a thatched roof. A hailstorm the night before, with pieces of ice as large as apples, had killed many small animals; the plains were strewn with the carcasses of deer, ducks, ostriches.

For supper at the eighth *posta* he asked:

"What am I eating?"

The officer in charge replied, "One of the favorite dishes of our country. . . ."

Charles put down his joint of meat. He knew that one of the favorite dishes was unborn calf.

"Calf of a cow?" he asked.

"No. Puma. Good white meat."

His stomach turned. The soldiers argued which was the best meat, jaguar or cat. Charles quietly put the meat behind him into the mouth of a waiting dog.

He began to reach settled country. The ninth *posta* was on the Río Tapalquen, surrounded by *toldos*, the ovenlike huts of the Indian families of the men serving with General Rosas. There were shops where he was able to buy biscuits, the first he had eaten since Bahía Blanca. He passed a small tribe of Indians going to Guardia del Monte to sell their hides and hand-woven clothes, yergas and garters of brilliant colors and fine workmanship.

They rode for long distances in water above the horses' knees, then came to an *estancia* where Charles saw cattle grazing and a white woman. After crossing the Río Salado he came to one of General Rosas's fortified *estancias* where he was treated as a special guest. The Guardia del Monte proved to be a pleasant little town with gardens filled with peaches and quinces. At a fresh-water lake near the town he found a perfect fossil of the Megatherium.

Then came rich green plains, an abundance of cattle, horses and sheep. Now that he was back in civilization he was warned that he must sleep at the *posta* because "There are so many robbers about, you can trust no one." The officer in charge seemed puzzled by Charles's passport. "What is a *naturalista?*" he asked, but was impressed by the title and allowed him to proceed.

He reached Buenos Aires with its agave hedges, its groves of olives, peaches and willows on the thirteenth day of his pilgrimage, safe and well, his saddlebags and leather pouch rich with specimens. He went directly to the home of Mr. Lumb, an English merchant he had met there. Mr. Lumb showed him into a bedroom with an English bed, an English bedspread matching the curtains and a real chest of drawers, then informed him that H.M.S. *Beagle* had reached Montevideo four days earlier. He led Charles to a rocking chair on a veranda overlooking the town, never for a moment taking his eyes off Charles's face.

"No one but soldiers ever travels those five hundred miles to General Rosas's encampment," he exclaimed in wonderment.

He sent a letter to Captain FitzRoy at Montevideo informing him of his safe arrival and asking if Syms Covington could be sent upriver to Buenos Aires. He recorded his expenses for the past year, cashed a draft at the bank and went shopping for fresh clothing and boots, pharmaceuticals, replacements of paper, ink, bottles, boxes.

Syms Covington arrived in rapid time, with a message from Captain FitzRoy that he would try to get away from the river Plata the first week in November, and with letters for Charles.

It was four months since he had received word from the family. Katty's letter was dated May 29, 1833. She was with Susan in London on their holiday:

> We see a great deal of Erasmus now as our lodgings are not very far from his. He is good-natured and pleasant and we enjoy it very much. He drives his cab so well even in a London crowd. He seems to be more in love than ever with Hensleigh Wedgwood's wife Fanny, and almost lives at their home. Papa has long been *alarmed* for the consequences and expects to see an action in the papers. . . .

Uncle Jos was also in London, feverish with influenza. . . . London looked as if it had the plague, all the theaters were closed because twenty-four of the singers were in bed. Many of the shops were closed; ninety clerks of the Bank of England were ill.

Poor Fanny Owen Biddulph looked deplorably ill and weak and was very lonely in her London house:

> For some extraordinary whim Mr. Owen would not let Mrs. Owen come up to her confinement so the poor thing was all alone. Mr. Biddulph seems fond and affectionate to her but he is a gay, dissipated man, and desperately selfish. . . .

Charles surmised that Hensleigh knew that Erasmus was no danger or threat; that Erasmus's love for Fanny was only a familial affection. As for Erasmus being more in love with Emma Wedgwood "than appears, or than he himself knows . . ." Charles heard his brother saying in Plymouth:

"I don't love myself or the world enough to enable me to love any woman."

He was genuinely sorry about Fanny Owen. Apparently she had made a bad marriage. She had selected her own destiny. Or had destiny selected her?

He was again perturbed that he had not heard from Professor Henslow about the safe arrival of his first shipment.

After reading his letters, Charles studied the calendar and said to Syms:

"It is now the twenty-third of September. If the *Beagle* does not leave Montevideo before the first week in November that gives me more than a month for a land trip to the north."

His eyes lighted with excitement. When Mr. Lumb returned from his business office for tea he found Charles on the veranda, a map spread out on an oval wicker table.

"Ah, my good host, help me plot a journey. I'd like to follow the Río Paraná for a goodly distance. . . ."

"Up to Santa Fe, right here." Lumb ran a long fingernail northward. "I will give you a letter of introduction to a good friend in Rosario who will take care of your needs. From Santa Fe you can cross the river to Entre Ríos. It's rich agricultural land watered by both the Paraná and the Río Uruguay. Once in Uruguay you can ride the river down to where it joins the Plata, follow it back to Buenos Aires, and then on to Montevideo. The entire journey? A fortnight to three weeks."

With the nearest thing to a smile that he could achieve, Syms asked:

"Mr. Darwin, could I come along on that ride? I could get you birds and smaller animals. . . ."

Charles was silent for a considerable time. He preferred to travel alone with a guide for a companion, one who would know the country but in no way intrude on him. He wanted the feeling of independence, as well as the freedom of not being responsible for someone who would look to him for orders. In fact it had become a need. . . .

Mr. Lumb read Charles's silence clearly.

"Covington, you won't need to be idle during Mr. Darwin's absence. I'll send you out to my *estancia* in the country. We have a plenitude of birds out there."

Syms's expression slid back to its blank acceptance of what came next. Charles went to the government offices to secure his visas for Entre Ríos and Uruguay. When he returned home after he had purchased a bag of shot for his larger pistol and a lens to replace the scratched one on his telescope, he found Mr. Lumb sitting with a bronzed, middle-aged Buenos Airean dressed in workman's clothes.

"Darwin, permit me to introduce you to Juan, the former guide for Captain Francis Head, who explored this country about a decade ago."

"Captain Head, who wrote *Rapid Journeys Across the Pampas*? In 1826, I believe. We have it in the *Beagle* library. I read it while at sea." He was as excited as a child.

"Captain Head he teach me leetle English," said Juan. "Few words. *Nos comprendemos.*"

"Yes, I'm sure we'll understand each other," said Charles. "Let's set-tle your fee, then draw up a list of what we'll need. Mr. Lumb, you are a good soul to help me with all this."

They got a late start the next morning and made only seven miles the first day into the town of Luxan. They were scheduled to stay at the mail posts along the way, where Charles and Juan would be charged so much a league between the post offices. However Charles decided to camp out for the night.

At dawn they crossed a fine wooden bridge over the Río Luxan. Their horses picked up speed in the open, level plains. The *estancias* were miles apart, the earth filled with thistles as thick as a miniature forest and so tall they reached up to the horses' backs. Juan warned him to keep his pistol ready and his gun strapped over his left shoulder rather than behind his back.

"Thistle good place for robbers. Live here."

At dusk they crossed the Arrecifes on a raft made of empty barrels lashed together, then put into the posthouse. The postman said in Spanish:

"You come from Buenos Aires? So. Then you pay for thirty-one leagues."

Charles knew he had not ridden any ninety miles. The league in South America by no means meant the three miles it was supposed to. But he was not inclined to argue. He paid for himself and Juan at about the same rate that was charged for parcels delivered between two post stops. The supper was sparse but tolerable, the camp beds clean. He was content.

By the next evening they had reached the town of San Nicolás located on a branch of the Río Paraná.

"Ah!" exclaimed Charles, studying the view. "It is a noble river. Worth coming to see. Look, there are large vessels anchored at the foot of the cliff."

Juan had seen vessels at the foot of the cliff before.

"Tomorrow enter province Santa Fe. Good people. Better thieves. No cut throat. Steal ears off head."

They did not steal Charles's ears but while he was in a crowded market square someone did get his pistol from its leather belt. He did not notice the loss until he had crossed the water of the Pabon with its spectacular twenty-foot cascade. While admiring the falls his hand brushed his pistol holder. It was empty. He uttered an oath used by failing Cambridge students when they were sent down. Juan grinned apologetically.

"Tell you steal ear. Pistol we more need than ear."

"You're right. It's too dangerous to travel without one. How far are we from Rosario? I have a letter to a Spanish gentleman there. Perhaps he will lend me one for the rest of our trip."

Juan shaded his eyes from the hot sun. "Few league. Ride quick."

Rosario was a striking-looking town built on a level plain about sixty feet above the Río Paraná in which were many low and wooded islands. The perpendicular cliffs of the Paraná were a bright red, broken by masses of mimosa and cacti. There were a number of ships moving up and down the river, providing priceless linkage with Buenos Aires and Montevideo.

They rode directly to the home of Mr. Lumb's friend. When he had read Charles's letter he said:

"Mr. Lumb is my good friend. He teach me English. Also how English do business. My poor house is honored."

He took Charles for a walk through the large town, served him a refreshing meal and asked how long he would have the pleasure of his company. Charles replied:

"Not for long. Thank you. But I want to cross the river to Entre Ríos and return through Uruguay to Buenos Aires. There is one favor I desperately need. Someone stole my pistol. Could you spare me one? I will return it to you by the post."

"Certainly. But please, do not send it by post. Leave it with Mr. Lumb."

They started out by moonlight, reaching the Río Tercero by sunrise. Charles had been told there were old bones in the cliffs nearby. He went searching and soon found a curious large cutting tooth. Juan said:

"Giant bones stick out cliff upriver."

"Take me there. We'll hire a canoe."

Juan had reported accurately. Charles landed at the base of a cliff from which he saw two groups of bones sticking out.

"What they?" Juan asked.

"I believe they belong to the mastodon."

The fossil bones, though large, had so completely decayed, he was unable to extract even one of the smaller ones intact. Frustrated, he returned to the canoe and made notes of what he had seen.

He began to feel feverish. The heat was intense. The road was pretty, with an abundance of birds and flowers. He enjoyed the little village of Coronda with its lush gardens, but from there the road led through a large wood of low prickly trees with abandoned houses where the inhabitants had been killed in an Indian raid. Juan took out his revolver, held it in one hand, reins in the other.

They arrived in Santa Fe at sunset. Charles felt exhausted. He rented a room with a bed in it and fell into an uneasy sleep.

He stayed in bed for two days, unwell. It was the first time he had been ill since the two tortured days on horseback with Mr. Lennon on the way to his coffee fazenda in Brazil a year and a half earlier. Now, however, he had a strange headache. There was a good-natured old woman attached to the house; she became his doctor and nurse. First she bound an orange leaf to each of his temples. When they fell off she bound a bit of black plaster. When the plaster did not hold, she split a bean into halves, moistened them and placed one half on each temple, where they easily adhered. It was, she assured him, a sovereign cure for headache.

On the third day he summoned the strength to go with Juan across the Río Paraná to Paraná, the capital of Entre Ríos. He arrived at the bustling port after four hours of winding about different branches of the river. He took his letter of introduction, also from Mr. Lumb, to an old Catalonian, who invited him into his home. However Charles changed his program.

"I planned to cross the province of Entre Ríos and return by the Río Uruguay to Buenos Aires. But I have not been quite well. I think I had best return immediately. Will I be able to hire a boat to take me?"

"If not, Mr. Darwin, you can always take passage on a *balandra*, one of the small coasting vessels. It will get you there just as well."

He sold the horses and found a *balandra* whose master said he would be going down the river the next day. However the weather turned bad and the owner was indolently happy not to be at work. Charles was delayed five days, staying with his Catalonian host. He took long walks and enjoyed the geology of the surrounding environs. Since the province was bounded on every side by the Paraná and the Uruguay rivers the land was fertile; the two rivers kept the Indians out.

It was not until the twelfth of October that he and Juan were able to embark on the *balandra*, a one-masted vessel of a hundred tons, which sailed downriver with the current. When the weather became bad again, the owner, a timid character, fastened the vessel to the trees on one of the islands every few leagues and waited for a calmer moment, bearing all delays with admirable resignation. He was an old Spaniard who had been in those parts for many years. He professed a liking for the English but stoutly maintained that the battle of Trafalgar had been won by buying over the Spanish captains. It struck Charles as interesting that the man should prefer his countrymen to be considered traitorous rather than unskillful fighters.

The passing islands, covered with willows, resembled a jungle with their rich profusion of creeping plants. At one weather stop Charles decided to explore the island but had not proceeded a hundred yards before he found the most indubitable sign of a jaguar. He got back on board in a hurry, to be told that the jaguar had recently killed several woodcutters and sometimes jumped aboard the vessels.

The next couple of days held a constant gale and rain. Charles remained in bed as the four-foot-high cabin was too low to sit up in. When the weather cleared he went on deck and fished; the river abounded with large and extraordinary varieties even Juan was unable to identify. Or he walked to the cliffs of the Paraná where he was able to pick up fossil shells.

The evenings were tropical, the thermometer around eighty degrees. The air was filled with fireflies and mosquitos which, within five minutes, had covered his hand solidly black. He spent a night sleeping on deck, his head bound with a narrow-mesh gauze curtain. Finally, anxious to reach Buenos Aires, he left the vessel at Las Conchas, obtained a canoe which he and Juan paddled downstream to the Punta de San Fernando.

When they reached the outskirts of Buenos Aires, Charles found to his consternation that a revolution had broken out; he would not be allowed to go into the city since Buenos Aires was under a blockade. He talked to the commandant about General Rosas's civility to him. Instantly the atmosphere changed. He was given permission to enter the city but without Juan, and without permission to secure a horse. He set out on foot and eventually found himself on the stones of Buenos Aires on his way to the house of Mr. Lumb. Mr. Lumb explained that there was a revolt of General Rosas's officers and soldiers who did not like the present governor, and intended to show the country that no one could rule in peace except Rosas.

"How shall I get Syms Covington back into the city? It is important that we catch a ship down to Montevideo as quickly as possible," Charles said.

"You'll have to bribe a certain man to bring him in through the belligerents."

Syms arrived two days later, badly frightened. He had very nearly lost his life in quicksand; one of Charles's guns had gone down completely. All of Syms's clothing had been stolen; Charles's tools and the specimens Syms had shot had been confiscated.

5.

They rejoined H.M.S. *Beagle* in Montevideo, the reunion with his surrogate family a hearty one. The poop cabin had become the nerve center of the ship. Not only Wickham and Stokes but several others from the two schooners were working there. The chart table was filled with maps, charts, logbooks, hourly sheets of figures. There was no room for him to work or to sleep.

"It will be a full month before we sail," Captain FitzRoy informed him. "That's how long it will take us to complete these studies and send them to London . . ."

". . . a full month! And I worried while we made that slow passage down the Río Paraná that you might sail without me!"

"Sail into the Pacific and South Seas without our naturalist? Who else could we find to dump such quantities of ancient bones and rocks onto our immaculate decks?" Wickham was pulling his leg.

Charles grinned sheepishly.

"For a moment there I forgot how invaluable I was to the *Beagle!*"

He surveyed the crowded activity in the poop cabin.

"Wouldn't it be easier all around if I spent the month ashore? I have a letter to an English merchant here who apparently has a bed for me."

But first he must ship back to England his fourth set of boxes and crates. The third batch had gone from Río de la Plata late in July. He and Syms cleared a space on the poop deck. Mr. May set up temporary sawhorses covered with planks on which to lay out the specimens. The revolution in Buenos Aires had ended and Mr. Lumb had been able to recover Syms's birds. Once again he was going to need at least three big boxes.

"Why not also use one of those kegs we bring aboard filled with sugar or spirits?" Mr. May suggested.

"Can you build compartments in a round keg?"

May lined one of the boxes with tin plate and then helped the cooper put strong bands of metal around the keg. With loving hands and infinite care Charles put into the tin-lined box his two hundred skins of birds and animals, and a representation of the mice of South America. In the larger of the two boxes went his fossil bones and geological specimens, all labeled and catalogued. Into the cask he put his jars of fish, pillboxes of insects, bottles of soft marine life, a bundle of seeds and a bag of sweepings from a granary. A packet was due to sail in a few days; his friends in the crew helped him move the boxes and keg onto the deck of the packet.

The packet also brought him a bundle of mail. The best news was that the family's daily *Morning Herald* had had an article telling about H.M.S. *Beagle* at the Falkland Islands; and that all was well on board. The second item took a tremendous burden off him. His first set of boxes had reached Cambridge safely. Apparently Susan had also visited Cambridge, for she reported:

> Professor Adam Sedgwick made a most wonderful eloquent speech upon resigning his office as president of the British Association.

Charles's lips twisted into a warm smile. Was he getting closer to having an academic brother-in-law with each batch of mail?

His father was very well. He had bought a new light carriage and enjoyed having Edward drive him around the countryside. But Aunt Bessy Wedgwood was dangerously ill. Professor Henslow had to give up his Friday evenings because Mrs. Henslow was lying in; Fanny Owen had borne a daughter. One message set the gears of memory churning for a lost love. Susan wrote:

> We stayed four days at Woodhouse. The hay was making so we took novels, a bottle of cider and fruit and spent two whole days upon the haycocks. . . . It was high strawberry season and Caroline Owen said that always put her in mind of when you and Fanny used to *lie full length* upon the strawberry beds grazing by the hour.

He made his way around the chart table in the poop cabin, put the letters into the chest, gathered the clothing he would be taking ashore. Now he must make up his mind about a journey up the Río Uruguay with its extraordinary geological formations. He had intended to return that way from Entre Ríos when fever and headaches precluded it. He told himself sternly that he should not undertake it since it would cost another fifty pounds and he had already spent his year's allowance. It would be an extravagance. Would his father become angry? He wrote to Caroline:

> . . . I have really now been struggling for a whole week but there is a very interesting geological formation on the coast of the Uruguay, & every day I hear of more facts respecting it. When I think I shall never be in this country again, I cannot bear to miss seeing one of the most curious pieces of geology. I wish any of you could enter into my feelings of excessive pleas-

ure which geology gives. . . . I have drawn a bill for £50. I well know that considering my outfit I have spent this year far more than I ought to do. I should be very glad if my Father would make a real accounting against me, as he often says jokingly. . . .

Then he wrote a sentence that genuinely startled him.

. . . the sort of interest I am taking in this voyage is so different a feeling to anything I ever knew before. . . .

He paused to think precisely what he meant by this. For the moment he was frightened. He could feel himself quivering. That youthful determination he had made so lightly only thirty days out of Plymouth while sitting at the base of a cliff on St. Jago eating a solitary lunch of biscuit and tamarinds, to write a book on the geology of South America, had become not only the focus of joy for him but in all truth an obsession.

"No," he thought, "not an obsession, a possession. I am possessed by the idea. Never would I have thought that I could love rocks and mountains and plains and ravines more than my beetles!"

His English host had recommended a *vaquero* as guide, and a stable for renting horses. He took whatever of his equipment he could from the *Beagle* to keep the costs down. It was a glorious morning when they set out. He had originally thought the pampas to be level; now he saw that the land was formed in a series of undulations of thick green turf.

They slept at the *vaquero's* cottage that night, rising at dawn with the hope of riding deep into Uruguay. However the rivers were flooded. Charles watched the peons as they took off their clothes, tied them in a bundle, mounted their horses. As soon as the horse was out of its depth the peon slid off backward, seized the tail and was towed across the river. Charles jotted in his notebook:

A naked man on a naked horse is a very fine spectacle. I had no idea how well the two animals suited each other. As they gallop up on shore, before putting their clothes back on, they remind me of the Elgin marbles.

They stopped at night at the post buildings or, when Charles had still another letter of introduction, at a ranch house where they were well received. The scenery and life of the people changed dramatically with each town and region reached. One ancient town presented the demolished walls of what had been a heavily fortified city; its original character destroyed by the war waged between the Spanish of Buenos Aires and the Portuguese of Brazil. The Arroyo de San Juan had a prosperous port for small vessels carrying wood for fuel to Buenos Aires. One night he slept at a house adjacent to a limekiln. On the road to Punta Gorda he found jaguar scratches on the trees, yet nary a sight of a jaguar though he kept his gun ready. On the next *estancia* he watched the *vaqueros* lasso, kill and skin the monkeys, the skins worth the astonishingly high price of five dollars each. At the next, the last before he reached the geological formation, the owner was away but he was received by a nephew and an army deserter. Charles found the dialogue at table enchanting.

"Are not the ladies of Buenos Aires the handsomest in the world?" he was asked.

"Charmingly so."

"Do ladies in any other part of the world wear such large combs?"

"I assure you they do not."

They started at sunrise, riding through immense beds of thistles and thistle artichokes as high as their heads. It was ten days before he came upon the prospect that had prompted the trip, the cliffs on the banks of the Río Uruguay. He found a formation of red earthy clay with nodules of marl covered by a white limestone containing large extinct oysters and other marine shells. He knew that each layer represented a specific time, a separate age. There were giant bones protruding from washed-out cliffs. He was convinced they were Megatheriums. In any event, an important addition to his fossil collection, though the nature of the rock in which they were embedded gave him considerable trouble in extracting the fragments. He made up for this the next day when he found, at an *estancia*, an almost perfect head of a Megatherium. He was elated; there was no such fossil in all England. He bought it for a few shillings.

They rode through grassy fields, then rocky hill country to the Río Perdido, his two leather bags full of rocks dug out of earth, riverbank, cliff. They slept in posthouses where the roof leaked and they were soaked by midnight; and in one post where the manager was so drunk he suggested, indicating Charles:

"He is *gallego*, worth murdering."

Charles did not think the manager, who had a companion with him, was serious. His guide did, keeping guard over him all night with his gun. At dawn, when Charles awakened, his *vaquero* made his first joke of the nearly two-week ride:

"Those stupid peons thought you were worth murdering. I know better."

He returned to Montevideo happy with his finds. Augustus Earle was returning to England by packet. He was no longer the boyish painter who had bounced into Charles's room at 17 Spring Gardens to deliver a message from FitzRoy and stay to tea. His face was thin and lined from his continued illness.

"We're sorry to lose you, Gus," Charles told him. "I'll come to your first exhibition after we return."

There was talk of sending George Rowlett home with Earle. Rowlett was the hard-working purser who had kept H.M.S. *Beagle* free of scurvy by scouring each port for fresh fruit and vegetables, pickles, lemons. . . .

"Rowlett won't come to sick bay," Mr. Bynoe reported, "but I've watched him go through a series of ailments. Fortunately no two symptoms yet arrive together. It might be the better side of caution to invalid him home."

Rowlett came to the captain's cabin, a little haggard but cheerful and energetic. When asked if he would like to go home for safety's sake, Rowlett cried:

"Never so, Captain. The *Beagle*'s my home. These passing bouts don't bother me. They come and go."

Captain FitzRoy would not proceed without an artist on board. He hired a Londoner named Conrad Martens, who had studied landscape painting under Copley Fielding. Martens had been on the sloop *Hyacinth* when, in Rio de Janeiro, he met Mr. Hamond, an ex-*Beagle* officer on his way home, who informed him that H.M.S. *Beagle* needed an artist for the rest of her trip around the world. He promptly left the *Hyacinth* and made his way to Montevideo. FitzRoy told Charles amusedly:

"Mr. Martens is a stone-pounding artist who exclaims in his sleep, 'Think of me standing on a pinnacle in the Andes or sketching a Fuegian glacier.' By my faith in bumpology I am sure you will like him and like him very much. His landscapes are really good compared with London men, though perhaps in figures he cannot equal Earle."

Charles found Martens a pleasant person with rather too much of the drawing master about him.

H.M.S. *Beagle* had been out for close to two years now. Charles's wardrobe was showing signs of being outgrown. He had lost some of his lanky thinness, developed muscles and thicknesses throughout his body. He weighed around a hundred and fifty pounds. After a protracted bout of seasickness, when he could hold nothing down but a few raisins and edges of hardtack, he lost as much as ten pounds, and looked it, his cheeks showing hollows, his shoulders thin and hunched. In good weather, and on his land expeditions, he had a hearty appetite and quickly gained weight. Dressing for dinner with the captain, he was aware that the seams of his long tan topcoat were strained, his tan trousers short and tight at the waist. Only the gold chain of his watch strung across his vest was immune to his new growth.

He scoured Montevideo for a good suit for Sunday services and for dining with the captain; for shirts and nightshirts, warm underwear and cool, heavy trousers and light socks and heavy boots . . . all a full size larger than his London outfits.

The ships were being restocked as well. It would be at least six months before they rounded the Horn and reached a large port on the west coast of South America. While in port, Captain FitzRoy turned the Sunday service over to Sulivan. The missionary Matthews, who was now working as a seaman, was determined not to return to England but to stick it out until the *Beagle* crossed the Pacific Ocean and he could join his brother, a missionary artisan stationed in northern New Zealand.

By December 6 the *Adventure* was ready to sail. FitzRoy had determinedly hired twenty extra sailors to work under Wickham's command though the Admiralty had not authorized him to do so. It would involve a sizable outlay. The *Beagle's* charts, maps and drawings were ready to go to London. The two ships left together, sailing south down the coast to Port Desire, a thousand miles on the way to Cape Horn. They had a fair wind, stood out of the river and by evening were in clear water. H.M.S. *Adventure* sailed ahead of H.M.S. *Beagle*. Charles exclaimed to Sulivan while standing on the poop:

"It is great entertainment having a companion to gaze at."

The two men stood talking as the *Beagle* gently pulsated over the water, her sails full. Charles told of his last trip up the Uruguay where the poor folk lived off the fruit on the trees and the fish in the river.

"When I asked two of the men who were most shabbily dressed why they did not work, the first replied: 'Because the day is too long.' The second answered, 'I am too poor.'"

Sulivan laughed, said, "Ah, Charley, me lad, that's a story with a fishbone in it." He turned serious. "We just lost two petty officers. They deserted. With two years' pay waiting for them at the Admiralty in London!"

Sulivan, still only twenty-three, looked sad.

"I wouldn't want this repeated, but there is a childish want of steadiness in seamen."

Charles had seen Captain FitzRoy only occasionally while living ashore in Montevideo, but had found him anxious or depressed. He became totally frustrated when the packet containing Charles's boxes and cask left suddenly for England without the *Beagle's* charts and surveys. He had been counting on the documents to justify his two years of work and the added expenses. He had finally to leave them all with the

British consul general, Mr. Hood, who did not know when they would reach the Admiralty. FitzRoy's face was flushed as he twisted the palms of his moist hands.

"They're obviously not going to pay for the *Adventure* or the twenty-man crew I hired," he said as he and Charles took tea together. "It's a subject made more galling by reflection. A ship as small as H.M.S. *Beagle*, employed in stormy southern latitudes, has more arduous duties to perform than any surveying vessel on foreign station, and can have the help of neither dockyards nor men-of-war. Captain King on our first voyage, with far less extensive orders, had three vessels: the *Beagle*, the *Adventure* and the *Adelaide*, a tender which was purchased in Montevideo by the government for two thousand pounds sterling. Then why won't the Admiralty spend two thousand pounds for my *Adventure* when we need her so desperately? Darwin, a good spring should bend and be elastic. I am a good spring. I hope I will not break."

Charles felt a shiver go through him.

During the seventeen-day run down the coast to Port Desire, FitzRoy ate his meals quickly, slept even faster, Charles guessed about four hours a night. He never for a moment rested, relaxed or refreshed himself. He worked with devastating intensity on his big charts and chronometers, rechecked his data a dozen times so that not the slightest detail should be incorrect. Sometimes he endured what Charles could only describe as "fits" of working, thinking, making decisions. During these seizures he would go through three meals in a day opposite Charles, neither looking up nor uttering one word. At such times Charles began eating in the gun room, where the noise was most welcome. He knew there was nothing personal involved; FitzRoy spoke to no one else on board either, except to spill "hot coffee" on the midshipmen when he went on deck before breakfast for inspection.

Charles was in an interim passage of his own. From his little red notebooks he wrote up his geology, plant and insect life; then rather quickly turned to subjects that would be considered outside the naturalist's sphere: the life and character of the people among whom he had traveled; the superiority of the gauchos to the town residents; their hospitality combined with high spirits; the bloodshed resulting from their frequent use among themselves of their ever present knives. He wrote of the wars, the destruction they caused; the constant revolutions; the lack of any concept of justice, which was entirely for sale; the carrying on of everyday life by bribes and corruption in all offices, including the post offices, which printed money at will. He wrote of the contrasting societies, the absence of education, the disregard of religion, except for the taking of holidays. He calculated how much *estancias* were worth, how many generals a war inflicted on a society; and how long a democratic form of government, ruled by corrupt men, could stave off a dictatorship.

He remembered Alexander Pope's dictum:

"The proper study of mankind is man."

He could not preserve "man" in bottles of spirits as he did fish and marine life, or mount him on pins in little boxes as he did beetles, but he found his horizon so enormously expanded by his inland travels as well as the ports of call that he was no longer content to write about the natural philosophies alone. While neither the Darwin nor the Wedgwood family subscribed wholeheartedly to the religious tenet that God created the earth and everything on it for the sole use and benefit of mankind, he did think that a specific race of man, such as the colorful gauchos, were at least as interesting as the Sierra de la Ventana range of mountains, and could reveal as much of origin and history as the rock specimens he dug out with his geological hammer.

Was he indeed a latent clergyman?


6.


With the bulk of the surveys off to London, the poop cabin was his own again. On one of the first mornings at sea he and Syms Covington spread out on their section of the chart table the fruits of the two-week trip up the Río Uruguay: fossils, rocks, thistles, reptiles; numbering and describing them in Charles's specialized notebooks. Twenty-year-old Syms turned on his stool and looked at Charles with a familial expression.

"Mr. Darwin, I can't tell you how glad I am to be back in our workroom. I like being your assistant."

Stokes, who was sketching on the other side of the table, looked up in surprise. Charles commented:

"God is good. He gives each of us something to be happy about. Particularly when He keeps the sea tranquil."

It was a seventeen-day sail south to Port Desire. The winds were generally light. When the weather became capricious, "foul," Charles called it, he tried to beat off any suggestion of seasickness by ignoring it. The stratagem did not work.

When the two ships reached port, Lieutenant Wickham informed Captain FitzRoy that "the Adventure did not sail well on a wind"; that he would need a few days to alter the sails. Charles and Ben Bynoe went for a long walk into the wilds of Patagonia, a sterile desert composed of gravel. On the surface of the plain they discovered oyster shells and blue mussel shells. Charles observed:

"It's certain that within no great number of centuries this was all beneath the sea. Did the waters subside or did this plain elevate?"

At that moment Charles spied two giant guanacos. He got his gun up fast and shot the one in front.

"Capital shot!" exclaimed Bynoe. "This fellow is so large the whole crew will have fresh meat for Christmas dinner."

At the order of the captain every man also had the day ashore. FitzRoy distributed prizes for the best runners, leapers, wrestlers, crew and officer alike. They romped almost as school children. Charles entered a foot race which he lost handily.

"Too bad we don't have long-distance walking matches," he said, "say twenty miles. I'd win the gold medal."

He spent the days geologizing in the sandy chalk and gravel country; walking for a full day to the distant hills without finding a tree for shade. It was desolate land yet he observed, "I feel a high pleasure which I can neither explain nor comprehend."

He obtained some new birds and animals, measured barometrically the height of the plain; it had an altitude of almost two hundred and fifty feet.

He shot another of the deerlike guanacos which must have weighed two hundred pounds.

Waiting for the *Adventure*, Captain FitzRoy decided to run down the hundred and ten miles south to Port San Julian and survey the intermediary coast. They floated with a strong tide out of the harbor, passed the narrows and made sail . . . and immediately struck twice rather heavily on a rock before they passed over it. FitzRoy, on the bridge, cried out:

"Damnation! That's the same rock we hit on the first *Beagle* voyage! How much damage has it done to our copper sheathing?"

Sulivan yanked off his boots, plunged over the side. It seemed to Charles that he was under water far too long, but surfaced on the other side, blood showing from scratches against the torn copper.

"Nothing serious, Captain. Some rough copper edges on the bow, no breakthrough or leakage."

"Thank you, Lieutenant. I'll go and have a look myself just to be sure."

To Charles's surprise FitzRoy went over the side. It was some minutes before he realized that the act was true to the captain's character. The skipper was responsible for everything that happened to his ship. FitzRoy announced that the damage would have to be repaired.

They anchored at the head of the harbor at San Julian, going ashore in a whaleboat. Early the next morning Charles went with FitzRoy and two crewmen to search for a fresh-water supply for the ship's tanks at the head of an inlet described on an old Spanish map as a "place of sweet water," *agua dulce*. The captain carried his double-barreled gun; the crewmen some heavy measuring instruments; Charles his gun and two water bags.

It was a bootless search. There was no *agua dulce*. The weather was extremely dry and after many hours the water in Charles's canteens was gone. When they reached the top of still another hill, FitzRoy lay down on the ground.

"I'm too tired and thirsty to move further."

"I can see two lakes of water about two miles off," Charles said. "I'll make my way to them and fill my canteens." And to the two crewmen, "You stay with the captain."

He pushed on relentlessly, not overly fatigued; he had gone longer than eleven hours on some of his inland trips. He walked the two miles to the first lake, eagerly scooped up a handful of water. It was a *salina*, the salt too strong to allow drinking. Disappointed, he trudged on to the second lake. Another *salina*.

Night was falling. Sore of bone, now, and unhappy that he had not located fresh water, he returned to find the captain had slept but could not travel. He took charge.

"I am going back to the ship; one of you must stay with the captain." He turned to the other crewman.

"Do you feel strong enough to walk back with me to the ship?"

"I'll manage, sir."

He found a shorter route but it was still a walk of many hours. It was dark now. When they reached the *Beagle* Charles had two men sent out to assist the captain, then insisted that a huge fire be lighted on the beach to serve as a beacon for the returning party. They stumbled into the lighted fire area toward dawn, none the worse for wear. However Charles spent the next two days in his hammock with a fever. Mr. Bynoe supplied lemonade, and cool cloths to his brow.

Charles thought little of the incident, particularly since he had failed to find fresh-water lakes. But the story of his strength and fortitude ran from bulkhead to bulkhead. A subtle but noticeable change came over the officers and crew, both.

Charles Darwin was no longer a dilettante, a "man who knows everything." He was a highly respected shipmate.

In March of 1834 H.M.S. *Beagle* completed its survey of the east coast of Patagonia and Tierra del Fuego. Because the *Adventure* was sharing the chores and the weather promised to hold, FitzRoy decided to go up the Beagle Channel to Ponsonby Sound to see how their three Fuegians were faring. They passed a chain of mountains three thousand feet high which terminated in sharp, broken peaks after rising abruptly from the water's edge, then came to a mountain which towered above them all. With a glint in his eyes, FitzRoy announced:

"This is the highest mountain in Tierra del Fuego, above seven thousand feet. It is herewith named Mount Darwin."

Charles was overcome, then murmured:

"First I became a Sound, now I am a Mountain. The Lord alone knows what I shall become next!"

"An ocean, perhaps?" Sulivan said slyly. "All you have to do is to discover a new one."

They anchored in the northern part of Ponsonby Sound.

When they reached Jemmy Button's country, there was no sign of the little settlement that had been started for Jemmy, York Minster and Fuegia Basket. The lookout called:

"Canoe approaching. Flying a flag."

When the canoe came alongside they recognized Jemmy, naked except for a bit of skin around his waist, his matted hair hanging over his shoulders.

FitzRoy, staring down at him, could hardly restrain his feelings.

"How wretchedly thin he is. I can see by your faces that I'm not the only one touched by his squalid appearance."

Mr. Bynoe, who had been Jemmy's closest friend on board, said, "It's a catastrophe! When he left us he was fat and fastidious, afraid of dirtying his shoes."

Jemmy climbed the rope ladder, stood on deck with the smile on his face mixed with embarrassment in his smoke-reddened eyes. The captain barked orders:

"Take Jemmy below. Give him a bath. Wash and cut his hair. Clothe him in the best we have."

The process of rehabilitating Jemmy took the crew only half an hour. The captain's steward brought a third chair into his cabin where Jemmy, Charles and FitzRoy sat down to dinner. Charles and FitzRoy exchanged glances at how properly Jemmy was using his knife and fork.

"I must congratulate you, Jemmy. You behave in every way as correctly as if you had never left us."

Jemmy grinned a full-toothed expression of thanks.

"Have you been getting enough to eat?" Charles asked.

"Plenty eat. Plenty fruits, plenty birdies. Plant turnips, potatoes. Me big man here."

FitzRoy asked, "Where are Fuegia Basket and York Minster?"

Jemmy's face went dour. He gritted his back teeth.

"Go 'way. Big canoe. Their country. York very much jaw. Pick up big stone. All men 'fraid. He send Fuegia catch my clothes. I wake up, they go. Leave Jemmy naked. York steal tool, blanket, seed . . . everything."

There was a silence. FitzRoy asked:

"Jemmy, would you like to stay on the *Beagle* and return to England when we do?"

Jemmy hung his head. He spoke without looking up.

"No. Stay here. My friend good people. Know English word. Good here for Jemmy."

He returned in the morning laden with gifts: two fine otter skins, one for FitzRoy, the second for quartermaster James Bennett, who had befriended him; for Charles, two fine spearheads which he had made expressly for him; gifts for Bynoe. He had with him a pretty young squaw who wept quietly until Jemmy said:

"No cry. I no go."

That, and the sudden appearance of shawls, ribbons, handkerchiefs, a gold lace cap, dried her tears.

Jemmy strongly opposed a second opening of the mission. It would do no good. Besides, he was certain Matthews would be in danger from the foot Patagonians who came over to steal . . . and from Jemmy's own people as well.

H.M.S. *Beagle* stood out of Ponsonby Sound. Jemmy lighted a farewell signal fire for them. Standing at the bow with Charles, Captain FitzRoy said somewhat sadly:

"I cannot help hoping still that some benefit, however slight, may result from the intercourse of these people, Jemmy, York and Fuegia Basket, with other natives of Tierra del Fuego. Perhaps a shipwrecked seaman may hereafter receive help and kind treatment from Jemmy Button or his children."

They made a short passage to the Falkland Islands by scudding before a gale of wind. Captain Beaufort had instructed FitzRoy to make his first-ever survey of their east coast. When they reached Berkeley Sound the acting governor, Lieutenant Smith, came on board with a tale of horror: three gauchos and five Indians had murdered five Englishmen, kidnapped some eighteen men, women and children and plundered their homes. Three of the miscreants had been caught. Would Captain FitzRoy put their leader in chains until a cutter arrived to take them to Rio de Janeiro?

The captain would.

To Charles's great joy there was a letter from Professor Henslow, the first he had received in his twenty-seven months of travel. It was dated the fifteenth of January *1833*, over a year in the arriving.

"By what fatality it did not arrive sooner I cannot conjecture," Charles mused as he prepared to study its contents.

My dear Darwin,

. . . I had intended writing by the Dec^r. packet, but just as I was about to do so your letter arrived stating that a Box was on its road, so I thought I had better delay till I had seen its contents. It is now here & everything has travelled well. . . . I would not bother myself about whether I were right or wrong in noting such & such facts about Geology—note all that *may* be useful—most of all, the relative positions of rocks giving a little sketch.

. . . So far from being disappointed with the Box, I think you have done wonders, as I know you do not confine yourself to collecting but are careful to describe.

Most of the plants are very desirable to *me*. Avoid sending *scraps*. Make the specimens as perfect as you can, *root, flowers & leaves* & you can't do wrong. You need not make quite so great a parade of tow & paper for the geolog. specimens as they travel very well provided they be each wrapped up & closely stowed.

Another caution I wd. give is to place the number on the specimen always inside and never outside the cover. The moisture & friction have rubbed off one or two. I shall thoroughly dry the different perishable commodities & then put them in pasteboard boxes with camphor & paste over the edges, & place them in my study or some very dry place. . . .

*Birds.* Several have no labels—the best way is to tie the label to their legs. *Quadrupeds.* The large one capital, the two mice rather mouldy. The minute Insects most excellent. The *Lichens* are good things as scarcely any one troubles himself to send them home. Every individual specimen once arrived here becomes an object of great interest, & tho' you were to send home 10 times as much as you do, yet when you arrive you will often think & wish how you might have (& had) sent home 100 times as much! Things which seemed such rubbish, but now so valuable. However no one can possibly say you have not been active, & that your box is not capital. . . .

Most affect^ly. & sincerely yr.

J. S. Henslow

There was also a letter from his sister Katty. It had been four months since her last one. He thought of home often, but it was not until he saw a letter with a sister's handwriting that a love for The Mount felt like a strangulating hand around his throat. He consumed the letter in one misty gulp.

His father was traveling more and working less. Erasmus followed the Hensleigh Wedgwood family wherever they went: to Hensleigh's parental home, Maer Hall; and to The Mount when the Wedgwoods came to visit . . . even after Mrs. Wedgwood had given birth to a daughter. Fanny Biddulph had come to The Mount for a visit, coloring prettily whenever she talked about Charles

> affectionately and warmly. She said how much she wanted to see you again and how very much she wished for your happiness. . . .

"Too late," he thought dryly; "much too late."

The most arresting lines were Katty's:

> I cannot help being rather grieved when you speak so rapturously of the tropics as I am afraid it is a still stronger sign of how long it will be before we shall have you again. *I have great fears of how far you will be able to stand the quiet clerical life you used to say you would return to.*

"I used to say?" he mused. "I always say. I know of no change in my mind. I'm a stayer."

Since H.M.S. *Beagle* would be busy surveying for at least two weeks, Charles decided that he would take a trip inland. FitzRoy warned against it. His shipmates looked askance.

"Since the murders there are no gauchos you can trust. And you must have a guide."

He found two Spanish gauchos who were recommended by acting governor Lieutenant Smith. They were willing to go out for a number of days. Charles rented six horses, prepared to leave the next morning. The weather was boisterous and cold, with heavy hailstorms, yet his little party moved along well. The gauchos proved to be amiable, and one of them, St. Jago by name, became attached to Charles, watching him with curiosity while he attacked with his hammer the main range of quartz rock hills, and while he wrote notes about the flocks of geese feeding in the valley.

At sundown St. Jago brought down a fat cow but had difficulty killing the furious beast. The ground was wet, there was little brushwood available to cook their supper. St. Jago solved the problem by bringing in the bones of a bullock; they made as hot a fire as coals would have.

The rain continued. Charles collected whatever the land had to offer but it was rough work. The ground was a bog without a dry spot to sit down on, let alone sleep. Yet sleep he did, with his saddle for pillow and the horse blanket for covering. The horses foundered in the mud, fell while trying to jump streams. To complete their misery they had to cross an arm of the sea which came up to the horses' backs. Violent winds broke waves over the three men.

"This is an endurance contest," Charles declared.

He arrived back at the *Beagle* still sopping wet. He looked in on Benjamin Bynoe in his sick bay, telling him to be ready for any emergency.

"Such as?" Bynoe asked.

"Double pneumonia."

"Prescription: a double allowance of rum. Take it with tea. Anybody try to murder you?"

"Only me."

7.

They were all eager now to get out to the Pacific Ocean and see the other half of the globe. But first the *Beagle* had to be beached at the mouth of the Santa Cruz River to repair her copper keel.

It was a six-day crossing from the Falkland Islands to the mainland against western breezes. Charles had never seen the ship under a greater press of sail. At the mouth of the Santa Cruz River she was laid on shore, her guns, anchors, small boats removed. It was found that a piece of the secondary copper keel under the "forefoot" had been knocked off.

Once in the Pacific, Captain FitzRoy explained to Charles, worms would eat their way through the unprotected planks. The work had to be completed in one tide.

There was a low tide twice in every twenty-four hours, after seven hours of the rushing of the river water through a confined opening into the ocean. They would have precisely five hours before the ocean tide roared in again and covered the estuary.

The armorer set up his forge. Mr. May and his carpenters set about cleaning the exposed planks. The ship carried extra copper sheets for just such an emergency. The armorer sized them, the carpenter crew cut away the jagged copper and fitted the new sheets snugly into place. Just after noon the ocean waters came in and floated H.M.S. *Beagle*, her guns, anchors, boats all back on board. Sulivan took her to a safe mooring.

Captain FitzRoy congratulated his craftsmen, then organized a three-whaleboat expedition to explore the Santa Cruz River. He took three weeks' provisions in the hopes of reaching and mapping the river's source in the Andes. Charles lowered himself down the rope ladder into the whaleboat commanded by the captain; it carried its own tent, blankets, surveying equipment. There were half a dozen sailors in each boat to do the rowing. They carried no sails. The other two whaleboats were in the charge of Edward Chaffers and John Stokes; twenty-five men in all, well armed in case of attack.

Mr. Bynoe, as well as thirty-three-year-old Conrad Martens, were in the captain's boat. Charles had found Martens to be a well-educated man with meticulously groomed side whiskers and mustache and a pleasant manner. His features and eyes were nondescript . . . until he started to sketch as they proceeded up the river. He drew all day with a sure hand and an excited expression the changing aspect of the river, setting down descriptive notes about the differing colors and land formations to be used later for his water colors. The water colors were done in delicate beiges and browns which caught the spirit of the country, even as he had captured H.M.S. *Beagle* beached and lying partially on her side while her copper bottom was being repaired.

When the Santa Cruz downstream current, running from four to six knots, was too strong to allow rowing upstream the three boats were fastened astern of each other; the men would go ashore, put on collars of canvas and canvas chest halters which had been sewn on board the *Beagle* by the sailmaker and were attached to long ropes, and pull the boats upstream. Each man's stint was an hour and a half. Captain Fitz-Roy said to Charles, Bynoe and Martens:

"You three specialists don't have to do the hauling."

"Will you do so, Captain?" Charles asked.

"Certainly. So will Chaffers and Stokes."

"Then why am I not good enough to wear the collar?"

Charles served a stint four times, actually enjoying the vigorous pull. His body had the strength of lean, sinewy men. He felt the challenge of using it on this tumultuous river. As always, at the back of his mind was the inarticulated thought:

"I am a landsman. I must sustain the respect of the seamen."

When night fell they found a level spot for their lodging. Three tents were erected; each boat settling into a tent containing its officer and crew. When it came time to draw lots for an hour's guard duty to safeguard the boats and watch for marauders, Charles volunteered for the midnight shift.

He relished the hour. He and Ben Bynoe never uttered a word. In the silent darkness they kept the fire burning and listened for the least sound of an intruder.

By the third day they were in *terra incognita*. They assessed it to be country never seen or penetrated by any except bands of Indians. Although the curse of sterility was on the land of Patagonia, with not even a fish in the water and hence no waterfowl, the country swarmed with guanaco, several herds of a hundred. They provided fresh food. For Charles the scenery was totally dependent upon the geology. As the river channel narrowed he came across blocks of lava which knocked two holes through the side of one of the boats. At last they hauled themselves and their boats so high they could see the snowy peaks of the Andes. They found great blocks of slate and granite in the river bed.

"Where did they come from?" asked Bynoe.

"From the Andes, Ben, in former periods of commotion."

"How did the lava get here?"

Captain FitzRoy had joined them as Charles pounded the lava rocks to secure specimens.

"My guess?" said Charles. "At some remote period these plains must have formed the bottom of an ocean, and this lava was poured down from an eruption in the Andes to the then ocean level. When the plains rose in an upheaval, or the ocean subsided, the lava rock we are looking at surfaced. Does that sound outlandish?"

FitzRoy shook his head in uneasy bewilderment. He was looking off toward another plain of diluvial detritus, stone and earth resulting from a general deluge or period of catastrophic action of water. When he spoke his voice was dry to the cracking point.

"This could never have been effected by a forty days' flood."

"Captain, does that mean you think these lava plains and diluvial plains go back before 4004 B.C.?"

FitzRoy did not appear to like what he was saying but the words came out simply enough.

"We're looking at sea-worn, rolled single stones and alluvial accumulations, water-worn pebbles. They compose the greater part of this plain. How vast and of what immense duration must have been the action of those waters which smoothed the stones buried in these deserts of Patagonia."

That night on his silent watch Charles pondered the captain's words and his conclusion that the geology of this earth is "of immense duration."

It was mid-May 1834 when they steered toward the Strait of Magellan. It took them four days of sailing to reach Cape Virgins at the mouth of the strait. The weather was "bad, cold and boisterous," and made Charles proportionately sick and miserable. Only a hundred and twenty miles from the coast of Patagonia where the weather had been dry, the sky clear, they were enduring hail, snow and wind. H.M.S. Beagle beat about the entrance of the strait obtaining soundings, finding and mapping one dangerous bank. The next morning at daylight they sighted the *Adventure* coming from the Falklands. A British man-of-war had taken away the prisoners from Berkeley Sound and handed over to Lieutenant Wickham a packet of mail from England.

Charles had four letters from his sisters, dated the previous October and November. They had received the first installment of his journal and were taking turns reading it aloud in the evening to their father, who sent Charles his affectionate love. Susan had knitted him a little purse which she hoped his foreign coins would fit into; she had also forwarded a novel she had just finished about Ceylon called *Cinnamon and Pearls.* Mr. Howell was sending the shoes he had ordered and Erasmus had already turned over to Captain Beaufort the several books on natural history that he had requested, including Lyell's third volume of *Principles of Geology.* His sisters informed him that his letters passed through a whole chain of hands and were being widely discussed.

"It's ridiculous," he complained to Bynoe while they exchanged news from home. "My collections and observations are becoming known while my journey is only half over!"

There was good political news. Slavery was being abolished in August 1834, with twenty million pounds' compensation to the owners. The family was reading pamphlets about Parliament taking up the Poor Laws of Ireland. Susan wrote that the Rev. Charles Langton and his wife, Charlotte Wedgwood, ". . . have their living" in charming country.

There was also questionable news. Hensleigh Wedgwood, who had been serving as a police magistrate for eight hundred pounds a year, was giving up his post because of religious scruples over the English system of administering oaths. He could not reconcile giving these oaths with his conscience. He and his wife and child would now have only the four hundred pounds a year which Uncle Jos had given him at his marriage. According to Katty, they would be wretchedly poor. Hensleigh once before had refused a fellowship at Cambridge by not subscribing to the Church of England's Thirty-nine Articles.

Caroline had also sent him a few little books which were being talked about by everybody in England, written by Miss Harriet Martineau. She had become a literary lion in London and was admired by Erasmus. If Charles found her books dull he was to throw them overboard. She was also sending by the same post the Archbishop of Dublin's book, *Scripture Revelations.*

The weather dropped below the freezing point. A lot of snow fell. He described this as "rather miserable work in a ship where you have no roaring fire and where the upper deck covered with thawing snow is, as it were, a hall in your house." However one aspect of life improved con-

siderably. He had been drinking water with a heavy brine for a number
of days. It was like drinking a physic and having none of one's thirst
quenched. Now, in Gregory Bay, they took on a six days' supply of fresh
water. Though he had not minded the stinking water, they had boiled
it thoroughly and made it into a generally acceptable dish of tea, he
had not realized what a joy fresh water was and how necessary to one's
well-being.

It took three more days of hard plowing through the strait to reach
Port Famine, so named after a Spanish colony settled there by King
Philip II of Spain in 1585, when most of the men died during the
first winter of disease and hunger. It was a cheerless place; the dusky
woods piebald with snow could be seen indistinctly through the rain and
fog, one of the most inhospitable areas of the entire world in which
the human race could live. Despite the weather the onshore survey
continued.

FitzRoy left the Strait of Magellan by the Magdalen Channel, only
lately discovered. They were running with fair winds behind them but
the atmosphere was thick. Dark ragged clouds drove over the mountains and jagged peaks, cones of snow and blue glaciers were outlined
on the lurid sky. In the midst of this wild scenery they anchored at
Cape Turn close to Mount Sarmiento. Here Charles had an opportunity to make a close study of the one marine production about which
he believed a great volume could be written: kelp. The plant grew on
every rock from low-water mark to a great depth and so thick in places
that it could cause death: Clerk Hellyer had died in it. Charles had observed not a single rock anywhere near the surface which was not
buoyed by the floating weed. With the help of several of the sailors he
gathered large quantities of the kelp, which they dumped onto the
poop deck.

"Darwin, you're incorrigible!" cried Lieutenant Sulivan.

"Don't be hasty, Sulivan. I'm about to unfold for you one of the
great miracles of nature. The number of living creatures of all orders
whose existence intimately depends on the kelp is wonderful."

He spoke quietly to the large circle of men gathered around him
while unraveling the seaweed. Almost every leaf was thickly incrusted
with the remains of corallines. He scraped loose shells, molluscs, bi-
valves. Innumerable crustaceans frequented every part of the plant.
Shaking the great entangled roots, a pile of small fish, shells, cuttlefish,
crabs, sea eggs, starfish, planaria, fell out. As he turned his attention to
another branch of the kelp he discovered creatures of new and curious
structure.

"Amidst the leaves of this plant," he went on, "species of fish live
which nowhere else would find food or shelter. If the fish were de-

stroyed the many cormorants, divers and other fishing birds, as well as otters, seals and porpoises, would soon perish also. The Fuegian savage, the miserable lord of this miserable land, would decrease in numbers and perhaps cease to exist."

Charles looked up at Sulivan, his hands and trousers wet and stained from the kelp and its inhabitants.

"So you see, this kelp is a universe unto itself. Each part of it bears a relationship to the whole. How many thousands of years do you suppose it took nature to bring about this intricate but delicately balanced structure?"

"That's for the man who knows everything to answer," grumbled Sulivan. "I'll give you exactly one hour to get all your prized specimens onto the chart table."

After a sufficient time for rating the chronometers, FitzRoy sailed from Cape Turn. The following day they beat westward through the Cockburn Channel. At dusk he said to the group of men standing with him on the bridge:

"I would have anchored for the night had there been a safe place offered."

"That looks like a safe cove at your right elbow," Lieutenant Sulivan observed.

"It's a small one and I prefer to leave it for the *Adventure*. We'll remain under sail in the *Beagle*."

Charles groaned. That meant constant movement.

FitzRoy smiled.

Remaining with his friends on deck, Charles found the night long and very dark. Light rain fell nearly all the time. Squalls from the west were frequent. There were only four square miles in which it was safe to sail to and fro. For fourteen hours they traversed the area in every direction. Captain FitzRoy had always been an advocate of short tacks under manageable sail because his ship was safer to handle while going through the water than while hove to. He kept them as much as possible near the same place. Those on board were also more on the alert than when the vessel herself seemed half asleep.

After over two years of watching, Charles remained intrigued by the crew's expert manipulation of the sails. On this still night he could distinctly hear the cracking and groaning of the great moving mass propelled by the glaciers of Tierra del Fuego. The same force which was known to uproot whole forests of lofty trees must tear from the flanks of the mountain many huge fragments of rock. Beneath each glacier, also, he heard a roaring torrent draining the upper part of the ice. In his specific notebook on the geology of South America, he wrote:

To these effects, which are common to all cases, there must be added, in this country, the wear and tear of the waves produced by each successive fall of forest and rock. Nor can this agency be inconsiderable when we remember that it goes on night and day, century after century. We must look at every portion of the mountain as having, during the gradual rising of the land, been successively exposed to the action of these combined forces.

When dawn finally broke, on June 11, 1834, the captain ordered a portion of rum served to the crew, then announced:

"The *Adventure* is coming out to us from the cove where she has passed the night. Both vessels will sail out of the channel, past Mount Skyring and all the Furies as fast as our sails can urge them. By sunset we should be near the Tower Rocks, not far from Cape Noir, and with a fresh northwest wind, stand out into the Pacific with every inch of canvas set which we can carry."

The Pacific! Charles felt a clutch at his heart. After nearly two and a half years of sailing since they had left Plymouth! It was a day for which he had long dreamed.

But he was not the same man who had sailed out of Plymouth two and a half years before.

Resting in his hammock in the poop cabin, with the sea moving gently beneath H.M.S. *Beagle*, he came to realize that he had made the transition from carefree youth to adult, to manhood; unwittingly something had come into his life to which he could devote himself though he did not yet see clearly how it could evolve into a responsible profession. He had a sense of growing excitement, with a tinge of exultation that there was a world into which he could fit and make, perhaps, a modest contribution. How rewarding were all these months, these years; on board the *Beagle*, and on shore making his naturalist's excursions, serving an apprenticeship for the future.

He understood for the first time that he had left behind forever his directionless youth and had come to man's estate not gradually but precipitously. He remembered the young lad who had boarded the ship in Plymouth, the even younger chap he had left behind in Cambridge, Maer Hall, The Mount. He felt an intense gratification that he had leapt a chasm, landed squarely on his two big feet in a land of infinite horizon. How marvelous to have charted through his hard-earned knowledge of the ship's ways, the survey's instruments, nature's multitudinous creations, a whole new existence he might have missed altogether!

All this he would take into the Pacific . . . which every man yearned to sail.

# BOOK SIX

*"What an Immense Variety of Life
Has Been Created Here"*

1.

CHARLES's jubilation at being in the Pacific was quickly thwarted. The ocean was anything but pacific. A succession of furious northerly gales provided H.M.S. *Beagle* with its worst weather since leaving Plymouth, worse than the storm which had nearly sunk her off Cape Horn. They stayed afloat by using their close-reefed top-, fore- and staysails. When the winds died down the great sea prevented them from moving up the west coast. Such weather utterly destroyed Charles for any useful purpose; he could not work, read, swallow food or find surcease in sleep.

George Rowlett suffered most; he had been going downhill steadily with periodic flare-ups which Mr. Bynoe thought might be tuberculosis or an infectious disease. Rowlett refused to take the medication the doctor believed might save the oldest officer on board: calomel, morphine, tartar emetic. The furious weather of the Pacific hastened his demise. He slipped into a coma, died. He was a stately and formidable thirty-eight years of age.

The body and lead shot were sewn in a hammock and additional canvas, covered with a flag, and placed on a plank. The officers and crew assembled on the quarter-deck. They mourned Rowlett's passing. Captain FitzRoy read the funeral service, intoning:

"We commit the body of our deceased companion to the seaman's grave, that 'ever-changing and mysterious main.'"

The plank was tipped up. The weighted body was "committed to the deep." There was a splash, an awe-filled and solemn sound, as the water consumed a shipmate.

"It's my responsibility," Bynoe said later. "I should have invalided him home from Montevideo."

"Rowlett knew he was dying," Charles said comfortingly. "He was unwilling to die in England. I never heard him mention having a home there or family or friends. He was out on the first *Adventure* for five years, and now two and a half years with us. The *Beagle* was his home, and we his family. That's why he wanted to die on board."

Captain FitzRoy had meant to sail up the coast to Coquimbo, considerably north of Valparaíso, the major port on the southwestern coast, but after six hundred storm-battered miles, he put into the protected harbor of San Carlos at the island of Chiloé. After eighteen days of being knocked about, Charles said:

"I hope the island is securely anchored to the bottom of the ocean."

The natives, who lived in tiny thatched houses on the point, rowed out in small boats to welcome the *Beagle* with unaffected joy, for few ships stopped in this remote port. They were a mixture of Indian and Spanish blood, and brought pigs, potatoes and fish to sell. There was a constrained moment when everyone realized that George Rowlett was no longer there to bargain and purchase. Edward Chaffers stepped forward, quietly assumed Rowlett's duties.

Charles took a short walk up winding creeks through beautiful woods. He noted in his book that nowhere except in tropical Brazil had he seen such an abundance of elegant forms. The volcanic ash soil was fertile, giving rise to a teeming luxuriance of the forests and bamboo which astonishingly twined through the trees to a height of forty feet.

The *Adventure* limped into port with a broken main boom, a result of the storm. The usually imperturbable Wickham was annoyed with himself.

"Gripes me soul," he complained.

". . . and on your immaculate deck, no less!" taunted Charles.

He found a clean bed in a cottage in the village of San Carlos, one surrounded by paddocks of grass and lofty evergreens. The natives were dressed in coarse woolen garments which each family wove and dyed with indigo of a dark blue.

First there were torrential rains, as befitted these winter months, then the weather turned balmy for three whole days. He examined the structure of the rocks, named his geological hammer "Old Thor" in honor of Adam Sedgwick, and was convinced that these were formerly submarine beds which had been elevated to dry land in a very recent period. How recent? Five thousand years? Five hundred thousand? Five million?

Late that afternoon he returned to the dock, had supper on board the *Adventure* with a reconciled Wickham, and viewed the new main boom.

"I feel as you do, John," he confided over their ham steaks and fresh boiled potatoes. "I was so bloody miserable after doubling the Horn that I vowed I would jump ship and return to the glories of Shropshire. But Chiloé has made it worth while."

Lieutenant Wickham chided:

"You can't become an authority on the geology of South America by sitting in front of a fireplace at The Mount playing whist with your sisters, charming as I'm sure all three young ladies are."

The ten-day sail north to Valparaíso was calm enough for Charles to put in long bouts of writing in his diary and scientific notebooks. The only digression was the sighting of several vessels and "speaking" to two of them.

"The ships look like great birds of the sea," he observed to Bynoe, who was at his side watching them through his spyglass.

When they arrived at Valparaíso, a port used by the Royal Navy as a South American station, and depot for the replenishing of supplies, receiving of official communications and packets of mail, on July 23 there were letters for practically everyone on the *Beagle* who had family in England. Charles had three, one from Caroline dated November 3, 1833, the second from Katty dated January 27, 1834, and the third from Susan, who wrote on February 12, his birthday, because the three girls and his father had remembered the date and wanted to send him "best love and blessings on reaching twenty-five years."

The family was well. As always, the romantic ons and offs and vital statistics of their communal life predominated: Dr. Henry Holland was about to marry Sydney Smith's daughter, as he had indicated to Charles in London. The Darwin girls were not happy about this. . . . Uncle Jos had persuaded Hensleigh Wedgwood not to resign his office. . . . Susan was happy "scrattling" with a long account book and innumerable bills; Katty was now quite the "junkety" person in the house, eager for balls and visiting of all kinds. . . . Erasmus had become everybody's available bachelor, spending his life in a round of visits about London. . . . Fanny Biddulph "looks the ghost of herself. . . ." The British papers reported the news of the Buenos Aires revolution. . . .

There was also a long letter from Professor Henslow dated the thirty-first of August 1833. Another consignment of boxes and crates had reached Cambridge safely:

> . . . excepting a few articles in the Cask of Spirits which are spoiled owing to the spirit having escaped thro the bung hole. The fossil portions of the Megatherium turned out to be extremely interesting as serving to illustrate certain parts of the animal which the specimens formerly received in this country & in France had failed to do. Buckland & Clift exhibited them at the Geological Section of the British Association's third meeting held in Cambridge under the presidency of Professor Adam Sedgwick, & I have just received a letter from Clift requesting me to forward the whole to him that he may pick them out carefully, repair them & return them to me with a description of what they are & how far they serve to illustrate the osteology of the Great Beast. . . .
> I have popped the various animals that were in the Keg into

fresh spirits in jars & placed them in my cellar. The more delicate things as insects, skins etc., I keep at my own house with
the precaution of putting Camphor into the bones. The plants
delight me exceedingly, tho' I have not yet made them out;
but with Hooker's work & help I hope to do so before
long. . . .

Henslow longed as much as Charles did for the day when they could
be together and discuss all the events of his voyage; but he hoped that
Charles would continue as long as possible.

If you propose returning before the whole period of the voyage expires, don't make up your mind in a hurry—but let it be
a steady thought for at least a month without one single desire
to continue. . . . But I suspect you will always find something
to keep up your courage. Send home every scrap of Megatherium skull you can set your eyes upon, & all fossils. Use your
sweeping net well for I forsee that your minute insects will
nearly all turn out new. . . .

He folded the letters and stacked them in the top drawer of his
chest and then sat down at the chart table to redigest their news. Susan,
who was a stickler for correct spelling, had written that in his journal
there were a number of little errors. He had misspelled *loose, lanscape,
higest, profil, cannabal, peacible, quarrell*. However she had added a
line that not only compensated for her admonitions but severely shook
him:

What a nice amusing book of travels it would make if printed.

His elbows dug into the wood surface of the table and his hands covered his eyes. Did he really have a potential second book? He had never
dreamed of publishing his diary. He had been presumptuous enough to
imagine that he could write a book about the geology of South
America, had worked hard and steadily to accumulate his materials,
and had now decided that book must be done. But his journal? Over
the years he had read many diaries of world travelers; it had never occurred to him that he might have even the faintest chance of adding to
that lore. He found it a heady idea. However he would not be foolish
enough to become self-conscious. During the past two and a half years
he had written several hundred pages with spontaneity and candor and
the kind of informality that Susan had spotted in his spelling. He
would keep on as he had, write about everything he saw and believed
and felt including the human condition in the various cultures and
countries he traversed.

Robert FitzRoy had not been so fortunate with his mail. When Charles joined him for the midday meal he found the captain in a severe state of depression, his skin sallow, one eye bloodshot. A letter from Captain Beaufort lay on his writing table. FitzRoy looked up sightlessly, then sighed.

"All of my news is bad. I must sell the *Adventure*. I must discharge the twenty seamen I hired in Montevideo and myself pay their wages and costs. The seven hundred pounds I spent on refitting the ship must also come out of my personal account."

He sprang up, walked up and down the small, elegantly appointed cabin.

"It's a bitter disappointment, Charles. The mortification will prey on me. If the Admiralty had allowed me to keep the *Adventure* we could have filled up all the blanks in the charts of the outer west coast of Patagonia, then carried a connected survey along the coast to the equator; after which the Galápagos Islands, Marquesas, Society, Friendly and Fiji islands. With both vessels we could have effected an examination of all of these during 1836 and part of 1837. . . ."

*Eighteen thirty-seven!* That would have made the voyage six years in duration! Charles's innards trembled; his expression remained calm.

"Your maps and charts will be your justification. You are performing one of the greatest surveying tasks the world has known."

FitzRoy was too deep into melancholy to nibble at the sweetmeat of encouragement.

"Now I have the Lords of the Admiralty down on me. They've gone to the length of refusing all three of the promotions I recommended: John Stokes and a boatswain among them. . . . However my work shall not suffer!

"I propose to remain here in Valparaíso during these winter weeks of July and August. I'll take up quarters ashore, bring Stokes and King with me. We'll need more room, more light and quiet than we can have on board. I'll leave Lieutenant Wickham to refit and provision the *Beagle*."

"Then I too can have more than a month ashore! To make a long trip to the Andes?"

He had not been able to keep the joy out of his voice. A ghost of a smile came over the captain's careworn face.

FitzRoy had earlier intended to make a week's excursion to Santiago, the agreeable capital city. Now he shook his head resignedly.

"I can't go. Santiago has a thousand attractive novelties which inevitably would divert my attention from the dull routine of calculations and the new data accumulated by our two vessels. I'll send Wickham to secure permission from the Chilean government to survey their coast."

"A thousand novelties is precisely what you need, sir," protested Charles. "They would clear your mind of your disappointments and refresh you for another year of work."

FitzRoy closed his eyes wearily. Charles took his misgivings to Benjamin Bynoe.

"Isn't there any way you can get him to slacken off, Ben? He's been working himself half to death. And now, being given short shrift by the Admiralty . . ."

"If the captain broke an arm," replied Bynoe, "he would allow me to set the bone. If he suffered a cut on his thigh, I would be permitted to cleanse the wound. But the things that go on in his head, there I may not intrude. Exhaustion and depression lie outside my authority as the ship's surgeon."

"Pity," commented Charles.

Since he was to have five weeks in Valparaíso, he went ashore to look for rooms and had the good luck to come upon an old schoolfellow from Shrewsbury, Richard Corfield. They had been acquaintances during those early years and Charles had visited Corfield's family home in Pitchford, a small village close to Shrewsbury. Richard Corfield, two years older than Charles, had come out to Chile several years before as a merchant representing English manufacturing firms and had prospered.

When the two young men had finished wringing each other's hands and expressing their amazement and delight at the chance meeting so far from home, Charles told of his position as the naturalist on board H.M.S. *Beagle*, then asked Corfield if he knew a friendly Englishman who would let him rooms.

Corfield laughed.

"Bet your last quid I do! I live in a charming house in the Almendral, a suburb built on a former sea beach. There's plenty of room. Come back with your things at eight o'clock. I'll drive you home for the evening meal and get you settled in."

The weather was fine, blue skies and a warm sun overhead. Charles liked the aspect of Valparaíso with its main street running parallel to the coast and houses piled on each other wherever a little valley straggled down to the beach. All the rooms in Corfield's house opened into a quadrangle with a small garden; there were English hunting prints on the walls, men in red jackets on sleek horses, a pack of well-groomed hounds barking in anticipation of the fox hunt. Another gentleman shared the expenses of the house which Corfield explained cost the modest sum of about four hundred pounds sterling for the year's rent, food, wine, two menservants and four horses. When Charles insisted upon paying his share, the blond, blue-eyed Corfield replied: "Very well, if you'll be more comfortable, though I'd be proud to have you as my guest. You took the same arithmetic courses as I did, so figure out any pro rata you please."

"Richard, Shrewsbury never taught me how to add or subtract. I learned that from watching my father's meticulous bookkeeping each day: how much he took in from which source, how much he paid out for which purchases and services."

The following day was Sunday. Corfield gave a dinner party for Charles, inviting the larger part of Valparaíso's English colony, as well as Captain FitzRoy. Charles found the guests generally superior to the English residents he had met in other towns in South America. Their interest was by no means limited to bales of goods, pounds, shillings and pence. An older merchant leaned across the table and asked:

"Mr. Darwin, would you be so kind as to give us your candid opinion of Lyell's *Principles of Geology?* We have connections with the London bookstores and have had a chance to read his first two volumes."

Surprised at finding people in Chile who read Lyell's work, Charles gave a rather lengthy answer.

Corfield said:

"You know, Charles, you'd make an excellent teacher. Ever think about becoming a don at Cambridge?"

"I trained for the clergy, Richard, and that's what my father expects of me. . . . But I must say I contemplate engaging in the communication of ideas."

Chile was a long narrow pencil of land held in a vise between the rugged Andes mountains and the equally rugged Pacific Ocean. Charles wanted to set out at once on an excursion to the base of the Andes, before the area was shut up by winter snows. But after the pounding he had taken from the sea, and the beautiful climate with one day as fine as the foregoing, he spent a lazy and relaxed two weeks basking in Valparaíso's hospitality.

On August 7 a packet put into the port on its way up the coast. There were letters for H.M.S. *Beagle* and for Charles. One from Caroline, dated March 9, 1834, contained a collection of strange announcements: The London *Times* had reported the arrival of:

> several packages of fossils, birds, quadrupeds, skins and geological specimens collected by the naturalist Mr. Dawson and sent to Professor Hindon at Cambridge.

"Ah well," he exclaimed, "it's the first time my name has appeared in an English newspaper; how could I expect them to spell it correctly?"

He was greatly relieved to learn that the third set of boxes had arrived safely, having decided that the story of their reaching England could be relied upon even though the *Times* had garbled Professor Henslow's name as well. There was a second piece of news in Caroline's letter that was equally surprising. Erasmus was working on Charles's behalf in London and getting results. He had written to Caroline:

> I called on Mr. Clift, the Curator of the Museum at the College of Surgeons to read him the passage in Charles's letter about the bones. You never saw a little man so delighted. I have written to Cambridge to get the fossils forwarded to London. The Curator has been working every spare hour for the past two months on fossils and it certainly does appear a strange coincidence that the College should possess the front portion of the skull of a Megatherium and that Charles should send home the remainder of it. This enables them to complete the drawing.

Caroline added:

> I give you joy, my dear Charles, on having found these bones that delight the learned so much.

Tom Eyton, on whose family estate he used to go shooting for a spell each year, had visited The Mount for several days, and then set out for Cambridge

> to hear what people said about the specimens you sent home.

How could Tom Eyton conceivably know that there would be discussions about his collections in Cambridge? There was a third startling statement in his sister's letter. Charles's father sent his kindest love and bade Caroline write that he did not growl or grumble at the last fifty pounds he drew. Charles must not fret about money but be as good and prudent as he could. Dr. Darwin had asked his daughter:

"Have you told Charles about his fame?"

Charles laughed heartily as he considered the fame of Mr. *Dawson* who had sent all those collections to Professor *Hindon* at Cambridge!

2.

Richard Corfield helped him secure horses for his trek to the Andes, and a reliable *guaso*, Mariano Gonzales, for his guide. He went with Corfield and Gonzales to buy the supplies for the projected three-week journey, for unlike the gauchos of the pampas, the *guaso* did not live off the countryside but carried chipped beef, maté, fruit and vegetables.

He went aboard the *Beagle* to advise Captain FitzRoy of his departure. He had seen the captain from time to time at dinner parties in Valparaíso, and he had appeared to be enjoying them as much as Charles did. Now Charles found FitzRoy's face ashen. They had dinner together in silence. Toward the end of the meal the captain looked up at Charles for the first time.

"I simply can't bear the idea," he complained bitterly, "but I must give a great party for all the inhabitants here who have entertained me."

Charles knew the energy Captain FitzRoy put into his "reciprocation" parties. He was already strained, painfully thin and in low spirits. Charles remonstrated in what he hoped was an ameliorating tone.

"I can see no such necessity, sir, under the circumstances."

FitzRoy burst into a fury, knocking his fragile dining chair backward onto the carpet. His face went purple.

"That's the sort of man you are, one who would receive any favors and make no return!"

Charles did not reply. He felt no sense of insult; the captain's outburst was a result of frayed nerves. He left the cabin without speaking and promptly went ashore. This was the first time in well over two years, since March of 1832, when Captain Paget had initiated a discussion of slavery, that Charles and the captain had quarreled. At that first upset he had feared that, less than three months out of Plymouth, he would be obliged to abandon the expedition. This time he had no such feeling of trepidation. He knew that when he returned to the ship the storm would have blown over. He was surprised when, a few days later, on boarding the *Beagle* Lieutenant Wickham cried:

"Confound you, Philosopher, I wish you would not quarrel with the skipper. The day you left the ship I was dead tired and he kept me walking the deck till midnight abusing you!"

He set out for the base of the Andes in mid-August. Gonzales was garbed in common trousers protected by black and green worsted leggings and brightly colored poncho over all. His chief pride was his enormously large spurs. He was expert with his lasso; the pampas *bola* could not be used in this rugged terrain. Charles had on his high boots, baggy sailor trousers, white shirt, and worn hiking jacket from home. They had strong horses under them.

Before long they came upon great beds of shells, elevated some yards above the level of the sea, which were so numerous that for years they had been quarried and burnt for lime. They slept under the stars after heating their chipped beef and maté over a brush fire. Gonzales refused to eat with Charles, insisting upon waiting until Charles had finished and retired.

"Why, Mariano? Traveling alone into the country, we eat together." Gonzales shook his head. "No proper. You boss. Me *guaso*. Hire man eat after pay man."

As the sun rose, having drunk their hot maté, they turned toward the valley of Quillota, with open spaces separated by smaller valleys and rivulets. Evergreen forests flourished in the ravines. When they reached the brow of the sierra they had the valley immediately below them, broad, flat, easily irrigated, its gardens crowded with orange and olive trees and every kind of vegetable.

They slept that night at a hacienda at the foot of the Andes. The next morning the major-domo loaned Charles fresh horses and an extra guide for his ascent of the Campana, or Bell, a six-thousand-four-hundred-foot mountain nearby. The second *guaso* tethered their horses.

"Bad path," he said. "Steep. Go slow. Come back in light."

It was perilous riding but the geological formations repaid the hours of rocky climbing. He rested for an hour at the crest, then came down the southern slope through a sort of bamboo rising to a height of fifteen feet, and palms growing at the unusual elevation of four thousand five hundred feet.

The hacienda *guaso* knew of a fresh spring. They unsaddled their horses in the glow of a glorious sunset, the snowy peaks of the distant Andes shining with a ruby tint. At dark they made a fire beneath an arbor of bamboo. Charles feasted on dried strips of beef, peaches, figs and grapes, then retired a few yards to where he had set up his saddle and horse blanket.

Only then would the *guasos* eat.

Charles fell asleep to the shrill noise of the *bizcacha*, a large mountain rabbit, and the faint cry of the goatsucker bird. His last thought was once again of the inexpressible charm of living in the open air.

With daylight they climbed to the highest ridge of a rough mass of greenstone shattered into angular fragments, some seeming, to his eyes, quite fresh, or recently upheaved, others old enough to hold growing lichens. He was convinced that this was an area of constant earthquakes; and unconsciously moved himself and his two *guasos* out from piles of loose rock. Without remembering the nature of his audience he asked the two Chileans:

"Who can avoid admiring the wonderful force which has upheaved these mountains, and even more so the countless ages which it must have required to have broken through, removed and leveled whole masses of them?"

Gonzales and his colleague stared at him uncomprehendingly.

Charles laughed at his folly, sat with his back against the rough bark of a tree, put the same penetrating question into his notebook.

That evening instead of going to sleep, he waited a little distance away until the Chileans had finished their supper, washed the pans and stored them in saddlebags, then joined them around the fire. They were not very communicative but they were conscientious, watching out for his safety. Talking in a kind of *lingua franca*, Charles learned that the *guaso* of Chile was more civilized than the gaucho of the pampas, which to Charles meant that they had lost some of their individual character and placidly accepted gradations of rank and wealth in their society. The gaucho, who was both a cutthroat and a gentleman, would not exert himself except on horseback; the *guaso* could be hired to work in the fields or the gold mines, every part of these mountains having been drilled in a rage to find the valuable metal.

They passed through the town of Quillota to the copper mines of Jajuel in a ravine of the lower Andes. The superintendent, a Cornishman married to a Spanish woman, invited Charles to stay the night. At the roughhewn supper table he asked Charles about the death of George IV, the news of which he had only recently heard:

"Now that George Rex is dead, do we have another Rex as King?"

"Assuredly," Charles replied with a tiny smile. "King William IV. I saw his coronation in London several years ago."

"In Valparaíso they know; no news climbs into these Andes," the man grumbled.

Charles had collected flowers, plants and shrubs possessing strong and peculiar odors, bamboo, palm, lichen, numerous cacti, acacia, marine shells with new forms. Among the birds he got *el turco* of the thrush family, *tapaculo*, or "cover your posterior," because it carried its tail erect; two species of hummingbird. Remembering Henslow's advice, he gathered spiders from under stones; snakes, scorpions, leeches, yellowish lizards.

He was moved by the hard lot of the Chilean workman. During the summer and winter alike he labored in the fields and the mines from first light to dark, with little time for meals. He was paid one pound sterling a month, and his food: sixteen figs for breakfast and two small loaves of bread. For midday dinner, boiled beans; for supper broken roasted wheat grains. He rarely tasted meat.

The miner had it worse than the field laborer. He was paid twenty-five shillings a month and given a little dried beef but was allowed to go down from the bleak mountain shack to visit his wife and children only once in two or three weeks.

He mixed the mores and the intimate way of life of the whole people with his collecting in the natural sciences. A heavy fall of snow prevented him from reaching the crest of the nearer ranges although he ascended to a great height before becoming involved in the drifts. He spent five days prospecting around the mines of Jajuel, scrambling in all parts of the huge mountains, the shattered and baked rocks traversing the dikes of melted greenstone always demonstrating the commotion that must have taken place during the formation of these ridges.

Charles and Mariano Gonzales continued across the basin of San Felipe, and across the Cerro del Talguen in a glaringly bright day on their way to Santiago and the inn where Richard Corfield had reserved a room for him.

That evening they slept at a little rancho where a wise Chilean explained:

"Comparing Chile to other countries, Mr. Darwin, I am very humble. Some see with two eyes and some with one. But for my part I do not think Chile sees with any."

Two days later they arrived in Santiago. For a week he rode in different directions into the plains around the city, seeking out geological phenomena. In the evenings he dined with Corfield's English friends. Among these was Mr. Alexander Caldcleugh, who had published in 1825 a book entitled *Travels in South America in 1819, 1820 and 1821*. Charles had found the book shallow.

Determined to return to Valparaíso by a longer circuit to the south, he and Gonzales found themselves at one of the peculiar suspension bridges made of hide. He watched it oscillate rather fiercely while he led his horse across. Their first evening they reached a nice hacienda where there were several very pretty señoritas.

When Charles amiably mentioned that he had seen many interesting churches, they turned up their eyes in pious horror.

"How could you enter a church just to look about you?" one of them asked. "Churches are sacred."

A second demanded, "Why do you not become a Christian? Our religion is certain."

"I am a Christian," Charles replied lightly.

"No, no. Do not your padres, your very bishops, marry? It's absurd for a bishop to have a wife! I scarcely know whether to be more amused or horrified at such an atrocity!"

Nonetheless they all curtsied and bade him a good night of rest.

As he traveled he was well treated, but nowhere did he receive the unbounded hospitality of the pampas. He was surprised to find each morning that his host, even if he was rich, expected a small payment to be given, as little as two or three shillings.

They turned up the valley of the Río Cachapol to the hot baths of Cauquenes, known for their medicinal qualities. He decided to soak himself out for a couple of days, but when he was ready to leave he was held in for another two days by extremely heavy rains. His only entertainment was to watch the condors wheeling at great height over a particular area.

Gonzales explained:

"Lion kill cow. Or one died. If condor light, many cry 'Lion' and all hurry to chase."

Lions and puma were frequently killed by small dogs who leaped at their throats.

On September 14 they reached the gold mines at Yaquil. Mr. Nixon, the owner, told Charles:

"This particular mine is altogether four hundred and fifty feet deep. Each man carries on his back a quintal weight of stone, considerably over a hundred pounds. They bring up their loads by climbing up alternate notches cut in trunks of trees placed in the shaft. We give them bread and beans. They prefer to live on bread alone but this weakens them, so the company forces them to eat the beans even though they don't like them."

Careful to keep any sense of criticism out of his voice, Charles asked:

"Isn't that meager compensation for hauling those heavy loads up from the depths?"

The owner was not perturbed.

"Sure it would be for you or me. But the Chileans accept it. They are desperate for work and the few shillings to feed their families."

He had a final devastating lesson in economics when he learned the system by which the land was tilled in Chile. The landowner gave so much land to a man, a number of acres on which he had the right to build, in return for which the man worked for the owner every day of his life without compensation. Until the laborer had a grown son who could substitute for him, the women and children cultivated the patch of ground. The family remained embedded in poverty.

In the dining room Charles found two other guests, an old Spanish lawyer and a German naturalist, Herr Renous. They both spoke English.

Renous turned to the elderly Spaniard and asked:

"What do you think of the King of England who sends out a young man to Chile to collect lizards and beetles and to break rocks?"

The old gentleman pondered over this, then replied:

"It is not well. There is a cat shut up here. No man is so rich as to send persons to pick up such rubbish. I do not like it."

Charles laughed while Renous said:

"Some years ago I left some caterpillars in a house in San Fernando, under charge of a maid, to turn into butterflies. This was talked about in the town. At last the padres and the governor consulted together and agreed it must be some heresy. When I returned to San Fernando, I was arrested."

He stayed with Mr. Nixon for four days, during two of which he was unwell. He started out again on September 19.

Then he came a cropper.

While at the gold mines he had drunk some *chichi*, which appeared to be a weak, sour, new-made wine. It turned out to be a powerful brew made from molasses and corn, a whiskey distilled by the South American Indians. He awakened several nights later and felt, during the long and painful hours until dawn, as though the lining of his stomach and intestines had dissolved in lime or acid. That morning his host, a rich *haciendero*, assured him that if he would eat eggs with bread and maté his stomach would heal. Charles got halfway through the egg and had to dash outside to throw it up.

He remained in bed for two days, unable to retain anything but a few drops of water. Flames of heat struck through his viscera. He was certain he had fever. On the third night he managed to sleep a little and on awakening was emboldened to set out for Valparaíso. He barely made it to the next hacienda, weak and nauseous, clinging desperately to the horse's sides with his thighs and boots. He suffered severe gastritis. He was frightened. His only hope was to preserve his strength sufficiently to reach the city.

The next morning after riding only a short distance he could not remain on his horse. Gonzales spread one blanket on the ground for him, put another over him. He ate nothing and slept that night only in feverish stretches, his mouth dry, his lips cracked. The following day he was fortunate enough to reach a rich *haciendero* who received him into his house close to the sea and gave him a local medication. He remained for two days under the kindly attention of his host and hostess. On the third day he got up and collected a number of marine remains from beds of tertiary formation of which the plains by the sea consisted.

It was nearing the end of September. He had been out six weeks. He considered himself well enough to start out again, but the following night was exceedingly feeble, though he had what he called the uncommon luck of obtaining some clean straw for a bed. How truly comparative all comfort was.

"If I were in England and very unwell," he told himself, "clean straw and stinking horse cloths would be thought a very miserable bed."

Necessity made him push on. He and Mariano Gonzales reached Casa Blanca that night, the guide frequently putting a hand on Charles's shoulder or around his waist to steady him on his horse. By daybreak Charles knew he had reached the end of his tether. He had been riding now for six days in a state of exhaustion but could not manage the last stretch into Valparaíso.

"Mariano, it's not possible for me to stay on the horse for even one more day. Ride into Valparaíso as fast as you can and come back with a horse and carriage."

He dozed, slipping into a phantasmagoria of nightmare and flashback to seemingly unrelated episodes in his youth; except for a case of scarlet fever at the age of nine, he had always enjoyed robust health.

Gonzales arrived with a carriage, wrapped him in clean blankets which he had obtained from Corfield's and drove him into Valparaíso on the rutted roads. Corfield came running out, took one look at Charles and exclaimed:

"My dear Charles, you're pale as a sheet and look half your size."

Corfield and Gonzales undressed him, put him into a long, warm nightgown and nightcap and tucked him into bed. The cook brought him a cup of hot milk. Charles fell into a sleep that was more like oblivion than rest.

Corfield sent word to the Beagle. Mr. Bynoe came as fast as a shot from one of the Beagle's cannons. He took Charles's temperature and pulse, listened to his heart and the tale of the raw wine, tapped his lungs, felt his stomach and intestines, causing Charles to exclaim with pain. He ordered Charles washed down with lukewarm water, summoned a barber to shave him and remove the straggly Patagonia beard, dosed him with calomel.

"It's a grievous loss of time, Ben," Darwin moaned. "I had hoped to collect many marine animals."

"You'll be a marine animal yourself," replied Bynoe, "if you don't watch your step. It's going to be several weeks before you'll be able to move about. I'll come in often as I can; and I'll tell you when you can get up."

Then he seated himself on the foot of the bed and told Charles that Captain FitzRoy had sold the Adventure. Managed to get a hundred pounds more than he paid for it. However when the monies for the refitting as well as the wages and provisions for the twenty crewmen had been added up, he had suffered a loss of some seven hundred pounds.

Charles shook his head sadly.

"How is he taking it?"

"Not well. The next set of charts is progressing slowly; they're not ready to send to the Admiralty in London. He complains that it's heavy work, all work and no play; and that is certainly true. John Wickham is back on the Beagle, which will bring you great pleasure. However because of constricting lack of space, Captain FitzRoy has had to let our artist friend Martens go."

The calomel caused diarrhea; the faba beans which Corfield's cook persuaded him to eat brought on nausea. However his stomach appeared to be healing. This buoyed him. What helped a great deal more was a letter from Susan telling him that the prestigious British Museum, which had been disinterested in the collection he had offered to send them, were now delighted with the section of the Megatherium skull he had sent to Professor Henslow and were saying publicly that it was an extraordinary piece of luck that Darwin's portion of the skull should fit so well with the segment they had on hand as to convince them that the two sections belonged to the identical animal! Charles was inordinately pleased, at the same time thinking:

"Not likely. There must be skeletons of thousands of Megatheriums buried in South America."

The next day Captain FitzRoy came to visit. Charles was shocked to see the dark circles under his eyes.

"You look overworked, Captain," he exclaimed. "I do wish you could complete the charts and get them onto a clipper for England."

FitzRoy pulled up a chair. His voice was hoarse.

"Troubles and difficulties harass and oppress me. I've been obliged to sell my schooner and crowd everything again on board the *Beagle*. We'll be able to do only half the work out in the Pacific that I had hoped to do."

He rose, paced around the room blindly as Charles had so many times seen him do in his cabin; then stopped and looked at Charles glassy-eyed.

"The Admiralty denies me everything. Continual hard work and heavy expense, these and many other things have made me ill and very unhappy."

It was not until October 13 that Charles was able to sit up in bed. It had taken him sixteen days to progress this far. The officers of the *Beagle* had visited as often as they got shore leave, as had Syms Covington.

On October 14, Mr. Bynoe, in his daily visit, reported that Captain FitzRoy had confided that he feared his mind was becoming deranged, that it was in his heredity, his uncle on his mother's side, Lord Castlereagh, had committed suicide a few years before. . . .

Charles was overcome. When Bynoe had left he allowed himself to become fully anxious. In the sharing of the captain's cabin, their long hours together, he had seen the process by which FitzRoy had plunged into the depths. Was it possible that he could feel it inevitable that he kill himself? Robert FitzRoy, his beau ideal of a captain, handsome, brainy, highly skilled, wealthy, from a royal family . . . a man blessed!

Charles tossed, beat his bolster into an unshapen mass, did not sleep that night.

The following noon Bynoe and John Wickham came to call. Wickham quickly announced:

"Bad news, Philos. The captain has invalided himself and stepped down. He appointed me to the command."

"Invalided himself how?" Charles asked.

"By writing a letter in my presence. Under ordinary circumstances he must be ordered home. This time, no. I have simply put the letter away."

Bynoe said, "We believe he needs an enforced rest. . . ."

Up from his turgid guts and mixed emotions Charles heard himself say, "Then I am determined to leave the *Beagle.*"

"Don't be in such a rush," Wickham intervened. "I believe much of the captain's depression comes from the exhaustingly long time we have spent on this coast. In his state of mind it has not occurred to him that the Admiralty instructions order him to do only as much of this west coast *as he has time for.* I will suggest that he proceed at once across the Pacific to the Galápagos Islands, Tahiti, New Zealand, Australia and across the Indian Ocean to the tip of Africa, and home."

"I know he deeply cares about surveying through the South Pacific," Charles proffered.

Wickham gritted his teeth.

"When I become captain of H.M.S. *Beagle* it will be because the Admiralty has chosen me; not because my commanding officer has been invalided."

"Ben, may I go on board?"

"You'll stay right here."

When the men left, Charles lay in the bed and reviewed his own outburst. He had often flinched at the length of the voyage, but he would never have left the *Beagle.* He was a stayer, yes. But he also knew that the pleasures of seeing Shrewsbury and his family could not compensate for having endured Tierra del Fuego and not explored and collected in the Pacific. He would have felt . . . cheated! For whatever reason, he had to admit, ill as he was, that he was not ready to go home.

The laggard days dragged their interminable minutes one by one while he could do little but worry about Captain FitzRoy. To fill time he wrote home, skimmed in desultory fashion a few novels which Richard Corfield borrowed from his English friends. At last he was able to put on his dressing gown and go out into the patio garden. At midweek Bynoe had one other encouragement.

"Wickham kept asking the captain what would be gained by his resignation. Why was he not content to do the most useful part of the survey here and return by the Pacific as commanded by Captain Beaufort? John is pretty shrewd; he knows how much FitzRoy admires Beaufort. The captain is listening more responsively. He is also resting . . . comparing no charts, ordering no maps, no inspection of the ship and crew. . . ." He added: "The grief on board the *Beagle* at FitzRoy's decision is universal."

"I hope our missionary knows the right prayers," said Charles.

"Or was it Wickham's low-keyed yet incisive campaign?" Charles asked himself when Benjamin Bynoe and John Wickham burst into his room at the end of the week crying, "The captain has withdrawn his resignation."

"I have torn it into shreds and sprinkled it over the waters," exclaimed Lieutenant Wickham triumphantly.

Charles was astonished the following afternoon to find Captain FitzRoy standing in the doorway of his bedroom in full-dress uniform: blue cloth coat with scarlet stand-up collar and cuffs, two rows of highly embossed gold buttons, gold epaulet, gold lace on the coat and around the cuffs. Single-breasted, white kerseymere waistcoat with buttons to match the coat; black silk cravat. Trousers of blue cloth with gold lace down the outside seams. Belt of blue morocco. Blue cocked hat bound with gold lace. . . . He was standing proudly erect, a friendly smile on his face.

Charles bounded up from his chair. FitzRoy extended his hands.

"Old Flycatcher, I must apologize for not having visited you oftener. Now I want to hear about your trip to the Andes."

Charles asked:

"How soon do we sail, Captain?"

"Not for another ten days. The *Beagle*'s refittings are not quite ready."

Charles laughed lightheartedly. "And my legs still have a tendency to wobble under me."

When Benjamin Bynoe came visiting the next day, Charles volunteered:

"I'm glad the *Beagle* isn't ready to sail for another ten days. I'll feel a lot more secure by that time."

Bynoe grinned mischievously. "The *Beagle* is ready to sail this very moment, Charley."

Charles was flabbergasted. "Then why . . . ?"

"The captain knows we cannot let you get seasick until your stomach is back to normal."

Tears smarted behind Charles's eyes.

"I am deeply touched. To think that he would hold up the voyage for ten days. . . ."

"It means that our skipper is back in good spirits again," Bynoe said happily, "showing the generosity we've all known these years. This benevolent gesture helps him recover his full regard for himself."

Charles studied the hunting prints on the walls, the sleek horses and dogs, the men in their red coats. He felt a resurgence of strength.

"It's a leg up for my psyche too, Ben," he said softly.

H.M.S. *Samarang* to Portsmouth was carrying his shipment of two casks containing bones and stones, a box with six small bottles and one large jar. With the help of Syms he now prepared two more boxes to go on H.M.S. *Challenger*, even though that ship would not sail until the following January. He sent a good many bird skins, a paper parcel containing pillboxes with insects, some brittle, dried roundworms, plants with their leaves stitched together and a bottle, securely corked, containing water and gas from the hot baths at Cauquenes, of which he hoped someone in Cambridge would make a chemical analysis. He sent a letter to Henslow on the same ship and, five minutes before closing the box, enclosed part of his diary, writing to his proctor:

> Of course you may look at any part of my hum-drum journal if you are inclined. Would you then be kind enough to direct it by coach to Dr. Darwin in Shrewsbury?

He was ready to return to the *Beagle*.

3.

H.M.S. *Beagle* lifted anchor and sailed out of Valparaíso Harbor on November 10, 1834.

Soon it was December and Christmas; three years of his journey had passed. They had no games this year, for there was nowhere to hold athletic contests. The New Year of 1835 roared in with a storm of stark ferocity. The *Beagle*, having retraced its steps south to Chiloé, slowly made its way north to the anchorage of Valdivia. Charles and Syms took long walks in the woods collecting everything that lived, animal, vegetable and mineral. Just before noon on one of their expeditions, Charles stretched out on the ground to rest.

He no sooner lay down than he felt the earth tremble. He was conscious of a rocking motion, an undulation beneath him, like the *Beagle* caught in a cross ripple. He thought it must be his own quiverings. He had no difficulty getting up but the rocking motion beneath his feet made him giddy. The grinding, twisting, heaving lasted a full two minutes.

"It was an earthquake, Syms. Let's get back into Valdivia and see what happened."

He found most of the *Beagle* officers in town. The wooden houses had been shaken violently, the nails partially drawn, but none of the simple dwellings had fallen. It was not until they reached Concepción after ten days of surveying up the coast that they learned the true consequences of the quake. The *Beagle* entered Concepción's port of Talcahuano. On the island of Quiriquina they were shocked by what they saw. Smaller vessels had been tossed on shore. The earthquake had destroyed every house in the village. The coast was strewn with timber and smashed furniture, as though great ships had been wrecked. Storehouses had been destroyed, bags of cotton strewn about. A tidal wave had swept away much of the ruins.

He went searching for cracks in the earth; the largest was near the cliffs on the coast, a yard wide. Masses of rock had fallen off the cliffs; other fragments, six feet long, which had been lying under water and still had marine life on them, had been cast up on shore.

It was a stunning experience in live geology! The most awe-full spectacle he had ever beheld. He wrote in his notebook:

> . . . For the future when I see a geological section traversed by any number of fissures I shall well understand the reason. I believe this earthquake has done more in degrading or lessening the size of the island than 100 years of ordinary wear & tear.

The next morning he went with Captain FitzRoy and several of the officers the seven miles up the Bío Bío River to the town of Concepción. The streets here too were piled high with debris and timber where houses had fallen outward. Only one arch and a piece of wall of the large church in the plaza were still standing. He could not believe this had once been a habitable community. Since the series of quakes had taken place at eleven-forty in the morning only a hundred inhabitants had perished; however the townspeople were still digging for bodies.

Mr. Rous, the British consul, had been at breakfast when the first motion began. He had reached the middle of his courtyard when one side of his house came thundering down. The trembling of the ground was so strong he had had to crawl on his hands and knees. The sky became dark with a great cloud of dust; his eyes were blinded and his mouth choked by the time he reached the street. . . .

Fires had started; the thatched roofs fell into the fires, the whole town burned. People were half crazed looking for relatives. Thieves pillaged valuables from the rubble crying, "*Miserecordia*," while continuing to filch silver and jewelry.

The townspeople were making plans to rebuild.

"Earthquakes are strong," FitzRoy observed; "human beings are stronger."

Mr. Rous nodded agreement.

"It makes a wonderful difference, the misfortune being universal. A man is not humbled. We are all without shelter; we have all lost our wealth. Of course the people know the cause of the quake: some old Indian women, two years ago, were discourteously treated; by the use of witchcraft they stopped the volcano and now comes the earthquake!"

The men chuckled. Charles observed:

"The townspeople are basically right; experience has taught them the relationship between the suppressed activities of volcanoes and the tremblings of the earth. There is reason to believe that the earth is a mere crust over a fluid, melted mass."

When he returned to the *Beagle* he sat writing in his diary until almost dawn, trying to capture the desolation of Talcahuano and Concepción. He ended with a value judgment.

> To my mind since leaving England we have scarcely beheld
> any sight so deeply interesting. The earthquake and volcano
> are parts of one of the greatest phenomena to which this
> world is subject.

H.M.S. *Beagle* returned to Valparaíso on March 11, on a cool autumn day. In spite of the fact that Captain FitzRoy had responded to Lieutenant Wickham's advice to move on across the Pacific, the captain chose to spend more time surveying, mapping and charting this important southwest coastal area since Captain Beaufort advised that it had never been adequately surveyed before.

"Indeed," he wrote, "the only general knowledge we have is from the Spanish charts which seem with the exception of certain ports, to have been merely the result of a running view of the shore. . . . The present state of science, which affords such ample means, seems to demand that whatever is now done should be finally done; and that coasts which are constantly visited by English vessels should no longer have the motley appearance of alternate error and accuracy."

It was all part of Britain's ambitious purpose, the selling of their manufactured goods and the importing of the essential raw materials needed for Britain's Industrial Revolution. South America had been under the dominion of Spain and Portugal but was now in political turmoil and open to British influence.

Charles was given a rousing welcome by Richard Corfield. Corfield obligingly cashed his draft for sixty pounds, all of which he needed for provisions, supplies and guides for his newly projected month's exploration of the Andes themselves . . . an expedition he coveted, to the despair of his friends on the *Beagle*.

Mariano Gonzales, his former guide, was in Santiago. Charles set out in a gig surrounded by his horse cloths, stirrups, spurs and other purchases. In Santiago he was taken in by Alexander Caldcleugh, the English travel author whose book he had found shallow, while Gonzales rounded up a muleteer, ten mules and a *madrina*, the female mule who wore a large bell around her neck. Gonzales explained:

"The mules all male. *Madrina* female. Mules follow female, not bell. Bell tells where female is. They come quick; stay close."

Six of the mules were for riding, four for cargo, a good deal of food, for they would not live off the precipitous Andes and if they got caught in a severe snowstorm they would starve without their own provisions. Charles laid in supplies of chipped beef, a variety of beans, dried fruits; nuts, hard toffee, coffee, maté, cocoa, condiments, sugar and rum. Caldcleugh introduced him to the President of Chile, Joaquín Prieto, who courteously wrote a letter of recommendation into Charles's passport.

Charles laughed at the sight they made leaving Santiago: himself, Gonzales and the muleteer riding mules, the other three tethered behind, and behind them the cargo mules with saddlebags bulging and strapped under their small bellies.

They rode over a burnt plain for a number of hours until they reached the mouth of the valley of the Maipo River, bounded by the high mountains of the first range. Just before evening they came to a Chilean customhouse where their saddlebags and firearms were inspected. At dusk they found a cottage where the owners were willing to rent them a couple of rooms for the night. The next evening they bought some firewood from a farmer and hired pasture for the animals, then bivouacked in a corner of the field, setting up their cooking apparatus. Charles was well again and happy; delighting in the freedom of his travel, never knowing when he set out in the morning where he would sleep that night. After being confined for four months to a hammock in a crowded corner of the poop cabin, it was freedom indeed.

At dawn they cooked their breakfast, the muleteer jiggled the bell on the *madrina*, the mules came patiently into line to be saddled.

They made slow progress; passed the highest house in the valley, about one hundred feet above the Maipo River, a mountain torrent, its water the color of the mud, and its roar like that of the sea. As they rode upward the steep cliffs, by Charles's measure, rose three thousand five hundred feet above them, utterly bare, purple in color, chillingly steep. When they passed troops of cattle being driven down from the higher valleys because of the approaching winter, he urged his muleteer to make as fast progress as possible. However he was frequently off his mule getting samples of rocks which he could not identify, and alpine plants which he packed in the cargo. He was disappointed that there was scarcely a bird or insect to be seen. This first range of mountains created a wild scene of vertical peaks. He had never observed such a massive, unbroken series.

As evening approached they reached the Valle del Yeso, which Charles decided must once have been a very large lake. He dug up samples of a pure white gypsum. That night they camped with a party of men who were loading mules with the gypsum to be taken down to Santiago along with a herd of cattle. Still following the Río Yeso, they came to the foot of the ridge which separated the snow and rain waters, part of which flowed westward into the Pacific Ocean, the other east into the Atlantic. Gazing upward from the pass between two principal ranges, about twelve thousand feet high, they found they were on a steep, zigzag track. Beyond these ranges there were higher peaks, perhaps to eighteen thousand feet, and covered by snow the year around.

The ascent of the great Andes was slow and tedious. The mules halted every fifty yards to catch their breath. All three of the men had difficulty in breathing the increasingly rarefied air.

"It's *puna*," declared Gonzales. "A disease. Where there is snow there's *puna*. See the crosses of graves? Here people die of *puna*."

Though his breathing was deep and difficult, Charles felt nothing more serious than a tightness in head and chest. He wondered how Humboldt and those who had followed him in the mountains hundreds of miles north had managed to breathe at all. On the highest ridge he found a supply of fossil shells which he dug out and put in his leather pouch. Near the summit, over fields of perpetual snow, the wind became violent and extremely cold. Charles saw the substance described by arctic navigators as "red snow." He collected a good sample which he would examine under his microscope when he got back to the *Beagle*. At the crest the air was totally clear, the sky an intense blue, the view glorious. Below them the valleys, the wild broken forms of the mountain structures, the colored rocks were seen against mountains of solid snow. Only an occasional condor survived. He could not imagine any part of the world presenting a more extraordinary picture of the breaking up of the crust of the globe than these central peaks of the Andes.

He moved away from the other two men, walked alone a mile or so on the ridge, savoring the moments. The magnificent panorama was like hearing a chorus of the *Messiah* in full orchestra.

They descended two thousand feet down the opposite side of the range, pitched camp at an elevation a little short of ten thousand feet. There was no vegetation whatever. Gonzales tried to boil potatoes over the thick roots of an unnamed plant but they remained hard and cold.

After an hour he cried to the muleteer about the pot Charles had bought for the trip:

"This cursed pot does not choose to boil potatoes!"

Charles made himself a bed between the horse cloths. He had a headache from the high altitude and awakened around midnight to see that the sky had become clouded. He shook the muleteer.

"Is there any danger of a storm?"

The muleteer studied the sky.

"No thunder. No lightning. Can no be bad."

At the earliest moment of dawn Gonzales and the muleteer assembled more roots to make their fire. They were able to warm the chipped beef a little as well as the beans, and had to drink their maté tepid.

They traveled to the foot of the Portillo range. Their climb once again became heavy and long between bold, conical hills of red granite. Numerous pinnacles closed in their zigzag trail so closely it was difficult for the cargo mules to get through. The men had to unload some of the provisions to flatten out the saddlebags. This pass in the Andes had derived its name of Portillo from the narrow cleft at the height of the range through which the trail passed. When they had achieved the ridge they were swallowed up by a cloud which rained minute frozen needle-like crystals on them.

It was a distinct relief to descend once again and to find vegetation and a good camping ground under the shelter of large rock fragments. The clouds cleared, the full moon and stars all shone with increased brilliancy at the high elevation and in the transparency of the air. The air was so extremely dry that the bread and sugar became hard. When Charles took out his hammer he was startled to find that the wood handle had shrunk.

It was a hard journey down the Atlantic side of the mountain range and into level country. In the succeeding days they crossed the low swamp and the dry plain which led north to the city of Mendoza. The mules managed to do forty-two miles to Estacado. The second day they did fifty-one. The sterile plain was hot and dull but on the second evening they came to green gardens around the village of Luxan. To the south rose a cloud of dark reddish brown. Gonzales thought it was smoke from a pampas fire. Charles perceived it to be a pest of locusts, traveling, as he estimated, at a rate of ten to fifteen miles an hour, the vast body of them reaching from twenty feet off the ground to perhaps two thousand feet. The noise they made was similar to a strong breeze passing through the rigging of a ship, and the sky appeared like a mezzotint engraving. When the locusts alighted the fields changed from green to a reddish brown; they stripped the trees of every leaf. The three men watched the cottagers light fires and, with smoke, shouts and waving of branches, try to drive the stream aside. Their growing things were eaten bare.

Luxan was a small but agreeable town at the southern tip of a fertile territory. Charles managed to rent a room in a house. He awakened some hours later with a sensation of disgust. On his hand was a ben-chuca, the great black bug of the pampas. He was revolted at watching the soft, wingless insect, about an inch long, crawl over his hand suck-ing his blood, the insect going from thin to bloated in ten minutes. He felt no pain and became vastly interested in the process. He wondered how long this blood would keep the insect fat. For a fortnight? For a month? He then squashed it and brushed it aside so he could go back to sleep. The next day he found a live specimen which he impaled on cotton and enclosed in one of his small boxes.

After two days of rest and an orgy of watermelon and peaches, the lit-tle mule train began its trip back to Santiago. Though they were still several thousand feet above sea level the sun was powerful on their backs, and they traveled through clouds of fine dust. Once again they had a mountain range to cross, the Uspallata, barren and without fresh water. From the ridge Charles saw white, red, purple and green sedi-mentary rocks mixed with black lava, as well as strata broken up by hills of porphyry of many shades of brown and bright lilac. They were the first mountains he had seen which literally resembled a colored geologi-cal section.

The next morning an unmanageable gale of wind and clouds of dust made it difficult to saddle the mules; for once they did not seem eager to fall in behind the *madrina*. By nightfall they had reached the Río de las Vacas, which was known as the most difficult, muddy stream in the mountains, dropping downward too rapidly for the mules to cope with. The muleteer insisted they camp by the side of the river until an hour after daybreak when the flow was less impetuous and they were able to cross safely.

The next day was one of concentrated geology, with large deposits of shell fossils. He concluded that in some remote era this grand chain of the Andes had simply consisted of volcanic islands covered with forest. He found tree trunks one of which was fifteen feet in circum-ference, silicified and embedded in the marine strata. The mountains had risen slowly, the change of climate had left them ultimately parched. A large part of the range might have been established only since South America was peopled. Perhaps ten thousand years, twenty? He would stand by that conclusion.

They finally took the high road to Santiago, crossing the Cuesta de Chacabuco and remaining that night in the quiet village of Colina.

Charles awakened suffering sporadic bouts of shivering both in his innards and outer skin. This time he had drunk no sour wine and had eaten much the same food for all the weeks they were out. Nor had there been any polluted water. He asked Gonzales:

"Have you seen other people sick in this region?"

"Maybe black bug that suck your blood. Many peoples at Luxan sick all time."

He counted back in his mind; it was two weeks since the benchuca had bitten him. It could be an incubation period. For the next two days he saw nothing and admired nothing, feeling robbed of the observations he might have made. However when he reached Santiago, at midday on April 10, he was already feeling better. He decided to remain at Mr. Caldcleugh's a day to make sure that he was entirely well before he set out for Valparaíso. Back in Valparaíso he observed to Richard Corfield:

"I was well repaid for my trouble but it is going to take a hundred men and a hundred years to understand that rugged chain."

He wrote to Susan that since leaving England he had never made so successful a journey, though it had been very expensive, and expressed the delight he felt at such a famous winding up of all his geology in South America:

> . . . to a geologist there are such manifest proofs of excessive violence; the strata of the highest pinnacles are tossed about like the crust of a broken pie.

He spent the next days having his hair cut, his clothes pressed, his laundry done, buying spirits for his specimens, replenishing articles of hardware, medications. Despite the long hard expedition and his long illness, he felt in excellent health, the color high on his cheeks and his eyes bright with accomplishment. As with most men, he never saw his eyes in the mirror when he shaved, or any other feature except the precise area of cheek, upper lip and chin to which he applied the razor. Catching an unexpected glance of his face in the good-sized guest-room mirror, he turned to the glass fully and realized that he no longer wore the young man's face he had sailed out of Plymouth with. His face had matured, his eyes were no longer those of an innocent, his mouth had set with such precise character that his nose was no longer out of tune. His hair had begun to thin a little, backward, which gave him a more formidable brow, in concert with his now fully rounded, strong-boned chin.

"I've changed," he thought; "though I didn't perceive it day by day. I have become a man. But what manner of man?"

H.M.S. *Beagle* returned to Valparaíso. Charles boarded, found mail from home and consumed the news like a starved creature. Even his oldest sister, Marianne, who had married Dr. Henry Parker when Charles was fifteen, and did not write her own letter, begged for a flap on Caroline's letter to put down a few lines saying that she had not forgotten him. One line in Caroline's letter made him scramble down the hatchway to the captain's cabin. He impetuously flung open the door without knocking. FitzRoy turned in surprise. Charles explained:

"You've been promoted! My sister saw the announcement in a London newspaper! At long last we know how valuable the Admiralty considers your maps and charts!"

FitzRoy's face flushed; he grasped the arm of his chair. After a moment he exclaimed:

"Mighty good news, Darwin. It means the Admiralty is no longer vexed with me; and that my sins over the *Adventure* and the schooners are forgiven. I no longer need to worry that I have hurt Captain Beaufort or made enemies in the Hydrographic Office." His eyes blazed with pleasure, his melancholia nautical miles behind him.

Charles prepared the latest cargo to be shipped home. He filled one box with his soft specimens, taking especial care, the second with his rock findings. His last trip had added half a mule's load of rock samples, for without plenty of proof he did not expect a word of his theories about the Andes to be believed.

They sailed the twelve hundred miles north to Lima with a steady trade wind. Charles took advantage of the quiet sea to spend thirteen days writing up his geological finds. He was ready for shore when they reached the port town of Callao, seven miles from Lima, but the town was a disappointment, "most miserably filthy, ill built, the atmosphere loaded with foul smells." Peru was in a perennial state of revolution, with four military sets vying for control. Mr. Belford Hinton Wilson, the British Consul General, fortyish, an impeccably dressed foreign servant who looked as though he were holding a permanent clothes peg to his nostrils, warned him:

"Don't go ashore alone, or into the countryside. Not long ago Lord Clinton, a Frenchman and I were out riding when we were attacked by a party of soldiers, robbers, in reality, who plundered us so completely that we returned naked except for our drawers. The robbers waved the Peruvian banner patriotically and intermingled cries of 'Viva la Patria!' with 'Give me your jacket.' 'Libertad! Libertad!' with 'Off with your trousers!'"

Charles could not stem his laughter.

"I have read that Lima is small but splendid. How do I get up there? I must see the city."

"There's a well-guarded coach which runs twice a day. I will join you."

Ten days later he was in Lima, which stood on a small plain formed by the gradual retreat of the sea. He found the city in a wretched state of decay, the streets unpaved and piled with filth. There was no air of business and few carriages, carts or even cargo mules to be seen; yet there were many beautiful churches. The Consul General gave a dinner party for him. The English and European residents were intelligent and well read. But mostly he fell in love with the young ladies, whose elastic gowns fitted their figures so closely that they were obliged to walk with elegant small steps, revealing white silk stockings and very pretty feet. Black silk veils worn around their heads were fixed to the waist behind, only one flirtatious eye remaining uncovered.

"But that eye is so black and brilliant," he exclaimed to the amused Wilson, "and has such powers of expression that its effect is very powerful."

"Remain and marry one of them."

"I can't do that, but at the rate my sisters write that the beautiful English girls are marrying, there can scarcely be one left for me when I get home."

Suddenly he felt a painful need of a warm feminine hand in his, a sweet face to look into. He had been out four months short of four years. It was a long time to live in a male world, without the giving or receiving of affection from young women.

4.

He looked forward to visiting the Galápagos, the Islands of the Tortoises, named after the giant land tortoises which had been discovered accidentally by Bishop Berlanga, sent out by King Charles I of Spain, whose becalmed ship had drifted six hundred miles from the mainland of South America . . . right up to the group of volcanic islands. Charles's major excitement, he told John Stokes, was "for the sake of climbing an active volcano."

After the bishop's unintended visit, no sailing ship had ventured near the Galápagos for a century and a half, although they were indicated on the maps of Ortelius and Mercator in 1587. The few who knew about them steered clear of their dangerous reefs; their uncanny appearance of being unhinged and floating about in the Pacific. Until the whalers and buccaneers found that they contained fresh water and literally thousands of giant tortoises which could stay alive stacked half a dozen high in a lower deck, providing fresh meat for months. The islands then became so traveled that a post office was set up, a barrel in the crotch of a tree, where sailors could leave mail to be taken and delivered by the first ship going to the required homeland.

They had sailed a thousand miles in eight days and were anxiously looking for land when the lookout cried from the masthead, "Islet dead on course, sir." He had spied the summit of Mount Pitt, at the end of Chatham Island. As the breeze and current carried them onward, the tops of other hills appeared. They paused momentarily at Hood's Island to lower a whaleboat so Mr. Chaffers and Midshipman Mellersh could go exploring for anchorages. In a cove at Chatham a whaleboat was lowered with Lieutenant Sulivan in charge of ten seamen to map the central islands of this group of eighteen volcanic relics. The men discarded their heavy clothing in the heat of the rays of the vertical, equatorial sun and sultry sea.

To Charles, at first sight, the islands appeared utterly desolate, sloping symmetrical cones of black lava completely covered with leafless brushwood and stunted trees. That was the end of his discouragement, for when H.M.S. *Beagle* anchored in St. Stephen's Harbor off Chatham Island, he found the bay abounding with fish, sharks and turtles popping their heads up out of the sea. His line went over the side with the rest of the crew's and he immediately began pulling up fine fish, two to three feet long, the heavy catch flapping all over the deck. After the midday meal he climbed ashore with King and Stokes; the day was glowing hot, the black lava resembling Annie's stove at The Mount. He was astounded by the enormous family of reptiles living on the lava, not only the hard-shelled, slow-moving tortoises, the tiny head stuck out on its short thick neck from a stone-hard plated carapace, but the slithery creatures on the low-lying rocks, thousands heaped upon each other five and six deep: "Disgusting, clumsy lizards, black as the porous lava they're lying on," he exclaimed. "I didn't know they were living creatures until I came within a couple of feet of them."

Stokes grimaced at the uncanny sight:

"I've heard them described as 'imps of darkness.'"

Charles turned away without attempting to capture one. He preferred to botanize, climbing the slope of a dead volcano and gathering ten different specimens, "so insignificant and ugly," he cried, "that Professor Henslow will think I have been gathering in the arctic instead of the tropics."

They also smelled unpleasant.

What did delight him that first day was the variety of birds, species he had not seen before.

"All new, all different! My ornithology friends in England are in for a treat."

The birds were so innocent of man, and unafraid, that King killed one with his hat, and Charles pushed a large hawk off a branch.

The finds on the following day, from a different Chatham anchorage, were equally overwhelming: the black rocks at the shore line crawled with an infinity of bright red crabs, the sandy areas were alive with sea lions honking great noises at each other between graceful swims in the sea.

He exclaimed:

"The island looked dead from a distance but what an immense variety of life has been created here."

He and Stokes walked to the top of a large but low crater. The country to the north was studded with small black cones which Charles described as ancient chimneys for the subterranean melted fluids. Using his hammer, he quickly ascertained that the volcano they had climbed had once been submarine. He chipped away samples of hard sandstone composed of volcanic dust.

Each day in the Galápagos provided separate adventures as the *Beagle* made its way from anchorage to anchorage surveying the different islands: Chatham, James, Charles, Narborough, Albemarle, the highest and boldest of the volcanic peaks, its east side black with lava, sterile and dry, studded with small craters which were appendages to the great volcanic mounts from which the black lava had flowed. Charles frequently took his bedroll and a tent ashore accompanied by one or more of his shipmates. They bivouacked under a miserable little spring of water in a small valley; crossed black sand which was disagreeable to pass over even in thick boots, and brown sand which registered 137° when they placed a thermometer in it, as high as the thermometer could register!

On James Island their walk was a long one. About six miles to an elevation of two thousand feet, very dry, very hot, the trees low and crooked and nearly leafless but of a larger size than he had thus far observed. At three thousand feet they found the only watering places on the island. Clouds hung over this highest land; the vapor condensed by the trees dripped down like rain. It was wonderfully refreshing. Sometimes they made "wet landings," onto narrow, shallow beaches, rolling their loose-bottomed trousers above the knees, tying their shoes around their neck by the laces, the socks stuffed inside, slipping off the side of the whaleboat after waiting out the incoming wave to wade ashore, the water high on their legs as they picked their way over pumice rocks and pebbles. Sometimes they approached a sharply inclining lava cliff, fingernails and toes holding onto weathered crevices in the near perpendicular walls.

Since the crew members had been bringing back ten to fifteen giant tortoises a day, he and Syms tried to lift one. All they got for their pains was a solid hissing before the enormous antediluvian creature pulled in its head and began to move pachydermously away. Charles stood on the tortoise's thick-crusted shell but this did not stop its inching forward.

"In fact," he said with a grin, "he hardly noticed! I wonder how old he is. It's said they can live for hundreds of years. This cactus they chew on must be Ponce de Leon's Fountain of Youth."

The geology was instructive and amusing: craters of all sizes and forms studded about in every direction; some so tiny they might properly be called specimen craters. There were layers of volcanic sandstone, streams of lava naked, black, rough and horrid, grand fields of trachytic lava containing large crystals of glassy, fractured feldspar. The streams were mostly naked of water, their age marked by the presence or absence of foliage; he now believed every plant or tree was in flower or leaf, brown being its prevalent color. Some of the craters were high hills, getting greener as one ascended the peaks, these upland green valleys frequently capturing a refreshing southerly trade wind.

He explored the black cones of craters which resembled the ironwork chimneys at Wolverhampton, large circular pits, "which were probably produced by a volume of gas at the time when the lava was liquid."

He exclaimed joyfully:

"It's always delightful to behold anything which has long been familiar, but only by description."

One night he slept on the beach, then spent the next day collecting a variety of black basaltic lava, volcanic dust, ancient shells, insects he could describe but not name; cactus, brushwood, birds, the marine iguana which he had at first found disgusting but now admired for the way it glided into the sea for sustenance, evaded its only enemy, the shark, and returned to bake in the hot sun. In this hot tropical sun Charles's hair became a goldish red, as in the cold of Tierra del Fuego the color had frozen out to leave it dark.

He had failed to anticipate the breath-taking beauty of the archipelago: the brilliant blueness of the sky and sea; the rich plumage of the myriad birds: frigates with their inflatable orange or red throat pouches, penguins, the clean white-masked and blue-footed boobies; the flightless cormorant with its truncated, useless wings, the waved albatross, lava and swallow-tailed gull, the red-billed tropic bird, the night heron, finches; the little pools where baby seals romped playfully, the massive bull sea lion flopping up to the best flat rock on the promontory, where his females could gather round him; the sea turtle digging a hole in the sand to deposit its eggs; the birds dropping their eggs on meager stick-nests on the hard lava ground or in their mating places high on the pock-marked, scarified pumice cliffs; the thick, stumpy-legged tortoises looking like inhabitants of another planet; the sounds of birds, reptiles, fish and sea animals. And very high up, the green foliage where the *palo santo,* the button mangrove, *matazarno* had taken hold in the earth that the winds had blown in over the aeons; the tall, distorted cactus trees, a peculiar rugged cactus whose large oval leaves formed connecting branches. The blowholes where the sea erupted like geysers; the submarine cliffs descending as far as two miles to the bed of the ocean; circular lakes, cliffs sculptured by wind and sea into fantastic columnar shapes.

The several hundred species of fish were incredible; and on the shore line, in addition to the Sally Light-foot crabs, were starfish, sea urchins, sand dollars, sea cucumbers, all shimmering in the intensely white heat.

He found only one live, smoking volcano. When he climbed the rim he observed that there was no flaming fire or liquid lava. It was obvious that neither the numerous volcanoes on each island, nor the islands themselves, had been formed at the same time, each island consisting of many separate and distinct lava flows which had poured down the flanks of the volcanoes, many reaching the sea. The weird, dramatic, multi-volcanoed structure of the islands, the tumultuous life in the sea, in the air and on the shell-crushed beaches, made them appear to have been created during one of God's early experimental stages, before He quite knew how He wanted to shape and populate the earth.

It was not until H.M.S. *Beagle* anchored in a cove of Charles Island that he got his first glimpse of the true significance of the Galápagos Islands. Part of it was his own discovery; by studying the finches he had caught on two different islands, he found that they unexpectedly had differently shaped beaks. The second half of the awakening was provided by Nicholas Lawson, the acting British governor who had been appointed when Ecuador claimed ownership of the islands only a couple of years before. Lawson's hair and face were fried red by the sun but he loved the islands for the beauty of their stark black cliffs, clear lagoons, the variety of wild life.

He was at the port of Charles Island to visit a whaling vessel and offered to show Charles the way to the settlement of some two hundred exiles who had been banished from Ecuador for political crimes against the state. During the four-mile walk along the cinder path to the center of the island, they passed a number of tortoises moving at the rate of four miles in twenty-four hours.

Lawson commented:

"I maintain that I can at once tell from which island any one of these tortoises was brought."

Charles pulled up short.

"Are you suggesting, Mr. Lawson, that each island produces its own kind of tortoise?"

"No question about it, Mr. Darwin. I learned how to identify them more'n a year ago. The tortoises of the various islands differ chiefly in their carapaces, different island forms having consistently higher or lower domes on their shells, and distinctive flared margins at the front and back. The carapaces differ too in color and thickness. The tortoises on different islands also grow to a different size, have longer or shorter necks and legs."

Charles was confounded by the phenomenon, and asked Lawson, "Why and how would they change their characteristics?"

The consul's voice sounded as though his throat too had been blistered by the implacable sun.

"I couldn't say, Mr. Darwin. I only know what my eyes tell me."

The puzzle stuck in Charles's mind the way burrs had stuck in the fur of Pincher when he walked him along the river Severn. During the several hours that he spent with Lawson in the *pueblo* of thatched roofs, makeshift dwellings resting on poles, with patches of sweet potatoes and plantains, the riddle of the differing tortoises bedeviled him. He sat on a log near the natural spring where the turtles and tortoises got their fresh water, a scarcity in the islands because the porous lava rock would not hold the rainfall. Many of the prehistoric monsters traveled upward with outstretched necks as another set returned, having drunk its fill. He watched the tortoises with their heads buried above the eyes sucking in great mouthfuls of water.

"I've been remiss," he decided. "I've put my finds from these islands in the same bag without identifying their place of origin. If there are differences in the beaks of the finches and the shells of the tortoises, I must exercise extreme care to label each island's collection quite scrupulously. In that way I can make comparisons, learn if all the species, birds, lizards, plants, vary from island to island. That could be the most important discovery of my journey. What causes these differences? 'Ay, there's the rub.' "

Of the thirty-six days the *Beagle* spent charting the Galápagos, Charles spent twenty ashore. The burrows of the land iguana, which was two to three feet long and so scaled with yellow, pink and purple shadings that its very ugliness appeared beautiful, were so numerous that the men sometimes had difficulty in finding a spot to pitch their tents. These oversized lizards lived entirely on berries, leaves, for which they frequently crawled up the trees, and the succulent cactus in place of water. The collecting over the days made his head spin: over twenty species of land birds which he was certain had never been identified.

Every plant was in flower, for it was the flowering season: coarse grasses, cacti, mosses, ferns, salt-loving succulents. When whaleboats went out to chart the other islands, one under Chaffers and Mellersh, and another under Lieutenant Sulivan, the men collected for him: small tortoises, snakes, birds: gulls, buzzards, owls, boobies, warblers, doves, a variety of finches; and all manner of plant life. He instructed them well; they kept the catch of each island in a separate bag.

The *Beagle* ran into trouble only once, from lack of water. The spring they had relied on, near the shore, had been overwashed by waves. Everyone was put on half rations. On Albemarle Charles climbed a crater at the bottom of which appeared a blue and clear circular lake surrounded by bright green succulent plants. He scrambled down its cindery inside, choking with dust, and upon scooping up his first handful found it as salty as brine, even as he had at Port San Julian when attempting to secure water for an exhausted and dehydrated Captain FitzRoy.

They were saved by an American whaler whose officers kindly gave them three casks of water and a bucket of onions as a present. Captain FitzRoy thanked the Americans, then said to Charles:

"That's not the first time the Americans have shown themselves at least as obliging as, if not more so than, our own countrymen would have been."

"What I admired most, Captain, was the hearty manner in which their liberality was offered."

"I wonder if their prejudices are as strong against the English as ours are against them?"

When Charles first went ashore on Chatham Island, Lieutenant Wickham had asked:

"What does the island feel like?"

"What we might imagine the cultivated parts of the infernal regions to be."

Now he had come full circle; every island he visited was not only gorged with beauteous abundant wild life but, with the exception of the giant tortoises which had been taken away by the thousands by the whaling vessels and pirate ships, all forms of life had proliferated, were intact, untouched by man, exactly as they had evolved over the millions of years since the series of eruptions had created the archipelago. He knew of no other place in the world where nature could be seen as it was on the day of Creation; a laboratory of primordial life, untouched, undefiled, unchanged, having boiled up from the bottom of the ocean millions of years before . . . and then, slowly, over the aeons been inhabited. But how had each of the islands developed its own, readily differentiated species? More urgently, why?

5.

For once the Pacific lived up to its name. Fair trade winds took H.M.S. *Beagle* from the Galápagos Islands to Tahiti in a little less than four weeks with studding sails on each side as they covered one hundred and fifty miles a day across the blue ocean. It was a happy time; Charles wrote descriptions of the plants, birds and reptiles collected on the Galápagos and did considerable theorizing as to which "center of creation" the beings of the archipelago had to be attached. After dinner each evening he and FitzRoy, interested in the role played by the English missionaries in the South Pacific, read aloud passages from William Ellis's *Polynesian Researches*, which was favorable to the missionaries; F. W. Beechey's *Narrative of a Voyage to the Pacific*, which was neutral in the matter; and Kotzebue's *A New Voyage Round the World*, which was severely critical of the white man's influence on the native.

At daylight of November 15 Charles was on deck to catch his first sight of Tahiti, land of sunshine, warm water and gentle breezes, which he observed "must forever remain as classical to the voyager in the South Seas." H.M.S. *Beagle* anchored in Matavai Bay. All the flags were strung from bow to stern. Charles found himself faced with a lush beauty and a curtain of stark, jagged mountains that rose before them like a wall of infinity. They were cordially received by the bronzed natives and guided to the home of the missionary for the district, after which Charles took an exploratory walk along winding paths, cool from the surrounding shade, among scattered airy houses. He exclaimed:

"This must be Paradise. Or would it be violating the Thirty-nine Articles of the Church of England to be experiencing Paradise here on earth?"

The only cultivated ground was a strip of alluvial soil accumulated at the base of the jutting mountains, completely protected by an encircling coral reef. He made his way through an orchard of tropical trees: bananas, coconuts, oranges, breadfruit, guava and, between them, plants of yams, sugar cane, sweet potatoes, pineapples. The Garden!

That afternoon the captain had the decks cleared so that the Tahitian men could paddle out in their outrigger canoes to hawk their wares. They swarmed over the *Beagle* like bees, turning the ship into a noisy bazaar: pigs, baskets of shells, fruit, fishhooks, rolls of cloth. When they saw that someone was interested, they cried out:

"One dola! One dola!"

They would not take English coins, wanting only American silver; and oddly enough the price for everything was the same, one dollar, for a pig or a fishhook. The men wore loose linen wrappers in place of trousers. Charles thought them the finest-looking men he had ever seen, tall, broad-shouldered, athletic, their skin a golden copper, their figures beautifully proportioned. They were lightly tattooed, the designs so gracefully following the lines of their bodies as to produce an elegant effect. One figure Charles deciphered as a branch of palm leaves, another the capital of a Corinthian column, the lines starting from the backbone and embracing each side. He realized that the simile was fanciful, but he considered the bodies of these men as being ornamented, like the trunk of a noble tree, by a delicate creeper. He could not help but remember the ugly painted savages of Tierra del Fuego, and commented to John Dring, a keen bird collector, who had come aboard to replace Rowlett:

"These men have only to pick their fruit off the trees and lift the fish, prawns and eels off the coral reefs. To me they seem like the blessed of God."

Dring, who had been on shore that morning buying pigs and fruit, paused long enough to reply:

"Then why aren't the Tahitian women beautiful too? They seem mighty plain to me. That's a heartbreaker!"

The following morning Charles climbed a nearby mountain, used his hammer to hypothesize about its origin. He stopped at the missionary's to secure the names of two guides who could take him and Syms on a journey of several days deeper into the mountain ranges. While there he asked the mild-mannered, big-bellied blond what effect the missionaries had had on the natives.

"They were pagans. Largely naked. Probably practiced human sacrifice. We put clothes on them, made them Christians. Taught them sexual morality. Stopped their drinking the juice of the ava root, which had a powerful intoxicating effect. We taught them English, how to read the Bible; put a stop to their heathen dancing and singing, except for hymns."

"Are they happy about all that?"

"Apparently. You see how pleasant and hospitable they all are. They come to church on Sunday. That's proof enough."

Syms packed a bag of provisions, a flask of spirits, and blankets, and they set out. The two young guides, who wore only loincloths, tied the heavy bag and the blankets to each end of a pole that they took turns carrying across their shoulders. Since the whole island appeared to be one group of mountains, the only way to penetrate to the interior was to follow the river valleys. They made their way through the woods which bordered the river; soon the valley began to narrow, the mountain walls became more precipitous. After four hours of steady climbing they found themselves in so narrow a vertically walled ravine that Syms said:

"Pity. This is the end for us."

"No, Syms. The guides say they can take us to the top."

The older of the two cried:

"We can do. See. Ledges. Use rope."

The Tahitians mounted the rock walls like mountain goats, then helped haul Charles and Syms up to ledges thickly covered by wild bananas and tropical plants; then on higher to the knife-edge ridges with profound ravines beneath them. They scaled a precipice a thousand feet high; came to a magnificent mountain gorge.

Late in the afternoon they reached a flat area where they made camp. When Charles had told the guides that they would have to provide their own food and clothing they had grinned and replied:

"Skin is clothes. Plenty food in mountains."

The Tahitians dove into the nearby river with a net, followed fish and prawns into their corners, emerged with a good catch. They wrapped pieces of fish and banana into small parcels of freshly picked leaves, made a fire of sticks, collected twenty small stones and put them on the burning wood, then laid each green parcel between two stones. The whole was covered by a layer of earth so that no smoke or steam could escape. They then laid out a tablecloth of banana leaves, broke open coconuts to use as cups for the fresh water of the stream. When Charles offered them his flask of spirits they put a finger in front of their mouths and whispered, "Missionary!" before taking a swig. Now ready to eat, the two natives fell to their knees and murmured Christian prayers.

"What does the mountain have for dessert?" Charles asked.

"Ti. We cut root."

The ti was sweet as treacle. The meal finished, Syms rolled out their blankets. They walked along the stream to a waterfall and back, then fell asleep as darkness lowered upon them in the shelters their guides had strung together out of banana leaves.

On Sunday morning FitzRoy invited Charles and several officers to accompany him to divine services in Papeete, first in the Tahitian language, conducted by Mr. Pritchard, the leading missionary on the island, and then in English. Mr. Pritchard was well educated, agreeable, sensible; altogether a good man, Charles decided. He met a third missionary, a Mr. Nott, who had lived in Tahiti for forty years and was completing the translation of the Bible into Tahitian, a kindly man and devoted scholar. Charles commented to Captain FitzRoy:

"Kotzebue was wrong in so savagely denouncing our missionaries. I've come down on their side."

Then, having had enough of formal religion, he hired a canoe and some men and spent the rest of the day studying the coral reefs which had created the lagoon. The corals were exquisitely flowerlike, and stretched for miles to form the reef through which Captain James Cook had found a single entrance back in 1769. The Tahitians slipped overboard from their outrigger and cheerfully broke off enormous chunks for his inspection.

Coral reefs appeared to be the poetry of nature's creation. The living organisms had achieved an incredible variety of size and structure: sponges, stars, clusters of flowers, staghorn that resembled intertwined stag antlers, organ pipes, bleached calcareous skeletons, stony seawood; polyp tentacles forming spires, vases, necklaces, fans, rosettes . . . There were fields of ripe stalks, tubes, trees with thick, bare branches, lava beds, richly woven carpets, bizarre forms that could be described by no known name; any composition the human mind could imagine was brilliantly present. The subtle hues of the coral from stark white through amber, pink, yellow, rose, blue, green, deep red, purple and black, with all the delicately merging combinations in between were an unimaginable phantasmagoria equal to the most exquisite flower garden in full bloom.

When he returned to H.M.S. *Beagle* he labeled the coral specimens, then wrote in his diary:

> It is my opinion that besides the avowed ignorance concerning the tiny architects of each individual species, little is yet known, in spite of the much which has been written, of the structure & origin of the Coral Islands & reefs.

He picked up the second volume of Lyell's *Principles of Geology* which had reached him in Montevideo in 1832 and read:

> The circular or oval forms of the numerous coral isles of the Pacific, with the lagoons in their center, naturally suggest the idea that they are nothing more than the crests of submarine volcanoes having the rims and bottoms of their craters overgrown by corals. . . .

Of one thing he was now certain. Charles Lyell was dead wrong! The coral reefs had been built in a quite different fashion. He was determined to find out what that process was before he reached home.

The officers and crew were in a happy mood when they left Tahiti, steering a course for New Zealand. The Queen of the Islands had lived up to its reputation. The natives had been warm and hospitable, hard working when necessary. John Stokes had stayed with a Tahitian family and enjoyed the experience; Captain FitzRoy had adroitly garnered the three thousand dollars Commodore Mason of Valparaíso had instructed him to collect for the plundering of the British ship H.M.S. *Truro* in 1831; Charles had become intensely alive to the possibility of creating an answer to Lyell's conclusions on the nature of coral.

After a comfortable dinner of fresh pork and Tahitian potatoes, FitzRoy lolled back in his chair, stretched his arms upward in a lazy body yawn, and said:

"Philos, you've been working away at that journal of yours for four years now and you've never shown me a page. Would you like to let me have a look at some of the passages?"

The captain's steward cleared the table. Charles set the latter sections of his diary in front of FitzRoy, then stretched out on the divan to read in Playfair and Hutton's *Theory of the Earth*, one of the books in the box that his brother Erasmus had sent to Valparaíso. He had been ingesting the author's theories for about an hour when FitzRoy rose from the table and said with a gratified smile lighting his saturnine face:

"You've kept a good record of our expedition, my dear Darwin. It is my opinion that it would be worth publishing."

Charles bounded up from the divan, saw that the captain was entirely sincere. It was true that Susan had admired it and suggested that it be published, but one's family had to be considered prejudiced. His loving sisters were reading his journal for news of him; the delight of sharing his adventures coupled with their longing for his safe return; that did not make them the most incisive of literary critics. But to be praised by Captain FitzRoy, who had read the world's travel literature, that was a different kettle of brilliantly hued coral reef fish! He had written his journal to keep complete notes on everything he did on this extraordinary journey. He had never consciously thought of publishing it.

"However," he admitted. "I've lived for four years just a few feet away from our poop cabin bookshelves filled with man's travels. I could read the titles in the dark from my hammock. Would it have been terribly pretentious to have imagined that I might write a book equally interesting and authentic?"

He knew that Captain FitzRoy was already getting his own narrative of the voyage in a forward state for publication. But that had been understood at the Admiralty before H.M.S. *Beagle* left Plymouth. Captain FitzRoy's book would become an important part of maritime history. But Charles Darwin's? A young man of twenty-six who had been signed on at the last moment as an unfinished naturalist?

"After all, I'm an amateur," he told himself. "I've never written anything except letters to my family and friends. Pity!"

Suddenly, he asked:

"Captain, would it be too early for me to read parts of your journal?"

"Not particularly." FitzRoy unlocked a drawer of his writing desk, drew out a bulky manuscript.

"Please read it here in the cabin and let me know when I can lock it up again."

When FitzRoy went about his duties, Charles had a good two hours of solitude. His first reaction was, "How amazingly well he writes! I shall tell him so, of course."

What he would not tell FitzRoy, when the captain returned to the cabin and locked up his manuscript, was that, to Charles's taste, the journal was deficient in energy and vividness of expression, the interests narrow.

Later that night, lying comfortably in his hammock, he ruminated on Captain FitzRoy:

"I have been for the last twelve months on very cordial terms with him. Only two quarrels in four years . . . in such crowded quarters. Remarkable! He is an extraordinary, noble character, unfortunately affected with strong peculiarities of temper. Of this, no man is more aware than himself, as he shows by his attempts to conquer them. I often doubt what will be his end; under many circumstances I am sure it would be a brilliant one, under others I fear a very unhappy one. . . ."

They had left Tahiti on November 26. As they approached their fifth Christmas on board everyone was homesick, Captain FitzRoy as severely as Charles. To make matters worse, the brig was pitching her bow against a head sea; in his seasickness Charles groaned to Stokes, trying to draw accurately on a chart table which pitched and heaved under him:

"Hitherto pleasure and pain, geology and seasickness have balanced each other. Now that we are approaching the meridian, I have moved all my pleasures forward to Shrewsbury, some eight months before I shall reach there."

There was a lot of sea still to be covered; but the brunt of their mission had been accomplished.

They came upon friendly fair winds. In twenty-five days they saw New Zealand in the distance and anchored safely in the Bay of Islands on December 21, 1835. Through his telescope Charles saw that the country was mildly green, hilly but smooth in outline, deeply intersecting the bay with outstretched arms of land. Only one canoe came alongside, with several silent natives whose faces were completely in-cised and tattooed with dark-lined whorls, curves, circles, curlicues from chin through nose to lined forehead.

"Not a prepossessing sight," said Lieutenant Wickham, who was never altogether happy to become involved with areas of land.

There were three whaling ships lying at anchor; beyond them, little clusters of square, neat-looking houses were surrounded by flowers.

"Looks English to me," said FitzRoy, "but from all my information the natives don't live in whitewashed houses with rose gardens."

Charles noted that all of the hills were steeply terraced. Once ashore, he learned that the terraces were fortifications. The New Zealand Maoris were among the most ferocious tribes on earth, and had spent centuries annihilating each other, taking slaves among the conquered.

That evening Charles went ashore with Captain FitzRoy and Mr. Baker, a missionary who had come aboard to welcome them. In the whaleboat Mr. Baker, who was more disillusioned than bitter, reported that, although some of the heathen tribes in the interior had been converted to Christianity, he had had little success here in Kororadika, New Zealand's largest village. When they landed they found that the English inhabitants were mostly convicts exiled from England, who had escaped from New South Wales. Mr. Baker said quietly:

"It grieves me to say so, and I know it's not a proper Christian sentiment, but these Englishmen are mostly worthless characters, addicted to drunkenness and vice of all kinds. We missionaries are held in little esteem."

At Mr. Baker's house permission was asked for Richard Matthews to join his brother in the northern part of New Zealand. After some consultation the other missionaries present agreed. Charles was happy for Matthews's sake. He had been a lonely man spending close to three years on the *Beagle*, listed as an able-bodied seaman on the books but unable to find a proper place for himself on board the ship.

Learning that a few of the missionaries had purchased land in the interior at Waimate for agricultural purposes, Charles asked if he might come for a visit.

"Delighted, dear boy. You'll come part of the way by boat, then it's a mere four hours' walk to the farm. Be sure to take guides; paths in this undeveloped country are hard come by."

The British resident, Mr. Busby, who served as consul, took Charles to meet a chieftain and former great warrior. He was completely tattooed. When Charles asked if he could provide two of his men for guides, the chief replied:

"I go. How much pounds pay?"

"No pounds. Two dollars."

"Two dola! Much good!"

Their long walk was over volcanic soil, impractical for cultivation, covered by tall ferns and low bushes. When they passed native villages, Charles saw that the hovels were filthy. Mr. Baker had told him:

"They never think of washing. From birth to death. Nor do they clean anything they use. It's simply not in their culture."

The natives appeared to be akin to those in Tierra del Fuego. The extraordinary manner in which every inch of their faces was tattooed puzzled Charles. Their expressions appeared to be rigidly inflexible, their eyes filled with cunning and ferocity.

"But as Mr. Baker says, that may not be a proper Christian sentiment," he told himself. "Possibly the incisions in their faces have made it impossible for them to do anything but stare implacably."

The farmland that had been cleared and planted by the missionaries was beautiful to his eyes: fields of barley, wheat, clover. Growing in the gardens he found most of the fruits and vegetables from home: kidney beans, cucumbers, rhubarb, apples and pears, gooseberries, currants, hops; gorse for fences and English oaks.

He reached the Rev. Mr. Williams's home late in the afternoon to find a large party having tea, the English children scrubbed and holiday dressed, chirping as spontaneously as birds speaking to each other from separate trees. The vivacity of the scene made Charles think of Maer Hall and his Wedgwood cousins. Tea was an institution, the chief common denominator which held the English people together. All present were fascinated by the attempt to establish Richard Matthews in Tierra del Fuego.

"It was a failure," Charles concluded, remembering Matthews's dangers and hardships.

"No, no," cried Williams, "it was the first step. Similar to our first step in New Zealand. But by God's blessing we have at last succeeded beyond our expectations."

The next day was market day in Waimate. The natives came in with their stock of potatoes, Indian corn and pigs which they traded for blankets, tobacco and an occasional bar of soap. It was a colorful sight, market days always were for Charles's absorbing mind. The return trip to the Bay of Islands was a disappointment, for he found few birds in the woods and even fewer indigenous animals.

Back in Pahia, Charles joined FitzRoy at divine services.

"Our fifth Christmas away from home," he murmured.

FitzRoy added quietly:

"And our last! Next Christmas in England!"

His last day in port, December 29, 1835, Charles took a long walk upriver. He ran into the funeral of the daughter of a chief; she had died five days before. The hut in which she died had been burned down, and her body enclosed in two upright canoes surrounded by the wooden images of native gods, everything painted red. The girl's hair was strewn at the foot of the enclosing canoes, her gown fastened to the upright coffin. The relatives of the dead girl had scratched their faces, arms and bodies so that they were covered with clotted blood, a ghastly sight.

If there had been few rewards in New Zealand for a naturalist, there assuredly were some for the anthropologist growing to mature stature within him.

## 6.

It was a thirteen-day passage to Sydney Cove, New Holland (Australia), a beautiful harbor filled with large ships and surrounded by warehouses similar to those in Plymouth. Philip King, who had just turned eighteen, was beside himself with joy. Sydney was his birthplace. After four years, he would be rejoining his father, Captain King, and his mother and brothers, whom he had not seen for ten years.

"Charley, you've got to save us some time," he sputtered; "come to our home, meet my family."

Charles laughed. "Worry not. I'll spend a couple of days with you as soon as I have made one expedition to the interior."

All aboard ship had eagerly welcomed the dropping of anchor in Sydney Cove as there was bound to be a feast of correspondence awaiting them. But when the tender came out from shore there was not a single letter for anyone on H.M.S. *Beagle*. Officers and crew were as crushed as though the mainmast had fallen. Charles returned with Captain FitzRoy to his cabin.

"In New Zealand I had guessed we were moving ahead of our mail instructions back home," Charles said glumly.

FitzRoy was not as badly stricken.

"Pity. But it brings us back to England that many weeks earlier."

In the late afternoon Charles walked through the broad, clean streets of Sydney. He was struck by how solid a town it was, with well-built homes, the shops amply provisioned. It compared with the suburbs which stretched out from London. Many large houses had just been completed, and many more were under construction. Sydney appeared to contain a great deal of wealth; passing him while he walked were gigs, phaetons and carriages driven by servants in livery.

"Astonishing," he thought, "for a colony that we founded only forty-eight years ago. It is a testimony to the power of the British nation. I can't resist the feeling to congratulate myself that I was born an Englishman."

His euphoria did not last.

He hired a man and two horses to take him on an exploration to the village of Bathurst, a fertile agricultural area about one hundred and twenty miles in the interior. The macadam roads were good, he passed two packed coaches of the type he himself rode in England, and an excessive number of alehouses. He was not prepared for a party of convicts, dressed in yellow and gray, working in irons under the guard of sentries with loaded guns. It was a chilling sight. He learned that the chained ones had been convicted of some trifling offense here in Australia. He had also heard of the convicted felons who had been shipped out of England to exile in this new country; a numerous and inevitably dangerous part of the population.

He returned to observing the landscape, its most remarkable feature the extreme uniformity of vegetation: open woodland, the ground partially covered by a thin pasture. For a country with such a prosperous main city as Sydney, he was surprised to find a countryside of such arid sterility.

At sunset a score of aboriginal blacks passed by, each carrying a bundle of spears. They were partly clothed and several spoke a little English. They appeared good-humored. He approached a splendidly built young man and said:

"If I pay you a shilling will you show me how accurately you can throw your spears?"

He took out the coin and passed it to the fellow. There was a shout of approval from the aborigines, who rarely saw a coin since they could not be persuaded to cultivate the ground, keep sheep which had been offered them or build houses and remain in one place. They preferred their walkabouts, apparently living off wild animals.

The young man cried, "Put cap."

One of his companions ran thirty yards ahead and placed the cap on a low branch. Each in turn threw his spear with the rapidity of an arrow from the bow, and each in turn transfixed the cap.

"Good show!" Charles exclaimed. "You are great spearsmen! Worth every ha'penny of my shilling."

With which he clapped his hands, and the aborigines clapped back, then moved on with much laughter. He slept that night in a comfortable inn at Emu ferry, thirty-five miles from Sydney.

During the next few days he made his way to the Blue Mountains to find them merely sloping foothills from which he dug out sandstone samples for his pouch. Although the roads were bordered by the ever present eucalyptus trees, he found no houses or cultivated land. He slept at the Blackheath Inn that night, and the next morning took the three-mile walk to Govett's Leap, with a striking view of forest below.

Back again on horseback, he detoured to Walerawang farm, which ran fifteen thousand sheep and raised the wheat necessary to feed its convict laborers. Charles had a letter of introduction to the superintendent from the man in Sydney who owned the farm.

"Why not spend the night? We'll go kangaroo hunting in the morning."

"I take that kindly. I would very much like to find a kangaroo and take a skin back to England with me."

After supper Charles asked quietly:

"Mr. Browne, are your convict laborers all exiles from England?"

"Every one."

"I see you don't have armed guards over them."

"Not necessary. A few run away but most want to serve out their time and become free men. Many of them then go into trade, make a lot of money. They're not accepted into respectable society, but they can buy everything they want."

Charles did not find a kangaroo but he saw flocks of white cockatoos feeding in a cornfield, beautiful parrots, crows, birds similar to the magpie and, later, in the dusk, the famous platypus, a rare egg-laying mammal with enormous lips, diving and playing about on the surface of a pond.

He spent ten days collecting whatever wild life was available and reflecting on the strange animals of Australia, the platypus, kangaroo, koala bear, spiny anteater, wombat and bandicoot. He mused:

"An unbeliever in anything beyond his own reason might exclaim, 'Surely two distinct Creators must have been at work.' A geologist perhaps would suggest that the periods of Creation had been distinct and remote the one from the other; that the Creator rested in His labor."

On the way back to Sydney, Captain King took him to his home in Dunheved, thirty miles from the city. Captain King thanked Charles for his kindnesses to Philip, then told him that the boy had decided to leave the service and become a farmer with them, at which the whole family was rejoicing.

"Captain FitzRoy tells me that he has read parts of your journal of the voyage," Captain King continued, "and they are quite good. I've been working on my own journal of the first *Beagle* journey, 1826–1830, but making slow progress. Captain FitzRoy has further said that he may combine some of your materials with his own."

Charles swallowed hard but did not comment.

The following day the King family took Charles to lunch at Parmetta, the home of King's brother-in-law. Charles found himself in a house which would have been considered superior even in England. He was plunged into a bevy of attractive young girls dressed to the nines in gowns of organdy, muslin, silken gauze.

"When were you last in London?" he asked.

Several of the young ladies answered at the same time.

"Oh, we are Australians. We know nothing about England."

And evidently could not care less!

Again in Sydney, he learned that the city was rancorously divided into factions on almost every subject. The servants were paroled convicts, their hatred deep seated and ill concealed. The only subjects discussed were wealth and wool. Wandering about the city, he found the bookstores empty of everything but trash. He also came upon artist Conrad Martens, who had had to leave the *Beagle* in Valparaíso for lack of space. Martens had made his own way to Tahiti where he had sketched for seven weeks and to the Bay of Islands in New Zealand. In April of 1835 he had sailed into Sydney harbor where the people decided that he was the first to discover the harbor's pictorial qualities and had taken him to their civic bosom as their official painter. Charles visited his comfortable home, half of which had been converted into a studio. The sense of acceptance and permanence had taken some of the stiffness out of his bearing. He threw an arm about Charles's shoulder, a gesture of which he would not have been capable two years before.

"I hated to leave you and the *Beagle*," he said, "but it worked out best for me. I'm selling well and I am cordially received by all the good families."

Charles walked about the studio room.

"These are paintings you did from the *Beagle* sketches," he exclaimed. "Marvelously good; our two little sailboats in a vast lagoon, under a smoking volcano; our sails among the others, with Valparaíso in the background. I really shouldn't spend the money but I would love to have a couple of these water colors to take home. This one with the *Beagle* laid ashore at the mouth of the Santa Cruz, having its copper keel repaired; and this one of Tierra del Fuego. What would they cost?"

"For you, Charles, my friend, a token price. Say, three guineas each. . . ."

"Done!" Then he asked: "Why is it, Martens, that you rarely put humans in your pictures?"

Martens was thoughtful for a moment.

"My bent is topography and landscape. I put in occasional figures as landscape accessories. I am of the family of Claude, the French landscape painter who used to say that he included figures with the price of the picture, and made no extra charge for them."

Just before H.M.S. *Beagle* sailed for Hobart Town in Tasmania, Charles wrote to Professor Henslow:

> . . . I must feed upon the future & it is beyond bounds delightful to feel the certainty that within eight months I shall be residing once again most quietly in Cambridge. Certainly I never was intended for a traveller; my thoughts are always rambling over past or future scenes; I cannot enjoy the present happiness for anticipating the future; which is about as foolish as the dog who dropt the real bone for its shadow.

To Katty he wrote:

> . . . I confess I never see a Merchant vessel start for England without a most dangerous inclination to bolt. It is a most true & grievous fact that the last four months appear to me as long as the two previous years. There never was a ship so full of homesick heroes as the *Beagle*. We ought to be ashamed of ourselves.

Hobart Town proved to be a geologist's dream. The first time he tried to ascend the three thousand feet of Mount Wellington he suffered one of his rare defeats, turned back after a number of hours by the thickness of the woods. The next day he hired a guide who took him up by the damp side of the mountain. Thickets of dead trees and branches made the climbing difficult; it took five and a half hours to reach the peak, but once there he cried:

"Worth it! Every stumbling step. What an intricate design of broken land and glistening bays."

He reaped a harvest of rocks: basalt which had flowed as lava, unstratified masses of greenstone, yellowish limestone which contained impressions of leaves, plants and trees no longer in existence. Bynoe found him stooped over his magnifying glass for such long stretches that he cautioned him:

"Get up each time you hear two, four, six or eight bells and walk about the deck. Otherwise you'll return to England a hunchback."

"Ben, look what came out of this small quarry; the only remaining record of the vegetation of Tasmania during a former epoch."

Bynoe studied the fossil leaves and plants under the magnifying glass. "How ancient?"

"Probably of the age of the Silurian system in Europe, millions of years ago."

They spent seventeen days sailing through the Indian Ocean charting along the south coast of Australia. It was during these long sails with the weather unobtrusive that he occupied himself with his old geological notes. In the rearranging he found that he had to rewrite them totally. Only then did he begin to discover difficulty in expressing his ideas on paper. He groused to Sulivan:

"As long as the writing consists solely of description it is pretty easy. But when reasoning comes into play, when I must achieve a modest fluency, this is to me a difficulty of which I had no idea."

Sulivan was taken by surprise.

"I should have thought you'd have the hang of it after four years of voluminous writing in your diary."

"Maybe one never does get the hang of writing. Maybe that's why we have so few great authors."

Captain FitzRoy was also busy setting down his accounts of the voyage. It was clear that he was daily becoming a happier man. He confided one evening when they had finished their supper:

"I look forward with cheerfulness to this writing work before me."

"Perhaps that's because you don't have to submit it to the Hydrographer's Office!"

FitzRoy flashed Charles one of his rare grins.

"Philos, I wish you would read my last few chapters. Then too, I'd like to read yours."

The two men exchanged manuscripts. Charles found FitzRoy's style for the most part simple and readable, if somewhat dull.

FitzRoy returned his own pages.

"Darwin, these two hundred pages are jolly well done! Fascinating, much of it. Now I have a proposal to make to you. Please feel free to reject it if it does not strike you right. . . ."

"All of your proposals are in season, Captain." Charles knew what was coming.

". . . I suggest that you join with me in publishing our accounts. That is, for me to have the disposal and arranging of your journal and to mingle it with my own."

Captain King had been right!

Charles's innards knotted at this dashing of his hopes, then sank like the lead taking a fathom. It was the worst of all possible situations. Not only would his own book be annihilated but the whole project would be a waste and a blunder. FitzRoy's journal was already some five hundred pages long, more than enough for a full-length publication. To add several hundred of Charles's pages would make it unmanageable; to add less would be to obliterate it. Nor would a publisher be willing to print a truncated version of his journal after the heart of it had already appeared.

Even more serious was the fact that the two texts could no more mingle than floating oil and the salt water beneath it. While FitzRoy's observer's eye was excellent, his book was technical, dwelling on the performance of H.M.S. *Beagle* and everything achieved in charting and mapping around the world, materials necessary and valuable, but dry. His own manuscript was warm, personal, covering a wider range of scientific interests because of his intensive collecting and because he had become involved in the whole life of the peoples he had visited, their anthropological mores and morals.

Yet there was no way he could refuse the proposal! It was Captain FitzRoy who had invited him on this voyage, who had encouraged, protected and even indulged him so that he could assemble a collection unique in the world.

He had rigidly controlled the expression on his face so that FitzRoy would not suspect the tenor or testiness of the thoughts flashing across his mind. He said quietly:

"Of course I am willing, Captain, if you want my materials. Or if you think the chitchat details of my journal worth publishing."

"Thank you, Darwin, most cordially. I knew you would respond that way."

Lying fully clothed in his hammock, not lighting the candle in the chart room, shivering, he asked himself:

"Was I a hypocrite? A coward? What else could I honorably do?"

But he did have his geology book! It was a rare piece of good fortune that of the many errant naturalists who went voyaging in ships there had been no geologists. He would enter that field unopposed. It would appease the loss of his newborn hopes for the journal.

He rose from the hammock, undressed.

"I look forward with no little anxiety to the time when Henslow, putting on a grave face, shall decide on the merits of my notes. If he shakes his head in a disapproving manner, I shall then know that I had better at once give up science, for science will have given up me. For I have worked with every grain of energy I possess."

King George Sound proved to be a new settlement of some thirty small whitewashed houses in the midst of such uninteresting and sterile country that the inhabitants lived on salt meat. The only adventure Charles could scrounge up was a walk with FitzRoy to Bald Head where they came upon a stand of petrified trees erect in the position in which they grew.

"Strange!" exclaimed FitzRoy. "You're the geologist. How do you explain such a phenomenon, a petrified forest standing stark upright, untouched?"

"Oh, it's been touched! By a good many forces of nature. Give me about an hour to work with the pick end of my hammer."

He thought out his conclusion, then explained to a patient, puzzled FitzRoy:

"These trees were turned to rock over a long period of time by the wind heaping up calcareous sand percolated into the trees by driving rains. In this way the trees and roots were completely enclosed. In time the wood of the trees decayed inside their rock shells. Lime was washed into the cavities, becoming hard as a stalactite. The weather has worn away the soft rock covering so now you have a hard cast of trees and roots, an exact imitation of a dead forest."

FitzRoy's eyes sparkled with pleasure at the adroitness of the analysis.

"Philosopher, your friend Adam Sedgwick was right. You are an 'unfinished' geologist!"

It was not until three weeks later, in the Keeling Islands, an eighteen-day sail northwest in the Indian Ocean, that he staked out his claim to be a professional.

For a very long time now he had doubted Lyell's theory that coral reefs were built on the rims of submerged volcanoes. The idea of a lagoon island thirty miles in diameter being based on a submarine crater of equal dimensions had appeared to him a monstrous hypothesis. In Tahiti he had seen coral reefs which extended for miles and miles. There was no way on earth, or under the sea for that matter, that a volcano rim could extend for such a distance. Since the early days of his South American studies he had attempted to put together a valid theory of how coral reefs were formed. Fragments of ideas had come through but nothing like a sound, coherent theory. Now came the revelation, not as an intellectual thesis, but in terms of solid proof.

On the steep outside of one of the Keeling Islands, a low, circular coral reef, Captain FitzRoy took numerous soundings with a layer of tallow affixed to the lead. Within ten fathoms, sixty feet, the tallowed lead invariably came up marked with the impression of coral polypifers, a colony of polyps . . . as clean as if it had been dropped on a carpet of turf! Proof that the polyps were alive.

When the depth of the soundings increased Charles saw that the impressions left on the tallow by the living coral grew less numerous as the adhering particles of sand became more numerous. Somewhere between one hundred and twenty feet and one hundred and eighty feet the tallow showed that the bottom consisted of a smooth sandy layer.

"Captain, could we go back to our soundings between thirty and sixty feet?" he asked excitedly.

After several hours of testing and note taking, the uncontrovertible truth came through. The utmost depth at which coral polyps could construct reefs was one hundred and eighty feet. Wherever there was now an atoll or coral reef, a foundation of ocean bottom of sand or stone must have originally existed within a depth of from twenty to thirty fathoms from the surface!

He perceived that reefs of living coral could extend for hundreds of miles, even thousands, just so long as there was a land base or sunken mountain base between those two dimensions for the polyps to build on, billions of them, trillions, piling on top of each other over the vast millennia, enclosing tropical bays and island coastlands in immense atolls and lagoons such as the ones he had studied at Papeete and here in the Keeling Islands, and the ones he had read about at Bow Atoll and Menchikov Island. It was not a volcanic crater under the surface of the ocean that formed the base of the coral structure, but mountains whose peaks had once risen above the surface and were gradually subsiding, providing a foundation, as they sank, for the growth of the polyps.

"I'm sorry about Lyell, but when I get back to London I shall have to tell him that his 'volcano rim' hypothesis is now obsolete," he observed to Captain FitzRoy. "I can also tell him several other things about coral polyps that I've observed."

His face flushed, he started to count on the fingers of his hand:

"First, corals can only live in warm water. Second, they grow on the windward side and flourish where most exposed to the waves, which bring them nutriment. Third, loose sediment in the water is injurious to the growing corals. Fourth, they cannot tolerate fresh water. Fifth, and this is going to take considerable work, reefs are made of several kinds of corals, differing shapes, sizes, structures, colors, depending on varying conditions of nature and the sea."

"The Eighth Wonder of the World?" suggested FitzRoy.

"Yes, Captain. How utterly insignificant are the Pyramids when compared to these mountains of stone accumulated by the agency of various minute and tender animals."

They broke their long passage across the Indian Ocean at Mauritius, a former French colony, since 1810 British, known for its beautiful scenery; houses scattered against a bright green background of sugar cane; at the center wooded mountains with ancient volcanic rocks at the summit. The town of Port Louis was delightful; clean streets, well-stocked booksellers' shops, a charming theater where operas were sung, shops filled with the finest of French merchandise. Charles climbed La Pouce, a mountain which rose two thousand six hundred feet behind the town, but that was the extent of his naturalizing. He met Captain Lloyd, the surveyor general, well known for his survey across the Isthmus of Panama, who invited him and Stokes to spend a couple of days at his country house, six miles from the port. They passed pretty gardens, sugar cane growing amidst lava rock, and rode on Captain Lloyd's elephant.

Sitting on Captain Lloyd's veranda, Charles commented:

"Mauritius has an air of elegance, of harmony. How pleasant it must be to pass one's life in such a quiet abode."

Captain Lloyd's leathered face made a grimace.

"Elegant, yes. Harmonious, no. Since England took possession from

France twenty-five years ago, we have used the macadamizing art to build the excellent roads you've ridden on and increased the export of sugar in proportion of seventy-five to one. Though on the neighboring island of Bourbon, still under French rule, the roads are miserable, and the French residents here have prospered from the increased productivity of our island, the British government is far from popular. Jealousy, envy and hatred are common."

Charles was thoughtful, then commented:

"Alas, there does not exist a terrestrial paradise where such feelings have not found an entrance. Reginal Heber, an English clergyman educated at Oxford, once wrote:

> "Though every prospect pleases,
> And only man is vile."

Before he left Mauritius, on April 29, 1836, he wrote a letter to his sister Caroline which revealed considerably his expectations for the future:

> I am in high spirits about my Geology, & even aspire to the hope that my observations will be considered of some utility by real geologists. I see very clearly it will be necessary to live in London for a year, by which time with hard work the greater part, I trust, of my material will be exhausted.

7.

They passed the south end of Madagascar, made the coast of Africa at Natal, sailed a length of the southern shore, lost a week because of contrary winds off Cape Lagullas and finally anchored in Simon's Bay the last day of May, at the Cape Colony on the extreme tip of Africa.

After nine months of an agonizing starvation for news from home everyone aboard H.M.S. *Beagle* once again expected to find a grand pile of mail awaiting them. The mountain of letters, alas, dwindled into a mere dozen, but at least there was one for Charles, from his sister Katty, dated only four months before. He thought, "Nine months of letters are wandering over the wide ocean."

It was heartening to learn that as late as January 29 everyone was well, his father taking long walks in Shrewsbury every day. Katty had been occupying Charles's bedroom at The Mount but would much enjoy turning out of his room to give it up to its dear old owner.

Then came a strange paragraph:

> . . . We have sent William Fox one of the little books with the Extracts from your letters; everybody is much pleased with

them, who has seen them. Professor Henslow sent half a dozen to Dr. Butler; we sent one also to your friend Tom Eyton. He says he has written to you at Sydney so you will have his opinion for himself of them.

He stared, glassy eyed and stunned. A little book of his! What little book? Extracts from his letters? Letters to whom? Professor Henslow had sent half a dozen of the little books to Dr. Butler, his nemesis, the headmaster of Shrewsbury School who had publicly reproved him for wasting his time over such useless subjects as chemistry and had labeled him before the school as "little caring." Then it must have been his letters to Professor Henslow. Published by the good professor himself? Which letters, and what was in them?

He sat down at his corner of the chart table and wrote to Katty in a state of perturbation:

> I have been a good deal horrified by a sentence in your letter where you talk of "the little book with the extracts from your letters." I can only suppose they refer to a few geological details. But I have always written to Henslow in the same careless manner as to you, & to print what has been written without care or accuracy is indeed playing with edged tools. As the Spaniard says, "No hay remedio." I have no remedy.

He then packed a small duffel bag, rented a gig and rode the twenty-two miles into Cape Town. It was June 1, 1836. He was diverted by the entirely new vegetation he saw on the ride, and arrived late in the evening to find that that morning several ships from India had come into port and disgorged their hosts of passengers to fill the one good hotel and several inns. He went searching for a boardinghouse and found a clean airy room.

The next morning he went for an early walk to see the city. He was struck by the number of bullock wagons in the streets, some of them being drawn by a herd of twenty-four yoked oxen. The town was laid out with the rectangular precision he had come to expect of Spanish cities. The streets were macadamized and lined with trees, the houses whitewashed. There were signs of the early Boer settlement. At the docks hides, tallow and wine were being loaded for export.

He stood beneath the well-known Table Mountain with his mouth slightly open, gazing upward to a height of thirty-five hundred feet of absolute wall reaching into the clouds. Composed of horizontal strata, it gave to Cape Town a grand character as a monumental backdrop.

He hired a couple of horses and a young Hottentot groom to guide him about the countryside. The Hottentot spoke English and was tidily dressed in a long coat, beaver hat and white gloves. He was lighter skinned than the African blacks. The landscape was uninteresting, with few animals and fewer plants to collect, without a tree to break the monotonous uniformity of the sandstone hills. He saw very few of the native blacks, learning that they lived away from the coast on their tribal lands. What he did see were hundreds of Boers leaving the Cape Colony, taking their women and children, household goods in great lumbering ox wagons headed north to carve out new settlements, driving their herds of cattle and sheep before them. Though he heard a good deal of English spoken he soon realized that, although the Dutch settlers had profited under the British government, the Boers disliked British rule, particularly the missionaries, who segregated the native blacks in reserves to protect them from exploiters. When the British Parliament emancipated the slaves, the Boers felt they were inadequately compensated for their losses.

That night he slept at the house of an English farmer and returned to Cape Town the following day by way of Sir Lowry's pass, a cut along the side of a steep mountain. He spent an interesting day with Dr. Andrew Smith, who had just come back from an expedition into the interior of South Africa, and subsequently took long geological rambles and exchanged with him knowledge about the rocks and mountains of distant parts. He dined out one day with Thomas Maclear, the Royal Astronomer; and then to his delight met Sir John Herschel, whose book *Introduction to the Study of Natural Philosophy* he had read with profound interest during his last year at Cambridge. No dozen other books had influenced him nearly so much as von Humboldt's *Personal Narrative* and Herschel's *Study of Natural Philosophy*. Sir John invited Charles and Captain FitzRoy to his home, surrounded by fir and oak trees in the open country, for dinner. After an apéritif he showed them his garden, full of Cape bulbs of his own collecting.

Sir John Herschel, forty-four, was a blunt man who spoke little, every word to the point. He was known in Cape Town society as a man whose eyes were always clear from gazing at the stars, but whose hands were always soiled from planting Cape Colony bulbs in his garden. By dessert he had unbent enough to reveal his more interesting discoveries in astronomy during the two and a half years since he had left England. Charles learned a great deal about the stars and galaxies he had been viewing from the decks of the *Beagle*.

As they were saying their adieus on the front veranda, Herschel turned to Charles with a personal warmth and interest he had not hitherto displayed, and said:

"Darwin, I hear we were collaborators during the November meeting of the Cambridge Philosophical Society."

Charles could only echo:

". . . we were? . . . how so, Sir John?"

"Extracts were read from some of my letters on astronomy as seen from the Cape Colony. Apparently extracts were also read from your letters to Professor Henslow about the geology of South America."

Charles was struck dumb, then managed to stutter:

"What a compliment to me, Sir John . . . to be read in your company. Mine were only rough notes sent to my friend and mentor."

Herschel liked the younger man's humility.

"Oh, I don't know," he said with a faintly mocking smile. "I hear the Philosophical Society published your extracts in a monograph. Can't say the Society was moved to do as handsomely by mine!"

On the drive back to Cape Town, Captain FitzRoy said earnestly:

"Congratulations. I didn't know you had a publication to your credit."

"Neither did I, Captain, neither did I."

It seemed to Charles a thousand separate and impatient miles to St. Helena, halfway between the gigantic African and South American continents. He found lodgings within a stone's throw of Napoleon's tomb, and wrote:

> In respect to the house in which Napoleon died, its state is scandalous; to see the filthy and deserted rooms scored with the names of visitors, was to my mind like beholding some ancient ruin wantonly disfigured.

He spent four days wandering over the small island, guided by a civil old man who had been a slave and a goatherd as a boy. The little world of St. Helena, situated in the midst of a vast ocean, excited his curiosity. He and his guide carried their dinner and a horn of water, walking through wild valleys, desolate and untenanted. The mountain rocks showed successive changes and complicated violence. He concluded that "originally it was raised in mass from beneath the waters." He enjoyed his rambles among the rocks and mountains and wrote Professor Henslow a note which, he realized, might forge still another link in his destiny. He described the degree to which he longed to be once again living quietly, with not one single novel object near him. . . . "No one can imagine it, till he has been whirled round the world, during five long years, in a ten Gun Brig. . . ."

But on rereading the letter it was the opening paragraph which revealed, even to himself, the main thrust of his mind:

> I am going to ask you to do me a favor. I am very anxious to belong to the Geological Society. I do not know, but I suppose it is necessary to be proposed some time before being balloted for. If such is the case, would you be good enough to take the proper preparatory steps. Professor Sedgwick very kindly offered to propose me before leaving England; if he should happen to be in London, I daresay he would yet do so.

The island of Ascension also lay halfway across the Atlantic Ocean, between the outthrusting humps of Africa and South America. It was inhabited solely by British marines. Nothing grew on the lava coast, but inland, near the summit of the central island, Green Hill, Charles found houses, gardens and fields. There were castor oil plants, grasshoppers, sheep, goats, cows and horses, all thriving. There was little to collect but land crabs, mice and guinea fowl. He took long walks, guided by the marines, into the frightening interior: layers of pumice, ash, volcanic sandstone and volcanic bombs which had been projected red hot from the crater and still lay strewn on the surface. He had never seen a sight of such naked hideousness; and remembered what the witty people of St. Helena had told him:

"We know we live on a rock but the poor people of Ascension live on a cinder."

On July 18, 1836, at Ascension he received a letter from Susan dated November 22, 1835.

> Eras says he hears that some of your letters were read at the Geological Society in London. Dr. Butler sent Papa an abstract of a letter from Professor Adam Sedgwick to him, which was as follows about you. "He is doing admirably in South America and has already sent home a collection above all price. It was the best thing in the world for him that he went out on the Voyage of Discovery. There was some risk of his turning out to be an idle man; but his character is now fixed, and if God spares his life, he will have a great name among the Naturalists of Europe."

He gripped the sheets of paper in his fist, then fell back into the chair behind the chart table, a dozen amorphous hopes, fears, puzzlements knocking about in his groggy head like bowling balls.

When quieter he asked himself, "How did those letters get to the Geological Society in London? To what passing juvenile theories have I been committed?"

Then he read again the words from the letter of Professor Adam Sedgwick:

> *There was some risk of his turning out an idle man.* . . .

Was that what people had thought of him? Because he had not wanted to be a doctor, had only under duress consented to enter the field of theology? He had always tramped the fields and hills collecting, and taken his specimens seriously. Was it the action of the Geological Society that made the difference in how he was now regarded?

With his notebooks and journals bulging with undigested observations and a new professional acceptance, what was the status of his promise to his father to become a clergyman?

His life was erupting like a live volcano. The room became stiflingly hot. He rose from the chair, stepped out on deck for fresh air.

8.

Instead of heading straight north for England, Captain FitzRoy decided to sail west to Bahia, Brazil, because of singular disagreements in the longitude. Though he was anxious to complete the circle in the Southern Hemisphere he retraced his steps along the line from which they had come out of England. Charles wrote to Susan from Bahia on August 4:

> This zigzag manner of proceeding is very grievous; it has put the finishing stroke to my feelings. I loathe, I abhor the sea, and all ships which sail on it.

They would make their last stop in Pernambuco, at the bulge of Brazil, then sail for home via the Azores. If he was impatient to be home, the good news never ceased coming.

He received a letter from Caroline dated December 29, another of the letters that had been floating over the wide seas, trailing H.M.S. *Beagle.* Stretched out on the sofa in the captain's cabin, he read with damp eyes:

> . . . You must now hear how your fame is spreading. A note came to my Father on Xmas day from Prof. Henslow speaking most kindly of you & rejoicing you would soon return "to reap the reward of your perseverance and take your position among the first Naturalists of the day." With the note he sent my father some copies of extracts from your letters to him, printed for private distribution. The little preface to the extracts says they were printed for distribution "among the members of the Cambridge Philosophical Society in consequence of the interest which has been excited by some of the Geological notices which they contain, and which were read at a Meeting of the Society on the 15th of November 1835." My father did not move from his seat till he had read every word of *your* book & he was very much gratified. He liked so much the simple clear way you gave your information. Your frank unmannered mode of writing was to him particularly agreeable! . . . My father has given away a few copies of the extracts to those friends who have all along felt the most constant interest about you. . . .

The tremor of an earthquake went through his long, lean body. Adam Sedgwick had said that he would have a great name among the naturalists of Europe. And here was Professor Henslow saying that he would take his position among the great naturalists of the day!

"Lord God in heaven, what has happened to me without my knowing it? Can it be true? Have I achieved a vocation? Must I no longer be buried among the trees surrounding a quiet country parsonage?"

He realized the full implication of his sister's letter. His father had read every word of his book and had respected his work. He had been so proud as to give away copies. Did that mean he would allow his son to work all his life as a scientist and not consider it still another broken promise? If he had his father's support he would have not merely the usual two years until he was assigned a deacon's post but all the years ahead to write up his geological notebooks, his journal, the monographs which he hoped could be published in all the fields of his collections. To continue his work as a naturalist, wherever it might lead him!

The prospect of a lifetime of creative work in the field he loved so passionately filled him with an ineffable joy. No longer would his father consider him a wayward youth, say, "You care for nothing but shooting, dogs and ratcatching, and you will be a disgrace to yourself and all your family." No longer would he be considered an "idle man."

"As one grows up nothing seems planned or charted," he mused. "Yet at some given point all the readings of the dip needle come together, the captain knows where he is in the sea and can safely make his way to the designated harbor."

He went out on deck. Night had fallen. There was a scimitar of moon and a galaxy of brilliant stars. He walked to the bow, watched H.M.S. *Beagle*, her sails billowing out before her, cut through the phosphorescent waters of the Atlantic with the sharpness of a carving knife.

There flashed into his mind the picture of himself sitting under Milton's mulberry tree in the Fellows' Garden at Christ's College of a warm and fragrant spring day, the dahlias in bloom, yellow, red, orange and pink in the garden beds, reading a poem of William Cowper's:

God moves in a mysterious way
His wonders to perform;
He plants his footsteps in the sea
And rides upon the storm.

His whole being was flooded with ecstasy at the thought of returning home to The Mount, to Maer Hall, to Christ's College, to all the dear ones of his family, his friends and associates in Cambridge and London . . . to his new stature.

# PART TWO

## TURN THE WORLD AROUND

# BOOK SEVEN

*Paradise Regained*

1.

THEY were all on deck to catch the first sight of England. A shout went up at the landfall, but to Charles's surprise seeing England aroused no warm feelings in him. Had he exhausted himself by anticipation?

They docked at Falmouth during a stormy night. His shabby great-coat was thoroughly drenched by the time he reached the Royal Hotel and procured a seat on the *Royal Mail* coach. It was twenty-nine hours into London, to the Swan with Two Necks, before boarding the *Tally Ho!* at seven forty-five in the morning. Syms Covington had asked if he could continue in Charles's employ until the work on the collections was completed. Charles gave him a holiday until their job should begin in earnest; then they parted company.

It was another sixteen hours of being jostled around, dozing inter-mittently, before the *Tally Ho!* reached Shrewsbury at midnight, stop-ping at the Raven Inn on Pride Hill. His family would be asleep. They would also be so excited they would want to talk all night. He himself was knocked up, having been riding in the coaches for forty-six hours. Best to get some rest, put on clean clothes.

He slept like a dead man but by six he was bathing in a big metal bath, shaving carefully with his honed razor, and putting on the last surviving shirt of the twelve Nancy had made for him. The vestige of his fine blue velvet waistcoat, the newer less well-made long coat and trousers he had bought in Montevideo; the tan boots he had donned five years ago to welcome Professor Adam Sedgwick before their trip through North Wales, were scuffed, worn and crumpled. There was no help for it. The family was going to have to recognize him inside his ill-fitting wrappings.

It was a typical early October morning in Shropshire, a little fog, a cool sun trying to clear itself of all charges, the air fresh and clean in his nostrils. Best of all, the good earth of Shrewsbury stood still beneath his feet with neither pitch nor roll while he walked the several streets downhill to the river Severn, crossed the Welsh Bridge and entered the lower garden of The Mount with its autumnal flowers, the trees just losing their russet and purple leaves.

Edward opened the massive front door to the sound of the knocker, promptly let out a great cry which reverberated through the house. His father, who had just returned from "The Doctor's Walk," was the first to reach him.

"My dear Charles! At long last! We've been waiting every day since the first of September for your arrival."

His sisters came flying down the broad staircase, hastily tying their dressing gowns. Their faces were a blur as they all tried to embrace and kiss him at the same time. After a moment he stepped back to gaze at them. They did not appear to have changed perceptibly over the five years: Caroline, at thirty-six, seemed to have rather deepened frown lines in her forehead yet her thick, glossy black hair had given nothing to the graying years; tall, high-spirited Susan had lost little of her beauty, though perhaps a touch of gold had been minted out of her shoulder-length tresses. The largest change was in Katty, who had matured from girl into woman. Her pert face was resolute. Charles thought the change became her, and told her so. His sisters had written that Katty was "junkety," going on visits to friends' homes, accepting invitations to balls, bazaars. She had had no offer of marriage . . . which made her not the least unhappy.

They all made an effort to hold back the welcoming tears but no one succeeded, not even Dr. Darwin, whom Charles had not seen cry since the death of his wife.

By now the staff had arrived. Annie exclaimed, "Mr. Charles, they didn't feed you good on that ship!" Joseph, the gardener, shook his hand warmly. Nancy, his old nurse, did not hesitate to hug him. Mark, his father's coachman, held by the hand his wife, the Darwin laundress whom he had married while Charles was away.

Practical Caroline asked:

"Charles, have you had breakfast?"

"The last time I can remember eating was yesterday morning in London."

Dr. Robert Darwin, seventy, and seeing few patients, was showing his age. He was bald, with only a patch of white above each ear. Frequent attacks of gout and lumbago had slowed his pace. The bottom half of his double chin had become a bit flaccid, yet he had lost few of his twenty-four stone (three hundred and forty pounds). His voice boomed through The Mount as heartily as ever.

"To the dining room, everyone! Annie, prepare the finest breakfast of your life for our prodigal son."

Charles took his regular seat at the right of his father at the mahogany table with its massive claw legs and was promptly assailed by the homely smell of beeswax. He gazed out of the window over the river

Severn and the green grazing fields with their munching Herefords. He wolfed his way through the steamed haddock, four boiled eggs, lamb kidneys and bacon, the triangular cuts of toast, mugs of hot coffee and milk poured simultaneously by Edward from silver pitchers.

His sisters gazed at him with misty-eyed satisfaction. Not one of them tried to eat. Erasmus seemed so little interested in the family that Charles was the brother in their lives. They had missed him sorely, as he knew from their letters; their love for him was very strong. As he settled back in the Chippendale chair, he cried:

"Sitting here, I have a sense of *déjà vu*. What happened before is repeating itself. I've never been away, and nothing has changed."

"One thing has," said Dr. Darwin.

"What is that, Father?"

"The shape of your head is quite altered."

Charles and the sisters were aghast for an instant, then burst out laughing.

Charles exclaimed:

"How could it not, with all the sights and materials I've crammed into it? Now the question is, do I have the key to unlock the treasure? And what do I do with it when I take it out of the storage bin?"

There was a moment of quiet, then Dr. Darwin leaned over, put his enormous hand over his son's lean one.

"Oh, I think you know the answer to that question. You also know what to do with your collections. Work hard, but never feel you have to rush. You have many years ahead to do the job that nature appears to have cut out for you."

Charles rose, hesitated, then kissed his father's brow.

He had been set free! His father had given him his life!

He next heard Katty cry:

"It would be nice if Edward would light a fire in the library. I'm sure Charles has stories to tell since he posted us his last letter from Brazil."

"The best of all possible news," he said. "I'm home to stay. Why don't we play a few games of whist before the fire? Then I'll really know I'm back in the bosom of the Darwins!"

At midmorning he went out to the backyard and shouted for Pincher. The dog came running and set off on their walk along the river, showing no more emotion or surprise than if he had walked with Charles the day before instead of five years earlier.

He spent nine days getting his land legs, gaining the pounds he had lost during the last heaving days on board H.M.S. *Beagle*, unpacking his gear and refreshing his clothing, luxuriating in the printed extract of his letters which he propped up on his bureau where he could see it most often. He wrote affectionate letters to his Uncle Jos Wedgwood, to William Owen at Woodhouse, to Professor Henslow and to Captain FitzRoy, who was still on board his ship in Falmouth and literally seething to get ashore to marry Mary O'Brien, the girl he had danced with at the farewell parties given for H.M.S. *Beagle* officers in Plymouth. Marianne, his oldest sister, came from nearby Overton with her four sons and her nine months' old daughter to welcome him.

Early the next morning Charles took a breakfast tray up to his father's spacious, many-windowed bedroom overlooking the river and green fields beyond. He poured coffee for them both, sat on the edge of the bed.

"Father, I've kept fairly accurate records of how much I spent during the journey. Would you like me to go over them with you?"

"I don't think that's necessary, Charles. You have been 'deuced clever,' to use your own phrase before you left, and spent only for constructive purposes."

"I'm glad you're not upset with me over the sums for expeditions into the interior. According to my figures, including the guns, telescope, microscope and compass I bought before we sailed, I've drawn a little over nine hundred pounds in the five years. I hope to prove to you that the money was well spent."

"My dear young son, I have celebrated my seventieth birthday; I'm planning to enjoy my last years and not get upset by anybody or anything. Your clothes look worn out, even if you don't. If you mean to be a geologist in the Adam Sedgwick tradition, you're going to need several new outfits of clothing. We can't have you disgracing the Darwin escutcheon. Draw what you must to continue your work. Your four hundred pounds allowance will be continued."

A warm glow of happiness settled over father and son. His father had in effect called him a scientist. And seemed enormously pleased by the transition. Dr. Darwin read the flow of thoughts behind his son's eyes and enjoyed the generosity of his own gesture.

"The past is gone, Charles. You've written a whole new text. Your five years of travel and work are the equivalent of the highest degree you could have earned at Cambridge. Now we, the girls and I, will be watching you with affectionate interest to see how it turns out."

He left in the stables of the Red Lion Inn the horse and carriage which he had been obliged to rent at Brickhill, and walked with his suitcase directly to the Henslow home in Cambridge where he had been invited to stay. The three-story dwelling of tan brick on Regent Street, with its bow windows and blue stone-arched doorway, seemed unchanged through weathering. The family itself had increased to three girls and two boys. He gave the door knocker its five fast knocks, then two slow ones. Harriet and John Henslow threw open their front door together and he was gathered into their familial arms. John Henslow's big, sympathetic face was more appealing than ever. The gray streaking through his thick curly hair made him appear more attractive at forty than he had been as a younger man.

It was a happy reunion. The two older children remembered him; he had to be made known to the three younger ones. The Friday evening soirees had been abandoned because of the rather steady flow of children, but Henslow had not been idle. He had just published *Principles of Descriptive and Physiological Botany*, which was being declared the authority in the field. He had the living of Cholsey-cum-Moulsford in Berkshire which paid him an extra three hundred and forty pounds per year. It was a trip of a hundred miles but Henslow took his family each summer to the comfortable parsonage, some fourteen miles from Oxford, where they stayed during the long Cambridge vacation. He no longer had to give private tutoring lessons for six hours a day in order to support them.

After supper the two men settled into the worn, oversized chairs in the library. Henslow put fresh logs on the fire, stirred it around ritualistically.

"My dear Henslow, I have so longed to see you," Charles declared. "You have been the kindest friend to me that ever man possessed. I am, and always will be, most truly obliged."

"I put you on H.M.S. *Beagle*. It was my responsibility to help you get off with your collections intact. When will I be able to see your plants from the Galápagos Islands?"

"As soon as Captain FitzRoy brings the ship up to Greenwich. I want to take the burden of those boxes off your hands, and I want to get to work as quickly as possible on my geology book."

"Come to Cambridge for a stay, arrange and group together the different families, then wait until people who are already working in the different branches may want specimens. By the by, Sedgwick and I signed your certificate for the Geological Society last month. You are to be proposed as a fellow on November 2. You should be elected shortly thereafter."

Harriet Henslow's brother, Leonard Jenyns, came in from his parsonage on the border of the Fens to spend the day. Here was the second of the two men who had been offered the job as naturalist on H.M.S. *Beagle*, and because of family and professional obligations had had to refuse. Neither man had an ounce of envy or spite in him; they were gratified that his trip had been fruitful. Jenyns's bushy whiskers came below his chin but he remained as Charles remembered him, with kindly, heavy-lidded eyes which missed little in the way of nature about him.

"I've brought you a copy of my new book, just published by the Cambridge University Press, the *Manual of British Vertebrate Animals*. It's not for me to speak of the merits of my own production but the leading zoologists are giving it a good character. I've delved into the habits of the animals as distinguished from their description, so I'm afraid it will attract only the scientific naturalists. . . ."

"We are neither of us Charles Dickens putting out *Pickwick Papers* installments," Charles ventured.

The next morning Henslow took him through his basement. Charles's chest heaved as the five years on the *Beagle* washed over him. He gazed at the assortment of boxes, barrels, crates; his eyes became filled with pictures of the seas, mountains, deserts he had adventured in, his ears filled with the sounds of endless market places and languages, of Carpenter May's hammering the first crates; Lieutenant Wickham crying for him to get his messy catch off his clean decks. . . .

The basement rooms were cool but dry; they smelled like a combination of an early morning fish market and a well-populated aviary. Henslow gave Charles a running commentary on everything from his marine life to his rock samples, including a compliment on his "gorgeous, extraordinary fishes, so well packed in spirits."

"The fossils, as you know, I shipped to Mr. Clift at Surgeons Hall in London to repair and preserve. Your cargo of skins was delayed but everything was aired and is safe. I was in the country when these sweepings of the granary arrived, and some of the seeds spoiled before I could get them planted. For goodness' sake, what is this number 233? It looks like the remains of an electrical explosion, a mere mass of soot. However you preserved your birds, reptiles, plants and ferns quite well. We've lost only an excellent crab, which has none of its legs, and this one bird which had its tail feathers crumpled."

Charles threw an arm fondly around his mentor's shoulder.

"No one else in the world would have examined and stored all these thousands of specimens, my dear Henslow."

"I'm bringing up five children," Henslow replied, gruffly, to hide his feelings. "Why not a sixth?"


2.


Erasmus welcomed him to his quarters at 43 Great Marlborough Street in London. Charles had taken the *Star* from Cambridge, then rode an omnibus from the Bell Sauvage on Ludgate Hill and was sur-

prised to find himself plunged into one of the most colorful and informal areas of the city, the houses posed in crazy juxtaposition to each
other, streets at all angles, shops, offices painted in bright, almost
garrish colors.

"It's bohemian, pure and simple," Charles exclaimed.

Even the people on the streets looked different, by no means dressed
in the staid and proper British businessman's style. Rather they were
the gypsies of London society, a number of them painters in corduroy
trousers and coats, reminding him of Augustus Earle. Others, writers or
actors, talked animatedly, gesticulating, walking with a slouch or stroll-
ing carefree.

"Ras has found himself an artists' colony right off Oxford Circus,
and a few doors away from expensive Cavendish Square."

The brothers voiced their pleasure at being together after five years,
then stood apart studying what the passage of time had wrought.

"My God, how you have filled out," exclaimed Erasmus. "And your
head has changed its shape. Or maybe it's your face that is fuller. And
your eyes, merciful heaven, when I looked into them last I saw Fanny
Owen or the latest partridge you had shot. Now they're enormous with
—what is it?—knowledge, ambition, plans . . . ?"

"Work, my dear Ras. That's what my eyes and head are stuffed with.
But let me look at you: a little less hair on your brow but still handsome in a roguish fashion. What are you doing in your dressing gown at
one in the afternoon?"

"I'm enjoying life and letting life enjoy me. I have found out that
taking one's pleasure, usually called idleness, is the busiest thing in the
world. I have no wife, mistress, children or other responsibility except
to be dressed for high tea, when my friends start to drift in. Today you
will meet Thomas Carlyle and his wife Jane; Harriet Martineau, the literary rage of London; the great wit and divine, Sydney Smith . . ."

"Good for you, Ras. You've been collecting literary lions while I've
been collecting crabs and snakes."

Erasmus was staring at him with a strange expression.

"You know, Gas, I do believe you're shorter than when you left!"

"Nonsense, men don't start shrinking until they're sixty or seventy
and I'm four months short of twenty-eight. I was an even six feet when
I left and I'm an even six feet right this moment."

"Want to wager? I saw that hammock of yours in the poop cabin.
Come into the back room. I have a tape."

Erasmus was right. The tape showed that Charles stood five feet,
eleven and three eighths inches in his bare feet.

"Well, damme," Charles whispered; "that *Beagle* voyage cost me more than half an inch in height. I can't give that half inch away for nothing."

He started immediately to make his rounds of museums and scientists. His first forays were disappointing; he met scarcely anyone who wished to possess the naturalist treasures he had gathered. William Yarrell, who had been so helpful five years before, was having business complications, and in addition was attempting to distribute his new book, *History of British Fishes*. Charles called at Yarrell's bookstore twice before deciding that it was selfish to plague him with his own concerns. Thomas Bell, just appointed professor of zoology at King's College, whom Charles hoped to interest in his reptiles, let it be known that he was so much occupied that there was no chance of his wishing for specimens. The Zoological Museum, which he had visited at 33 Bruton Street, had upwards of a thousand specimens still unmounted. He had no respect for the British Museum; his materials would simply be dumped there, neglected or lost. He learned that no collection cared to receive unnamed specimens.

"When I got back to England," he told Erasmus, "I thought I had finished my job. Now I know I have barely started."

"That's what I don't like about work," Erasmus replied; "it has a tendency to perpetuate itself."

"I'll simply have to go back to Cambridge where I can get help in identifying the collection."

He was invited by George Waterhouse, who had recently been named curator of the Zoological Society, to attend an evening meeting. The first man to greet him when he entered the building just off Berkeley Square was John Gould, long-time taxidermist of the Society, who expressed an interest in seeing his birds. That was the last pleasant experience of the evening, for when the members began reading their papers they snarled at each other. He soon found himself out of patience with the zoologists, and what he considered their quarrelsome spirit. The Society would have no desire for his zoological collections; whereas Professor Henslow had wished Charles had collected even more botanical specimens! Just before departing from the hot, fur-flying lecture room, he thought:

"I wish I had known that the botanists cared so much and the zoologists so little; the proportional number of specimens in the two branches should have had a very different appearance."

But just as the rising sun changes the darkness to light, and the ocean tides reverse themselves, sweeping in and out of shore, so Charles's fortunes made a magnetic shift of one hundred and eighty degrees. He had risen early and just finished dressing when he heard a knocking at

Erasmus's door. He was astonished to see the craggy figure and face of Adam Sedgwick.

"Located your address yesterday and walked here in as direct a line as the mountain goat traveling uphill," exclaimed Sedgwick.

"My dear Professor, what a great pleasure. You taught me more than you knew on that trip through North Wales."

"Knowledge pours out of me like water out of a sieve. Come along, we'll find the best breakfast in London, and you can take me on your tour through the Andes."

"I'd be delighted. And if your ears are still holding up, I'd like to tell you about my proposed geology book."

They spent hours over the breakfast table. Sedgwick was past fifty now, handsome, virile, full of stories and quotations . . . and still complaining about his rheumatism. During Charles's stay at The Mount, Susan had only mentioned Adam Sedgwick in passing. He mentioned her not at all. Charles was resigned.

"What is important now," concluded Sedgwick, "is that I arrange for you to meet Charles Lyell. He can guide you through any forest of facts. Do you know what he wrote to me last December? 'How I long for the return of Darwin. I hope you do not mean to monopolize him at Cambridge.' "

Charles felt that his mouth had dropped open; it had not, it was just his stupefaction. His voice when he spoke sounded hollow, though coming from deep down in his chest.

"Charles Lyell wrote that to you? But how . . . why . . . ?"

"He liked what Henslow and I published from your letters. He thinks you may have a fresh grasp on geology."

The simple yet cordial note, written in a woman's hand, but signed by Charles Lyell, invited him to drop in any time the following afternoon. He donned the handsome dark waistcoat with its high stiff collar and flaring lapels, the double-breasted jacket and strapped trousers which his tailors, Hamilton and Kimpton on the Strand, had just made for him; the new boots cut to measure by Howell. Nancy had sent down a couple of the white shirts she so lovingly sewed for him; Erasmus lent him one of his quieter cravats. He was freshly shaved, with only the long light sideburns reminiscent of the full beard of Patagonia. His reddish-gold hair was brushed back smartly from a part low on the left side. Erasmus's brown eyes lighted with pleasure.

"Handsome devil, aren't you! Please dress that well for my guests, whom you've been too busy to meet as yet."

"Another time, Ras. Right now I have to meet the 'Great Men of Science.' I desperately need help with my collection."

It was not a long walk to 16 Hart Street, a small brick town house of three stories which Lyell rented, off Bloomsbury Square, an unfashionable neighborhood. Lyell's fellow scientists wondered why he, whose family was wealthy, and his wife Mary, who was the daughter of a wealthy Edinburgh merchant, chose to live so simply, without horses or carriage, and without a retinue of servants.

Charles hesitated in front of the Hart Street home for a moment, then raised the knocker and was welcomed at once by Charles Lyell himself, thirty-nine years old, long-legged, with worn-looking eyes.

"My dear Darwin, what a pleasure this is. I've been waiting for your return. Do come in. May I introduce my wife, Mary. She does all my social correspondence, as you probably noticed from the note you received yesterday."

Lyell ushered Charles into a fair-sized drawing room. He had brought the furniture he had used while a bachelor in Raymond Buildings, the remainder had come from his father-in-law, Leonard Horner. The effect was a jumble but the Lyells cared little about making an impression. The walls had been recently repapered; they had a fresh look about them.

"It's a nice airy situation, as near to Somerset House and the Athenaeum as my purse will permit," said Lyell.

Charles studied his prospective friend. The broad sideburns growing close to the corners of his mouth, the clean-shaven face and smooth chin; the big head becoming a touch bald, hair turning a tousled gray at the temples. His eyes may have been poor in looking out but they were superb for anyone looking into them: a warm gray with tawny specks. His strong, jutting nose was not able to overshadow a slender and sensitive mouth.

Mary Horner Lyell had a patrician head, flawless skin, a deep bosom, fine-textured nut-brown hair which she swept back past the corner of her eyes to cover all but the pearl-earringed lobes of her ears. She invited Charles to take the armchair across from Lyell's littered desk, asked if he liked his sherry sweet or dry. She had been only twenty-three when she married Lyell, four years before, had become his traveling companion when they went abroad to France or Germany for geological studies and, to save his weakened eyes for reading, his amanuensis.

"Professor Henslow tells me that you are a beetle enthusiast," said Lyell. "Formed a Beetle Club at Cambridge. In fact, found a totally rare beetle which Stephen's *Illustrations of British Insects* lists with the magic words 'Captured by C. Darwin, Esq.' "

Charles blushed a high red.

"That was the first time I saw my name in print. More intoxicating than brandy."

"But not the last, I'll wager. I too entered science through insects. I was taken home to Hampshire from school for health reasons. My father, a short time before, had taken up the study of entomology, a fit which lasted only long enough to induce him to purchase some books on the subject. At first I confined my attention to butterflies, moths, the like, as the most beautiful, but I soon became fond of watching the singular habits of the aquatic insects and used to sit whole mornings by a pond feeding them flies, and catching them if I could. . . .

"Now, tell me what your plans are. I want to help in any and every way."

Charles was shy about revealing his intentions in the presence of the master geologist. He told Lyell that he had filled some nine hundred pages of a geology notebook, in addition to the geology he had written into his diary.

"I made long overland trips through the pampas and into the Andes. It is one of my great hopes, after I finish transcribing my journal, that I may write a book on the geology of South America."

Lyell approved.

"No one has a monopoly on geology. The more books we get, particularly those that are accurately observed, the stronger our science will grow. One thing I envy you is your opportunity to have been out to Tahiti and the other tropical atolls where you could make a firsthand study of the coral reefs. I have never seen corals in great abundance. Tell me about them."

Charles scanned Lyell's face seriously, studying him for several moments. This was his first meeting with a man whom he found gracious and liked enormously, and with whom he apparently was going to have a fruitful relationship. Could he offend him by revealing what he had found on the Keeling Islands? His confidence that he now knew how coral atolls were formed, and that it was not as Lyell had written?

He decided to tell the truth, that it would be unworthy of him to truckle.

"With respect, may I tell you my theory about corals? It differs from your view that atolls are built on the rims of submerged volcanic craters. Perhaps you will point out its weaknesses or fallacies."

Lyell's compassionate eyes grew somber.

"Fire away."

Ready to become absorbed in thought, Lyell took the strange position of resting his head on the seat of a chair while still standing, his eyes closed tight, a contortionist's art for so tall a man; it sent the blood rushing to his head. Charles proceeded step by step, telling of his observations of the reefs and lagoons in the South Seas, particularly Tahiti, then his controlled experiments in the Keeling Islands where he proved to his own satisfaction that corals could live only in warm water, the polyps thriving on the seaward side from which they took nourishment; that they could not exist below a one-hundred and twenty- to one-hundred and eighty-foot level.

"In no instance, Mr. Lyell, was there a volcano rim involved. Nor does it seem to me that a volcano rim can be as many miles long as it is broad as at Bow Atoll. No crater can be sixty miles long as at Menchikov Island. The volcano theory will not explain the existence of the New Caledonia barrier reef, which is four hundred miles long, or the Great Barrier Reef of Australia, which is twelve hundred miles long. And, considering the depths at which coral polyps must live, it is impossible to believe that submarine volcanoes raised the rims of their craters to within one hundred and twenty feet of the surface of the sea over vast stretches of ocean. It is my theory that it is not volcanic craters under the surface of the ocean that form the base of the coral structure but submerged mountain ranges, continents that once had their peaks above the surface and, gradually subsiding, provided a foundation for the growth of the polyps."

When Charles finished, there was a silence while Lyell remained with his face on the chair, digesting the points of departure. Mary Lyell sat quietly in a far corner, watching her husband. After what seemed an endless time, Lyell sprang up to his full height and cried:

"I am overcome with delight!"

Whereupon he danced about the drawing room, throwing himself into the wildest postures. Mary said quietly to Charles, who was standing in the center of the room unable to believe his eyes:

"My husband always gives this demonstration when he is excessively pleased."

Lyell ceased his gyrations, pumped Charles's hand in congratulations, crying:

"I am very full of your new theory of coral islands. I shall urge William Whewell, who takes my place as president of the Geological Society next February, to make you read it at our next meeting."

"Mr. Lyell, I must exclaim that you are a man of astonishing good will and hearty sympathy to beginning amateurs such as myself."

"In matters of science I proceed with caution. Had I not seen your case so clearly, I would have advanced all possible objections. My training as a lawyer at Lincoln's Inn taught me that. Now I see that I must give up my volcanic-crater theory forever, though it costs me a pang, for it accounted for so much."

Lyell also wanted to hear stories about the zoological collection. Charles described it in some detail. He then thought it would be polite to excuse himself. Lyell exclaimed:

"This afternoon has been a veritable cornucopia of science. You must come on Saturday at eight for a tea party. I'll invite Richard Owen. He's just been appointed Hunterian professor in anatomy and physiology at the Royal College of Surgeons. He's one of the best men in London to advise you about the disposition and publication of your zoology."

"I must go to Greenwich on Saturday morning to collect the rest of my specimens, including the plants from the Galápagos Islands, and my scientific instruments. But I'll assuredly be back in time."

3.

It was a happy reunion with his friends on H.M.S. *Beagle*, for Captain FitzRoy had already been accepted by Mary O'Brien, and they were planning an early marriage. Lieutenant James Sulivan had been accepted by Admiral Young's daughter; they were planning to be married in January of 1837. Lieutenant Wickham was happy because he had intimations from the Admiralty that he would be appointed to the command of H.M.S. *Beagle* on its next surveying journey. John Dring, who had come on board as acting purser at Valparaíso, introduced Charles to an agent who agreed to ship Charles's last four boxes to Professor Henslow on *Marsh's Wagon*. Charles decided not to risk his Galápagos plants; he carried them into London himself and then sent them to Henslow on the *Fly Coach*.

That evening he attended the party given by the Lyells. Here he met Richard Owen, five years older than himself, with large eyes and a swath of jet-black hair combed close to his aristocratic head. He had been educated in Edinburgh, completed his medical course at St. Bartholomew's in London, accepted a position as assistant to William Clift, conservator of the museum of the College of Surgeons, married Clift's daughter, prepared an important series of catalogues at the Royal College and, dissecting the animals that died in the Zoological Society's gardens, became an expert. He had a cool standoffish nature but did say, quietly:

"I've seen the mammal fossils you sent home from South America, Mr. Darwin. My father-in-law, Mr. Clift, is impressed by them. He says that a couple of your heads fit the ancient bones he has collected before."

"Since Mr. Clift finds them valuable, I should very much like to contribute them to the museum."

"As for myself," Owen continued, "when your collection is ready, I should very much like to dissect your animals."

Charles had visions of having acquired a collaborator in the zoology publishing plan he was beginning to hatch, but had better sense than to say so. Instead he replied:

"They will be ready in a few months, catalogued and classified."

Lyell then introduced him to Roderick Murchison, a geologist and Sedgwick's and Lyell's collaborator on expeditions to North Wales and abroad. Murchison had degrees from both Oxford and Cambridge. Charles found himself grasping the hand of a tall, wiry, muscular man with a commanding presence.

"So you're the young man my two companions speak so highly of."

Mary Lyell's tea party turned out to be a light supper. The group helped themselves from the dining-room sideboard; there was a kedgeree (fish in rice), scrambled eggs with bacon, tea and a chocolate blancmange. Everyone wanted stories about places they had not been: the Andes, Patagonia, Tierra del Fuego, New Zealand, Keeling Islands, the Cape of Good Hope; and about their good friend, Sir John Herschel, whom Lyell had urged to take the presidency of the Royal Society. Instead he had fled to the tip of Africa. The discussion got around to where Charles should do his work. Lyell responded:

"London is the best place when you start to write your geology. But right now, Cambridge. There you can concentrate."

"You are spurring a willing horse," said Charles with a grin.

William Yarrell, realizing that he had been brusque with Charles, sent him a note inviting him to dinner at the Linnean Society the following evening. The Linnean Society was one of the most prestigious in the life of British scientists, having been founded by royal charter in 1788. Yarrell picked him up in a gig and took him down Oxford Street to the handsome dark stone building in Soho Square.

"Here you'll meet all the Great Men," Yarrell told him as they entered the door with its white stone curving arch.

The first of them was Professor Thomas Bell, fifty-six, but youthful and easygoing. He had come up through dental surgery at Guy's Hospital, had been attracted to zoology, and was now completing his volume to be called A History of British Quadrupeds.

"Naturally I'm interested in your crustaceans and reptiles, Mr. Darwin. I can't imagine who could have told you I was too engaged. I'm fascinated to see what you've gathered around the world."

Charles sipped his sherry, told Bell of his budding idea:

"As soon as I get my specimens separated, I'd like to plan for a series of books on fossil mammals, birds, fish, reptiles, plants, each done by an expert in the field . . . once they become convinced the specimens are new and interesting. I will do the geology myself."

"Capital! I might just be your man for the reptiles."

The next day Lyell took him in a hansom cab to dine at the Geological Society, which had its spacious quarters in Somerset House, off the Strand. Charles was awed by the building's noble entrance: two wide, terraced, red and gray marble-roofed walks, each with eight fluted columns and, in the center, an ample carriageway. Once inside, he saw that the complex had two very long three-storied buildings, each graced with a six-columned entrance; straight ahead was the connecting building, just above the river Thames.

Lyell paid off the cabby. They walked through the high-ceilinged entrance hall with its marble columns and semicircular many-paned windows.

"I'm impressed," Charles murmured. "Our architects certainly built on the grand scale."

"Why not?" replied Lyell heartily. "Aren't we a grand nation? Don't we mean to conquer the world? Our Geological Society quarters are grand as well. You're going to enjoy working and meeting here."

He was welcomed by William Clift, who thanked him for the gift of his fossils. William Whewell, the incoming president, shook his hand, saying, "I well remember our walks home from Henslow's after his Friday evenings. Congratulations on your nomination. We should have you voted in by the end of the year."

Whewell and Lyell took turns introducing him to the members who had come to dine together; for the Society was known to have an excellent chef and wine cellar. He was offered a glass of sherry from a silver tray which a butler was circulating. From what Charles could observe in the library, and then in the paneled dining room, these men liked and respected each other. He recalled the disputatious evening at the Zoological Society, asked Lyell, sitting next to him at the massive mahogany table:

"Why is it that men who work with fishes, birds, insects, reptiles, dislike each other and quarrel, while the men who explore mountain ranges and gather minerals behave like gentlemen?"

Lyell laughed:

"It's all the climbing that does it, Darwin. Those long expeditions into the Alps, the Pyrenees, the Apennines, North Wales, strengthen our legs and our psyches."

When he returned to Great Marlborough Street he found Erasmus with his long nose slightly out of joint because Charles had not yet been home of an evening to meet his literary friends. He muttered:

"Appears to me, Gas, that these geologists have got you hooked as thoroughly as some of those big fish you caught in the Galápagos. Are you happy?"

"As our cousin Emma says, 'Happiness is like heaven, more a state than a place.' Yes, the geologists have accepted me; there is nothing like a little vanity to buoy the spirits."

He had been home for over a month and had not yet visited his Wedgwood family at Maer Hall. Since there was nothing more he could do in London until his collections were ready, he packed and decided to go directly to Maer. He carried with him his eight-hundred-page diary.

He took the Liverpool *Royal Mail* coach to Newcastle-under-Lyme, an all-night trip, refreshed himself at an inn, rented a horse to carry him the remaining miles. A tolerably deep snow covered the flowering bushes, the multilimbed Spanish chestnuts. The limes, elms, oaks and copper beech stood out white against the late autumnal sky; a few wild ducks were paddling about the fresh spring lake. On the hill opposite cattle were trying to graze through the snow under the green beech and scarlet oak. A sigh of accumulated tension escaped him.

He found Josiah Wedgwood in his library. The two men threw their arms about each other.

"Uncle Jos, my First Lord of the Admiralty!"

"And you are the embodiment of my brother Tom."

When Charles stepped back he found Josiah much aged, yet he was only sixty-seven.

"At the moment I am fatigued, Charles; perhaps from my two tumultuous terms in Parliament, living away from home. . . ."

There was a cry of joy from the stairway. Emma burst into the room, curls flying.

"Charles, at last! We've been waiting every hour for your arrival."

They found themselves in an embrace of reunion not at all cousinly. When they separated, their feelings went skittering between astonishment and awe. They sat side by side on the leather divan.

"We all thought we ought to get up a little knowledge for you," Emma said; "but I took to no deeper study than Captain Head's gallop, which I had never read before."

"*Rapid Journeys Across the Pampas*," murmured Charles, grinning. "Quite a lot too rapid. I had one of Head's guides to make trail for me along the Río Paraná."

"Charles, I do hope you brought your diary. Your sister Caroline—she's here by the by—has told us about some of your adventures."

"Are she and your reluctant brother Joe making any substantial progress?"

"We keep hoping." Emma smiled conspiratorially. "Did you get any sleep on that Liverpool *Royal Mail?*"

"No. Unfortunately my legs are too long. No place to put them."

Uncle Jos volunteered, "Your old bedroom is prepared for you. Emma will have some food and hot chocolate sent up. Sleep soundly, for we have been very handsome in inviting all the outlyers of the family to meet you."

"How is Aunt Bessy faring?"

"Badly, Charles. We agonize for her and with her."

"I'll hold her hand for a while."

It was late afternoon before he awakened, refreshed. Hot water was brought up, he sponged, shaved, then donned his smart new clothes and boots. When he came downstairs he heard Emma playing the pianoforte. A picture flashed into his mind of the last time he had visited Maer and heard the Doveleys singing duets. It was over four years now since Fanny's death. He thought:

"I must let Emma know, without kindling fresh sorrow, how badly I felt for her when I received the news in Montevideo."

In the drawing room he was immediately besieged, his sister Caroline reaching him first. Joe Wedgwood wrung his hand. Elizabeth Wedgwood kissed him; Harry and Frank Wedgwood had ridden over with their wives and children. Dr. Henry Holland was also there, with his second wife, Saba Smith. It was in this room that Dr. Holland had advised him to refuse the *Beagle* voyage because no details were spelled out and Charles would be in servitude to the ship's beck and call. The only one missing was his good friend Charlotte Wedgwood, the artist, who had married the Rev. Charles Langton. They had waited for his arrival for two days and then had had to go home.

The family plied him with questions without mercy. Emma linked her arm through his, whispered:

"Charles, I've asked that supper be served at six. That will give us a long evening to hear you read from your journal."

Charles put his arm lightly around her waist.

"What has happened to our Little Miss Slip-Slop? Apparently you're managing Maer Hall these days. I must say the house never looked more beautiful."

Emma flushed with pleasure.

"Elizabeth and I divide up the jobs. It's strange how one's attitudes change when one takes on responsibilities."

When they had finished a festive meal of roast lamb, applesauce and a treacle tart served by candlelight, Uncle Jos suggested they repair to the library. The wicks in the paraffin oil lamps had been trimmed and raised high. The quite large lampshades of milk glass, clear alabaster and saffron, created pools of congenial light. Josiah insisted that Charles take the leather chair in which he himself spent the better part of his life reading. When everyone was seated Charles unwrapped the stout packing in which he protected his diary. When he exhibited the seven hundred and seventy-nine pages there were gasps of astonishment.

"I am going to choose what I think are some of the more colorful passages."

The room was utterly still. Charles's voice was pleasant to listen to, with variation of tone and excellent articulation. He started with the pages early on: the luxuriance of the Brazilian jungle; the incredible setting of Rio de Janeiro; the moon shining on the glassy waters when they were becalmed; the schools of porpoises crossing the bow of their vessel; the luminous sea with the vessel driving between two billows of liquid phosphorescence; the ferociousness of the waves and wind at Cape Horn, the savages of Tierra del Fuego and their failure to leave a missionary there; his description of the gauchos and their independent way of life; the catastrophic earthquake at Concepción; his twenty-three-day trip with Mariano Gonzales through the staggering ranges of the Andes; the eccentricities and lavish wild life of the Galápagos Islands, where man could see nature exactly as it was thousands of years before; the beauty of the wildly colored coral reefs and the fish that lived among them. . . .

It was midnight when he finished his excerpts. Between scenes there was little whispering; no one broke the mood by asking questions. He was heartily complimented.

"How long have I been reading?" he asked.

"About four hours."

"The rest of the material is no better and no worse."

He explained that Captain FitzRoy had asked permission to interweave the journal into his own publication.

Dr. Henry Holland spoke up, though not unkindly.

"My dear Charles, a diary is always a diversion while cut off from home. But its value ends there. I must in all honesty tell you that those jottings are not worth publishing. I am an experienced judge of travel literature; there is nothing you have read us that is amusing or interesting."

A hush fell over the library, a silence that could have been cut with a knife. Everyone felt it except Dr. Holland, who began a story of one of his own travel adventures. His wife, Saba, was more sensitive. She went to her husband's side, said:

"Dear, it has grown late. Might we retire?"

With the Hollands gone, the room broke into an uproar:

". . . I don't believe he's any judge. . . . He didn't want you to go on the trip in the first place. . . . You bring everything to life: the land, the sea, the peoples of those exotic countries. . . ." From Emma:

"I'm convinced it will make a beautiful book." There were several murmurs of "Hear! Hear!"

Charles turned to his Uncle Jos. Josiah Wedgwood's eyes were flashing; he looked twenty years younger than he had that morning.

"Charles, you must not allow your journal to be mixed in with Captain FitzRoy's. That would destroy it. You have accomplished something important here. Every phase of the naturalist's science is movingly portrayed. In addition you have observed as an anthropologist by studying the life and nature of distant races. It is splendid."

Charles kissed his uncle and Emma, both. Too emotionally overwrought to speak, he bowed his "good night," went upstairs and to bed . . . to stare sightlessly at the ceiling until dawn.

After a couple of days at Maer Hall, he and Caroline rode straight west some twenty-five miles to Overton to visit with their sister Marianne. Charles had never been close to the Parkers but he had sometimes ridden the twenty miles to visit his nephews, Marianne's four sons. He especially liked eleven-year-old Packy, who had studied geography by following his uncle around the world.

He had promised the family a two-week stay at The Mount before leaving for Cambridge and plunging into what could be a year or two of work on his specimens, journal, geology of South America. He wanted a quiet stay but his father and sisters insisted on giving "welcome home" parties and taking him on calls to friends in Shrewsbury and outlying areas of Shropshire, much of the fortnight "grievously destroyed by visits to stupid people who neither cared for me, nor I for them," he mourned. He did not complain; his father and sisters were so proud of him, eager to show him off, the least he could do was be amiable. He mimicked his younger years when he had little on his mind but beetles and shooting, when to be sociable was an indigenous part of his character.

He knew what had happened to him! He was desperately eager to begin *work*. Work could suck more blood out of a man than the benchuca bug in Luxan.

4.

He needed considerable space to house his several thousand specimens and could not impose on the already crowded Henslow home. His friends among the fellows of Christ's College invited him to dinner and urged him to lease rooms in the college for the academic year.

"I don't know how long I'll be here," he responded. "What I must find are quarters that I can take by the month, with the few basic pieces of furniture I need."

He found just that on a charming cul-de-sac, Fitzwilliam Street off Trumpington Road, closed at the top end by Tennis Court Lane. He guessed there were a dozen attached houses on each side of the quiet, genteel street, some with window boxes of colorful flowers. There was only a little variation in size, color or style. He went to the office of the Fitzwilliam House Trust, which owned many of the houses as well as the large piece of land across Trumpington on which the Fitzwilliam Museum would be built as soon as the architectural competition had been decided. The museum would house the same art collection which he had enjoyed in its original home, the Perse Grammar School close by.

"Pleased to have you as a tenant," the elderly renting clerk said; "but you'll be obliged to post three months' rent in advance. You may take immediate possession."

The narrow four-story house was dandy for his purposes. He exulted as he went through the rooms deciding what each would be used for. The basement room facing the street had one window and a fireplace, "good for a kitchen where Syms can cook my meals." The main floor had a fair-sized front room, its big window admitting the east sunlight. At the rear was the best room in the house, ten feet by twelve, with two windows on each side overlooking a garden. In the room was a bed and a knocked-about chest of drawers.

"My bedroom," he decided. "Syms can have one of the rooms off the hallway."

He ascended a hairpin curve of stairs, narrow and steep. Here he found two small front rooms. The one on the right could house his marine life, the crustaceans, jellyfish, sea slugs, fish; the other, his insects and reptiles. He would have Syms build trestle tables.

The larger rear room he decided to use for his animals, vertebrate and invertebrate. The next floor, the third, had two rooms with dormer windows.

"One for my birds," he murmured aloud; "the other for the botany collection: plants, flowers, grasses, seeds, the parasitic growths on the jungle trees."

His shells would go into one of the smaller side rooms. The attic had a sharply sloping roof, but there were again two rooms.

"My rocks, of course!" he exclaimed.

He summoned Syms Covington from his modest hostel, instructed him to hire a horse and wagon and two porters at the Red Lion Inn and meet him at the Henslows'.

It took Syms and the porters two days to repack and seal the twenty-

one crates, boxes and casks he had shipped to Henslow as well as the
five additional ones he had brought with him on the *Beagle*. Most of
the boxes had to be taken from the Henslow basement. The others
were in a storehouse on the edge of town. The ample-sized front room,
which he intended to use as a study and office for the editing of his
journal, took several of the heavier crates and smaller boxes. The two
storerooms behind the basement kitchen held several more, as did the
small room off the entrance hall. The two workmen managed to juggle
the lighter casks and boxes sideways up the steep, curving stairs. The
remaining ones were lined in a row, like wooden soldiers, along the
downstairs hallway.

"I'll empty these first," he reasoned, "so we can move around. Then
I'll tackle the crates in the front room. I'll buy a couple of inexpensive
baskets and use them to carry the smaller items upstairs. Covington has
already conquered these corkscrew stairs; and he can read my labeling."

Moving the thousands of specimens, so many of them in spirits, into
their designated rooms was a task and a half. While carrying the hundreds of geological specimens up to the attic, he cursed himself:

"Idiot! Why didn't I put the rocks in a ground-floor room? Then we
wouldn't have had to break our backs carting these confounded
weights up three flights."

But he was inordinately pleased to have reached this forward point.
Now his professional work could begin. Syms, a better fiddler than a
carpenter, had cut himself a couple of times while sawing rough planks
into sturdy workbenches; he had a low-key grin on his broad, flattened-
out face.

"Like a little museum, it is. Be a pleasure to work here, Mr. Darwin."

There was little that needed doing for the house itself, and nothing
that Charles would have wasted his time on. There were faded curtains
at the windows, linens and blankets for the two camp beds; but no
towels, pots, dishware. When he mentioned this to the Henslows over
supper that night, Harriet Henslow told him:

"We can surely spare you a pot and pan, a few dishes, spoons, forks."

"That's motherly of you, Harriet dear. But be sure you lend me the
most battered utensils you can find. I'll guarantee to return them in
much worse shape than they come out of your kitchen."

The following days and weeks proved to be an adventure in the
recapitulation of his five years around the world. He emptied the crates
of the small, dark blue jellyfish and sea squirts from his first sea-net
catches on the way from Teneriffe to St. Jago; the cuttlefish from the
Cape Verde Islands which had squirted him in the eye; spiders and the
insects from Rio de Janeiro: brilliantly colored butterflies, beetles, ants;
the strange reptile he and FitzRoy discovered outside Montevideo

which looked like a snake but had two small hind legs or fins. There
was his bird collection from Maldonado: parrots, turkey buzzards,
mockingbirds, woodpeckers; the duck which had been the cause of Edward Hellyer's death in the Falkland Islands; the animal skins including
the guanaco, remembering how at Port Desire he had seen two guanacos chasing each other and had shot the one in front; plants and
finches and fish from the Galápagos, each carefully identified by the island from which it had come. The comprehensive collection of rocks:
volcanic rocks from St. Jago; gravel mixed with recent shells from Bahía
Blanca where he had found his first fossils; specimens of lava from the
voyage up the Santa Cruz River. From the Andes excursion: pure white
gypsum from the Valle del Yeso, rocks from the summit where the air
had been so dry that the wooden handle of his hammer had shrunk; the
white, red, purple and green sedimentary rocks from the Uspallatas; the
black lava from the Galápagos. . . .

Syms brought him breakfast shortly after first light. Then, dressed in
their rough, warm, seagoing clothes, they worked with infinite care in
each box and crate, careful not to damage the slightest specimen;
grouping together the different families.

Once emptied, the box was set in its chosen room to serve as a bench
or table for the close-packed orderly rows of specimens. The hours fled
by. Charles commented to Syms:

"It's like traveling on land all the way. After that first moment when
we opened the box with the sea-net capture from Rio de Janeiro, *I
haven't been seasick once!*"

The first two weeks were leading into Christmas and Cambridge was
quiet, the faculty staff and students of the colleges away for the holidays. That suited Charles perfectly. After an early supper he turned to
his journal. He had written the diary with considerable care; his chief
labor now was to make an abstract of the more interesting scientific results. To this end he eliminated the first twenty-nine pages of the manuscript, everything relating to his sometime misery and heart palpitations in Plymouth during the two months of vexatious delay before the
winds allowed H.M.S. *Beagle* to sail out of the harbor.

He received a letter from Lyell confirming his election as a fellow of
the Geological Society and urging him to write a paper on a subject
they had discussed: Observations of Proofs of Recent Elevation on the
Coast of Chile. The paper was almost completely written in his comprehensive geological notebook; he had only to clarify and put the article
into more formal language. He kept it short, about six pages, and sent
it down by the *Royal Mail* to Lyell's house.

For relaxation he took an hour's walk with Henslow before supper. It
was cold along the Backs, passing Peterhouse, Queen's College, King's,

Clare, Trinity, St. John's. They bundled up in greatcoats, mufflers and Charles's woolen sea caps. They talked science, the wind blowing away phrases, but they did not mind. Charles told Henslow:

"I just received a letter from Lyell saying that he had read my paper with the greatest pleasure but that several passages require explanation. He wants me to come down to London on January 2 for half an hour of corrections, and then to read the paper at the Geological Society meeting."

"By all means do so!" Henslow exhorted, with so much emphasis that the wind could carry away not the tiniest syllable. "I'd like them to know not only the quality of your work but of your person, as well."

"I'll do it, of course. Lyell has also proposed me for the Athenaeum. He says I may dine at the club, if I like. There is no vacancy but I stand the first of those who are knocking at the door for admission."

"That is decidedly for the good. The Athenaeum is the best private club in London. There you'll meet scientists, literary men and artists of eminence, as well as noblemen and gentlemen, patrons of science, literature and the fine arts. You'll be a member in a matter of months, as soon as one of their elderly members goes to his reward."

His work on the journal became the more pleasurable when he received a letter from Robert FitzRoy bringing him the best possible news.

> While in London a few days since I consulted with Henry Colburn, a reputable publisher on Great Marlborough Street, about Captain King's Journal and my own. He recommended joint publication, one volume for King, another for you and a third for me. The profits, if any, to be divided into three equal portions. Shall I accept the offer, or wait and talk the matter over with you when we meet?

He ended with an affectionate salutation:

> I wish you a happy Christmas, my good Philos, ever sincerely your friend. . . .

He shot off an acceptance with the speed of the marines firing one of the *Beagle*'s cannons.

He reached Lyell's promptly at 5:00 P.M. as suggested, and spent half an hour rewriting sentences and rearranging paragraphs as he quickly saw how right Charles Lyell was in his every suggestion. At five-thirty he sat down at table with Mary Lyell's parents. Mr. Leonard Horner greeted Charles cordially; he had met him in Edinburgh at one of the meetings of the Plinian Society where Charles had read a paper, On the

Ova of the Flustra. Interested in this gangling, burgeoning lad of eighteen, Horner had taken Charles to a meeting of the Royal Society of Edinburgh.

Later that evening he went with Lyell and Horner to the Geological Society where he read his paper. It was the first time he had spoken in public since that Plinian Society meeting in Edinburgh, some ten years before. He was nervous as Mr. Lyell, president, introduced him but, once started reading about the elevation of the coast of Chile, he was back in South America and completely at ease. His voice, tight during the first sentences, became full-toned and precisely articulated as it filled the big lecture room of his peers.

He was well applauded. Lyell beamed. Though only twelve years younger than Lyell, Charles had become a surrogate son.

"Let's sail ourselves over to the Athenaeum. We'll take a glass together."

Charles had never been inside the club, founded in 1824 by Sir Walter Scott and Thomas Moore. The mansion, located on the northeast corner of Pall Mall, was almost deserted at this late hour. Charles was able to move through the elegant rooms and to spend a few moments in the book-rich library on the second floor. After a couple of glasses of brandy, just before the porter announced, "Closing time, gentlemen," Lyell leaned forward and said with considerable earnestness:

"Charles, you're launched now in the Society, and at the outset I must offer you some serious advice."

"I'm all ears."

"Don't accept any official scientific place if you can avoid it, and tell no one that I gave you this advice. I fought against the calamity of being president as long as I could. Work exclusively for yourself and for science for many years, and do not prematurely incur the honor or penalty of official dignities. There are people who may be profitably employed in such duties because they would not work if not so engaged. You are not one of these."

By the time he returned to Cambridge the term and the social season had begun. Charles was invited to numerous parties, many in his honor, one by Adam Sedgwick to repay the hospitality he had received at The Mount; another by George Peacock, newly elected Lowndean professor of astronomy, who, along with Henslow, had recommended him for the post of naturalist on H.M.S. *Beagle*. Except for the Sedgwick party, which ran well past midnight, Charles made the proviso that he be permitted to leave at ten in order to get in a couple of more hours on his journal before retiring. On Sunday mornings he went to Little St.

Mary's with the Henslows, or to hear the choir sing in King's College Chapel.

Aside from his work, his greatest pleasure came from the companionship of the fellows of Christ's College. Most of the officials whom he had known were still in office: the Master, the Rev. John Graham; the tutor, the assistant tutors. There were also fourteen fellows who had their own beautiful house at the back of the Fellows' Garden, with Milton's famous mulberry tree at its center. The Rev. Joseph Shaw, senior dean, invited him to join them for the evening meal in Hall. Charles exclaimed:

"I didn't know how deep an affection I had for the college until I was a couple of years at sea."

The following evening he entered the first quad just as the bell rang and the butler threw open the big wooden door announcing that dinner was served. The senior dean was waiting for him with a black gown. He sat at the high table on the dais. The room struck cold. He waited impatiently for the long grace to end. Sitting below him were the undergraduates and over sixty M.A.s in residence. At the end of the meal he was glad to move to the combination room where the faculty staff met for wine, walnuts and informal joshing. The room was right up from the dining hall, across the screening; a square room with lower, more intimate ceilings and a large fireplace which already had the room warm. There were two big windows with window seats overlooking the second quad and a long serving table set against the entrance wall with shining glasses and bowls of nuts.

Mr. Shaw cried, "I propose a bottle to celebrate the return of young Darwin."

"I too!" said the Master. "Yours is to be port as usual, Shaw? Then I propose a bottle of manzanilla."

Charles was moved by the depth of his reception. No one seemed surprised that he was back, nor did they seem to think that he would leave again.

It was the beginning of an extraordinarily happy period. He was invited to dine at the college several times a week, though he remained skinny and seemingly undernourished. After a few helpful glasses of wine in the combination room, he entered into the betting games, losing his first wager on the height of the ceiling from the floor.

"I shall pay my bottle this very night," he exclaimed.

The fellows began dropping in on him at the Fitzwilliam Street house to see his collections. He explained that he had been trying to think his way through the zoology of the *Beagle*.

"In London, Thomas Bell has agreed to look at my reptiles and crustaceans. Richard Owen, my fossil bones. John Gould, the birds. Only this morning Leonard Jenyns agreed to examine my fish. If I can find a way to raise a substantial amount of money for the color plates, I'm hopeful that each of these men will do a book on his findings."

The senior dean asked:

"Darwin, are you sensitive about your journal? I would relish to see a few pages."

"I would be honored. Please come with me."

An hour later Charles glanced up from his work to see the man gazing at him wide-eyed.

"Who would have suspected that 'The man who walks with Henslow,' only five years ago gathering toads in the Fens, can write like an angel?"

Charles blushed. When he crossed to the combination room the following evening he found himself a hero. All of this, of course, got back to John Henslow. When Charles was breakfasting with him the next Sunday morning before church, Henslow said gently:

"Charles, you're happy at Christ's, aren't you?"

"Extremely. They're a superb group."

"Do you think you might like to join them? . . . By becoming a permanent fellow, teaching and lecturing? The future is long and a man needs a power base. There's none better than here."

Charles felt as though the breath had been knocked out of him.

"Do you imagine they'd have me?"

Henslow smiled. "Perhaps not tomorrow morning when the eight o'clock bell rings. But when you've published your journal and geology of South America. A man who writes books intends primarily to instruct. Changing the subject, about the books you're planning for the zoology, why not apply to the Chancellor of the Exchequer for a grant? After all, it would be a culmination of the work accomplished by a Royal Navy ship. The Geological Society would back you, so would Sedgwick, Peacock and I. Please don't be timid. Try it."

Winter came down with a tremendous snow. For days there was slush in the roads. At night the moon shone with icy brilliance on the rooftops of Fitzwilliam Street. The house grew bitterly cold. Charles threw shovelfuls of coal to the back of the fireplace in his bedroom so that it would burn all night.

At the beginning of March he decided that this particular aspect of his work was finished. Professor Henslow took the botanical specimens, exclaiming with pleasure every time he found a plant intact with roots, flowers and leaves. Mineralogy professor William Miller asked if he could keep in Cambridge some of the rock samples. With the preserved fish safely in Jenyns's parish in Swaffham Bulbeck, he and Syms repacked the reptiles and crustaceans and sent them by *Marsh's Wagon* to Thomas Bell at the University of London. That left several of the rooms empty.

The Master of Christ's College, learning that Charles was about to depart for London, invited him to dinner. In the combination room he found all fourteen fellows as well as Professors Henslow and Sedgwick.

"I ask permission to present a bottle," Adam Sedgwick called. "I believe we all prefer claret these days."

Charles felt a perceptible change of mood. He was solemnly offered a cigar, which he lighted. He had picked up the habit from the gauchos of the pampas. The Master stood rather solemnly before the fireplace.

"Mr. Darwin, would you be so kind as to come forward?"

All eyes were riveted on him as he crossed the room and stood facing the blazing coals.

"Mr. Darwin, as titular head of Christ's College, and in earnest discussion with my colleagues, we have come to the conclusion that your work in the five years since you left our august halls has entitled you to the degree of Master of Arts. This is not an honorary degree. It has had to be earned. In the considered judgment of Christ's College, you have indeed well earned your higher degree. The scroll will be presented to you tomorrow in the Senate House."

Tears welled behind Charles's eyes.

"This is an honor of which I never dreamed. I shall cherish your good opinion of me and try to live up to it."

He got a good many poundings on the back. More bottles of wine were ordered, and drunk to his good health.

The next morning, while packing his valises, he received a note sent by the registrar of the university. The Master's degree had not been totally free. He was obliged to pay the government six pounds for stamp duty, and another five pounds four and six to the senior proctor of the university. He remarked to Henslow, wryly:

"I'll be lucky if I earn that sum back in royalties from my two books."

5.

Erasmus enjoyed an occasional outburst of energy. He spent hours scouring the neighborhood for Charles, bounding up and down flights of stairs, inspecting the layout of various flats, rejecting them as unsuited to his brother's needs. After several days of searching they found what Charles wanted, just a couple of doors down from Erasmus's house, at 36 Great Marlborough Street, over a shop. The flat had five rooms; the two facing Great Marlborough Street had blue curtains left from the last tenant, otherwise it was bare. The owner wanted something under one hundred pounds a year. Charles signed a paper, paid two months' rent in advance. He was troubled about the money it would take to furnish the place.

"Then don't. Furnish only two rooms, say your parlor-study and your bedroom."

Erasmus knew the neighborhood. He took Charles shopping for a desk, chairs, a comfortable sofa, inexpensive rugs against the London cold, used but respectable bookcases, a comfortable bed, a few sheets, blankets and pillows, a wardrobe for his clothes. His father had told him to let the luxuries go but never to deprive himself of the necessities. He gave Syms money with which to furnish the kitchen; if he was going to live as frugally as possible he would be obliged to eat at home.

He placed his books on the shelves, hung one Martens water color in his living room-study, the one of H.M.S. *Beagle* laid ashore at the mouth of the Santa Cruz River; the other in his bedroom, the scene of Tierra del Fuego with H.M.S. *Beagle* safely anchored in Ponsonby Sound. Erasmus loaned him two prints of the English countryside with its refreshing green fields. The rooms were beginning to look homelike.

"When you tire of Covington's cooking," said Erasmus, "my daily does a good mutton chop. There's always a bottle of champagne to make it taste better."

"Mutton chops and champagne! My last luncheon in Plymouth before the *Beagle* sailed. How life does go round in cycles."

Syms furnished the kitchen, bought himself a bed and small chest of drawers for one of the back rooms, settled into the role he enjoyed as servant and assistant. Charles rose early, shaved with his ebony-encased razor and white mug with its little blue flowers which he had brought from his room at The Mount. He had one of Syms's hearty breakfasts of porridge, a kipper, boiled eggs, brown bread and butter, then went to work on his journal. After the first week or two of dinner parties his social whirl quieted, to his infinite relief.

He went to the Zoological Society for a meeting with George Waterhouse, its curator, and John Gould, who had expressed an interest in the birds. While the three men had coffee together they came to an agreement that Charles's collection of bird skins, as well as his mammals, should be turned over to the Zoological Society where they would be cared for and put to use for scientific purposes. Charles was happy that they had found a proper home.

Before many weeks George Waterhouse agreed to write the material on the collection of mammals as well as some papers on the insects. John Gould, famous for his published volumes on the birds of Europe, brilliantly illustrated with lithographic plates made by his wife, Elizabeth, volunteered to do the work on Charles's unknown birds; Thomas Bell, professor of zoology at King's College, had been studying the reptiles.

"Fascinating collection, Darwin. You've picked up a dozen specimens I never knew existed."

"Then you'll do the book on the reptiles?"

Richard Owen informed Charles that he was no longer interested in the animals in spirits which he had asked to see. However he had been captivated by the fossil bones. That was the study he would like to prepare for the zoology series.

Charles's good fortune held. Word spread in the scientific world that young Charles Darwin had brought back as large, varied and interesting a collection in the natural sciences as had yet been collected by any world voyager. A specialist named M. J. Berkeley studied Charles's fungi and wrote several articles for the *Annals of Natural History;* G. B. Sowerby studied the shells and wrote up the material; Frederick William Hope, founder and past president of the Entomological Society, offered to research Charles's collection of insects.

During the month of May he read two more papers before the Geological Society, the first on the fossil bones of the Megatherium he had dug out of the cliffs at Punta Alta, the second on his theory of how corals were formed. The papers made a stir.

Now that he had his five contributors to the zoology project—Jenyns, Owen, Bell, Gould and Waterhouse—he tackled the problem of getting the monograph-books published. Since many plates would be required for the texts, and all of Gould's birds in color, he knew it would be difficult to find a publisher to risk the venture. John Gould had published his own books successfully. Charles dropped into the Gould house off Berkeley Square and asked about the process.

"It's simple, Darwin. The naturalists of London have taken a good deal of interest in your collections. Why not let them back you? By taking subscriptions. Publish the work in short installments, as long as the funds last; that way you will not lose money by it."

Charles took Gould's plan to William Yarrell, sitting at his desk in the middle of his bookshop. Yarrell exclaimed:

"I don't like the idea of you going around soliciting subscriptions."

"Do you think I should try Henslow's idea of applying to the Chancellor of the Exchequer for a grant?"

Yarrell sprang to his feet.

"Of course! The Treasury! You have now turned over your collections to our scientific societies. Your work was done for the British government; therefore it should pay the costs of your zoology of the *Beagle*."

"How does one approach the Chancellor of the Exchequer?"

"First you write up a précis of the plan. Then you take it to the Duke of Somerset, president of the Linnean, and Lord Derby, former president; and to William Whewell, president of the Geological. They will write letters for you. The five contributors are respected by the government, which also knows how expensive color plates and even black and white drawings are. Properly presented, you could get a grant of a thousand pounds."

He could feel his heart pounding in his chest.

"Mr. Yarrell, I hope you're a prophet."

The three men suggested to sponsor his grant were sympathetic but warned that those affairs had to go through channels; that he must be patient and keep the work going forward.

During the night of June 20, 1837, King William IV, seventy-two, whose coronation parade Charles had impulsively paid a guinea to see, died. William's niece, Victoria, daughter of the Duke of Kent, was the heir apparent. The last Queen who had ruled on her own was Elizabeth, some two hundred years before. Victoria, living in Kensington Palace, had no time to dress, receiving the Archbishop of Canterbury and the Lord Chamberlain in a dressing gown at five in the morning. The Lord Chancellor administered the royal oaths. For weeks to come there were whole columns in the London *Times*, the *Morning Advertiser*, *Morning Chronical* and the *Standard* about the grace and dignity of the eighteen-year-old Queen, the fine impression she made during the royal ceremony. There was universal rejoicing in the romantic concept that a greater epic in the history of the English monarchy was about to take place; and that all of Great Britain would benefit.

For Charles the royal hoopla served to delay for months any action on his grant application.

He received a letter from The Mount telling him that there was good news and would he not come home to help celebrate? It was seven months since he had visited his family! Toward the end of June, with his journal completed except for a summation chapter, Advice to Collectors, he decided he had earned a visit with his father and sisters and a stay at The Mount. He would take the early morning *Tally Ho!* and enjoy the English landscape. He invited Erasmus to go with him. Erasmus declined; he considered it a dreadful journey only to be undertaken once a year.

The news was indeed good. Joe Wedgwood had at last proposed to Caroline. Joe was forty-two, Caroline thirty-seven. Caroline was radiant when she greeted him in the broad hall of The Mount.

"We're to be married on August first. Only five weeks away."

Shropshire was beautiful in its spring gown, the clear sunlight glistening on the green fields of clover, wheat and barley, with intersecting quadrangles of yellow mustard. He slept late, gorged himself on goose, duck, pigeon, herring and potato pie. He took the girls fishing on the river Severn and horseback riding through the countryside. After the evening meal they gathered at the card table for a game of whist. Emma Wedgwood came to visit Caroline, returning Caroline's visit of five months before. When Charles handed her down from the Wedgwood carriage he exclaimed:

"What extraordinary good luck to have you here for my last two days of holiday."

"Coincidence, isn't it?" Emma replied sweetly but with a gleam in her eye. Caroline pursed her lips in a discreet smile of approval.

It was in the middle of July, with his Journal sent to the publisher, that he began assaulting a subject which had intrigued and puzzled him for a considerable time. He started to put his thoughts on paper, yet he knew it would be difficult, for he was moving into a closed area of investigation: the transmutation of species. When he sailed out of Plymouth Sound he had believed, as did most scientists, in the immutability of species. God had created all the creatures in the heavens, on earth and in the sea, "grasses and herbs and fruit trees; great whales, fowl and every living creature that moveth; cattle and creeping things: and God said, 'Let us make man in our image.'" From that day of creation to this in July of 1837 God had created no new species. There had been catclysms, such as the Flood, but every living thing was precisely as it was when God created it!

"That is patently not true," he now exclaimed.

He remembered back to when the Beagle was anchored in a cove of Charles Island in the Galápagos, how he had discovered that the finches he had caught on two different islands had different forms of beak. He remembered his four-mile walk with Nicholas Lawson, and Lawson's observation that he could tell from which island any one of the giant tortoises had come. He had asked then:

"Are you suggesting that each island produces its own special kind of tortoise?"

Lawson had replied confidently:

"No question about it, Mr. Darwin."

Then there were the fossils he had unearthed in the cliffs of Punta Alta, the Megatherium, the Mastodon, the Toxodon, other gnawing animals; some of the species had disappeared, while others appeared significantly modified.

Why? When? By what process? He did not know. But he felt he was on to something . . . important.

He had become accustomed to living with notebooks on the *Beagle*, recording in them nearly every day not only what he had seen but his emotional and intellectual reaction as well. It would be good to have another notebook as a confidant and companion.

"The seed has to be planted in my mind first, but after that my mind and writing hand form a team."

He walked on the warm July day amidst the throngs of people on Great Marlborough Street, found his favorite stationers, bought a brown-covered notebook six and a half inches by nearly four, with some two hundred and eighty pages, and returned home to write that he had been greatly struck since the previous March on the "character of S. American fossils & species on Galápagos Archipelago."

He wrote in this notebook, which he labeled "B," each day, not on a disciplined basis but to catch up on the ideas he had already formulated; and to ask himself questions:

"Why is life short? Why does individual die? We *know* world subject to cycle of change, temperature and all circumstances which influence living beings. We see the young of living beings become permanently changed or subject to variety, according to circumstances. . . ."

He went back to his grandfather's *Zoonomia* to study it this time, and was gratified to see how much insight Dr. Erasmus Darwin had had about man and the living creatures of the world. Dr. Darwin had come to believe in some form of evolving life and was convinced that the earth's crust was millions of years old. Yet he had had neither time nor temperament to prove these heretical conclusions. He was a full-time practitioner of medicine as well as a voluminously published poet. He had not gone out to observe the world or brought back irrefutable facts to sustain his theses.

He also returned to Charles Lyell's Chapter X of the second volume of *Principles of Geology* in which Lyell had written about the "Distribution of Species." Lyell acknowledged the movement of all forms of life under changes of climate or geographical position; yet he had written:

> It is idle to dispute about the abstract possibility of the conversion of one species into another when there are known causes so much more active in their nature which must always intervene and prevent the actual accomplishment of such conversions.

He enjoyed writing in his species notebook in a different way from the rewriting of his journal and the first experimental pages of the geology of South America. In these two manuscripts he was leaning on what he had already written. In the species notebook he was digging into his own mind for new ideas, hypotheses, calculations, abstract trains of thought, for a correlation and cohesion that he had not found in any printed matter or in the mind of the most informed scientists he knew. As a result, the work of querying himself was exhausting, whether he spent the whole day at it or only a few hours. When he finished his jottings his head would be spinning.

Propagation explains why modern animals same type as extinct, which is law almost proved. They die, without they change, like golden pippins; it is a *generation* of species like generation of *individuals*.

If *species* generate other *species* their race is not utterly cut off.

On a later page he wrote:

Astronomers might formerly have said that God ordered each planet to move in its particular destiny. In same manner God orders each animal created with certain form in certain country. But how much more simple and sublime power,—let attraction act according to certain law, such are inevitable consequences,—let animals be created, then by the fixed laws of generation, such will be their successors.

His brother Erasmus stopped by to complain about him.
"Gas, you're naughty. You're making a virtue out of a vice."
"Which vice?"
"Work. It's a narcotic to you. A drug."
"Not really. I'm exploring an area of thought, not very clearly as yet, which fascinates me."
"That's no excuse for becoming a hermit. Come to supper tonight, I'm having some of the most celebrated writers in London."
"I'll be there."

But of course he was not. After writing in his species notebook until dark he could not get himself to go into company. His head was thoroughly charged, his body poisoned with fatigue. He had an egg, some toast and tea, went to bed.

In the midst of his concentration came an offer from President Whewell to become one of the two secretaries of the Geological Society. It was one of England's important scientific posts though it paid no salary. The second secretary, William Hamilton, who had trained in geology under the outstanding Roderick Murchison, would bear the brunt of answering the letters that came to the Society from all over the world. Charles's task would be to make abstracts of each paper chosen to be read before the Society; to give the papers careful study if he were obliged to read them himself; attend all meetings of the council and of the Society. Lyell had held the secretaryship for three years before he became president. Charles immediately recalled Lyell's warning not to accept any official scientific place if he could avoid it.

"I'm proud that you want me for the post, Mr. Whewell," he responded. "But am I not too young for the position, and inexperienced? I've been a fellow for only seven months. . . ."

"We prefer young men in that post, Darwin." President Whewell had purposely seated Charles next to him at the Geological Society dinner. "You'll learn fast; our fellows agree that you have that capacity. You won't be taking over the office until February. That will give you half a year to prepare."

His first step was to check the office more closely. Dr. John Royle, a surgeon and naturalist and previous secretary, told him:

"The office consumed much of my time, three days and more out of every fortnight."

Charles could not deny that he was flattered by the offer, but could he spare the time and energy when he had so much work on his shoulders and so far to go in his new profession?

It was not until mid-August that he was summoned by the Chancellor of the Exchequer. He thought:

"I'm in for an awful interview."

When he reached the office of Chancellor Thomas Spring-Rice he found there George Peacock, who was making sure that the young man he had recommended as naturalist on H.M.S. *Beagle* would be certain to get his grant. He pumped Charles's hand animatedly, introduced him to the Chancellor. Thomas Spring-Rice had not the slightest intention of putting Charles through an "awful" interview. He beamed at him with satisfaction.

"Heartiest congratulations, Darwin. I must first inform you, in formal language . . ." and began reading from his notes:

> "It having been represented to the Lords Commissioners of Her Majesty's Treasury, from various quarters, that great advantage would be derived to the Science of Natural History if arrangements could be made for enabling you to publish, in a convenient form, and at a cheap rate, the result of your labours in that branch of science, my Lords will feel justified in

giving their sanction to the application of a sum not exceeding
in the whole one thousand pounds in aid of such a publication."

An emotion halfway between relief and exultation knocked about in
Charles's breast. Anxiety as well. The Chancellor broke into the skein
of feelings he was winding around himself.

"We impose no restrictions, Darwin, only that you make the most of
the money from the public funds. Payments will be made from time to
time on a certificate that progress has been made in the engravings."

Charles expressed his deep gratitude for the opportunity. He walked
George Peacock to his club, thanked him for being "a friend in court."
Peacock replied simply:

"We must all help each other in science. That is what our age is
about."

He was now able to sign a contract for the volumes of the zoology of
the *Beagle* with Smith Elder and Company, publishers who were interested in scientific texts. It was agreed that Charles would superintend
the emergence of the work, edit the various installments as they were
ready as well as the completed volumes, and write a geographical introduction to each volume, and a preface to the whole work to be printed
in Part One of Fossil Mammalia. The five contributors would receive
nominal royalties. Charles would have no compensation. At the same
time, Smith Elder also agreed to publish his geology of South America.
For this book he would receive royalties.

He did not know what caused it, but he awakened in the middle of
the night at the beginning of September feeling sick to his stomach,
and with palpitations of the heart. His mind immediately went back to
the palpitations he had suffered in Plymouth during the last two dreary,
overcast and cold months while he waited for H.M.S. *Beagle* to sail.
Why had they come back now, six years later? He was comfortable in
his flat, eating and drinking simply. He was pleased with the way his career was going, even proud. He was making good progress in his notebook on the transmutation of species, sorting out his thinking in directions where few ventured. Only that day he had written:

We have absolute knowledge that species die and others replace them.

What he had begun by calling "*this* view of propagation," he was now
calling "*my* view" and "*my* idea of propagation." He had not had to
evict the Deity from the framework of his theory. God had created
laws; the laws themselves governed the working of natural processes.

The discomfort did not go away; the palpitations recurred and so did the "shock" to his stomach. Not on any regular schedule, sometimes during the day, sometimes at night. The one consolation was that it did not seem to get any worse; he was kept partially miserable even though he was able to continue working.

In late September he felt sufficiently unwell to visit Henry Holland in his consultation room. Dr. Holland had become Physician Extraordinaire to Queen Victoria. Although Victoria had not yet been crowned, Dr. Holland's official position made him the most sought-after doctor in London.

Dr. Holland found gastritis and soreness in Charles's digestive tract. After Charles had recounted his work schedule, including the offer of the secretaryship, "which haunted me all summer," Dr. Holland took off his pince-nez, which he carried on a black cord around his neck, tucked the glasses into an outside pocket with an air of self-satisfaction.

"Now I understand and can cure you. Two or three days of continued anxiety will bring disorder and debility into all the actions of the digestive organs, however healthy their previous state. Even urgent intellectual exertion, unattended by any emotion, interferes for the most part with easy and perfect digestion."

"Are you saying that intellectual exertion is my enemy?" cried Charles in dismay. "However would I get my work done?"

"You won't. Not until I effect a cure with my well-known diet. As a general rule animal food is the most proper; the most tender muscular parts are to be used. Mutton and all kinds of game are of easy digestion. Oily articles are most difficult. Venison is the best. New bread is exceedingly difficult. Fried articles of food are intolerable. Cheese, milk and butter are generally oppressive. Fresh vegetables are injurious, particularly cabbage, peas and beans, as are cucumbers, pears, melons. . . ."

Unsatisfied by Dr. Holland's diagnosis, Charles visited Dr. James Clark, whom he had met at a Society meeting. He learned that Clark was writing a book to be called The Sanitive Influence of Climate. Charles disclosed that he had not been feeling well, with uncomfortable palpitation of the heart. Dr. Clark put his stethoscope to Charles's heart, then his chest and back.

"Darwin, I find nothing amiss. Your heartbeat is strong and regular. You're simply suffering from fatigue. I most strongly urge you to cease all work and go and live in the country for a few weeks. The improvement produced by a change from the city to the country, even for a short period, and the great amelioration of various diseases effected by a removal from one place to another, are matters of daily remark."

Two days later he rode the coach from London to Maer Hall. The Wedgwoods were both surprised and delighted to see him. He laid the cause of his malaise at the door of the impending secretaryship of the Geological Society.

"It's not just a one-year job," Charles grumbled; "it will take me years to get out."

Emma opened a window of the library for some cool air, then slipped gracefully beside him on the sofa, took his worried face in her hands.

"You're being fainthearted, Charles, and that's not like you. Get yourself a piece of stout rope and tie a knot in it every time you record another scientific accomplishment."

"My suggestion," said Uncle Jos, "is that you sit down at my desk and write your major objections to accepting the secretaryship. . . ."

Charles studied the faces of his favorite uncle and cousin, then his own lean face broke into an embarrassed grin.

"You're teasing me out of my reluctance, aren't you?"

"We're trying, Charles," Emma and Josiah said almost simultaneously.

"I will write a letter to Professor Henslow and ask him to give me a fair judgment."

"You know what he'll answer, don't you?" asked Josiah.

"Yes. Stop whining and go to work."

"Bravo, Charles," Emma cried. "Now you're making fun of yourself. That's the Charles I love."

After Uncle Jos retired, Charles and Emma went into the drawing room where she played him some Mozart and Haydn. He confided in her about the palpitations.

"I'm sorry to hear about that, Charles." There was genuine concern in her voice. "You should take more time for leisure."

"Trouble is, Emma, I don't enjoy leisure. Who was it that said, 'We suffer as much from our virtues as from our vices'?"

"You just did. Do you think that living in London is too pressure laden?"

"Yes, but I need London for the proximity of scientists I consult with, for the libraries at the Geological Society, the Linnean . . . publishers . . ."

He spent three weeks of idleness at The Mount, moving about his home landscape of Shropshire, in the family boat on the river Severn, on horseback and on foot. His only work was correcting printer's sheets of the journal and poring over Henslow's corrections of errors of spelling and fact which invariably creep into a long manuscript. There was little serious family discussion aside from whether the entire family should go to London the following June to watch the coronation of Queen Victoria. His father did ask for news of Erasmus, making a wry face at the intelligence that Erasmus, at the age of thirty-three, found the coach trip from London to Shrewsbury too exhausting.

"Ras calls you Governor. Governor, he likes good company. That's about all he lives for. But he also likes his guests to leave at the stroke of midnight. He doesn't want to have to face anyone over breakfast the next morning."

"Including a wife?"

"Particularly a wife."

"Charles, I hope you don't feel the same way."

"Not at all. It's just that I'm too preoccupied to give marriage even a passing thought."

"You are approaching thirty. It should be soon. If you marry late you miss so much good pure happiness."

## 6.

He returned to London toward the end of October, refreshed. The corrected press sheets of his journal had been sent to the publisher Henry Colburn. Henslow had demolished all his objections to taking the secretaryship, as had Josiah Wedgwood. He had only one final recourse, Lyell. The Lyells had been on the Continent, geologizing. There was a note at the flat suggesting that Charles come to dinner the night he returned to London. As he entered the Lyell hall, Lyell slapped him jovially on the shoulder.

"Congratulations, Charles! You were my first choice for the post. It will open the scientists of the world to you on a personal basis."

"But you warned me not to accept any office."

"Indeed! But that did not include the Geological Society. That's the one time you must permit yourself to be burned at the stake!"

"But it's going to be a massive job to transform my nine hundred pages of geological notes and observations into a coherent and readable book."

"I can tell you one way to simplify the task, the way I ultimately had to do it when attempting to cram all the materials of my *Principles* Books Two and Three into one volume. Break up your project into several parts, work at only one of them at a time. It will make the work less formidable."

"You mean break the overall book into the several organic units and publish each when it is completed?"

"Precisely. Each volume will kindle interest in the next."

Charles threw his arms in the air.

"My dear Lyell, you have just reduced my work to a third. I'll do my first book on coral reefs. The next on volcanic islands. The third on the elevation and subsidence of the coast of South America."

Lyell grinned.

"I've probably increased it because you can now be more thorough in each area."

On the first of November, just a month over a year since he had set foot in England, a messenger from Henry Colburn brought him a set of clean and corrected pages of the *Journal of Charles Darwin, M.A., Naturalist to the Beagle*, together with foldover maps showing the entire journey of H.M.S. *Beagle* around the world. The six hundred pages had no binding or cover, that would have to wait until King's and FitzRoy's volumes of the set were ready for publication. Nevertheless he wrote to Henslow:

> I sat the other evening gazing in silent admiration at the first page of my own volume when I received it from the printer!

He tossed restlessly in his sleep, rose several times to gaze out of the window at Great Marlborough Street, dark and deserted. He did not know what the connection was but his mind returned to The Mount, to his father's saying:

"When should you marry, soon or late? Son, it should be soon. . . . One's character is more flexible . . . you miss so much good pure happiness . . ."

He read by lamplight until dawn, then went to his desk. Over the past six years he had done his writing, except for letters home, in sturdy, well-made notebooks. Since his jottings now would be about his personal life, he picked up two old envelopes which he had opened a considerable time before, scribbled across the top of one: *If Not Marry*; on the top of the other *If Marry*. Since there was no young woman whom he wished to marry, or who wanted to marry him for that matter, he started on the negative side of the problem.

> If *not* marry TRAVEL? Europe—Yes? America???
> If I travel it must be exclusively geological.
> If I don't travel—? Work at transmutation of Species— Microscope—simplest forms of life.
> Live in London—in small house near Regent's Park. Keep horses— Take summer tours— Collect specimens, some form of Zoology. Speculations of Geography and geological works —systematize and study affinities.

He heard Syms padding about in the kitchen. He picked up the second used envelope, wrote:

> If marry—means limited— Feel duty to work for money.
> London life, nothing but Society, no country, no tours, no large Zoological collection, no books.
> Cambridge Professorship. Either Geology or Zoology.
> But better than hibernating in country—and where? I could not indolently take country house & do nothing— If I were moderately rich, I would live in London, with pretty big house— But could I act thus with children & poor? No.
> Then Cambridge Professorship, and make best of it. Do duty & work at spare times.
> My destiny will be Cambridge Professor or poor man.

He was not particularly pleased with his analyses. Neither one appeared to be incisive or conclusive. Ah well, he would tackle the marital problem another day. He went instead into one of the "lumber rooms" where Syms had set up a workbench. On it were a blowpipe, a large candle with flat wick, some rocks. While in Cambridge he had learned from William Miller, professor of mineralogy at St. John's, the method of determining the nature of any mineral by blowing hot air from a lighted candle through the blowpipe, heating the minerals, some of which melted at low temperature, some at high. Miller had said:

"All minerals are crystals, except things like coral or lava rock. All mineralogy is crystallography. The rate at which minerals melt is an authentic clue to their character and identity."

Professor Miller had kept some of Charles's rocks in Cambridge and sent down reports to Charles as to their nature and category.

"But it is helpful to me to be able to perform experiments here and now so that I can make my own identifications," Charles explained to Erasmus.

"We didn't name you Gas for nothing," Erasmus said.

January 1838 started out in a blaze of work. He kept a month-by-month journal recording the books he read to flesh out his own experience and the writing of the geology. At the end of each week he could remember little that had happened aside from the work itself. The days, weeks and months blended together in a storm of exertion; he stopped only long enough to be stoked by food and sleep.

In January he finished his account of the geology of the Galápagos Islands and of Ascension; in February the work on St. Helena and the small islands of the Atlantic. In February he also used up the last pages of his notebook on the transmutation of species; promptly bought a second notebook and continued writing.

March was devoted mostly to mammalia for a zoology study; he also did a paper on earthquakes for the Geological Society that brought him praise.

In April he helped John Gould with the bird collection for the zoology of the *Beagle*, gave the Goulds some money from his grant for plates. John Gould had already made fifty sketches of the birds. Elizabeth Gould executed them on stone. The plates came out brilliantly, for the most part of natural size.

"Your monograph is going to be gorgeous," cried Charles; "as beautiful and authentic as Audubon's."

Gould looked up from his taxidermy table, said a touch sadly:

"Darwin, we're going to finish the text on the first installment and all the color plates but we're leaving soon for Australia to collect and sketch and make notes. Could be as long as two years. . . ."

At Charles's crestfallen expression, Elizabeth Gould hastened to add: "We've spoken to George Gray, the ornithologist at the British Museum. He will complete the texts for you."

He started work on the Cape of Good Hope, King George Sound and Sydney. He also spent considerable time on the second notebook of his species, but felt unwell. The palpitations returned as well as considerable flux and movement in his intestinal tract. May was primarily geology, for he was writing his sections on Hobart Town and New Zealand, St. Jago and the Cape Verde Islands.

To his surprise he took pleasure from his secretaryship, editing the papers that came in from geologists, making abstracts for the bulletin, attending meetings, reading to the assembled membership those papers submitted by authors who could not leave their positions in distant parts of England. He soon learned that the two secretaries ran the Society. It was a heady experience. Instead of resenting the time spent at meetings he was grateful for the opportunity to get away from the flat and his intense concentration there into the amiable companionship of his fellow scientists.

He received an amusing letter from Captain FitzRoy, who said:

> The work on my book is going on steadily, though not on a railroad. I am rather old fashioned in habits as well as ideas, ergo, a slow coach.

Lyell combed his hand through his curly hair.

"I didn't know the good captain had a sense of humor."

Richard Owen's first installment of *The Zoology of the Voyage of*

*H.M.S. Beagle, Fossil Mammalia,* was released. It was a handsome oversized folio with a large readable type face. Charles had worked steadily
with the printer to accomplish this, for the first folio would set the pattern for those to follow. It had seven plates, thirteen pages of Charles's
preface and introduction and twenty-seven of Owen's writing. It cost
eight shillings, the modest price schedule for all the installments varying from eight shillings to twelve depending on the number of plates
and the length of the text. When Charles went into Yarrell's bookshop
on the corner of Bury and Little Ryder streets, he asked tremulously,
as do all authors with their first publication:

"How is it going?"

"What do you mean, going? It's gone. I'm sold out."

Charles heaved a long sigh of relief.

"I feel like a mother who has been told her newborn child has the
normal five toes, and not six."

"It bodes well for your future installments."

The scientists at the Linnean, Zoological and Geological societies
were pleased with this beginning work, bought copies, applauded him
for his clearly written descriptions of the localities from which the specimens were obtained. The Geological Society promptly awarded Richard Owen their coveted Wollaston Gold Medal. Owen was thrilled at
this acceptance of what he called "Darwin's Fossils."

"What a send-off for the series!" Charles exulted.

The government, which had provided the money for the plates, was
satisfied with their own good judgment.

Robert Brown, the Linnean Society librarian and botanist, invited
Charles for Sunday morning breakfast. Charles had supplied him with
pieces of fossil wood from King George Sound which Brown had cut
and ground to ascertain its ingredients. Brown, now sixty-four, shuffled
through his laboratory in slippers, no longer thinking it necessary to act
young. His underlip was outthrust like that of a bulldog.

One of the Linnean porters brought up breakfast, which they ate in
Brown's laboratory surrounded by his hundreds of botanical specimens.
Brown said in his deep, gruff voice:

"Pleased to see you publishing, Darwin. About time, too."

"Mr. Brown, you astonish me! When I visited here six years ago you
said you never wanted to see your words in English print, that a mistake in print is condemnation to the gallows. I also can make mistakes."

Brown set his squared-out jaw.

"You'll survive them." His puffy eyelids shot open. "I was born to
build a strong base under the science of botany, as was your friend
Henslow. Neither of us will publish beyond descriptive catalogues. You

were born to reach a large audience with creative discoveries. Write, publish; you will make mistakes. Accept your fate gracefully."

He limited himself to one dinner party a week, and on a second evening paid his debts to hosts. He and Erasmus had a midday meal occasionally. Other than that he confined his social life to the meetings of the Geological Society and his confreres there. In May he wrote rather steadily in his second notebook but was unwell much of the time, so much so that in mid-June when his sister Katty, Emma and several other members of the Wedgwood family came into London from a holiday in Paris, he saw the girls only once, and then for just a few moments to make his apologies. He was hurt to learn that Emma thought he had purposely neglected her.

"Why would I do that?" he asked himself. "I just couldn't bear to have her see me ill for a whole week."

To cure himself he went by packet to Edinburgh, took a solitary walk on Salisbury Craig, remembering back to his two years at the university there and how much he had disliked Professor Robert Jameson's lectures on geology. Yet how much Robert Grant and William Macgillivray of the Natural History Museum had taught him of the natural philosophies. He spent some time in Glasgow, then moved on to Glen Roy where he wanted to compare the terraces, roads, benches and shelves to those he had seen in Chile. After a week he returned by sea to Liverpool and from there to Shrewsbury.

"How well you look after your outing," Katty cried, seeing his suntanned face. "Emma and I were worried about you in London."

"I shall go to Maer and show her, on my return to London."

He was rested after the sixteen-day holiday but for the first time the image of his London flat struck a kind of terror in him.

"My God, how barren it is! Only Syms there to cook my food and bring me the rock samples I need for my chapters. That's living as a hermit in a cave, not as a normal being. I can't bear the thought of going back to that sterile silence."

He had wanted it for the past twenty months. But another twenty? A hundred and twenty? He would begin to feel imprisoned, in exile. He remembered the notes he had made on the backs of two old envelopes: *If Not Marry. If Marry.* He would try again.

He went into the library, took a couple of sheets of paper out of a desk drawer, began to write:

### This is the Question

He paused, reminded himself that in London he had put *If Not Marry* first. This time he set down *Marry* first.

"I wonder if that reversal means anything?" he asked himself; then started writing rapidly:

Children, (if it pleases God)—constant companion, (friend in old age) who will feel interested in one—object to be beloved and played with.
Home, and someone to take care of house. Charms of music and female chit-chat. These things good for one's health.
My God, it is intolerable to think of spending one's whole life like a neuter bee, working, working and nothing after all— No, no won't do— Only picture to yourself a nice soft wife on a sofa with good fire, and books and music perhaps—compare this vision with the dingy reality of Grt Marlboro' St.
Marry—Marry—Marry.

He left the library, walked along the paths of the extensive Darwin gardens in full summer bloom. Then returned to the desk, wrote *Not Marry*.

No children, (no second life) no one to care for one in old age—
Freedom to go where one liked— Choice of Society *and little of it*. Conversation of clever men at clubs.
Not forced to visit relatives, and to bend in every trifle—to have the expense and anxiety of children—perhaps quarrelling.
*Loss of time*—cannot read in the evenings—fatness and idleness, anxiety and responsibility—less money for books etc.— If many children forced to gain one's bread.

On the reverse side of the page he wrote his summing up:

But then if I married tomorrow, there would be an infinity of trouble and expense in getting and furnishing a house—fighting about no Society—morning calls, loss of time every day. . . .
Cheer up— One cannot live this solitary life, with groggy old age, friendless and cold and childless, staring one in one's face, already beginning to wrinkle.
Never mind, trust to chance—keep a sharp look out. There is many a happy slave.

He had always loved the land between Shrewsbury and Maer, particularly in late July, with the green and yellow fields almost ready for harvesting. On this ride he saw little, for his thoughts were turned inward. Except for the Lyells, Brown, Yarrell, a few others of his scientist friends, he had cut himself off from all social life. He had not met an attractive or amusing young woman, or even an interesting one, since his return to England. He knew there were plenty of them in London; he saw them go by in carriages. . . .

Everything except concentrated work had gone by. He had always been a companionable person, now he was a semi-recluse. Nor did he find Erasmus's bachelor life attractive. As his father had reminded him, the following February he would be thirty years old, no longer a youth. If he did not marry and have children, that would be the end of the Darwin line, which could be traced back to the fifteen hundreds. It was not an imperative duty; however he had taken much felicity from his own large family, that of the Wedgwoods, the Henslows. Marriage, a home, children were the normal way of life. He was a normal man.

What to do? Put an announcement in the London *Times:* Wife Wanted? Begin to look at every available young woman at dinner parties with interested rather than preoccupied eyes? Ask his scientist friends and acquaintances to introduce him to charming young ladies? He had only been in love once, with Fanny Owen, and had got over her fairly caustically on the *Beagle.* Should he have his sisters introduce him to young women they knew? Go to Maer Hall, ask Elizabeth and Emma if they knew anyone. . . .

The treadmill inside his brain stopped short. Emma! Good God Almighty, Emma! Of the warm brown eyes and the soft brown curls, the melodious voice and lovely figure, the sympathetic personality, his closest friend and confidante from childhood. Emma, who had asserted his right to go on the *Beagle,* to publish his journal, who had been tender when appropriate, discerning when necessary. . . .

Emma! He had always loved Emma. Emma had loved him. As cousins? But he had espied Caroline and Emma exchanging knowing glances!

"Ah, there is my answer," he exclaimed aloud to the unlistening fields of growing potatoes. Emma had been meant for him over all the years!

Now he remembered that she had turned down four eligible suitors, one of them a young clergyman who had burst into tears when she rejected him. Why had she done so? Did she not want love or marriage? That could not be. She had a warm and loving heart. She gave affection to all manner of child and adult. Had she decided herself unsuited for them? No, she had a very healthy opinion of herself. Had she been waiting? . . . For whom? He had not heard any names mentioned though there were many eligible young men in Staffordshire. The Wedgwood family was one of the very best in the district to marry into.

"For me?" he asked himself timidly. "If so, how could she have been so patient?"

Suddenly he increased the horse's stride.

"Good gracious! Have I waited too long? Am I out in the rain without a sailor's black oilcloth to cover me? I must try. Soon. Now! I must not build up any hopes but I must try. I'll use twenty-two chronometers and when I have my position exactly charted, sail straight for the harbor."

He reached Maer in high spirits. He and Emma were happy in each other's company. A dozen times in the next two days he braced himself to the sticking point only to back off.

"What if she rejects me? After all, I am not self-supporting, I have a plain face. We would both be so terribly embarrassed."

When he departed, Emma kissed him demurely, said:

"We've had such lovely times, Charles. Do come back soon."

"I will, Emma."

He kicked himself all the way into London for being a coward.


7.

When he returned to Great Marlborough Street he found it hard to concentrate, for he could think of little but Emma Wedgwood. He carried the image of her around with him during the day and most of the night. He had been a total fool not to have proposed to her. He was going to have to do it anyway, and mighty soon, for he was now totally in love with her and had decided that she was the only woman for him. He was determined to go back to Maer Hall just as soon as he could figure out exactly what words and sentences he would say, and could be certain that he would not bolt again.

He achieved surcease from his anxiety only by concentrating on geology. He began an article about the roads or benches he had observed in Glen Roy. In May the first installment of George Waterhouse's *Mammalia* had come out, with sixteen pages and ten plates. In July the first number of John Gould's *Birds* had been published, with ten magnificent color plates. His zoology series was well on its way.

A copy of Lyell's newly published *Elements of Geology* had been delivered to his desk at the Society. Lyell was in Scotland, at Kinnordy, visiting his parents. After devouring the volume, Charles wrote immediately to his friend:

> I have read it through every word, and am full of admiration of it. . . . I must talk to you about it. There is no pleasure in reading a book if one cannot have a good talk over it. I felt in many parts some mortification at thinking how geologists have labored and struggled at proving what seems, as you have put it, so evidently probable. . . .

A line in Lyell's preface disturbed him, however. It declared that the publication of Darwin's Journal of Researches had been delayed, "to the great regret of the scientific world," by the failure of Robert FitzRoy to complete the companion volumes to it. He realized that Lyell was paying him a compliment but he was uneasy about FitzRoy's reaction. He could hope that FitzRoy would not see it but knew that the captain bought all the important science books. . . .

It was only a few days before there was a brusque knock at his front door. Syms admitted Captain FitzRoy, tall, lean, aristocratic in his long dark blue coat and trousers and pearl-gray waistcoat. His collar was turned down over a loosely knotted tie, a new fashion; he also had on a new-style Homburg hat. Although still in the Navy, he was on half pay and without a command. His face was several shades darkened by what was undoubtedly fury.

"Captain FitzRoy! How good to see you after this long time," greeted Charles.

"I'm not here for pleasure. I have been insulted and my integrity attacked." He thrust forward a copy of Lyell's book. "You have seen this bitter attack against me."

"Yes, Captain, and deeply regretted it."

"Regretted it? You probably prompted it."

Charles's eyelids flared.

"Why would I do that?"

"To prove to the scientific world that you are a zealous worker while I am a laggard and desultory in my duty."

"No man could think that of you, sir. You are one of the most devoted and conscientious men I know."

"Yet you allowed Lyell to attack me in public print."

"I give you my word that I never saw the preface. If I had, I would have persuaded Lyell to take out all mention of our books. Syms, see if there is some brandy." To FitzRoy he said placatingly, "Please sit down. Let us talk this over like long-time friends. You know that I would never offend you. I don't know why Lyell wrote those lines but I will counteract them."

"How can you do that?" stiffly.

"By letting it be known that you are writing both Captain King's and your own books and that if I had had to write two volumes it would have taken me a year or two longer."

Mollified, FitzRoy accepted the brandy from Syms, whom he belatedly recognized.

"Very well. But I want you to tell Lyell I resent his implications and I want that passage deleted from any further editions."

Charles smiled for the first time since FitzRoy had stormed in.

"There won't be another edition before our three books are out . . . in another year, would you say?"

FitzRoy's voice returned to normal.

"I have only a few months of work to complete both volumes. Our books should be in the bookstores by this time next year."

"We'll be on a smooth sea with a gentle wind in our sails," said Charles.

FitzRoy sipped his brandy, said with one of the quick smiles Charles remembered so well:

"I have a temper, as you had occasion to find out. I know that you had nothing to do with Lyell's belittling remark, and that you would have expurgated it had you seen the manuscript. So . . . I apologize for my accusation."

"Accepted."

They chatted amiably for a while. Then FitzRoy shook hands and left. Charles wrote to Lyell:

> I have seen FitzRoy, who has bought your book. He looked rather black at the preface . . . but then came smooth again. Some part of his brain wants mending. . . .

He continued writing his Glen Roy paper. It was a long and detailed article which took him the better part of six weeks, though at the same time he had been writing steadily in his third notebook on species. As early as June he had written to his cousin William Darwin Fox:

> I am delighted to hear you are such a good man as not to have forgotten my question about the crossing of animals. It is my prime hobby, and I really think some day I shall be able to do something in that most intricate subject, species and varieties.

Now, in September, with the Glen Roy article completed for publication and the second number of Waterhouse's *Mammalia* published, he concentrated full time on his species notebook. He talked to his friends about such technical matters as crossbreeding. He did not divulge a purpose for his interest. To Lyell he wrote:

> I have lately been sadly tempted to be idle, that is, as far as pure geology is concerned by the delightful number of new views which have been coming in thickly and steadily on the classification and affinities and instincts of animals, bearing on the question of species. Notebook after notebook has been filled with facts which begin to group themselves *clearly* under sub-laws.

The September and October weather was good enough to allow him rambling walks through the city. His destination was usually a bookshop, Yarrell's, John Tallis's, or Hatchard's. He roamed among the tables, buying something for a good read that night, for he was reading in random fashion for pleasure and to get his mind off Little Miss Slip-Slop. His taste was catholic; in September and October, in addition to starting his book on corals, he read John Ray's *The Wisdom of God*, Lister's *Husbandry*, Horne's *History of Man*, Lisiansky's *Voyage around the World*, Abercrombie's *The Intellectual Power*, Harriet Martineau's *How to Observe*. Through a combination of accident and curiosity he picked up a copy of Thomas Malthus's *Principles of Population* which, in 1838, was exactly forty years old. Charles had not met Malthus during his short stay in London before H.M.S. *Beagle* sailed but a number of his friends had. Malthus had been educated at Cambridge and had taught for over twenty years at the East India Company's college at Haileybury.

He walked home in a smoke-discolored sunset, the new book comfortingly under his arm. Syms fed him a light supper before the cheery fire in the front parlor. He flipped open to the first chapter, which was headed: "Ratios of the Increase of Population and Food."

He started reading and, by Malthus's second page, felt as though he had been hit by a bolt of lightning, an intellectual flash that left him dizzy, so staggering was its import to him. It was a full fifteen months since he had begun his systematic inquiry into the origin, changes and deviations in species, animal and vegetable, and only now had he come across the key to the riddle. He read:

> The cause to which I allude is the constant tendency in all animated life to increase beyond the nourishment prepared for it.
>
> It is observed . . . that there is no bound to the prolific nature of plants or animals but what is made by their crowding and interfering with each other's means of subsistence. . . .
>
> That is incontrovertibly true. Throughout the animal and vegetable kingdoms Nature has scattered the seeds of life abroad with the most profuse and liberal hand; but has been comparatively sparing in the room and the nourishment necessary to rear them. The germs of existence contained in this earth, if they could freely develop themselves, would fill millions of worlds in the course of a few thousand years. Necessity, that imperious, all-pervading law of nature, restrains them within the prescribed bounds. The race of plants and the race

of animals shrink under this great restrictive law; and man cannot by any efforts of reason escape from it.

. . . population has this constant tendency to increase beyond the means of subsistence. . . .

He could not contain his exultation at finding this key to the locked and inviolable world of the origin of species. He paced the two front rooms, images from the journey of the *Beagle* and his studies since he had returned flooding through his mind. Exhausted but unable to bring himself to undress and go to bed, he threw himself down on the sofa.

Now he had a theory by which to work! He was anxious to avoid prejudice and determined that for some time he would not write even the briefest sketch. He would wait until he had it thoroughly documented.

He reached Maer Hall on Friday evening, November 9. Some of the family had already gone to bed, including his sister Katty, there for a visit. Emma went foraging in the kitchen and brought him a bite to eat, along with a pitcher of hot cocoa. Fatigued and rumpled as he was, he had no intention of proposing to Emma that night. He wanted all the next day to be with her, walking in the woods, mufflers around their throats to keep out the chill; re-establishing the comradery they had enjoyed during his visit in July.

The moment arrived after they returned from church on Sunday, after listening to the vicar of Maer, Emma's cousin, John Allen Wedgwood, preach a sermon, "Thanksgiving after a Storm to Be Used at Sea," which Emma whispered to Charles was being done particularly for the returned "Old Salt" of the family.

The drawing room was cool but pleasant. Charles and Emma sat together on the piano bench. She played for him, softly, some Mozart Lieder. Charles sighed with infinite relief, for Emma had struck precisely the right note.

"Emma, I would like permission to speak to you."

Startled, she replied, "Why, Charles, since when do you have to ask permission to speak to me?"

"I'm serious. This is something important."

"I can see by your expression that it is."

"Emma, we've been friends for a long time. . . ."

"As long as we've been cousins."

"I don't know how you are going to receive this. Frankly, I'm frightened out of whatever wits I have left."

Emma turned to him. She had become a little pale.

"Charles, when you came to stay with us last July you were in high spirits and I was very happy in your company and had the feeling that if you saw more of me you would really like me."

The strain went out of his face. He took her two hands in his. "My dearest Emma. I have always liked you more than any other. Now I know—forgive me for being so slow and so late; that appears to be part of my character—that I have long loved you. Please don't be afraid of hurting my feelings; I know I'm not a handsome man. Above all tell me the truth."

"I promise, Charles."

"Then I want to ask if you will marry me."

There was neither hesitation nor silence on Emma's part.

"Why of course I will, Charles. I've been waiting for years for you to propose. Everyone in both our families has expected us to marry. Didn't you know that?"

"No. I didn't know . . . anything. . . ."

She laughed quietly at how miserable he looked.

He said quietly:

"I love you. You've said you would marry me, but do you love me?"

She put her arms tightly about him and kissed him.

He murmured:

"What a beautiful answer. We are going to have a fine life together. I hope you are as happy as I am."

"I'm much too bewildered by this suddenness to feel my full happiness. But I will. You are the most open, transparent man I ever saw. Every word expresses your real thoughts. You are affectionate and very nice to your sisters, and perfectly sweet-tempered."

"Like a child that has something he loves beyond measure, I long to dwell on the words *my own dear Emma*."

It was his turn to kiss her, a deep, passionate kiss, the second they had known. It stirred them both and gave a breast-warming confidence that their love would be good. When she separated herself from his embrace, she asked:

"Shouldn't we tell Papa and Katty?"

When Josiah and Katty came into the room, Emma said with a radiant smile:

"Surely you can tell by our faces? Charles has proposed. We are going to be married."

Josiah Wedgwood's eyes shone with unashamed tears of joy. He embraced Emma, then Charles.

"This is one of the happiest moments of my life." His voice was husky with emotion. "I have hoped and prayed for years that it would happen. Charles, you know that I have always had a high regard for you."

"And I have always looked up to you, Uncle Jos, with the greatest respect and affection."

A number of the Wedgwood relatives had been invited for Sunday dinner. Hensleigh and his wife Fanny had come from London. Despite the fact that he had finally resigned as a police magistrate and had been out of work for close to a year, Hensleigh and Fanny were in good spirits, as was the rest of the party.

"In fact, hilarious," Charles whispered to Emma, sitting next to him at the dining table; "I don't think we want to announce our engagement in the midst of this babble, do you?"

"I agree."

He squeezed her hand under the table.

"I'm so happy and relieved that my uncertainties are settled and we understand each other that I have a headache."

"So do I, dear Charles."

He was about to undress for bed when there was a knock on the door. He opened it to find Hensleigh Wedgwood standing there.

"Come along to our bedroom, there's a do under way."

Charles walked down the hall. He could hear the excited voices. When he entered the room Emma sprang up from a chair by the fire.

"Charles, we looked so dismal at supper that both my Aunt Fanny and Harry's wife Jessie wondered what was the matter. Fanny guessed. Our secret is out."

"Your secret is several years old," Fanny exclaimed. "Only it is we who have kept it."

Charles was heartily bussed by his female relatives. He felt a glow of well-being, a heady sensation that all was now right in his world. Emma pulled him down on the chair beside her.

"Charles, my dear, it is a match that every soul has been making for us."

"Nevertheless Katty and I will ride to Shrewsbury tomorrow to tell Father and Susan," he said. "I'm sure Father will be as happy about it as Uncle Jos was."

Emma's eyes sparkled.

"Hensleigh, I'm hungry. Please forage for us."

They found themselves in the midst of a discussion of the advantages of a long or short engagement.

"Short!" Charles cried. "I've already forfeited a sufficient amount of happiness."

"Long," said Emma quietly. "I can't leave Elizabeth alone to care for Mama."

"And why not?" demanded the pain-ridden Elizabeth. "I'll take my happiness from yours."

Hensleigh came in with a platter of bread, a carving knife and two pounds of fresh butter. They pitched to and had what Emma declared to be "an elegant refection."

Josiah and Charles were the first up the next morning. There was a fine crystal-like snow falling over Maer. After having coffee Josiah suggested they saddle horses and go for a ride through the woods. The air was sharp, cold, delicious in the nostrils and to the senses. They rode along the lake and then into the woods where they had spent so many happy Septembers shooting partridge and other game. Josiah's voice carried in the white stillness of the early morning.

"A good, cheerful and affectionate daughter is the greatest blessing a man can have, after a good wife. I could have parted with Emma to no one for whom I would so entirely feel as a father." His deeply lined face broke into a hearty smile. "Let us take care of the practicalities for a moment, Charles. I propose to do for Emma what I did for Charlotte and for my sons, give a bond for five thousand pounds and allow her four hundred pounds a year as long as my income will supply it, which I have no reason for thinking will not be as long as I live."

Charles flushed. He had not given a thought to any possible dowry for Emma, though of course there would be one; the Wedgwoods had become wealthy from their internationally famous potteries at Etruria.

"That's generous of you, Uncle Jos. I'll want your advice and my father's too on how to invest Emma's five thousand pounds. I should be earning soon, and it would be my hope that we could keep Emma's capital as well as its earnings intact for our children, the way my father did for us."

Emma was still at breakfast. They kissed, their eyes shining, then Emma helped him to porridge, a kipper, boiled eggs in little blue Wedgwood cups, a pile of sliced toast, coffee with hot milk. Charles ate prodigiously.

"Emma, could we have a fire laid in the library? It is such a good place to have a quiet talk."

Once inside the book-lined room, he said:

"I'm afraid we're going to have to live in London for several years, until I get my geological works published. Shall you mind?"

"I'll be happy in our home wherever we live. I have a capacity for happiness."

"It's one of your many talents. Would you prefer the center of London or the suburbs?"

"I should think central London would be more convenient since you are secretary of the Geological Society."

"I should also like to be close to the Lyells; he is of the most extraordinary help to me, in both geology and economics. It's not a fashionable neighborhood but a rather good one, near the British Museum and the new London University."

"When you find a few houses that suit, I'll come to London and help you choose."

After some discussion Emma set their wedding date for January 29, 1839, some two and a half months off. The wedding ceremony would take place in their church on the hill above them.

8.

Erasmus was more amused than surprised.

"My commiseration, Gas. But then, you don't have the talent to be a bachelor. As long as you're taking the fatal step it is as well you are keeping the problems in the family."

They roamed the streets, covering the several square miles of Bloomsbury, the areas around the British Museum and London University from Euston Road to Great Russell Street, from Tottenham Court Road to Gray's Inn Road. Charles kept notes in his St. Helena notebook on every house they saw, addresses, rentals, sizes, furnishings, interspersed among his jottings about volcanic dust and the skeletons of pigeons. Mr. Fuller, at 8 Albany Place near Regent's Park, wanted two hundred pounds a year. On the same street they found an unfurnished house at seventy pounds per annum which was too small; for another the agent wanted a hundred-pound premium paid at once. They found more houses to let on Montague Place behind the museum, another on Russell Square near Lyell's house on Hart Street, still more at Gordon Square, number 40, built that year; a rather nice house at 20 Woburn Square, but too expensive; two more new ones on Tavistock Square; one at 12 Upper Gower Street which was ugly in a pleasant way, with a back garden and some remnants of furnishings.

He got no work done, which exasperated him, and ended the week with a feeling of frustration. He wrote to Emma:

The landlords are all gone mad, they ask such prices.

Lyell had finally got him admitted into the Athenaeum in August 1838. He wrote to Emma in high glee:

I go and dine at the Athenaeum like a gentleman, or rather like a lord, for I am sure the first evening I sat in that great drawing room, on a sofa all by myself, I felt just like a duke. I am full of admiration at the Athenaeum, one meets so many people there that one likes to see.

On Saturday evening he dined with the Lyells. He wrote to Emma:

Lyell grew quite audacious at the thought of having a geological companion and proposed going to dine at the Athenaeum together and leaving our wives at home. Poor man, he would as soon eat his head as do such an action.

On Sunday evening Erasmus took Charles to drink tea with the Thomas Carlyles. Erasmus had taken Emma to visit the Carlyles when she was in London the previous June. Carlyle had told Erasmus that Emma was one of the nicest girls he had ever seen. Thomas Carlyle was forty-three, already well known in English literary circles. He had published *Sartor Resartus*; just the year before his intensive study, *The French Revolution*. A dedicated scholar of German, he had also translated Goethe's *Wilhelm Meister* into English. The Carlyles, who had been married for twelve years, were childless, had a pleasant house and grounds overlooking the river Thames in Chelsea. Erasmus heroworshiped them. Jane Carlyle sent messages to Charles over their teacups and cakes but Charles found her difficult because of a "hysterical sort of giggle which makes her remarks not very intelligible."

It was decided that Emma had better come to London and help to select a proper house. She could stay with Fanny and her brother Hensleigh in Notting Hill.

Charles met her at Euston Station. It was a restrained public reunion. He took her by carriage to Hensleigh's home. Once there she took off her wide-brimmed bonnet; they threw their arms about each other and kissed warmly.

"Do you know what Papa is going to give us as a wedding present?" she exclaimed. "My choice of any piano in London! Mama takes our marriage very comfortably and entertains herself a good deal with planning about houses, trousseau and wedding cake, which I was in hopes she would not have thought of as it is a useless trouble and expense."

Early each morning he picked her up in a carriage, took her to see all the houses he and Erasmus had visited and a dozen others. The only one they truly liked was at 12 Upper Gower Street, a five-story red brick house, one in a line of attached buildings, all of them scrupulously maintained. It had what Charles described as a "spacious and beautiful garden" at the rear. The location was perfect; across the street from the garden was London University, the British Museum was only a short walk away, Lyell's home another street or two; magnificent Regent's Park, with its boating lake, a ten-minute walk.

"The landlady insists on our buying her ugly shutters, curtains, scraps of carpet and some mediocre furniture at a ridiculously inflated price," Charles explained to Emma.

Emma expressed her pleasure in the layout of the house. There was a good-sized basement, lighted both front and back by open enclosures; ". . . good for a kitchen at the rear," she decided. The ground floor provided a hallway and staircase with rooms front and back. It was the first floor that appealed to them both, a large room overlooking Upper Gower Street with three fine windows for light and air, suited for a drawing room; another spacious room at the rear also with three windows, overlooking the garden with its trees and flowers. Both rooms had green marble fireplaces with dark marble mantels.

"This could be our sitting room," Emma said, "for the piano."

The bedrooms on the second floor were equally attractive. "Even the attic can be useful," Charles said. "I can bring over my workbenches for the geological and zoological specimens."

They could get nowhere with the landlady. When Charles offered her a hundred pounds a year rental, with an immediate deposit, and an adequate price for her used furnishings, his offer was categorically refused. They returned three separate days, guaranteeing a two-year lease if she would either take out her furniture or bring the price down to a sensible figure. She perceived how eager they were to have the house.

"Take it or leave it," she declared.

Sadly, they had to leave it. Emma's two weeks were up. She had to return to Maer Hall to prepare her trousseau and arrange for the wedding. It was already December 21. Charles drove her in a fly to the railroad station.

He spent the next eight days looking at more houses than he could remember. On the ninth day a messenger brought a note suggesting that he return to Upper Gower Street as soon as possible; it was from the landlady. Charles put on a coat and hat, walked the mile plus up Great Portland Street, cutting across Howland Street and Tottenham Court Road. He was excited and hopeful.

The landlady's brusque expression had changed completely.

"Mr. Darwin, I've decided that you and that ladylike Miss Wedgwood would make good tenants. You can have the lease for a hundred pounds a year. As for the furnishings, you can have them at valuation. Would you say Pearsall and Jordan will set proper prices?"

"Yes, they're acceptable."

"Then the house is yours."

He took some bank notes out of a notecase, handed them over, signed the lease and in return received the key to the house. To his surprise he had also inherited an old woman who would be his house-keeper until after his marriage.

He raced back to Great Marlborough Street, made for his desk.

My dear Emma, I cannot let a post go by without writing to tell you Gower Street is ours, yellow curtains and all. . . . How glorious it will be to see you seated by the fire of our own home. . . .

That night he was so possessed with thoughts of his happy future that he did not close his eyes until long past two o'clock. He woke again at five, his head too busy to let him sleep; got up, decided to spend a quiet day, then rang for Covington.

"I'm very sorry to spoil your Sunday, Syms, but begin packing."

"Pack up, sir, what for?"

"I'm flitting. I rented the house on Upper Gower Street. You arrange the specimens to be moved in their proper containers. I'll sort my multitude of papers."

Erasmus came by to help. At half past three they had two large wagonloads full of goods.

"I am astounded at the bulk of your luggage," exclaimed Erasmus.

"So am I."

The porters carrying the geological specimens down the stairs to the wagons were equally surprised at their weight.

"What you carry in these boxes, gov'ner, rocks?"

By six o'clock everything had been transferred. Elated, Charles went walking around his garden. At eight Margaret, the woman left behind by the landlady, fed him eggs, bacon and tea, for which he was grateful. Before going to sleep he wrote, "12 Upper Gower Street!!" on a sheet of paper and told Emma:

I sit down just to date this letter that I may enjoy the infinite satisfaction of writing to my own dear wife that is to be, the very first evening of my entering our house. There never was so good a house for me. . . .

He wanted the house to be as attractive as possible for Emma. He brought in charwomen to clean the windows, had the curtains washed, the hall and stairway carpets cleaned, the walls washed down, the floors scrubbed and polished, the furniture thoroughly dusted and waxed. The colors inside the house clashed: red blinds, yellow curtains, walls a depressing mustard, gaudy green or faded blue. He named the house Macaw Cottage after the multicolored parrot.

He labeled the front attic "The Museum" for his collections. He took the back bedroom for his study, arranged his bookshelves, desk, hung Martens's water colors on the walls along with several earlier etchings, placed his *Beagle* instruments on a table. He wished he could make the drawing room as comfortable.

Fanny Wedgwood called at the house to inform him that she had inquired into the qualifications of a cook, Jane, and advised Charles to hire her.

"She'll cost you fourteen pounds ten per year, with tea and sugar."

Charles hired the woman, instructed her to see that the fires were blazing in all four main rooms for Tuesday evening when he and Emma would arrive after their wedding. Syms Covington moved into his own lodgings with Charles's assurance that he would give him a high recommendation for a new job.

He ordered in coal, sent Margaret shopping for a supply of groceries, then set off for Shrewsbury. His new tailor, Mr. Stewart, wanted to make him a blue coat and white trousers for the wedding but Charles vowed that he would wear only what he could travel in decently. Clothing was unimportant. He had just been elected a fellow of the Royal Society, a distinction which England bestowed on its talented scientists, the most prized honor in academic and professional circles! It was a wedding gift he was proudly carrying to Maer to share with Emma.

He spent two days at The Mount, then with his father, Susan and Katty rode to Maer Hall, arriving the afternoon before the wedding to find the house filled with a host of both their relatives. Emma was so busy having her gown fitted that she hugged him just once and murmured, "See you in church in the morning." By evening the noisy, laughing, drinking group was quieted by the news that Emma's mother would not be strong enough to be carried up to the church; Caroline's and Joe's first baby, ill for two months, had taken a turn for the worse.

Nevertheless the wedding went off stoutheartedly. Emma was beautiful in her wedding gown of gray-green silk and a remarkably lovely white chip bonnet trimmed with blond flowers. The church was cool but hospitable with the winter sun coming through the stained-glass windows. John Wedgwood, Vicar of Maer, read the marriage ceremony in a resonant voice that filled the little chapel.

"Dearly beloved, we are gathered together here in the sight of God, and in the face of this company, to join together this Man and this Woman in holy Matrimony; which is an honourable estate . . ."

Charles was so nervous that on the first of two marriage certificates he had to sign he managed to run an ink line through his middle name, partly obliterating it. The ensuing laughter broke up the intensity of the ceremony.

It was midmorning when they trooped down the hill, Charles and

Emma arm in arm, to have punch and spongecake. Emma changed from her wedding gown, sat for a few minutes before the fire in the dining room with her two sisters, then went upstairs to her mother's room to say good-by. She was relieved to find her asleep, saving them both the pain of parting. She returned downstairs and said to Charles:

"I'm ready to leave now."

They were driven to the new railroad station at Whitmore, a mile and three quarters from Maer, in the family carriage. On the train they enjoyed the chicken, cucumber and tomato sandwiches Elizabeth had made up for them, and were refreshed by the bottle of cool water she had included.

They arrived at Upper Gower Street rather late in the evening. Fires were burning brightly in the drawing room, the sitting room behind it, upstairs in their bedroom. They were overwhelmed to see Edward, The Mount's long-time butler and Charles's friend, appear in a doorway to congratulate them.

"Edward," Charles exclaimed, "what are you doing in London?"

"Dr. Darwin sent me down. Thought I might be helpful for a couple of weeks while Mrs. Darwin gets settled in."

Emma cried, "Oh, Edward, you are as welcome as the flowers in May. What a nice thing for Dr. Darwin to do."

They wandered from room to room, Emma's hand snuggled in Charles's.

"Perhaps it's because the lamps are turned low and the fires blazing, Charles, but the house looks very comfortable and I am getting to think the furniture quite tasteful."

"So do you look tasteful, Mrs. Darwin."

"Mrs. Darwin. My, my! It sounds extra special."

Edward served them supper before the fireplace in Charles's study, then bade them a discreet good night. Charles put a shovelful of coal at the back of the fireplace in the bedroom so that it would burn all night.

They retired early, for it had been a long day. While they lay clasped in each other's arms, he spoke against Emma's lips:

"When Fanny married her cousin Hensleigh, Fanny's maid was asked her opinion of the marriage. She replied, 'Well, ma'am, I think it won't make much difference.'

"Emma, my dearest, that maid was wrong. It makes all the difference in the world."

# BOOK EIGHT

*"Love Is a Fever in the Blood"*

## 1.

AFTER a leisurely breakfast Emma, fully dressed, said:
"Dear Charley, we'll have to buy me a morning gown. I didn't want to get one in Staffordshire for fear you might not like it."

"I'll like you in anything . . ." He suppressed the desire to add, ". . . or nothing."

He found marriage companionable.

They slipped into an easy pattern. Because there was only one arm-chair in the Gower Street house which Emma found comfortable but Charles did not, they hired a fly which took them the short distance to Hewetson, Milner & Thexton on Tottenham Court Road, known as Furniture Row. In the third shop they came across an oversized mahogany chair upholstered in stamped red velvet. Charles asserted:

"It was made for oversized readers, for bookworms. It supports my back at the same time that it releases my long legs."

The day was cold, the streets slippery and snowy; they did little else but stop at a library and bring home a novel which they read aloud before the fire in the study.

The next morning they slopped through the melted snow to buy Emma's morning gown, a claret-brown satin with a high collar.

"Do you like it, Charles? I find it unobjectionable."

"It's beautiful on you, though I doubt the satin is going to keep you warm."

"I'll let you do that, dear one."

Dinner that night was poor. Emma was not impressed by Jane, a saucy young redhead.

"The cook is not very good, is she?" she asked.

"Not very."

"I shall have to face her in her own region. Which part of the dinner did you like the least?"

"The potatoes. Overboiled."

"Very well, I shall find fault with the boiling of the potatoes. That will make a good beginning and set me up a little."

The following day they went together to Broadwood's, which sold pianofortes. Emma looked around the floor for the one selected for her by the Rev. Thomas Stevens, a friend of the Wedgwood family who had given her piano lessons. She found the piano with Mr. Stevens's card on it. It was in a beautiful mahogany case; literally a grand piano. When Emma sat down and played snatches of her favorite pieces her face was wreathed in smiles.

"Oh, Charles, it gives out such a marvelous sound. It has none of the faults of touch that ours has at Maer. Trust the Reverend Mr. Stevens to choose the best for me."

Charles gave the manager of the shop the order to deliver the instrument to 12 Upper Gower Street as quickly as possible.

They had received a charming water color of Barmouth painted by Emma's sister Charlotte, and hung it in the sitting room on one side of the fireplace. The other side was bare. Not wanting to ask Charlotte directly for a companion piece, Emma wrote to Elizabeth, saying:

> If Charlotte should have any curiosity about the size of her Barmouth, it is 13 inches by 8½. Ahem!

In a remarkably short time they received a second water color of precisely the same size as the Barmouth. It went up on the other side of the fireplace. The blue wall looked better with their additional prints and drawings complimenting Charlotte's landscapes.

Their next outing was by carriage to Lambert and Rawlings at 11 Coventry Street just off Regent Circus to purchase their silver, plate and cutlery. Emma liked best the King's pattern made by Harrison Bros. & Houson, a Sheffield firm, Cutlers to Her Majesty. It was a shell and leaf design with a shell embossed on each handle on the back and on the front. She bought a service for twelve, twelve enormous soup spoons, twelve smaller spoons for tea and twelve a bit larger for dessert; there were twelve steel knives with silver handles, the blades sharp for cutting meat; and twelve bread and butter knives. They selected heavy forks for the main courses and smaller forks for the puddings. They also acquired a fish set with ivory handles and a big fish slice and fork. For apples, pears and other fruits there were smaller silver knives and forks with pearl handles. Each set came in its own velvet-lined slotted chest. When Emma added up the cost she whispered to Charles:

"We've half ruined ourselves!"

"Let's go the other half," he said magnanimously. "Choose your silver bowls. Father gave us two hundred pounds as a stopgap wedding present until we find a home in the country. That will be his earnest gift."

Other members of their families had also given gifts of money with which to buy their plate. Emma took infinite care in selecting her silver platters, soup tureens, jam pots, tea set, making sure that Charles was accepting her choices. She chose her cutlery on the basis of what she knew of the Maer Hall kitchen. At the end of a number of hours of comparing and questioning they had completed their purchases for the dining room and the kitchen and had spent a hundred and eighty pounds for the silver and cutlery, another sixty for the plate. Seeing it all assembled, shining and luxurious, Charles commented:

"This stock should last us a lifetime."

"It will. I somehow feel more married now that I can set a proper table."

They were happy as they rode home in the carriage, laughing and kissing like the newlyweds they were, knowing they were out of sight of the driver who sat high up on his box in front.

Edward admitted them. There was a letter on the hall table. Emma exclaimed:

"It's from Elizabeth. I'd recognize her handwriting in a desert sandstorm."

She opened the letter, read a few lines, burst into tears.

"It's Caroline's baby. The poor little thing died. She is taking it very hard. She will be desolate."

"Only until she has her next child, a healthy one, which is bound to happen," he said in an attempt to console Emma.

On Saturday while out walking, Charles spotted a piano wagon near their home. He followed it back to the house, watched the moving men, experts at their craft, turn the pianoforte on its side in order to haul it up the one flight of stairs and install it in the niche between the back and side walls of the first-floor sitting room. Emma immediately sat down and ran through some Handel and Haydn.

"I shall give you a large dose of music every evening," she cried.

"Didn't William Congreve say that music hath charms to soothe the savage breast?"

"You should have taken a pianoforte with you to Tierra del Fuego."

Emma decided to try her hand on family for her first dinner, serving an oyster soup, lemon sole, roast turkey and "vitings," a seasoned stuffing. Hensleigh and Fanny arrived early the following Tuesday evening. Hensleigh was floating with happiness:

"A wonderful piece of good fortune. I've obtained the position of Registrar of Cabs. No oaths need be administered. I am to receive five hundred pounds a year, three hundred less than I earned as a police magistrate, but we can get along."

Charles wrung his hand, kissed Fanny's cheek. He knew how much she had suffered during the past year.

"I'll be employed from ten to four, four days a week," Hensleigh went on. "That will leave me leisure for my research and writing. During the entire year that I had no employment I couldn't concentrate on my etymology. The origin and derivation of words seemed so meaningless when I had no place in the world. Now I do; humble as it may be."

Hensleigh was the closest of the Wedgwood sons to Josiah; not as tall, but slim, with a mass of dark curls and wide-spaced intelligent eyes. He had been bookish since childhood and encouraged by his father to read widely; he had become a high wrangler at Christ's College and been offered a fellowship. He had rejected the offer because of the giving and taking of oaths at Cambridge University.

Fanny, who was a first cousin to Emma on her mother's side, was an ash blonde, with gray eyes and a patient "I can stand anything" air. She had backed Hensleigh in his resolution to resign his highly paid position as police magistrate; and moved the family from their spacious home in Clapham to the one on Notting Hill.

Since Hensleigh and Fanny were staying overnight, Emma showed them to their bedroom. When she returned to the study, Charles asked:

"Where do you suppose Hensleigh picked up this fetish against oaths?"

"Papa tried to find out but Hensleigh considers it an integral part of his privacy."

"So it is. Yet he ardently yearns to be a scholar and to publish. The fellowship at Cambridge would have given him that opportunity."

Edward, who appeared an Adonis in his best livery from The Mount, set the table with the Wedgwood china and crystal from the plant in Etruria. Emma's father and two brothers at the pottery had selected the floral motif, a red and dark blue border with roses on a white background. Their silver service, bowls and platters gleamed on the none too handsome sideboard that had come with the house.

Erasmus arrived at seven, meticulously garbed in a long-tailed, wide-lapeled coat and waistcoat, his black stock tied tight around the white collar. His hair was receding from his brow so he grew thick patches of it above each ear. His eyes held a bemused smile. Wandering through the house for the first time, he came upon the dining room and exclaimed:

"Ah, you've done yourself proud!"

The five family members sat down to dinner. Outside the windows the garden was dark but it gave the room a sense of spaciousness. Edward brought in a bowl of the steaming hot soup which was ladled into the deep plates, the platter of sole, then the roast turkey, "vitings" and roast potatoes. Erasmus said with a sardonic grin:

"Ha! A base imitation of my Marlborough Street dinner."

Emma was amused.

"I must admit, Ras, that the likeness is very striking."

Then a bowl of plum pudding appeared. Erasmus tasted several mouthfuls, capitulated:

"Emma, I'm sure I appear knocked under. I confess myself conquered."

Charles allowed himself an eight-day honeymoon. He spent his time with Emma, shopping, taking long walks in good weather, attending concerts, including Blagrove's. On the ninth day he bounded out of bed so resolutely that he woke her. She rubbed her eyes, saw him standing over her, tall, broad-shouldered in his striped nightshirt, his auburn hair night-mussed over his forehead.

". . . Charles . . . what's wrong?"

"I got out of bed."

"So I see. Were you fleeing from someone in a bad dream?"

"That's the way I always get up when I start work."

He leaned over, kissed her good morning.

"I learned that from Sir Walter Scott, who said, 'Once turn on your side and all is over.'"

He closed the study door behind him, plunged into his book on corals, setting forth the argument that atolls were not based on craters. Emma summoned him for breakfast at ten, serving him the foods he had liked at Maer. They ate and chatted in leisurely fashion until eleven when Charles returned to work, writing and checking in his reference books until two, five hours of concentration which Lyell had advised him was sufficient for a day.

"I'll have to spend the afternoon at the Geological Society," he told Emma after their midday meal. "There must be a bundle of papers awaiting my reading and abstracting. I've neglected them ever since you accepted me. Neglected everything else as well. I hadn't realized love was such a fever in the blood."

"You'll make up for it," she replied serenely. "You'll save time by not being obliged to court other girls."

"I began and ended my courting with you."

Emma became serious.

"I think we ought to send Edward back to The Mount in a day or two. I know how dependent your father is on him. I managed Maer Hall, with Elizabeth, of course. This house is simple by comparison. We often had as many as a dozen guests. Here, you're my only guest, and a most cooperative one, I might add."

"I'll give Edward a nice gift from the two of us. Shall we walk in Regent's Park before I immolate myself at the Geological Society?"

"I'll wear my best bonnet."

She did, but it started to rain while they were in the park. They were fortunate to find a gig on Euston Road, immediately outside, which saved Emma's hat. Charles continued on to the Geological Society and plunged into the pile of scientific papers.

He went back to his fourth notebook on species, which he had begun in October 1838. He had quoted from Malthus:

> "It accords with the most *liberal!* spirit of philosophy to believe that no stone can fall or plant rise without the immediate agency of the deity. But we know from *experience!* that these operations of what we call nature have been conducted *almost!* invariably according to fixed laws: and since the world began, the causes of population & depopulation have been probably as constant as any of the laws of nature with which we are acquainted".—I would apply it not only to population & depopulation, but extermination & production of new forms. . . .

He started reading seriously again, putting in three to four hours a day on Pope Eugenius IV's *Observations on Morals,* John Phillips's *A Treatise on Geology.* Yet it was by no means all work; they walked the short distance to the Lyells' for tea, where Mary Lyell exclaimed:

"Charles, I'm so happy you found yourself a wife. Now I won't have to listen to you and my Charles spout all that geology. Emma and I will have a jolly visit about human affairs."

Dr. Henry Holland and his wife Saba gave an elaborate dinner party in their honor. Holland said:

"Marriage agrees with you, my boy. Emma, you've done us a great service."

Charles answered:

"I've turned over my digestion and my heart to my wife."

He left Emma alone only when his paper on Glen Roy was read at the Royal Society, and when he went to the Geological Society to help celebrate its thirty-second anniversary and hear President Whewell's address on fossil shells.

In January the second installment of John Gould's *Birds* had been published, with ten color plates. Richard Owen's second section of *Fossil Mammalia,* illustrated with ten lithographs, was ready for distribution. George Waterhouse was the fastest worker; he had already published three installments for his *Mammalia* and had a fourth under way. At ten shillings each, the installments were selling well. Charles visited the writers frequently, kept meticulous account of the government money he was expending.

Wanting a change from corals, he plunged into a chapter on earthquakes which intrigued him at the moment even though it would not appear until a later volume of his trilogy. Emma, coming to summon him for his two o'clock meal—he rarely consulted his own gold watch—and seeing the sheaf of notebooks filled with his hieroglyphic scrawls strewn over his desk, said:

"My dear old Charles, I never knew how hard you really work. Your visits to Maer Hall were for rest or holiday. I'm happy to see how much satisfaction you take from your writing."

He sat her down on his lap, kissed her.

"Emma dear, there are only two important elements in life, love and work. Or work and love, in whichever order you prefer."

"Let's put love first." She returned his kiss. "Wash all that ink off your fingers. I have a lemon sole for you."

"You're a very nice girl to always serve the foods I like best."

"I'm not a girl, dear, I'm a woman," she retorted. "Besides, I don't think a fellow of the Royal Society should split an infinitive."

He had fallen into his father's lifetime habit of keeping a detailed account book of all monies spent: so much for food, for wine and beer, for coal, for his haircuts, for gigs and carriages, for books, for clothing, everything down to the last ha'penny; for the wages of the cook and housemaid and their new man, whom Emma did not much like.

"He serves well enough but that's about all he does, except order Margaret and Jane around. I particularly resent his getting twice as much salary as our women for half their service."

"If you don't like him, hire another. But we'll still have to pay thirty-five pounds a year. That's the standard wage."

"I know that in London it's considered proper to keep a manservant," Emma said; "but I would be much happier with only women."

Late in February he began browsing in the bookshops again. From Yarrell's shop he bought a book on the lives of Haydn and Mozart for Emma; for himself, William Herbert's *Amaryllidaceae*, dealing with hybrid mixtures, in which he made marginal notes; the three volumes of Carlyle's *French Revolution*, which made Erasmus happy for his friend; Wells's lectures on *Instinct*; Cline's *On the Breeding of Animals*; a treatise on domestic pigeons and, to refresh his memory, the first volume of his grandfather's *Zoonomia*.

On Sunday mornings, regardless of the weather, they went to a not too distant church for services and to hear the choir sing. Charles knew that Emma was religious by nature. Most of the Wedgwoods were Unitarians, as Charles's mother had been. His grandfather, the redoubtable Dr. Erasmus Darwin, once said, "Unitarianism is a featherbed to catch a falling Christian." Charles could not think of anyone in either the Darwin or Wedgwood families who was devout. He now realized that his wife was an intense believer. He resolved to take her to church every Sunday. In early March they walked the mile and a half to the church at King's College, found only half a dozen people in the unwarmed chapel. Midway through the service he felt a chill run through him.

"Emma, it's bitterly cold in here. Could we go?"

"As soon as the service is over."

They were fortunate to find a carriage outside Somerset House, next to King's College, and were very quickly home. She put him to bed, fed him tea with lemon; was relieved when he had entirely recovered after a few days.

He also supported Emma's love of the theater. He took her to the new play, *Richelieu*, starring the famous actor Macready. The pit was crammed full of people, "listening with all their ears," Emma whispered. Charles found himself applauding heartily. On the way home he commented:

"The story was interesting and well acted. I do thank you for reconverting me into a theatergoer. I had resigned from the order."

In mid-March Charles noticed that his usually imperturbable Emma was fretting.

"I have a desire to part with Jane," she explained. "I have the genuine feeling that she is too cute, and is rather making the most of us."

"Is she pilfering?"

"I particularly wish not to find any dishonesty. I want to be able to give her a character."

"You should not have anyone in your home with whom you feel uneasy," he declared.

Emma smiled happily.

"Thank you, Charley, you old gentleman. I shall take courage tomorrow and tell her she does not suit. Your sister Susan has heard of a woman in Shropshire she thinks will do. It will be quite refreshing to have a countrified person."

"Not to mention countrified food!"

Susan's countrified Sally arrived very shortly. She was plump, middle-aged, happy about her first chance to live in London. Emma liked her, was comfortable having her in the house.

Their good fortune continued. Emma had tried two manservants, neither of whom suited.

"I'll try only once more," she told Charles determinedly; "then I shall defy convention and do without."

Joseph Parslow was recommended. He seemed to fit into the family from the moment he came in the front door. He was twenty-seven, slight of build, homely in an inoffensive way, as fast on his feet as a cat. He had tried several trades, for which he had no talent, then gone into domestic service. He had not liked the two previous homes in which he had worked; they were cold, the people aloof.

"What I'm wantin', ma'am, is a family I can join. Like, say, permanint. Be a member. Liking my people. Being treated decent, not looked down on. Takin' good care of their house, their persons. . . ."

"Joseph Parslow, you are hired. If you mean what you say, you have found a family."

Parslow got along well with Margaret and Sally, polished the silver, trimmed the wicks and filled the lamps, served the meals, ran errands for Charles, shopped for Emma. He was indefatigable, good-natured, loving Charles and Emma and their friends when he opened the door to them and served tea in the sitting room.

"Parslow is a young Edward," said Emma. "We now have a smooth-running household."

Adam Sedgwick came to call one Thursday at teatime toward the end of March. He was happy with his church work as the canon of Norwich combined with his geology professorship at Cambridge. He made no bones about being proud of his protégé. He and Emma had never met and so he set out to entertain her during his three cups of tea with tales of how he conquered mountains with Old Thor. When he left, complimenting Emma on the cucumber and watercress sandwiches and sweet cakes, Charles said:

"Still the unconquerable mountain climber and spouter of yards of English poetry."

"He is a remarkably fresh man, but there is something odd about him."

"Odd? That's because he's a confirmed bachelor. All confirmed bachelors are odd. Look at Ras. That's why I married you, so I wouldn't appear odd."

2.

Charles received a letter from John Henslow; he and Harriet were coming up to London and hoped to visit them. Emma had never met the Henslows but she knew the critical part they had played in Charles's life.

"Why don't we invite them to stay with us?" she asked. "The spare room is presentable now with the new prints on the walls."

He wrote the invitation and promptly started worrying.

"How are we to entertain them? Can we have a party with scientists whom Henslow will enjoy? Perhaps I should reserve a carriage for several days . . . ?"

Emma laughed.

"You sound like a son who is inviting his demanding parents into his home for the first time. Not to worry. All will go well."

There never were easier guests. They arrived at four in the afternoon. Harriet took herself off to the guest room to rest; Charles and Henslow vanished into the study. Emma was released to supervise the final details for her first big dinner party. The table was beautiful with its elegant Wedgwood service, the shell-and-leaf-patterned silverware, the sparkling crystal and fine linen damask cloth, another wedding gift. She was then free to bathe and dress leisurely in an off-the-shoulder blue velvet gown which complimented her coloring.

The Lyells were the first to arrive, bringing Mary Lyell's sister Leonora. The Henslows and Lyells were old friends. Soon after, Robert Brown arrived; Henslow and Brown, two of the most famous botanists in England, fell upon each other with high glee. Dr. William Fitton, eminent geologist and past president of the Geological Society, was quite late. Emma became disturbed. She went into the kitchen to make sure that Sally did not let the dinner burn.

"Trust it to me, mum. I always allows for laters. Got 'em all the time in Shropshire, partic'lar when roads was bad."

William Fitton apologized over a fast glass of sherry, then the party took to table. Emma had done them proud with the menu.

"You don't mind if I show off a little bit, do you?" she had asked Charles.

Parslow, in his new frock coat, black trousers and boiled shirt provided by the Darwins, brought in a puree of artichoke soup, a cod's head in oyster sauce, Provençal cutlets and sweetbreads in white sauce; then a saddle of mutton followed by fruit and cheese, an ice pudding; sweetmeats and sugarplums from a silver dish, small cakes. There was a good claret.

In spite of the delicious food, the atmosphere was heavy. For some reason Lyell, who had an outpouring voice when discussing geology in his home, did not once speak above his breath, so that the others lowered their tones to match his. No one could hear a thing. Robert Brown, whom Humboldt had described as "the glory of Great Britain," was so shy that he appeared to shrink into himself and disappear entirely.

"Dear, oh dear," thought Emma, "with those two dead weights this learned dinner party is going to fall as flat as a cold soufflé."

The women saved the day. Harriet Henslow had a good, loud, sharp voice. She began to tell the newest tales about the Cambridge faculties. Mary Lyell, astonished at her husband's breathlessness, revenged all the hours she had sat mute while he ranted technical geology, and took over with a vigorous repartee. Charles, seeing what had happened, dove headlong into the conversation, drawing out each of his friends in turn. Lyell and Brown had to speak up to be heard. Everyone had a good time and congratulated Emma on her sumptuous meal.

The next morning Henslow took himself off for a day of consultations. Harriet ordered a gig and went to pay social calls. Charles was fagged out from having to help the women save the party.

They gathered together for tea. Harriet and Emma had taken to each other at once. Harriet confided:

"You know, Charles, I used to be concerned about you. Would you pick the wrong kind of wife? Or would you remain a bachelor like Adam Sedgwick? I must compliment you."

"I agree," responded Charles heartily.

The Henslows stayed only a few days. On Wednesday the Lyells gave a dinner party for them, and the next day William Fitton entertained. When they were about to depart John announced:

"I've saved the real news for last. We're selling our home in Cambridge and moving out to a Crown living at Hitcham in Suffolk where I am rector of the parish. I'll return to Cambridge each spring to teach my botany course."

He leaned forward on the sofa, his hands clasped intently before him.

"There's much to be done in Hitcham. The parish of upwards of a thousand people is poor, uneducated. Baptism and the marriage ceremony are regarded as superfluities or luxuries. The church is empty. With regard to food, clothing and the means of observing the decencies of life, the inhabitants are far below the average scale of the peasant class in England. It's a serious challenge which I am determined to accept. These people have to be brought back into the Church. One way will be to introduce modern methods of agriculture which can raise their standard of living. As a self-professed man of God, I can do no less."

There followed a happy and productive month of map making and drawing to illustrate sections of the Keeling Atoll and the reefs of Mauritius, revealing new materials on the rate of growth, depth at which corals live, submerged and dead coral reefs. He worked most of the day. This was agreeable to Emma, for it gave her privacy, the time to get used to living in London. In the evenings she read to him from the humorous lines of *Mr. Slick of Slickville's Sayings*, or played a soothing piano recital.

Toward the end of April, wanting a change from the concentration on corals, he turned to his continuing search in the realm of species. In his fourth notebook he set down:

When two races of men meet they act precisely like two species of animals: they fight, eat each other, bring diseases to each other &c., but then comes the most deadly struggle, namely which have the best fitted organization or instincts (i.e. intellect in man) to gain the day. . . .

It is difficult to believe in the dreadful but quiet war of organic beings going on [as] the peaceful woods & smiling fields. We must recollect the multitude of plants introduced into our gardens (opportunities of escape for foreign buds & insects) which are propagated with very little care, & which might spread themselves as well as our wild plants, we see now full nature, how finely each holds its place.

Then he made a generalization about all variation:

My principle being the destruction of all the less hardy ones, & the preservation of accidental hardy ones.

He made a serious error in judgment. He had no one with whom to discuss his species work except Charles Lyell, who was already a believer in change and modification. He saw no reason why he should not tell Emma why he was buying books on animal breeding and reproduction, why he was writing letters to stock men who were crossbreeding to obtain new and useful strains. Sometimes, while writing in his current notebook and checking back for materials in the earlier three, he would comment on this work, unformed and hesitant as yet, which fascinated the whole of his mind.

"It was Malthus who gave me the final link in the chain," he explained, "by writing that there is a constant tendency in all animated life to increase beyond the nourishment prepared for it. My theory that the amount of change within historical times has been small cannot be objected to; change in one form is a result of change in circumstances. It makes sense that when a species becomes rarer, as it progresses toward extinction, some other species must increase in number where there is this gap."

Emma did not question his statements but went on with her crocheting, her head down in a silence which Charles, in his enthusiasm for the subject, took to be assent.

Another evening he told her:

"Every structure is capable of innumerable variations as long as each shall be perfectly adapted to the circumstances of the times."

Still Emma did not respond. Had he not been so caught up in his own involvement, he might have detected that this silence of Emma's was different from any other he had heard. What brought the problem to a climax was a long discussion he had late one afternoon with Lyell which he reported in his notebook and, later that evening, to Emma:

"Lyell remarked that species never reappear when once extinct. He suggests that from the remotest periods there has been ever a coming in of new organic forms. My own studies and observations substantiate this. Lyell also suggests that there has been an extinction of those forms which pre-existed on the earth. Such as the Megatherium fossils I found in South America."

Emma looked up with a disturbed expression.

"Are you suggesting that there is no God?"

"I am suggesting that God, in the beginning, created certain laws. Then He retired, allowing His laws to work themselves out."

It was the first time he noticed Emma's concern. But he was not prepared for the sequel. The following night, as they were undressing for bed, she said quietly:

"Charles, my dear, I have put a letter on your desk. Well, not really a letter, rather a communication. Would you prefer to read it tonight, or perhaps tomorrow morning?"

"It's the first time since we've been married that you've written me a communication. I had better get to it at once."

He donned a robe, went into his study, picked up Emma's "communication," written in her precise manner.

"Too precise," he thought. "Emma must have rewritten this several times."

> The state of mind that I wish to preserve with respect to you, is to feel that while you are acting conscientiously and sincerely wishing and trying to learn the truth, you cannot be wrong, but there are some reasons that force themselves upon me, and prevent myself from being always able to give myself this comfort. I daresay you have often thought of them before, but I will write down what has been in my head, knowing that my own dearest will indulge me. . . .
>
> May not the habit in scientific pursuits of believing nothing till it is proved, influence your mind too much in other things which cannot be proved in the same way? And which if true are likely to be above our comprehension? I should say also there is a danger in giving up Revelation which does not exist on the other side, that is the fear of ingratitude in casting off what has been done for your benefit as well as for that of all the world, and which ought to make you still more careful, perhaps even fearful lest you should not have taken all the pains you could to judge truly. . . .
>
> I do not wish for any answer to all this—it is a satisfaction to me to write it. Don't think that it is not my affair and that it does not much signify to me. Everything that concerns you concerns me and I should be most unhappy if I thought we

did not belong to each other forever. I am rather afraid my own dear will think I have forgotten my promise not to bother him, but I am sure he loves me, and I cannot tell him how happy he makes me and how dearly I love him and thank him for all his affection which makes the happiness of my life more and more every day.

He felt the tears roll down his cheeks at Emma's expression of love for him as well as her anxiety over his danger if he lost God and the promise of everlasting life. She had written of her fear of his "giving up Revelation" and his "casting off what had been done for his benefit, as well as that of all the world," obviously by God Almighty.

His mind was awhirl. He sat at his desk for an interminable time, then paced his study. When he looked into the bedroom he saw that Emma was fast asleep. She had done her duty as she saw it; it enabled her to achieve tranquillity. He kissed the letter for the intensity and wholeness of her love, then stood at the window of his study overlooking the dark garden. What was he to do? He could not go on with his work on the origin and fallibility of species if that work frightened his wife. It would be a sword in the side of their marriage, with perhaps a serious enough wound to destroy it.

"I cannot impose such a crushing burden on her. She deserves better from me. She wants only to save me from eternal damnation!"

He had made no sacrifices for Emma; he had merely accepted the wholeheartedness of her love and the goodness of life it would bring him. It was proper that he live happily as a geologist and give up the pursuit which questioned the Thirty-nine Articles of the Church of England, not one of which his mentor, Professor John Henslow, disbelieved.

This must be the end of his apostasy. At least he had had the good sense not to spread his heretical findings at the Royal and the Geological societies, and perhaps be drummed out for his efforts. He had placed himself in danger without realizing the ultimate consequences.

Emma had awakened him to his responsibilities. In the morning he would burn the notebooks. She would never mention the subject to him again. The door was closed. "Permanently."

He got into bed and lay shivering in the dark. He could have warmed himself by snuggling close to his wife but he felt he had no right to do so. Not on this night. He felt each minute and hour struggle by. At dawn he was still awake. He rose, went back into his chilly study, sat down at his desk . . . and wrote eight more pages in his species notebook.

It may be said that wild animals will vary according to my Malthusian views, without certain limits, but beyond them not. Argue against this. Analogy will certainly allow variation as much as the difference between species, for instance pigeons; then comes question of genera. It certainly appears that swallows have decreased in numbers; what cause?

He did not tell Emma that he was impelled by a force stronger than himself to drive forward with his questioning. He dipped into two new books, On the Influence of Physical Agents and A Familiar History of Birds. Then he could do no more. Several days went by in troubled idleness. He did not consider that he was brooding, or being willful. He just could not work.

He became ill. Ran a fever, had palpitations of the heart, vomited.

"Charles, what can it be?" Emma asked. "The food; not enough exercise? Worries about your father or sisters? The household?" She came close to him, put a hand in his.

"Do you find anything wrong with me?" She had her letter to him in mind.

"Yes. I love you exceedingly well."

Emma kissed his warm brow.

"We'll just live with it as painlessly as we can, until it goes away, as mysteriously as it came."

3.

They followed the advice Dr. Clark had given Charles some time before. On April 26 they left for Maer. It was one of the loveliest times of the year in Staffordshire. The pink cherry and white almond trees were beginning to bloom. Tulips of every hue were breaking through the soil. The elms were full along the roads and in the fields. The green hills moved back like waves, starting one behind the other.

They found Elizabeth, alone now to take care of both ailing parents, working in the garden, in a patch of crocuses, when they arrived. She raised herself from her knees with difficulty.

"I was planting the flowers when a feeling took me by surprise that I was doing it all alone, and for nobody else. I took a fit of sadness; but one should like gardening, like any art, for its own sake. . . . I am so happy to see you; I shall enjoy three weeks of your company and go with you to Shrewsbury for your last week. One of our cousins will take care of Mama."

Although his own volume of The Narrative of the Surveying Voyages of His Majesty's Ships "Adventure" and "Beagle" would not be officially released until sometime that summer, he had picked up freshly bound copies to take to Maer and The Mount. Josiah Wedgwood would hardly speak to anyone for the three days he was engrossed in the book.

"For you in particular, Uncle Jos, it has to be worth while," said Charles. "You risked a lifetime friendship with my father to rescue the voyage for me."

Josiah rose from his leather chair with an effort, and put a hand on Charles's shoulder.

"I knew I was depriving Emma of a prospective husband for a few years. But I judged the journey would set you on the right track. It all worked out. Good fortune? The will of God?"

A fortnight later, in mid-May, they rode the twenty miles into Shrewsbury. Dr. Robert Darwin examined his son and arrived at a plausible answer to his continuing sense of being unwell.

"I believe you are feeling the effect of too much exertion in every way during your voyage. Let us say that during those five years of exploration you lived and worked as intensely as you would have in twenty years in England. You must be careful not to work your head too hard."

That night, after Emma had fallen asleep and he could hear her gentle breathing, he probed his mind. On the entire five years' voyage of the *Beagle* he had been ill on only three or four occasions, the worst time when he had drunk raw Indian whiskey in Valparaíso. Considering all the brackish water he had drunk, the strange native foods he had eaten, the insects that had bitten him, he had been extremely healthy. Why now, for no apparent reason, was he ill? He thrived on work.

"I don't think Father is right about my noodle being exhausted," he muttered aloud. "I had more than enough days on deck, or reading on FitzRoy's sofa, relaxed and resting. I felt wonderfully strong during my months at Cambridge and while living in Great Marlborough Street . . . until that first attack in September of 1837. What was I doing at the time?"

He rose gingerly so as not to awaken Emma, went downstairs, lighted a lamp in the warm, airless library. He reviewed all he could remember about that period. He had been employed on his journal, had written two papers for the Geological Society, one on corals, the other on extinct mammalia; and was also working on getting his government grant for the zoology books.

Then, not suddenly, but wound down, somewhat as a ball of string finally becomes unwound, he had stopped all that and had begun his first species notebook, attempting to organize the thoughts aroused by the Galápagos tortoises, the finches from four different islands, the South American fossils he had uncovered at Punta Alta. He had found that exhilarating if, in a strange way, more exhausting than his other writing. The geology was based largely on observation; even for the radical theory which contradicted Lyell about the growth of coral atolls he had proof that his findings were sound. But the speculation on how species were born, changed, adapted, either died out or flourished, here he was on marshy ground and could be covered with mud up to his eyebrows. Almost all was supposition, conjecture, surmise, hypothesis. He had stumbled upon a handle with no biological Old Thor with which to carve out specimens from the life stream. Besides, he was tinkering with problems and answers which had been divinely revealed and settled for all time.

He sipped a cool lemonade he had rescued from a cellar room.

"But I never intended to publish my thoughts, or to speak about them to anyone except Lyell, who wouldn't resent my questioning. It was just an exercise for me, really, to keep my head straightened on."

He went back up the broad staircase and turned left to their bedroom. Sleep still did not come. As he fitted himself gently against Emma's back for comfort, he continued to ponder on his curious condition.

An answer came to him, bringing relief in its wake.

"But of course! My feeling unwell has nothing whatever to do with my four notebooks. The truth is that I never turn to them until I am literally exhausted from long stretches of my other work. I pick up these notebooks and fill them with jottings only after I have reached a surfeit with geology and zoology. *I escape to the species notebooks.*"

With which, he fell into a sound sleep. In the morning, warm and fragrant for mid-May, he awakened refreshed and feeling fine. When Emma returned from the bathing room with its deep metal tubs and pots of hot water, he announced:

"Emma dear, I'm completely recovered. Now I'm eager that we return to London so I can get on with my work."

"I'm happy for you, Charley, my old soul. You had us all worried, you know."

The farewells were boisterous; Charles told the family that they would be back in August or September.

They returned home to find from their newspapers that London was much perturbed about a scandal at the court of Queen Victoria. Accusations of immoral conduct against Lady Flora Hastings, a lady in waiting to the Queen's mother, were being bruited about. Lady Hastings was extremely popular in society circles. When the source of the scandalous rumors pointed to Queen Victoria herself—and were later found to be totally false—the press and the public came down hard on the monarch and her Prime Minister, Lord Melbourne.

The following day he was walking across Trafalgar Square when a familiar face came toward him. He stopped short, cried:

"Dr. Robert McCormick! I haven't seen you since you invalided yourself home from Rio de Janeiro; that must be almost seven years ago. Do you still have that gray parrot you wanted to bring back to England?"

"Charles Darwin! What a memory you do have. Yes, that blasted parrot is still talking his head off. May I introduce Joseph Hooker? He's coming with me as my assistant surgeon on H.M.S. *Erebus* to explore the Antarctic." McCormick's face wore a triumphant smile. "*I am named the naturalist this time.*"

"You loved the expedition to the cold climate and barely survived the tropics, Doctor," Charles responded. He turned to Joseph Hooker, a pleasant-looking chap of about twenty-two, wearing steel-rimmed spectacles which slightly enlarged his already big and alert brown eyes.

"Are you going on the *Erebus* as assistant naturalist as well?"

"No, Mr. Darwin, as the botanist of the four-year journey. I want to follow my father's profession. He's the professor of botany at Glasgow University."

"Then you must know the work of my good friend Professor John Henslow."

"Naturally. I also know the work of Charles Darwin."

"My work? How? There is so little of it published."

"I've read the proof sheets of your *Journal*. Charles Lyell sent the set to his father at Kinnordy, who was taking a kind interest in my projected career as a naturalist, and let me have them. I was taking my medical degree at Glasgow University and was so pressed for time that I slept with your pages under my pillow so that I could read them between waking and rising. They impressed me profoundly . . . and despairingly as well with the variety of requirements, mental and physical, demanded of a naturalist who wanted to follow in your footsteps! You stimulated my desire to travel and observe."

Charles liked the young man, not only for the complimentary sentiments but because he had a wonderfully open, disingenuous manner.

"Hooker, come to see me when you return from your journey. The Geological Society will have my address. Dr. McCormick, bring back a marvelous collection. Good luck, gentlemen."

He was pleased by Hooker's enthusiasm but by late afternoon found himself frustrated by the publisher, Henry Colburn. The first flyer or advertisement had his volume listed at the bottom of the sheet, in small letters, as though it were an addendum to King's and FitzRoy's volumes; was, in fact, the least valuable of the three, an afterthought.

Henry Colburn, in his second-floor office in Great Marlborough Street, was evasive, or at least vague. Yes, he had printed fifteen hundred copies; no, he had not bound them all. How many had he bound? He was not quite sure. The bookstores would have enough sets to begin with. What would happen if this first group did not sell well? He did not know, perhaps the remainder of the sheets would be pulped, storage space was scarce, there were new books coming. . . .

Returning home, he found Syms Covington awaiting him. He had not seen Covington since his marriage though Syms had sent a letter of congratulations along with a modest wedding present. Covington was neatly dressed but Charles noticed that his manner had reverted to the downbeat. However a bright smile came over his face when he saw Charles. Charles greeted him heartily. Syms had been clerking, keeping account books in a big office.

"From your expression, I would say you don't care much about the job."

"No, it's too confining after hunting and collecting with you. I've been saving my wages, miserlike, and I have almost enough for my passage to Australia."

"Australia. So that's the country that impressed you the most."

"Yes, Mr. Darwin. It's big . . . and near empty. Looked to me like a place a man could make a life for himself . . . out in the open. I came to ask would you be so kind as to write me a character?"

"Most certainly."

He wrote:

> I have known Syms Covington for more than eight years; during the whole of that period his conduct has been perfectly satisfactory. He assisted me then as Clerk and this has been his chief employment since that voyage. In circumstances of difficulty he has always behaved with prudence. I have constantly been in the habit of trusting him with large and small sums of money. . . .

Syms thanked him for the letter. Charles said:

"When you get settled be sure to write to me and tell me how you landed."

"Rest assured, Mr. Darwin. If you ever need me I'll come sailing back fast as the winds can carry me."

Charles returned to his work schedule, writing in the coral book as well as his species notebook and reading voraciously. Sir Charles Bell's *The Bridgewater Treatises. The Hand, its mechanism and vital endowments as evincing design*, from which he made comments in his species notebook; Pliny's *Natural History of the World*; the second volume of Lamarck's *Philosophie Zoologique*.

On the first of June a messenger boy brought him the bound volumes by King and FitzRoy and the first notice, which appeared in the *Athenaeum*, one of the most respected magazines in Great Britain. Only King's and FitzRoy's volumes were quoted and described; no criticism was included. A note informed the reader that Charles Darwin's volume would be reviewed soon.

Some few weeks later the *Athenaeum* observed:

> The defect of these volumes is that, consisting not of a single narrative but of several journals of persons viewing the same countries together or in succession, they exhibit occasionally a want of unity and continuous interest and contain frequent repetitions. . . .

Charles had to admit that this criticism was cogent; he was unprepared for the personal approach to himself:

> . . . We must not, however, be supposed to intimate that Mr. Darwin's journal ought to have been dispensed with, or absorbed in the body of the preceding narrative; we only mean to express our regret that by appending it to a work composite in its nature, and diffuse in execution, he should have been obliged to abridge his remarks for the purpose of confining himself as much as possible to his peculiar province, and, even on topics of natural history, to omit many details. . . .

The *Athenaeum* then proceeded to blast his observations that the South American continent had risen from the depths of ocean, a foot at a time. That at least one million years had elapsed since the waves of the sea washed the feet of the Andes. This was patently impossible since Bishop Ussher had pronounced in the seventeenth century that the world had been created in 4004 B.C. Vigorous as they might be, Mr. Darwin's observations and generalizations were without credibility or merit. After that, the book got what Charles described as "real good abuse": the *Journal* was presumptuous, "made up of the scraps and rubbish of the author's portfolio."

Lyell laughed away his exasperation.

"What was it Henslow told you about the first volume of my *Principles?* 'Study the book but on no account accept the views Lyell advocates.' But it's Henslow and the other believers in successive cataclysms created by God to punish man who are sitting on the sharp horns of a dilemma, not us geologists."

Emma had news of her own which she considered much more important.

"I want you to hear something from me before nature begins announcing it to all the world," she said with a smile at the corner of her mouth.

Charles stared at her, wide-eyed.

"Yes, dear, you are going to become a father. Before the end of the year likely."

"Emma, are you sure?"

"Now isn't that a standard reply? Of course I'm sure. Have been ever since that morning sickness at Maer Hall."

He kneeled before her chair, took her face gently in his hands.

"Emma, my dear, I'm so happy for you. For me. For us. For everybody." He kissed her tenderly. "I'll take loving care of you."

"No need," she replied. "I am a Wedgwood; there is bone in my porcelain. I have another bit of news. Hensleigh and Fanny have found a house just four doors away on Upper Gower Street. However Hensleigh doesn't want to sign the lease until he has your approval. I would find it a great comfort, now that I'm in a family way. What do you think?"

"I think it just fine. Neither you nor Fanny are idle people who would fall into the error of running in and out at all hours."

"Thank you, dear. It's like giving me a present."

"You're giving me one, aren't you?"

Despite the "communication" from Emma and his ardent desire not to hurt her in any way, he was powerless to ignore his growing concept of the origin, modification and coming into being of evolving species. He was a man possessed; an actual count showed that since he had started his first notebook in July of 1837, two years before, he had read and annotated hundreds of articles, pamphlets and books, and subscribed to most of the useful journals: the *Transactions of the Linnean Society*, the *Quarterly Journal of Science*, the *Edinburgh Philosophical Journal*, the *Annals and Magazine of Natural History*. Though he was able to concentrate on corals, make certain that the number three monograph of *Birds* maintained its splendid color-plate level, or edit Waterhouse's final sixty-page study of modern *Mammalia*, the moment this work was accomplished his mind returned to the thought processes that had begun in the Galápagos Islands and moved forward with new observations and insights every day. He was off on a treasonable course and traitors were publicly executed as was . . . in effect, Galileo Galilei. He wrote in his notebook:

> The weakest part of my theory is the absolute necessity that every organic being should cross with another. To escape it in any case we must draw such a monstrous conclusion, that every organ is become fixed and cannot vary—which all facts show to be absurd. I utterly deny the right of anyone to argue against my theory because it makes the world far *older* than what even geologists think. What relation in duration are planets to our lives?

He finished his fourth notebook in July, determined to acquire substantiating materials and plow his way to tentative conclusions inside the privacy of his own head. He would not set down another line but in his mind he would formulate an articulate theory which he knew he would one day have to write. To be published as well?

Emma would give birth to her baby, bringing joy to their families. But the material with which he was pregnant . . . to whom would it bring joy?

4.

The weather was lovely over the summer. He and Emma walked in their garden; she was carrying easily. For pleasure they read aloud to each other *The Life of Cowper* as well as a volume of his letters. Emma played the piano each evening for an hour. By himself in the study he read Walker's *Intermarriage*, an article on the East Indian archipelago which gave him information on both corals and certain examples of transmutation. He felt conscience-stricken at his duplicity.

During the warm days of August he took himself on cooling voyages: books by Turville, Marion, Dixon and Dampier. Each had something to teach him about earthquakes, volcanoes, geology, distant lands. He immersed himself in the technical journals and the seven volumes of the *Transactions of the Horticultural Society*. Sometimes he skimmed or practiced "skipibus" when the material was dull or distant from his field.

In late August he left Emma at Maer Hall, then traveled to Birmingham for the meeting of the British Association for the Advancement of Science, where most of Great Britain's scientists were assembled to read papers, exchange ideas and intellectual blows. They included university professors, librarians, archivists, researchers, talented amateurs making their living in some other area. Charles knew many of the men, others he was meeting for the first time. A few had already read the *Journal*; they praised his writing style and descriptions of strange countries and peoples. They categorically rejected his geological theories about subsidence and elevation, the concept that over millions of years not only great bodies of water had risen and fallen, and perhaps risen again, but land masses as well. They accepted his observations while rejecting the resulting hypotheses even as John Henslow had rejected Lyell's.

He was having a beer with Lyell in a pub next to the meeting hall. Lyell wiped suds from a corner of his mouth.

"As an anonymous sage once said, 'Don't hope to convert your peers; the next generation will believe you.'"

Returning to the uncombative quiet of Maer, seated on the front steps of the Hall watching the great-crested diving grebes hunting food, he reflected:

"I'm in purgatory. Just how do I get purified that I may enter heaven?"

They were back in London by the end of October. He found a note from Yarrell. Could Charles drop into the shop?

The old man, wearing a woolen cap against the cold air, was beaming, the upturned corner of his lips making him look like the Greek symbol of happiness.

"Your book has sold out, Darwin. Congratulations. I ordered a second stock. So are the other shops sold out."

Charles was stunned. The notices following the *Athenaeum* review were little more than a line, only occasionally favorable.

"The King and FitzRoy volumes are not moving nearly as well," continued the bookseller. "Now is the time for you to demand that Colburn bind your other sheets. What's more, you should have a proper title page. Your name doesn't appear until the subtitle page."

Henry Colburn readily agreed to bind another five hundred sets for a second issue.

"Remember," he told Charles, "it's not a second printing, still the first one; when we put in your new title page that will change it to another issue."

Charles thought, amused:

"Splendid! Between Emma and Colburn I'll have two new issues this year."

The new title page read *Journal of Researches into the Geology and Natural History of the Various Countries Visited by H.M.S. "Beagle," Under the Command of Captain FitzRoy, R.N. From 1832 to 1836* by Charles Darwin, Esq., M.A. F.R.S. Secretary to the Geological Society. He ordered thirty copies to be delivered to his home as soon as they were ready. At long last he was going to earn some money from his writing. He would earn nothing from the eleven already published installments of *The Zoology of the Voyage of H.M.S. "Beagle"* though he had put in hundreds of hours on the editing and on the illustrative plates. Jenyns's first installment on Fish was due in January. Charles was cautiously conserving the thousand-pound government grant but the maps and plates were astonishingly expensive. At tea before the fire at Lyell's, he asked:

"If, when the entire *Zoology* is out, I have a few pounds left over do you suppose I might use what's left for the ten or so maps and woodcuts I'll need for the coral book?"

"I don't see why not," Lyell answered. "The Chancellor of the Exchequer, not to mention the scientists of London, agree you've done a marvelous job of superintending the output."

"I'll ask permission, of course. I'd hate to lay out the money from my own purse when no human being will ever read the book . . . though there is a growing rage for geology."

"Ah, my young friend, we shall fan the flame. Between the two of us we are going to convince the world that we are all living on the top of a slippery ball of mud."

The days passed. At the end of November they fitted up the smaller front bedroom for the expected child. Margaret asked to be released as being too old for a house with a newborn babe. Mary Lyell recommended a tall, reedy, flat-chested girl with a set of teeth juxtaposed to each other at odd angles. Bessy's clothes seemed not altogether tidy but Emma liked her earnestness and her need for a permanent place to live. Josiah Wedgwood and Elizabeth came to stay until the baby was born. Erasmus was perplexed at his own excitement about becoming an uncle.

"It just never occurred to me that there'd be another male Darwin . . . if it's a boy, I mean," he exclaimed.

"But this is only the opening race at Ascot," blurted Emma, suppressing a self-conscious giggle.

The Wedgwood family decided to consolidate the Christmas festivities at 12 Upper Gower Street. Elizabeth and Fanny shopped for the Christmas tree, Parslow set it up in front of the window of the sitting room. Everyone helped clip the small wax candles in their brass holders to the branches. On Christmas morning the three Wedgwood children emptied their stockings with shouts of glee at each new toy or bit of sweets. Then the servants retrieved their gifts from under the tree: a warm dressing gown, a handsome wool waistcoat, handkerchiefs, eau de cologne. For the men of the family there were new books and boxes of cigars; for the women, gold trinkets, a locket on a chain, a jeweled bracelet; for Elizabeth, packages of exotic seeds to take home to Maer for spring planting. After church they returned to sing Christmas carols with Emma at the piano, then trooped downstairs to the dining room, Charles standing up to carve the obligatory Christmas goose.

Dr. Henry Holland had recommended an obstetrician. The baby was born two days after the Christmas party. Emma rode the crest of the wave with considerable pain but no complications. As Charles wiped the perspiration from her brow with a damp cloth, she murmured:

"That's the most *travail* I've ever worked through."

Charles grinned. "I like your spirit. As we said at Cambridge, even a bad pun is better than none."

They had chosen two sets of names in advance. The applicable one was William Erasmus Darwin.

"It's a good omen, William Erasmus's being born on December 27, the eighth anniversary of my sailing out of Plymouth Sound," Charles exclaimed. "Everything that has happened to me since that day has been good."

Emma gazed down at her first-born in his cradle made of turned and joined wood and fitted with a clock spring to swing it gently for forty-three minutes, a gift from her father.

"I like his dark blue eyes, otherwise he looks such a poor little wretch. . . ."

"He'll improve with age," quipped Erasmus. "Like wine . . . and cheese."

Emma's father and sister remained for another few days, so happy with Emma and the baby that they had trouble wrenching themselves away. Though William Erasmus was baptized, as the Book of Common Prayer said he should be, no godparents were named because neither the Wedgwood nor the Darwin families subscribed to the idea.

Emma remained in bed much of January. She had hired an excellent wet nurse and made arrangements for asses' milk to be delivered. She exclaimed to Charles:

"Papa and Elizabeth went away too soon, before William's appearance began to improve. He's very nice-looking now, with a pretty, small mouth. His nose I will not boast of but it's harmless as long as he is a baby."

Charles grinned sheepishly.

"All Darwin noses are too long."

Becoming a mother brought a fresh beauty to Emma's warm brown eyes. She felt so well that she took Fanny Wedgwood and her three children to see the illuminations a week before the marriage of Queen Victoria to her first cousin, Prince Albert of Saxe-Coburg-Gotha.

"Are you sure you don't want to come, Charles?"

"Thank you, no. I attended the illumination for the coronation of William IV. If you've seen one illumination . . ."

With the birth of his first son, Charles began to watch carefully and make notes on the infant's emotional reactions, when and why he cried, when the tear ducts were activated, how long the crying continued; the emotion of excitement or happiness in the little one's eyes, his reactions to food and play, to being picked up and fondled by his parents. He had never seen or read anything about the emotions of children from the day of their birth and decided it was an area worth studying.

Aside from the abstracts he made for the papers sent into the Geological Society for publication in the *Proceedings*, he was writing not a word. For some reason he had gone stale on the coral book.

"Happens to the best of us," Lyell reassured him. "Let it set for a year, like plum pudding."

The only concentration he could achieve was reading, stretched out on a sofa in his study: Johannes Müller's Elements of Physiology, Carlyle's Chartism, which all of England appeared to be reading, including Emma. The book put her out of patience.

"It's full of passion and good feeling, but utterly unreasonable," she exclaimed.

Charles looked up, perplexed:

"Carlyle is pleasant to talk to, he is very natural. . . ."

". . . but his writing is not at all so," Emma added.

"Maybe it's best that I don't write any more. Why don't I just be pleasant to talk to?"

She ventured to ask:

"Charles, my dear, why are you not writing?"

"I don't know. It's painful to me to be idle."

"I know that. It is a great happiness to me that when you are most unwell you continue just as sociable as ever."

He held her close, rubbed his cheek against hers.

The weather during the early months of 1840 was bad, with wet soot-colored slush underfoot. They rarely ventured out. Susan came for a week's stay, swinging her golden curls as she told animated stories of the people around Shrewsbury. Charles continued to be fascinated by his son; they called William Mr. Hoddy-Doddy, a nickname for a short, stout person. Queen Victoria and Prince Albert were married on February 10 in the Chapel Royal at St. James's. The Queen wore a white satin dress trimmed with English Honiton lace and a sapphire brooch, a present from Prince Albert; the Prince was in his Saxe-Coburg uniform. After the ceremony they left for a honeymoon in Windsor Castle. By late March news came from the palace that the Queen and Prince Albert would be parents by the end of the year, producing an heir to the English throne.

Charles's secretaryship of the Geological Society proved to be a blessing, the one job of work he managed to get done, perhaps because the reading and abstracting of other people's scientific papers required no creative energy. He also assisted in the publication of three numbers of his Zoology, two by Jenyns on Fish, the final installment on Fossil Mammalia by Richard Owen. Colburn had sold out the second issue of the Journal and had bound the final five hundred copies, changing the date on the title page to 1840 for this third issue.

Late in March he obliged himself to resume writing the coral book.

"I only want vigor," he said to Emma; "in wanting which, however, one wants almost all which makes life endurable."

"Why don't we plan to take a long summer holiday at Maer Hall and The Mount?" she suggested.

"I'd like that. My present castle in the air is to live near a station in Surrey about twenty miles from town. Let's plan for early in June."

"That fits perfectly. My Aunt Jessie Sismondi and her husband are coming to London for a month's stay. They're the ones I lived with in Switzerland. They can stay here while we're away. I'll be sure the house is perfectly set up for them."

As they packed to leave for Maer, London was shocked at an attempt to assassinate the Queen. She and the Prince were on their way up Constitution Hill from Buckingham Palace in a low open carriage when a seventeen-year-old boy shot at the Queen with pistols in both hands. The crowd shouted "Kill him! Kill him!" but he was sent to a lunatic asylum for life.

They left London on June 10, taking Bessy with them to watch over the boy. Elizabeth was overjoyed to have them.

"You have no idea how silent these rooms are with you and Joe married out."

Emma's mother and father perked up with their arrival. Her hour of playing the old piano on which she had been taught was a tonic to them, as was the presence of their grandchild. Charles dug into Josiah's library, which contained not only Josiah's books on natural history but his father's extensive collection as well, with the original Josiah Wedgwood's four volumes on fossils. He read avidly, in particular those books which related to his species theory. A nine-volume translation of Buffon's *Natural History* served as a reference base as he worked his way through eight travel books from countries as divergent as Siberia, the Levant, Bengal and North America. He read Montague's *Ornithological Dictionary*; two books on roses, one on peat, Jones's work on fruited forms.

He did not jot down a single note yet his mind was moving to viable conclusions. As he walked around the fishtail lake, or rode alone on one of the Maer horses through the woods, he refined his thoughts, rewriting and editing them in his head as clearly and fully as he would have on a sheet of blank paper:

"There is much grandeur in looking at the existing animals either as the lineal descendants of the forms buried under a thousand feet of matter, or as co-heirs of some still more ancient ancestor. . . .

"It is derogatory that the Creator of countless systems of worlds should have created each of the myriads of creeping parasites and slimy worms which have swarmed each day of life on land and water on this one globe. We cease being astonished that a group of animals should have been directly created to lay their eggs in bowels and flesh of others. . . .

"From death, famine, rapine, and the concealed war of nature we can see that the highest good, the creation of the higher animals, has directly come. . . .

"There is a simple grandeur in the view of life with its powers of growth, assimilation and reproduction, being originally breathed into matter under one or a few forms, and that whilst this our planet has gone circling on according to fixed laws, and land and water, in a cycle of change, have gone on replacing each other, that so simple an origin, through the process of gradual selection of infinitesimal changes, endless forms most beautiful and most wonderful have been evolved. . . ."

Charles's father and two sisters drove up to Maer in the Darwin carriage eager for a sight of the new Darwin. Susan and Katty were hilarious; Dr. Darwin was a little awe-struck.

"Why are you looking at the boy so seriously, Father?" Charles asked.

"It suddenly came to me. Your sister Marianne has five children but they're all Parkers. This is my first grandchild with the name of Darwin. I suppose it's oriental of me but I've worked hard to create a good name for myself, and I wanted it to be perpetuated. Thank you, Charles."

"Emma did all the work."

They promised to bring William to The Mount for a fortnight so that he would come to know his father's home.

"You've always loved it, haven't you, Charley?" asked Susan.

"My years were happy there. Except that blasted Shrewsbury School."

"Now, now, Dr. Butler brags on you as his most brilliant student."

"Gas!" exclaimed Charles, then laughed at himself.

They received a letter from Emma's Aunt Jessie and Jean Sismondi, the renowned Swiss historian:

> . . . Your roof, my Emma, brought us good luck while there, everything went to our hearts' content; be it observed that Parslow is the most amiable, obliging, active, serviceable servant that ever breathed. I hope you will never part with him.
>
> I just found Sismondi in an ecstasy over your husband's book, the *Journal*. He said it was the most attractive reading he had met with; that notwithstanding his ignorance of natural history he found the greatest interest in it. . . .

In mid-July Charles took Emma, William and Bessy along the familiar road to Shrewsbury, with green fields lying below densely wooded hills. The house was filled with flowers to welcome them. Dr. Darwin had abandoned "The Doctor's Walk" before breakfast each morning;

he no longer took leisurely jaunts about the colorful town of Shrewsbury.

"I stroll about the garden for an hour each afternoon," he told
Charles. "It just seems that after seventy-four years my legs have grown
conscious of my twenty-four stone. But we're supposed to be talking
about your health, not mine. Perhaps the vomiting is what is draining
your strength. Emma assures me you have a good cook. You are obviously not throwing up your breakfast or dinner."

"Then what am I heaving?"

"You tell me. Is there anything unhappy in your life? Sometimes I
have found my patients throwing up their hardships, or rejections, or
sadness about their work. . . ."

"That couldn't apply to me."

"Then we'll have to find something else. I'll put together the best
possible soothing formula."

At the beginning of August Emma announced that she was pregnant
again.

"Won't it be pleasant for William to have a playmate?"

Charles embraced her.

"Now that there's life in you I have better hopes for myself."

In October he was shocked out of his lethargy by the receipt of an
issue of the *Scotsman* with an article on Glen Roy entitled "Discovery
of the Former Existence of Glaciers in Scotland, Especially in the
Highlands," by Louis Agassiz, a professor of natural history in Switzerland whose work Charles knew from the monographs Agassiz had
been publishing since 1833 in which he had gradually raised the number of identified fossil fishes to close to one thousand. What disturbed
him was that Louis Agassiz claimed proof that the roads and benches of
Glen Roy, which Charles had claimed were former marine or sea
beaches, were valleys that had been filled with lakes, dammed back by
glaciers. Neither he nor Lyell had heard scientific claims made for the
geological influence of moving glaciers.

"If Agassiz is right, then my paper on Glen Roy is dead wrong! That
would be terrible. It would impugn my judgment and undermine the
value of my other work. Agassiz can't be right. I shall marshal my arguments against it. . . ."

Charles decided they must return to London. Dr. Darwin had converted the room next to the main bedroom into an office. He was at his
desk when Charles climbed the broad staircase.

"I have your formula prepared. A goodly package of it. You must
take some each day."

"What is this magic potion, Father?"

"You'll recognize most of the ingredients: potassium bicarbonate for your acidity; logwood and cinnamon to make the brew palatable. . . ."

They were happy to be back in their own home even though it was only a five-story box closed in on both sides by other five-story boxes. The house was scrupulously clean, their favorite foods on the stove.

He continued to read widely, mostly on species, but also on political economy, philosophy, Christianity, history. For reading aloud he and Emma turned to literature: the poems of Grey, Shakespeare's *Midsummer Night's Dream*, Goldsmith's *Vicar of Wakefield*, Dante's *Divine Comedy; Gulliver's Travels.*

He longed to begin a fifth notebook on species with the new confirmations racing through his head. It took an act of ongoing determination, painful to both mind and body, to keep himself away from the job he most wanted to do, and which in his opinion was by far the most important contribution any scientist could make. From the reaction to his minor geological heresies he could not doubt the risks he ran of losing his growing acceptance and position, endangering his beloved friendship with John Henslow, with his confrere and admirer Adam Sedgwick; and, for all he knew, the entire body of the Geological and Royal societies! It would be humanly impossible for him not to publish . . . one day. That would bring the Church of England down on his head: the government, the universities, established society.

Three short papers kept him reasonably content, one of which he could use later when preparing his book on the geology of South America, one concerning a block of rock embedded in an iceberg which threw light on "erratic boulders" which had long perplexed geologists because they showed up in areas where they did not rightly belong. He spent considerable time at the Geological Society making up for the months he had been in the country, getting the accumulated papers abridged for the *Proceedings,* answering the correspondence which had piled up. He wanted everything shipshape because on February 19, 1841, he would have served as secretary for three years and would relinquish his post at that anniversary meeting.

He was considerably jarred when his good friend Charles Lyell in November and December of 1840 read to the assemblage a two-part paper in which he strongly supported Louis Agassiz's theory of glaciers and their role in the geography of Scotland. Adam Sedgwick attacked Agassiz's glacier theory vigorously; Charles did not speak but listened until almost midnight to what would have turned into an acrimonious quarrel had it taken place at the Zoological Society.

That Sunday Emma said:

"Charles, Mary Lyell has been inviting us regularly for tea. I think I'd like a little outside company."

He and Lyell heatedly discussed Louis Agassiz and his glaciers. Lyell said:

"When Agassiz and William Buckland completed their tour of Glen Roy and the highlands, Buckland came to visit us in Kinnordy. He showed me beautiful clusters of moraines, accumulations of earth and stones carried by a glacier and deposited within two miles of my father's house. I accepted their theory. It solves a host of difficulties that all my life have embarrassed me."

"Wasn't that a rather instantaneous conversion?" Charles asked quietly.

Lyell laid his face on the seat of his favorite chair, then straightened up, his face flushed, a wicked gleam in his eyes.

"Yes, as instantaneous as my conversion to your revolutionary theory of coral reefs, which proved me to have been wrong!"

"As now you are convinced that I am wrong about Glen Roy."

"Precisely."

"You wish me to retract?"

"You'll have to eventually. The sooner the better. Let me lend you Agassiz's *Études sur les glaciers*, just published."

Lyell linked his arm through Charles's affectionately.

"In art or literature one never has to admit he has been wrong. In science, yes. Our friend Robert Brown therefore refuses to publish in English. But science cannot grow that way. We must dare to explore and to theorize from our findings, to learn as we go along. There's Mary signaling us for tea. She has some of your favorite cold meats and a caraway cake."

Charles smiled, shyly, as they walked to the dining-room table.

"That's an area where people can make no mistakes. High tea. With thin sandwiches of tomato, watercress and cucumber, hot scones buttered inside and served with strawberry jam!"

5.

By the turn of 1841 he began to sort out his transmutation of species notes and observations.

"I can't put down my excitement over it," he told himself.

He also decided to set up a dissecting laboratory again; perhaps the dormer up under the roof, which he could keep locked. To his cousin Fox, who had now been the rector at Delamere Forest for several years, the configuration of clergyman and naturalist which Leonard Jenyns also pursued and which had been Charles's apparent destiny before he sailed on H.M.S. *Beagle*, he wrote:

> I continue to collect all kinds of facts about "Varieties and Species," for my some-day work to be so entitled; the smallest contributions thankfully accepted. Descriptions of offspring of

all crosses between all domestic birds and animals, dogs, cats, very valuable. Don't forget, if your half-bred African cat should die that I should be very much obliged for its carcass sent up in a little hamper. It, or any crossbred pigeons, fowl, duck &c., will be more acceptable than the finest haunch of venison or the finest turtle.

Emma's second child was born on March 2, their first daughter. They named her Anne, promptly corrupted to Annie. From the beginning Annie was an adorable baby. Emma confessed to Charles:

"Before my confinement I took so little notice of Doddy that he got not to care a pin for me. It used to make me rather dismal sometimes."

"I spoil him for you," he comforted.

They seldom disagreed, even more rarely did they quarrel. There was one bone of contention, young Bessy, the housekeeper turned nursemaid. He complained:

"Bessy is not wearing her cap. That's not proper."

"She hates caps. Let her be. I want her happy with the children."

"It's more important than that. Bessy actually looks soiled. Her dress, I mean. Can't you persuade her to launder her things more often?"

"She does. It's just that she messes herself up so fast. Little Miss Slip-Slop of London."

The *Zoology* series continued to be well received. The final issue of *Birds* came out in March, the third installment of *Fish* in April. These folios were transformed into hard-bound books with a gray-green binding so that Charles was now credited with three more books as editor and superintendent: *Birds* by John Gould, *Fossil Mammalia* by Richard Owen, *Mammalia* by George Waterhouse. Only a few more installments were due on *Fish* and *Reptiles* before the series would be completed. He still had money left to help illustrate his own coming volumes.

May was a good month for them. Charles read his paper on "Erratic Boulders and Unstratified Deposits" before the Geological Society where it was commended. Emma returned to her piano for an hour a day, the music filling the house, but mostly devoted herself to her son, wooing him back to love and confidence in her. Charles continued his short pieces; kept up his detailed expenditure accounts, amused himself by making value judgments on the books that poured into and out of his hands, as they do of any omnivorous reader: Peter Tallas's *Travels*, wretched. Abraham Tucker's *The Nature of Light Pursued*, intolerably prolix. . . .

Wordsworth still gave him pleasure. However the heart of his reading was in research, absorbing knowledge from studies of reindeer, noxious insects, silkworms, foliation of trees, economy of nature, the Swedish pine, Peruvian sheep.

Charles and Mary Lyell were jubilant; he had been invited to give a series of lectures at the Lowell Institute in Boston, with an honorarium sufficiently large to allow them to travel North America as they had always wanted to do.

"First I want to study the Great Lakes area, Niagara Falls. I have some radical theories about its geological source."

"You have radical theories about many things," Charles said. "That's what makes you a great man."

Emma had learned that, although Mary sometimes professed boredom with her husband's technical talk, she had absorbed a good deal of geology.

"The geologizing trips abroad are the best times for me," she told Emma. "Charles talks his observations, I jot them down in my notebook from which he can write later. That's when we enjoy a true partnership. In London, life is so fragmented."

When Sir William Hooker was appointed director of the Royal Botanical Gardens at Kew and moved down from Glasgow in late spring of 1841, Charles took Emma and the two children there in a carriage for an outing. Sir William had met Charles only casually at a British Association meeting but he knew of his son Joseph's intense admiration for the *Journal*, which Joseph said was his unfailing guide on H.M.S. *Erebus*. Sir William was fifty-six but he had the look and vitality of a much younger man, with a strong face and enormous tan eyes. He took the Darwin family for a tour of the fifteen acres in which few commoners were allowed, and which were even then under heavy guard.

"That's the first thing I'm going to change," the new director confided. "As soon as I can tear down these dividing brick walls the public will be invited in at all times. I feel certain there will be no depredations, particularly when I acquire the surrounding lands and convert them into beautiful gardens with walks and fountains and flower plots."

"What are you going to do with all the glass white elephants?" Charles asked, looking toward a series of glasshouses, functional perhaps but without charm.

"We're going to redesign and enlarge them, put in modern heating, create a network of hot-water pipes for the cactus glasshouse, as well as the houses for the orchidaceous plants and ferns . . . in fact, all tropical plants. Then we'll join them together, put in ponds with water lilies, bright greenswards. I'm certain that Joseph will bring us back a superb collection from the *Erebus* expedition."

"Please send him my greetings. I'm looking forward to his return."

"So am I." Wistfully. "I'm hoping he will become my assistant director. It would be a natural place for him to work and live."

They returned to Maer at the end of May. Their reception was always a happy one. The family fell in love with Annie. Elizabeth murmured:

"Each spring or summer you bring a new infant. That's thoughtful of you. We've come to expect it, you know."

Emma linked an arm through her sister's, smiled a little poignantly.

"I dare say you'll achieve your expectations, Elizabeth dear."

Elizabeth stroked her crooked spine.

"I can tell you haven't heard about Charlotte. She's pregnant. After ten years of marriage to Mr. Langton. Isn't that a miracle? He is resigning as the pastor at Onibury. They're coming to live here. She will help take care of Mother and Father."

Emma kissed her sister with affection.

"Oh, Elizabeth, I've felt such a traitor, living comfortably in London while you were alone with the sole care of Mama and Papa."

"Each has his role, dear Emma. I'm happy doing the work which the Lord assigned me. I'm happy for you, taking care of our darling Charles and bringing combined Wedgwood-Darwins into the world."

Toward the end of June, although he had thrived in the clear air of Maer, Charles confided to Emma:

"Sometimes about four in the afternoon I begin to feel shivery."

A week before, they had sent their son, accompanied by Bessy, in a carriage to Shrewsbury.

"Why don't you fetch William and see your father? He helped you last year."

Dr. Darwin never wished to discuss his own health with his son.

"I'm all right. The life spark in me is going to keep me ignited for a few more years."

But he listened thoughtfully as Charles described his latest bouts of feeling "bad and shivery."

"Charles, I scarcely expect that you shall become strong for years. I underestimated the exhaustions you suffered on your long voyage. You poured out fifteen, perhaps twenty years of energy on that trip. That may be how long it will take you to recoup."

Charles was heartsick. To be pronounced an invalid . . . His voice was strained.

"Father, it is a bitter mortification to me to digest the conclusion that 'the race is for the strong' and that I shall probably do little more than be content to admire the strides others make in science. I long to be settled in pure air, out of all of the dirt, noise and misery of that 'great wen,' as William Cobbett described London in *Rural Rides*.

Your offer to buy us a house in the country as our wedding present is still good?"

"Of course."

"Then we'll start looking in Surrey and Kent."

"I suggest that you rent in a neighborhood for at least six years before buying. That way you'll both be sure you are at home in that particular area."

"Six years! Father, that's too long to be a renter in the country. We want to buy soon, though not rashly."

After dinner they gathered in the coolness and mossy scents of the solarium. Despite Katty's barrage of lively chitchat the atmosphere seemed throttled; Susan was glum. His father began it, after Bessy had come in to announce that Willy was asleep. When she left, Dr. Darwin said:

"It's disgraceful, Bessy not having a cap. Besides, she looks dirty!"

"Like a grocer's maidservant," exploded Susan.

His father added with considerable wrath, "The men will take liberties with her if she is dressed differently from every other lady's maid."

Charles was not going to betray his wife.

"We'll tidy her up when we return to London."

"She is also giving Doddy half a cup of cream every morning," Susan complained.

"That's one of the most injurious things you can give him," Dr. Darwin added. "He already looks a delicate child."

"Delicate?" exclaimed Charles. "We've never found him so."

Susan was relentless. "Last night I went into his bedroom and found no water by his bedside. Really, Charles, Bessy, or any housekeeper or nursemaid, should be meticulously trained to care for a child."

Numbly, Charles muttered, "She shall be."

The next morning the sun sent bright rays into The Mount. After breakfast the family strolled through the Darwin flowers, in full summer bloom, while each in turn taught Doddy the name of a different plant. Katty steered Charles aside:

"I'm sorry I didn't have a chance to warn you, Charley. It's all a tempest in a teapot. I'm not so sure half a cup of cream could hurt Doddy. If he wants water during the night, his door is open and he can call out."

Apparently abashed at the abuse he had heaped on the only son who came to visit him, Dr. Darwin said, later that day:

"You were right about the house you want to buy, Charles. Six years is too long to debate whether you like a particular countryside. When you find the house you and Emma want, let me know. The money has been set aside."

Charles put an arm lightly about his father's broad but stooping shoulders.

In London a message reached him which had gone through three hands, or rather three mouths, apparently originating with John Henslow, carried forward by Adam Sedgwick, then transmitted to Charles Lyell. The message? That it was time to begin arranging for his permanent attachment to Christ's College. Perhaps he would rather wait until he had completed his geology trilogy? But he could put off no longer the time when he must make an extended visit to Cambridge, renew his allegiances there, make his intentions clear. Some of the Christ's College people were beginning to observe that Charles Darwin had not visited them since the winter of 1837, some five years before, with Cambridge only a few hours away from London by comfortable coach.

He had heard how proud the faculty and administration of the college had been of his *Journal* and his numerous published papers. They had also indicated their respect for the five volumes of the *Zoology*. They were pleased at his being selected as the secretary of the Geological Society, his election to the Royal Society, an honor quite rare even for Cambridge University professors. There was little question that he had been accepted at Christ's, from the Master down to the fellows, as a member of their family. Nor was there any doubt, according to Henslow and Sedgwick, that they expected him, at the proper time, to join their roster on a permanent basis.

He and Emma had discussed the question, albeit not very seriously. Now the moment had arrived when Christ's College apparently wanted an earnest of his intentions.

"I could go up to Cambridge easily enough," he told Emma as they sat in their dressing gowns before the bedroom fire; "but the question is, do I want to spend my life at Cambridge University?"

He slumped into his chair, ran a hand distractedly over his broad forehead and through his darkening hair.

"Cambridge is a charming medieval town with its magnificent architecture and vast lawns and flower gardens, the punts being poled on the river Cam at the Backs, the glory of King's Chapel and its Sunday morning choir. The salary is only a hundred pounds a year, perhaps two hundred later, but since we have private money I would not have to spend my hours in tutoring as poor Henslow had to do. There would be enough intercourse with my peers to satisfy me. I would have to give only a moderate number of hours in guiding the students and helping administer the college's affairs; I would have the better part of my days and years for my own work. That is the way the college as well would want it."

Since there was nothing abrasive in his personality, since he was not aggressive, self-centered, boastful or uninterested in the affairs of others but was, rather, outgoing and warm, he had made no enemies at Christ's College that he knew of. He had been liked as a student, though not conceived of as a scholar. Now he had turned his life around. With luck and fortitude, he might eventually become a scholar.

"You are giving it serious consideration," Emma observed.

He kept his voice low.

"Life at Cambridge could be good. It has some of the world's best minds, finest libraries and research projects. It is an excellent place to raise children, with good educational opportunities for them."

It was a community where gregarious Emma Darwin, in a busy, invigorating social milieu, could continue the Wedgwood tradition of hospitality.

"You could become in time the *doyenne* of Cambridge society."

Facing his wife more squarely, he continued:

"Surely you have the training and inclination, Little Miss Slip-Slop, with your capacity for happiness and gift of liking people."

Emma gazed at him wide-eyed, not knowing in which direction he was going. Charles very definitely did.

"However, I am convinced that, as attractive and rewarding as that kind of life would be, *it is simply not for me.* I want and need quiet, privacy, isolation really, in the country, with only enough social life to keep us from feeling cloistered. I have my reasons, which I want to suggest to you in simple terms. I have books to write, theories to prove and promulgate that do not allow of college functions, university affairs, social activities."

Emma returned his confrontation.

"I can be happy in either place or either life. The only important matter to me is my family: my husband, my children, the well-being of all of us. I can accept that in London, if that's where you need to be; in Cambridge, if that's what you prefer; or deep in the country, if that's the best for you and your work. I am happy and will remain happy, even if you take us all to Tierra del Fuego!"

"Not Tierra del Fuego!" he cried, laughing at himself. "But I need solitude, away from busyness, I need an opportunity for uninterrupted work with total concentration. Dinners, formal affairs, long and spirited discussions drain me. I am good for nothing the next day."

"I've observed that, my dear."

"I have spoken to my father about buying a house in the country. I will be happiest in a rural area, to hear only the song of the birds and the wind soughing through the trees. I have these as yet unexplained bouts of being unwell. I don't know when they are coming or how long they will last. If I am at the college and one of these attacks comes upon me I will be unable to fulfill my obligations, which would embarrass me and make me feel guilty. If I am unattached, with a duty only to my work, then if I do not feel well I can play with the children, walk among the trees, read, listen to your music, and not fail anyone. Does that make sense to you?"

"Yes. You want . . . freedom from set obligations in order to fulfill what you conceive to be more important obligations."

"Quite. Much as I love John Henslow for his ability to teach young students as individuals—and I am grateful for what he did for me—that simply is not my cup of tea. I want the findings I put into my books to teach . . . perhaps an entire generation. I want my books to be my power base. Does that sound presumptuous?"

"Each of us must discover the best way to do the work which the Lord assigned us. My father became a 'reading' naturalist; your father a 'listening' doctor. You will become a 'writing' scientist. Is that what you want?"

"Devoutly."

## 6.

He picked up his long-neglected manuscript on coral reefs, read through what he had already written, found his materials and conclusions sound.

"Thirteen months of neglect!" he thought. "But I won't waste any emotion looking backward. I'll get the book finished by the end of the year."

He put in two hours of concentrated writing that morning on the upward growth of reefs. Each day he increased his work quota. His eyes had a sparkle which had been missing. When Emma commented on this, Charles replied:

"My father scared me witless with his prediction about my health. I've got to prove him wrong. As well as prove that I'm not a hypochondriac."

"Whoever thought you were?"

"I did."

Emma got a cap on Bessy's head, bought her two new uniforms and a whole box of white aprons which the girl learned to change during the day when they became even slightly soiled. Parslow, the very antithesis of the stiff-lipped formal English butler, made not the slightest effort to conceal his joy at having found a good home. He kept busy all the day serving meals, moving rugs so the floors could be waxed, polishing boots, going early to the nearest bookshop to pick up the London

*Chronicle* and *Times* for Charles to peruse after breakfast. Sally was following the recipes brought back from Annie at The Mount with modest success.

After their midday meal Charles and Emma took the children in a pram to Regent's Park where they strolled under the shade trees. Charles taught William, now a sturdy year and a half old, how to sail his boat along the winding lake. They went across the long greensward to the Zoological Gardens to see the rhinoceros kicking and rearing, the elephant trotting about with his trunk curling and uncurling, frequently braying at the onlookers. William was most fascinated by the ourangoutang who threw herself on her back, kicked and cried like a naughty child when the keeper showed her an apple but would not give it to her. When she finally got the apple she jumped into an armchair and began eating it.

"With the most contented expression imaginable," commented Charles.

He set down sections on the various structures of the coral reefs and drew rough sketches to make his observations more comprehensible. On Sundays after church they took the train a short distance into Surrey or Kent to look at houses that were for sale. They could find nothing that suited; they were either too large or too small, much too expensive or too cheap. Some were too ornate, others had been left unoccupied for so long they had deteriorated badly. At length they found an attractive house called Westcroft on several acres of land an hour and three quarters from Vauxhall Bridge, some six miles from Windsor Castle. However the owner was asking at least a thousand pounds beyond what Charles felt justified in spending.

"It's more than the house is worth," he said on their way home. "Certainly more than I would allow my father to spend. On Friday I'll take a valuer out with me."

The valuer declared the property overpriced. Charles submitted an offer in line with his estimate.

There was only silence from the owner.

They continued to search all through the autumn, sometimes taking a carriage at the station and inspecting several houses in a day. Nothing suited.

"Somewhere there is a particular house and some land that is meant for us," Charles said.

"Why, Charles, I do believe you're becoming a fatalist," she replied teasingly.

Several events occurred at the end of the year. Emma became pregnant for the third time. She gave Willy a party to celebrate his second birthday. Charles finished his coral book and prepared to deliver it, along with six woodcuts and three folding maps showing atolls in dark blue, reefs in pale blue and fringing reefs in red. This enabled him to delineate the previous elevation and falling away of different areas of the earth's surface.

Before sending it to Smith Elder and Company Charles wrote an introduction in an attempt to achieve clarity:

> The object of this volume is to describe from my own observation and the works of others, the principal kinds of coral reefs, more especially those occurring in the open ocean, and to explain the origin of their peculiar forms. I do not here treat of the polypifers which construct these vast works, except so far as relates to their distribution, and to the conditions favorable to their vigorous growth. . . .

Emma asked if she might read parts of the manuscript. She locked her fingers behind Charles's neck, murmured:

"My dear, you are a poet. I thought so when I read your *Journal*, but feared for rocks and corals."

"There's poetry in nature too, my love."

He corrected the printed proofs. Although the color plates and drawings for the nineteen parts of the five volumes of the *Zoology* had been expensive, he emerged with one hundred and thirty to one hundred and forty pounds and secured permission from the Lords Commissioners of the Treasury to apply the sum toward the maps and drawings of the South America volumes. The illustrations for *Coral Reefs* alone used up the residue. He said to Emma plaintively:

"The government money has gone much quicker than I thought."

"All money does," she replied with a mischievous grin.

When it came to the second volume on volcanic islands both Charles and the publishers would have to contribute money of their own for the plates. The books would be bought by the libraries and the men of British science, or so Yarrell told him.

"Unfortunately," moaned Charles, "there are not enough of them. We are not going to sell out the edition."

"You will," Yarrell replied sympathetically, "as soon as you bind the three volumes into one complete whole."

"Oh well, I'm not complaining, really. If I wanted to become a rich man I should have followed my grandfather and father in the practice of medicine."

Emma felt uncomfortable from the outset of her pregnancy. Charles spent his spare hours with her, reading the current romantic novels, chattering away with a series of anecdotes. She insisted on dressing for dinner. Willy frequently sat at table with them, astonishingly well be-

haved for a two-year-old. The boy was having a speech problem with his
w's.

"My name Villy Darvin. . . . Vipe Doddy's own tears avay. . . .
Open the vindow."

"It's the London air that's doing it," remarked Charles. "But then
I'd blame the end of the world on falling coal dust."

For some inexplicable reason little Annie would not come to him.
Emma comforted Charles.

"It's a passing phase. I'm beginning to understand that childhood is
an endless string of passing phases. Leave her be. Use your time to
teach Doddy how to say Darwin instead of Darvin."

He also spent his time shamelessly canvassing votes for Erasmus's
election to the Athenaeum, attending the Monday evening soirees since
most of the literary and scientific men of London were members.
Erasmus's only two qualifications were that he maintained a literary
salon and that he was Charles's brother. Charles went off to the election meeting with high hopes knocking against legitimate fears.

"I hope that no one asks what Erasmus has written," he confided to
Emma. "It takes only one adverse vote to keep a man out and it would
mean so much to him; give him the place in London society for which
he yearns."

He returned rather late, having picked up his brother on the way
home. They were laughing and jabbering like a couple of youngsters.

"No need to ask what happened," commented Emma dryly; "it's
written all over your faces."

By a stroke of fortune they acquired an excellent Scottish nursemaid
by the name of Brodie. Her strong features were deeply pitted with
smallpox; she had carroty hair, china blue eyes and, in spite of the pock-
marks, a delightful smile. She seemed as happy to have acquired a new
family as Parslow had been. She took over William and Annie with
skill and gentleness; the boy began to pronounce his w's; Annie came
running to her father.

With their staff of four now caring for the house and the children,
Emma asked Charles if she might go to Maer for a week; her sister
Charlotte had had her baby in November but was still languid.

On his thirty-third birthday Charles walked in the slush of the February snow to Great Marlborough Street for a meeting with the publisher
of the *Journal*. After an hour of undistinguished talk he returned home
to write ruefully to Susan at The Mount:

> Talking of money, I reaped the other day all the profit I
> shall ever get from my *Journal*, which consists in paying Mr.
> Colburn £21.10s. for the copies which I presented to different

people; 1337 copies have been sold. This is a comfortable arrangement, is it not?

At that moment a messenger delivered a note from Roderick Murchison, former army officer turned geologist, close friend of Adam Sedgwick and Charles Lyell. The note said that Murchison was entertaining Alexander von Humboldt, who had expressed the desire to meet young Charles Darwin. Would Charles grace his board at breakfast the following morning.

"Humboldt, the god of my youth, wants to meet me!" cried Charles. "Now that's the mountain coming to Mohammed for a certainty."

Murchison was a wealthy man who lived in a mansion in Belgrave Square, with liveried servants. Since he was a past president of the Geological Society, Charles knew him well. Seventy-three-year-old von Humboldt was cheerful and energetic, even after publishing a thirty-volume work. He had a fine shock of tousled blond hair, an enormous forehead round enough to be half a globe, observant and penetrating blue-gray eyes determined to pry out and understand all of nature, a large warm mouth, obviously a man who loved his life and was determined to make the most of it for his beloved science. He was handsomely dressed in a long velveteen coat with wide lapels, a stiff white cravat tied flamboyantly and flowing into his well-cut waistcoat.

"Altogether an appealing man," Charles thought.

He found von Humboldt wringing his hand for a considerable time while complimenting him on his *Journal*, the volumes of the *Zoology*, as well as the pages of *Coral Reefs*, which the publisher had sent him hoping for a line of praise. He was particularly interested in the plants Charles had gathered on the Galápagos Islands.

Charles stuttered, ". . . But . . . it is I who should . . . I mean you've been the greatest of scientists to me. . . . I admire your . . ."

Murchison had thoughtfully placed Charles next to his honored guest so that they could converse. Charles never got to say another word. Humboldt started on a three-hour monologue, all of it interesting: his travels, his newest theories, his collecting that remained unbroken even though he was at the same time putting away a hearty breakfast. When Charles left the great scientist again wrung his hand.

"I was so happy to meet you, Darwin, and to come to know something about you."

On his way home, Charles wondered:

"How could he know anything about me; I never got a chance to open my mouth. . . ."

Emma's week at Maer helped her considerably though she had grown thin. At the beginning of May she returned to Maer, taking the two children and Brodie on the train to Whitmore Station, then in a fly to the Hall. Charles remained behind to "do a deal of printing business." His sister Katty came in from The Mount to keep him company.

He joined Emma at Maer late in May.

"Please give Papa all the time you can," she pleaded. "Elizabeth says she hasn't seen him smile more than twice in the past months."

His father-in-law, now seventy-three, could not keep his hands from shaking with palsy; his cheeks had hollowed out, his dark eyes were pools of pain and embarrassment over his condition. Charles got a half-smile as he slid his arm shyly around Uncle Jos's shoulder. Aunt Bessy, after two strokes, barely recognized him.

He spent the first weeks walking the public footpaths across the fields, concentrating on an attempt to structure an essay on his species material. He would begin with the basic questions: How were species born? How did they change? Why did they change? Why do some flourish and others die off? Were there laws which governed all things that lived . . . and died? What are those laws?

He stayed at Maer Hall for a month, then asked Emma if she could spare him for a few weeks while he visited some of the places in North Wales that he had covered with Adam Sedgwick eleven years before. Since reading Louis Agassiz's book he was interested in observing the effects of old glaciers which Agassiz claimed formerly blocked all the larger valleys. It was four years since he had gone on his geological trip to Glen Roy.

"It's the first time I've wanted to, actually. I'll stop at The Mount to visit the family and borrow a horse."

The Wedgwood stableboy drove him by carriage into Shrewsbury. His family expressed their pleasure at how well he looked. They also handed him the tax papers they had received for him from the British government in London. It was the first time that an income tax had been imposed since the Napoleonic Wars of 1803–1815. The tax was seven shillings in the pound. Charles calculated that his income for the previous year had been one thousand and thirty pounds. Therefore his tax would be about thirty pounds. He hoped the rates would go no higher, there were so many things he and Emma needed, particularly now that they had children to raise.

After three days he left on the North Wales road just below the house, using his horse only to get him to the places he wanted to explore. He then stabled the animal at a convenient inn, climbing the mountains around Capel Curig, Caernarvon, Bangor, taking all-day walks through the long valleys, searching out signs of old glaciers. His legs were strong under him, his wind durable.

"It may be that Agassiz is right about the effects of old glaciers. But I still don't think he's right about Glen Roy."

For ten days he routed himself much as Adam Sedgwick had led him on the earlier trip. He tried to stay at the same inns where he and Sedgwick had had their evening meals and slept overnight. Sometimes he remembered the owners, sometimes they remembered him. As he climbed into a high bed at the inn of Capel Curig he again had a sense of *déjà vu*, as though it had all happened before.

"Fortunately for me, it did!" he mused.

He returned to Maer Hall determined to begin writing about species, their origins and their laws, to formulate the answers to the questions he had been asking himself the past three years. He sequestered an unused bedroom, moved a table into it, spread out his four species notebooks. He was prepared to take on established religion, even as Galileo had done to prove that the earth revolved around the sun, and for his pains was tried for apostasy, given the choice of retracting his sacrilegious findings or being put to death.

Galileo had retracted. What would he, Charles Darwin, do in a similar situation? That was a question only the future could answer. In the meanwhile he would take his first coordinated and rational step. He could do no less.

The quality of paper available was poor but he did not mind. He took up a soft pencil, wrote slowly, carefully, painlessly, making corrections as he went along. For Part One of his essay he used the title, On Variation Under Domestication, and on the Principles of Selection.

> When the organism is bred for several generations under new or varying conditions, the variation is greater in amount and endless in kind . . . holds good when individuals have long been exposed to new conditions. . . .

For his second section he used the title, On Variation in a State of Nature and of the Natural Means of Selection.

> Our experience would lead us to expect that any and every one of these organisms would vary under new conditions. Geology proclaims a constant round of change, bringing into play by every possible (?) change of climate and the death of preexisting inhabitants, endless variations of new conditions. . . .

Each day he closed the door of the workroom behind him; no one intruded on his privacy. Day after day he tapped the vast resources he had piled up during the *Beagle* journey as well as his years of reading in the world of plants and animals, the swimming fish, the soaring birds, the crawling insects and reptiles; and as a frame of reference, aged fossils; attempting to build his volume of fact into a disciplined theory about the myriad changes in species since the beginning of time.

He was surprised to find himself entirely well. There was no sign of the nausea that had dogged his days. In a concluding section he wrote:

> . . . The affinity of different groups, the unity of types of structure, the representative forms through which foetus passes, the metamorphosis of organs, the abortion of others cease to be metaphorical expressions and become intelligible facts. We no longer look on an animal as a savage does at a ship, or other great work of art, as a thing wholly beyond comprehension, but we feel far more interest in examining it. . . .

The essay, when completed after several weeks, ran only to thirty-five pages; yet he now had a compact beginning.

"For what?" he asked himself.

## 7.

At first sight he was not overly impressed by the house on the fifteen acres of chalk fields that lay beyond it. Yet it had been described to him as "a very possible place for your country home, extraordinarily rural though only sixteen miles from St. Paul's." The price was reasonable, two thousand and two hundred pounds, a sum which he could in all conscience ask his father to pay. He had taken the train for ten miles to the station at Sydenham, then rented a fly to drive the eight and a half miles through the rolling hills, green valleys and superb forests of Kent with a warm late July sun in a flawless blue sky.

He stopped for some minutes in the tiny village of Down, the house that was for sale being a third of a mile up the lane. The village had about forty houses, with one butcher, one baker, one grocer, a post office, an infant school, a carpenter's shop, and small inn above the grocer's shop. No main thoroughfare went through the village, whose center was a cleared area in which stood a giant walnut tree and a small church and graveyard where three lanes crossed. The church had been built of the local flint stone, whose segments looked like huge, empty oyster shells, the center a light gray, next an intensely dark to black area and a white outer border. He liked what he saw of the inhabitants of Down; they appeared very respectable. The men touched their hats to him, as had been the custom in Wales.

He got back into the fly and drove up the narrow lane to the vacant house situated on rather high tableland. It was now known as Down House, though at an earlier time it had been known as the Great

House. His first impression was that it was ugly, constructed of brick with a fading coat of whitewash. It had been built much too close to the lane, and the ground floor had been built on the very level of the lane itself, precluding privacy.

"But how busy can this lane be?" he wondered. "An occasional plow horse clop-clopping by, a carriage now and then?"

The house was in good repair, with fifteen hundred pounds having been spent only a few years before to provide a new, tight roof and other repairs. At the far end was the site of the original farmhouse, built around 1650. The kitchen, a rather large space, was in the basement. Next to it was a cool room for keeping the butter, cheeses, milk and wine. In this area there were also a scullery and meat storehouse. Somewhat apart was a small rustic cottage, a stable with a number of stalls, a ratty vegetable strip. The rear of the house, overlooking the fifteen acres of fields, mostly in hay, was attractive, with a clump of trees: old cherry, walnut, yew, Spanish chestnut, pear, larch, Scotch and silver fir, a big mulberry.

He went into the house prepared to take careful notes for Emma. The hall was spacious. One of the fair-sized rooms facing the lane could serve as his study. The room next to it was well suited for a dining room. The sitting room overlooked the clump of trees and the hayfields. It would be adequate for a while; he saw how it could be extended into the garden by building out with large bow windows.

"What pleases me most," he told Emma when he returned home at dusk, "is the number of bedrooms; there are enough to house Hensleigh and Fanny Wedgwood, Susan, Katty, Elizabeth, Erasmus, all at the same time." He hesitated for a moment. "The location is ideal, so quiet and yet so close to London. The surrounding countryside of Kent is glorious; the house leaves something to be desired, yet we can improve it and make it distinctly our own."

"I'll go out with you tomorrow. It would be an enormous relief if we could like this Down House and settle in."

The day dawned gloomy and cold, with a strong northeast wind. Emma insisted on making the trip anyway. They took a small valise so they could stay overnight at Down. Emma was disappointed at the nature of the country immediately around the house.

"Charles, isn't this area rather . . . desolate?"

"Yes. All chalk areas are. I'm used to Cambridgeshire, which is ten times worse."

However she liked the building and hayfields rather more than he had. It was situated the way she wanted, not too near and not too far from other houses.

The next morning the sun was out. After a second inspection of the house and grounds they drove in their carriage back the eight and a half miles to the railway station. Emma was delighted with this scenery.

"I'm coming around, Charles. The green rolling hills, the narrow lanes with the high hedges, they bring me a sense of peace and contentment. Perhaps it will be Down House for us, after all."

"There are lovely public footpaths across the fields," Charles cried, buoyed by Emma's encouragement. "It means we can cut diagonally to some of the most charming forests and green valleys in England. We'll have years of splendid and private walks, you and I and the children."

Dr. Darwin readily agreed to the purchase of the property in Down since Charles assured him that the price was "cheap" for the house, outlying buildings and fifteen acres of fields which, surrounded and protected by good hedges, would bring in some forty pounds or more a year for the hay, which the purchaser cut and the owner did not have to fertilize. Now ready to buy, Charles got the price reduced to two thousand and twenty pounds, which left him one hundred and eighty pounds leverage for the carpentry work that would have to be done in his study to build solid walls of bookshelves and filing cabinets.

The purchase was completed, the papers signed, the money paid over within a few weeks. Charles said:

"Emma dear, the house is ours now, but don't you think we ought to wait until after the baby is born and you recover before we make the move? There's a lot of work, you know, or at least a lot of movement. Are you sure you want that?"

"I'd rather do it as soon as possible. Have the baby in our new home. I think it would be easier on me, all around, if we were settled in and I could take my time recovering."

He made arrangements with a moving company to pack their possessions and transfer them to Down. Since the movers could not do the job for a week or more, Charles sat at his desk for the last times on Upper Gower Street and wrote his article on the effects of glaciers on the terrain in North Wales, conceding that glaciers had indeed existed there, but still maintaining that the roads or benches at Glen Roy had some other cause than glacial blockage of lakes. The articles were readily accepted by the *London, Edinburgh and Dublin Philosophical Magazine and Journal of Science,* which pleased Charles because this particular publication would broaden his audience. There was good news also from Smith Elder and Company about *Coral Reefs;* the book would be seriously reviewed and, for so technical a volume, the sale was good. The publishers assured him that they were looking forward to putting out his volume on volcanic islands.

Charles sorted his papers, packed and filed them carefully before they went into boxes. His books he wrapped in old newspapers with loving care. Most of his remaining specimens he packed separately but there were some items which he no longer needed, and so he sent a parcel of paints with which the Fuegians colored their bodies, two spears with which they speared porpoises, fish, otters and guanaco, and a Pacific dolphin's hook, to Professor Henslow for his collection.

In the afternoon, while Emma napped, Charles toted up his punctiliously kept accounts, which were on a September to September basis. Adding all of the hundreds of items together, he found that they had spent for the year on 12 Upper Gower Street for rent, food, cook and maids £465, another £24 for coal, £14 for beer, £40 for their man-servant, £200 for doctors, £11 for stationery and postage, £65 for furniture and repairs, £22 for the renting of horses and carriages, £76 for traveling, £142 for taxes, £53 for charities . . . so many pounds for books, scientific instruments . . . Altogether £1,062, which was, he saw, £67 more than they had spent the year before. However, their income had been large enough for them to have on deposit in their bank account £475 11s. Adding this to his savings from the previous year, he was now able to purchase £600 worth of Consols, government securities, for £538 5s., which would earn them roughly another £50 a year. He told himself sternly that there would be many expenses of moving into and changing Down House from an ugly duckling to a white swan; but they must not spend one pound more on the house and its equipment than he took in. Debt was anathema.

There was sad news from Maer. Uncle Jos's palsy was now out of control; he was bedridden. Dr. Darwin made the trip from Shrewsbury every few days to afford what help he could. Dr. Holland would not allow Emma to make the long trip to Maer Hall. She was sadly distressed.

Charles hired the biggest and most comfortable carriage he could find, and on September 14, 1842, Emma moved out to the house in Down with nearly three-year-old William and eighteen-month-old Annie. Along with her went Brodie, the Scottish nursemaid who was now indispensable to the family; Parslow, who would manage the installation at Down House, and Sally, the cook. Bessy decided she wanted to remain in London. She stayed for a couple of days to take care of Charles while he attended to the dozen odds and ends before he turned the house back to its owner.

The bedroom, immediately above the sitting room, which Emma moved into, was pleasant and comfortable except that the windows overlooking their fields were too small to admit much light or sun.

Charles reassured her.

"Worry not. I have plans for this whole wing. By this time next year we'll be flooded with light and air and have a good view of the hills beyond."

Emma had her third child, a girl, whom they named Mary Eleanor, just nine days after she moved into their new home. Dr. Edgar Cockell, a member of the Royal College of Surgeons, who had come from London to Down two years before and had bought a property only two fields away from the Darwins, had met Charles on the little street of the village and introduced himself. They found that they had friends in common. The villagers respected Dr. Cockell highly. Charles engaged him to deliver Emma's baby.

The birth was normal. Emma suffered rather less than in the other two births, perhaps because there was so much relief mixed in with the terrible pain. However Mary Eleanor was sickly from birth. She never ceased to cry except when asleep. Dr. Cockell found them a good young wet nurse in the village but the infant would take little nourishment. The doctor came every day to visit Emma and the baby. He could find no way of determining what was wrong with the child.

"Charles, I'm worried," Emma confided. "She's so pale. She isn't gaining at all; her face is pinched. I don't think she ever has an easy moment. . . ."

Charles sat on the edge of the bed, kissed her brow comfortingly.

"Now, dear, we can have a turn for the better any day."

"I love her so much, Charles. She has my mother's face. I hoped during the first days that she would also have my mother's beauty and character."

"There's another doctor close by. I'll bring him in for consultation."

Emma was mending by the hour. The baby was not. The little one was suffering from some kind of internal disturbance. To occupy his mind and keep from worrying about her, Charles went into a cyclone of work, hiring the carpenter who owned the pothouse above the grocery where he and Emma had spent the night, taking measurements in the study, making drawings for shelves of varying heights for his books, and for the space between the end of the shelves and the door, where the carpenter installed a set of drawers, all of which Charles would meticulously label.

Emma hired a thirteen-year-old nurserymaid, Bessy Harding, whose family she knew from Staffordshire. Little Bessy Harding had an amiable disposition. She was a help to Brodie with her chores. Charles hired a gardener-coachman by the name of Comfort, which he was. Comfort very quickly tore up the miserable garden patch with its lime and fragments of flint stone; moved it to a better location, brought in a load of rich topsoil. During the ongoing days Charles bought a phaeton and horses, cows and pigs, which Comfort took care of, and shopped for a saddle, a bridle, corn, oats and a large set of clippers for Comfort's use.

Mary Eleanor died at the end of nearly a month. They buried her in the little graveyard alongside the flint-stone church in the village. Charles was grief-stricken, dreading the funeral. Emma took the blow with sad calmness. It was she who consoled her husband with the words he had used to her when Caroline's baby died:

"You will be disconsolate only until we have our next child, a healthy one; that is bound to happen." She added, "We must put the child out of our minds and work our way back to our normal lives. Our sorrow is nothing compared to what it would have been if the baby had lived longer and suffered more. We have our two other dear children. We must not let them suffer from this blow. I feel well and strong today. I am coming downstairs for dinner."

"That's the best news possible. We haven't done much with our house yet, hardly become acquainted with it. Now we must begin to live in it and enjoy it and make it very specially our home."

Emma put on a dressing gown. Charles led her downstairs. They walked arm in arm through the rooms, deciding where they would need new rugs or articles of furniture and where they would want a fresh coat of paint on the walls, or perhaps an agreeable wallpaper. Charles then took her for a short walk along the footpath which crossed their field. Although it was already late October, the weather had remained warm. They turned and looked back at the building.

"This will really be the front of the house," Charles told her, "where we can sit out in good weather under the trees. I have plans for this first acre or two. We'll plant flowering shrubs, a lawn, and next spring we'll build bow windows on all three floors. That will add a deal of space to our sitting room and bedroom, and will give us a view of the countryside. Admittedly, the house was ugly when we bought it. Bleak. Now we'll have the opportunity to make it as beautiful as Maer Hall or The Mount, and it will be ours. . . . And everything that happens in it will be beautiful too."

He took her in his arms, kissed her. They walked slowly back into Down House, arms about each other's waists, love and tenderness in their eyes and a strong hope for fulfillment in the years ahead.

# BOOK NINE

*The Whole of Life*

1.

D OWN House was to be a family home. Its creative core, however, was Charles's study, a spacious room with a handsomely decorated white marble fireplace, a tallish marble mantelpiece and full-width gold-framed mirror above. There were now bookshelves along the wall opposite the fireplace with compartments for periodicals and monographs; at the corner near the door some thirty drawers of varying sizes to accommodate notes, clippings, correspondence. Emma hung the window wall and the area around and above the fireplace with a figured light gray and blue cloth.

When Charles entered the study at eight in the morning to begin his first workday, he found the grate filled with red-hot coals which Parslow had lighted an hour before to warm the room against the crisp autumn air.

"Where might you like your desk placed, Mr. Darwin?" Parslow asked. "Between the two big windows with the lane at your back?"

"Parslow, new home, new habits. I shan't want the desk in here at all. I'm going to write in my favorite armchair from Upper Gower Street."

Parslow cut a piece of plain board which fit across the two arms of the chair, wide enough to allow for pencils, pens, ink, paper and notes, and covered it with green cloth. He placed the chair in the rear corner of the fireplace wall, next to another set of filing cabinets, bookshelves high up, and a low built-in cupboard with a projected surface to hold a jade glass lamp. On a light red carpet woven in diamond-shaped squares sat the stand with Charles's yellowed world globe, his circular table with its dozen or so drawers holding his treasures from the *Beagle*; specimen bottles, interesting stones, powder mixtures, tubes, bottles of chemicals.

Emma came in to wish him good fortune.

"I see you've recreated your corner of the poop cabin," she observed.

"So I have! Ah well, I did some good work in that cramped space."

"You're going to be comfortable here, Charles."

"For many years, I hope. Your new wall covering gives the room an air of floating . . . on a quiet sea."

Emma smiled, pleased.

"I don't see how you can float anywhere, my dear, barricaded behind a writing plank . . . except of course to South America for your volcano book."

Emma settled the family into the rest of the house. The sitting room and their bedroom became less commonplace as she recovered the walls with a handsome fabric, set her exquisite Wedgwood vases on the mantelpieces, bright carpeting on the floors, added small coffee tables and chairs to their possessions from Upper Gower Street, hung the two Conrad Martens water colors of the *Beagle*. The exterior stucco of the house got a coat of pearl-gray paint.

"I've only one problem," she confided to Charles, "that basement kitchen, with Parslow having to bring the food up a flight of stairs and through a hallway into the dining room. We have enough bowls and covered platters to keep it reasonably warm, but eventually we ought to have our kitchen upstairs. There's plenty of room on the old foundations to give us a spacious kitchen and fireplace."

"Within the year, my dear. We must allot only so much rebuilding money from each calendar income."

"Neither Sally nor Parslow is complaining. They seem to be as happy to be living in the country as we are. I was looking toward the future, a more interesting place to look than the past."

"Is it, my dear?" He gazed out his near window. "I have a problem as well. It's that lane outside my study. Anyone passing on horseback, in a farm wagon or carriage, can see in."

"Are you planning to raise your study or lower the road?"

He chuckled. "Lower the lane. About two feet. Also build a wall on our side."

"How does one go about getting a lane lowered in Kent? Apply for a permit at Maidstone, the county seat?"

"We apply the palms of several hands to the ends of several shovels."

Emma gazed at him quizzically.

"Mightn't someone object?"

"Not if we leave the lane in as good or better shape than it is now."

They established a routine into which everyone fitted harmoniously. Charles arose before seven, careful not to waken Emma, shaved, dressed, donned a cloak and went for a walk among his gardens and fields. This walk through the dark before sunrise sometimes surprised foxes making for home after their night's foraging. At seven forty-five he ate a light breakfast alone and by eight had closed the door of his study. Cold winds blew in from the north. In spite of Parslow's abundant fire, he frequently needed a shawl around his back and shoulders. He began writing about volcanic islands. No one knocked on his door, nor did he look up from his work until nine-thirty. At this point he walked across the hall to the sitting room where Emma awaited him.

"Where are the little ones?"

"Bessy is taking them for a walk. It's dry out, and they're bundled against the cold."

"Any letters?"

"One from Maer Hall, one from The Mount."

If there was no post Emma read him a chapter from an advance copy of Charles Lever's *Jack Hinton, the Guardsman*, a medley of harum-scarum exploits in Ireland, or William Bulwer's melodrama *Night and Morning*. At ten-thirty he returned to his study, picking up his narrative where he had left off, quoting from other travelers or geologists, setting down theories and hypotheses. When he stopped at noon, Emma could tell from the expression on his face how the writing had gone.

"I've had a good day's work!"

"Splendid. Now have a walk, all that sitting won't give you an appetite for dinner. We're having mutton pie, caper sauce and suet pudding."

He put on his cape, soft black hat, picked up his walking stick, a piece of ash which had a spiral indentation its full length where a wire or honeysuckle had wrapped itself into the growing wood, and set out for a brisk two-mile walk first to the end of his own acres, then, following footpaths, into Cudham Wood in the long green valley.

Dinner was served at one o'clock, the substantial meal of the day, usually with a glass of light wine. After lunch Charles read the London *Times* which Parslow had picked up in the village along with the post, then returned to take care of his correspondence, which was growing rapidly in response to his inquiries to farmers and stock breeders, seeking information for his species concept.

At three he went to his bedroom, lazed on a sofa, smoked one of the two cigarettes he allowed himself for the day, rested, dozed occasionally, then returned to his study for another hour. This broken-up workday was a technique Charles Lyell had recommended.

Later he wanted only a simple tea with an egg or a slice of meat. Then came the real contest of the day, two games of backgammon with Emma, a pastime they had had little time to engage in at Upper Gower Street. When she won he was genuinely exasperated, exclaiming:

"Bang your bones!"

After the backgammon, Emma played the piano for an hour; then he read in the German or French scientific books and journals while she crocheted until their bedtime at ten-thirty.

It was a period of quiet, contentment and stability. He was deeply attached to his children, played with William and effervescent Annie dur-

462        THE WHOLE OF LIFE

ing his periods outside his study, and never missed a good-night visit
when Brodie tucked them into bed.

Every second week he rode up to London to attend meetings of the
Geological Society, on whose council he was serving, and the Royal Society, keeping up his friendships with his colleagues.

When in London he stayed with Erasmus. They had tea or dinner
together at the Athenaeum.

"Emma keeps asking when you're coming down, Ras. We've bedrooms galore."

"As soon as spring breaks. But you'll have to promise not to take me
on any of those long walks through the woods. That country air upsets
my circulation."

Emma could not be persuaded to come to London with him. He was
concerned that she might find life dull in their rural retreat. The villagers knew who they were and treated them with respect; John Willott,
the rector, and the congregation of the small church at the crossroads
were civil, but they made no friends in Down. In the English countryside friends were made slowly, cautiously, over a period of years.

"I asked you this when we lived in London, Emma, and now it's a
hundredfold more important: are you happy in this isolated spot with
no family or friends close by creating gaiety . . . ?"

Emma laughed low in her throat.

"There are as many varieties of happiness, my dear old gentleman, as
there are individuals. I would not like to get cemented into the center
of any one of them."

By November there was considerably more activity in the house.
Hensleigh Wedgwood had come down with a severe illness which could
not be diagnosed. Fanny was acting as Hensleigh's nurse. Emma said:

"It will be too much for Fanny, nursing Hensleigh and taking care of
five children with only one nursemaid on hand. Charles, do you think
we could bring two or three of the children down here for a while? It
would ease life for them."

"Naturally. Comfort will take your note into town and get it on the
afternoon mail coach."

Two days later the Wedgwood nursemaid, Isabella, arrived with
Snow, the nine-year-old Wedgwood daughter; Bro, the eight-year-old
son; and Erny, five. The Darwin children were rapturous. Emma put
the youngsters in two bedrooms across the hall from her own. All went
well until Emma allowed fourteen-year-old Bessy Harding to take all
five of the youngsters for a walk through the adjacent valley and
Cudham Wood. The ground was covered with mud, the woods were
quite dark; young Bessy was unable to keep the five children together,
in part because she was carrying two-year-old Annie. Snow and William

got separated but Snow had a sense of direction. She brought William to the house. The others were overdue. Emma and Charles went out to search for them, along with Parslow and Comfort, all expecting to find the children sitting in a puddle somewhere, lost, crying. Instead the owners of the first farmhouse they stopped at said that the children had inquired for directions, and a few moments later they came across Bessy, still carrying Annie, standing in front of a second farmhouse with the other two boys.

They returned to Down House and huddled for warmth in front of a crackling sitting-room fire.

For their first Christmas in Down House Comfort found a symmetrical fir tree in the forest and set it up in the sitting room. On Christmas Eve Charles and Emma draped the pictures with holly, as well as the mantelpiece. Since the three Wedgwood children were still visiting, there were five stockings hanging from it. Charles surprised Emma with a brooch he had bought for her on one of his trips to London; Emma had ordered out two books which Charles had spoken of admiringly. It was cold outside but clear.

When Hensleigh Wedgwood returned to work in early January his three children left for their own home. Emma announced that their families now considered the Darwins had settled in and would be coming to visit.

Charles was pleased to receive a copy of the *Edinburgh New Philosophical Journal* which contained a long review of his *Coral Reefs* by a competent critic, Charles Maclaren, who said: "This theory explains the phenomena under consideration better than any other which has been proposed. . . ." He then went on to outline astutely the major content of the book before taking exception to some of its theories.

Never one to refuse a challenge, Charles wrote to Maclaren. His letter was modest, even admitting that one of Maclaren's criticisms was "a weighty and perplexing one."

Both the review and his reply were read in England's scientific circles, attracting attention to the book. On his next trip up to London he was congratulated by his friends. Lyell, who had returned from his trip to North America with considerable enthusiasm for the country, was the most pleased of all.

"It's a jolly good start for your trilogy, Darwin," he said, having taken Charles to the Athenaeum for a nightcap. "How is the Volcanic Islands coming?"

Charles sipped his brandy.

"I should finish by the end of this year and have the volume in the bookstores early next year."

March broke surprisingly warm. Charles called in carpenters and bricklayers to build large bows out from the sitting room, master bedroom and the bedroom above, with wide windows. The extension gave the rooms almost a third again as much space and light and converted the modest sitting room into a proper drawing room. The brick bow structures were covered with stucco and painted to match the rest of the house. Comfort planted wisteria creepers which would have mauve flowers to cover the new walls. Emma found a draper in the nearby town of Orpington to cover her three new bow windows. She selected lace curtains and floral-designed hangings of velvet. They were to be held back by cords during the day to admit the maximum of light and sun; closed at night to keep out the cold.

"Our ugly duckling is coming round," she cried happily.

Charles took a holiday from his study to supervise the workmen. A second crew was building a large kitchen on the ground floor, as Emma had suggested. A group of workmen from Down were lowering the lane outside the house the two feet Charles required. No one objected since no difficulties were created for those traveling over it. The excavated material was taken in wheelbarrows to the back garden where it was deposited to form two ornamental mounds. The study seemed more comfortable with the lowered country lane. He next called in masons to construct a ten-foot-high wall along the front drive with the indigenous colorful flint stone, the flat irregular surface extending out, the rounded part buried in the wall; it shut out some of the cold wind and increased his privacy. He was delighted with all the changes until his account books showed that the extension of the three rooms, the new kitchen, with its large stove, and the lowering of the road and building of the wall had cost him over four hundred pounds.

A kitchen garden was staked out at the side of the house where the soil was good so that the Darwins would be eating their own green vegetables and potatoes. They were getting enough milk from their cows for the children, as well as butter and cheese, all of which was stored in the cold room of the cellar along with Charles's wines.

He returned to his study. The manuscript on Volcanic Islands moved along felicitously. He plunged back into his reading, bought Richard Hinds's The Regions of Vegetation which had just been published, abstracted several volumes of the Linnean Society Transactions, made notations on William Spence's book on insects.

When he went up to London in April he called on the FitzRoys in their elegant home on Belgrave Square to say au revoir to the family, since Captain FitzRoy had just been appointed governor of New Zealand. He and FitzRoy had gotten along amiably since the scene on Great Marlborough Street when FitzRoy had been angered over Lyell's comments about the journals. Charles had been amused when he heard what happened when FitzRoy had run for Parliament from Durham and been elected. FitzRoy had become involved in an acrimonious exchange of letters and pamphlets with a Mr. William Sheppard which resulted in a "duel" in the Mall outside the United Services Club. Sheppard strode up to FitzRoy and, waving a whip, cried:

"Captain FitzRoy, I will not strike you but consider yourself horsewhipped."

FitzRoy had felled Sheppard with his umbrella!

Surprisingly, after so many years of being at home on the sea, FitzRoy had done well in Parliament, serving on important committees and pushing for legislation on matters concerning the Royal Navy.

After taking tea with FitzRoy and his wife Mary, Charles walked from Belgrave Square to Erasmus's newly rented house on Park Street. It had a feeling of lightness, for Erasmus had covered his windows with bright chintz. He stayed the night.

Emma, several months pregnant, walked with Charles while he studied the geology and jotted descriptions of the local countryside. He pointed out interesting aspects of the terrain as they strode across the hilly chalk country with its valleys of steep rounded bottoms, valleys which were in all probability ancient sea bays.

"Are you planning to write about Kent?" she asked.

"Just keeping my hand in."

In early July Emma had a letter from Elizabeth telling her that their father was sinking rapidly. When they reached Maer Hall after the grueling nine- to ten-hour trip by way of London, Uncle Jos was able to speak few words but his eyes showed his relief at having them at his bedside. He died four days later in his sleep, at the age of seventy-four. Funeral services were held in the chapel above Maer Hall where Emma and Charles had been married. Aunt Bessy was unable to leave her bed for the services. There was no weeping, no outward show of grief. When Charles returned to the house with the Wedgwood family and his own—Dr. Darwin had been making the twenty-mile drive from The Mount every few days, attempting to ease Josiah's waning hours—they sat out under the shade trees sipping cool lemonade. Joe Wedgwood commented:

"He never really liked the potteries. Any more than I do. His happiness came from his books and his family."

Charles added: "He was a naturalist at heart and was always alive to the beauties of Maer and the forests."

After a short visit to The Mount they arrived back in Down in mid-July. Elizabeth came for a visit a week later. Since Emma had company, Charles decided to attend the British Association meeting in Cork, Ireland, in August. He met a number of the younger men working in the life sciences, particularly in biology, and now had new colleagues with whom to correspond when he needed special information.

Late summer struck hot. The house itself was cool. After work sessions on the Volcanic Islands Charles read in the first four volumes of Gibbon's *History*, some volumes of the *Annals and Magazine of Natural History*, and a travel book on Salmone, on the eastern point of Crete. He also dug at the far end of his property where the workmen found a clay pit fourteen feet deep, as well as a large sand pit.

"What is all this sand doing here?" he asked himself. Had the area been a beach when Kent was under the sea?

A Scotsman named Kemp sent him a parcel of seeds which he had found in the bottom layer of a very deep sand pit with the comment:

"No geologist will pretend to guess how many thousands and thousands of years must have elapsed since these seeds were embedded with vegetable matter at the bottom of the sand."

Charles sent some of the seeds to Henslow and others to the Horticultural Society. To everyone's astonishment they germinated freely! The growth turned out to be a Rumex which neither Charles nor Henslow nor the Horticultural Society had ever seen. They were all agreed that what was sprouting before their eyes was not a British plant. But if it was not British, where did it come from? If indigenous, where was it now? Had there been a very different England here eons before? He remembered the tropical shell the workman had handed him out of a gravel pit years before. If there were tropical shells under the surface of England this island must once have had a tropical climate. The documentation on earlier ages was growing. Louis Agassiz had been finding fossil fish that went back many thousands of years. All life was evolving, perhaps also the continents and the sea. He was fascinated.

In September the gardener, with a modest assist from Charles, finished the work of laying the gravel paths from the house through the gardens and down the fields to the edges of the property. The orchard with its cherries, pears, plums, apples and quince was doing well. Charles added peaches and apricots.

Emma gave birth to their second girl. They named her Henrietta; both mother and daughter flourished. Charles said:

"There's never been such a good little soul as Miss Henrietta Emma Darwin."

Susan came down from Shrewsbury to spend a month, whereupon Charles dug in for the last pages on the Volcanic Islands and completed the manuscript. He wrote to Lyell:

"I hope you will read my volume, for if you don't, I cannot think of anyone else who will."

THE WHOLE OF LIFE 467

In October, with Susan to keep Emma company, he decided to spend a few days with his father and Katty in Shrewsbury. Dr. Darwin was now seventy-seven, hale and hearty, but not walking as much as he used to. When Charles told him about a sometime numbness in his finger ends, Dr. Darwin said with a nonchalant smile:

"Yes, yes, exactly, tut-tut, neuralgic, exactly, yes, yes. It will go away."

Charles showed him his account books and how much money he had spent for the rebuilding at Down House.

"Perhaps I have been extravagant? I certainly don't want to face ruin. . . ."

His father waved a dismissing arm through the air.

"Stuff and nonsense, Charles. Not to worry about money. You still are not spending more than your income; how can you be ruined? There is sufficient for all of us. Concern yourself with your scientific books and not your account books."

Autumn was without a cloudy day. Charles watched the birds congregating in groups of ten to thirty in the trees. The nuthatches were numerous as well. His cousin, the Rev. William Darwin Fox, came for a visit. Charles enjoyed having a colleague in the house and planned to invite his London friends, meeting them with the trap at Sydenham station, eight and a half miles away. The family was visiting regularly now. When Emma found that Brodie and Parslow were growing a bit subdued at the lack of available entertainment, she sent them by carriage to Bromley, some four miles distant, to hear a concert or watch a play. They came to know Lady Lubbock, whose family owned a nearby estate, High Elms. There was an occasional visit back and forth.

"In short," Charles declared, "we are digging in. I'm satisfied that this is our anchorage."

2.

The minutes and hours ticked by on the tall pendulum clock in the entranceway. The calendar leaves dropped off effortlessly as the leaves off the maples and elms. Time rushed by like a torrent; or sometimes stood as stagnant as a dry creek.

After the turn of the year 1844 Charles delivered his Volcanic Islands manuscript to his publishers. In February, having corrected the last of the printer's sheets, he brought out his nearly nine hundred pages of observations on the geology of the places visited during H.M.S. Beagle's voyage, as well as the loose-leaf notes written on board, in ink, on uniform sheets approximately eight by ten inches in size.

"It's already a book and a half," he exclaimed aloud. "It needs extensive organization."

He read through the pages, then put the wrapped packages away.

"It's too soon to start," he explained to Emma as she was about to play him an hour of lieder. "I need a stretch of time between volumes."

"Why hurry?" she asked, loosening her fingers on the keyboard. "You have time for dozens of books."

He did not tell her that he was aching to get back to the transmutation of species. He had written nothing since he completed the thirty-five-page essay at Maer Hall in the summer of 1842, which was safely resting in one of his locked drawers. This time he wanted to get a book written based not only on his discoveries around the world but his correlations of the life sciences about which he had been experimenting for the past seven years. Lyell knew a little about it, as did his cousin Fox. He chose a new young friend to confide in, Joseph Hooker, to whom he had first been introduced by Dr. Robert McCormick when Hooker was about to embark on H.M.S. *Erebus* as botanist for the voyage. Hooker had been away for four years but he had written Charles a brilliant letter about his growing collection. Charles considered Joseph Hooker, eight years younger than himself, as having the enthusiasm, dedication and depth of perception to become a superb botanist and a first-rate naturalist. The men had exchanged letters since Hooker's return, with Charles encouraging Hooker to write fully about the plants and flowers gathered on his journey.

"You wouldn't be liking him," Emma twitted, "because he admired your *Journal* so much that he slept with the galley sheets under his pillow?"

"It helps. I'm going to invite him to have lunch with me at Ras's house next time I go up to London."

On January 11, 1844, when he moved intently back into his species work, he had written quite openly to Hooker:

> I have been ever since my return engaged in a very presump-
> tuous work, and I know no one individual who would not say
> a very foolish one. I was so struck with the distribution of the
> Galapagos organisms, and with the character of the South
> American fossil mammifers, that I determined to collect
> blindly every sort of fact which could bear any way on what
> are species. I have read heaps of agricultural and horticultural
> books. At last gleams of light have come, and I am almost
> convinced (quite contrary to the opinion I started with) that
> species are not (it is like confessing to a murder) immutable,
> unchangeable. . . . I think I have found out (here's presump-
> tion!) the simple way by which species become exquisitely
> adapted to various ends. You will now groan and think to
> yourself, "On what a man have I been wasting my time and
> writing to." I should, five years ago, have thought so. . . .

Before the end of the month he received an encouraging reply from Joseph Hooker.

> . . . Vegetation was undoubtedly once very different on the same spot to what it is now. . . . There may in my opinion have been a series of productions on different spots, and also a gradual change of species. I shall be delighted to hear how you think that this change may have taken place, as no presently conceived opinions satisfy me on the subject.

Charles knew from his extensive reading that as far back as 1749 the French naturalist Buffon had estimated that the earth could be seventy thousand years old. In 1755 the German philosopher Immanuel Kant believed that the earth could be millions of years old. Neither man had attempted to document his beliefs. The first to come up with an intelligible theory of evolutionary change had been the French naturalist Lamarck, who in 1809 wrote about the nature of change of all organisms from plants to animals to man. Charles had first learned about Lamarck's theories from his mentors in the Natural History Museum of the University of Edinburgh. Where Lamarck was wrong, Charles had long ago perceived, was in ascribing evolution to a natural instinct embedded in all organisms *of an inescapable drive toward perfection of its own species.*

During the cold and blustery weather of January and February Emma read him several novels by the Swedish writer Fredrika Bremer, as well as part of Lord Chesterfield's letters. For his thirty-fifth birthday she gave him Henry Hallam's *Constitutional History of England.* For their fifth anniversary he gave her a handsome set of Sir Walter Scott's Waverley novels but begged off from her big family celebration dinner. It was impossible to single out just a few to join them. Instead they had the two older children to the dinner table and placed four-month-old Henrietta in her crib beside it. Parslow laid on their finest silver, linens and Wedgwood service. Sally worked in the kitchen for two days preparing a feast of clear soup, oyster soufflé, chicken Marengo, roast lamb with mint sauce, new potatoes dressed in butter, pineapple and rice. They could merely sample each course. Sally had also baked a special Dundee cake with currants, chopped raisins and peel, nutmeg, brandy and almonds.

"Took two hours to mix and bake," she said triumphantly; "but might be worth it."

There were six candles among the sprinkled almonds.

"One to grow on," Emma said under her breath. "I suppose I shall. Three children is hardly our full quota. But it would be helpful for me to rest a year or so."

Charles took her hand in his.

"I do think it cruel that the woman has to bear all the pain, that the man cannot assume his rightful share."

"You do, my dear old soul. Your pain at the lying-in is almost as intolerable as mine." She gazed at William, Annie and Henrietta. "They gladden our lives."

Fanny Wedgwood was going to have her sixth child very soon. Emma asked permission to bring her five children to Down House.

"My dear, those five are not only your nieces and nephews, they are also mine through my Wedgwood mother."

Hensleigh sent them down in a large carriage with their governess. William and Annie were happy to have a whole school of playmates descend upon them. They ran out of doors in woolen scarves and knitted hats, literally playing "Here we go 'round the mulberry bush," around the huge mulberry just outside the new bow window. In bad weather Emma arranged games for them in an upstairs playroom. She learned how well built the old house was when the screams, shouts and laughter of seven children playing at "Up Jenkins," a guessing game with a marble clenched in a child's fist, or "Snakes and Ladders" with a pair of dice rattled on a board to determine whether the thrower went up a space or hit a snake and moved down, rocked the very furniture, floor and walls of the room without penetrating the rest of the house.

Charles did not mind the general hubbub in the halls and family rooms. He as well as Emma had spent weeks, sometimes months, in the homes of their aunts and uncles, living and playing with an equal number of cousins. He was captivated by the play of emotions that he watched in his own children and the Wedgwood young, and wrote to his friends asking them to observe their little ones. His volume of notes grew; then his inquiring mind reached out to the field of animals. Did they not have emotions too? Pleasure in eating, running games, affection for their owners and keepers, for each other, alertness to attack, fear, pain? He began scribbling notes on the discernible reactions he had seen in animals during his land journeys off the *Beagle*, from his visits to the London zoo; and began looking for recorded animal lore in his library. There was material aplenty, but no one had conducted a search for the causes or delineated the extent of the expression of animals. He felt certain there was illuminative material here; and perhaps some valid connection between the emotions of children and animals.

He was writing steadily now on species, on loose pages, sometimes dividing a wide sheet into three columns, working strictly from memory. He retained the basic chapter headings of his Maer Hall essay: using for his first chapter, On the Variation of Organic Beings Under Domestication, but each day plunged deeper, ranged wider:

. . . The effects of external conditions on the size, colour and form, which can rarely and obscurely be detected during one individual life, become apparent after several generations: the slight differences, often hardly describable, which characterize the stock of different countries, and even of districts in the same country, seem to be due to such continued action.

. . . As different races of men require and admire different qualities in their domesticated animals, each would thus slowly, though unconsciously, be selecting a different breed.

He expanded his second chapter, Natural Means of Selection, to read:

De Candolle, in an eloquent passage, has declared that all nature is at war, one organism with another, or with external nature. Seeing the contented face of nature, this may at first be well doubted; but reflection will inevitably prove it is too true. The war, however, is not constant, but only recurrent in a slight degree at short periods and more severely at occasional more distant periods; and hence its effects are easily overlooked. It is the doctrine of Malthus applied in most cases with ten-fold force. . . . Even slow-breeding mankind has doubled in 25 years, and if he could increase his food with greater ease, he would double in less time. But for animals, without artificial means, *on an average* the amount of food for each species must be constant; whereas the increase of all organisms tends to be geometrical and in a vast majority of cases at an enormous ratio. . . .

He thought:
"Everything that is born is born to eat and be eaten."

In late March the banks around Down House were covered with pale blue violets. Primroses grew everywhere. When they walked through the neighboring copses they found them entwined with wood anemones and a white stellaria. Large areas became brilliantly colored with bluebells. With the flowers came the birds. Larks abounded, calling their notes agreeably on all sides. Nightingales were common; a large number of doves made their cooing sound in the woods.

"Something like the purring of a cat," Emma observed.

She slipped her hand into his as they walked.

"Oh, Charles, the land seemed so desolate when we bought our house . . . it was almost an act of desperation. Yet now I think it's the loveliest place I've known."

All the land around Down had burst into flower. The traffic increased along the footpaths, the townspeople became more friendly and hospitable. The Darwins accepted several invitations to dinner. Charles was happy for Emma to have some adult society.

In April Charles planted lilies, larkspur, portulacas, verbenas, ga-zanias "scientifically and unscientifically." Comfort worked alongside. In the warm weather of June they sat on benches in the secluded area outside the drawing-room bow, Parslow setting out tea, the children gathering for red currant tarts in the rose-purple glow of the Kentish sunset.

By July 4 he had completed close to a hundred and ninety pages of a species treatise. He used much of his earlier phrasing but added new ob-servations and insights.

. . . How interesting do all instincts become when we spec-ulate on their origin as hereditary habits, or as slight congeni-tal modifications of former instincts perpetuated by the indi-viduals so characterized having been preserved. When we look at every complex instinct and mechanism as the summing up of a long history of contrivances, each most useful to its pos-sessor, nearly in the same way as when we look at a great me-chanical invention as the summing up of the labour, the expe-rience, the reason, and even the blunders of numerous workmen . . .

. . . For we see in all this the inevitable consequences of one great law, of the multiplication of organic beings not created immutable. . . .

Even as he exulted, ensconced in his protected nook, he decided:

"I have no intention of publishing this work in its present form, yet I must protect it in case of my death. Why do I think of death at this particular moment when I've been feeling well for months? We're all mortal. Men go to sleep in England and wake up in the nether world. And then . . .

"I don't know whether Emma realizes what I have been writing since the turn of the year. Probably so. Women are prescient about such things. Yet she will one day have to know, for I must entrust this man-uscript to her."

At eight the next morning he settled into his big chair in the study, put the cloth-covered board across its arms, began to write a letter to Emma.

"As they said on the Beagle," he reminisced, "I shall steer by the light of a volcano."

I have just finished my sketch of my species theory. If, as I believe, my theory in time be accepted even by one competent judge, it will be a considerable step in science.

I therefore write this in case of my sudden death, as my most solemn and last request, which I am sure you will con-sider the same as if legally entered in my will, that you will devote £400 to its publication, and further, will yourself, or through Hensleigh, take trouble in promoting it. I wish that my sketch be given to some competent person, with this sum to induce him to take trouble in its improvement and enlargement. . . . I also request that you will hand over to him all those scraps roughly divided in eight or ten brown paper portfolios. With respect to editors, Mr. Lyell would be the best if he would undertake it; especially with the aid of Hooker. . . .

He put the letter in the locked drawer which would be opened only after his death, the drawer in which he intended to place his last will and testament. That done, he took the manuscript to a scrivener by the name of Fletcher who would give him a fair copy without bothering to understand what he was copying.

Charles was involved in his work. Emma's concern was the raising of her children. William was past four and Annie three, Henrietta, whom they called Etty, was nine months old. Though both she and Charles had been raised in families which did not punish their childish errors or pranks, in all too many homes throughout England the nannies and governesses were sadists, mean-tempered, taking out on their wards their own frustrations and unhappiness, striking them, locking them in cupboards or dark rooms. Emma had vowed when their first child was born:

"None of that is ever going to happen to our young."

During the day she visited the children's playroom, told them stories or read to them. The baby was brought down to the little room off the kitchen where she could be spoiled by Sally, Parslow and Brodie. Brodie was a cheerful and competent nursemaid in her early thirties. Emma had chosen her because she perceived neither unhappiness nor throttled violence in her eyes. Her stricture to Brodie when she hired her early in 1842 had been:

"If you don't genuinely like children, or are taking this job out of desperation, please don't start."

"It's not like that with me," Brodie had replied with a Scots burr. "To be in a pleasant home, treated with respect, there come my pot of gold."

"Very well, Brodie, you are engaged at forty pounds a year. But remember, the disciplining of the children will be my sole responsibility."

Emma brought the children into the dining room for breakfast; in the evening if they were not yet sleepy she sat them on pillows at the dining table to have an egg and tea, with a slice of cake. For the main meal at one, they joined their father if he was not too fatigued. If they ate alone, earlier, Emma sat with them.

The atmosphere at Down House was as tranquil and productive as the countryside.

In spite of his several years of walks into the Fens of Cambridgeshire and his collecting of plants and flowers during the *Beagle* voyage, he considered himself an amateur in botany. It was a defect he would have to remedy because a good deal of his proof of the evolution of species would come out of the vegetable world. Since he considered Joseph Hooker the brightest young botanist in Great Britain, and having already confided in him some part of his species theory, he now turned to him for help.

He asked Erasmus if he could invite Hooker to breakfast in Park Street. Erasmus summoned his daily to prepare a breakfast of grilled kidneys and bacon, scrambled eggs, watercress, strawberries. Erasmus was too sleepy to join them; besides he could not understand much of what his two guests were discussing. He excused himself and went back to bed. When they had finished eating Charles and Hooker transferred from the small dining room to the drawing room. Though the house was unpretentious, Erasmus had made the move from colorful Great Marlborough Street and the adjacent Carnaby Street to the more expensive, higher social status of Mayfair.

Despite the difference of only eight years in their ages, Joseph Hooker seemed to Charles to belong to a younger generation. He wore steel-rimmed spectacles, the sidepieces of which went into hiding under his rich black hair, which he parted neatly and combed down conservatively. He had grown long, thick sideburns while on H.M.S. *Erebus*. During the voyage his face appeared to have become leaner, El Greco-ish, except that there was no sadness in his eyes, only absorption in his subject. He had a large dimple in his chin. All in all a plainer face than that possessed by most of the scientists Charles knew.

Hooker carried with him the air of a student on his way to becoming a scholar. His clothing appeared younger, with narrower lapels on his shorter coat, the black silk stock covered a lowered white collar which did not cut into the jowl. He had a delicate constitution, a tendency toward consumption ran through the family. As a child he had been known as "Croaky Joe" owing to a croupy hoarseness. Yet he had endured the long rough *Erebus* journey extremely well. It was the first time Charles had a young confrere. All the others, Henslow, Sedgwick, Lyell, were ten to fourteen years older than himself, as were the contributors to the *Zoology*. He found it a refreshing experience.

The two men talked botany all morning.

Both of Joseph Hooker's grandfathers had been interested in or practiced botany. In his childhood he had collected mosses as Charles had collected beetles, returning home from botanizing in the highlands to build loose stones into a miniature mountain and placing his specimens at heights relative to those at which he had collected them.

"That was the dawn of my love for geographical botany," he told Charles as the two men sat side by side on Erasmus's elaborately upholstered sofa. "Among my contemporaries I neither court popularity nor am I constitutionally fitted to practice the art of popularity. Indeed, I suffer from a nervous irritability of the heart which from my schooldays brought on palpitations when I stood up to construe in class."

Charles thought:

"He is a delightful companion and most kindhearted. One can see at once that he is honorable to the backbone. His intellect is very acute, and he has great power of generalization."

Charles knew that Lyell had sent Hooker a copy of the *Journal*. Hooker had written to Lyell, "Your kind present is now a well-thumbed book, for all the officers sent to me for it." To his mother Hooker had written: ". . . Clouds and fogs, rain and snow justified all Darwin's remarks. They are so true and so graphic wherever we go that Mr. Lyell's kind present is not only indispensable but a delightful companion and guide."

He now told Charles of how he was almost refused the post of botanist on the *Erebus* because Captain Ross wanted "someone well known in the world, such a person as Mr. Darwin. . . ."

"Here I interrupted him with 'What was Mr. Darwin before he went out? He, I dare say, knew his subject better than I now do but did the world know him? The voyage with FitzRoy was the making of him.'"

They differed only twice, and both times with an ample show of emotion. When Charles suggested that coal plants had lived in shallow waters of the sea, Hooker repudiated the idea savagely. When Hooker said that a continent might formerly have existed between Australia and South America, Charles rejected the concept with scorn. Both men recovered quickly from their outbursts, laughing at their indignations.

"It's better this way," Charles said; "now we know that we'll never agree out of politeness. That would make for a porridge; what we want is rare roast beef."

He was now well into his geology of South America, Lyell's encouragement pushing him along. He continued to read widely but at random: books on deerstalking and salmon fishing, on an extinct gigantic sloth, on the philosophy of natural history, on agriculture, Linnaeus's *Reflections on the Study of Nature*, which he labeled "nothing." He deposited notes and abstracted quotations in dozens of precisely labeled file drawers.

Now that the repairs and extension to Down House were completed he called in the Sun Insurance Office Ltd., whose representative studied the property before a policy could be issued. He paid four pounds sixteen shillings for a year's coverage totaling twenty-one hundred pounds of insurance.

When he next went up to London he had dinner with the Lyells in Hart Street. Lyell's new book, *Travels in North America*, was at the printer.

"Interesting country, the United States," he proffered. "The people are very good-humored and full of jokes."

"I remember that from the American sailors who supplied the *Beagle* with fresh water and other victuals when we ran short. Incredibly generous."

"I found it so. The great throng of them are from fifteen to twenty years younger than those playing the same active part in England or Europe. I am surprised at the little that is known in England about matters over there, where there is so much worth imitating as well as avoiding. You and Emma should visit North America sometime; the publication of your *Journal* in the United States insures you a warm reception."

Charles threw up his arms in mock horror.

"What, and cross that Atlantic Ocean again!"

They fell to discussing the geology of the United States, as well as Charles's geology of South America, of which he now had sixty pages. He told Lyell:

"I always feel as if my books come half out of your brain, and that I never acknowledge this sufficiently. I have always thought that the great merit of the *Principles* was that it altered the whole tone of one's mind, and therefore, when seeing a thing never seen by you, one yet saw it partially through your eyes."

"Be very careful, my dear Darwin, or one day, particularly after the publication of your origin of species book, some young scientist is going to throw that charming compliment right back in your teeth."

Charles did not tell Lyell that he did not intend to publish his species book. He would work on it steadily and accumulate exhaustive evidence over so wide a field of the life sciences that no one would be able to disprove his claims. But he would not take on the establishment; anyone who went against the revealed word of the Bible would not be met with logic or reason, but rather by "the faith that passeth all understanding." To abandon the project out of fear of this reaction would indeed be faintheartedness. He would complete the job even if it took a lifetime . . . and he would arrange for its publication after death. Then let the hurricane roar.

3.

For some reason inexplicable to Charles, the publication of his book on volcanic islands was postponed until November though printer's sheets were read much earlier by Lyell and by Mary Lyell's father, Leonard Horner. Horner wrote Charles a flattering letter. Charles told Emma:

"If one third of what Horner says be really true and not the verdict of a partial judge, then I should be contented with my small volume." To Horner he wrote:

Small as it was, it cost me much time. The pleasure of observation amply repays itself; not so that of composition. It requires the hope of some small degree of utility in the end to make up for the drudgery of altering bad English into something a little better.

Emma was exasperated.

"Whatever are you talking about, *bad English?* Technical material, yes; but please remember what I said when I read your *Coral Reefs.* I called you a poet. I'd take it kindly if you would never forget that."

"I'll try not to," he answered meekly, amused at the fire in her eyes.

During the months he had spent writing the species manuscript he had felt well. Now, having corrected the fair copy and tucked the longer version of his manuscript with the shorter into his locked drawer, he began to feel uncomfortable, then a little unwell, particularly at night when he would be awakened several times by cramps.

"What am I doing differently that should cause the distress?" he asked Emma as they sat over a light supper.

She thought for a moment.

"Nothing that I can think of. You get an hour's walk in the woods every day. You dig in the warm sun of the garden. I am serving you the same foods."

"In heaven's name, what goes on in me?" he cried.

It was at this point in October 1844 that a book was published anonymously with the title *Vestiges of the Natural History of Creation.* The volume caused an uproar. It also upset Charles considerably. Had this anonymous author usurped his species manuscript? Nonsense! Nor was he much comforted by the early denunciation of *Vestiges,* as the book was commonly called. One critic compared it with an accomplished harlot who could sing as sweetly as a siren but who was in her person "a foul and filthy thing whose touch is taint, whose breath is contamination." The *British Quarterly* denounced it as rank heresy; the *Athenaeum* included it among such kindred humbugs as alchemy, astrology, witchcraft, mesmerism and phrenology. Charles read the volume carefully, pinning a list of questions and observations to the pages. He thought the book well written but the geology bad and the zoology worse. He was alternately amused and horrified to learn that *Vestiges* was being attributed to him, among others. He told his friends in London:

"I ought to be much flattered and unflattered."

*Vestiges* continued to be widely read because of its radical concept of natural evolution. The abuse continued to pour in; Charles considered most of it out of season but was not surprised at the vehemence of the reaction.

"The book is weak and inconclusive," he told Hooker, who had come to visit at Down House early in December, bringing with him the first installment of his own book, *Flora Antarctica*, "for the same reason as my grandfather's book, *Zoonomia*. Both men read the available literature but neither went into the field for close study and observation as I did on the *Beagle*. *Vestiges* is a closet study."

"I was more amused than disturbed by the book," Hooker replied.

"I'll agree that the idea of a fish passing into a reptile is monstrous." He hesitated, then made a bold decision.

"My dear Hooker, I have a manuscript of my own, some two hundred and thirty pages, on the evolution of species. No one has seen it except the scrivener who gave me a fair copy. Would you like to read the manuscript? You could then make a comparison to *Vestiges*. I know I can rely on your absolute discretion."

"You may, indeed."

Hooker read the manuscript behind the closed door of the study. On the afternoon of the second day they went for a long walk. Hooker's voice was gentle albeit full-bodied.

"I particularly relished your references in my field, such as 'Will anyone say, that if horticulture continues to flourish during the next few centuries, that we shall not have numerous new kinds of potato and dahlia . . . ?'"

"What about my principles of selection, the gradual appearance of new species, the extinction of old species?"

Hooker took a long breath.

"I agree with your assumptions . . . up to a point. You are of course right about the infinite variability of species, the manner in which they are moved and placed. I accept the relationship of varying species, their relationship to their fossil antecedents. But when I come to your focal issue of transmutation, the conversion of one species into another, there I am not convinced."

The sun was beginning to abandon the wintry sky. Charles wrapped his wool scarf tightly around his neck.

"You will, my dear Hooker, in good time."

They turned their steps homeward, to the blazing fire in the sitting room with Emma awaiting them with pots of tea.

Along with the New Year of 1845 came the knowledge that Emma was pregnant again. In February she went to Maer Hall to visit her mother and sisters, leaving Charles at home with the three children. The days were so thick and wet with fog that they could not play out of doors. Charles spent hours playing "Snap," with two packs of cards, having romps with Etty. Occasionally when they all grew quite out of rule, jumping on furniture, playing tag around the chairs, Charles cried:

"I shall jump for joy when I hear the dinner bell."

William added:

"I know when you will jump much more: when Mama comes home."

Despite frequent digestive upsets he completed his first draft of the geology of South America in late April. At the same time he earned his first respectable sum of money from his writing, a hundred and fifty pounds for an outright sale to the publisher, John Murray, of the permanent right to issue the *Journal* in his Colonial and Home Library series.

"However I shall have to work for the hundred and fifty pounds from John Murray," he told Emma, "as we both believe the book could use extensive revisions and shortening."

The *Journal* would now reach the general public at a low price, half a crown, though it would be a miserable piece of printing, with small type and mean margins. Murray was omitting the maps, which Charles regretted, but the number of woodcuts was increased. The series had a considerable following. It was a kindness he owed to Lyell, who had influenced Murray to buy the book.

He went to work at once on the revisions, adding a good deal about the Fuegians; cutting in half the descriptions of climate and glaciers. His most valuable addition, he decided, was a muted discussion of the extinction of species; for he had learned a great deal since the *Journal* had been published six years before. He allowed a stronger tinge of his belief in evolution to seep through the pages.

The Lyells were coming to Down House for a visit. Charles received in the post Lyell's *Travels in North America,* which he read immediately. His critical eye saw structural flaws as well as moral lapses; Lyell, for example, appeared to condone slavery. Charles told Lyell so when the two men walked in the woods. Lyell was startled. Later in the year the Lyells were leaving for a second trip to the United States, to be gone nine months. He promised to take a closer look at the subject.

"Mary has peremptorily stopped me from working too much," Lyell confided. "Does Emma keep a tight rein on you?"

"No need. My miserable digestive tract does that." He shot a quick glance at Lyell's face. "Many of my friends, I know, think me a hypochondriac."

They had returned to the little area outside the drawing room overlooking the gardens and the hayfields. The summer sun had left a legacy of color from light rose to deep purple. Lyell inched a chair closer to his friend.

"No, Darwin, we don't think you are a hypochondriac. We're simply nonplussed that the doctors can't diagnose the cause of your attacks."

"No more than I!"

Shortly after the Lyells returned to London, Emma was delivered of a second son, George Howard Darwin, born on July 9, 1845. She was slow in garnering her strength. Charles was as tender with her as she was patient with him during his attacks. They both adored the chubby baby and were happy when Emma was again walking with Charles in the woods and garden.

At the end of August he sent his revised *Journal* to John Murray, then plowed ahead on refining his South American geology. Erasmus came for his second visit. The children adored him, fastened on him all day. Emma commented:

"Ras bears the children with wonderful patience."

Erasmus was indeed in good form. Early the next morning he took Charles out to the mound under the yews on which the evergreens they had planted were doing badly.

"I told you so, more than a year ago," Erasmus exclaimed; "I've always insisted that this mound is a great blemish in hiding part of the field. It will simply have to go!"

To Charles's astonishment, Erasmus peeled off his coat, waistcoat, cravat, picked up a shovel and began tearing down the mound, transporting the earth in a wheelbarrow to a spot at some little distance from the back door, between two lime trees.

"Ras, you amaze me. I haven't seen you work like this since we were children."

"Everybody must help. This new mound will cut off some of that intolerable wind from the north, yet you will retain your view."

In the days that followed, Erasmus planned the new layout, dug, drove stakes. No job was too much for him.

"You're positively glowing with health," Emma commented. "Why not move down here with us?"

Erasmus sighed, plaintively.

"Once I got your garden straightened out I'd be bored to death. Just invite me down once a summer; that'll get the coal dust out of my lungs."

John Murray published his *Beagle Journal* in three separate parts, in July, September and October. The segments did moderately well. He then bound five thousand copies of the complete book. It had taken Colburn some four years to sell his fifteen hundred copies.

"That is a big jump in numbers," exclaimed Charles. Then, ruefully, "'Cheap' he calls the series in his advertisements. I wish he had used the word 'inexpensive' instead."

He went up to London to roam the bookstores and to lunch with Lyell at the Athenaeum, already feeling the weight of Lyell's coming absence. The two men walked along the Thames embankment on the way to the club, talking so steadily, heads bent into the wind, they barely noticed the majestic government buildings they passed. At the Athenaeum they selected a corner table and sank into the deep leather chairs of the morning room.

"I have continued reading and collecting facts on variation of domestic animals and plants," Charles declared. "On the question of what constitutes species I have considerable data and I think I can draw sound conclusions."

"That all species are mutable, subject to change over the millennia?"

"Quite. And that allied species are co-descendants from common stocks."

"Are you still not planning to publish these findings?"

"Not for a long time . . . if ever. I've been working on the subject for nine years now; it has been the greatest amusement to me."

Lyell's brow was creased.

"Amusement? Are you certain of that?" He drained his hock, asked, "How is Emma taking this continued attack on Revelation?"

Charles searched through his feelings with care.

"She must suspect what I'm doing, for she sees the interminable flow of letters, technical journals and books from breeders, botanists, zoologists . . . and I am a geologist! Yet she says nothing. I never bring up the subject."

It was during one of these one-day trips into London that he learned that Captain FitzRoy had failed to get along with the settlers of New Zealand and had been recalled after less than two years as governor. It was not the only depressing news. Despite their isolation in their secluded rural spot, Charles knew from his daily reading of the London *Times* that England was going through its worst period in many a year. Wages were at their lowest in a century. The detested Corn Laws, against which both the Darwin and Wedgwood families had fought, kept the import duties so high that grain was prevented from coming into the country, and domestic prices were high. The poor were in great alarm, for their earnings were barely sufficient to supply food for their families. Farm output had been seriously slowed because of the Industrial Revolution. Farmers, particularly the young ones, were abandoning the land and flocking to the cities to earn real wages in the factories. To make matters worse there was a poor corn harvest and a fungus attacked the potato crop, destroying most of it. When Charles looked over his own potatoes he found that a good many had rotted in the ground.

"How are we going to get a crop next year," Emma mourned, "if we have no seed potatoes?"

"I garnered a small bunch of good ones. I am drying sand in the oven today and shall store them in baskets of sand."

He did not tell Emma, who took little interest in the daily newspapers, that in the opinion of some of the journalists England had never been nearer to revolution. He wrote to John Henslow:

> My laborer here complained that when flour rose once again his family consumed fifteen pence more of his twelve-shillings earnings a week on flour for bread. This would be nearly as bad as if one of us had to pay an additional £50 or £100 for our bread. Those infamous Corn Laws must be swept away!

It was a dreary winter throughout the land. The following June the Corn Laws were repealed. Charles reported:

"The fungus accomplished what twenty years of agitation failed to do."

Emma's mother's health deteriorated at the beginning of 1846. She went to Maer Hall to comfort her. When she returned to Down House, Charles went to The Mount because of Dr. Darwin's faltering strength. Bessy Wedgwood died at the end of March. Elizabeth wrote:

> How thankful I am that her death was so gentle. In the evening I heard her say, as I had before, "Lord, now lettest thou thy servant depart in peace."
> I think we shall come to the conclusion that we must break up and sell Maer Hall.

Emma was shattered at the idea.

"Maer Hall will be gone out of our lives," she mourned. "It was a glorious place to grow up."

Dr. Darwin was hardier than Aunt Bessy. He recovered, went about his daily life with Susan and Katty caring for him.

William was going on seven. With four young ones growing up, it was evident that Down House was going to need a schoolroom, and a governess to instruct them.

"I'd like to put off the governess as long as possible," Charles commented, "but you're right about the classroom. We'll remodel a couple of the outbuildings so that we can put a complete floor above them with a sizable schoolroom overlooking the garden, then behind it, living quarters for a governess."

"While you're about it," Emma added, "Sally is complaining of what a nuisance it is to have the passage from the outside for everyone who needs to come in, delivery boys or workers, go straight through her kitchen. Couldn't we brick up that door and cut through a new one this side of the kitchen by the pantry?"

Charles massaged his eyebrows as he pondered the reconstruction.

"Parslow's pantry is also too small. I'll add some space for him. It's too bad the original owner bricked up that pantry window to save window tax. I'll have the bricks torn out and glass put in."

"Can we afford all of that?"

"Barely. I hope the Shrewsbury conclave will not condemn me for extreme extravagance, though now that we are reading Sir Walter Scott's life I sometimes think that we are following his road to ruin at a snaillike pace."

Dr. Henry Holland, on one of Charles's visits to London, had recommended his giving up his occasional cigar and two cigarettes a day as injurious to his health. As a result he had taken to snuff, which he enjoyed; it cleared his head and seemed to sharpen his faculties. He kept the dark green pottery jar on the cabinet next to his right hand where he could reach it easily.

"Too easily," Emma cried when he fell ill again. "Snuff is just as bad for you as cigarettes. For my sake as well as yours, I want you to give it up for a month."

He gave up the snuff but he went around muttering:

"My cruel wife! She persuaded me to leave off snuff and I am most lethargic, stupid and melancholy in consequence."

At the end of the month they compromised.

"Why don't I put the snuff bowl out in the hallway?" he asked. "That way it'll be so much trouble setting aside my writing board and crossing the study into the hall that it will cut the habit greatly."

"To a third? Very well. That much can't hurt you. But I'll never reveal to your children that you had to put temptation out of reach."

Joseph Hooker arrived for a stay, bringing his work with him. He had become Charles's closest friend and confidant. Charles fed him his most recent ideas on the life and death of species. Because Hooker looked pale and thin, Charles exclaimed:

"You ought to have a wife to stop your working too much."

Hooker smiled wanly.

"I'm only twenty-eight. You weren't married until you were thirty. I want one more voyage of exploration before I settle down."

When Hooker returned to Kew, Charles made a resolution.

"I've decided to build a walk," he told Emma, "like 'The Doctor's Walk' at Shrewsbury. At the end of our property, by the boundary that separates us from the Lubbock lands. I feel the need of a walk that's peculiarly my own. Call it a 'thinking path,' where I can have the encouragement to raise questions and probe for answers. Monographs and books are conceived first in the mind before being written on paper." He hunched his shoulders forward. "I'll establish it at the south end of our fields. The first half will be out in the open, the other through the woods beyond the far hayfield, a kind of roundabout. We've discovered a sand pit in the woods. The supply of sand is plentiful. When Comfort and I have established the route I'll hire a couple of laborers to clear the area of rocks, tree stumps, weed growth, do a little leveling, then put down a bed of sand."

"Your own cogitation empire. About how big?"

"Let's say seven or eight feet wide, perhaps a third of a mile over all."

He found that he did not have enough land beyond the woods for the path he envisioned. It would encroach by a few feet on his neighbor, Sir John Lubbock, banker, astronomer and mathematician. The strip was a distance from Lubbock's large estate, High Elms, and was not used for anything though it topped a lovely green valley where the Lubbock cattle grazed. The Darwins and Lubbocks had become acquainted, had dined in each other's homes a few times. Lady Lubbock was particularly friendly with Emma.

"I don't like to ask favors of neighbors," Charles said.

"Offer an annual rental," Emma replied matter-of-factly.

Charles walked over to High Elms, stated his problem concerning the proposed sandwalk.

"Might I rent that land from you?" he asked. "We will pay any reasonable fee."

"I believe that particular area is part of my wife's estate," Sir John answered. "Let me ask her about it."

Two days later Lubbock rode to Down House on his favorite stallion, told Charles and Emma over tea:

"Lady Lubbock says you are more than welcome to use that narrow strip. She declined any rental fee but I suggested that you might prefer to pay a token amount so that you won't feel beholden."

They rented from the Lubbocks one acre, two rods and ten perches of land. Along the open section Charles had the gardener put in a long line of hollies, then hazel, alder, lime, hornbeam, privet and dogwood. An oak and beech tree were planted just inside a wooden gate in a high hedge at the farthest edge of the kitchen garden. This open part of what the family came to call the Sandwalk, which lay between the Darwin and Lubbock meadows, was fenced for privacy. It was the light side, at the end of which Charles had the carpenter build a little summerhouse. From there the Sandwalk turned into the dark side, through a thickly forested wood, the path traveling across its sides and back before returning to the light corner of the open path. Within this cool, forested oblong the undergrowth was thick with moss and low-lying plants.

At last the Sandwalk was completed, to Charles's intense satisfaction. The soil was rich, virginal in fact; his newly planted hedges, flowers and trees would grow rapidly.

"Now," he confided to Emma with an effusion of pleasure, "I must evolve a way of keeping track of how many times I have walked around the wooded loop."

"Couldn't you just walk until you are tired?"

"That's too simple. I must work out a formula."

Emma laughed but he was in earnest. At the corner where the light side of the Sandwalk reached the woods, he set out a series of small flint stones, anywhere from one to seven. Each stone represented a turn about the oblong. When he completed each tour he would kick one stone out of the way. When he came upon the last, he kicked it away, walked down the light side to the little gate in the hedge and returned home through the vegetable and flower gardens for his midday meal. He loved his Sandwalk with a grave intensity, never missing a daily walk no matter how tired he might feel.

"One thing puzzles me," Emma commented while accompanying him on the walk. "How do you know in advance how many of these pebbles you want to put in your pile?"

"Depends on a variety of factors," said Charles with mock seriousness. "Just as Captain FitzRoy had to balance his variables to decide whether to find a cove and heave to, or ride out a storm. It is a mathematical equation. How long must I walk to expel the body poisons caused by intensive mental work? How good is the weather? How good did Sally's roasting leg of lamb smell when I went out of the garden door? You see, my dear, now that I am no longer walking to a destination, say Cudham Wood or Holmsdale, I have to have a routine. Relaxes me, at the same time that it keeps me organized. Make sense?"

"For you, yes. I'm always glad when we come round to the last flint."

4.

In June Emma took William and Annie to visit their Aunts Elizabeth and Charlotte now staying in Penally on Carmarthen Bay in
South Wales, leaving Charles with the two youngest, Henrietta and the
baby, George, almost a year old. Etty, with whom he played between
work sessions, proved to be charming, though she frequently preferred
playing with her dolls.

The flower gardens had been looking very gay with roses, multicolored snapdragons and blue lobelia. The next few days turned
stormy and gloomy. Despite an odd gnawing at his innards, Charles
wrote five letters a day to his correspondents, giving as well as asking for
details on the nature of living and growing things. He ranged widely in
Wagner's *Elements of the Comparative Anatomy of the Vertebrate
Animals*, Steenstrup's *On the Alternation of Generations*, the American
John Charles Fremont's *Expedition*, his friend Richard Owen's *A History of British Fossil Mammals and Birds*.

For relaxation in the evening, when he sorely missed his hour of
music and two games of backgammon, he read Carlyle's *Oliver Crom-
well's Letters and Speeches*, marveling at the fecundity of Carlyle's
research and writing. As far as his own work was concerned, he felt like
a Galápagos tortoise to Carlyle's hare. To Emma he wrote:

> I am an ungracious old dog to howl, for I have been sitting
> in the summerhouse, whilst watching the thunderstorms, and
> thinking what a fortunate man I am, so well off in worldly cir-
> cumstances, with such dear little children and far more than
> all with such a wife.

The Lyells returned from the United States and moved from Hart
Street to Harley Street, a more fashionable neighborhood. The seventh
edition of his *Principles of Geology* was released, a salute to Lyell's authority in the field. He asked Charles for help with his ongoing project,
"Changes of the Organic World Now in Progress."

Sir William Hooker was halfway through building at Kew Gardens
the Great Palm House, which would be the largest plant house in the
world. Joseph Hooker published another portion of his *Flora Antarctica*, which Charles found eminently useful for his own work. He sent
Hooker a laudatory letter, adding:

> You will find this letter unique, considering that it comes
> from a man who hardly knows a daisy from a dandelion!

He decided to attend the British Association meeting in Southampton in September and asked Emma if she would accompany him. Emma pondered for a moment, then asked:

"Could we also make some excursions, to Portsmouth and the Isle of Wight . . . ?"

To their joy, they found the Lyells in Southampton as well as Leonard Jenyns, who presented Charles with a copy of his newly published *Observations in Natural History*. Charles met a number of his friends from Edinburgh, and a group of Irish naturalists. Those naturalists who lived close by took the Darwins sightseeing and to festive, argumentative dinners at their homes. After a particularly dry technical paper had been read, Charles turned to Emma.

"I'm afraid that was very wearisome to you."

"Not more than all the rest," she replied resignedly.

Charles laughed heartily, passing on the story to his closest friends. He took her on the excursions he had promised. On the way home he remarked:

"I enjoyed my week."

Emma studied her husband's face, the high color in his cheeks, the sparkle in his eyes, the spirit he emanated of robust good health.

"Perhaps we ought to spend the rest of our lives attending dry meetings," she said; "and going on excursions. You would never suffer another sick moment."

"I know you're speaking in jest," he retorted. "Life for me would be unbearable without work."

Toward the end of the year *Geological Observations on South America* was to be published. He shook his head in disbelief that ten years had passed since he had taken on the task. John Henslow had predicted early on that it would take twice the number of years to describe that it took to collect and observe. He had been right. It had been a productive decade but what about the future? He asked himself:

"How do I want to spend it and what might I hope to accomplish?"

His mind turned to the world's barnacles, known by the group name of Cirripedia. When on the coast of Chile he had come upon a most curious form which differed from all others he had known. To understand the structure of his new Cirripedia, he decided to examine and dissect many of the common forms, but found the state of knowledge concerning barnacles deplorable. It was not until Joseph Hooker came for a few days' visit that he began to formulate a work schedule.

"The barnacles will last me some months, perhaps a year," he told Hooker. "Then I shall begin looking over my ten years' long accumulation of notes on species and varieties. The writing, I dare say, will take me another five years. If published, I dare say I shall stand infinitely low in the opinion of all sound naturalists."

"Your friends, who have witnessed the thoroughness of your research," replied Hooker, "will go along with you. Your enemies, or the enemies of your ideas, are your natural attackers. That is their role in life."

October 1846, the start of his second professional decade, ushered itself in with a crisp clear day. He whistled up his dog, strolled down to the Sandwalk and placed seven stones in the starting corner because he felt in vigorous good spirits. At their one o'clock dinner he told Emma:

"I found a curious form of Cirripedia off the coast of Chile. It's different from all other forms of barnacles in that it has developed an organ which enables it to burrow through the shell of Concholepas, a mollusc, which is probably its only source of food. Without this burrowing instrument, its particular variety would have died out. I'm going to dissect this barnacle under the microscope to learn how it functions."

On the second window seat, the one away from his writing chair, he laid out his microscope and tools: a long, delicate dissecting scissors with a wheel to open or widen the cutting area, a triangular file with sharp needle point; a group of tiny brushes; a long ivory stick at the end of which was inserted a hooked piece of steel; a probe or teaser needle; a small knife. The barnacle which interested him had been preserved in spirits of alcohol along with the dozen more ordinary types which he had collected. He went down to the cool cellar, retrieved one of the few bottles of specimens he had kept in his possession these ten years, took it up to his study, and extracted the small barnacle from the jar. He carefully removed the shell, found its insides still soft, and placed them in water in a clear glass saucer. He then put the dish on the microscope's one-inch platform, attached his right eye to the microscope, adjusted the reflecting mirror below to catch the maximum of light.

The result was disappointing; the soft innards of the barnacle, though less than a tenth of an inch long, were thick enough to be opaque. He could not bring the individual organs, even thin layers of them, into focus on the unsteady platform to give him the detailed information he wanted: the distinction between the upper and lower end of the animal, whether or not the small orifice was toothed; whether it could be withdrawn; the color of the muscles and other internal parts. The microscope was inadequate for his needs. If he were to study this strange *peruviana* which lived by boring through the shells of molluscs, and dissect other barnacles which attached themselves to ships, logs, rocks by cementing themselves to their base and kicking food from the sea into their mouths by means of feathery legs, he was going to need a large and fixed stage for the saucer. He had taken the most advanced micro-

scope available for the *Beagle* venture; it had served him well. Now that
he wanted to get into the dissection of both vertebrate and invertebrate
animals, he would need something superior.

London was the only place he could find it. Parslow packed his old
blue bag; he would stay overnight with Erasmus. Comfort drove him to
the station at Sydenham. Ordinarily he enjoyed this long carriage ride
along the narrow, winding roads; he was able to relax and rest while
watching the elms, ash and beech trees drop slowly behind him. But
today he was impatient to get on with his task. He hired a cab at London Bridge Station to take him to Covent Garden, particularly Garrick
Street, also Newgate and Coleman streets where the optical shops were
clustered, as was the habit in the city for everything from hatters to tailors to tea merchants to fishmongers.

He went to a half dozen of the best shops, explaining what he
needed. The owners were polite but regretful.

"We've only the same microscope you had in 1831, Mr. Darwin. We
know of no improved model."

In one of the larger shops, Smith and Beck of 6 Coleman Street, near
the Bank of England, the owners offered to make anything he would
design if he would furnish them a set of plans or specifications.

"Thank you, gentlemen, but I have no set of plans; and alas! I am
unqualified to draw them."

At dusk, discouraged, he made his way to Erasmus's house. He arrived at Park Street in time to find Erasmus's salon in full blast, with a
fire on the hearth, the little tables laden with tea sandwiches, buttered
brown bread, potted meat, a chaudfroid of chicken, jams, hot scones,
pots of tea and hot water covered with cozies. The drawing room was
noisy but cheerful.

"Gas!" Erasmus cried, greeting Charles at the door. "You've arrived
on exactly the right day. My daily has done me proud. Must have
sensed you were coming. Let me introduce my guests."

Erasmus's face was shining at this happiest hour of his day. Charles
thought, as he greeted Thomas Carlyle, "Ras was born to be a host. It's
his trade. No one does it better." He was introduced to a couple of lady
novelists whose names he recognized from the popular novels Emma
read him, skipibus style; and several men, one an architect, another a
sculptor. He took a chair in a corner, had a dish of tea, listened with
half an ear to the dialogue swirling around him. When the last guest
had left, Erasmus asked:

"Why so glum, Charley?"

Charles told him.

"Don't be fainthearted. We'll have luncheon tomorrow at the Athenaeum, then dinner at one of your societies. We'll tell everyone what

you are looking for. Establish a network to spy out any better microscope in existence anywhere."

He did not keep track of how many scientists he and Erasmus inquired of the next day, twenty, perhaps; no one had heard of any but the simple one they were all using, including Hooker, Owen, Bell, the reptile expert, and Gould, the ornithologist. They were having a late glass of port at the Athenaeum when William Carpenter, already at the age of thirty-three being called "a great physiologist," arrived.

"Darwin, I've heard about your search. A few days ago I stumbled across a set of plans just in from Paris, drawn by a man named Chevalier. I only glanced at them but I think they may contain some of the features for which you are looking."

The librarian at one of the historical societies located the plans the next morning, unrolled them, anchored each end with a heavy book. Charles read Chevalier's comments in French on the inked lines leading out from each new aspect of the instrument. He was an artist who was interested in scientific design and was commissioned to draw the plans for a Mr. Brucke.

"It's beautiful!" Charles cried. "This platform will hold a saucer three inches in inside diameter. It's fixed and steady."

He asked permission to borrow the plans long enough to have Smith and Beck make a copy.

The owners at Smith and Beck summoned a draftsman from their workshop, spread out the drawings on the showcase from which they removed binoculars and eyeglasses. Charles made a number of additional suggestions. When the draftsman had his copy ready, Charles asked:

"How long will it take to construct?"

"Hard to tell, Mr. Darwin. We'll have to make molds for the castings, grind and fit the new lens. Three to four months."

Charles groaned. "The cost . . . ?"

"That we can't tell either. But we'll keep an account of materials and labor, then add our regular shop profit. Agreed?"

"Agreed."

Impatient, he went up to London several times to inspect the progress being made at Smith and Beck. At home he plugged away with his *Beagle* microscope. During the waiting period he invited to Down House for a few days' stay his companion from the *Beagle* James Sulivan and his wife; George Waterhouse, who had written the *Mammals* for the *Zoology* series, and Thomas Bell, who had done the *Reptiles*. Sulivan had been named to command the brig *Philomel*, and had spent years surveying the Falkland Islands, with a home on shore where his wife had given birth to the first British citizen born there. Sulivan was highly regarded at the Admiralty and was posted for another promotion.

"England shall rule the seas, and then the world!" he cried.

Joseph Hooker came frequently, always bringing his own work with him. In February he had accepted a job as botanist for a geological survey to establish the British flora in relation to its geology. The salary was a hundred and fifty pounds with traveling allowances. He did much of the work at home. After breakfast each morning the two men would repair to Charles's study where Charles declared:

"Now I shall pump you for a half hour."

He would bring out a handful of slips with botanical questions on them.

Hooker commented:

"I always leave with the feeling that I have imparted nothing and carry away more than I can stagger under."

Hooker worked in the bedroom over Charles's study. At noon he heard Charles's mellow voice calling his name under his window to join him in his walk around the Sandwalk.

It was shortly after New Year's, 1847, that Erasmus arrived for a weekend, triumphantly carrying the completed microscope.

"Smith and Beck want your permission to make another model and asked that you recommend it to the naturalists you know. Your crotchety friend Robert Brown, who was at Smith and Beck's when I arrived to fetch it, asked me to tell you, 'It's a splendid plaything.' "

They went into the study where Charles lovingly lifted the shining microscope out of its sturdy wood box. He put a layer of barnacle in a dish of water, placed it on the three-inch platform, adjusted the lens.

"It is indeed a splendid plaything!" he cried. "It is infinitely easier to adjust. I will see parts of valves and scrotum muscles I never knew existed. Nor did anyone else! Look at the beautifully contrived teeth, the subtle purple colorings. I feel the way Galileo must have when he first gazed at the heavens through a telescope."

"Are you equating barnacles with the stars in the heavens, Gas?" queried Erasmus.

Charles cocked his head to one side.

"Perhaps not, Ras. The study of barnacles is not an end in itself, but a means. If I dissect and observe the internal structures of hundreds of barnacles from all over the world they may reveal to me how gradually nature makes its changes and forms new species."

The two-foot-deep sill of the second window was too small to hold the new microscope. He summoned the carpenter from Down to install a shelf, fitted securely into the window seat. When completed it measured forty inches deep at the window and jutted out twenty inches from the original sill, and fifty-three inches along the window and wall at each side.

"Splendid," Charles exclaimed when the carpenter had finished. "I now have an adequate workbench."

He set up the microscope, which had been fitted into a base of stout oak. One of his own innovations was a slight crossarm attached to the top of the upright stem to carry the magnifiers; it was fitted for rotation and could be moved backward and forward. From his bedroom he brought down a sturdily built revolving stool which his father had sent to Down House as a present. It was a little more oblong than square and was topped with a comfortable cushion several inches thick. It proved to be exactly the right height for work at the microscope.

He read the existing literature on barnacles. It was scant; there were two books available, one in French, *Mémoire sur l'organisation des cirripèdes*, the other in German; and a few scattered monographs.

He found two extraordinary facts. The first, that with very few exceptions none of the naturalists had bothered to distinguish the valves and soft organs of the Cirripedia but named and classified them by the *external* appearance and differences in their shells. The second, that the nomenclature of the hundreds, perhaps thousands, of different varieties was in total chaos, the same barnacle being given different names by different naturalists. Charles declared:

"I intend to remedy both those unscientific situations, even if it takes me a year or more. It's a job worth doing, once and for all, to introduce some methodology into the field."

5.

The earth turned on its axis, the Darwins turned on their close family life and Charles's concentrated work on his barnacles. Though he was dissecting, discovering, describing in minute detail, and cataloguing a field which had been neglected, it was largely a mechanical operation, absorbing while he was at his microscope but making no demands upon him once he closed the study door at the end of the day.

He watched the development of each child's personality, so remarkably different one from the other. William, eight, was totally independent, inclined to keep his thoughts and activities to himself. Annie, almost seven, was his favorite, a sensitive child, affectionate and joyous. Frequently she would come into the study with a stolen pinch of snuff, smiling because she was giving her father pleasure. When Charles was at leisure she would sit on his lap, spending half an hour "making his hair beautiful." She would accompany him to the Sandwalk, sometimes holding his hand, at others pirouetting ahead. Her parents agreed that she was the love of the household.

Henrietta, Etty, going on four, was the exact opposite. She was a quiet, studious child who could already read and chose to sit close by Emma while she read to Charles, astonishing them both on how closely she could follow the story. She was also the only jealous child. She had become unhappy when George was born and she had had to give up the attentions of Brodie, who always devoted her time to the newest born. In good weather the children skipped their way to the Sandwalk. Here Brodie would sit in the little summerhouse knitting, Scottish fashion, with one of the needles stuck into a bunch of cock's feathers tied at her waist to steady it.

Down House became a center for the Darwin and Wedgwood relatives, as Maer Hall and The Mount had been; there was nearly always some part of the family visiting: Emma's sister Elizabeth; her brother Hensleigh with Fanny and their children; her brothers Frank and Harry with their wives and children; Joe Wedgwood and Charles's sister Caroline, who with their three children had moved to Leith Hill Place near Wotton in Surrey, not far distant; her sister Charlotte and the Rev. Charles Langton with their one child, Edmund. Charles's sisters Susan and Katty came from Shrewsbury, one at a time. Charles was happy about all this for Emma's sake; her bonds to family were her roots in the earth. They did not disturb his work, nor did he have to talk at table if he did not wish to. The visiting family required less of him than he felt obliged to give when he was out to dinner parties or entertaining friends.

"You have become materfamilias," he observed to Emma. "Both families bring you their troubles and problems for solution."

"Their happiness and joys as well." Her smile was matronly. "I enjoy being surrogate mother to the Darwins and Wedgwoods, despite the fact that I am the youngest of them all, excepting Katty."

"Wisdom has nothing to do with age."

"I don't have wisdom, merely patience and affection."

There were changes in their appearance as they neared the end of their thirties. The light reddish color had fled from Charles's hair, turning it dark. His bountiful crop, which had begun to recede at the time of his marriage, had now, at the age of nearly thirty-eight, greatly retreated. By way of compensation he was wearing his sideburns long, wide and thick. His eyebrows too had turned dark, the structure of his brow had grown heavier.

"I should not have aged so much in eight years," he groused to Emma. "When you married me I was a light-haired, light-complected, amiable-looking young man. Look at me approaching forty; beetling brows, almost bald. . . ."

"It's the hard thinking that did it," she teased. "I think you are a much better-looking man now than when we married. Your face has considerably more strength, and your head, which your father said changed its shape on the *Beagle,* is more massive. Early on you were pleasant-looking. Now you are powerful."

"Ah, love! So charming, so blind."

"As a person grows older," he ruminated the following morning while shaving, "the face reflects more accurately what he is within himself."

Though Emma had borne five children by 1847, she had aged only moderately. Her hair still had its brown sheen, her skin was smooth, with healthy coloring. Neither the Wedgwoods nor Darwins ever considered her beautiful. Nor had they ever considered her plain. Her luminous eyes still wore the sympathetic brown velvet cloak which fitted her sanguine nature. She had a face that people could be happy with, from day to day and year to year. Nor had she lost her figure.

If his outward visage had indeed become more powerful as Emma said, he could not say as much for his physical health. He was a long way from the man who could ride fourteen hours a day, sleep on the damp ground with his saddle for a pillow, eat guanaco . . . all enhanced with the flavor of freedom and independence. He told Joseph Hooker:

"I have nothing to say about my health, being always much the same, some days better and some worse."

He was constantly concerned that his friends might consider him a hypochondriac.

Emma had told him that it was a great happiness to her that when he was most unwell he continued as sociable as ever, and as warmly affectionate, so that she felt a comfort to him.

Dr. Henry Holland commented:

"Emma, you are the perfect nurse for the ideal patient."

"Are you accusing us of catering to Charles's ailments?" she demanded spiritedly.

Charles was used to their cousin's ineptitude. He had commented to Emma early on:

"Our distant kinsman seems destined to play the adversary role in our lives. If I had listened to him I would be buried in some remote country parsonage pursuing beetles."

He had only a few specimens left from the collection of Cirripedia he had turned over to Richard Owen when he returned from Cambridge, enough of the genera Conia, Balanus, Acasta and Clisia to provide him with study material for perhaps three months. These barnacles which he had gathered throughout the tropical and warmer temperate seas had a small orifice, diamond-shaped or oval, the color nearly white or purple, occasionally black or a pale peach. The scuta valves were subtriangular. The soft bodies had compartments with thick walls and numerous tubes. He became increasingly unhappy about the specimens he had given away.

"I shall have to ask Owen if the Royal College of Surgeons would return my collection for study at Down," he decided.

In February 1847 he took a short break to visit his father in Shrewsbury and the Royal Society on his way through London. The newspapers were crying with great satisfaction that the Commons had passed the Ten Hours Bill limiting women and children to ten hours a day in the factories, probably the most liberal act to be passed since the repeal of the Corn Laws.

When he returned home Emma confided that she was pregnant again.

"But it's almost two years since George was born," she said. "We wanted a large family, so we should thank God for getting one. . . ."

He kissed her on the forehead, murmured:

"I'm afraid we have no choice, unless I take the vows and enter a monastery."

Because his next day's work was already laid out at the microscope he no longer had to think about it. His mind ranged instead through the realms of the many sciences he had been surveying, the material that was coming in to him on the variations in species derived from selected breeding. He constantly regrouped the known facts to arrive at provable hypotheses.

Ten years before he had jotted in his notebook:

> If we choose to let conjecture run wild, then animals may partake our origin in one common ancestor. We may all be melted together. . . . We are led to endeavour to discover causes of change.

In thinking about the increasingly rare ostriches of Patagonia it had struck him that "favorable variations would tend to be preserved and unfavorable ones to be destroyed." Malthus's chapter on the checks to population had buttressed this original and intuitive belief.

He was enjoying both aspects of his work, the practical labors in his study, the theoretic speculations on his rounds of the Sandwalk. In June he went to the British Association meeting at Oxford. It seemed all his colleagues were there: Adam Sedgwick, George Peacock, Richard Owen, Charles Lyell, Whewell, Buckland, Murchison, Michael Faraday, Sir John Herschel, and John and Harriet Henslow with their oldest daughter Frances, now a ripe twenty-two and something of a beauty. Or so Joseph Hooker thought, for as he told Charles when they walked together to hear Lyell speak to the geological section:

"Odd thing, I've seen Frances many times in the Henslow house and always liked her. But last evening at the dinner table the whole sense of her lovely being struck me between the eyes . . . or was it in the pit of the stomach? It was like unto a revelation; I knew for a certainty that I loved her and wanted to marry her. I spoke to her this morning. The Henslows have approved. . . ."

"I should think so! They're getting the most brilliant young botanist in the country. Interesting how we interbreed, either by family or profession."

Compliments fell off Joseph Hooker like raindrops off a seaman's oilskin.

". . . however we won't be married for several years. The Admiralty is planning a scientific voyage to Borneo and may appoint me as naturalist. The Woods and Forests Department has offered me a cruise to India."

Hooker brought the news that the Royal Botanical Gardens at Kew were now open for the public, as was Sir William Hooker's new Museum of Economic Botany. John Henslow's botanic garden outside Cambridge had finally been funded and the first trees planted.

Charles spoke at the geological section, along with Adam Sedgwick and Robert Chambers, who Charles had decided was the author of the violently opposed book, Vestiges. When he returned home he told Emma:

"I enjoyed the meetings but I took the most pleasure from the way the specialists in crustacea received the news that I'm concentrating on the dissection and description of all genera of barnacles. Henri Milne-Edwards, author of three volumes on crustacea to which I have long owed much pleasure and instruction, has offered to let me examine his collection and to spread the word that I need the loan of specimens."

Emma's approval was polite but restrained.

"Forgive me if, at this moment, I'm more interested in babies than barnacles."

A daughter was born on July 8, whom they named Elizabeth, their third daughter to accompany their two boys. Emma felt well from the moment the delivery was over. Charles went back to work on *Tubicinella coronula* and the anatomy of pedunculated Cirripedia. He observed:

"When I completed my book on coral reefs I complained that no human being would ever read it. Now who in the world is going to read my book on the anatomy of Cirripedia?"

"All the literate barnacles! Haven't you said you were interested in creating source books?"

"But I enjoy selling too. John Murray has already sold out his copies of the revised *Journal*. I realize I gave the book outright and can receive no further royalties but it salves my pride to know that my books can sell."

In his first four books published, and the five he edited, the scientific truth of relatively few of his theories had been questioned, and always in a quiet, scholarly manner. Now in September of 1847, in the *Transactions of the Royal Society of Edinburgh*, there was published an article on the roads and shore lines of Glen Roy which was such a severe attack on Charles's earlier paper for the Royal Society of London, and on his personal integrity as a scientist, the dearest and most valuable part of his reputation, that, as he confessed to Hooker, it "made me horribly sick."

The controversy was not all that earth-shattering, yet Charles cursed the day he had taken off for Scotland nine years before.

"I cannot take criticism," he cried to Emma. "I'm sure it's a weakness in me. I should be stronger, more able to do battle when I'm attacked."

He retired to his study and wrote a nine-page letter of refutation to the editor of the *Scotsman*. His pages were blackened with corrections; he rewrote almost every sentence. The editor of the *Scotsman* did not publish the letter.

In October Charles and Mary Lyell came for a week's visit, Lyell bringing a collection of barnacles for Charles, Mary a fine picture of Lyell, already framed. Charles promptly hung it over the mirror on the center wall of the chimneypiece. He brought Mary into his study to show her the result.

"I'm uncommonly glad to have it, and thank you for it."

Lyell read Charles's accumulated notes on the Cirripedia, watched him dissect under water, bringing forth the soft, rounded, baglike portion of the body.

"Well done, Darwin. You're becoming an expert in the use of those tiny cutting edges. But what I admire most is the infinite detail of your descriptions. That is the way of the specialist, the thoroughgoing man of science whom everyone must revere. It's scholarship at its best."

Charles permitted himself a sigh, put the cap on his microscope, said:

"Shall we get our coats and go some rounds on the Sandwalk? How many stones shall we place? Shall we make it ten? I haven't done ten rounds all year."

Somewhere about the eighth circuit Charles said:

498 THE WHOLE OF LIFE

"Lyell, I never imagined how many different barnacles there were in the world. I knew hundreds. But thousands? To do a complete job of dissecting and describing will take years of my life."

Lyell's amiable face broke into planes of a gigantic grin.

"Isn't that what the years of your life are for?"

Charles chewed on that root for a bit. Lyell kicked the next flint stone out of the way. They had only one traverse left. It was getting cold, with the scent of rain in the air.

"Admittedly, barnacles are a bore," Lyell added. "All they do is foul up the hulls of ships. But nature put them here for some reason or purpose. As you study the adaptations of their anatomy to climate, differing seas, changing food supplies, you may discover something relevant to that mystical theory of yours, the transmutation of species . . ."

He paused long enough to throw an arm roughly but affectionately about Charles's shoulders.

". . . of which I believe only half of what you say!"

When he had finished dissecting Lyell's barnacles he went to London to see Richard Owen. Owen's offices at the Royal College of Surgeons were in complete contrast to each other: one room was a warm book-lined study smelling of scholarship and pipe tobacco. The other was a cold laboratory with an operating table and all of the scalpels, curved knives and cutting scissors needed to anatomize the live animals in cages, the dead ones in ice-packed drawers. Charles asked:

"Owen, could I borrow back the collection of barnacles I gave the College? I need infinitely more genera to interpret the variabilities within their structure."

"Of a certainty. Your collection is sitting in the museum doing little more than collecting dust."

"I misspoke when I used the word 'borrow.' They will be destroyed in the dissection process; I haven't found any way of putting them back in their shells."

Owen smiled at Charles's attempt at humor; his aloof manner had long since proscribed laughing aloud.

"We'll take your monograph as more than ample return."

What surprised him was the amount of concentrated time involved, his eye alternately on the microscope and on his recording page. He kept strict account in his diary of the time spent on each genus.

"I unwillingly found it indispensable to give names to several valves and to some few of the softer parts," he told Emma.

"No one had named them before?"

"No one has *seen* them before."

One particular genus occupied him for thirty-six days, ending with twenty-two pages of description. Still another took nineteen days of observation but he was rewarded with twenty-seven pages of fresh material.

"At this rate there will be no end for me," he groused as he sat in the sitting room before a wood fire. "I've already been on the little beasts for over a year."

"Work is work," Emma replied. "You like what you're doing, don't you?"

"On my beloved barnacles? I'm captivated."

6.

After several attempts on the part of the Admiralty to send Joseph Hooker to Borneo, the Malay Islands or India for a botanizing survey had evaporated, it was a letter from Baron von Humboldt which made the dragged-out affair a sudden reality. The aging but ever active Humboldt outlined so persuasively the good that could be done for science by an expedition into India and the Himalayas, where fossil deposits proved indisputably that this double mountain range, with some of the loftiest peaks on earth, had once been under the seas, that the Chancellor of the Exchequer gave Hooker a grant of four hundred pounds a year for the Indian mission. Hooker, who was still on half pay from the Navy, was granted free passage on H.M.S. *Sidon*, which was carrying the new British governor general of India to his post. Charles told his young friend:

"I congratulate you heartily. It will be a noble voyage and journey but I wish it was over. I shall miss you selfishly and all ways to a dreadful extent."

A note arrived from Sir John Herschel asking if Charles would dine with him the next time he came to London. Herschel had been the first to inform him of his little monograph published by the Cambridge Philosophical Society. Sir John had returned to England from Capetown in 1838, two years behind H.M.S. *Beagle,* and had spent the next nine years writing his magnum opus, *Cape Observations.* He was soon to become president of the Royal Astronomical Society. On seeing Herschel a feeling of warmth and nostalgia crept over Charles for his five years at sea.

"I've called you in to do an important job for the Lords Commissioners of the Admiralty," he said over dinner. "They've asked me to compile, and I quote, 'A Manual of Scientific Enquiry for the officers of Her Majesty's Navy, and for naturalists, travelers in general.' We are going to have many chapters, including astronomy, hydrography, meteorology, and of course zoology, to be written by your friend Richard

Owen, and botany by Sir William Hooker. We are all agreed that you are the one to write the chapter on geology. What do you say?"

Though it was only two years since he had finished his manuscript on the geology of South America, and he had been heartily sick of it by then, he did not believe it would be difficult to mint what he had learned into some twenty-five or thirty pages which would be helpful to generations of officers and naturalists.

"The Admiralty will publish," said Sir John; "John Murray has agreed to distribute. No royalties or honorarium have been suggested. I doubt that will deter you."

"I owe the Admiralty a great deal; in fact, everything. I am proud to be included in the same volume with you, Richard Owen and Sir William Hooker."

Riding home in the rattling smoke-belching train through the wintry Kentish countryside he mused half aloud over the noise of the clacking wheels:

"This makes up for the attack in the *Transactions of the Royal Society of Edinburgh*. That hurt; this heals."

He covered his microscope, put away his tools and resumed his accustomed place in the corner chair with the cloth-covered board across its arms . . . glad to be back in the real poop cabin for a spell. The chapter wrote itself, off the top of his head, the geological experiences and insights gained from his five-year *Beagle* voyage. The writing took him only two to three weeks; he was afraid he might have included too much material but Sir John was happy with both the industriousness and the quality. Buoyed in spirit, he plunged at once into a paper which Lyell and the Geological Society had long wanted: On the Transportal of Erratic Boulders from a Lower to a Higher Level.

In the evenings Emma played for him medleys from Bellini's *Norma*, Rossini's *William Tell*. One of Charles's favorites was, quite understandably, Auber's *Emma*. It was also a good year for books to read aloud, for there appeared in London Charlotte Brontë's *Jane Eyre*, the first installments of Thackeray's *Vanity Fair*, Emily Brontë's *Wuthering Heights*.

The number of treks to the station at Sydenham also increased as his colleagues from London became familiar with Down House.

On April 19, 1848, he had dinner at the Geological Society with Lyell, Murchison, Horner, Whewell. He had not attended the Society in some time and took a lot of jollying about having become "a retired country squire given up to the somnolence of rural life."

"You wouldn't think Darwin retired," protested Lyell, "if you could see his study. He's going to come out the other end of his cave as the world's authority on barnacles."

During the reading of his paper Charles offered proof of his theory that it was coastal ice that moved boulders to an elevation higher than their parent rock. The paper was well received, his hand shaken warmly by most of the members present in the lecture hall.

Walking back to Lyell's home on Harley Street, Lyell asked quietly: "Darwin, wouldn't you rather live in the city? There's a lot to be said for London. Such as your reception tonight. That should have warmed the cockles of your heart."

"It did. I must agree, London has its charms and compensations. But I am completely committed to country life. It will work out best for me, you will see."

The next morning he had breakfast with Erasmus, then went to see John Gray, the zoological keeper at the British Museum. The museum had a considerable collection of Cirripedia deposited there over the years by naturalists, including Gray himself, but they were unclassified and hence could not be catalogued.

"We have no real need for them here," Gray said; "nobody ever bothers to examine them. I'll speak to the trustees about letting you have them."

He went up to London again that spring to hear Gideon Mantell give a paper on the fossils found in ancient rocks. He met Lyell for an apéritif and dinner in the Royal Society's rooms at Somerset House. Sitting across the dining-room table was Richard Owen. Owen, Charles knew, considered himself the outstanding English authority on geological fossils. He was becoming, in fact, quite famous.

Charles enjoyed Mantell's paper, considered it not only interestingly written, a rarity in scientific circles, but closely reasoned as well. To his shock, when Mantell took his seat, Richard Owen sprang to his feet, his face flushed with fury, and began to shout at Mantell.

"This paper is beyond contempt! Its research is shallow and its conclusions spurious. I denounce this kind of skeetbug posturing as unworthy of the Royal Society. It should be condemned out of hand!"

Dr. Gideon Mantell, a fifty-eight-year-old medical practitioner, respected in England for his *The Wonders of Geology, The Medals of Creation,* and his establishment of a museum containing his remarkable collection of fossils, sat stunned. From the embarrassed fellows a silence drummed through the hall like the humming of night insects in Bahia which Charles had listened to from the deck of the *Beagle.*

Charles and Lyell walked to the Athenaeum wrapped in silence. Over a glass of port, ensconced in deep leather chairs, Charles finally opened up.

"What wretched doings come from fame! The love of truth alone would never make one man attack another so bitterly."

Lyell studied Charles's face intently, asked:
"You've maintained a friendship with Owen, haven't you?"
"Yes."
"He has visited at Down House?"
"On more than one occasion."
"But you have not disclosed any of your species theories to him?"
"Assuredly not. Why do you ask?"
"Beware of Owen. He will turn on you. He turns on everyone. It's an
imperative of his nature."

Charles taught the older children how to use the microscope, which
fascinated them, particularly when gazing at some hidden organ which
their father's scalpel had uncovered. From hearing Charles use the word
"crustaceous" so often they described "Papa's barnacles" as "crustaceous mummies." William, the loner, wandered the neighborhood's
footpaths, coming to know every house for miles around. One day he
returned for dinner puzzled about something.
"Papa, do you know Mr. Montpicher who lives a ways south of the
village? He sits at the open window of his cottage all morning long
puffing on his pipe and doing nothing."
"Perhaps he's retired, Willy."
"But when does he do his barnacles?"
Emma laughed heartily.
"You see what has happened, Charles? Watching you these past couple of years, the children have come to think that every man works at
dissecting barnacles. They don't know any different."
"They will, if I can somehow finish this eternal job. But I doubt it.
I've had a letter from a Mr. Stutchbury of Bristol offering me his life-
time gathering of Cirripedia, reputed to be a splendid one."
Other collections kept coming in. Hugh Cuming, a naturalist and
sailmaker, sent his own fine group; the Rev. R. T. Lowe posted his
collection from Madeira; August Gould sent his private specimens from
Boston, as did Louis Agassiz, recently appointed professor of zoology at
Harvard. Even Syms Covington, now working in Australia, sent a good-
will box of barnacles. Letters poured in from France and Germany,
from people who wanted him to have the fruits of their experience . . .
followed by boxes, crates, a jar containing another hundred specimens
formerly unknown to him. He studied each classification from its earliest larva stage through its growth process to its final adult form. By
diligent dissection he proved that without exception barnacles were
crustaceans related to crabs, shrimps, lobsters.
The post brought other news. Captain Robert FitzRoy, some three
years after his fiasco as governor of New Zealand, had been appointed

to the post of superintendent of the Woolwich Dockyard. Charles Lyell was to be knighted by Queen Victoria at the royal castle of Balmoral in Scotland. He would now be Sir Charles Lyell and his wife Lady Mary. The Darwins opened a bottle of champagne and drank a toast to them.

The newspapers brought less cheer, reporting revolutions in Germany, Austria, Italy. In London the Chartists, members of a working-class movement calling for universal suffrage, the secret ballot, annual elections, organized plans for a massive demonstration. Queen Victoria's ministers persuaded the royal family to move to the Isle of Wight to avoid possible violence. It seemed not altogether a happy time to be alive in England.

It was a pleasant summer; the heat not too oppressive. Ivy had grown up the garden side of Down House, making it look cooler, the azaleas were in bloom, the apple trees in the orchard were heavy with fruit. Charles spent several hours a day in the open. His jaunts around the Sandwalk were also fruitful, new ideas for his speculations sprouting in his mind as the flowers in the fields. Emma gave birth to Francis, their third son, in August.

Then why, from the beginning of July, had he been "unusually unwell," as he jotted down in his diary? With a swimming head, depression, trembling, black spots before his eyes, attacks of nausea and vomiting?

In spite of Emma's constant attention, and her carefully prepared bland diet, his condition worsened. His nervous system began to break down; his hands trembled, there was an involuntary twitching of his muscles. Toward the end of the year he suffered incessantly. He decided to himself:

"I am going the way of all flesh."

He had the kindness not to tell Emma that he thought he was dying, but took his 1844 species manuscript and the letter to her out of its locked drawer and put it where she would more readily find it.

A letter from his sister Katty jolted him out of his lethargy. Dr. Darwin could no longer walk. He was now in a wheel chair and slept on a bed placed in the library. The gardener wheeled him out to the greenhouse each morning, for he seemed to be most content under the banana tree he had planted after receiving Charles's description of them in Bahia, Brazil. Katty's letter left no doubt in Charles's mind that his father was dying. He left for The Mount immediately. He would not let Emma accompany him, for the baby was only a few months old. He stayed overnight with Erasmus in London, reached Shrewsbury the following afternoon, so worried about his father on the long coach journey that he forgot to worry about himself.

He was shocked at the first sight of Dr. Robert Darwin in the wheel chair in the library, eating a sparse tea off a tray with Susan sitting by, reading from one of his favorite poets. A good deal of flesh had evaporated from his huge frame. When Charles kissed him on both cheeks tears came into the old man's eyes.

"I'm planning to stay with you for two full weeks, Father. I have wonderful news. The Ray Society, which was founded four years ago in honor of John Ray, the renowned English naturalist, has as their primary purpose the publishing of scientific reports and books. The Society has agreed to publish my book on the barnacles when it is finished. They have over seven hundred and fifty members, among them some of the most distinguished scientists in Great Britain. Truth to tell, I was never sure I'd ever get the book published."

A smile came over Robert Darwin's face. He put out his arm to touch his son, too emotionally overcome to speak. Later that evening when he had fallen asleep, with Susan watching over him, Charles and Katty talked at the dining-room table while his old friend Annie cooked supper.

"What do you think, Katty?"

"There's no way to tell, Charley. Father is perfectly collected and placid in his mind. He is so sweet and uncomplaining, so full of everybody else, the servants, the servants' children. Susan was up all last night. She is wonderfully able to go through the most trying part, all his directions are given to her."

The two weeks went by quickly, for Dr. Darwin seemed buoyed by his son's presence. His strength increased as he listened to Charles's tales of the Sandwalk, of Emma and the children, of how close he and little Annie had grown; the new microscope. He felt well; he told himself that he had to in order to keep his father from worrying about him.

However all his symptoms returned as soon as he entered his study at Down House. He could do no work at all. At the back of his mind was also the debilitating thought that bad news was imminent. It came only nineteen days after his return home. Dr. Robert Darwin died quietly at the age of eighty-two.

Charles wept unabashedly. The older children, particularly Annie, who could grasp the nature of death, came to him to kiss him and join their tears with his. He had loved his father, doubly so after he had been able to convince the older man that he cared for something besides shooting, dogs and ratcatching, and would not be a disgrace to his family. A note from Katty said:

> God comfort you, my dearest Charles, you were so beloved by him.

He was too ill to get out of bed for a couple of days.

"But I must be in Shrewsbury for the funeral," he told Emma.

"Do you have the strength?"

"Strength comes with doing. Please have Parslow lay out my clothes."

The ride to London did him good. He did not feel exhausted until he got near Erasmus's house. Erasmus was already in Shrewsbury but his daily fixed Charles some tea and toast for luncheon. By now it was three in the afternoon; there was neither coach nor train to get him to Shrewsbury that night. He posted Emma a note to assure her that he felt "pretty nearly at my average."

He caught the earliest morning mail coach the next day. He was too late for the simple service in the Montford churchyard where Dr. Darwin was laid to rest beside his wife. However he was at The Mount to join the family and his father's friends, to whom one of the young maids was serving coffee, when they returned to the house. The obituary of Dr. Robert Darwin published in the Shrewsbury *Chronicle* was a laudatory one, and of help to the mourners. However Charles saw that Susan and Katty were desolate. Dr. Darwin had been their whole life and now they were like two pilotless sailing vessels floundering at sea. Charles decided that he would remain with his sisters for a week and persuade them that they must continue to live at The Mount for the rest of their lives. When Dr. Darwin's will was read it was learned that they had inherited a sufficient fortune to sustain them there quite gracefully. Erasmus's share of the inheritance was generous. He was now secure. Charles would receive something over forty thousand pounds, enough money to educate his children, start them in their professions, make Down House more spacious and further beautify the grounds.

Dr. Robert Darwin had remembered all his children very well indeed.

7.

After the turn of 1849 he heard from Sulivan and William Fox about Dr. James Gully's water cure at Malvern. Intrigued, he sent to London for Dr. Gully's book, *The Water Cure in Chronic Disease*, read it thoroughly and came to the conclusion that Dr. Gully wrote like a sensible man. He made further inquiries; learned that almost everyone who had taken the cure had been helped.

"I think I ought to try it," he told Emma.

"If it is helping others."

"But we'll have to stay for six to eight weeks at Malvern for it to do me any substantial good."

"That's too long to leave the children. We must take them with us, and the servants as well."

It was no problem. Malvern had a large house called The Lodge which they could rent by the month. After further correspondence The Lodge was rented and Dr. Gully alerted to Charles's arrival. They made the long journey north in the direction of Shrewsbury, mostly by train, then by the Cheltenham coach, their three sons, their three daughters, Parslow, Brodie, Sally, Miss Thorley, the governess, and a housekeeper. Comfort was left behind to tend the gardens. The Lodge proved to be comfortable in a rustic fashion, with enough bedrooms for everyone. It had a little field and woods opening onto the mountain.

"This will be a capital place for the children to play," Charles exclaimed.

The following morning he went for his first appointment with Dr. James Gully. Dr. Gully was a few months older than Charles, already bald, with a big plain face which he kept professionally compressed, his eyes shuttered, his lips tight. He was dressed in a rich black velvet coat and matching black stock. The walls of the plush office were hung with framed diplomas from various medical schools including Edinburgh and Paris, and honorary medical societies. His early practice in London had been successful; he had published widely on medical subjects. However Dr. Gully had become disillusioned with the route of medication as "effete and inefficient, if not positively harmful." When his friend and confrere, James Wilson, returned from the Continent "filled to the brim with hydropathy" and the wonderful power of water treatment in both acute and chronic diseases, Dr. Gully was convinced. Together with Wilson, he opened his Hydropathic Establishment in Malvern, which prospered.

The Hydropathic Establishment had originally been a Benedictine priory long famous for the curative value of its waters, having been favored by Queen Victoria and Tennyson. It consisted of a very large Tudor House and a Holyrood House, connected by what was called "The Bridge of Sighs," possibly because Dr. Gully kept the unmarried of each sex in their own house. Behind the little community, with the priory church in the center, were the Malvern Hills.

Dr. Gully examined Charles, said in a noncommittal voice:

"I am prescribing a cold scrubbing in the morning, two cold foot baths a day and a cold compress on your stomach. Here is also a diet for you. We will start slowly."

"Do you think this will help, Doctor?"

Gully compressed his lips even tighter.

"Time will tell, Mr. Darwin, time will tell."

Each day he felt a little better, ate a little better, took the children on long walks toward the mountains to gather flowers and plants for Joseph Hooker. They exclaimed:

"We have more of Papa's company than at home."

There was fog and haze but fortunately no March rain. The only disagreeable result of the treatment was an excessive irritation of the skin over his whole body which came on every evening so that after seven o'clock he could not sit quiet for one minute. Dr. Gully commenced a sweating process which helped. Emma was happy with his progress.

"You are already stronger, my dear, and your stomach is somewhat better. At least you are eating more."

At the end of a fortnight Dr. Gully said:

"I think I can help you more and more. I rarely tell that to a patient. Now you are ready for the full course."

The "full course" consisted in getting up at six forty-five and being scrubbed at the washhouse with a rough towel and cold water, which, he told Emma, "makes me look like a lobster." He had a quiet washerman who scrubbed him behind while Charles scrubbed in front. He then had to drink a tumbler of water, get his clothes on as quickly as possible and walk for twenty minutes . . . "all of which," he told his family, "I like very much."

His next instruction was to put on a compress of a wet folded linen covered by a mackintosh. The compress was dipped in cold water every two hours. Charles wore it all day, except after the midday meal. After his early morning walk he returned home, shaved, had breakfast which consisted solely of toast, an egg or meat. No liquid was allowed. When Charles could not swallow the dry toast, Dr. Gully gave permission to have a little milk in which to sop it. He was permitted no sugar, spices, butter, tea, bacon. . . .

"Or anything good," he grumbled. "But I must say I am feeling better. The tremulousness has gone from my hands, there are no more muscle twitchings, and my stomach seems to have settled down."

At noon he had to put his feet in cold water, with mustard added, for ten minutes. Then his washerman rubbed his feet down violently. The coldness made his feet ache but on the whole they were less cold than when he had been ill at home. He walked for twenty minutes, had dinner at The Lodge with Emma and the children, rested until five o'clock, took the cold water treatment for his feet again. Dr. Gully recommended horseback riding so he bought a gentle mare and rode for an hour in the afternoons. His supper at six o'clock was the same as his breakfast.

He made such good progress that Dr. Gully stepped up the treatments. At six each morning he was wrapped in a blanket for an hour and a half, with a hot water bottle at his feet, then rubbed with a cold dripping sheet. By the end of April he was well enough to write to his cousin Fox:

I shall have to go on with the aqueous treatment for many months at home under his direction. With respect to myself I

believe I am going on very well, but I am rather weary of my
present inactive life & the water cure has the most extraordinary effect in producing indolence & stagnation of mind;
until experiencing it, I should not have believed it possible. I
now increase in weight, having escaped sickness for 30 days,
which is thrice as long an interval as I have had for last year; &
yesterday in 4 walks I managed 7 miles: I am turned into a
mere walking & eating machine.

In the increasingly good weather Malvern was filling up with patients. Charles learned that the summer before Dr. Gully had had a
hundred and twenty patients in attendance.

"He must be making an immense fortune," he commented.

"It's worth every guinea," Emma said flatly.

"Dr. Gully tells me he has little doubt but that he can cure me in
time. I have experience enough now to be certain this water cure is no
quackery; it's a great and powerful agent and upsetter of all constitutional habits. But how I shall enjoy getting back to Down House
with renovated health to resume the beloved barnacles!"

The Darwin entourage returned to Down House early in July 1849.
Charles hired a young farm boy to ride the mare back to Down, continued his riding on most days and taught William to ride bareback. He
brought in the carpenter from the village to build an outside douche
where he could sluice himself with cold water from an assortment of
pitchers and jugs Parslow brought to him, as part of Dr. Gully's continuing cure.

He also decided to start a health diary, keeping track of his condition
during the hours of the day and the long nights in which he was so frequently awakened by flatulence.

"I've been haphazard in my attention," he told Emma; "kept no regular or sustained record. Now I shall. It's the scientific way to go about
it. I will discover a pattern, see what hurts and what helps."

Emma had just played for him one of Mendelssohn's Songs Without
Words and was going to read aloud an installment of Dickens's David
Copperfield.

"You're good at keeping daily records; you and your father both.
Some four times a year you've even recorded the children's height and
weight, with clothes and without. Also that of Hensleigh's children.
You're a professional diary keeper and I'm sure your health diary will be
therapeutic."

"I have the feeling I'm having my leg pulled."

"You know me. Little Miss Slip-Slop. All my records are in my
head."

THE WHOLE OF LIFE

He found himself a little better every month. He continued his cold showers, frost or no frost. He used a lamp five times a week, followed by a shallow bath for five minutes afterward. He also used a dripping sheet daily. He found the treatment wonderfully tonic.

Dr. Gully permitted him to work only two and a half hours a day at his barnacles. He concentrated so hard that even the short stint exhausted him. He wrote to Joseph Hooker, still exploring plant life in India:

> You ask about my cold water cure. The greatest bore I find in it is the having been compelled to give up all reading except the newspapers; for my daily two and a half hours at the barnacles is fully as much as I can do of anything which occupies the mind. I am consequently terribly behind in all scientific books. . . . I confess I often feel wearied with the work, and cannot help sometimes asking myself what is the good of spending a week or fortnight in ascertaining that certain just perceptible differences blend together and constitute varieties and not species. . . . What miserable work, again, it is searching for priority of names. I have just finished two species which possess seven generic, and twenty-four specific names!

Despite his complaints he made some extraordinary discoveries. Contrary to the word of former authorities who maintained that Cirripedia had salivary glands, they were ovaries; the actual cellular content of the ovarian tubes passed into the cementing material. In fact Cirripedia made glue out of their own unformed eggs. Earlier students had maintained that the barnacle had no head. He proved that the whole of the Cirripedia, externally visible, consisted of three anterior segments of the head.

Another startling observation was that, with the exception of one genus, all Cirripedia were bisexual, the males microscopically minute. He wrote:

> Here comes the odd fact: the male or sometimes two males, at the moment they cease becoming locomotive larvae, become parasitic within the sack of the female and thus fixed and half embedded in the flesh of their wives, where they pass their whole lives and can never move again.

If he himself had slowed down, word from John Henslow indicated how much progress his friend had made in his poverty-stricken, illiterate, godless parish in Hitcham. He had built a schoolhouse and hired a teacher. He taught the farmers how to get a better yield from their land, secured some fifty quarter-acre allotments for the impoverished laborers, took his parishioners on natural history trips, even as he had

Charles and his class group; and at last had the parish coming to church for marriages, baptisms, death services, holiday sermons.

"There is a truly great man," Charles thought reverentially.

Dr. Henry Holland and his wife came for a weekend at Down House; he had heard of Charles's miraculous cure. At a late supper he commented:

"You certainly look well. You have good color, your eyes are clear and bright. Now tell me about the hydropathy discipline."

At the conclusion he proclaimed:

"The cold water sheets and cold foot baths didn't cure you, my dear Charles. You cured yourself. By giving yourself close to four months of holiday in a beautiful spot in the hill country. Did you do any work there?"

"Not a whit."

"Did you study?"

"No."

"You were not anxious or worried about anything? You were not attempting to conceive new scientific theories?"

"On the contrary, the water cure brings complete stagnation of mind."

"You carried on no considerable correspondence?"

"A few brief notes to Henslow, Hooker, Susan."

"You walked a great deal?"

"Seven miles a day."

"Went to sleep early? Slept the entire night?"

"Yes."

"After a week or two the nausea never returned?"

"Never did. I was reminded of the Gamlingay trips in the Fens with Henslow's students: one had no such organ as a stomach then; only a mouth and masticating appurtenances."

Dr. Holland's face was wreathed in a triumphant smile.

"Don't you see the implications of what you're saying? Those cold wet sheets, the buckets of cold water for your feet, were just theatrical properties."

"Are you suggesting that Dr. Gully is a fraud?"

"Not at all. I knew James Gully when he practiced in London. He is an honest man who believes implicitly in the value of hydropathy. Why not, when hundreds of people like you are cured by taking long holidays at his spa? It's a question of his credulity. He also believes in mesmerism, spiritualism and homeopathy."

"What are you trying to tell me, Henry?"

"That those four months of complete rest and relaxation in beautiful country without care, worry, anxiety; the long walks and horseback rides, the being away from home and work, that's what cured you!"

A bit angry, an unusual emotion for even-tempered Charles Darwin, he retorted tartly:

"Some ten years ago when I consulted you, you said, 'I shall be able to set you going again.' You gave me two prescriptions for medication, which I took as you instructed, and remained as ill as when I visited your office."

Saba Holland laid a restraining hand on her husband's arm; but Henry Holland blustered on.

"Of course you were. Because you returned to work immediately!"

"I beg to differ. The water cure is assuredly a grand discovery. How sorry I am that I was not somehow compelled to try it five or six years ago."

"Pity. Before the end of your lifetime hydropathy will be as discredited as mesmerism is today."

In their bedroom that night, Emma said emphatically:

"It's a good thing Henry Holland is in both the Wedgwood and Darwin bloodlines or one of us could blame the other for him."

Charles took Emma in his arms; he had regained his good humor.

"Not to worry."

In February of 1849 Sir Charles Lyell had been re-elected president of the Geological Society; Charles Darwin was elected one of the vice-presidents of the British Association for the Advancement of Science for the summer meeting. When Charles and Emma met the Lyells at Birmingham, Lyell teased:

"You must exercise extreme caution, Darwin, or you will succeed me as president of the Geological Society; and before long, be knighted."

Lyell's attitude toward Charles was quite different from Adam Sedgwick's. Sedgwick treated him as a son or disciple, as did John Henslow. To Lyell, who saw no difference in age, only in mind and discipline, Charles was a companion and confrere.

Emma celebrated the first month of 1850 by having her seventh child. Charles had heard about the discovery and use of chloroform as an anesthetic. Since the doctor at Down had not yet used the spirits to save the pain of childbirth, Charles ordered a supply from London. The doctor agreed to use the chloroform and discussed with Charles how many drops were to be poured onto a gauze pad, how often the drops should be renewed. However Emma went into labor rather suddenly. It would be a time before the doctor could be summoned and make his way to Down House. Emma entreated Charles to use the chloroform. He got out a gauze pad, poured ten drops onto it, held the pad over Emma's nose and mouth.

She relaxed, the pain lessened. Charles added drops of the chloroform, slowly, one at a time. The doctor arrived ten minutes before the delivery. When Emma awoke and was shown her fourth son, she said: "I remember nothing from the first pain until I heard that the child was born."

"Is that not grand?" Charles exclaimed.

When the doctor congratulated him on his handling of the dangerous chemical which he had never seen used before, Charles replied with a touch of false modesty:

"I do come from a medical family!"

The boy was named Leonard. Various members of the family intimated that Emma had done her patriotic duty and should have no more children. Dr. Robert and Susannah Darwin had had six children, Uncle Jos and Aunt Bessy had had nine. Emma and Charles were reconciled to Henry Holland's pronouncement:

"Nature has its own schedule for mothers. A certain number, yes; after that, no more."

He returned from six rounds about the Sandwalk to find a group of men from Down dressed in their Sunday suits, waiting for him. They had founded the Down Friendly Club which gathered monies to assist its members when they became ill or permanently disabled, and to bury them when they died.

Would the Honorable Mr. Darwin become their treasurer and keep their books?

He did not hesitate for an instant.

"Indeed I will. Keeping books is one of my few virtues, instilled in me by my father. Bring me your accounts next Sunday. Then you can officially induct me as your treasurer."

The intelligence came through that Captain FitzRoy, who had been moved the year before from his position at the Woolwich Dockyard to the command of the Navy's first screw-driven steamship *Arrogant*, had resigned from active service, the stated reason being health and the need to attend to private affairs.

"Something went wrong again," Charles suspected.

He joined with Francis Beaufort, still the Royal Navy's Hydrographer, to get Robert FitzRoy elected a fellow of the Royal Society.

Then came an immensely rewarding event. The University of Oxford instituted its first degrees in science. Cambridge University followed suit, an acknowledgment that science was no longer despised as vulgar, heretical, useless. Not only was science tenable, it was indispensable! Charles's great friends, and his own efforts, were beginning to turn the world around.

8.

During the summer of 1850, when Emma was forty-two and Leonard was still a babe in arms, Emma realized that she was pregnant again. At the same time Annie took ill. A number of times in the past years she had been what the family called "poorly" but had made a reasonable recovery. Emma and Charles had not been very worried because of the child's robust animal spirits. This time she did not recover as rapidly as before. Her fever increased, her appetite fell off; the doctor could not diagnose the cause.

"It's an infection, I presume. But from what? She has no open cuts or festering sores. I'll order some medication to bring the fever down."

Annie's eyes began to glaze. She ate little but never complained. Then something in the vitality of her spirit defeated the fever and she was able to get up, eat more normally, play outside with the other youngsters. However each attack left her increasingly listless.

"We've bested the result but not the cause," said the doctor. "We must keep watching."

Charles and Emma decided to take the family for a holiday to Ramsgate, a seaside resort on the southeastern corner of England. It was October, the holiday crowds were gone, the sea-salt air was brisk. The walks along the beach with her father seemed to help Annie. But the improvement did not hold after they returned to Down House; the fever came and went, depriving her of any genuine recovery. When Henry Holland came for a visit over Christmas, he too examined Annie.

"I confess myself baffled," he admitted. "It's not like anything I've ever seen before."

By the beginning of March 1851 there could no longer be any doubt about the seriousness of Annie's illness.

"Shall I take her to Malvern for the water cure?" Charles asked Emma. "Put her under the care of Dr. Gully?"

"He's the only doctor who has ever helped you."

"It's worth trying," he agreed. "I'll take Etty to keep her company, also Brodie. Miss Thorley can join us there. I'm afraid, my dear, you're much too close to delivery to travel."

Charles and his party of four were installed in a series of rooms in the main building.

"I'll do all I can for her," said Dr. Gully sympathetically. "We'll start the cure very mildly. I shall attend her every day."

Buoyed by Dr. Gully's pledge and the arrival of the governess to watch over the two girls, Charles went to London to stay a couple of days with Erasmus. On Sunday, March 30, he and Erasmus dined with Hensleigh and Fanny Wedgwood in their new home on Chester Terrace, a better location for their children than the one on Upper Gower Street. The Thomas Carlyles were there, as well as other friends and relatives. Ruskin's *Stones of Venice* was the book of the day, being widely praised. Answering Erasmus's question about *Stones of Venice*, Carlyle replied tartly:

"The entire book is a moral preachment: that you must be a 'good and true man' to build even a common dwelling house!"

Charles and Erasmus engaged in banter with Carlyle. Emma's Aunt Fanny Allen commented:

"There is something uncommonly fresh and pleasant in you, Charles. I do not know which of you two brothers is the most agreeable."

He returned to Down the following morning, reassured Emma about Annie, resumed work. He had been home sixteen days when he was brought an electric telegram which had been dispatched from Malvern to London, then brought out to Down House by special messenger.

Annie had been taken by a vomiting attack which Dr. Gully had at first thought to be of little importance. Then it assumed the form of a dreadful fever. Charles was to return to Malvern at once.

Fanny Wedgwood joined him in London for the balance of the trip to Malvern. When Charles walked into Annie's room he could not recognize the child; the hard sharp pinched features.

She opened her eyes, said, "Papa," quite heartily. That helped him to picture his daughter as she had been.

Brodie took Etty to London in the Cheltenham coach. That night at eleven-thirty Dr. Gully saw Annie asleep and said:

"She is turning the corner."

With that renewed hope, Charles went to bed in an adjoining room. The following morning he found his daughter in too tranquil a state and was plunged into despair when the doctor said her pulse was tremulous. However she was taking a little gruel every hour. That afternoon she sipped some water. She was still uncomplaining. When Charles told her he thought she would be better, she replied meekly:

"Thank you."

She then asked Fanny for an orange. When Fanny gave her a sip of tea, and asked if it was good, Annie replied:

"It is beautifully good. Where is Etty?"

The next day when Charles fed her some water she said:

"I quite thank you."

Those were the last words addressed to her father. Annie died at midnight on the twenty-third of April.

Charles and Emma exchanged letters of consolation. He sent Miss

Thorley to London. Fanny Wedgwood remained for the funeral. Annie was buried in the little cemetery at Malvern. Charles then went home as quickly as possible to be with Emma. They were, in fact, inconsolable.

Miss Thorley, the governess, returned to Down House but Brodie, who had taken care of each of the babies in turn, was too sorely afflicted to rejoin the grief-stricken Darwin family. She returned to her home in Portsoy, Scotland, coming occasionally to Down House for a visit.

Less than a month after Annie's death, Emma's fifth boy, christened Horace, was born. Her sister Elizabeth came to keep her company. Charles hoped that the birth of the child would relieve some of their sadness.

When it was learned by the Palaeontographical Society in London that Charles was working on fossil Cirripedia, a field in which little was documented, the Society offered to publish his monograph in their annual journal. Charles had completed the first part in 1850, but the eighty-eight pages, under the forbidding title A Monograph of the Fossil Lepadidae; or, Pedunculated Cirripedes of Great Britain, were not published until June 1851. Later in the year the Ray Society published the first half of his work on modern Cirripedia, with detailed anatomical plates, for its members. No copies were sold in the bookstores, there was little or no public notice, the text was far too technical for the general reader. The work was however appreciated in scientific circles. He was able to secure twenty-two copies from the Society, his sole compensation, to be distributed among those generous collectors and researchers who had helped him.

Now that he was reading the newspaper again he found that a row was going on about the building housing the Great Exhibition of the Works of Industry of All Nations in Hyde Park, already being called the Crystal Palace because it was constructed of prefabricated girders and columns with close to a million feet of glass frames. Lyell was working on the committee, striving to give the exhibition an educational turn and insisting that galleries be set aside for great works of art. Joseph Hooker, recently returned from India, was a juror of the botanical section.

The Crystal Palace exhibition had been conceived by Prince Albert and approved by Queen Victoria. Yet as the immense galleries neared completion, covering the whole of nineteen acres, the London press and a voluble section of English critics took out after it: Hyde Park had been ruined. . . . It would become the bivouac of all the vagabonds of London. . . . Foreign visitors would plot to assassinate the

Queen. . . . Rats would start a bubonic plague. . . . Infiltrating
papists would spread idolatry. . . . The whole edifice would collapse at
the first thunderstorm. The loudest outcry came from a Colonel Sib-
thorpe who declared:

"It is the greatest trash, the greatest fraud, and the greatest imposi-
tion palmed off on the people of this country."

Charles was amused. Both Lyell and Hooker had assured him that
the structure was sound and that hundreds of thousands would go
through the galleries, which reflected the highest accomplishments of
modern civilization. He told Emma:

"We'll spend a week with Ras and see the Crystal Palace. Take a
couple of the children with us. They'll adore it."

At the end of July they rode into London with Henrietta and
George. Erasmus brought in an extra daily to keep his brother's family
comfortable. The next morning they set out in two cabs, Charles in his
high silk hat, long dark coat and light trousers; Emma in a new bonnet,
three-tiered hoop skirt of lightweight cotton which covered her shoes, a
large enveloping shawl of the same fabric over her shoulders. The
children were also rigged out like full-masted sailing ships, with large
bonnets tied under their chins, long velveteen coats of dark navy and
white lisle stockings.

Charles was enchanted with the rich color of the galleries. There
were over a hundred thousand exhibits from all over the world: Turkey,
Tunisia, Russia, the United States. In the sculpture gallery they gazed
at the American Hiram Powers's *Greek Slave*, Boston's *Wounded Indian*, Belgium's *Crusader King*; and the *cause scandale* of the show, the
sculpture of a nude Bacchus wildly and hilariously drunk, lying lascivi-
ously on a bed of vine leaves.

"The French contribution," said Emma, turning the children away
from the nude.

Etty, nearly eight, and six-year-old George were far more interested in
a display of stuffed animals, a family of cats sitting on chairs drinking
tea and one frog shaving another. They enjoyed even more the ices and
sweet cakes. Charles led his family from gallery to gallery explaining the
latest prize-winning mechanical inventions; as well as the harvester
pulled by a "Puffing Billy" engine, a knife with eighty blades, a floating
church for seamen, from Philadelphia. The device all four Darwins got
the most fun out of was a silent alarm bed: the owner set the alarm for
whatever hour he wanted to arise; when the alarm rang the sleeper was
ejected from the bed and dumped into a cold bath.

They spent the entire day at the Crystal Palace. Finally the children
grew tired.

Charles returned several times during the week but it was with Lyell or Hooker rather than his family. Charles and Joseph Hooker met several times in the gardens of the Pavilion, enthusiastically renewing their friendship after Hooker's four years of hardship and exploration in India and the Himalayas, including imprisonment. He had tracked through the vast mountain ranges eighteen thousand feet high, in areas that had never before been trod by anyone except the native aborigines. The man who seemed so delicate had shown, as had Charles on his five-year voyage, enormous resources of strength, courage and endurance. He had brought back a marvelous collection of plant life, much of which had not only not been seen before in England but had not even been heard of. On Hooker's return he and the Henslows' daughter Frances had been quietly married in the church at Hitcham and gone to live in Kew Gardens.

Unexpectedly, Charles encountered John Henslow shepherding a group of his parishioners whom he had brought down from Hitcham, using the money he had saved by abolishing the annual drunken brawl in which the parish males indulged prior to Henslow's arrival. This was only one of the numerous excursions on which he took groups of his people to broaden their horizons. They were neatly dressed and carried themselves with an air of having been rescued, reborn, and rightly so, for Henslow had won his fight with the large landowners to sell their former peasants parcels of their own to make them self-sustaining.

John Henslow was now fifty-five, his superb stand of hair was turning white. Charles exclaimed:

"My dear Henslow, when I see what you've accomplished, my words on paper become insignificant."

Henslow replied sternly:

"Each of us does God's work according to his own bent."

It was at the Crystal Palace that Charles met, in the company of Joseph Hooker, twenty-six-year-old Thomas Huxley, who had been out for a four-year cruise of the Indian Ocean and Australian waters as assistant surgeon of H.M.S. *Rattlesnake*. During the latter part of the cruise he had written and mailed to London three zoological articles which Charles had read in the *Proceedings of the Zoological Society*, the *Philosophical Transactions of the Royal Society*, and the *Annals and Magazine of Natural History*. All three had been of such penetration, clarity and freshness of eye that Huxley found, when he returned to London, that he was already well known. Charles had been so engrossed in his Cirripedia that he had not met Thomas Huxley, but only that June he had had the pleasure of helping vote him into the Royal Society.

Joseph Hooker introduced Thomas Huxley to Charles with considerable warmth.

"I know you don't make friends easily, Darwin, but Huxley is a man you'll like, from start to finish."

Huxley blushed as he put out his hand.

"I know of no man in England, Mr. Darwin, I admire more. I've been studying your books since the *Journal*, including your recent volume on fossil Cirripedia."

Thomas Huxley was of exactly the same height and figure as Charles, dark of complexion with dark dramatic eyebrows, and wore his thick black hair long, covering his ears and massed at the back. He had a personality that captivated all who knew him; but not because of his desire to please. His compelling face, with piercing dark eyes, straight jutting nose and wide mouth, spoke of an inner strength and determination to be a productive man.

"I am very pleased to meet you, Huxley, and have looked forward to it," said Charles, "after all that my friends have told me about you."

Hooker excused himself and Charles invited Huxley to join him for an ice.

"My children say they are excellent."

When the cool dish had been served, Charles studied the young man across the small round table from him. He was neatly dressed, with a big velveteen coat which fitted him loosely, a high almost clerical collar with a widespread butterfly bow instead of a stock. He was clean-shaven except for a narrow strip of sideburn that ran under his wing collar. There was a lightness about his manner, and good spirits.

"Huxley, tell me about yourself. Where were you educated?"

Huxley grinned.

"I wasn't. Though my father was assistant master of a school in Ealing where I was born, I had only two years of schooling, from my eighth to tenth years. Then my father lost his position. We moved to another village where we were on the poor side. The society I fell into at school was the worst I have known. We were average lads, with much the same capacity for good and evil as any others, but the people who were set over us cared as much about our intellectual and moral welfare as if they were baby farmers." Huxley's smile generated the radiance of an early spring sun.

"I suppose that's how I knew, instinctively, that I was going to have to educate myself. At the age of twelve I would wake up at dawn, light a candle, pin a blanket around my shoulders and read Hutton's *Geology* . . . followed by Lyell's *Principles of Geology* the following year."

Charles remembered his own two years with his scientist masters at the museum in Edinburgh, and then three and a half years at Cambridge encouraged by the friendship of such men as John Henslow, Adam Sedgwick, George Peacock, William Whewell.

"Surely you must have had some scientific training."

"In a fashion. Both of my sisters married doctors. One of them took me 'walking' through the hospital wards with him. From there I received a three-year scholarship at Charing Cross Hospital, then spent time at London University where I received my M.B. That's how I got my job as assistant surgeon on H.M.S. *Rattlesnake*, and a chance to visit faraway lands. I'm not a collector, you know. What I really wanted to become was a mechanical engineer. That, in effect, is what I am as a zoologist. I study the internal mechanics of invertebrate animals, as you have the Cirripedia."

"Where do you go from here?"

For the first time Huxley's face fell.

"Richard Owen was kind enough to intervene with the Admiralty and get me a nominal appointment so that I can complete my writings from the *Rattlesnake* expedition. The stipend is modest; I live with a brother. No job in science has opened for me. I've tried all the colleges and institutions that employ lecturers. What makes it worse is that I fell in love with an English girl whose parents moved out to Sydney. We have been engaged for over three years. How many more it will be before I can bring her back from Australia so that we can marry, I don't know."

Charles was not about to offer false optimism.

"A few years. When you have published your papers and books from the *Rattlesnake* journey you will be wanted somewhere."

The subject got around to species. Huxley believed in lines of demarcation between natural groups, and in the absence of transitional forms. Charles answered gently, with a humorous smile:

"Such is not altogether my view."

Joseph Hooker found them an hour later. Charles extended his hand to Huxley:

"I hope I will see you again."

"Oh, you will!" cried Huxley. "I'm frequently at your brother Erasmus's house. The Carlyles take me. They're perfecting my German, a study I started so that I could read European scientific journals."

As Hooker and Huxley walked away, Charles thought:

"I like that young man. I am deeply touched by him. I have the feeling that we could become allies."

He had not thought that about anyone since he had met Joseph Hooker.

Charles and Thomas Huxley did meet at Erasmus's and Lyell's in London and the Hookers' in Kew. When Charles had a complex problem in zoology he would ask Huxley about it. His mind cut to the heart of the material as a knife through a pancake. Often their conversation got around to Richard Owen, England's most famous anatomist and zoologist. Huxley had tried to thank Owen for helping him become a fellow of the Royal Society but Owen had replied: "You have nothing to thank but the goodness of your own work." Huxley commented to Charles:

"Owen has been amazingly civil to me but he is a queer fish, so frightfully polite that I don't feel thoroughly at home with him."

Charles was tempted to tell Huxley that he never would but decided it would be better for the young man to find his own way through the jungle of London's scientists. It did not take him long. After a meeting of one of the societies, Charles took Huxley to the Athenaeum for a nightcap. Over his glass of brandy Huxley mused:

"It's strange about Richard Owen; he is both feared and hated. I've seen him do some very ill-natured tricks. To my mind he is not so great as he thinks himself."

"He hasn't played one of his 'ill-natured' tricks on you?"

"Not yet."

It was not long in coming. Huxley wrote a memoir for the Royal Society, On the Morphology of the Cephalous Mollusca, which he considered the best paper he had done, and of some importance. Richard Owen attempted to keep it out of the Philosophical Transactions. Huxley exclaimed:

"He is determined not to let anyone else rise. Why is he so greedy? I do so long to be able to trust men implicitly."

Charles was deeply moved by Huxley's pain.

"For the last twenty years Owen has been regarded as the authority in his field," he explained. "There has been no one to tread on his heels until you came along. Unfortunately he has come to look upon the natural world as his special preserve. . . ."

". . . and we are all poachers!"

"That is right. But you are not to worry unduly. He cannot stop your endeavors. Confidentially, my friends and I have proposed you for the Royal Medal."

For a moment it looked as though Thomas Huxley was going to weep. He grasped Charles's hand in his own two hands, exclaimed:

"With men like you and Joseph Hooker and Charles Lyell in the world of science I will withstand a dozen Richard Owens."

"You may have to," Charles answered with a grimace. "And so may I."

He had perhaps a year or two of work left on what he had called "my beloved barnacles" but now thought of as "my hated barnacles." There was no help for it, he had the two remaining volumes to write, the one consolation being that publication was assured. He did his best to conceal his irritation from the family, plunged into a search for the best school for William, going on to twelve. After considerable scrutiny he selected Rugby, on the road to Shrewsbury. Hensleigh Wedgwood's two older boys were already there. The cost would be between a hundred and ten and a hundred and twenty pounds a year.

Twice each twenty-four hours, once for the daylight hours, once for the nighttime, he made a report in his health diary of how many "fits of flatulence," he had had, including times when he was awakened by "ft.," his shorthand for flatulence; how many headaches, toothaches, colds, rashes, boils; the medicines he was taking, his hydropathy treatments; how frequently he had spells of retching, depression, fright, shivering, sinking sensations, bouts of oppression; when he felt unwarrantedly heavy and fatigued. He had started the record of his physical condition in July of 1849. At the end of each month he also recorded how many days of grace he had enjoyed, when he felt perfectly well. These good days in each month varied from two to five at the lower end of the log to as high as twenty to twenty-nine. After a good day he put a double dash.

He realized that his health record, in addition to something built into his nature by his father, was a kind of confessional. When he wrote it all down it was similar to telling it to someone. By this means he could keep his own counsel and not burden those around him. As time moved on he used Dr. Gully's hydropathy only fitfully, dropping the douches and foot baths. However in his search for sound health he was still credulous, trying new "cures" which he read about in the London newspapers. In October of 1851 he tried the newly espoused hydroelectric chains, wrapping around himself alternating brass and zinc wires, first about his waist, then around his neck. When moistened with vinegar these chains were supposed to give off annealing electric shocks. On the nights that he used the chains he felt well but could not go to sleep. He decided they were of questionable value and discarded them.

The trees bordering the Sandwalk grew miraculously; the holly, bramble and privet were now tall hedges. The children grew apace. The manuscripts grew apace. They thanked heaven that Emma did not. They now had seven children. Smith Elder and Company combined his three separate books, *Coral Reefs, Volcanic Islands* and *Geological Observations on South America,* into one volume, bound in blue or purple cloth, at the reasonable price of ten shillings and sixpence, which his aging friend William Yarrell informed him was selling well and expanding his general public.

The hours were absorbed into weeks, the weeks into months, the months struggled into years. They visited William at Rugby. He was

doing well in his classes, as well as any young lad wrenched out of his
home and family to be set down amidst a group of older bullies. The
six children at home were well and robust, the older ones studying
under William's former tutor, to whom Charles paid one hundred and
fifty pounds a year for "teaching nothing on earth but the Latin
grammar."

Down House was full of relatives and friends. He welcomed them
but the fatigue of constant communication frequently sent him rolling
downhill in pain. Then he would see no one except his own clutch.
When, after a time, he began to feel like a hermit he would send out
distress signals, as he did to Joseph Hooker, to get him into the Philosophical Club to be formed in London:

> Only two or three days ago I was regretting to my wife how
> I was letting drop and being dropped by nearly all my ac-
> quaintances, and thinking of the Club which, as far as any
> one thing goes, would answer my exact object in keeping up
> old and making some new acquaintances. . . .

In November of 1853 he was awarded the Royal Medal for his publications, the highest honor in the power of his peers to bestow. He wrote
to Joseph Hooker:

> In a year or two's time I shall be at my species book, if I do
> not break down.

He knew he would not break down.

And when he completed his final two volumes on the barnacles he
would be a free man.

"Or will I? Shall I simply be moving into another penitentiary?
Without bars, but still a place where I shall be self-incarcerated. Perhaps for the rest of my life."

# BOOK TEN

*"All Geniuses Are Idiots,
in One Way or Another"*

## 1.

By May 1855 the second volume of *Living Cirripedia* had been distributed, and now the second volume of the monograph *Fossil Cirripedia* was being released by the Palaeontographical Society.

"I am unutterably relieved to have finished with my last barnacle," Charles confessed to Emma. "If I ever stumble across another I shall simply turn my back and walk away."

Emma's knitting needles clicked with a familiar sound as they sat warming themselves before the bedroom fire.

"Now I'm eager to get on to the next project."

"What might that be?"

He was startled; she had never inquired about his work plans. Not since he had read her letter sixteen years before had he discussed with his wife his theory about the origin of species. There was no longer any way to conceal his intent, since he had decided to spend the rest of his life on the pursuit. He did not wish to make Emma unhappy; but he considered it a more serious offense to dissemble.

He had been staring into the flames. Now he turned full face to Emma, put her knitting aside, took her hands in his.

"My dear one, I'm going to tell you what my plans are for the coming years; the full truth as I am able to perceive it. I hope and pray you will not be distressed."

Her warm brown eyes met his, head on.

"I promise I shall not permit myself to be disturbed."

He rose from the divan, stood with his back to the fire.

"I shall set our studding sails on each side to catch the trade wind. I feel that if you know whither I am tending you might not think me so wild and foolish in my views. I arrived at them slowly enough, and I hope conscientiously. Yet these views are bound to meet opposition. To give you an example: the last time I saw my botanical friend, Hugh Falconer, in London, he attacked me most vigorously, though not unkindly, and told me, 'You will do more harm than any ten naturalists will do good. I can see that you have already corrupted and half spoiled Hooker!' "

Emma showed no reaction.

"Let me give you the briefest abstract of my notions on the means by which nature makes her species. Why I think that species have changed depends on general facts: embryology, rudimentary organs, geological history and geographical distribution of organic beings. Do you follow me?"

"Vaguely."

"I would like to make myself clear." He paused for a moment. "Let's take the subject of organs, rudimentary, atrophied or aborted. Organs or parts bearing the plain stamp of inutility are common throughout nature. It would be impossible to name one of the higher animals in which some part or other is not in a rudimentary condition. In the mammalia, for instance, the males possess rudimentary mammae. In snakes one lobe of the lungs is rudimentary. In birds the 'bastard-wing' may safely be considered as a rudimentary digit in that it cannot be used for flight. What can be more curious than the presence of teeth in fetal whales which, when full grown, have not a tooth in their heads? Or the teeth which never cut through the gums in the upper jaws of unborn calves?

"It is wonderful what the principle of selection by man, that is the picking out of desired qualities and breeding from them, can do. Even breeders have been astonished at their results. I am convinced that intentional selection has been the main agent in making our domestic races. Man, by his power of accumulating very slight or greater variations, adapts living beings to his wants. He may be said to make the wool of one sheep good for carpets, another for cloth."

"This kind of animal breeding has taken place only of late times, has it not?" she asked.

"Yes. Yet I think it can be shown that there is an unerring power at work, or *natural selection*, which has long selected exclusively for the good of each organic being. Reflect that every being, even the elephant, breeds at such a rate that in a few years, at most a few centuries, the surface of the earth could not hold the progeny of any one species. I have found it hard constantly to bear in mind that the increase of every single species is checked during some part of its life. Only a few of those annually born can live to propagate their kind. What a trifling difference must often determine which shall survive and which perish."

Emma turned pale.

"Is all this not anti-Christian?"

"No, it's anti-dogma; a set of dogmas superimposed upon the Church rather late in life. It does not impugn the existence of God. Nature simply follows His laws."

"Are you not attributing cruelty to God when you say that only a small number of those who are born can remain alive?"

"It would be far more cruel if everything that was born in plant or animal life were to remain alive. This earth of ours would have been choked to death millions of years ago. Only by natural selection, by the dying off of the less fitted, can our world remain inhabitable."

Emma was leaning toward him intently, her elbows on her knees, chin held firmly in her two hands. She was not only sincerely religious but definite in her beliefs. She went regularly to church and took the sacrament from the Rev. Mr. Innes. She read the Bible to their children, and discouraged all social activities on Sunday which required the use of the family carriage. It was a question in her own mind whether she should embroider, knit or play patience on Sunday, though she believed that England would be morally the better for permitting some amusement on Sunday. In her early married life it had distressed her to know that Charles did not share her faith. However that sense of distress had passed; in her mind Charles lived such an exemplary life that he must have a sense of God within him.

"It is hard for me to accept that all living things are not as God made them, and are not blessed by Him and meant to flourish."

"I know. It was difficult for me as well, until the evidence appeared irrefutable. Lyell does not accept it fully, nor does Hooker."

"I must respect your convictions. But how will you buttress such an unacceptable idea?"

"In order to write about the mutability of species, their change, growth, departure, I am going to have to learn about and document all living creatures: plant and animal, insect, fish, bird, reptile, the earth's crust with its mountain ranges, valleys, plateaus, the encircling seas. It's an impossible task, no one man can know all the secrets of our world back to each beginning organism. But someone has to start! There is a Hebraic saying: 'It is not encumbent upon thee to complete the work, but neither art thou free to desist from it altogether.' . . ." Suddenly his spirits tumbled; he felt despondent.

Emma's brow was lined with concentration. Her voice was not unsympathetic.

"You feel you are the one chosen for this task?"

"I chose myself," he replied, a self-mocking smile at one corner of his mouth.

"They are the same, Charles. If you are chosen, then you must accept your fate. Since you are quoting proverbs take solace from Matthew in the New Testament. 'If it be possible, let this cup pass from me: nevertheless, not as I will, but as thou wilt.' "

He lifted her from her chair and embraced her.

He settled into his barricaded poop-cabin corner, the green cloth-covered board across the arms of his comfortable chair. It was good to begin expanding and speculating again on the work that enthralled him. It was good to be settling into his study again. The previous January, with two of their sons ill with fever and bronchitis, the Darwins had rented a house in London, at 17 York Place, Baker Street, partly for amusement, partly for a change of air which they hoped would help the boys. The moment they moved into the rented house the city suffered a severe frost so that half the time they were unable to go out. It was also the winter of the dreadful Crimean War, the English and the French fighting the Russians to prevent the Czar from taking over strategic parts of Turkey. England was depressed at the loss of so many of its young men; and although Tennyson's poem *The Charge of the Light Brigade* had lifted the people's spirits, Lyell observed:

"Remember what the French general Bosquet said? 'It was magnificent, that charge, but it is not war.' "

The outrage over the mismanagement of the Crimean War caused Lord Aberdeen's ministry to resign; Lord Palmerston became Prime Minister. The tax on newspapers was at long last abolished, more of the poorer people could now afford to buy them, in particular the newly founded mass-circulation *Daily Telegraph*. Messrs. Straham, Paul and Bates, prominent bankers, were caught appropriating twenty-two thousand pounds' worth of bonds for their own use. Because they were highly educated men who should have known better, or so said the Court, they were given the severe sentence of fourteen years of exile in Australia.

"Australia!" exclaimed Charles, remembering the country from H.M.S. *Beagle*'s visit there. "Good country. Rich in potential. They'll do well. Own vast sheep ranches, marry pretty Australian girls. They should have been sentenced to fourteen years in exile in the poorest and most degraded parts of London: Bermondsey, Holborn, the East End. That would have been punishment, indeed!"

There was a smattering of good news. Florence Nightingale and a band of women nurses landed at Scutari to take care of the sick and wounded of the Crimean War. Letter boxes appeared for the first time on the streets of London, curtailing the need to go to a post office to post a letter. Queen Victoria and Prince Albert were entertained at a ball at Versailles; Victor Emmanuel, King of Sardinia, who had joined England and France during the war, visited Queen Victoria and Prince Albert, being invested with the Order of the Garter, presaging a unity of diplomatic relations between countries.

When the weather permitted they visited Joseph and Frances Hooker in Kew. They took twelve-year-old Henrietta to the concerts conducted by Louis Jullien, the portly Frenchman who had done so much to popularize symphonic music in England, and who was equally famous for his gorgeous waistcoats. The first Sunday in London they hired an enclosed brougham to take them to luncheon at the elegant four-story house Erasmus had bought some time before, at 6 Queen Anne Street, just a short distance from Cavendish Square with its charming park. The house stood resolutely guarding a corner in a secluded cul-de-sac with only two handsome buildings beyond it, the last being Chandos House, headquarters of the prestigious Royal Society of Medicine; close by was Harley Street with the best, or at least the most expensive, surgeons in London. Another street beyond was Wimpole Street, where the poetess Elizabeth Barrett had been brought up by her tyrannically possessive father, whom she fled to marry Robert Browning and live in Florence, Italy. She had published the much-admired *Sonnets from the Portuguese* five years before. Erasmus was now a short walk from All Souls' in Langham Place, with its beautiful circle of pillars and exquisitely pointed spire.

The Darwins stood in front of Erasmus's house admiringly for a minute in the penetrating February cold. Emma murmured through a wool shawl wrapped about her mouth:

"Our brother hath come up in the world. He is enjoying his inheritance."

"Oh, indeed. The younger members of Parliament attend his Sunday luncheons quite often. Since he became friends with the playwright, Charles Reade, whose *Masks and Faces* was so popular, his guests frequently include a number of our most dashing actors and beautiful actresses. His favorites are still authors: Charles Kingsley, whose new *Westward Ho!* you are reading, Anthony Trollope, whose novel *The Warden* is in process of being published; Wilkie Collins, whose *Antonina* and *Hide and Seek* you read to me at home . . ."

They climbed the front steps. A butler handsomely attired in a black suit, starched white shirt and white tie admitted them at the first sound of the door knocker. He took their coats. They made their way to the marble fireplace in the spacious high-ceilinged drawing room with its carved wooden frames and filled brass coal scuttles on either side. Emma stood with her face to the fire, arms outstretched to be warmed. Charles stood with his backside hearthward. Emma remarked:

"How tastes change. Ras's earlier house was light in atmosphere. Since Queen Victoria has been setting the style, the drawing room is much darker in tone. His windows are covered over with heavy plush curtains, his wallpaper is a dark satin patterned in somber hues."

Erasmus's elaborate drawing room was even more marked by the quantity of furniture that crowded the room, displaying his collection of china boxes, small filigreed screens, large and small vases and figurines, ornamented clocks, plants. Embroideries hung over the backs of the hand-carved chairs. There was an occasional simple English piece, beautifully crafted, a cabinet or drop-leaf table, for Erasmus had taken to haunting the London antique shops.

"Do you like it?" Erasmus asked his brother. "It's quite finished now. Took me two years to get it precisely right."

He had slipped into the room smelling of eau de cologne, fastidiously garbed in a blue velvet smoking jacket and well-cut gray trousers held precisely by being strapped under his shining boots.

"It's charming, Ras," Emma murmured. "You have a fine flair."

"What I don't understand," said Charles, pretending to be serious, "is where you put your numerous guests with all this modish furniture cluttering up the place."

"The chairs are expendable. The divans are contractible." Erasmus had a grin on his usually melancholy face. "You'll see how miraculously it all works out. Besides, my guests will be famished after listening to the two-hour sermon at All Souls'."

The first to arrive was Thomas Huxley, with the vibrant personality that shook walls as well as beliefs. He made a courtly bow to Emma, pumped Charles's hand.

"I've come early on purpose, Darwin," he confided. "I hoped to catch you alone so that I could apologize."

"In heaven's name, for what?"

"For being an idiot. When I met you I expressed my belief in the sharpness of the lines of demarcation between natural groups and in the absence of transitional forms. I spoke with all the confidence of brash youth and imperfect knowledge. Your gentle answer that such was not your view long haunted me and puzzled me. Years of hard work have enabled me to understand what you meant."

"I'm pleased to hear that, Huxley. Species need friends."

"Please don't inscribe me as a convert quite yet, Darwin. I haven't the smallest objection to raise to the account of the creation given in *Paradise Lost*, in which Milton so vividly embodies the natural sense of Genesis. *Far be it for me to say that it is untrue because it is impossible*."

While Charles laughed deep in his chest, Emma asked solicitously:

"What news of your fiancée, Miss Heathorn?"

Huxley's broad, handsome face broke into a radiant smile.

"She and her parents are on a ship en route home from Sydney. Having waited seven years, I plan that we should be married immediately. I can support her now, though barely, on my two hundred pounds a year pay as a lecturer at the government School of Mines, in addition to my fee from the Geological Survey."

His enormous eyes became hooded, an expression of anguish settled over his face.

"I am really worried half to death. Nettie's father wrote to me that her health had broken down. Apparently Australian doctors believe in bloodletting and giving doses of calomel, nothing more."

Erasmus's guests began to arrive. It was a parade of fashion such as the Darwins rarely saw. The women were elaborately gowned, wearing bonnets trimmed with flowers, lace and velvet ribbons, set far back on their heads to show more of the face. They filled the room with their gathered bodices, tightly nipped in at the waist, and widely flounced skirts. The new lighter colors had been adopted by the most daring, blue, greenish gold, pink and yellow; the more conservative clung to dark browns and greens with fancy braid and sprigs of flowers on their lightweight woolens and printed muslins. The even newer shot silk skirts over crinoline frames drew the most attention. Each arriving lady carried her reticule of Berlin woolwork or steel beadwork, wore the short white kid gloves which had become fashionable and black or white satin pumps.

"Upon my word," exclaimed Emma to Charles, "these elegant women make me feel like a country bumpkin."

"In nature," Charles murmured, "it is the male peacock who has the most colorful plumage. Will you look at the double-buttoned, tight-waisted overcoats in which they arrive . . . the frock coats with the fronts sloped away to the sides!"

The men were trying to outshine the women in cashmeres, silks and velvets, navy and dark greens mixing with popular plaids. Their brightly colored waistcoats were bound in braid and finely embroidered. The collars of their pleated shirt fronts were turned down over loosely knitted ascots. Their short ankle boots of soft leather shone like mirrors. A few of Erasmus's artist friends wore the new loose lounging jackets and smoking caps of velvet or cashmere.

"Clothing marks the gentleman," Charles observed with an amused smile; "or at least his exterior. In a few hours we'll know what's inside these elaborate waistcoats. You must admit they're decorative."

He moved from group to group listening to the repartee. It was bright, animated, witty, sometimes naughty, occasionally vicious as the newest books, plays, music were dissected, the politics of Whitehall incisively analyzed, the latest gossip about the court and scandals among the gentry wholeheartedly aired.

Luncheon was announced. Erasmus's dining room was also elegant, with vertically striped wallpaper and curtains of green striped silk. There was a carved white chimneypiece, a bright fire, a long rosewood table under a crystal chandelier spreading soft candlelight. He had a well-trained staff to serve the luncheon buffet of hors d'oeuvres, turbot with shrimp sauce, chicken in casserole, cold pheasant, galantine of veal, salad, apple tart with cream, fruit in jelly, caramel cream.

"Quite a change from the 'daily' who served a mutton chop!" Charles muttered in an aside to Emma.

The cold outside, the gaiety of the conversation in the drawing room, the fact that it was three in the afternoon gave Erasmus's guests heroic appetites. Charles and Emma were surprised to find themselves eating along enthusiastically. Incredible as it seemed, all of the copious dishes, washed down with seemingly endless bottles of a fine white wine, were not merely conquered but devastated, the long Chippendale sideboard as empty as a battlefield with the troops withdrawn.

Erasmus walked them to the door.

"You've achieved your life ambition, Ras," Charles said.

"Now don't condescend to me, Gas. I'm just as much a perfectionist as you are. I work meticulously to make each gathering a memorable one. The right people, the right food and drink, the correct ambience in which conversation and friendship can flower. You would be surprised how many first-rate, creative men and women meet here for the first time, establishing relationships that enrich their lives."

"I'm sure they do, Ras," Charles replied placatingly.

2.

They had returned to Down House in mid-February, before the snowfall of that year had melted. The children, wrapped in greatcoats, scarves and woolen caps, walked about on a level with the top of the iron railings enclosing the lawn while Charles wrote an article on the power of moving icebergs to make grooves and scars across any landscape they traversed. It was published in the *Journal of Science*. He then dug into his friend Thomas Wollaston's recent book on the insects of Madeira, in which he found the descriptions admirable but the reasoning as leaky as an old river Thames scow. Wollaston was an entomologist and conchologist, a graduate of Jesus College, Cambridge. He had made assumptions about a large breed of insects with elementary wings which Charles had not been able to dislodge from Wollaston's mind. When Joseph Hooker came for a visit, Charles showed him the chapter in dispute.

"Hooker, are not these a jolly set of assumptions?"

"Jolly indeed. And not one of them true."

The breed of insects which had elementary wings took Charles's mind back to the flightless cormorants of the Galápagos Islands. He had been sorely puzzled, as had Captain FitzRoy, John Wickham, Benjamin Bynoe, about these birds which could no longer fly. No one on H.M.S. *Beagle* could vouchsafe an explanation and only now through his research on rudimentary organs had the explanation come through to him.

He told Hooker of his day on Albemarle, reliving it vividly in his study. The ship's water supply had been so low that everyone was on half rations, half a gallon per man, an intense hardship at the equator with its vertical sun. Charles had gone ashore determined to find a supply of fresh water but had scooped up only brine. It was here on Albemarle that he had seen the cormorants feeding off the low-lying rocks, their wings mere stumps with a ragged fringe of feathers. There was a prodigious food supply on the rocks; they had no need to fly over the waters to fish; nor had there been predators. There were no animals to destroy them, no big birds of prey. The cormorants' wings had atrophied because there was no need for them! Unused, the sedentary wings had shrunk from what must have been a span sufficient to carry their large bodies through the air, as any unused organ in any living creature virtually disappeared if it lost its function.

Joseph Hooker pulled caressingly on the hairs of his eyebrows, which were luxuriating like the tropical plants at Kew.

"No way to dispute you on that point."

"No, Hooker, you cannot. God would not have created a stump-winged bird that could not fly! Time and change have created the flightless cormorant."

At the beginning of 1855 he had abandoned the health diary he had kept for five and a half years. He enjoyed keeping records for their own sake but his daily jottings had failed to reveal any pattern to his chronic upheavals.

He spent only part of his time in his study; the other half he worked out of doors with the skeletons of chicks, ducks, turkeys, attempting to determine how many varieties there were in each species. To his cousin Fox he wrote:

> I should be very glad for a seven days duckling, and for one of the old birds, should one ever die a natural death.

While working with little chickens he began a system of measuring limbs by feeling their joints. He recorded the skeletons of old wild turkeys; he had cart horses and race horses carefully measured. He learned that one of his fellow naturalists had collected forty varieties of the common duck. He began investigating both the eye and ear structure of hundreds of birds, fowl, reptiles and animals, constantly aware of their subtlety and complexity.

"I'm getting out of my depth," he groaned.

He began boiling ducks over a wood fire which the new gardener, young Lettington, who had replaced the now retired Comfort, kept stoking in their outside shed. His seven children, for William was home from Rugby for a stay, were intrigued by his work with the fowls; they had grown fatigued with barnacles long before their father had. They teased him by crying:

"Oh, the smell of well-boiled, high duck!"

Instead of protesting the stench, Emma asked if he would not like to build a little boiling shed at the far end of the kitchen garden.

"I'm going into a new phase now, the study of pigeons. Yarrell will educate me so that when I go to the breeders to buy I won't be excessively liable to be gulled. No," he grinned, "I am not going to boil them."

From the main dealer in London, Bailey, he bought several pair of choice birds, fantails and pouters, in a grand cage. Though he had never cared much about pigeons, he now became enchanted with them and, to the children's delight, built a pigeon house.

In the spring Joseph Hooker was appointed assistant director of the Royal Botanical Gardens at Kew. Joseph and his wife, Frances Henslow, who already had two children and were expecting a third, were also given the gatehouse by the entrance to the gardens in which to live. Charles told Hooker, who was looking leaner and more academically wide-eyed behind his rimless spectacles:

"I am most sincerely and heartily glad about the appointment. I realize that the income is a poor one yet it must lead in future years to the directorship."

Hooker felt toward Charles much the way Charles felt toward John Henslow. Though he was overworked trying to eke out a living from such jobs as botany examiner for medical service candidates and concluding his labors for the publication of his New Zealand and Indian flora, he was never too preoccupied or fatigued to answer Charles's letters with their dozens of queries in the vast area of botany.

In early June Charles and Miss Thorley, the children's long-time governess, made a collection of all the plants growing in a field that had been allowed to run waste but which before had been cultivated. Then they collected the plants in an adjoining cultivated field to learn which were recently arrived, which had died out.

"How dreadfully difficult it is to name plants," Charles exclaimed, looking over their booty. "We shall want a bit of help from Hooker in naming puzzlers."

When he was able to distinguish his first grass among the numerous grasses, he cried, "Hurrah! Hurrah! I never expected to make out a grass in all my life. I must tell Hooker."

He had discovered during the *Beagle* journey as well as the subsequent years of intensive reading that species of plant life as well as animal and bird life could be found on remote islands when it was impossible for the plant or animal to have traveled there, or for any but the largest bird to fly there. The traditionalists had a tidy explanation:

"Spontaneous creation by God of all forms of life on all areas of the earth."

Charles did not believe this. He had theorized his way through to a partial answer: the movement of seeds and eggs across the seas on timbers, conglomerate rafts of logs or weed stuffs, in the claws or bowels of long-flying birds who had dropped their mainland excrement on the islands.

He asked Hooker:

"Can seeds and eggs or sperm stay alive for hundreds of miles in salt water, for days, weeks, months, and still reproduce on some distant shore?"

"Possible," replied Hooker, "but it will be up to you to demonstrate it."

"I mean with my utmost power to prove the facts. I know you will not sneer at me but view the experiments like a good Christian. I am going to secure seeds of every kind, newly laid eggs as well, put them in bottles and tubs of salt water, keep records on how long they stay alive, can be taken out of the containers, planted and grow in a normal fashion. That is, without you demur."

"Damme, no!" Hooker cried. "Would you mind if I conducted a few of the same experiments in Kew Gardens? I too want to see if seeds can float."

"Experiment along with me. Float they will, and float they must."

He bought bottles and old tubs of wood in all sizes, set them in rows alongside the kitchen garden, filled them with salt water, keeping the temperature between thirty-two and thirty-three degrees Centigrade, the temperature he figured the ocean waters would be on an average over the years. The children liked this new game which they secretly believed Papa was playing for them. Emma, who had wanted no part of his dissection of animal, fowl, bird, let alone barnacle, was now interested. The children labeled the outside of each bottle and tub, telling which seeds were in each. Emma offered to keep records on the condition of the seeds day by day. She had no notion that it could be one of the keystones of her husband's treatise on the origin of species.

He started with seeds of radish, cress, cabbage, lettuce, carrot, celery and onion. For one week they were kept in the tubs, then taken out to be placed in the ground. The children kept running into his study, calling:

"Papa, Papa, come and see, the celery and onions are sprouting."

He watched the cress and lettuce grow at an accelerated rate, but the cabbages came up irregularly.

"I think many of them are dead."

The children groaned their disappointment.

After three weeks the cress and lettuce were still growing strongly. Charles said:

"Upon my word, I can hardly believe our success."

The children asked, "Shall you beat Dr. Hooker?"

His next batch of seeds to go into salt water were French spinach, oats, barley, canary seed and beets. After two weeks of immersion, and then three, he took them out and planted them. He knew these time spells were too short for the seeds to have drifted on rafts to far places. But when the hardy celery and onion seeds germinated after eighty-five days of living in salt water, he cried:

"This is a triumph! It means that certain forms of life can float across the oceans and re-establish themselves on islands; also on other, distant, mainlands."

He wrote to Henslow asking his old teacher to offer the little girls of his parish sixpence to collect seeds for him. Plenty poured in, for which he paid in stamps. He conducted another experiment in conjunction with the Zoological Society in London. He wrote to Hooker:

> The fish at the Zoological Society ate up lots of soaked seeds. In my imagination they had been swallowed by a heron, had been carried a hundred miles, been voided on the banks of some other lake and germinated splendidly. Alas the fish ejected all the seeds vehemently.

His cousin Fox sent him fantail and pouter pigeons. He banished Emma from the rough workshed but let the older children stay. He wrote to Fox:

> I have done the black deed and murdered an angelic little fantail, and a pouter at ten days old. I tried chloroform and ether for the first. For the second I tried putting lumps of cyanide of potassium in a very large damp bottle, half an hour before putting in the pigeon, and the prussic acid gas thus generated was very quickly fatal.

He needed to learn whether newly laid lizard and snake eggs could float in sea water long enough to populate other lands. He asked Fox:

> As you live on sandy soil, have you lizards at all common? If you have, should you think it too ridiculous to offer a reward

for me for lizard's eggs to the boys in your school; a shilling for every half-dozen, or more if rare, till you get two or three dozen and send them to me? If snake's eggs were brought in by mistake it would be very well, for I want such also; and we have neither lizards nor snakes here.

As the weeks and months passed he filled hundreds of pages of random notes on any handy piece of paper, even old envelopes, with the results of his experiments. The dozens of file drawers which he had built into his study began to fill. They were his mine of observations and information. He was only rarely despondent when theory and fact did not harmonize.

He made a fruitful relationship when he met the American, Asa Gray, at Kew Gardens, introduced to him by Joseph Hooker. Dr. Gray, professor of botany at Harvard University, author of *Manual of the Botany of the Northern United States*, provided valuable information about American plants. Charles also went up to London to join the Southwark Columbarian or Pigeon Fanciers Society which met at seven o'clock at the Yorkshire Grey Tavern at 4 Park Street, Borough Market, approximately a ten-minute walk from London Bridge station, and close to the Thames. It was a part of London he rarely saw since he had moved to the country. The public house was located between a baker's and coffee rooms.

Moving northward to Rugby to visit William, who had been down with the measles, he told his oldest son:

"I met a strange set of odd men in a tavern run by a woman, oddly enough; a Miss Victoire Arden."

"Which does Miss Arden prefer," William asked with a mischievous grin, "the odd men or the pigeons?"

"The odd men; they have more money for ale than the pigeons do. Mr. Brent, one of their leaders, was a very queer little fish; after dinner he handed me a clay pipe saying, 'Here is your pipe,' as if it was a matter of course that I should smoke. I am going to take a lot more pigeons back with me on Saturday, for it is a noble and majestic pursuit and beats moths and butterflies, whatever you may say to the contrary."

His boys were butterfly hunters. Like most young and ardent lepidopterists, they despised the beetle collectors. It was also a way of pulling their father's leg. By precept and enthusiasm he had instilled in his children a taste for natural history but he knew better than to give them specimens. Youngsters had to collect for themselves to acquire the fervor. Emma had brought up her brood to be dutiful and well behaved, yet each child had cultivated a sense of independence. Once when he wandered into the sitting room Charles found five-year-old Leonard jumping up and down on their red velvet sofa.

"Leonard, I've told you I didn't want to see you jumping on that sofa."

"Well, Papa, if you don't want to see me, I suppose you'll just have to leave the room."

During the summer and autumn he got onto cocks and hens, trying to establish the differences in bone structure, weight, number of tail feathers in order to establish authentic varieties. He had difficulty getting specimens for, unlike the barnacle collectors, people seemed unwilling to box or send him dead game. He had found that the putting to death of young birds distressed Emma and the children. Now he offered payment for dead pigeons, rabbits and ducks to a Mr. Baker, who bred and sold them. His most faithful supplier was his cousin Fox who, though in constant pain from lumbago, sent him old and good Cochin, Dorking and Malay fowl. Charles also wrote twenty letters to well-known breeders and professional skinners to acquire poultry and pigeon skins.

He ruminated:

"About thirty years ago there was much talk that geologists ought only to observe and not theorize, and I well remember someone saying that at that rate a man might as well go into a gravel pit and count the pebbles and describe the colors. How odd it is that anyone should not see that all observation must be for or against some view if it is to be of any service."

3.

It was in the autumn of 1855 that he picked up his recently arrived copy of the *Annals and Magazine of Natural History* to which he subscribed, and began reading an article by Alfred Russel Wallace called, On the Law Which Has Regulated the Introduction of New Species. The title itself jolted him. He had not even suspected that anyone else was working the unconventional acreage which he himself had begun to till some eighteen years before, in 1837. He was in for additional shock after he took a pinch of snuff from the green and tan pottery container in the hallway and began to read:

*Geographical Distribution dependent*
*on Geologic Changes*

Every naturalist who has directed his attention to the subject of the geographical distribution of animals and plants must have been interested in the singular facts which it presents. . . .

. . . A country having species, genera, and whole families
peculiar to it, will be the necessary result of its having been
isolated for a long period, sufficient for many series of species
to have been created on the type of pre-existing ones, which,
as well as many of the earlier-formed species, have become extinct, and thus made the groups appear isolated. . . .

He rose from his footstool and paced the room, thoroughly perturbed.
Riffling back to the table of contents, he saw that the article had been
written by a young man he remembered slightly from a brief encounter
at the British Museum some two years before. He had also read a chapter or two of Wallace's *Travels on the Amazon* at Lyell's house, thinking that Wallace was a discerning, disciplined naturalist. Alfred Russel
Wallace, now thirty-two years old, had been about to embark then on
an expedition to Singapore, Bali, the Celebes, Malacca: the area of the
Malay Archipelago which had not yet been explored by naturalists, or
scientifically collected. Charles remembered Wallace saying:

"It is due to my study of the Insect and Bird Departments here in
the museum that I decided on Singapore as a starting point for my natural history collecting. I'd like to stay out a number of years, as you did
on the *Beagle* and Hooker on the *Erebus*. I'm not married, so my time
is unlimited."

He recaptured the picture of Wallace in his mind: plain-looking,
built in a chubby fashion, with heavy shoulders and chest, a mop of
black hair, dark sideburns and a pair of rimless spectacles much too
small for his enormous, inquisitive yet non-aggressive eyes. Charles remembered him as shy of manner, soft spoken and well educated,
though not through formal schooling since a collapse of the never
affluent Wallace family finances had obliged the boy to leave school at
the age of fourteen.

The trail of Alfred Wallace also unwound in his mind. Charles recalled that, since Wallace had no money, he had laid his plans before
Roderick Murchison, then president of the Royal Geographical Society,
and it had been through Murchison's application to the government
that passage was provided on a Pacific and Orient ship going out to Singapore, leaving early in 1854.

Charles picked up the article again. It had been published only eighteen months after Wallace's departure from England!

"Incredible that he should have perceived so much in so short a
time," he declared, his heart pounding; and then read straight through
to the concluding paragraph of the nineteen pages of Wallace's observations and examples:

It has now been shown, though most briefly and imperfectly, how the law that *"Every species has come into exist-*

*ence coincident both in time and space with a pre-existing closely allied species,"* connects together and renders intelligible a vast number of independent and hitherto unexplained facts. . . .

He simply could not believe his eyes. Alfred Wallace had come up with this revolutionary theory and stated it in almost precisely his own words. It was indeed incredible! During the reading he had been vexed, nonplussed, disappointed, angry, then frustrated. He strode out of the study, gathered up his cloak, soft hat and ash walking stick and made for the Sandwalk. He did not bother to count out flint stones but took two turns around the walk before he began to feel a sense of relief. Wallace had observed the facts and grouped them into a theory about species, but he had not found the mechanism of *natural selection.*

He used his scissors to cut the other articles out of the magazine and discarded them, leaving Wallace's intact between the two covers. He put it in a cabinet drawer. With that act of filing away, he resolutely put the article out of his mind.

But not for long.

Having dinner with Lyell in London prior to a Society meeting, Lyell asked:

"Did you read that article by Alfred Wallace in the *Annals?*"

"I did."

"Well done, didn't you think?"

"Capitally."

"Rather treading on your toes, was he not?"

"On my toenails. But he has no concept of what causes the change of species."

"Do you?"

"I'll answer that later."

"I started my own notebook on species after reading Wallace's article."

"You started! . . . After all the years that I discussed species with you, it was not until Wallace's article that you began a notebook?"

"When you were alone in the field I saw no need to. Now that there are two of you . . ."

The second reminder came from a naturalist friend, Edward Blyth, curator of the Museum of the Asiatic Society of Bengal, an authority on Indian birds and mammals. In his letter sending Charles information on Indian flora, Blyth asked:

What think you of Wallace's paper in the *Ann. M.N.H.?* Good! Upon the whole! . . . Wallace has, I think, put the matter well; and according to his theory, the various domestic races of animals have been fairly developed into *species*.

This letter was rather more disturbing to Charles than his conversation with Lyell, for Blyth described Wallace's deduction as "A triumph of a fact for friend Wallace to have hit upon."

Would Wallace also come upon the principle of natural selection? What then would happen to his own years of work and discovery? Was he about to lose priority for his important concept?

"Of course not!" he exclaimed half aloud to the bookshelves of his study. "That's utter nonsense. And utter self-centeredness as well. Wallace is a dedicated and brilliant young naturalist. I shall help him all I can, just as Lyell helped me."

January 1856 was a disagreeable month for the family. Emma was racked by unfamiliar headaches. The children had colds which kept them indoors. The snowbanks were high in the fields so that Charles could do little work in his outdoor sheds. He cornered himself in the study in front of Parslow's warming fire, annotating newly arrived books, writing correspondence and digesting his letters, storing up the particulars on the world's differing eggs, the varying colors of ducks and sheep. Few could work out what he was doing with these thousands of uncoalesced facts about animal and plant life or what purpose they served.

Only he knew of his grand design. Sometimes he faltered, brooded because he was not having success in one line or another of investigation. Yet his fundamental faith in his concept of the developing, changing and adapting of species from the beginning of the earth's time, from its first form of life millions of years before, rarely wavered. He believed strongly that his theory was a sound vessel and would hold water. But he would be cautious, candid, and avoid dogmatism.

There was distressing news from London when a dead body found on Hampstead Heath turned out to be that of John Sadleir, M.P., a suicide because he had been involved in bank frauds amounting to half a million pounds. It came as a severe shock to the British people and was the beginning of a series of exposés of high society figures who were found guilty of dipping into the communal till, causing incalculable misery to depositors, farmers, tradespeople. Later in the year a Leopold Redpath robbed the stock register of the Great Northern Railroad, misappropriating a quarter of a million pounds sterling. Charles nearly got burned on that embezzlement, for he had seriously considered buying Great Northern Railroad stock with their savings.

"I'll wait until they have recouped their losses," he determined. "But it's a good investment and we shall have some."

There were those who said that these scandals undermined the faith of the British people in their upper classes. To add to the general anguish, the beloved Covent Garden Theatre burned down during a drunken orgy at a masked ball. By way of partial compensation, a new opera called *Piccolomini* opened triumphantly. Charles promised Henrietta he would take her to hear it. Even as he was now frequently taking the children to the Crystal Palace, which in 1854 had been purchased for seventy thousand pounds by the Brighton Railway Company and moved to Sydenham, eight and a half miles northwest of Down. The children grew enamored of the varying exhibitions.

At the end of March a peace treaty was signed ending the Crimean War; but on its heels came a declaration of war against Persia, followed by the shelling of Canton, which marked the beginning of a war of conquest against China by the Royal Navy.

"That old saying, 'There is nothing certain except death and taxes,'" groused Charles, "has to be expanded to death, taxes and war." Would Malthus claim that wars were necessary to keep the population figures down?

He had become a conduit for the daily news, which he edited carefully to fit the ages of the children who happened to be listening. He did not spare Emma because she did not become emotionally upset, as he did. Somewhere in the back of her mind was the idea that newspapers were an inky toy, concocted each day for the entertainment of guileless males. The day passed, the news passed; other patter took its place. It was so ephemeral! What was permanent and important for Emma was the well-being of her husband, children, home.

It was during the latter part of April 1856 that he resolved to join all issues and set forth his premise to be tested in an ordeal by fire. He invited to Down House Charles Lyell, Joseph Hooker, Thomas Huxley and Thomas Wollaston, with their wives. It had taken weeks of letter writing to manage to have the four men convene at Down House together. He sent Lettington with the carriage to the station at Sydenham, where he had hired a second vehicle to bring them all out. He was not looking for agreement from his four friends; rather for the challenge of all possible criticism of his fundamental thesis.

So far in 1856 Lyell had published only one paper, but his *Principles of Geology* was in its ninth, expanded edition. Joseph Hooker was continuing his work on the flora of Tasmania. Thomas Huxley had been married less than a year. A prominent doctor had given Miss Henrietta

Heathorn six months of life. Marriage to the robustious but at the same time gentle Thomas Huxley had cured her. For two years now he had been a lecturer at the government School of Mines on Jermyn Street and head naturalist to the Geological Survey. He had turned down the chair of natural history at the University of Edinburgh because he preferred to work in London and had just been asked to give a series of lectures at the Royal Institution. Thirty-four-year-old Thomas Wollaston had devoted himself to a study of the beetles of Madeira, the Cape de Verdes and St. Helena, whence he deduced evidence in support of the belief in the submerged continent of Atlantis, his favorite fantasy. His first scientific paper had been written when he was an undergraduate at Jesus College, Cambridge.

By late Friday afternoon the guests and their luggage had been deposited on the steps of Down House. Emma had doubled up the children to make four bedrooms available. She had also hired an extra woman from the village to help with the cooking. When all of the guests had refreshed themselves and come down to the sitting room for a glass of sherry, she told them:

"I reasoned that during such a busy day you might not have had time for a substantial midday meal. If you'll cross the hall to the dining room I believe I can make it up to you."

The dining table was beautiful with the light of half a dozen candles. Sally had prepared a grilled salmon, curried veal with potato balls, apple marmalade pudding covered with bread crumbs. The guests ate their way enthusiastically through each course. Unlike her first dinner party for Charles's confreres at 12 Upper Gower Street, where the men had spoken in so low a key as to kill all conversation, this evening everyone was speaking and laughing at the same time, in festive mood. No sooner had they finished their salmon than they broke into a discussion of the ice age; whether it was possible for northern plants to migrate south as far as the equator, even as tribes of humans had; whether the only creatures who survived after the ice had melted were those which had been able to crawl, generation after generation, up the mountains, as in Ceylon, Java, the Organ Mountains in Brazil. The women cut underneath the men's excited voices and carried on a homely interchange.

After supper the party returned to the sitting room where Emma played for them. Charles set up two backgammon boards with alternating contestants. They retired early, for Charles had asked his associates to be downstairs at seven for breakfast. By eight o'clock the five men were closeted behind the closed door of the study. Since Charles Lyell was the senior member of the group, at fifty-eight, Charles insisted he take the armchair in the corner. At forty-seven, Darwin seated himself on Lyell's right, Hooker, thirty-nine, was on the left and Huxley, the youngest at thirty, was content with the padded footstool Charles had been using all the years of dissecting barnacles.

Charles's gaze observed the clean-shaven faces, the alert eyes, the set of the heads carrying inquisitive minds. All five had traveled to distant and exotic lands, had braved danger, had returned with treasures of scholarship.

"I'd like to ask your opinion first about geographical distribution of plant and animal species around the world. I believe there is an explanation for the similarities of living things on lands or islands quite distant from each other."

"There is," replied Joseph Hooker, "and it is *not* your theory of seeds floating across oceans. At some time in our geological history there were vast continents that connected such faraway places as New Zealand and South America. There were other continents, since lost, that provided an entire circle around the world; hundreds of small islands are the tops of submerged continents."

"I agree," said Wollaston stoutly. "I am convinced that Plato's continent of Atlantis was a connecting land mass that enabled the varying species of beetles to move with safety and be found in widely separated areas."

Charles decided to answer Hooker.

"My experiments with seeds has proved that some can stay alive in salt water for as long as eighty days, and germinate when washed ashore. This is also true of the eggs of lizards and snakes. I have seen that the excrement of long-flight birds can contain seeds which will flower once they are deposited on fertile soil, no matter how far from their homeland. The same is true of big birds which fly with mud-encrusted claws. Inside that mud are living seeds."

"Makes sense," growled Huxley; "or at least better sense than inventing a continent every time we are confounded by the appearance of a plant or bird or reptile thousands of miles from its nearest kin."

"Let us get on with your species theory," suggested Lyell. "Darwin, what about human beings?"

Startled, Charles answered:

"What about them?"

"Aren't they a species?"

"Of course."

"Then what is the history of their evolution?"

"Oh no!" he exclaimed vehemently. "Man is an untouchable area."

"How so?" Lyell asked blandly. "Could we not have come from an ourang-outang? En route from Borneo and Sumatra? The males were over four feet in height, not too much shorter than the exquisite bull dancers of Crete. You will one day be forced to tackle the descent of man. That's why I cannot accept your approach, for man does not fit into the pattern. The generally received opinion is that all the leading varieties of the human family have sprung from a single pair, a doctrine against which there appears to me to be no sound objection."

Charles refused to take the bait, asked instead:

"Is there anyone in this room who agrees with my theory that the struggle for existence is the *modus operandi* for the evolution of our modern forms of life?"

His four guests looked at one another. Lyell and Hooker then said that Charles would need a body of authenticated information to prove his contention about the disappearance of former varieties and species. Thomas Huxley claimed that he, himself, would have to do more work in the field. Thomas Wollaston was the only one disturbed by Charles's statement. Charles's approach offended the sanctity of Genesis. His manner was a little reproachful.

"True, there have been changes in our world and its creatures. We all agree that there was an ice age, as well as many ages before it. Yet they are logically explained. When God determined to make a dramatic change in our earth, for reasons best known to Himself, He simply created different continents, seas, fish, birds, flowers, trees. If He could create a world in the first place, in six days, why could He not re-create that world in as many different forms as He wished? It makes sense."

Their arguments lasted until noon, when Charles took his friends for a five-flint-stone walk around the Sandwalk. After dinner they went their separate ways to rest. At three o'clock they returned to the study, where Charles told them about his work among fifteen varieties of the common pigeon.

"This is where the work of classification is done so well by men like Henslow, Brown, you, Hooker, and Asa Gray at Harvard. The job is enormous because over the surface of the earth, in the air and in the seas there are hundreds of thousands of minute variations in all living things brought about, I claim, by the harsh, ofttimes cruel need to change, to adapt to immediate surroundings in order to survive. It is on the basis of this classification that my concept of natural selection must stand or fall."

On Sunday morning, while the others attended the Rev. Mr. Innes's church service in the village, Charles asked Lyell to remain behind so that he could reveal his growing weight of evidence.

"Lyell, doesn't natural selection have to be defined as the preservation of favored races in the struggle for life? In this contest any variety of a species has the best chance to survive if it has made organic adjustments to changes of food supply, predators, environment, overcrowding.

Those varieties or species which do not make the imperative adaptations die off. You've seen enough fossils in your lifetime. Why did they become extinct while variants lived on?"

Lyell looked about for a proper chair to lay his face on, then settled for striding about the room.

"I cut my wisdom teeth on Lyell's *Principles of Geology*," said Charles emphatically. "A great master does not produce thickheaded students."

Lyell had the grace to blush. He hunched his big shoulders forward.

"What I want to suggest most strongly, Darwin, is that you begin a book about your views, a great deal more detailed than the essays you wrote some years ago."

Charles did not respond.

Lyell persisted.

"Use the materials that best symbolize your departures. You should begin very quickly, before someone parades in and is given the credit for the whole concept."

Charles answered reluctantly:

"I certainly should be vexed if anyone were to publish my doctrine before me."

After midday dinner there was time for one more session in the study before it was necessary to drive the guests back to the station.

"What I need," he told the men, "are specific reactions to my theory. Please be so kind as to throw hard questions at me."

They did, demanding: What were the stages by which an insectivorous and terrestrial animal acquired the capacious wings of the bat? What of the penguin, which used its wings exclusively as paddles when diving? How explain the formerly flying reptiles? Or the frequency in the lower animals in which the same fluid and tissue served for digestion, nutrition and respiration? How could six hundred caterpillars in a uniform part of the valley of the Amazon evolve into six hundred different species of butterflies?

Quietly he responded, stressing his natural-selection-for-survival theory, the mutability of species. Quietly he listened to their rebuttals.

As he handed his guests into the carriages, he told them:

"It has been a heady experience. I have much to thank you for, particularly your patience."

Joseph Hooker put his wife into the brougham standing in front of the house, then turned and said:

"As I suggested once before, I always leave with the feeling that I have imparted nothing and am carrying away more than I can stagger under."

"Do you also urge me to publish my species work?"

"I do, Darwin."

"But how? I will not expose an editor or council to heretical materials for which they might be abused."

"All new concepts bring abuse," replied Hooker. "Editors and scientific societies know this; they have the right of refusal. Or they can publish with a note saying that the views expressed are those of the author and not of the society or publisher."

"I don't know that I have the stomach to start what Lyell describes as 'an enormous book.' It would be easier for me to start with the idea of a thin volume. . . ."

"Start any way you like," said Hooker urgently; *"but start immediately!"*

4.

He assembled his materials, a chore that took more than two weeks, and on May 14 settled into his big chair, put his writing board across its arms. For note making he had used any scrap of paper available. However this was to be a proper manuscript. He took from the sideboard a folio of paper eight inches by twelve in size, set up his inkwell and pen, began to write:

No one ought to feel surprise at much remaining as yet unexplained in regard to the origin of species and varieties, if he make due allowance for our profound ignorance in regard to the mutual relations of the many beings which live around us. Who can explain why one species ranges widely and is very numerous, and why another allied species has a narrow range and is rare? Yet these relations are of the highest importance, for they determine the present welfare and, as I believe, the future success and modification of every inhabitant of this world. Still less do we know of the mutual relations of the innumerable inhabitants of the world during the many past geological epochs in its history. . . .

Pen and pages flew. He wrote on only one side of the paper, but sometimes went back and wrote between the lines. If a thought displeased him he ran his pen through it. He used symbols for interpolations, added phrases in the margins, sometimes turned the sheet over to add a new paragraph. He scrawled pencil reminders to himself, such as "Get Huxley to read this." He also pinned or pasted slips of paper onto the pages.

His handwriting, as he himself said, was "dreadfully bad," but he knew that he was thinking and organizing coherently. A scrivener would give him a fair copy. He also realized his spelling and punctuation were inconsistent. That did not trouble him. His one task was to make a strong and lucid case, while at the same time admitting its drawbacks, reservations and difficulties, to prove his assumption about what the philosophers called "the mystery of mysteries."

In his hours of relaxation he worked about the grounds, watching plants come up enclosed in the roots of trees. He confounded his children by showing them that twenty-nine plants had sprouted from a tablespoon of mud he had dug out of his little pond. He wrote to Fox the number of folio pages he already had from his month's effort. When Fox replied with high enthusiasm about the value of the contribution, he replied:

> . . . What you say about my Essay, I daresay is very true; it gave me another fit of the wibber-gibbers. I hope that I shall succeed in making it modest.

His serious reading was affording him more heartburn than edification. Thomas Wollaston's recently published *On the Variation of Species* had theology rather than nature at its base. Wollaston also denounced anyone who went beyond his own thinking as "most mischievous" . . . "absurd" . . . "unsound."

"You are like Calvin burning a heretic," Charles told him when they next met in London.

"Ultra-honesty is your characteristic," Wollaston retorted.

He received a letter from Samuel Woodward, an assistant in the Department of Geology and Mineralogy at the British Museum who had previously published a capital book on shells. Woodward also maintained that all the islands in the Pacific and Atlantic were the remains of continents, submerged within the period of existing species. Charles fairly exploded. He protested to Lyell:

> Summing up all the continents created of late years by Woodward, Hooker, Wollaston and yourself . . . a nice extension of land they make altogether!

To Hooker he wrote:

> I must cease being rabid and try to feel humble, and allow you all to make continents as easily as a cook does pancakes!

It was now five and a half years since Emma had given birth to Horace. She and Charles were convinced that Henry Holland was right in saying that nature had its time to stop conception. In June 1856, at forty-eight, she found that she was pregnant again.

They were sitting together in the window bow of their bedroom. He put his arm about her shoulder. A dozen apologetic sentences came halfway to his lips. At length he murmured:

"We'll do everything possible to make life easier and happier for you."

She laid her head on his shoulder.

"It's not my way to quarrel with God's will."

The French say, "The appetite comes while eating." The English state, "Thinking comes while writing." Before the middle of July, when he had been writing consecutively for two months, he solved a thorny problem. He wrote to Lyell:

> I have just finished in great detail giving evidence of coolness in tropical regions during the glacial epoch, and the consequent migration of organisms. . . . It harmonizes with the modification of species.

To Hooker, he observed:

> What a book a devil's chaplain might write on the clumsy, wasteful, blundering, low and horribly cruel works of nature.

It was singular, the relationship he had developed with Joseph Hooker. They loved and admired each other, were together as often as possible, wrote to each other long letters every few days; yet continued to wage war on each other's beliefs. Curled up in his comfortable chair in the study, Charles bombarded the ever patient Hooker with queries:

> You speak most truly about multiple creations by direct act of God, versus my notions. If any one case could be proved, I should be smashed; but I try to take as much pains as possible to give the strongest cases opposed to me.
>
> And now I am going to beg almost as great a favor as a man can beg of another: It is to read, but well copied out, my pages (about forty!!) on Alpine floras and faunas, Arctic and Antarctic floras and faunas, and the supposed cold mundane period. It would be really an enormous advantage to me, as I am sure otherwise to make botanical blunders.

His forty pages accounted for almost half of what he had originally thought would constitute his "thin volume." As the weeks passed he watched his pile of manuscript inch taller and taller.

"Very well," he buttressed himself, "the nature of my material does not permit it to be contained within a small book."

Lyell's letters indicated that he "was coming around at a railway pace on the mutability of species."

In mid-July he authorized Charles to put into the preface of his proposed book the fact that he approved the work. Charles was overjoyed. Sir Charles Lyell's approval of an approach to the origin of species which went infinitely beyond the exploratory work of Dr. Erasmus Darwin, the French scientists, Lamarck and Cuvier, and Robert Chambers's *Vestiges*, now out for twelve years without having gained respectability, what a shock that would be to his fellow scientists! It would give the book credence. But when would he publish? He was already into his second hundred pages!

Whatever spare time he could conjure up he spent in the garden with the children, even five-year-old Horace working as one of his helpers, attempting to crossbreed flowers. He had little success with sweet peas, orchids or hollyhocks. To Joseph Hooker, showing the Darwins the new lake being created in Kew Gardens, to be fed from the river Thames, he complained:

"I was so ignorant that I did not even know that you cannot castrate sweet peas without doing them fatal injury."

"Neither did anyone else. But I'm not going to let you carry this alone. I'll start crossbreeding at Kew. By the by, I found when I had finished your pages that all the individuals of the same species which you refer to seem to have a continuous distribution."

"In short, they have . . . evolved?"

"It would appear so."

Charles's lean face broke into a gratified grin.

"It does me a world of good to see you come round, even partially."

Thus fortified, he decided it would be helpful if he could make a single, succinct statement on what his lifework was about. For this purpose he chose to answer Asa Gray at Harvard, who was becoming America's outstanding botanist. He wrote to his friend:

> . . . Either species have been independently created, or they have descended from other species. . . . I think it can be shown to be probable that man gets his most distinct varieties by preserving such as arise best worth keeping, and destroying the others. . . . As an honest man, I must tell you that I have come to the heterodox conclusion that there are no such things as independently created species, that species are only strongly defined varieties. . . .
>
> I must say one word more in justification (for I feel sure that your tendency will be to despise me and my crotchets), that all my notions about how species change are derived from

long-continued study of the works of (and converse with) agriculturists and horticulturists; and I believe I see my way pretty clearly on the means used by nature to change her species and *adapt* them to the wondrous and exquisitely beautiful contingencies to which every living being is exposed. . . .

He said to Hooker, when next they met:

"What a science natural history will be when we are in our graves, when the laws of change are thought one of the most important parts of natural history."

Partly as a result of his letter, he received an invitation from Asa Gray to come to the United States to lecture on his findings, free passage provided back and forth on the steamers.

His study was blocked out of his mind for the moment and he was back on H.M.S. *Beagle*, young, in his hammock in the poop cabin, the oceans roiling beneath him, nibbling on his father's prescription of biscuit and raisins.

Emma was having a difficult summer. He read to her every evening. Fortunately it was a rich year for popular literature. From the London bookshops he secured *Callista* by John Henry Newman, *Aurora Leigh*, a novel in verse by Elizabeth Barrett Browning, *John Halifax, Gentleman* by Dinah Maria Mulock, *The Shaving of Shagpat* by George Meredith.

He took her around the Sandwalk when she wanted fresh air and exercise, a three- or four-pebble journey. They received good news about their second boy, George, now eleven; he was doing exceptionally well at a school in Clapham run by the Rev. Mr. Pritchard, an admirer of the sciences. George, described by his father as "an enthusiastic entomologist," was not confined to the study of Greek and Latin but was given a good deal of arithmetic, taught drawing and modern languages, and encouraged to build a collection of beetles and insects. He was allowed to return home for one day each month.

Charles went nowhere. In addition to his burgeoning manuscript, he floated plants in salt water, worked with his pigeons and rabbits. He took notice of the differences in the skeletons of domestic rabbits and thought it odd that no zoologist had ever considered it worth while to look at the very real differences in the skeletal structures of domestic animals and birds. He became convinced that botany had been followed in a much more philosophical spirit than zoology. He scarcely liked to trust a general remark in zoology without the botanists concurring.

He was putting in a full workday and had not been indisposed for a considerable time; his only physical problem was a touch of lumbago which made his back feel rigid. He decided that in the spring he would try the hydropathic establishment at close-by Moor Park for a fortnight; he could not bring himself to go back to Malvern with little Annie buried in the graveyard there.

Over the autumn months he continued to pile up hundreds of carefully documented pages; writing such an incredible number of long inquiring letters to breeders, crossers, travelers, that the correspondence alone would have exhausted almost any other man in England.

He had started with the subject he knew most about, variation under domestication. He pointed out how, under a principle of selection, breeders had modified their breeds of cattle, sheep, race horses, fantail and pouter pigeons.

> At the present time, eminent breeders try methodical selection with a distinct object in view, to make a new strain or sub-breed superior to anything of the kind.

The same situation was true in the botanical world, where the increased size and beauty of rose, dahlia, heartsease and other flowers was considerable when compared with the parent stock. The vegetables in the kitchen garden, the pear and apple trees, strawberries, had been vastly improved because of the wonderful skill of gardeners who, when a slightly better variety chanced to appear, selected and cultivated it.

By October 13 he had completed his chapter on Variation under Domestication and part of his discussion on Geographical Distribution. Needing reassurance, he took this part of the manuscript to Hooker's house and enjoyed a pleasant evening before running to the station at nine-thirty, barely making the train home. Hooker sent a lengthy letter of appraisal:

> I have finished the reading of your MS. and have been very much delighted and instructed. Your case is a most strong one and gives me a much higher idea of *change* than I had previously entertained. . . . The first half you will be able to put more clearly when you polish up. I have in several cases made pencil alterations in details as to words, &c., to enable myself to follow better; some of it is rather stiff reading. I have a page or two of notes for discussion, many of which were answered as I got further on with the MS. . . .

He had a spell of working with hawks; then turned his attention again to the dissemination of seeds across oceans. The seeds which an eagle had had in its stomach for eighteen hours were so fresh that when Charles planted them two oats, one clover and one beet came up. During his walks he examined the excrement of small birds, finding six different kinds of seeds. One partridge he discovered had enough of dry earth on one foot to carry a quantity of live seeds. When he thought of the millions of migratory quail, it seemed to him strange indeed that the seeds of any plants would not have been transported across the arms of the sea. Another of his seeds had germinated after two and a half hours in an owl's stomach. His ornithology friends assured him that the owl could carry the seeds "God knows how many miles; in a storm perhaps four to five hundred."

His exclamation upon hearing this was a triumphant "Hurrah!"

Though he tried to condense, it was a tiresome drawback to his satisfaction that every chapter ran to an inordinate length. His present chapter, number three, on the causes of fertility and sterility and on crossbreeding in nature, had actually run out to a hundred manuscript pages, and yet he did not think any of it superfluous.

Emma gave birth to her tenth child on December 6, another boy, whom they named Charles Waring. Their doctor administered the chloroform now widely used in England because Queen Victoria had approved of it and had been put to sleep with the anesthetic while bearing her fourth son and eighth child. For Emma it had been such a sudden and explosive birth that the doctor exclaimed:

"It was a good thing I was sitting by or your new son would have been born without any help from me."

By mid-December Charles had finished his third big chapter, which he entitled, On Possibility of All Organisms Crossing: On Susceptibility of Reproduction to Change. One reason he was moving ahead fast was that he was employing useful pages he had written in the 1837 notebook, as well as good references from his second notebook of February to July 1838.

"Plagiarizing myself," he mused. "I couldn't write these passages any better today so why not use the originals?"

One evening when Emma was feeling pert again, he sat on the edge of their bed holding her hand.

"Half a dozen boys! Good heavens, to think of all the sendings to school, and the professions afterward."

"Not to mention dowries for our two girls!" she teased gently. "Do you think we'll be able to afford it all?"

He brought his account books upstairs, turned up the wick of their oil lamp. He had kept these accounts since their first year on Upper Gower Street. He was still breaking down the expenditures into some twenty separate categories: food, oil, soap, tea for servants, books, dresses for Emma and the girls, clothing for the boys, wages for the help, tuition . . . His income was also recorded in accurate amounts so that the family never spent as much as it took in from various railroad bonds, London Dock bonds, the Wedgwood factory.

"We'll manage all right. In 1854 our income was £4,603, from which we saved £2,127 for investment. We took in a little less in 1855, £4,267, but we saved and invested even more, £2,270. Last year we had an income of £4,048, managing to invest £2,250. Without I am convinced of my error, our income should continue to rise as the children get older and our annual surplus earns its own return."

"I thank you heartily for the reassurance," Emma murmured in mock relief. "For a moment there I feared we were going to raise uneducated Darwins."

"That would grieve me beyond anything."

They laughed together.

He spent the month of January 1857 completing his fourth chapter, Variation under Nature. The intensity and strain of putting the material together in a tightly logical structure wore him out. He confessed to Emma:

"I'm not so well as I was."

"You are working too hard."

"Is there any other way? The book will be very big. I mean to make my manuscript as perfect as ever I can. I am like Croesus, overwhelmed by my riches. I've been taking some mineral acids I read about, with some effect, I think."

Emma suggested he take a holiday at the hydropathy spa at Moor Park, only forty miles away, now, instead of waiting for the spring.

"How I can leave all my writings and experiments, I know not."

She searched his face carefully.

"Charles, my good soul, would there be a touch of egoism in all this? Are you perhaps seeking after a great fame from your book?"

Charles dipped a shoulder, as though asking, "Who can tell?"

"I have got most deeply interested in my subject, is all. Though I wish I could set less value on the bauble fame, either present or posthumous, than I do. But not, I think, to any extreme degree. As I know myself, I would work just as hard, though with less gusto, if I knew that my book would be published forever anonymously."

One of his reasons for isolating himself in the country had been to avoid the competitions and jealousies of the scientists of London. He had observed this phenomenon in his earliest days of attendance at the meetings of the Zoological Society, and in particular at the meeting of the Royal Society in the spring of 1848 when Richard Owen had attacked Gideon Mantell. Now in 1857 a virulent quarrel broke out between Richard Owen and Thomas Huxley. Upon Huxley's return from his four-year journey on H.M.S. *Rattlesnake*, Owen had written to the

First Lord of the Admiralty to secure Huxley a paying appointment on H.M.S. *Fisguard*.

"Owen is, in my estimation, great," Huxley had told Charles, "from the fact of smoking his cigar to singing his song like a brick."

Owen had also joined with Charles and others in getting Huxley elected a fellow of the Royal Society. Even so, Charles had felt compelled to pass on to Huxley the counseling he himself had received from Lyell:

"Be careful about Owen. He will turn on you. He does on everyone. It is a need of his nature."

It had not taken Huxley long to learn of the dual nature of Richard Owen, who was both feared and hated by most of his contemporaries for his ill-natured tricks and the pillorying of his subordinates. Owen was a superior man and did not conceal that he knew it. He was civil to Huxley until he learned that the younger man was capable of unhorsing him as the undisputed master of the field of zoology. The first incident occurred when Owen blocked the publication in the Royal Society's *Transactions* of Huxley's, On the Morphology of the Cephalous Mollusca. Huxley commented:

"Owen has come to look upon the natural world as his special preserve, and no poachers allowed."

Charles had watched the growing antagonism between the two men come to a head in the early part of the year when Owen, taking advantage of his position at the School of Mines, unwarrantedly assumed the title of Professor of Palaeontology, seriously undermining Huxley's position there. Huxley broke off all relations with Owen, exclaiming:

"Owen is determined not to let me or anyone else rise if he can help it. Let him beware. On my own subjects I am his master, and am quite ready to fight half a dozen dragons. Although he has a bitter pen, I flatter myself that on occasion I can match him in that department also."

Charles perceived that these two antagonists, the embattled Old Guard trying to maintain the status quo, the younger man bruising his way upward toward leadership, would one day engage in a monumental battle, one that would shake the entire scientific world and leave an indelible imprint on history. What he could not know, or even wildly surmise, was that he would be not only at the epicenter of the eruption but its actual provocateur.

5.

He had frequently invited now Rear Admiral Robert FitzRoy and his wife to visit Down House. FitzRoy's first wife, Mary O'Brien, had died, leaving him with four children. He had then married a cousin's daughter. The FitzRoys accepted and Charles looked forward to reliving once again their companionable years aboard H.M.S. *Beagle*. FitzRoy quickly revealed that he had come for another purpose. The two men retired to the study, Charles drew up a ladder-back chair for FitzRoy, who had aged very much. His hair had grown gray, his eyes looked hard. Yet he was still a handsome figure of a man.

"Darwin, do you recall the trip we took up the Santa Cruz River in April 1834 in our whaleboats? When we crossed some plains composed of rolled stones embedded in diluvial detritus about a hundred feet in depth, I said to you, 'This could never have been effected by a forty days' flood.'"

"I remember. The story is in the last chapter of your book."

"That was because of my knowing extremely little of the Bible; because of my ignorance of Scripture. I've learned about some of your theories. You are repudiating the literal truth of the Book of Genesis, are you not?"

"Nature disproves it. I merely record what I observe. Nature never lies."

"But the Bible does! That's shocking of you."

"Evidence is growing all over the world that this planet of ours is many millions of years old. That all life on it has evolved, changed, adapted to circumstances of overpopulation, food supply, predators, climate. Many species could not adapt in time and they became extinct. You saw the fossil bones in Punta Alta. Some species have adapted so radically because of need that their internal organs, let alone their external appearance, have altered so greatly over the millennia that they are hardly recognizable. Whatever life we have on earth today constitutes the survival of the best adapters."

FitzRoy's face flushed.

"And do you conclude that man could have been first created in an infant or a savage state? That appears to my apprehension impossible. After a few hours of apathetic existence he must have perished. The only idea I can reconcile to reason is that man was created perfect in body, perfect in mind, and knowing by inspiration enough for the part he had to perform."

FitzRoy went on to explain that the first wanderers who left Asia Minor in a civilized state were before long lacking writing materials, clothes, their children taught only to provide for their daily wants, degenerating further from the traces of their early perfection to become savages!

His face became grim.

"Have we a shadow of ground for thinking that wild animals or

plants have improved since their creation? Can any reasonable man believe that the first of a race, species or kind was the most inferior? Then
how for a moment can false philosophers imagine that there were separate beginnings of savage races, at different times and in different
places? . . ."

He could not contain himself.

"The Mosaic account of the Creation is intimately connected with
that of the Deluge. The knowledge of Moses was superhuman. His
declaration that light was created before the sun and moon was divinely
inspired. Does not the first chapter of Genesis say, 'God divided the
light from the darkness. And God called the light Day, and the darkness he called Night. And the evening and the morning were the first
day'? And was it not until the sixteenth verse that God made two great
lights, the greater to rule the day, the lesser to rule the night? . . ."

Charles had no desire to quarrel with his house guest, let alone his
former captain and friend. He spoke in a conciliatory tone:

"My friend, I have no wish to take away from the marvelous poetry
of the Old Testament. I value it on that basis as much as any
man. . . ."

It was no use. FitzRoy plunged on for a full hour, good wind in his
sails, quoting Scripture, chapter and verse, to prove that the Book of
Genesis was correct in every detail. The workings of God were perfect.
Charles sank deeper into his chair, using it as a sheltered cove in a
storm. FitzRoy's first wife had been intensely religious. Was he honor-
ing her memory by fighting for her beliefs?

FitzRoy abruptly ended his sermon. Charles sprang up.

"Come, sir, let us take a walk. This countryside of Kent is one of the
most gently rolling greenswards in England. Then we can return for hot
buttered scones and tea before the fire in the sitting room. I should like
to get better acquainted with your Maria."

His amiability saved the day. He kept the conversation going through
tea and supper. Sensing something wrong, Emma too held the conver-
sational roof up over their heads. The next morning the FitzRoys returned to London, Charles sending them in his carriage to the new, and
closer, railway station at Beckenham. FitzRoy briefly and unsmilingly
shook Charles's proffered hand at the front door. When they had gone
Charles said to himself:

"I have the unhappy premonition that I shall never see my beau
ideal, Robert FitzRoy, again."

The work progressed. On March 3, 1857, he finished his fifth chapter,
"Struggle for Existence," and only four weeks later had completed his
sixth and pivotal section, "Natural Selection." His inability to stabilize
the amount of work each day distressed him. He said to Emma:

"I never know when I wake up how much material I will have completed before nightfall."

"Why not use your Sandwalk technique?" Emma vouchsafed. "Decide before you start how many pages you want to achieve, put a number of flint pebbles together, and kick one out of the way each time you complete a roundelay. When there are no more pebbles left, your day's work is done."

"Emma, you're a genius. If only it were as easy to circumnavigate an idea as it is to walk around a sandpath. . . ."

Yet, metaphorically at least, Emma's idea worked for him. Each time he felt he had proved a point and had footnoted the reference work to buttress it, he kicked a little stone away from his self-assigned work pile.

Neither Charles nor Emma remembered when they first began noticing that there was something unusual about the new baby. It was not that he was ill or in pain, for he rarely cried. He took nourishment, grew physically at what appeared to be a normal rate. However he was lethargic. He did not move his fingers in front of his eyes to study them as had the other children. Nor did his eyes sparkle when Charles or Emma picked him up to fondle him.

"His face is expressionless," Charles commented as they stood on either side of the crib. "I've watched the play of emotions on our little ones' faces, made notes on their wide variety. I wish Miss Thorley had not retired. I do not care for this new governess, Miss Pugh."

"It's the nursemaid who takes care of the baby, not Miss Pugh." Emma's jaw was firmly set.

"I know children develop at different rates. Maybe he finds the crib confining. On a warm day we must put him out on a rug and let him move about."

"I'll dangle musical toys and brightly colored cards to awaken his interest," Emma suggested. "Can a four-month-old be bored?"

"None of ours has been."

Henrietta was also a worry. She had developed an interest in ill-health. She was sometimes listless, without appetite. With the loss of Annie ever fresh in their minds, Etty received loving care and constant attention. When on one occasion she was told that she must take breakfast in bed she got so enamored of the idea that she never relinquished it. She told her parents:

"Even when I marry I'm always going to have breakfast in bed."

During the last week of April Charles went to the hydropathy spa at Moor Park in Surrey near Aldershot. He liked Dr. Edward Lane, his wife and her mother, who were the proprietors. They made him welcome. The treatment was a mild one, a daily shallow douche and sitz bath. Dr. Lane was very young; Charles found this his only fault. But he was well read, and Charles preferred him to Dr. Gully because he did not believe in as many eccentric theories, nor did he try to explain that which neither he nor any other doctor could explain.

The countryside was agreeable for walking. At the end of the first week he was surprised at how much good the passing days had done him and became convinced, all over again, that the only thing for chronic cases was the water cure. Having brought no books with him, and having embroidered not one stitch into the fabric of species, he felt so well that on May 1, beginning his second week at Moor Park, he decided to answer the letter he had received from Alfred Russel Wallace which had been written in the Celebes, across the Macassar Strait from Borneo, on October 10 of the year before, and reached Down, after some five and a half months in transit, just as Charles was leaving for Moor Park. He wrote to Wallace:

> My dear Sir,
> . . . I can plainly see that we have thought much alike and to a certain extent have come to similar conclusions. In regard to the paper in the *Annals*, I agree to the truth of almost every word of your paper; and I daresay that you will agree with me that it is very rare to find oneself agreeing pretty closely with any theoretical paper; for it is lamentable how each man draws his own different conclusions from the very same facts. This summer will make the 20th (!) year since I opened my first notebook on the question how and in what way do species and varieties differ from each other. I am now preparing my work for publication, but I find the subject so very large that though I have written many chapters, I do not suppose I shall go to press for two years. I have never heard how long you intend staying in the Malay Archipelago; I wish I might profit by the publication of your "Travels" there before my work appears, for no doubt you will reap a harvest of facts. . . .

During his second week he did a deal of vigorous hiking about the Surrey countryside, observing the effects of animals on vegetation. Eight or ten years earlier a part of the common, with clumps of old Scotch firs, had been enclosed. Inside the enclosure young trees were springing up, looking exactly as if planted by man, so many being of the same age. In that part of the common not yet enclosed, he could find not one young tree within a matter of miles. Walking a distance away, and looking closely in the heather, he again found tens of thousands of young Scotch firs, thirty in one square yard, with their tops nibbled off by the cattle which occasionally roamed those heaths. He commented to Joseph Hooker:

"What a wondrous problem it is, what a play of forces determining the kind and proportion of each plant in a square yard of turf! And yet we are pleased to wonder when some animal or plant becomes extinct."

At the end of the second week he felt rested and refreshed, and said good-by to Dr. Lane and his family.

His own coach had come to pick him up, arriving the evening before; but by the time he reached Down House at the end of the day he had caught cold. When he entered his study the following morning he felt as unwell as he had before he had left for Moor Park. He began to vomit. He had to admit to Emma:

"Our cousin-adversary Dr. Henry Holland appears to have been right. It is striking how well I feel when I am on holiday, at a pleasant spa, with gracious hosts and a countryside suited for walking. The moment I start work again my health tumbles downhill."

"What can you do?"

"Grumble. I fear that my head will stand no thought, but I would rather be the wretched contemptible invalid which I am, than live the life of an idle squire."

His wide-ranging interests were inexhaustible. He tried to learn whether any breed of pig, crossed with the Chinese or Neapolitan pig, was able to breed true. Then he did a study of the coloring and marks of the ancient grandfathers of the horse, ass and zebra. In his meadow, out of sixteen kinds of seed he had sown, fifteen germinated; in a bit of ground two by three feet he daily marked each seedling weed as it appeared over a period of three months. Three hundred and fifty-seven had already been killed, chiefly by slugs.

Who ate the slugs, those slow-moving, slimy gastropods? Small land animals, reptiles, birds? . . . It was indeed a struggle for existence, as he had titled his fifth chapter. Rippling through the manuscript pages of this section, he came across his subtitle, Mutual Checks of Animals and Plants. He read from his own sheets:

> We have considered as yet almost exclusively the manner in which animals check the increase of other animals. But plants & animals are even more importantly related; as are plants with plants. . . . All animals live on plants either directly or indirectly; & their breath is the plants' chief food; so that the relation of the two kingdoms on a grand scale is very obvious. One at first supposes that grass-eating animals devour all plants nearly alike; but of Swedish plants it has been ascertained that oxen eat 276 kinds & refuse 218; goats eat 449 & re-

fuse 126; swine eat 72 & refuse 271, &c. Southward of La Plata
I was astonished, as others have been, at the change effected
in the appearance of the plains by the depasturing of the cattle, & could not for some time believe but that there must
have been a change in the geological nature of the country.
What plants the many small rodents live upon is seldom
known, but everyone must have heard of the destruction of
whole plantations by mice & rabbits. . . . I have sometimes
fancied that the very common prickliness of the bushes of desert plains was chiefly due to the greater protection from animals requisite for any bush to live. . . . It has also been
shown in detail by Forskahl that those plants which are not
eaten by cattle are attacked in an extraordinary degree by insects; from 30 to 50 species sometimes preying on a single
plant. I presume a plant preyed on by both insects & quadruped would be exterminated. . . .

In June of 1857 he received a pleasant turn; the Rev. Mr. Innes and
the Lubbocks, father and son, came to Down House to ask if he would
accept a newly vacated magistracy, or Keeper of the Peace. Charles exclaimed:
"Me? A judge? I know little about the law."
Sir John Lubbock smiled, said:
"There will be no serious crimes brought before you. No adjudication
of large property disputes. It's mostly quarrels among neighbors over
borders, fencing, stray cattle, fights while drinking, poaching. I doubt
there will be any serious law involved; more likely your common sense,
listening to the facts on both sides and then helping the parties reach
an acceptable compromise."
Charles felt vaguely flattered.
"Where would I sit?"
"At Bromley," the vicar replied. "It's the closest. Perhaps sometimes
at Maidstone, the Kent County seat. They've agreed to group the disputes in this area and set the hearings for any one day you would be
available."
Charles did not hesitate for his answer; for he had developed a sense
of loyalty to his chosen area, had received gratification from his position
as treasurer of the Down Friendly Club. He had managed their funds
as carefully as he had his own, so that in the seven years of his subscribing and regulating, they had built to a most heartening sum.
"I accept, of course," he told Innes and the Lubbocks. "When would
I be sworn in?"
"July 3 has been set as the tentative date."

Emma and the children were titillated. They insisted upon coming *en famille* to the ceremony, dressed in their Sunday best. Henceforth when their father made promulgations about what the Darwins must do on a given occasion, one or the other would inquire:

"Is that a final decision handed down from the Bench? Or do we have the right of appeal?"

When they got into a dispute over toys or games or precedence at table, one of them would be bound to say:

"Magistrate, we neighbors have a thorny issue. . . ."

Charles enjoyed the ribbing. His duties in the magistracy were not demanding, nor did they interfere with his work. There was no emolument attached to the office, it was purely honorary, but it paid an oblique dividend in the area by converting him from a remote figure working in some incomprehensible field into an intimate member of the community to whom men respectfully touched their hats as he went by, and to whom the women of the neighborhood, young and old, curtsied. He made no enemies and remained a magistrate to the end of his days.

He took Henrietta to spend the summer with Dr. Lane's family at Moor Park, and while visiting her there learned to play billiards. He was beguiled by the game, the first to so engross him since his sessions of twenty-one at Christ's College. He was so taken by the precise skill of eye and hand needed to run up points that he vowed to install a table in Down House.

The infant Charles was not interested or amused by Emma's songs, games, toys. He did not make the early groping movements or sounds so universal in children. Put out on a rug, he did not attempt to crawl, or bring himself to a standing position by climbing the sides of his small bed. More disturbing, his eyes remained nearly blank. Charles and Emma were deeply concerned, though they distressed each other as little as possible. The doctor who had delivered the boy insisted that there was nothing to worry about.

"He's normal physically and growing well enough. He'll walk and talk when he's ready."

As the weeks and months succeeded each other and he himself reached forty-eight, Charles strove to get the Royal Medal awarded to young scientists to encourage and facilitate their experiments, rather than to older men as a reward. Research was an uphill road, rock strewn and filled with muddy potholes. He made a study of how ineffectual insects were in pollinating female holly and other plants, a life-giving rather than a life-consuming process within the intricate scheme of nature. Where no lists as yet existed in a field of animal or plant life, he made the compilations himself, long and tedious tasks in which it was easy to fall into error. When Joseph Hooker pointed out that one of his flora lists was incomplete, he answered woefully:

"I sometimes despise myself as a poor compiler as heartily as you could do, though I do not despise my whole work."

In dividing the New Zealand flora he evolved what he believed to be a proper technique of classification only to be shown by his astute neighbor and informal pupil, the twenty-three-year-old banker-naturalist son of Sir John Lubbock, that he had confused some genera. He cried:

"What a disgraceful blunder you have saved me from. It is enough to make me tear up all my manuscript and give in to despair. I heartily thank you."

The ever alert and peripatetic Thomas Huxley caught him favoring, fallaciously, a pet theory. He told the dynamic Huxley:

"Alas! A scientific man ought to have no wishes, a mere heart of stone."

When it was Charles's turn to catch out the usually thoroughgoing Huxley in an error of assumption, he exclaimed laughingly:

"It humors me to see what a bugbear I have made myself to you; when having written some very pungent and good sentence it must be very disagreeable for you to have my face rise up like an ugly ghost."

He learned that he had offended his American friend, Asa Gray, by suggesting that Gray might despise him when he heard about his theories. Gray felt his sense of loyalty and friendship had been impugned; and told Charles so. Charles responded:

> My dear Gray,
>
> I forget the exact words which I used in my former letter, but I daresay I said that I thought you would utterly despise me when I told you what views I had arrived at, which I did because I thought I was bound as an honest man to do so. . . . I did not feel in the least sure that when you knew whither I was tending, you might not think me so wild and foolish in my views (God knows, arrived at slowly enough, and I hope conscientiously), that you would think me worth no more notice or assistance. . . .
>
> As you seem interested in the subject, and as it is an *immense* advantage to me to write to you and to hear ever so briefly, what you think, I will enclose the briefest abstract of my notions on the means by which Nature makes her species. . . .

He went on for ten solid ink-packed pages, ending with:

> . . . This little abstract touches only the accumulative power of natural selection, which I look at as by far the most important element in the production of new forms. . . .

6.

It was a year, 1857, in which they could abjure their romantic novels in favor of some superb serious literature. When anyone, family, neighbor, asked, "What can I bring you for a good read?" they were able to name *The Professor, Barchester Towers, Madame Bovary, The Romany Rye, Tom Brown's School Days, Missionary Travels.*

His most relaxed period of the day remained the quiet hour after midday dinner when he stretched out in the sitting room with the copy of the daily London *Times* which arrived at the Down post office by noon. He had become a confirmed addict of the newspaper, consuming its savories as well as its sludge. The *Times* cost him a guinea for a four months' subscription, rather expensive but, to him, well worth the price. It was his way of keeping in touch with the outside world and its peregrinations. The *Times*'s coverage enabled him to follow the incessant wars being fought in distant lands and the nefarious doings of governments. For years he had been in the awkward sitz-bath position of a chauvinist believing in the beneficent greatness and the expansion of the British Empire while at the same time disagreeing with its exploitation of India. When in June of 1857 Queen Victoria had appeared before a vast crowd in Hyde Park and decorated sixty-one Crimean War survivors with the newly established Victoria Cross "For Valour," Charles tossed the newspaper onto the floor crying:

"Who decorates the dead? All those men killed in that suicidal war!"

Yet there was usually a scintilla of good news. The reading room of the British Museum, with its domed rotunda, opened with accommodations for over three hundred readers; two rows reserved for women. The first Court of Divorce was inaugurated, making divorce for the lower income classes available. New schools were opened for pauper students. The S.S. *Great Eastern* was launched on the Thames, a vessel five times larger than any afloat and reputed to be able to cross the Atlantic so smoothly as to abolish seasickness.

"Now maybe you'll accept Asa Gray's invitation to visit the United States and lecture at their universities," Emma volunteered.

At the end of September when he had finished Chapter VII, "Laws of Variation," he spread out their account books on the dining-room table to see if they could afford another expansion of Down House. For each of the years since 1851 their income had been well over £4,000; this year again they had over £2,000 surplus for investment. Along with their savings, there was Charles's inheritance from his father and Emma's inheritance of £2,000 as well. Their portfolio of investments came to approximately £50,000. When Charles looked up from the figures, he commented:

"I'm a frugal man but, by Jove, I do believe we can afford the new rooms. What do you think?"

Emma had long thought they could well afford the expansion but had preferred to let Charles make the decision in his own good time. She replied with a tiny smile at one corner of her mouth:

"Providing you don't think we'll need all our assets for the coming lawsuits."

"Who in the world would want to sue us?"

"Everyone from our Heavenly Father down to His lowliest deacon in the Church of England."

Charles burst into uproarious laughter. He threw his arms about his wife.

"Emma, how wonderful to see that you have retained your sense of humor about things of which you disapprove."

"That is when it is most necessary."

Was there a suggestion of grimness in her retort?

Charles called in the carpenter to build a new and larger drawing room on the side of the hall away from the old sitting room, with the comfortable proportion of nineteen feet by twenty-eight, and with three good-sized windows overlooking the back garden all the way to the Sandwalk; and moved the entrance door, which had opened immediately into the foyer and the staircase, back several feet to give themselves a vestibule before one reached the foyer. They divided the space above the new drawing room into two equal bedrooms; and on the floor above that, into extra children's rooms. When the new wing was plastered to match the plaster of the older section, and the new fixtures were installed, they found they had spent five hundred pounds.

"Well worth it!" Emma exclaimed, as the newly covered chaise and four varicolored, comfortable armchairs were strategically placed around the marble-topped table; her piano, expertly scraped and shellacked to look new, set in its permanent far corner by the last of the garden windows. There was a long, gold-framed mirror over the marble mantelpiece, a new end table and lamp by the sofa. She had chosen light gray and pink striped wallpaper.

"Without meaning to appear pretentious," Emma said, "we now have what looks like a drawing room, handsome and spacious. A few more pictures, a small hanging bookshelf for our leather-bound books. . . ."

They moved the dining-room furniture from the room facing the road, the darker side of the house, into the sunnier, earlier sitting room with its three-windowed bow. It was now considerably brighter.

They agreed that Down House and its grounds had become as beautiful as Maer Hall or The Mount. They had created their life, their particular place in the world, and had come home to the style of their antecedents; but with their own distinct flavor. That was what both had set out to accomplish.

When Charles Waring was ten months old and still had not attempted to walk or talk, the Darwins asked Dr. Henry Holland to come to Down House at his first opportunity. Sir Henry had long since been knighted and was busier than ever as Physician in Ordinary to Queen Victoria. He utilized a national holiday to take the train to Beckenham where Charles and his coachman met him. He asked many questions as they drove the six miles along the winding elm-, oak-, beech- and horse-chestnut-lined roads of Kent. At Down House he spent an hour alone with the little boy in an upstairs bedroom, then descended the angled staircase to find Charles and Emma in the new drawing room, pale and silent. They looked up quickly when he entered. Their usually gauche cousin wore a compassionate expression.

"I'm afraid the news is unfortunate," he told them. "The child is seriously retarded. Mentally, that is."

"But how? Why?" Emma cried in anguish.

"The how and the why are the same question, my dear cousin. His brain either failed to form or was damaged. Did anything unusual happen during his birth?"

"Our local doctor described it as explosive," Emma replied, tears in her eyes.

"There are a hundred causes that we know nothing about. Alas, I cannot see inside the little one's head."

"What is the prognosis?" demanded Charles. "What must we learn to live with?"

"Taking fastidious care of a child who may never recognize you. Also, accepting the will of God."

"I can do that." Emma was crying. "But is there no hope at all for the future?"

"There is always hope. Sometimes there are miracles. But you must reconcile yourselves to the reality. You have, how many, six, seven children? All well, normal, happy. Count your blessings. Do not dwell on what cannot be changed or rectified."

"We'll try, Cousin Henry," said Charles somberly. "Our greatest appreciation from Emma and myself for making the trip down. I'll accompany you to the station."

"No need. I'll nap en route."

He kissed Emma, shook hands with Charles, and was gone, leaving behind a confused, frightened and saddened set of parents who could not help asking themselves, albeit silently:

"Of what sin are we guilty that our littlest one should be so tragically doomed?"

Because of Charles's cordial response in October 1856 to Alfred Wallace's letter from the Celebes, Wallace wrote to him several times, long and detailed communications, so that Charles began to perceive that Wallace had come to believe that Charles Darwin was his confrere and friend, particularly since Charles was willing to discusss his species theory, though in a limited way. By the end of 1857, when Charles had been working on his book for a year and a half, he realized how right Lyell, Hooker and Huxley had been when they urged him to set down his findings. Wallace's latest letter, written on September 27, 1857, said:

> The mere statement and illustration of that paper in the *Annals and Magazine of Natural History* is of course but preliminary to an attempt at a detailed proof of it, the plan of which I have arranged, and in fact written. . . .

Wallace had proof of his species theory! He had already written it down! But surely not natural selection, or the preservation of favored races in the struggle for life? It would be an impossible coincidence, after several thousand years of man's thinking and writing about the laws of nature, that two individuals should come upon the same penetrating conclusions at the same moment in history. If Wallace had actually arrived at the results Charles Darwin had, and his essay was already written, might not some journal reach Down House in a matter of months with Wallace's solution to the "mystery of mysteries" spread over its pages?

He stood at the study window looking out at his enclosing flint-stone wall, but not seeing it, gradually achieving an emotional calm.

"I must answer Alfred Wallace immediately, he told himself. "And show quite plainly my admiration for him. Courageous fellow, to expect to remain out in that primitive country another three or four years!"

December 22, 1857

> My dear Sir,
>     I thank you for your letter of Sept. 27th. I am extremely glad to hear that you are attending to distribution in accordance with theoretical ideas. I am a firm believer that without speculation there is no good and original observation. Few travellers have attended to such points as you are now at work on; and indeed the whole subject of distribution of animals is

dreadfully behind that of plants. You say that you have been somewhat surprised at no notice having been taken of your paper in the *Annals*. I cannot say that I am; for so very few naturalists care for anything beyond the mere description of species. But you must not suppose that your paper has not been attended to; two very good men, Sir C. Lyell, and Mr. E. Blyth of Calcutta, specially called my attention to it. Though agreeing with you on your conclusions in the paper, I believe I go much further than you; but it is too long a subject to enter on my speculative notions. . . .

He had spent three months on his chapter on hybridism. At the beginning of 1858 he started Mental Powers and Instincts of Animals. There was a mountainous mass of material to sift through and collate; not only from his own years of observation but from the publishings of authors in a dozen or more languages. A curious field, instincts. Amorphous, as well. He told Emma:

"I find my chapter on instincts very perplexing. Authors have not agreed on a definition of instinct. This is not at all surprising, as nearly every passion, and the most complex dispositions such as courage, timidity, suspicion, are often said to be instinctive."

The more deeply he became involved, the worse he felt, particularly at night when he should have been sleeping. He commented to Hooker:

"Oh, health, health, you are my daily and nightly bugbear; and stop all enjoyment in life."

Then, not wanting to be guilty of self-pity, he added:

"But I really beg pardon, it is very foolish and weak to howl this way. Everyone has got his heavy burthen in this world."

Harriet Henslow died toward the end of January. Charles was greatly saddened, for she had been a surrogate mother to him during his years at Cambridge. He wrote to Henslow, saying:

> Those old days when I used as an undergraduate to be so much at your and dear Mrs. Henslow's house were certainly amongst the most happy and best days which I have ever spent.

He also sent an affectionate and consoling message to the Hookers, and particularly to Frances, whom he had known since she was three.

A way to take his mind off his physical plight was to read the new, popular literature and to mine the London *Times*. Each week when the Down courier went into London the Darwins gave him a list of books to buy or borrow from the lending library. The members of their family,

Erasmus and the Hensleigh Wedgwoods in London, Susan and Katty at The Mount, Elizabeth Wedgwood and Charlotte and Charles Langton in nearby Hartfield, continued to bring or send to Down House every book they themselves enjoyed. In this fashion as the year wound by as inexorably as the river Thames they read aloud *The Three Clerks* and *Doctor Thorne* by Anthony Trollope, the first two volumes of *Frederick the Great* by their prolific friend, Thomas Carlyle, *Scenes of Clerical Life* by George Eliot. They also received sheet music from the operas, Donizetti's *Lucia*, Méhul's *Cora*, Weber's Rondo and Haydn's Sonatas. Thus did the country Darwins keep abreast of London's cultural life.

As arbiter of the news, Charles was able to give his family an overview of the world's activities from the sage to the savage. Property qualifications for members of Parliament were abolished; a law was enacted by Parliament providing for better government for India, control of the administration being transferred from the East India Company to the Queen's Cabinet. Queen Victoria's first-born was married in the Chapel Royal of St. James's Palace to Prince Frederick William of Prussia. The stench from the river Thames was now so bad that Parliament had to be draped with curtains soaked in chloride of lime. Mr. Benjamin Disraeli, leader of the House of Commons, solved the obnoxious problem by getting a bill for three million pounds through Parliament to purify the river and complete a drainage system for the city.

Lord Elgin, appointed Ambassador to Japan, signed a treaty with that country to open five Japanese ports to British trade. England also signed the peace treaty of Tientsin with the Chinese Emperor which guaranteed the admission of English subjects to China and the teaching of Christianity. The Emperor agreed to pay part of England's expenses in the waging of the war against China!

Henrietta, nearing fifteen, was being tutored, along with her younger sister Elizabeth, by a new governess, a Miss Grant, in the light and airy schoolroom they had built above the kitchen area in 1845. The spacious room, twenty-five feet by fifteen, with its large book cupboard built into the back wall and the front wall mostly window overlooking the garden, was reached by a staircase with a fine mahogany banister . . . which the younger children adored to slide down. Emma and Charles tried to set up a disciplined work schedule for the two girls, whom they wanted to be as well educated as their brothers who went away to school. When Henrietta professed herself too unwell to study, Sir Henry Holland assured them that it was a common type of illness in growing girls. It was something they outgrew. That Etty would live to be a hundred.

Charles's chapter on instincts was one of the most exciting and puzzling in the book to write. He shared many of the stories with his family, for they were truly wondrous: The incredible mathematical judgment in the wax cell construction of hive bees. The power of communication among ants; their ability while in deadly strife with nests of similar species to recognize their own comrades. The wisdom of snails in searching out better pasture, returning for weaker members, and guiding them to food along the deposited layer of slime; and of the oyster, which shut its shell when taken out of water, enabling it to live longer. Of the beaver accumulating pieces of wood, even in dry places where no dam making was possible. The instinct of the ferret to bite the back part of the head of the rat at the medulla oblongata, where death was most easily achieved. How digger wasps dropped their prey and inspected their burrows before bringing in food for their young. How young sheep dogs, without instruction, naturally ran round the flock and kept it together. The astonishing migration of young birds across wide seas; and of young salmon from fresh into salt water, and the return to their birthplace to spawn. The lava-colored marine iguanas of the Galápagos who went into the sea only long enough to feed on submerged algae and quickly returned to the shore rocks out of harm's way of the sharks.

By early March his chapter, Instinct, was completed.

He went up to London occasionally, had dinner at the Athenaeum with his friends and Erasmus. The rage in his circle at the moment was Buckle's *History of Civilization*, which Charles found "wonderfully clever and original."

Toward the end of April, with his massive manuscript running to almost two thousand pages, he felt a genuine sense of depletion.

It was time for some hydropathy.

7.

The Linnean Society had scheduled its last meeting of the spring for June 17, with five papers to be read. However, when Robert Brown, librarian of the Society and subsequently its president, died on June 10, the meeting was postponed until July 1, at which time Brown, with whom Charles had become friends before H.M.S. *Beagle* sailed, would be eulogized and a new member elected to the council as well.

It was eight days after the death of Brown, on June 18, that Charles received a fat envelope from Alfred Wallace postmarked from Ternate, a small island in Malaysia. He used his letter opener to slice through the top of the envelope. It contained not only a letter but a long article as well: "On the Tendency of Varieties to Depart Indefinitely from the Original Type."

The print swam before Charles's eyes as he absorbed Wallace's early pages. Sick at heart or stomach, he knew not which, he collapsed into the nearest chair and read Wallace's text with blurred vision.

> . . . The life of wild animals is a struggle for existence. . . . There is a general principle in nature which will cause many *varieties* to survive the parent species, and to give rise to successive variations departing further and further from the original type. . . .
>
> . . . A simple calculation will show that in fifteen years each pair of birds would have increased to nearly ten millions! whereas we have no reason to believe that the number of the birds of any country increases at all in fifteen or in one hundred and fifty years. With such powers of increase the population must have reached its limits, and have become stationary. . . . It is a struggle for existence in which the weakest and least perfectly organized must always succumb. . . .

If Wallace had had Charles's 1844 manuscript he could not have made a better abstract!

What Charles had feared had happened. He went through a series of emotions from the deepest incredulity to bruising anger, to a forlorn sense of betrayal by a cruel fate. It was only by sheer will power that he brought himself under control. He picked up Wallace's letter, which had fallen to the floor, and read that Wallace hoped he would like and approve the piece, and if so, send it to Charles Lyell, who had spoken well of his first article in the *Annals*.

He walked out of his study, pale and totally distracted. From the hall wardrobe he took his long black cape and black crush hat; from the umbrella stand he selected a stout cane, and strode through the gardens and fields to the Sandwalk. He set out no collection of flint stones to determine how many times he rounded this rectangular portion of the woods, and returned home only when he felt physically exhausted. In his mind his lifetime work became analogous to the wreck of H.M.S. *Thetis*.

Emma saw at once that something was wrong.

"Charles, what has happened?"

They sat on the secluded bench in the sun; he told her of Wallace's paper.

"Even his terms now stand as heads of my chapters!" he exclaimed.

"How can that be? Had you written him details of your work? Could Lyell or Hooker have unwittingly revealed your materials?"

"He would hardly plagiarize me and send me the manuscript for my comments."

"What shall you do?"

"Send the article to Lyell as he requested."

Along with the manuscript he wrote a note to Lyell:

> Your words have come true with a vengeance—that I should be forestalled. You said this when I explained to you here very briefly my views of "Natural Selection" depending on the struggle for existence. . . . Please return me the MS., which he does not say he wishes me to publish, but I shall, of course, at once write and offer to send it to any journal. So all my originality, whatever it may amount to, will be smashed. . . .
>
> I hope you will approve of Wallace's sketch, that I may tell him what you say.

He was upset and fretful, unable to work or sit still, swallow much food or sleep. He accommodated more than his usual retching.

That Sunday, in midmorning, Charles Lyell and Joseph Hooker stepped out of a carriage at Down House. Lyell had asked Hooker to accompany him to Down, suggesting that their good and great friend was caught up in a crisis; that they must work out a practical solution which would be fair to both Charles Darwin and Alfred Wallace. Charles was so astonished to see them at the front door that the image of the two men was fixed forever on his mind as vividly as though it had been a daguerreotype on his fireplace mantelpiece. Hooker, now forty, had gone scraggily bald at the top of his pate. Although his remaining hair was still dark, his long side whiskers, flowing luxuriantly under the clean chin, were white. There were two deep work-creases in his cheeks, running from his nostrils down past each corner of his mouth; his rimless spectacles seemed smaller than ever below his big eyes and bushy flowering eyebrows.

Lyell, now past sixty, had turned white altogether, also with broad white side whiskers reaching almost to his chin. There were poignantly dark circles under his eyes denoting stress, which was unusual for him, for he was not a man to be disturbed by passing storms.

"I'm not going to ask, 'To what do I owe this honor?'" Charles said. "On the dozenth guess I'm sure I could figure that out."

"You'd be an idiot not to," growled Lyell. "But then, all geniuses are idiots in one way or another."

"We haven't come for a theoretical discussion," exclaimed Hooker, his voice more than usually hoarse. "I've read the Wallace material. On the train from London, Lyell and I mapped out a viable plan."

Charles had difficulty getting his own words out.

"You're both most kind to help me out of my ridiculous plight. I'll have coffee brought into the study."

The book-lined room, with its multitude of file cabinets, with its microscope on its shelf and tables laden with bottles, pillboxes and jars, magnifying glass and stacks of notes, embraced them in a womblike security.

Charles took a deep breath.

"There is nothing in Wallace's fifteen-page article which is not written out more fully in my 1844 sketch, which runs around two hundred and thirty pages, and was read by Hooker some dozen years ago. About a year ago I sent a short précis of my views to Asa Gray, so that I can most truly prove that I take nothing from Wallace. I should be extremely glad now to publish a sketch of my general views in about a dozen pages or so; but can I do so honorably? Wallace might indeed say, 'You did not intend publishing an abstract of your views till you received an outline of my doctrine. Is it fair to take advantage of my having freely, though unasked, communicated to you my ideas and thus prevent me forestalling you?' The advantage which I should take being that I am induced to publish from privately knowing that Wallace is in the field. I would far rather burn my whole book than that he or any other man should think that I had behaved in a paltry spirit. Do you not think his having sent me this sketch ties my hands?"

"Certainly not," snapped Hooker; "you are the older man and have been pioneering in this field two decades longer than Wallace."

Charles thanked him with an appreciative nod, but persisted.

"Though Wallace says nothing about publication it seems hard on me that I should be thus compelled to lose my priority of many years' standing, but I cannot feel at all sure that this alters the justice of the case."

Lyell and Hooker were singularly unimpressed.

"Do you have that 1844 sketch on hand?" Hooker asked.

"Of course. It has your pencil scrawlings all over it." He went to one of his larger file drawers by the door. "Here it is."

Hooker took the sketch and plunged into the pages. Lyell asked:

"May I see the letter you wrote to Asa Gray?"

He took a copy of the letter out of Asa Gray's file, handed it to Lyell, who began reading.

Charles muttered:

"I cannot persuade myself . . ."

"Be quiet," said Lyell; "or your father will have been right when he predicted that you would be good for nothing but shooting, dogs and ratcatching."

Charles laughed for the first time in days. Then he began pacing the room and finally slumped onto his hassock. Lyell and Hooker looked at, then nodded to each other.

"It's going to work," Hooker cried.

"No question," Lyell agreed. "This Asa Gray essay, plus the 1844 presentation, will make a perfect combination."

"For what?" Charles demanded.

"For delivering before the July 1 meeting of the Linnean Society."

"I cannot do that," Charles cried. "It would take me months . . ."

Lyell ignored the protest.

"We will also read Wallace's paper at the meeting . . ."

"We don't have his consent," Charles spluttered, "and mine will be too late."

"Not at all," Hooker replied blandly. "Lyell and I will extract a coherent and convincing statement from your 1844 treatise and the letter to Asa Gray. We'll make it approximately the same length as Wallace's."

Charles sat openmouthed.

"You plan . . . to do all that work . . . for me?"

"It won't kill us," said Hooker. "You've been pasting our ears back about species for a long while now."

Charles was silent for a spell, then murmured:

"You are the two kindest men I know. How are we going to explain to the Linnean Society this strange coincidence?"

"We will tell them the truth," Lyell proffered. "Hooker and I wrote out our explanation on the train." He took a folded piece of paper from his inside coat pocket and began to read:

> "The accompanying papers, which we have the honor of communicating to the Linnean Society, and which relate to the same subject, viz. the Laws which affect the Production of Varieties, Races and Species, contain the results of the investigations of two indefatigable naturalists, Mr. Charles Darwin and Mr. Alfred Russel Wallace.
>
> "These gentlemen having, independently and unknown to one another, conceived the same very ingenious theory to account for the appearance and perpetuation of varieties and of specific forms on our planet, may both fairly claim the merit of being original thinkers in this important line of inquiry. Neither of them having published his views, though Mr. Darwin has for many years past been repeatedly urged by us to do so, and both authors having now unreservedly placed their papers in our hands, we think it would best promote the interests of science that a selection from them should be laid before the Linnean Society."

Charles chewed on this presentation, found it eminently nourishing. "Splendid! I'll need only a little time to correct my earlier discourse. . . ."

"You must move speedily," Hooker warned. "We have only a few days before that meeting on July 1."

"I'll have Parslow deliver the package to you at Kew."

Parslow knocked to announce that dinner was served. Charles said: "Parslow, go down into the cellar and find the two best bottles of champagne we have." To Emma and his friends, as they crossed to the sunlit dining room, he said:

"I don't know how the future will judge us but we are most certainly going to celebrate the present."

He awoke on Monday to a week of chaos. Scarlet fever had broken out in Down. Several small children in the village had caught it. When they checked on their own brood they found that their baby had developed a fever, and Henrietta's sore throat had blossomed into a full-scale diphtheria. They sent for the doctor while Emma's sister Elizabeth, who had come to visit, suggested taking the other children home with her to Hartfield.

Charles kept vigil on one child, then the other. It was not until Thursday that he braved his study. He could not bear to look at his papers.

"Have a cup of coffee with me," Emma said.

The next day they received a report of the death of a child in Down of scarlet fever. Their emotions moved from apprehension to fear. However they did not accept Elizabeth's offer; the other six children, from William, now eighteen, down to Horace, age seven, were in good health.

Not so their nurse, who had been caring for Henrietta. She came down with an ulcerated throat and quinsy. Charles arranged for her to return home and engaged a second nurse. On that same evening Henrietta's fever was down and she was breathing more easily; the baby's ran very high.

It was a miserable Sunday. Emma said:

"I want desperately to go into Down for church services and to pray for my young."

"You don't dare!" exclaimed Charles. "There are half a dozen children in Down with the fever."

It was now a whole week since Lyell and Hooker had been there.

The doctor returned before sundown, exhausted. Scarlet fever had become epidemic in the entire area. He emerged from little Charles's room looking very concerned.

"I'm sorry to have to report this but the boy has scarlet fever. There is little we can do. I'm afraid your nurse is also coming down. I strongly advise that no one go into the boy's room. Scarlet fever is very contagious."

It was a long, dreadful night. Charles and Emma slept fitfully, rising frequently to stand outside the stricken child's room listening for sounds.

The doctor returned early on Monday morning. The nurse had indeed developed scarlet fever and had to be transferred to another bedroom. The doctor said:

"I'll sit with the little one. I've been exposed to so much of the disease that I must be immune."

It was a forlorn, bitter day; the baby died that night. They buried him the next morning in the little churchyard in Down where they had buried three-week-old Mary Eleanor sixteen years before.

They returned home inexpressibly saddened, as were so many families in the area. The other children had not been permitted to attend the funeral because of the plague. Charles gathered them around the marble-topped table in the drawing room. Emma did not want them hurt any more than had to be.

"It is God's will," she told her brood. "We must accept it with grace. Little Charles is gone; the rest of us are here to bring love and comfort to each other."

They decided to send the children to their Aunt Elizabeth's where they would join them later.

It was on the afternoon of that same day that Charles received an emergency message from Hooker reminding him that there were only two days left before the Linnean Society meeting, and that he must get all papers to Hooker immediately if he and Lyell were to prepare the joint Darwin-Wallace reports. After an hour of indecision, Charles gathered in one package Wallace's article, his own 1844 essay and his letter to Asa Gray. He summoned Parslow.

"Please dress immediately. I want you to deliver personally a package to Dr. Hooker at Kew Gardens."

Charles sat in his writing chair, dated the note Tuesday night, June 29, 1858.

> My dear Hooker,
> I daresay all is too late. I hardly care about it. But you are too generous to sacrifice so much time and kindness. . . . I really cannot bear to look at my sketch. Do not waste much time. It is miserable in me to care at all about priority.
> God bless you, my dear kind friend. I can write no more.

The hours became interminable until the first of July and the meeting of the Linnean Society. He could not stay in the house and galloped around the Sandwalk like a horse with a burr under its saddle. Emma's valorous efforts to divert him were unavailing. His mind spun with questions. How would the members react to his and Wallace's papers? They were both revolutionary, fortifying each other. Would they rise in wrath and denounce him as sacrilegious? Or an idiot? Would they suspect collusion between himself and Wallace? Would they demand his resignation from the Society? He had hoped to keep his conclusions quiet until after several more years had buttressed his case to the point where it would be incontrovertible. But Fate, in the guise of Alfred Russel Wallace, had forced his hand.

The waiting period began to be less endurable than the most dire results. He would not go to London for the meeting. He did not think it seemly with his little child buried only two days. Instead he coaxed some extra music out of Emma, put aside his books, went to bed, tossed and turned most of the night. How soon would Lyell and Hooker write, giving him a report?

On July 2 a rather pale-faced Joseph Hooker turned into the driveway in a carriage.

"Hooker, why didn't you let me know you were coming? I would have sent my phaeton for you."

"I wanted to bring you a report as quickly as possible."

A shiver ran through Charles.

"Don't spare me."

"Nothing happened." Flatly.

"What do you mean? Weren't the papers read?"

"They were read, all right. Yours was first. Lyell and I tried to impress the necessity of profound attention to the papers and their bearing on the future of natural history. But there was no semblance of discussion."

"No discussion?" Charles was shocked. "Was their interest not excited?"

"I think it may have been. But the subject was too novel and too ominous for the Old School to enter the lists before armoring. There was some scattered talk after the long evening but Lyell's approval, and in a small way mine, rather overawed those fellows who might otherwise have flown out against the doctrine. At the close of the meeting there was a thin scattering of applause. Then everyone went home."

Hooker shook his head bemusedly.

"It was as though the bloody French Revolution were taking place in Paris but none of the sidewalk café habitues bothered to look up from their brioches and coffee."

Charles stood stunned, then burst into uncontrolled gales of laughter. When he finally got himself to subside, he exclaimed:

"Days of self-drama wasted! I might just as well have been out with John Henslow gathering toads in the Fens for toad pies!"

Hooker was not amused.

"Lyell and I agreed last night that it is essential you now get something in print besides this first brief report. An abstract of your materials that is organized and integrated with the best examples to prove your points. You must establish your rights in the field."

Charles sobered up quickly.

"I'll do it."

# BOOK ELEVEN

*"Here Is a Pleasant Genealogy for Mankind"*

1.

O N July 9, 1858, Emma and Charles set out to join their children at Elizabeth's home in Hartfield. The Darwins had a familial week in the warm Sussex sunshine, then left for the Isle of Wight off the south coast of England, blessed with a mild climate, with beautiful scenery and high chalk downs. Charles remembered the island from his youth, when he vacationed there with William Darwin Fox, walking along the sandy bays and swimming in the protected coves. He had made reservations at the King's Head Hotel at Sandown, one of the more attractive watering spots. The nine Darwins, with one governess to take care of the four younger children, Horace seven, Leonard eight, Francis ten, and Elizabeth eleven, occupied six adjacent rooms at the end of a ground-floor corridor, one of them a sitting room for the clan. They ate their midday dinner on the wide wooden veranda, went inside for a light supper during the cool of evening. The five boys, led by eighteen-year-old William, who would be gone soon for a month of wandering about Europe before entering Christ's College, ran on the beaches, boated, fished, their faces burnt from the sun. Charles and Emma recuperated from the tensions of illness and death in the quiet health-giving atmosphere, walked with their two daughters or sat on the cool side of the veranda while Charles read aloud to them and Emma knitted a scarf for William.

Charles relished these days of surcease from strain, feeling as well as he had at Moor Park. After several days he was about to open a small valise in which he carried the first parts of his species manuscript from which Hooker insisted he abstract a thirty-page *Linnean Journal* article, when a hotel employee delivered a package with Joseph Hooker's name on the outside, sent down from London. He opened it and found the proof sheets of his own and Wallace's papers as presented to the Linnean Society by Lyell on July 1. It was nineteen days from reading to printer's sheets.

He dropped into a chair in the sitting room, took up the Lyell and Hooker introduction, which he remembered as a model of parental protection for their wayward child. There were a few changes from what the men had stated at Down House, and again made clear that they were not considering the relative claims to priority of Mr. Darwin and his friend, Mr. Wallace, but the interests of science generally; "views founded on a wide deduction from facts, and matured by years of reflection, should constitute at once a goal from which others may start."

Charles set the page proofs on the center table, prepared pen and ink to make corrections, then found that Lyell and Hooker had done such a concise job of editing his material that there was nothing to correct . . . except his own style. He cried:

"I'm disgusted with my bad writing. I cannot improve it without rewriting it all, which would not be fair or worth while."

"You wear that attitude the way certain monks wear a hair shirt," said Emma.

Charles flushed, put an arm about her.

"I'll do better with the writing when I do the thirty-page abstract of my manuscript, which already runs close to two thousand handwritten pages. Though how I will manage that, I know not."

"Can the *Journal* accommodate no more space?"

"Possibly, I could cover the extra costs if it is too long."

He returned the proof sheets to Hooker and asked for a set to send out to Wallace.

That morning the Darwins were disconcerted to learn of a scandal involving Dr. Lane of Moor Park and one of his patients, a married woman, who committed the unparalleled act of publicly detailing their adultery. Dr. Lane coldly denied any wrongdoing; there was an absence of corroborative evidence.

"It's cruel," Charles declared. "All those around him believe in his innocence. Yet he may have to stand trial. I fear it will ruin him."

"If a married woman makes public such a charge, where would those sensuous details of intimacy come from?"

"Hallucination, perhaps. She may believe her charges to be true though they happened not in fact but in the back of a disordered mind."

Charles's belief was generally shared. The woman's husband refused to press charges.

He worked for a couple of hours each day abstracting his chapters on Variation under Domestication. He found the effort diverting but unsatisfactory inasmuch as he had no room to give the sources for his conclusions. He complained:

"I have used a hundred and sixty footnotes, quoted from a round hundred authorities, given volume and page references to sixty-five periodicals and sixty books. Now they will have to be left out. No trained scientist would stand for such a process."

Emma had learned not to treat all of his problems as though they were fatal. She said with a mischievous gleam in her eyes:

"Couldn't you sprinkle a few names here and there, like specks of salt on a boiled egg?"

They spent ten days at the King's Head Hotel at Sandown, enjoying the sea, then moved by carriage to Shanklin where there was a row of simple houses on the beach. Charles told his children:

"This place has sprung up like a mushroom. When my cousin William Fox took me on a walking trip around this island it was a solitary sandy bay. Look at it now; three hotels, many charming villas . . ."

William had gone off for his tour of Europe. George, at thirteen, was the oldest son present and hence the one to take on his father.

"That was centuries ago, Papa. *Tempus fidgets.*"

"*Tempus fugit,* George. Nevertheless you're right, the world can't stand still. There are too many living forces knocking at its gate."

They settled in Norfolk House. Charles continued abridging his manuscript. Occasionally he felt his stomach begin to rumble but it was nothing to complain about. As he and Emma walked along the beach arm in arm, watching streaks of orange and purple fade slowly in the sunset, he said:

"I am most heartily obliged to Hooker and Lyell for setting me on this abstracting task. I shall, when it is done, be able to finish my big work with greater ease." He shook his head in despair. "However I'm already five pages over Hooker's suggested thirty pages with eight or nine long chapters still to go."

"You often say about the novelists we read that they wander down a garden path."

"I try not to put in anything that is not of scientific interest; and which was once new to me. It seems a queer plan to abstract an unpublished work. . . ."

"Follow my Papa's advice: do what you must and wait for fate to overtake you."

On August 5 he received a note from Hooker which lightened his burden. Hooker had spoken to George Busk, zoological undersecretary of the Linnean Society, who sent word that Charles could expand his abstract if the extra pages were imperative to his purpose.

"It will make the labor far less, not having to shorten so much every single subject," he exclaimed as they lingered over dinner on the dining veranda of the hotel. "But I will try not to be diffusive. Other members have rights to space in the *Journal.*"

Hooker had also suggested that perhaps each chapter could be read and published separately in the *Journal* over a year or two.

He wrote to Hooker telling him of his relief:

> The Abstract will do very well divided into several parts. Thus I have just finished "Variation under Domestication" in forty-four MS. pages, and that would do for one evening at the Linnean. But I should be extremely sorry if it all could not ultimately be published together.

They returned home on August 13 refreshed by sea and sun and settled into their normal life, gardening, sitting out of doors on warm evenings, Charles returning twice a day to his Sandwalk. He received a copy of Thomas Huxley's Croonian Lecture to the Royal Society entitled On the Theory of the Vertebrate Skull, in which Huxley unhorsed Richard Owen and, some claimed, "put a large dent in Owen's massive reputation." No one could detract from Owen's achievements; however he had made the mistake of committing himself to the theory that the skull was an extension of the vertebral column. Huxley, following the work of other embryologists, proved that the bones of the skull were derived from structures which preceded the vertebrae in development, thus eliminating the cranial theory.

Charles learned that Huxley, without remuneration, was giving lecture courses to workingmen's groups who had no other means of educating themselves. Huxley explained:

"I want the working classes to understand that science and her ways are great facts for them."

Four days after their return Charles began structuring his pivotal chapter: "Natural Selection." Although eliminating all sources and footnotes and peripheral material, he was at the same time adding paragraphs and pages of new material and deductions. By the time he had readied his sections On Possibility of All Organisms Crossing and Variation in Nature the idea of a small book had taken hold of him. Emma was amused.

"My, how one does grow! From a thirty-page abstract to a small book in less than three months. How long will it take for the little book to be converted into a big book?"

Charles laughed softly.

"Not too long. Let's just say that I have more talent for making a big abstract than a small one."

When his and Wallace's articles were published in the *Journal of the Linnean Society* toward the end of August, and were engulfed in silence, he cried:

"Who in the world is going to read my new, longer abstract? Why am I writing it?"

Joseph Hooker felt stimulated by working in the bedroom above Charles's study, concentrating on the final part of his book on the botany of the Antarctic voyage, completing sections on the flora of Tasmania and the plants of Ceylon, after which he would begin on a multivolumed encyclopedia about the world's seed-bearing plants with his friend George Bentham. Before dinner, when they went to the Sandwalk for exercise, Charles commented:

"Because you see only isolated sections of my manuscript you may feel that my speculations are a jam pot."

Hooker stopped in the sunlit stretch, gazed at Charles with guileless eyes.

"My dear Darwin, how could I ever conceive of you confecting a jam pot?"

Charles apologized.

"The truth is that I have so accustomed myself to expect opposition and even contempt that I forgot for the moment that you are one of the few living souls from whom I have constantly received sympathy and assistance."

Hooker ducked his head between his shoulders deprecatingly, took off his spectacles and wiped them.

"I could not stomach your theory of natural selection at first, but I have become largely a convert. A reading of your book in sequence should take me the rest of the way. How much longer do you have?"

"Three or four months. To make my views clear, I cannot make it shorter."

They made their seventh journey around the heavily wooded rectangle, then returned briskly to the house. Charles was writing more rapidly now, eager to publish, to establish himself and, more importantly, to establish his concept of the evolution of all living things. All the bearings fell into place, making the engine run smooth. Into his manuscript went the incisive study of living things during his *Beagle* years, and the editing of the *Zoology* books, building the ten-foot wall of his theory flint stone upon flint stone as he abstracted the results of his years of dissecting and classifying barnacles; the study of butterflies, beetles, the instincts of pigeons, the anatomy of rabbits, ducks and fowl, the measurements of horses; the planting of seeds and floating of them in salt water, speculating on the transportation of all growths to distant lands; the learned observation of natural scientists from every country with whom he carried on an incessant correspondence; the annals of crossbreeding. All the years of his hard-earned yet loving knowledge and perception came into focus for him. He stood at the very center of the universe, the spokes of his creativity radiating in all directions.

By the end of October he had completed Section V, Laws of Variation, and was now preparing Section VI, Difficulties of the Theory. The strain of penetrating the jungle of his hindrances brought on a nervous stomach which he described as "bad enough."

Though reticent about his early years with those outside the family, as a natural storyteller he bewitched his children with tales out of Shrewsbury, expeditions into North Wales, Cambridge and the Fens, in particular his wild yarns of exploration while on land journeys away from the *Beagle*. The younger children, in turn, used his study as the family storeroom, raiding it even though Papa was at work, for the necessary pins, scissors, string, sticking plaster, rulers, tools. Once when the younger boys, Horace, Leonard and Francis, dashed in for supplies for their ongoing game, Charles said patiently:

"Don't you think you could not come in again? I have been interrupted very often."

Emma suggested he indulge himself with a week at Moor Park.

Dr. Lane welcomed him back. He took long walks, idled, had mild hydropathy, worked some on his abstract for the section on instinct. He returned home on November 1. Emma asked:

"How is the digestive tract?"

"Remarkably normal."

In early November Charles Lyell was awarded the Copley Medal by the Royal Society, the highest honor in English science. Hooker offered to give the eulogy. Charles spent the evening jotting down notes on the merits of his friend. He completed the rough sketch the next day, filled with "horribly bad metaphors," but a deliberative impression of Lyell's merits, and sent it on to Hooker.

Their son William managed, after some delay, to secure the rooms Charles had occupied at Christ's College; he also inherited Charles's old gyp, Impey. It brought Charles a sense of continuum, as did the collecting of beetles by his third son, Francis. Then too he was looking forward to a visit by John Henslow toward the end of the month. With Frances Henslow married to Joseph Hooker—she had sat up half the night making a fair copy of the species paper for Lyell to read—the bond was all the closer. Henslow's science lectures in Suffolk had proved so popular that he was invited by H.R.H. the Prince Consort to give a short course on botany at Buckingham Palace for the junior members of the royal family. John Henslow surely knew about the book he was preparing on the origin of species by natural selection. Henslow was a pious man, a rector in the Church of England; did he consider it a defection by his bright young toad-pie maker, whose burgeoning career he had literally created by placing him on H.M.S. *Beagle*?

Unlike the *Beagle*'s captain, FitzRoy, John Henslow, now sixty-two, his long hair a pure white, dark evening circles setting under his eyes, a lonely man since the death of his wife, had not come for controversy but to bask in the warm affection of Charles and Emma. They passed several companionable days before Henslow broached the subject at morning coffee in the study. Charles's scrutiny of Henslow's face was so intense that Henslow smiled.

"Be reassured, nothing can affect our friendship. I shall stick up for you as well as I can when you are attacked."

Charles heaved a sigh of relief.

"My dear Henslow, you leave me in a fit of enthusiastic admiration of your character."

By the day before Christmas he had three hundred and thirty folio pages written; it would require another one hundred and fifty for a good-sized volume. He celebrated the completion of his chapter on Hybridism and Geological Succession by taking the whole of Christmas Day off and spending it with the family, his two older boys being home from school. Parslow, who was married now and had children of his own, set up a tree in the drawing room, draped the mantelpiece and pictures with holly, arranged the presents under the tree. Charles had been too preoccupied to buy any gifts; at the last moment he was crestfallen.

"Worry not," Emma reassured him. "I gave lists to the Down courier, who shopped for us in London. There might even be a little token for you."

At the Christmas dinner, centered around a plump bird and a plum pudding, Charles told how much of his opus was completed.

"The Linnean Society's *Journal* is out. I've run much too long."

"Does that mean you will publish yourself?"

"Not a good idea. One needs a reputable house to distribute the copies."

"Joseph Hooker offered to help you get a publication grant from the Royal Society or the Geological. Or the government. You did get a thousand pounds for your *Zoology of the Beagle*."

"Impossible. Not one of the societies, or our national government, will want to be saddled with my content."

In the middle of January 1859 he was surprised to be informed that the Geological Society had awarded him the Wollaston Medal, given to the individual who best promoted researches concerning the mineral structure of the earth. Among the former recipients were Louis Agassiz, Richard Owen, Adam Sedgwick. Lyell offered to give the eulogy, a generous gesture since he himself had never received the award!

He now had the Royal and Wollaston, the second and third most important medals of British science.

He had been uneasy about how Alfred Wallace would react to their

two papers being read simultaneously. Now two letters arrived from
Ternate, one for himself and one for Hooker. He quickly opened his
own. Wallace was more than delighted with what they had done! The
key paragraph, however, was in his letter to Hooker:

> Allow me in the first place sincerely to thank yourself & Sir
> Charles Lyell for your kind offices on this occasion. I cannot
> but consider myself a favoured party in this matter because it
> has hitherto been too much the practice in cases of this sort to
> impute *all* the merit to the first discoverer of a new fact or a
> new theory, & little or none to any other party who may, quite
> independently, have arrived at the same results a few years or
> a few hours later. . . .

Charles commented to Hooker:
"He must be a most amiable man."

Emma had started planning their twentieth anniversary celebration
on January 29 at the beginning of the New Year, wanting to make it a
complete family reunion. Happily it fell on a Saturday so that she was
able to invite everyone for the weekend. Her sister Elizabeth and the
Langtons came together from Hartfield, Charles's sisters from The
Mount, picking up Erasmus in London. Hensleigh and Fanny Wedgwood brought their older children, as did the rest of the Wedgwood
brothers.

When Charles saw the extent of her preparations—she had even engaged puppeteers for the children, to be set up in the schoolroom—and
the enormous quantities of food and drink pouring into Down House,
he exclaimed:

"This is going to be quite a do. Since I will have a fiftieth birthday
on February 12, why don't we celebrate the two events together?"

"Splendid idea. I'll have two cakes, one for Saturday for our twentieth, the second for Sunday for your fiftieth."

Sitting around the festive table, Charles realized:

"We are now the older generation. The children are growing up
around us as we grew up at The Mount and Maer Hall. We have taken
the places of my father, Uncle Jos and Aunt Bessy . . . and before long
these young ones will be taking our places. There's satisfaction in that
thought."

He was pushing himself hard now.

He had not intended to publish, not in his lifetime. He had allowed
his friends to persuade him, right here in this study, three years before. . . . He told Hooker:

"How glad I shall be when the abstract is finished and I can rest."

His health deteriorated, with severe vomiting and a distressing swimming of his head. He sometimes doubted whether he would ever get

the volume done, though so nearly completed. He was obliged to stop all work and go back to Moor Park.

He played billiards, started taking pepsin to implement his gastric juices. The first week he felt better, then the charm of the billiards and the pepsin began to wear off. He did not remember his birthday until he was already in bed and had read for a couple of hours. He laid down his book, *The Ordeal of Richard Feverel,* its pages spread open on the blanket, and asked himself wistfully:

"What have I accomplished in my fifty years on earth?"

2.

He decided to give himself a billiard table for a birthday present; it could stand in the old dining room, next to his study; and found what he wanted at Hopkins and Stephens on Mercer Street in London, with a lime or Canadian green felt covering. The rail caps were made of the hardest wood available, the underpart of a highly burnished rosewood. The price was fifty-three pounds eighteen shillings, which startled him.

"We're going to have to sell some of our possessions to raise that money," he told Emma.

"But why, Charles? Our income last year was almost £5,000. We had a surplus of close to £1,200. Our stocks alone must be worth about £70,000."

"We must not dip into capital to pay for such a luxury as a billiard table. I'm going to sell my father's gold watch. I'd also like to sell a couple of your Wedgwood pieces."

Emma was pained by his penury. Why should she give up her grandfather's exquisite vases, medallions, figurines? But she quickly quieted any thought of rebellion. The Wedgwoods were valuable to her, particularly since she would never use the billiard table, but not nearly as valuable as keeping peace in the family.

"As you wish, my dear."

He proceeded to finish his last chapter. In his summary he wrote defiantly:

> . . . The several classes of facts which have been considered in this chapter seem to me to proclaim so plainly that the innumerable species, genera and families with which this world is peopled, are all descended each within its own class or group, from common parents, and have all been modified in the course of descent, that I should without hesitation adopt this view even if it were unsupported by other facts or arguments.

He went back to his first chapters, of which he now had a fair copy from the scrivener, to make corrections and to polish his style. He wrote to Fox:

I am now finally correcting my chapters for the press and I hope in a month to have proof sheets. . . .

He stopped abruptly, put aside his writing board and began to pace the study.

". . . for the press . . . proof sheets . . . What press? What proof sheets? I couldn't sight a publisher if I used my *Beagle* telescope."

Fate overtook him just four days later. In a note from Lady Mary Lyell he gathered the impression that Lyell had spoken about the book to John Murray, who had bought the rights to his *Journal* for the Home and Colonial Library and was doing well with it. He decided to go to London the next day.

He knocked on the door at 53 Harley Street several times. A housemaid showed him into Lyell's study. When Lyell looked up and saw him there a beam of light flashed across his face the way the sun, suddenly appearing from behind a cloud, floods down on the earth.

"Ah, Darwin. You've come on exactly the right day. Give me ten minutes to finish this passage. I'll have a glass of sherry brought in for you."

Charles stood before Lyell's extensive bookshelves running his fingertips over the volumes. Soon Lyell had finished, motioning him to a comfortable chair.

"I gather from Lady Lyell's note that you have spoken to John Murray about me."

"I have."

"Does he know at all the subject of the book?"

"I imagine I conveyed a fair impression."

"He is willing to publish?"

"Quite willing. However he wants to see some manuscript."

"Naturally. I'll be able to send him the first three chapters in about ten days."

"That will do nicely. Murray is by far the best publisher of scientific books. You will recall that he did my first volume of *Principles of Geology* back in 1830."

"Would you advise me to tell him that my book is not more unorthodox than the subject makes inevitable? That I do not bring in any discussion of Genesis but only give facts and such conclusions from them as seem to me fair . . . ?"

Lyell smiled indulgently at his friend's combination of hope, excitement and anxiety.

"I'd say nothing. Let the manuscript speak for itself."

Charles gnawed away at the prospect of publication like a dog at a bone.

"Can you advise me then whether I had better state what terms of publication I should prefer, or ask him to propose the terms?"

"Let's see how Murray reacts to the manuscript. He seems to have second sight about how many copies a book will sell."

"Yes, of course. Would you be so kind, then, as to look at my title page?"

Lyell studied it. It read, "An Abstract of An Essay on the Origin of Species and Varieties." He went through the maneuver of bending himself in half in front of a chair, burying his face in its upholstered seat. After what seemed to Charles an interminable time, he straightened himself up.

"You should not use the word 'abstract' in the title. It will frighten readers away. They will think it's just a summary."

"It's the only possible apology for not giving references and facts in full."

"No apology is needed. Let Murray decide. If he wants it out, you can be certain the word 'abstract' will reduce your reading public."

The following day Charles wrote to Murray, giving him the headings of his chapters. Murray replied immediately, offering handsome terms. Charles excitedly took the letter to Emma, who was sitting with Henrietta in the drawing room, basking in the brittle spring sunlight.

"Emma, listen to this. Murray has agreed to publish! Without seeing my manuscript! Offering profit sharing."

He withdrew a little from his explicit joy.

"I'm going to tell him that I accept his offer solely on condition that, after he has read part or all of the manuscript, he has full power of retracting."

He also added to Murray:

. . . It may be conceit but I believe the subject will interest the public, and I am sure that the views are original.

John Murray read the three chapters, then showed them to one of his consultants, the Rev. Whitwell Elwin, editor of the *Quarterly Review*. Elwin recommended that Charles scrap the book and write about pigeons. Murray next gave them to George Pollock, a lawyer friend, who thought it "probably beyond the comprehension of any scientific man then living," but recommended its publication on the ground that "Mr. Darwin had so brilliantly surmounted the formidable obstacles which he was honest enough to put in his own path."

Murray himself liked the chapters and, since he had the strong recommendations of Lyell and Hooker, told Charles that he did not need to see any more manuscript but would like the entire book as quickly as possible to be sent to the printer. He was putting in an order for twelve hundred and fifty copies as a first edition. However he did take the word "abstract" off the title page. The revised title now read: On the Origin of Species by Means of Natural Selection, or the Preservation of Favoured Races in the Struggle for Life.

"That's a large print order for a scientific book," Charles exulted. "Henry Colburn only bound five hundred copies of the Journal."

"That was twenty years ago, my love," replied Emma. "When you were unknown. Didn't you tell Joseph Hooker that you thought your book would be popular to a certain extent among scientific and non-scientific men?"

He blushed.

"I'll read and correct printer's errors if you'd like me to," she offered.

He stared at his wife in bewilderment. She was offering to correct proof pages of which she disapproved, and in which almost every conclusion would go against her lifetime convictions! He picked her up out of her chair, threw his arms around her, bussed her heartily on the mouth and held her tightly to him.

"My dear Miss Wedgwood, I've been married to you for twenty years but never have I admired or loved you more."

Piles of manuscript sat on the far table of his study. The instruments for his research, the bottles, jars, boxes, tubes, bowls, measuring devices, filled the room and gave it a unique character; even as the material for his book, in which he had been involved for twenty years, gave full play to his cycle of belief in his inferiority, his humbleness, as well as his confidence in his inherent talent to see and understand more than the ordinary mortal. He went round and round, thoughts of supreme confidence giving way to thoughts of abject defeat, bouts of joy countermanding bouts of melancholia. He wanted publication desperately and also knew that he did not want his book published in his lifetime. He declared publicly that it would be successful and popular, then became convinced that it must fail. No one would buy it or read it. He sweated over what he told his friends was his wretched style, yet continued to let the words flow from his pen until the pages reached into the thousands, delighted with what he was getting down on paper, certain that his uncovering of nature's universal law would revolutionize the approach to science.

There was hardly a letter to his friends in which he did not complain that he had little strength left, that he was an invalid, even as he put in strenuous stretches of writing, researching, planning, often taking less than a month to organize and set down sequentially a long and detailed chapter in a technical area never before researched; a Herculean accomplishment to match his climb of the highest Andes mountain range. His writings had been authentic, laboratory tested in the "Darwin lab." His books had sold modestly, but as well as those by any other author in the field of experimental science. His volumes were known as seed copies; he believed he would never do any better. Yet he surveyed these results coolly, feeling assured that his ideas, documentation and perceptions had not been equaled since 1543 when Copernicus published his shattering book which proved that the sun was in the center of a celestial system with the earth only one of the planets revolving around it.

He possessed both hard common sense and gullibility. In the depths of his brain he knew that Dr. Henry Holland was right in declaring that it was the rest and change that brought him health rather than the water cures he searched out and submitted to at the hydropathy spas; that Charles Lyell was correct in saying that taking Emma for a vacation on the Continent, Italy, Spain, France, would bring him an equal amount of tranquillity. Every so often he would give up the ghost, only to return to work a few days or weeks later in full fettle.

He spent with a free hand for research materials, for books and specimens, for microscope and postage, for scriveners to give him a fair copy, investing eight years of time and capital in tracking down the life of the barnacle, not really expecting a proper return. Yet he watched penuriously over his account books and held back abstemiously on small personal pleasures, demanding an accounting he expected nowhere else . . . vacillating between pride in his substantial monetary worth and certainty of his imminent ruin.

There was his need for friendship and his avoidance of all social intercourse; his entrenchment in the isolation of Down House and his running up to London on innumerable pretexts. His obligation to call any idleness a period of incubation. He quivered over the reaction of critics to his work, insisting on its importance by writing long letters of rebuttal and explanation, even while believing completely that critics vanish and creative work endures. His love of praise was meteoric, his rejection a cause for deep despair. He was eager for acceptance by his contemporaries and peers, yet in his pursuit of the unconventional, the radical, the difficult to believe and understand, he fed them that which would most surely be condemned. His practice of thanking people for well-earned favors, his fulsome praise of the work and worth of other scientists was habitual, yet he himself sought only knowledge where none had existed before . . . humbleness and arrogance going hand in hand.

Did he know he was going round and round like the hands on the tall grandfather clock in his hall? That just as surely as the clock hands would indicate that it was twelve noon, so they would also release the chime at midnight? He must have had at least a glimmering, though those faint and fleeting moments, those sparks of intuition like those from the whetstone of the street grinder sharpening knives and scissors, would have done him little good. He had said:

"I would rather be the wretched, contemptible invalid which I am than live the life of an idle squire."

Herein lay the truth as Charles Darwin acknowledged it! Why then was his work making him ill? Almost all men worked, sometimes at more difficult and demanding jobs than his, and rarely of their own choosing. He had genuine concerns. In the dark of a troubled night he was properly anxious and frightened about what his theories, as written in the notebooks between 1837 and 1839 and his essays of 1842 and 1844, would unleash in a Christian nation such as Great Britain, whose history had frequently been plagued with religious upheavals. He had grown up as a friendly, uncontroversial, easygoing chap, popular at the Shrewsbury School, at Christ's College, on H.M.S. Beagle. He had been born without any appetite for conflict. He had not even participated in competitive sports, preferring to walk along the river Severn, go horseback riding, catch toads in the Cambridgeshire Fens. Though he had become convinced with Agassiz that nature never lied, it had made a ghastly mistake in choosing him for the role of the anti-Christ! Not that he was; but the world would think him so, which amounted to the same thing.

The dizziness, the palpitations, the flatulence, the retching, was the price he paid in order to turn the world around. In the precise scheduling of expenditures he was addicted to, he did not consider it too high. To most of England's scientists, and some of his friends, this would label him an incurable hypochondriac. So be it. He knew that he would pursue the origin of life as long as he lived. His brain was searching for ultimate truths about nature; his body profoundly resented that occupation! There was no cure for it. His omnipresent physical ailments would not lessen the incredible amounts of research, voluminous correspondence, published manuscripts, any more than his penury had kept him from investing eight years of life and capital on four volumes of Cirripedia. When his courage ebbed, as did the waters of the Santa Cruz River in Patagonia where they had beached the Beagle for repairs to its copper bottom, one tide of accomplishment would be all that was necessary to refloat his ship.

What kind of man did that make him? He did not want to know.

3.

Everyone pitched in. Frances Hooker, who was indeed John Henslow's daughter, made "fair copy from foul" any time the manuscript was in too rough a shape for Joseph Hooker to edit. Hooker made the trip to Down House for a final discussion on the geographical distribution of species. When they spread out the ninety pages of the chapter on the dining table, Charles said:

"I'd like to know which parts you most vehemently object to. I should also like particularly to know whether I have taken anything from you which you would like to retain for your own publication."

Now that Joseph Hooker had passed the august age of forty, his luxuriant side and under-the-chin whiskers had taken on a botanical flourish worthy of one of his father's greenhouses. He stroked them affectionately, as though they were a rare flora he had brought home from the Himalayas.

"You have taken chiefly from my published works. That's what they are for. However we do differ on several heads. Let's get at them and thrash out our views. . . ."

By the end of March he began to see daylight. A friend of Emma's and the Wedgwood family's, Miss Georgina Tollet, who had lived at Betley Hall just eight miles from Maer Hall, had by coincidence moved into 14 Queen Anne Street, a couple of buildings from Erasmus's, whose salon she frequented. She was a favorite with authors because of her willingness to read manuscripts for their spelling and grammar, in which field she had been trained. Since Charles had met her at Maer Hall and at Erasmus's, he had the temerity to ask if she would read his work.

"I should be honored, Mr. Darwin. Though you must realize that I know little about science. Style is my forte."

"Clarity is what I am seeking, Miss Tollet."

John Murray sent her the first three chapters. While she was undertaking the task of perfecting Charles's English, Charles sent Chapter IV, Natural Selection, to Murray, saying:

I presume you will want to read this section, which is the keystone of my arch.

John Murray found "Natural Selection" fascinating. He sent the chapter to Miss Tollet, who informed Charles that thus far she had found only three obscure sentences, which she had corrected. But Joseph Hooker, still working on Charles's last chapter, wrote that he still found much obscurity of style, that Charles must rewrite and rewrite until he had perfectly conveyed his meaning.

Charles knew Hooker to be a perfectionist, as relentless in his demands on himself as on his friends. He was not too worried about this; but when Frances Hooker admitted that she too found many passages obscure, it made him tremble. He worked so hard to clarify the deeply intricate concepts that his health quite failed . . . but not until he had sent the balance of the manuscript to John Murray.

"It's Moor Park for you," Emma commanded. "Take George Eliot's *Adam Bede* with you. You'll find it even better than billiards to relax your mind."

The *Journal of the Linnean Society* containing his and Wallace's articles had slipped by unnoticed. Now he received his first criticism and wished he had not. Emma was in the schoolroom teaching her two youngest boys penmanship.

"Here's a taste of the future," he cried, bursting in. "It's the Rev. Samuel Haughton's address to the Geological Society in Dublin.

"This speculation of Messrs. Darwin and Wallace would not be worthy of notice were it not for the weight of authority of the names Charles Lyell and Joseph Hooker, under whose auspices it has been brought forward."

The beauty of Moor Park, the rest, occasional douches, walks and *Adam Bede*, all were salutary. In his spare hours Dr. Lane played at billiards with him. He needed only a week to feel sufficiently well to return home.

When, very quickly, the printer's proof sheets came and he started to read them in his big chair, he was not merely shocked but horrified. The difference between the familiar handwritten pages he had sent to Murray and the formal printer's sheets before him appeared as great as the sun at noon and a storm at midnight. He told Murray, in as humble a manner as he had ever achieved:

I get on very slowly with proofs. I remember writing to you that I thought there would be not much correction. I was most grievously mistaken. I find the style incredibly bad . . . the corrections are very heavy. How I could have written so badly is quite inconceivable. . . .

He spent the following weeks so thoroughly interlining the printer's proofs with pen and ink corrections, writing additional material in the margins, top and bottom, that he thought the pages undecipherable. He offered to enter into some arrangement with John Murray that would allow all excess over a fairly moderate charge for corrections to be deducted from his profits.

To Hooker he wrote despairingly at the end of June:

> . . . I have fairly to blacken them and fasten slips of paper on, so miserable have I found the style. You say that you dreamt that my book was entertaining; that dream is pretty well over with me. I begin to fear that the public will find it intolerably dry and perplexing. . . .

Emma, who had been spending parts of her day searching for typographical errors, hated to see him writhing and agonizing so intensely. She asked:

"Are you not indulging in self-pity?"

In July his nausea returned, which he blamed on "the accursed proofs." He held out until July 19, correcting almost half the pages, then returned to Moor Park for a week. This time he took with him a few sheets of Hooker's introduction to *Flora Tasmaniae* to correct, as well as seven sheets of his own. For evening reading he had Henry Kingsley's *Geoffrey Hamlyn* and Fitzgerald's translation of the *Rubáiyát* of Omar Khayyám, both recently published. After a few days he wrote to Murray:

> I think I have got the style fairly good and clear, with infinite trouble. But whether the book will be successful to a degree to satisfy you, I really cannot conjecture. I heartily hope it may.

Murray replied that he had corrected so heavily as almost to have rewritten the book. He knew this to be true, but it had to be done. Finally the day came, on September 10, when he had finished the last proof, with little left to do but an index.

To Lyell he made an unexpected confession:

> . . . I cannot too strongly express my conviction of the general truth of my doctrines, and God knows I have never shirked a difficulty. I am foolishly anxious for your verdict, not that I shall be disappointed if you are not converted; for I remember the long years it took me to come round; but I shall be most deeply delighted if you do come round, especially if I have a fair share in the conversion. I shall then feel that my career is run, and care little whether I ever am good for anything again in this life. . . .

On the second of October he went alone to Ilkley, a health resort and mineral spring north of Leeds. The family would follow in a few weeks. Though he took three leisurely days for the journey, and the management had reserved him a commodious living and bedroom suite, he did not like the place. The food was good, his appetite increased, he took baths, walked . . . and then sprained his ankle, which sequestered him. His leg became swollen. There followed a rash, then boils. The weather turned bitterly cold.

His only consolation was his correspondence forwarded from Down House. He received outgoing letters from Lyell, Hooker and Huxley, which he answered at length. He asked Huxley for a list of foreign scientists to whom he might send copies of his book, though he did not know how many he could afford because John Murray had not yet set the price. His family arrived, and they managed to find an available house; but Charles's misfortunes continued. He developed a swelling of the face, with his eyes almost closed. Dr. Edmund Smith, the resident surgeon, told him that he was undergoing a unique crisis.

"It feels more like living in hell," he snorted.

Emma caught a baffled expression on Dr. Smith's face which seemed to say, "Whatever can be wrong with this man?" Charles too must have caught the fleeting glance, for when the doctor left he observed:

"I don't think Dr. Smith is as much interested in his patients as he is in his fee."

Henrietta agreed with her father about Ilkley.

"This place is a frozen horror."

Emma did her best to act as dissipater of gloom. Charles realized that his considerable ills were caused by the waiting time; anxiety over the possibility that his book would be an out-and-out failure, precluding any possibility of the publication of his much larger book on species; that it would be neglected or totally ignored; or attacked, beaten, vilified, and he himself drowned in a Noachian flood of contempt and damnation.

A source of relief was Charles Lyell's speech to the British Association at Aberdeen in September 1859.

> A work will very shortly appear by Mr. Charles Darwin, the result of twenty years of observations and experiments in Zoology, Botany and Geology, by which he has been led to the conclusion that those powers of nature which give rise to races and permanent varieties in animals and plants, are the same as those which in much longer periods produce species, and in a still longer series of ages give rise to differences of generic rank. He appears to me to have succeeded by his investigations and reasonings in throwing a flood of light on many classes of phenomena connected with the affinities, geographical distri-

bution, and geological succession of organic beings, for which no other hypothesis has been able, or has even attempted to account.

Lyell's public support made him feel "cockered up." What he did not allow himself to dwell on was that at the end of a long letter Lyell told him:

> I still see the necessity of continued intervention of Creative power.

Charles was nonplussed. Lyell was still unconverted. He still needed some kind of personal God to make the decisions!

He replied at once:

> I cannot see this necessity. Its admission, I think, would make the theory of natural selection valueless. Grant a simple archetypal creature, like the mud-fish or one with both gills and lungs, with five senses and some vestige of mind and I believe natural selection will account for the production of every vertebrate animal!

The day dawned, toward the end of the first week in November, when he received at Ilkley an advance copy of the *Origin of Species* from John Murray. He ran his hands tenderly over the volume, bound in green cloth, five hundred pages of solid and, he thought, beautiful print. Murray's note informed him that of the first edition, after distribution of fifty-eight copies to Charles, to critics and to Stationer's Hall for copyright, the eleven hundred and ninety-two copies which were left had been entirely sold out to the trade at Murray's autumn sale. Murray added, "We need another edition immediately!"

The news made Charles supremely happy.

It also made him well. The puffiness left his eyes and face, the swelling vanished from his leg, his sprained ankle healed. The weather turned warmer, so that he could take the children for long expeditions. He became a tornado of activity, writing to Murray that he wished to share the formidable cost of resetting the type, seventy-two pounds and eight pence, ordered another twenty books for himself, and drafted a long list of people to whom books should be sent, then proceeded to write letters to each, telling them that he would welcome their reactions.

In mid-November his spirits were raised even higher by a letter from young John Lubbock, strongly praising the book. This letter also made him feel "cockered up"; though in a hiccough of humility he wrote to Lubbock:

> I'm glad you have read my book, but I fear you value it too highly.

Two days later he received a note from William Carpenter, the physiologist who had led him to the plans for his new microscope. Carpenter wanted Charles's permission to review the book for the *National*. Charles wrote back saying that he would welcome the review.

When Dr. Edmund Smith next examined Charles he took note of his patient's transformation.

"There!" he exclaimed. "Didn't I assure you that your crisis would pass, and that you would be the better for it?"

"You did, Doctor, you did."

Three days later he received the first published review, in the *Athenaeum* of November 19. The anonymous reviewer was hostile; passing over every argument in favor of Charles's thesis, he spoke of the "author's evident self-satisfaction" and of his disposing of all difficulties "more or less confidently." After touching on the theological implications of the book, he left the author to "the mercies of the Divinity Hall, the College, the Lecture Room and the Museum."

Chagrined, Charles wrote to Hooker asking if he could find out who the reviewer was:

> . . . the manner in which he drags in immortality, and sets the priests at me, and leaves me to their mercies, is base. He would on no account burn me, but he will get the wood ready, and tell the black beasts how to catch me. . . .

A very few hours later he had a letter from Rear Admiral Robert FitzRoy. FitzRoy was now Meteorological Statistician for the Meteorological Department of the Board of Trade, which kept reports made by British ship captains on winds, atmospheric pressure, temperature, humidity. Charles had not seen or heard from him since his discordant visit to Down House. FitzRoy was writing at once to express his alarm at Charles's extreme views:

> I presume that your whole time for some years has been so much engrossed by your own avocations, your pigeons and rabbit breeding and your microscopic investigations that you have scarcely used a *telescope* for a wide range, and comprehensive view; and that you have hardly read the works of later authorities *except* those *bits* of them which you could use in your own work. This *used* to be your habit, and the consequence was partial instead of fair results.
>
> I, at least, *cannot* find anything "ennobling" in the thought of being a descendant of even the *most* ancient *Ape*. . . .

For a moment the paper in Charles's hand quivered. His book never discussed the origin of man! He had asked, "Why have apes not acquired the intellectual power of Man?" and stated, "Various causes could be assigned, but as they are conjectural, it would be useless to give them."

He returned to the *Athenaeum* review, obviously FitzRoy's source, and found the offending sentences:

> . . . Lady Constance Rawleigh, in Disraeli's brilliant tale, inclines to a belief that man descends from the monkeys. This pleasant idea, hinted in the *Vestiges*, is wrought into something like a creed by Mr. Darwin. Man, in his view, was born yesterday—he will perish tomorrow. In place of being immortal, we are only temporary, and as it were, incidental.

"Ah, well," he said half aloud, resigned now, "that idea has been talked about for quite a while. Doubtless some will give me credit for being its sole author."

November 24, publication date, found the family still at Ilkley. It was a day of joy: John Murray was printing a second edition of three thousand copies; there were congratulatory letters from Lyell and Hooker, a fine, totally supportive letter from Thomas Huxley.

"Our close and intimate family," Charles declared after he had read the letters to Emma. "With those three as our phalanx, we shall persevere."

There was a deprecatory note from Sir John Herschel, who had always been cordial, saying that he had received the book but that he leaned to the side opposed to it.

Charles was surprised.

"Herschel helped create the science of astronomy but doesn't allow the creation of a quite different science. Do you know what I think? I think men's brains are divided into compartments, like desk drawers or files. Open one, and they are receptive, intelligent. Open another, they are obdurate, close-minded. I wonder if we shall ever understand the human brain."

"Enough to survive," Emma replied caustically; "but not enough to rejoice over."

A more heartening surprise was a communication from Hewett C. Watson, the reputable botanist:

> Once commenced to read the *Origin*, I could not rest till I had galloped through the whole. . . . Your leading idea will assuredly become recognised as an established truth in science, *i.e.* "Natural selection." It has the characteristics of all great natural truths, clarifying what was obscure, simplifying what was intricate, adding greatly to previous knowledge. You are the greatest revolutionist in natural history of this century, if not of all centuries. . . .

4.

From Ilkley they went to Shrewsbury. It was good to be back at The Mount, in the house in which he had been born, wandering through the familiar quarters, the furniture unchanged since his earliest memories. The enormous library with its marble columns appeared baronial, making Down House seem a simple country seat. He had sent Susan and Katty a copy of the *Origin of Species*, which his sisters had added to his other books on an inlaid-wood table, the volumes held in their place of honor between pink-veined marble bookends. Neither Susan nor Katty had yet read the book.

He slept well, ate goose and potato pies in the dining room overlooking the river Severn, made some corrections and additions for John Murray's next edition, took his two boys for walks along the paths of his childhood. It was a good week, cut out of time. He wrote to Erasmus telling him that the family would arrive in London on December 6 for a few days' stay with him. Erasmus responded at once, saying that he would give a dinner party for Charles's closest friends on December 7.

Erasmus had been suffering from the ague, which he said "made me feel weaker in the head." Yet there was nothing weak about his reception of the Darwins. He kissed his nieces and nephews affectionately, pecked Emma amiably on the cheek, then threw his arms about his young brother and gave him a bear hug.

"Well, Gas, you did it! Every sentence derived from the training I gave you in chemistry in that little tool house at The Mount. Remember the day we stunk up the neighborhood with our sulphurous acid?"

While the servants were settling Emma and the children in their rooms, Charles and Erasmus sprawled in lounging chairs, close to each other.

"Did you read the whole of the *Origin*, Ras?"

Erasmus took a deep breath, began slowly:

"I think it is the most interesting book I ever read, and can only compare it to my first knowledge of chemistry. It's like getting into a new world, or rather, behind the scenes of an old one. To me the relation of islands to continents is the most convincing of the proofs, as well as the relation of the oldest forms to the existing species. I dare say I don't feel enough the absence of older varieties; but then I don't in the least know whether, if everything now living were fossilized, the palaeontologist could distinguish them. . . ."

There were two messages for Charles, one from Dr. Henry Holland, the other from Richard Owen. Henry Holland received him in his luxurious office in Harley Street.

"Ah, Charles, you look fit. Ilkley must be a better health resort than I had supposed. I have not read much above half of your book so I can give no definite conclusions. . . ."

"You appear to be in a rare state of indecision," Charles twitted.

"Well . . . yes . . . I am. I simply am not tied down to either view, yours or the clergy's."

"Don't you find it uncomfortable to be skewered on both horns of a dilemma?"

"What am I to do? I read your chapter on the evolution of the eye. It took my breath away, the daring of the concept. But it won't wash, you know, it's utterly impossible to trace the structure and function from the first fishes. . . . Yet . . . it's partly conceivable. . . . Anyway, I wanted to shake your hand, Cousin, and congratulate you on the book whether its content be right or wrong."

Charles left the office, half amused, half grumbling. He took a carriage to the British Museum where he found Richard Owen in his office. Glancing at Owen's face before the eminent anatomist and naturalist had looked up from the laboratory report he was studying, two scenes flashed into his mind: his first meeting with the withdrawn, elegant, brilliant man to whom he had been introduced shortly after his return from the *Beagle*; and the wild-eyed infuriated Richard Owen of the Royal Society who had torn to shreds the paper and reputation of a fellow member.

Richard Owen greeted him with civility, an urbanity which Charles had always suspected of covering an attitude of bitterness and sneering. Then his face went crimson. He said savagely:

"I deeply resent your putting my name with defenders of immutability."

"That was my honest impression, and that of several others."

"Your Huxleys, I suppose? My outstanding position among the scientists and naturalists in London is not to be questioned. At bottom, Darwin, I go an immense way with you."

"There is no one whose approval I would value more," Charles responded.

The anger seeped out of Owen's eyes as though through a meshed strainer.

"Your explanation is the best ever published of the manner of formation of species. But you must not suppose that I agree with you in all respects."

"It is no more likely that I should be right in nearly all respects than that I should toss up a penny and get heads twenty times running."

"Then I should say, we do not want to know what Darwin believes but what he can prove."

"I agree most fully and truly that I have probably greatly sinned in this line; but I do defend my argument that it is possible to invent a theory and see how many classes of facts the theory would explain."

Owen coldly rejected this approach.

"Another of my objections is that your book attempts to explain everything. It is improbable in the highest degree."

"Granted. One can only try. I am seldom more than one jump ahead of my facts, and it is precisely because I am one jump ahead of my facts that I have made progress. Without the making of theories, based on facts at hand, I am convinced there would be no observations. When I am speculating without a firm basis of fact I am careful to warn myself, 'Pure hypothesis—be careful.'"

Owen seemed to think this was an apology. He relented, shook Charles's hand with a modicum of warmth, then ended the interview with, "The charm of the book is that it is Darwin himself."

Riding back to Erasmus's house, Charles once again felt how insulting Owen's flattery could be.

Charles and Mary Lyell were at Erasmus's when Charles and Emma returned from a visit with Hensleigh and Fanny Wedgwood. Mary Lyell had a broad smile on her face; Lyell threw his husky arms about Charles, crying:

"Right glad I am that I did my best with Hooker and Huxley to persuade you to publish the book without waiting for a time which probably never could have arrived though you lived to the age of a hundred."

Charles could feel the flush rising red in his cheeks.

"I was going to have the manuscript turned over to you and Hooker for editing after my always imminent death."

Mary Lyell laughed at him.

"It's those of you men who are chronically ill, forever taking good care of yourselves, who live forever."

Erasmus's butler served them champagne. Lyell clinked glasses with Charles, took a generous swallow of the wine.

When Thomas and Nettie Huxley arrived, Huxley said exultantly:

"Since I read Von Baer's essay on embryology nine years ago, no work on natural history has made such a great impression on me as your book. As for your doctrine, I am prepared to go to the stake for it. I trust you will not allow yourself to be in any way disgusted or annoyed by the abuse and misrepresentation which, unless I greatly mistake, is in store for you. Depend upon it, you have earned the lasting gratitude of all thoughtful men. And as to the curs who will bark and yelp, you must recollect that some of your friends, at any rate, are endowed with an amount of combativeness which, though you have often and justly rebuked it, may stand you in good stead. I am sharpening up my claws and beak in readiness."

Joseph and Frances Hooker were the last to arrive. Hooker's usually serious expression was on holiday. His eyes danced and his lips murmured joy as he gripped Charles's shoulder.

"How different the book reads from the manuscript. We were staying with the Lyells when we both read *Origin*. Lyell, here, was perfectly enchanted; absolutely gloating over it! For my own part, I think it a perfectly glorious book, capitally written. It will be successful. I must accept your compliment to me in the introduction and acknowledgment of my assistance as the warmest tribute of affection from an honest though deluded man."

While Hooker was greeting the others, Charles took Frances Hooker aside.

"Has your father read the book?"

"Yes, he has."

"How has my dear old master taken it? I fear he does not approve of his pupil in this case."

"Some parts, yes, others . . ."

"Does he hate me for it?"

"He loves you like a son . . . and forgives you your sins against God."

Charles searched Frances's face, so like, in miniature, Professor Henslow's.

Dinner was announced. The butler filled their glasses with a chilled white wine. With a sly expression, Erasmus rose, raised his glass in a toast.

"To the Origin of Our Species!"

Charles Lyell responded:

"As the American, Emerson, said, 'Beware when the great God lets loose a thinker on this planet.' "

The family returned to Down House two days later. There, as John Milton, Charles's fellow graduate of Christ's College, had written in *Paradise Lost*, published almost two hundred years before:

"All Hell broke loose."

The real shocker came from Adam Sedgwick, his long-time friend, and at one stage, seemingly, his sister Susan's suitor. Sedgwick was now Canon of Norwich and an important man in both the Church of England and the University of Cambridge. The letter was obviously a rehearsal for a piece which Sedgwick would publish in the most influential British journal to which he had access.

After a first obeisance toward friendship, Sedgwick wrote:

> If I did not think you a good-tempered and truth-loving man, I should not tell you that . . . I have read your book with more pain than pleasure. Parts of it I admired greatly, parts I laughed at till my sides were almost sore; other parts I read with absolute sorrow because I think them utterly false and grievously mischievous. You have started us in machinery as wild, I think, as Bishop Wilkins's locomotive that was to sail with us to the moon.
>
> . . . I call causation the will of God; and I can prove that He acts for the good of His creatures. Here, in the language, and still more in logic, we are point-blank at issue. There is a moral or metaphysical part of nature as well as a physical. A man who denies this is deep in the mire of folly. . . . You have ignored this link; and, if I do not mistake your meaning, you have done your best in one or two pregnant cases to break it.
>
> Passages in your book greatly shocked my moral taste. . . .

Charles put the letter on the table beside him, deeply hurt. The diatribe pained Emma so greatly that she refused to allow even the older children to see it. When they had retired for the night, Charles agonized to his wife:

"I am wounded most when he says, 'Parts of it I admired greatly, parts I laughed at till my sides were sore.' That line, in spite of the affection he professes for me, is written to make me appear a fool, a ludicrous fellow who would spend years of his life publishing something which he declares 'utterly false and grievously mischievous.' He knows I have been a serious student of natural history all my life. There can be no greater insult than ridicule."

It took him two full days, writing innumerable replies in his head but not setting anything on paper, before he could make a simple reply.

> I do not think you would wish anyone to conceal the results at which he has arrived after he has worked according to the best ability which may be in him. I do not think my book will be mischievous; for there are so many workers that, if I be wrong, I shall soon be annihilated; surely you will agree that truth can be known only by rising victorious from every attack.

The next confrontation came in the *Edinburgh Review*. It was again an anonymous review; but as Charles, Lyell, Hooker and Huxley agreed when conferring at the Athenaeum over the extremely long article, there was no way for a known scientist to remain anonymous in Great Britain. All of the internal evidence indicated that the attack had been mounted by Richard Owen. They wondered why he had chosen to attack anonymously.

Joseph Hooker smiled wanly.

"Human nature is enormously difficult to understand, far more so than rare tropical plants or seriated mountain ranges."

"The article is extremely malignant, clever," Charles murmured, "and I feel it will be very damaging. He is atrociously severe on you, Huxley, and very bitter against you, Hooker. Lyell, he left you out of his fulminations. You should be flattered."

"Not at all," Lyell replied, with his hearty grin. "I feel deprived. The severest critique of Richard Owen is that, in all the years, he has never reared one pupil or follower."

The four men were in the morning room of the club having a sherry before their midday meal. Charles turned the page of the *Edinburgh Review*, read aloud to his companions in their deep leather chairs:

> ". . . The scientific world has looked forward with great interest to the facts which Mr. Darwin might finally deem adequate to the support of his theory on this supreme question in biology, and to the course of inductive original research which might issue in throwing light on that 'mystery of mysteries.' But having now cited the chief, if not the whole, of the original observations adduced by its author in the volume now before us, our disappointment may be conceived . . ."

Huxley cried:

"Jealousy! Pure jealousy! His entire system is as filled with the pollutants of jealousy as is a tubercular with bacilli."

The attacks followed hot and heavy, frequently in unexpected places. A slashing review in the *Daily News* accused him of stealing from his master, the author of *Vestiges*. The *Gardeners' Chronicle* carried an unfriendly article, which surprised Charles since he had been contributing short notices to them for years. Then came a broadside from the *Proceedings of the Royal Society of Edinburgh*; a yes and no review from the *Canadian Naturalist*; and in the *North British Review* one which everyone agreed was "savage," written by a Rev. John Duns, a Free Kirk minister and dabbler in natural history.

"I am dumfounded at the impression my book has made on many minds," Charles exclaimed to Emma. "Theology has more to do with the attacks than science. That was to be expected. Yet I have had some hearty kicks from my best friends. Asa Gray writes that the weakest point in the book is the attempt to account for the formation of the organs, the making of eyes, ears, by natural selection. Even Hooker tells me I make a hobby of natural selection, and probably ride it too hard."

However Joseph Hooker wrote an expository article for the *Gardeners' Chronicle*; Asa Gray wrote a strong commendation in the *American Journal of Science and Arts*, and later a longer and more incisive piece for the London *Times*, followed by a signed piece for *Macmillan's Magazine*. Thomas Wollaston published a hostile review in the *Annals and Magazine of Natural History*, a clever résumé which misinterpreted Charles's conclusions. Samuel Haughton, who had dismissed Charles's and Wallace's paper in the *Journal of the Linnean Society*, published a sharp attack in the *Proceedings of the Natural History Society of Dublin*. Oddly enough, he was praised in the *English Churchman*, though the author patronized the doctrine of natural selection. To balance the equation, old J. E. Gray at the British Museum, an authority on zoology, said:

> You have just reproduced Lamarck's doctrine, and nothing else, and here Lyell and others have been attacking him for twenty years and because *you* say the same thing, they are all coming round. It's the most ridiculous inconsistency!

Both he and the book were pounded and damned from pulpits all the way from Glasgow in the north to Plymouth in the south. He had become famous and infamous, seemingly overnight. The *Origin* was discussed feverishly over the dinner tables of Great Britain, frequently by people who had never read a line of the book. Yet he received an admiring letter from Charles Kingsley, famous cleric and novelist, recently appointed chaplain to Queen Victoria:

> Dear Sir,
> I have to thank you for the unexpected honour of your book. That the Naturalist whom, of all naturalists living, I most wish to know and to learn from, should have sent a scientist like me his book, encourages me at least to observe more carefully, and think more slowly.
> . . . All I have seen of your book *awes* me; both with the heap of facts and the prestige of your name, and also with the clear intuition that if you be right, I must give up much that I have believed and written.
> In that I care little. Let God be true, and every man a liar! Let us know what *is* . . . and follow up the villainous shifty fox of an argument, into whatsoever unexpected bogs and brakes he may lead us, if we do but run into him at last. . . .

He also received support from the Rev. Brodie Innes in Down. Innes was maintaining his loyalty to his friend with a grim determination, shunting aside any of his congregation who wanted to raise a dispute over the book. They shared a glass of port after a light supper at Down House. Innes explained:

"Even before I knew you, Mr. Darwin, I publicly expressed the opinion that natural history, geology and science in general should be studied without reference to the Bible. That the book of nature and religion proceeded on parallel lines and would never cross."

Charles nodded assent, then handed Innes an abusive pamphlet by a clergyman. Innes began to laugh at the charges levied against Charles's character. He stopped abruptly when he saw the expression on Charles's face.

"Ah, Mr. Darwin, you are bitter about this pamphlet."

"I am. I have never directly attacked religion or the clergy. Why do they vilify me?"

"Because they're frightened. They fear that your book may cost them their comfortable rectories."

Huxley responded to Charles's outcries of indignation:

"Ah, but you don't give proper attention to the amount of space *Origin* is getting, all of which stimulates discussion. Even the adverse reviews cause comment."

It was an advantage he could survive without.


5.


The violent changes in the weather of criticism, from storm to sunshine to hurricane, took him back to the voyage of H.M.S. *Beagle*. He was seasick from the violent rolling of the theological and scientific seas. He yearned for the isolated hammock in the chart room where he could stretch out, nibble on raisins and biscuit while the ship pitched beneath him.

Emma resented the hostile reviews as deeply as Charles did. She was wounded by the attacks on his capacity as an objective scientist and on his character, for he was being called most of the unfortunate names in the English lexicon; and was equally happy about the favorable reviews. Yet within her own being she agreed with the charges made by the theologians, convinced that Charles's concepts would undermine the people's faith in God.

"If they lose that," she told herself, "they will lose all hope. People cannot live without faith. Life would be too difficult, impossible, really, without it. I would be totally distressed to see materialism win over spirituality."

No one suspected this, of course. She had no confidant, for she would not reveal her immersed thoughts to her sisters, brothers, children, friends. She went to church regularly, took the sacrament, read her Bible every day, instructed her children. Charles was not insensitive to her dilemma, indeed it had been his basic fear despite the fact that she had volunteered to correct the printer's proofs of the *Origin*. He did not know how much she suffered over what he had written because the worse she felt the more stoutly she maintained a solid family front, backing her husband with intense loyalty. Her gratitude toward Charles's fighting phalanx of Lyell, Hooker, Huxley, Lubbock, his brother Erasmus, was unbounded. Yet mixed into her gratitude were deep pangs of doubt, reluctance. Her own health demanded that she set forth her beliefs, yet at the same time she had to maintain Charles's health and sense of well-being.

She wrote him a letter. Tore it up. Wrote another a few days later. Threw it into the wastebasket. The attempts, written in differing moods, failed to convey her need to console him and at the same time make her feelings clear that he must direct his thoughts upward to God. At length she placed the letter in his study while he was at the Sandwalk. This was the second letter she had left for Charles. The first, just after their marriage, twenty-one years before. Basically it carried the same message.

> I cannot tell you the compassion I have felt for all your suffering for these weeks past that you have had so many drawbacks. Nor the gratitude I have felt for the cheerful and affectionate looks you have given me when I know you have been miserable.
>
> . . . I am sure you know I love you well enough to believe that I mind your suffering nearly as much as I should my own and I find the only relief to my own mind is to take it as from God's hand, and to try to believe that all suffering and illness is meant to help us to exalt our minds and to look forward with hope to a future state. When I see your patience, deep compassion for others, self-command and above all gratitude for the smallest thing done to help you I cannot help longing that these precious feelings should be offered to Heaven for the sake of your daily happiness. . . . It is feeling and not reasoning that drives one to prayer. . . .

What pleased him greatly was the fact that French and German translations were in process. The American publisher, D. Appleton, was selling his version well. They had actually printed a first edition of twenty-five hundred copies, double the amount of John Murray's first printing. "A daring people, the Americans," he thought. His opinion was confirmed when he received a check from Appleton for twenty-two pounds, more money than he had ever expected to earn in a foreign country. Murray confided to Lyell that fifty copies of *Origin of Species* had been sold in the last forty-eight hours. Indeed a man who had been inquiring for it at the railway station at Waterloo Bridge had been told that there were none till the new edition was out. The bookseller said he had not read it but had heard it was a very remarkable book.

It appeared to Charles that the denunciations and vilifications of his character and his book outnumbered the acceptances a hundred to one. His mail indicated that. It also seemed that nearly everybody was reading at least part of the book, and no one was neutral. Was abuse a more natural form of human expression than praise?

It was Charles Lyell who gave him the simple insight with which to endure the lashing.

"Do not attempt to convince your contemporaries," he advised. "The next generation will believe you. People are afraid that you are attacking God and the Church. You would have been infinitely better off had you spent your energies attacking the British Empire."

Charles went to London more often now that he was a national scandal, to test the temperature of the water of the many societies to which he belonged: the Royal, the Linnean, the Zoological, Entomological, Royal Geographical, and the Geological, sticking his big toe inside their various doors. Aside from the Entomological Society, which opposed him as a body, most of his associates inferred that his opinions were his own, that they should be studied and evaluated. He found it a particularly fine display of loyalty. Those who mentioned his book merely said they were reading it, found it interesting and congratulated him on the success of penetrating a general public with a highly specialized scientific volume. Those who had not read the work treated him exactly as they had before the publication.

"I'm not loved," he told Charles Lyell as they were leaving the Athenaeum Club. "Neither am I hated. I find that an eminently satisfactory state."

"Basically we are civilized people," replied Lyell wryly. "In London a man can dislike your point of view and still not spill a cup of hot tea in your lap."

Charles glanced around his dinner table, then explained to the children:

"Lately I have had more kicks than halfpence. The attacks have been falling thick and heavy on my case-hardened hide."

The whole family knew better. Charles was a thin-skinned man, with no appetite for controversy. Each of the rare good reviews brought him as much pleasure as if it were the first kind word he had heard in his professional life. Each new attack caught him by surprise, as if he had never before suffered rejection.

He went back to work in his study, the first time he had done so, aside from correcting the second edition of *Origin*, since he had finished correcting the printer's proofs on the first day of October of the year before. In the passing months a deal of information had poured into Down House, correspondence from experts in their chosen fields, articles in scientific journals, newly published books which had an immediate bearing on the eleven chapters of the two-thousand-page manuscript from which he had extracted the *Origin of Species*.

He began integrating his newly found materials, feeling quite well. The retching had vanished, as had the flatulence which awakened him several times a night.

"Why am I so much better?" he wondered as he kicked away flint stone number six of an eight-trip tour of the Sandwalk on a cold January afternoon. "Was my anticipation of the infernal row over publication worse than the actuality? Am I relieved to have it in the open? Or am I so caught up in the excitement of the battle, with my long letters to my detractors as well as my backers, that I keep forgetting my ailments?"

As punishment for thinking such unorthodox thoughts his stomach acted up. Having been recommended to a London practitioner, Dr. Frederick W. Headland, who had won a prize for his book, *An Essay on the Actions of Medicine in the System*, Charles went up to town for a consultation. Dr. Headland ordered him to drink a sufficiency of wine every day, abstain from all sweets, in particular the chocolate candies of which he and Emma were so fond; and prescribed a routine of nitromuriatic acid.

The prescription worked fine.

In the continuing cold of March he came down with a touch of pleurisy, with coughing, difficulty of breathing and fever. He recovered in a very few days, writing to Hooker:

"It came on like a lion and went out like a lamb."

He enjoyed excellent health right up to the Oxford meeting of the British Association for the Advancement of Science, scheduled for June 27, 1860, at which Bishop Samuel Wilberforce, known as Soapy Sam for his mellifluous voice and his ability to slide from High Church to Low Church during their internecine quarrels, had promised to "smash Darwin."

Feeling so hearty, his mind clear and eager to be at work, he made a decision which would determine the course of his productivity for the following twenty-two years. As late as January 1860 he had still been trying to implement the two-thousand-page manuscript for publication. Finally realizing that this was impractical, he planned to bring out a separate volume for each of the chapters of the long footnoted work, with a preface and index for each. In that way he would be able to complete his research and expand all the chapters of the original manuscript.

There was plenty of company at Down House in the late winter and early spring months. John Henslow was happy to be with his favorite though errant pupil. They went for walks in the woods, collecting rare mosses and ferns.

"The only thing I miss in Kent are the Fens of Cambridgeshire with their magnificent collection of living creatures; the world in miniature," said Charles. "I always enjoyed collecting but it was in the Fens that you made a naturalist of me."

Henslow's long head of hair was snow white. Although only sixty-four, his cheeks had begun to sink a little. Yet to Charles he was still one of the most beautiful of men: kindly, giving of himself, saintly. A *rara avis* in a world of conflict and turmoil.

Henslow helped Charles achieve the emotional balance he needed to retain his equilibrium in the hurricane surrounding him. When Dr. William Whewell, now Master of Trinity College at Cambridge, refused to allow a copy of *Origin of Species* to be placed in the library, Charles was shocked.

"It's difficult for me to understand the duality of man's nature. In spite of censoring the book, the ultimate crime at a great university, he wrote me a friendly letter saying he had not, yet at least, become a convert but there was so much of thought and fact in what I had written that it was not to be contradicted without careful selection of the ground and manner of the dissent."

Henslow nodded his gnarled head, added:

"Then why not give his students the same privilege of careful selection? Censorship is always temporary and self-defeating. I'll discuss the book in my classes."

"How are my old friends at Christ's College taking this disreputable conduct on the part of one of their graduates?"

Henslow's fading blue eyes twinkled.

"Philosophically. With a bit of pride. Why don't you go back for a visit?"

"It's twenty-three years since they granted me a master's degree."

"Why not come when Adam Sedgwick gives his university lecture against the *Origin*? You're the best prepared to answer him."

Charles was aghast at the idea.

"I haven't the courage to defend my ideas in public. Only in the quiet of my study."

Henslow murmured, "Then I shall."

Emma was particularly happy to have the Lyells with them. Mary had been a good friend since their three and a half years at Upper Gower Street, with the Lyells on Hart Street only a few squares away. It was raining upon Down in slanted sheets so Charles settled Lyell in the comfortable writing chair, even as he had on that day almost four years before when Lyell and Hooker had convinced him that he must start writing immediately and publish as quickly as possible. Though plagued by a receding hairline, at sixty-two Lyell was still a handsome man, his wide, white sideburns coming down to his cheekbones, his big eyes and determined mouth those of a young man.

Lyell was bursting with excitement over his own new project.

"Darwin, I've made up my mind. I'm going to write a book about the descent of man. My proposed title is 'Geological Evidences of the Antiquity of Man.' "

Charles was as pleased as he was taken aback.

"Glory be to God! You have released me from that frightening burden. You are very bold in this and I honor you. Yours will, no doubt, be a grand discussion; but it will horrify the world. It was in this room that you cautioned me on writing about man. I suspect I must return that caution a hundredfold."

"I'm aware of the dangers. It is the last outpost on the road to hell. I shall protect myself by asking you to read every page of the manuscript."

Charles winced.

"I believe man is in the same predicament with other animals. It is in fact impossible to doubt it. . . . Our ancestor was an animal which breathed water, had a swim bladder, a great swimming tail, an imperfect skull, and undoubtedly was an hermaphrodite. Here is a pleasant genealogy for mankind!"

It was a treat to have Joseph Hooker and Thomas Huxley at Down House together with their wives. Emma, Frances Hooker and Nettie Huxley shared common burdens as well as joys. The three men were about as creative a trio as could be found in British science, for all three were digging into nature's unrevealed secrets and searching for primary causes. They overworked themselves, and as a consequence were frequently ill and had to be nursed; all three pursued their iconoclastic views and brought the tension into their family lives; all three were self-generating personalities. When the men were clustered around the table in the drawing room, the early spring sun still warm and the flower beds showing their first touches of color, Hooker said:

"I expect there will be before long a great revulsion in your favor to match the senseless howl that is now raised; and that as many converts, upon *no* principle, will fall in, as there are now antagonists upon *no* principle. Owen has done himself great damage in the eyes of independent literary men . . . whether for the gratuitous attempt to insult Huxley or the utter baseness of his conduct to you, his pretended friend."

Hooker was wrong, or at least premature. His introductory essay to *Flora Tasmaniae* had originally been well received by the critics. Now Charles's opponents entered into an agreement not to in any way call attention to it because parts of it buttressed the case for natural selection.

"It is incredibly paltry," cried Charles. "I look at their attacks as a proof that our work is worth doing. We must not give up hope. The time will come, I believe, though I shall not live to see it, when we shall have every fairly true genealogical tree of each great kingdom of nature."

The three men chose walking sticks from the umbrella stand near the garden door, stepped out into the brisk April gloaming toward the Sandwalk for a ritualistic seven-pebble jaunt around the darkening oblong of woods. When they had matched into an even stride Huxley said in a voice filled with inner strength:

"What exists now is an internecine war in which personal feelings rather than logical arguments dominate the field. Nothing can open a closed mind except a dose of strong physique. The irony is that our opponents are beginning to quarrel among themselves . . . accusing each other of using the wrong weapons against us."

"All the same," Charles vouchsafed, "it is painful to be hated in the intense degree to which Owen hates me. The Londoners say he is mad with envy because my book is being talked about. What a strange man to be envious of a naturalist like myself, immeasurably his inferior. It's as John Henslow says, 'I don't think it is at all becoming in one naturalist to be bitter against another, any more than for one sect to burn the members of another.'"

Hooker took off his glasses, waved them around in a circle before him.

"Botany is not a controversial field. Bentham's and my encyclopedia will contain only facts. Facts are not disputable."

"Ha!" exclaimed Huxley. "One man's fact is another man's fiction."

Darkness was filtering down like powdered ash. They left the Sandwalk, went through the little gate, walked along the path of the kitchen garden toward the lamplighted house. Hooker asked:

"You'll come with us to the British Association meeting in Oxford, won't you? Lyell has promised to be there."

"No, I will not."
His voice left no room for doubt.

6.

For each poison there had been an antidote. When Louis Agassiz, world-renowned naturalist, now teaching at Harvard, declared *Origin of Species* to be "poor, very poor!" and wrote an article for the *American Journal of Science and Arts* detailing his annoyance at the book and his repugnance as well, Asa Gray, also at Harvard, wrote an excellent reply, and in addition offered to transfer Charles's corrections for the English second edition to Appleton's second printing.

When his friend Thomas Wollaston launched a bold attack in the *Annals and Magazine of Natural History*, and William H. Harvey, the botanist, chastised Charles in the *Gardeners' Chronicle*, a long supportive article appeared in the New York *Times*. When the geologist Sir Roderick Murchison told Charles that he was disappointed in *Origin of Species*, a letter arrived from Leonard Jenyns, clergyman and naturalist, saying that he went with Charles "much further than he had expected."

While Richard Owen, hiding behind the screen of anonymity, published his brutal assault in the *Edinburgh Review*, there came very enthusiastic and explicit reviews from William Carpenter, physiologist, in the *National*, and a perfectly fair and just review in the *Bibliothèque universelle* of Geneva by Professor F. J. Pictet, a palaeontologist, which would go a long way to stimulate interest in France and Germany. Alfred Wallace wrote a highly laudatory letter from Malaysia, where he had finished the reading of the book. Charles told his friends:

"Wallace's letter was too modest, and admirably free from envy or jealousy."

Each reviewer had a favorite bee in his bonnet. The assaults by Samuel Haughton of Dublin and William Harvey, professor of botany at Trinity College, Dublin, convinced him that he must be a very bad elucidator. Then he learned that the great Henry Thomas Buckle, author of *History of Civilization in England*, highly approved of the book. Once again his spirits soared. The *Christian Examiner* of Boston gave him good space and grades; but in *Fraser's Magazine* the reviewer despised the reasoning power of all naturalists!

However there seemed to be no antidote for the fact that Adam Sedgwick had become rabid. Anonymously, he published an abusive article in the *Spectator*:

. . . I cannot conclude without expressing my detestation of
the theory, because of its unflinching materialism;—because it

has deserted the inductive track, the only track that leads to physical truth;—because it utterly repudiates final causes, and thereby indicates a demoralised understanding on the part of its advocates.

Not that I believe that Darwin is an atheist; though I cannot but regard his materialism as atheistical. . . .

Each series of facts is placed together by a series of assumptions and repetitions of the one false principle. You cannot make a good rope out of a string of air bubbles.

Huxley asked:

"How does it feel to be lauded to the skies one day, then flagellated the next?"

Charles searched for a simile.

"Like the sailors on the *Beagle* who got hilariously drunk as soon as we came into port, then were lashed over the bare back by the boatswain's mate with a cat-o'-nine-tails to pay for their pleasure."

The storm over *Origin of Species* had been largely confined to scientific and theological circles. Adam Sedgwick converted it into a wind-lashed hurricane whose purpose it was to sink the book as H.M.S. *Beagle* had very nearly been sunk in the nightmarish blow off Cape Horn. Charles learned from Henslow that Sedgwick was going to launch an attack before the Cambridge Philosophical Society.

"Now there's a staggerer for you," he told Emma. "It was Sedgwick who launched my career by presenting my letters from the *Beagle* to the Philosophical Society, and publishing them. He now intends to sink me using the identical Society."

The contest was waged before a large and distinguished audience. Henslow wrote about it to Joseph Hooker, who forwarded the letter to Charles. He read it aloud while he and Emma sat out at noon in the sun of the fragrant May day. Sedgwick's address was

". . . strong enough to cast a *slur* upon all who substitute hypotheses for strict inductions and, as he expressed himself in regard to some of Darwin's suggestions, as *revolting* to his own sense of right and wrong. Dr. William Clark, Prof. of Astronomy, who followed him, spoke so unnecessarily severely against Darwin's views, I got up, as Sedgwick had alluded to me, and stuck up for Darwin as well as I could, refusing to allow that he was guided by any but truthful motives, and declaring that he himself believed he was exalting and not debasing our views of a Creator in attributing to him a power of imposing laws on the Organic World by which to do His work. . . ."

Adam Sedgwick's stone, thrown into the academic seas, caused outspreading ripples that reached considerable distances. While Henslow defended Charles in his Cambridge lectures, the Rev. Baden Powell, professor of geometry at Oxford, adopted Charles's conclusions to prove his own scientific views. Outraged, Sedgwick took out after Powell. Richard Owen, trying to put a damper on all this publicity for Charles Darwin, went about London saying:

"The *Origin* is merely the Book of the Day. Next week, or next month, there will be a quite different Book of the Day."

Huxley cried exultantly:

"The Book of Today . . . and Tomorrow . . . and Tomorrow."

When Charles was accused of being an atheist he retorted in a letter to Asa Gray:

> The theological view of the subject is painful to me. I am bewildered. I had no intention to write atheistically. I own that I cannot see as plainly as others do, and as I should wish to do, evidence of design and beneficence on all sides of us. There seems to me too much misery in the world. I cannot persuade myself that a beneficent and omnipotent God would have designedly created the Ichneumonidae with the express intension of their feeding within the living bodies of Caterpillars, or that a cat should play with mice. . . . I am inclined to look at everything as resulting from designed laws, with the details, whether good or bad, left to the working out of what we may call chance. Not that this notion *at all* satisfies me. I feel most deeply that the whole subject is too profound for the human intellect. A dog might as well speculate on the mind of Newton. . . .

From Asa Gray he learned how hotly the battle was raging in the United States. But young John Lubbock came on horseback from High Elms to report that his father said there was an excellent piece in the French *Revue des deux mondes*.

"Europe will soon be as aware of *Origin* as England and the United States. By the by, Father has learned from an editor at the *Athenaeum* that your former captain, Robert FitzRoy, is hoping to join forces with Bishop Wilberforce at the British Association meeting in Oxford to . . ."

". . . blow me to atoms?"

"Of course you will want to answer FitzRoy."

When Lubbock rode off, Charles slumped into his study chair nursing the glass of cool lemonade that Emma had sent in.

"Answer them, be damned!" he swore.

The 1860 meeting of the British Association at Oxford was shaping up as a prestigious one. Two of the papers already announced made it clear that the focus of several sessions would be built around "The Book of the Day," which even the enemies of the book conceded to be the most important publication to emerge from the world of science in recent years. The Oxford professor of rural economy, Charles Daubeny, a learned and popular man, was to read a paper titled "On the Final Causes of the Sexuality of Plants, with particular reference to Mr. Darwin's work on the *Origin of Species*." The second paper, by William Draper, former professor of chemistry and physiology and now president of the medical school of the University of the City of New York, was called "The Intellectual Development of Europe considered with reference to the views of Mr. Darwin."

Richard Owen would be there. Also the Bishop of Oxford, Samuel Wilberforce, who had announced that he would reply to the main address on Saturday, having assumed the official position of the Church. Wilberforce had taken a first class degree in mathematics, which gave him the assurance that he could understand all things scientific. He was one of England's most popular public speakers, with a native wit, and drew enormous crowds wherever he appeared. He had had no training in natural history, or any known interest in it; his attack would be a masterpiece of misinterpretation and ridicule. The audience would be made up almost entirely of his followers. Debating with Wilberforce was like attempting to catch fleeting clouds with a flycatcher. Charles did not believe that anyone would attempt to answer him.

Emma studied her husband, her eyes shrewd but not unsympathetic.

"Since you will not go to Oxford, why not try a few days of hydropathy? Dr. Lane's new establishment in Richmond is so close now, only fifteen or twenty miles . . ."

Dr. Lane and his wife were happy to see him. He found a short walk, took a little of the water cure . . . and was wretched. On earlier visits to Malvern or Moor Park his distress left him very soon. Now he ate little, suffered from insomnia, found the hours protracted. He tried to divert himself by reading Dr. Lane's copy of the London *Times* but the paper held little that was inspiriting. While he was pleased to note that the City of London Gas, Light and Coke Company was providing gaslight to the city, there would be none available in Down for years to come. Charing Cross Station had been opened as the West End terminus of the railroad line the Darwins used, shortening their trip; and Big Ben, the thirteen-ton bell placed atop the clock tower of the Houses of Parliament, had been declared a great success as it rang across London. However the British had renewed their war with China, sending a force of thirteen thousand men to bombard Peking. The Maori tribesmen of

New Zealand, some of whom Charles had seen when H.M.S. *Beagle* was anchored off the Bay of Islands, rose in wrath over a land dispute and attacked the English strongholds, driving away the settlers from outlying districts. . . .

He abandoned the newspaper, attempted instead to read in two newly published novels, *The Mill on the Floss* by George Eliot, and *Great Expectations* by Charles Dickens. He recognized the quality of both but was unable to concentrate for more than a few minutes at a time. Deep in despair, he came to the conclusion that his predisposition to illness was hereditary, and that he had passed it on to his children.

"All Darwins ought to be exterminated," he thought, chewing the bitter cud of culpability.

The Darwin children had had their share of the illnesses of childhood: measles, mumps, whooping cough, winter-long colds, diphtheria . . . The younger ones had found the older ones contagious, or were imitating them as the highest form of flattery. Or, desolating thought, were they imitating their father, the chronic invalid almost since they were born? Perhaps they might have considered it poor taste for a parcel of seven children to be robust around so delicate a father.

Yet he remembered how strong, healthy, indefatigable he had been in his youth, walking for miles and collecting for days on end; how vigorous he had been during his Cambridge years, and on the *Beagle* voyage, on his land trips and mountain climbing, on the pampas of Patagonia, the Andes of Chile, the forests of Brazil. He recalled his long days of work when he returned to London at twenty-seven, his Herculean tasks in the little house on Fitzwilliam Street in Cambridge where he separated and classified his collections, sound and hardy until he had started delving and writing in his notebooks about the obscure secrets of nature.

If his illness was congenital where did it come from? Assuredly not from the Darwin side. Dr. Erasmus Darwin and Dr. Robert Darwin had enjoyed good health and longevity. From his mother's side then, the Wedgwoods? Had his mother not become bedridden and died before he was nine years old? Uncle Jos Wedgwood had shown no signs of illness early on. Aunt Bessy was confined to her bed for years . . . but no! She was an Allen, not a Wedgwood. It was all very confusing in his troubled state.

All this lasted for five days, until he received a letter from Joseph Hooker written in Oxford early that morning and sent by mail coach to Sudbrooke Park. By the time Charles finished reading it his stomach had settled down, his headache had miraculously disappeared. He was also overwhelmed at Hooker's audacity. Reading the letter for a second time, he felt a sense of exultation:

. . . Huxley and Owen had had a furious battle over your absent body, at Section D, before my arrival. Huxley was triumphant; you and your book forthwith became the topic of the day. . . . On Saturday Soapy was to answer Draper of New York University. The meeting was so large that they had adjourned to the Library, which was crammed with between 700 and 1000 people. . . .

Well, Sam got up and spouted for half an hour with inimitable spirit, ugliness and emptiness and unfairness. I saw he was coached up by Owen and knew nothing, and he said not a syllable but what was in the Reviews; he ridiculed you badly and Huxley savagely. The battle waxed hot. Lady Brewster fainted, the excitement increased as others spoke; my blood boiled. . . . I swore to myself that I would smite that Amalekite, Sam, hip and thigh if my heart jumped out of my mouth. I handed my name up to Henslow, the presiding president, as ready to throw down the gauntlet. There I was cocked up with Sam at my right elbow, and there and then I smashed him amid rounds of applause. I proceeded to demonstrate (1) that he could never have read your book, and (2) he was absolutely ignorant of the rudiments of Bot. Science. . . .

Sam had not one word to say in reply, and the meeting *was dissolved forthwith*, leaving you master of the field after 4 hours' battle. Huxley, who never before, (Thank God) praised me to my face, told me it was splendid, and that he did not know before what stuff I was made of. I have been congratulated and thanked by the blackest coats and whitest stocks in Oxford.

He slept peacefully that night, for the first time in weeks, ate a hearty breakfast and took a long walk over country paths. He had no further word about the Oxford meeting until he reached home four days later. Sir John Lubbock invited the Darwins to tea.

7.

Their gardener-coachman, Lettington, drove them the few miles to High Elms, an estate of fourteen thousand acres, with rolling greenswards, pools with jetting fountains, statuary, descending terraces, trails that led through formal gardens riotous with July colors. The mansion was a boxed oblong, three stories high with a ground-floor ceiling that rose twenty feet in the drawing room and library. The Lubbocks had been in the banking business in Lombard Street for several generations.

John Lubbock, the son, welcomed them. For a twenty-six-year-old, he was a remarkable man. At the age of fourteen while at Eton he had been taken out of school and brought into the bank because several of Sir John's partners had fallen ill, and it became obvious that Sir John Lubbock's son would one day have to manage the business. Sir John had also been an experienced naturalist. Now the youngster educated himself in anthropology and archaeology, and was researching and writing two manuscripts, "Prehistoric Times, as illustrated by Ancient Remains" and "The Manners and Customs of Modern Savages." He had a powerful forehead, large wide-spaced eyes, and the modest beginnings of a beard. He brushed his hair back in curling waves from his brow.

The Lubbocks, father and son, had attended the Oxford meeting. They were eager to know what Hooker had reported and were anxious to give their own report.

The son opened his notebook, observed by way of introduction:

"Thursday was a day of sun and cloud at Oxford, warm, soft, bright, far too beautiful a day in that lovely town for a war to erupt. But erupt it did. Oh, not right away. First, your friend Professor Henslow was appointed president of the zoology and botany section. Next we had to listen to a rambling paper by the Rev. Mr. Carpenter 'On the Progress of Natural Science in the United States and Canada.' Then Dr. Daubeny read his paper. And Professor Henslow called on Thomas Huxley for a commentary on the two papers. He declined, feeling that a general audience in which sentiment would unduly interfere with intellect was not the public before which such a discussion should be carried on. . . ."

"That doesn't sound like Huxley," Emma suggested.

"There was no challenge as yet," said Sir John.

"Next we heard from a Mr. Dowden of Cork who related several anecdotes of a monkey to show that, however highly organized the Quadrumana, the monkey, ape, gorilla, baboon, lemur, might be, they were very inferior in intellectual qualities to the dog, the elephant and other animals."

"We think it may have been a signal," Sir John again interpolated.

"A Dr. Wright then got up to report on the habits of the gorilla. Wright barely had time to sit down before Richard Owen was at the rostrum. At first he was all honey and sweetcakes, telling the audience that he wished to approach the subject in the spirit of the philosopher. Whilst giving all praise to Mr. Darwin for the courage with which he had put forth his theory, he felt it must be tested by facts in order to come to conclusions with regard to the truth of Mr. Darwin's theory.

"That was the point at which Owen went on the attack! He inferred that the whole of the *Origin* could be overthrown by proving you wrong in suggesting that man is descended from the ape . . ."

"I suggested no such thing!" Charles was furious. "I purposely avoided that area of speculation. All I wrote was that in the distant future I see open fields for far more important researches. That light will be thrown on the origin of man and his history."

". . . Owen said that he would refer to the structure of the highest Quadrumana as compared with man. Taking the brain of the gorilla, it presented more differences as compared with the brain of man than it did when compared with the brain of the lowest and most problematical form of the Quadrumana."

"Now Huxley had his challenge!" observed Charles.

"Right!" said the younger Lubbock. "Owen claims to be England's greatest anatomist and zoologist. Huxley, twenty years younger than Owen, asked permission to reply. He refuted altogether the idea that the difference between the brain of the gorilla and man was so great as represented by Professor Owen, and referred to the published dissections of Tiedemann and others. From the study of the structure of the brain of the Quadrumana, Huxley maintained that the difference between man and the highest monkey was not so great as between the highest and the lowest monkey as Owen claimed, that the feature which distinguished man from the monkey was the gift of speech."

Charles sat quietly gazing from the upland advantage of High Elms over the Lubbock pastures with their grazing cattle, and beyond to the gently undulating landscape of Kent, which he had come to love as much as Maer and Staffordshire, and his own Shropshire with its river Severn. He declined a third cup of tea, his long lean frame poised to hear the rest of the report.

"That was prologue," continued Sir John. "The real drama unfolded, as Hooker wrote to you, at the Saturday meeting when Bishop Samuel Wilberforce was the main speaker. Since he had earlier announced his intention to 'smash Darwin' his followers turned out in full force. There must have been up to a thousand people jammed in there, standing in the aisles, the youngish women in their bright summer frocks and hats, with white handkerchiefs which they used as fans. The university was not in session but there was a small group of undergraduates, and a quite large group of the clergy massed in the center to give Wilberforce support.

"He attacked you and Huxley viciously, with Huxley seated only a few feet from him. Then, spurred on by the applause of the audience and the waving of the white handkerchiefs, he made a great blunder. He turned to Huxley and asked with a smiling insolence:

" 'Mr. Huxley, I beg to know, was it through your grandfather or your grandmother that you claim to have descended from a monkey?'

"Huxley turned to the man next to him and, smiting his own knee with his hand, exclaimed, 'The Lord hath delivered him into my hands!'

"Then Huxley rose and said:

" 'I assert that a man has no reason to be ashamed of having an ape for his grandfather. If there were an ancestor whom I should feel shame in recalling, it would rather be a *man*, a man of restless and versatile intellect who, not content with a success in his own sphere of activity, plunged into scientific questions with which he has no real acquaintance, only to obscure them by an aimless rhetoric, and distract the attention of his hearers from the real point at issue by eloquent digressions and skilled appeals to religious prejudice.'

"Huxley was applauded and Wilberforce booed by the undergraduates. Thereafter when the various clergymen and amateurs rose to their feet to spout religious dogma, President Henslow quickly set them down with:

" 'Only scientific observation is permitted at this meeting!' "

How wonderfully Henslow too had taken on the Wilberforce challenge.

"The rest you know from Hooker's letter," Sir John concluded. "That evening at a reception given by Professor Daubeny the sole topic of conversation was the confrontation between Huxley and Wilberforce. Someone asked if Huxley had not injured himself irreparably, but the Vice-Chancellor of Oxford declared that the bishop got no more than he deserved."

The sun was completing its long slow arc of the summer sky, the western horizon a riotous blend of sunset colors from shell pink to a blue-dye indigo. Charles felt emotionally exhausted and exalted. How to thank his good friends? Yet gratitude was obviously neither needed nor wanted. The members of a close-knit group did not thank each other for loyalty and devotion. Those qualities were implicit in the structure of a family.

Thomas and Nettie Huxley came to Down House to spend a long weekend. Nettie had already borne three children. She was in good health and more in love with her husband than when she had married him five years before. Huxley had been letting his rich dark hair grow longer at the back, over his collar. As the two men walked around the Sandwalk they were both talking so excitedly about the Oxford meeting they never knew how many rounds they had made.

Charles noted that Huxley seemed more confident of his own potential in a frequently hostile and fractious world. "Rightly so," he mused; "he has made himself known in popular estimation as a dangerous adversary in debate; and established himself as a personal force in the world of science, having prevented the theory of evolution from being buried under misrepresentation and ridicule."

Huxley's eyes sparkled with satisfaction. Charles said as they emerged into the hot July sunshine of the Sandwalk's open stretch:

"You fought nobly."

"I assured you early on that I had sharp claws."

When they reached the little gate Huxley asked:

"Did the Lubbocks tell you about the antics of Captain FitzRoy at that fateful meeting?"

". . . FitzRoy?"

"John Henslow tried to stop him from addressing the audience, but to no avail. First he named you 'his poor friend and five-year messmate on H.M.S. *Beagle*,' then he told about how constantly you argued and quarreled about the earth's structure, the plants and creatures living on it."

Charles stopped short.

"We had precisely two quarrels in five years; the first about slavery, the second about the need for hospitality on board ship. . . ."

"His mind has locked," Huxley said, shaking his head. "He stood on the platform holding a huge Bible over his head, begging the audience to accept the word of God rather than man; implored us to reject with abhorrence the attempt to substitute human conjecture for the explicit Revelation which the Almighty Himself had made when it pleased Him to create the world and all that it contained."

Charles walked along in silence, sad, recalling the grand adventures and perils he and FitzRoy had shared. He was always grateful for the opportunity FitzRoy had given him to become a naturalist, and always feared for him.

They walked up the path by the kitchen garden. Huxley, wanting to lighten Charles's mood before they entered the house, exclaimed:

"Now I will tell you the best joke of the meeting. The Lubbocks told you that I replied to Wilberforce that a man has no reason to be ashamed of having an ape for a grandfather; if there should be an ancestor whom I should be ashamed of recalling . . ."

"I remember."

"I must tell you how England has translated my little speech. I am now being quoted as having said, '*I'd rather have an ape for a grandfather than a bishop!*'"

Charles stopped in sheer astonishment on the little porch outside the garden door. Then he burst into hearty laughter, threw an arm roughly about his defender's shoulder.

"My dear Huxley, that one deliciously garbled line has assured us both a place in history."

# BOOK TWELVE

*"I Am Like a Gambler,
and Love a Wild Experiment"*

1.

I N 1860 Down House became a citadel under siege. Charles had a mirror attached obliquely to the front wall of his study between the two windows overlooking the road so that he could see who was coming up the drive. He was not obliged to have his post picked up each day at the Down post office but when the packet became unwieldy some kind soul delivered the accumulated letters to the front door. Each passing month seemed to bring more letters, many of them from members of the family, for the Darwins' favorite couplet was:

> Write a letter, write a letter.
> Good advice will make us better.

However the bulk of the post was from strangers. He vowed that he would read only those letters which came from friends but this resolve was out of character. He read everything that came in, even the bitterly hostile tirades. Emma and his daughters Henrietta and Elizabeth also perused them. He began to feel like a seasoned campaigner, his chest covered with medals for bravery under fire, his body crisscrossed with scar tissue. Only occasionally did he allow the boiling lava of wrath which lay concealed beneath his pleasant exterior to erupt. To William H. Harvey, the Irish botanist who was making it a crusade to discredit him and the *Origin of Species* by a series of fallaciously reasoned letters, he finally wrote:

> . . . I should think you would as soon take an emetic as re-read any part of my book.

"I should like to retire to the Elysian Fields where never a voice is raised in anger," he exclaimed to the family. He was sitting in a rocking chair in the drawing room, his knees drawn up close to the wood fire. "I know how to get there. By writing natural history that is non-controversial. Such as the variation of animals and plants under domestication. Or a thesis on the fertilization of orchids by bees, moths and other winged insects. . . . I've never heard it said that orchids are fertilized by bees. . . ."

"Then, isn't that a bold assumption?" Emma asked.

His smile was half grimace.

"I am like a gambler, and love a wild experiment."

At his autumn sale John Murray had sold seven hundred copies of the second edition of the *Origin* but had only half that many on hand. Charles quickly made his corrections for the third edition and, when delivering them in London, visited Lyell. The late November rain was threatening to change to sleet. Lyell was dictating to a newly hired amanuensis, his stockinged feet stretched out to the coal fire. When the housemaid ushered Charles into the study, Lyell looked up with a scowl.

"Confound you, Darwin! The Oxford professor of geology, John Phillips, has been attacking you by citing passages out of my *Principles of Geology*. I will have to modify what I said for my next edition to prove that you had arrived while I was still snowbound in a halfway house."

Charles grinned sheepishly.

"Hooker says you are the sole sexagenarian philosopher who can change his position on good ground."

Lyell grunted at the left-handed compliment, went to his desk and showed Charles the flint instruments he had unearthed in the valley of the Somme at Amiens, and in the valley of the Seine.

"These tools indicate that the human race goes back to the time of the Siberian rhinoceros and other extinct animals. . . . But you obviously have something on your mind?"

Charles took a chair by the fire, murmured:

"I want your advice. It has occurred to me that it would be a good plan for the third edition of the *Origin* to use a set of footnotes devoted exclusively to the errors of my reviewers."

"Absolutely not! Why immortalize your adversaries?"

Charles shook his head, bemused.

"You're right, of course. I can perhaps answer the criticisms with an extra paragraph here and there. It will add only some twenty pages."

The Oxford meeting had advanced the subject of evolution by getting the discussion out into the open. A new word entered the English language: *Darwinism*. It spread through Great Britain, then through the academic circles of the United States and Europe. A second German edition of the *Origin* was on the press. A German naturalist visiting Down House told him that the German scientists were fascinated yet frightened that they might lose their positions if they came out for natural selection. The French translation had been released. Reports from Holland demonstrated a wave of interest there.

At Charles's suggestion, Asa Gray had his three articles from the prestigious *Atlantic Monthly* bound into a monograph. He sent Charles two hundred of them since Charles had shared the expense of publication. Charles distributed his copies to the newspapers, magazines and scientific journals.

John Henslow, accused in *Macmillan's Magazine* of December 1860 of being an adherent of evolution, published in the same magazine an abstract of a letter he had received from the Rev. Leonard Jenyns which said that, if he did not go along with Darwin totally, he did

go to the length of imagining that many of the smaller groups, both of animals and plants, may at some remote period have had a common parentage.

Charles was pleased.

"It indicates to the outside world," he commented to Emma, "that there is a growing unity in our scientific family."

His "scientific family" was often ill from overwork. Hooker was frequently down; Huxley had to be kept in bed for ten days with a combination of exhaustion and influenza. The Lyells went to Bavaria for reasons of health. He himself moved from subject to subject like the bees from flower to flower fertilizing the orchids in which he had become seriously interested. He began the study of the ground orchids that grew in Kent, and those that Hooker could send him from Kew Gardens. Other associates to whom he appealed provided him with flowers from Peru, Ecuador, Brazil, Madagascar, the Philippines, places that were four to eight thousand feet high, frost free, and where the fog set in. In the lush jungles of Brazil one could find thirty to forty different species on a single tree. He focused on the sepals and the pollen, protected at the top of the blossom by an overlap or umbrella.

From September to November he had taken his family to Eastbourne because Henrietta, with whom he had been playing backgammon for an hour each day, was ill. When not keeping vigil with Emma, he studied a strange phenomenon concerning the genus *Drosera* of which naturalists had taken little notice. He sometimes thought the insect-eating plant to be a disguised animal from the way its leaves caught flies and insects and devoured them. He learned that in the marshy areas of the United States there existed a plant called "Venus's flytrap," its circular leaves coming together like a bear trap when any prey touched its triggerlike hairs. The bladderwort and other insectivorous plants operated like a mousetrap; crustaceans and even small frogs tripped the saclike chamber whose door opened and captured the prey for feasting.

Strange world! Wondrous world!

He studied the pistils and pollen of the primrose and cowslip, finding that they required the action of insects to set the fertilizing process in action. To his children he explained:

"Observing the intricate functionings of nature is sheer pleasure; writing is sheer pain. But if we don't set down on paper what we have observed, how are we going to document the miracle of evolution and the life cycle of birds, beasts, flowers, plants, man?"

Back in Down House he became fascinated by the evolution of the modern dog from several varieties of wolf and jackal, and from other species. This field too seemed an untouched line of investigation. Answering the flow of letters from friends wanting to know what he was up to, he replied:

"I am at dogs."

Time contracted with age. Earlier on he had viewed the passage of months as episodic; now he took a philosophic approach to the wholeness of the year as an integrated design. His first move was to write a thirty-page historical sketch for the third edition of the *Origin* giving credit to those naturalists who had made the first, fragmentary steps toward the concept: men like Lamarck, Geoffroy Saint-Hilaire, W. C. Wells, Von Buch, Herbert Spencer and such contemporary exponents as Richard Owen, the author of *Vestiges*, still thought to be Robert Chambers, Alfred Wallace. He left out his grandfather, Dr. Erasmus Darwin, for fear of being charged with practicing nepotism in reverse. This review created for the reader a background and perspective for his own work.

Thomas Huxley too was looking for perspective. To drown his sorrow over the death of his first-born, a four-year-old boy, he plunged into a new job as chief editor of the *Natural History Review*. He brought his first copy to Down House for Charles to read. Huxley had become the acknowledged dynamo of British science. In addition to being secretary of the Geological Society, supplying Lyell with anatomical information for his "Antiquity of Man," lecturing weekly to workingmen on "The Relation of Man to the Rest of the Animal Kingdom," he was also in line for two additional important college posts.

Charles read Huxley's article in the *Review*, On the Zoological Relation of Man with the Lower Animals, and complimented him on its excellence, then observed:

"I am rather a croaker. I do rather fear that the merit of the articles will be above the run of common readers."

"So are your books!" retorted Huxley. "I haven't noticed that that impeded you at all."

Joseph Hooker was deeply immersed in continuity. In addition to preparing the first volume of his encyclopedia *Genera Plantarum*, on the world's seed-bearing plants, he was spending his days following his father about Kew, trying in vain to shore up Sir William Hooker's diminishing judgment about the management of the gardens. When Charles visited Hooker, he pleaded:

"Try to be idle sometimes."

"I am. In my sleep. Which doesn't give me much scope."

"I know I'm a pretty man to preach, for I cannot be idle, much as I might wish it. I am never comfortable except when at work. The word 'holiday' is written in a dead language for me."

Senior of them all, Sir Charles Lyell, at the age of sixty-three, had plunged into his most difficult and, for Charles, his most meaningful book, The Geological Evidences of the Antiquity of Man, sifting through the raw material he had accumulated over a lifetime, writing sections on Danish shell mounds, borings in Egypt, marine shells, flint instruments, the age of the Natchez fossil man. . . .

To Charles's surprise, Lyell did not send him a page or chapter of his new work, though the year before he had asked if Charles would read the pages in order to make suggestions. Nor did Lyell discuss his conclusions when they were together. Charles wondered why his friend had changed his mind but was not disturbed by Lyell's reticence. He was certain that Lyell would go the full way in revealing that man was in the same predicament as other animals in the evolution of all living things, the aspect Charles himself had avoided in the Origin of Species. Lyell's knighthood, his position at the top of British science, would enable him to bring it off without suffering the badge of infamy which had been pinned on Charles's lapel.

He told Lyell, as the highest form of compliment:

"Yours will be a grand discussion, but it will horrify the world at first, more than my volume of the Origin."

"I'm not seeking to horrify the world," Lyell replied with quiet dignity. "I'm trying to inform people. The hard facts are indisputable; but my conclusions will be my own. I have deferred what I am to say about you to the last chapter."

All five boys were home from school for the New Year's holiday, which made it a jolly beginning to 1861. After his noon tour on the Sandwalk and the midday meal, Charles stretched out on the chaise in the drawing room to read Olmsted's A Journey in the Back Country, a lively picture of man and slavery in the southern United States. His interest was increased by the dispatches in the London Times which reported that a civil war was impending between North and South over slavery.

"I simply don't believe these articles in the Times," Charles declared vehemently. "Such a war would be suicidal. Surely both sides will recognize that fact?"

"Stands to reason," replied William dubiously. "But are governments controlled by reason?"

He was moving along on the volume on the Variation of Animals and Plants under Domestication, sensing that once again his manuscript would be too long and detailed. He had completed a study of the pigs, cattle, sheep and goats of the world, their origin and the results obtained by breeding under controlled conditions. However he found the fertilization of the world's orchids such a series of miracles that the writing of this thesis was sheer joy. His sense of wonder at nature's ingenious marvels of evolution within the orchid family was so enormous that at no time did he feel any sense of fatigue, being able to write for a number of hours every day, his feeling of elation growing as rapidly as the pile of manuscript pages before him. He was even emboldened to gamble on a hypothesis he could not yet prove. A star orchid of Madagascar which had been sent to him by a friend had a foot-long nectary which contained nectar only in its bottom inch and a half. How could a bee, moth or other insect insert itself deep enough to get the nectar? He reasoned that it could be a sphinx moth with a proboscis a foot long. No one had ever seen a moth with a proboscis a foot long but that did not matter. If such a moth did not exist, the star orchid of Madagascar would long since have disappeared!

He calculated that he would be able to complete his monograph in something over a hundred pages, which the *Journal of the Linnean Society* had agreed to publish. He went to London to have dinner at the Society with Thomas Bell, who had done the book on reptiles for the *Zoology of the Beagle*, and caught the last train home. Emma was waiting up for him.

"How did the evening go?"

"Dining out is such a novelty to me that I enjoyed it."

"I'm glad. Perhaps you have built too many fences around yourself?"

Word reached him that Syms Covington had died of paralysis at the age of forty-seven. He was saddened by this totally unexpected loss of his former assistant during the *Beagle*, Cambridge and Marlborough Street years. They had exchanged occasional notes, Charles had sent him a new ear trumpet; Syms had collected for him boxes of barnacles from various parts of Australia.

Almost immediately after, he learned that Joseph Hooker and Frances were at the rectory in Hitcham caring for John Henslow on his deathbed. Hooker was badly stricken, for he dearly loved his botanist-preacher-father-in-law as a man. Charles wanted to make the journey to say farewell.

"I owe that to John Henslow," he told his wife.

It was about a hundred miles to Hitcham. He would have to take his carriage to Beckenham, the train to London, coach to Ipswich, then hire a fly to Hitcham, twelve hours of journeying. His attacks of retching came about three hours after eating. Would there be an inn in the village of Hitcham?

He found that he could not gird himself to make the trip. He asked himself why he lacked the physical strength to undertake the journey, and wrote to Hooker:

> . . . I should never forgive myself if I did not instantly come, if Henslow's wish to see me was more than a passing thought.

Apparently John Henslow took this as farewell.

When Henslow died in mid-May, Charles was engulfed in a wave of guilt. Providentially, he was offered a release; the Rev. Leonard Jenyns began to write Henslow's biography. Would Charles set down his memories of Henslow during the early years at Cambridge? Charles fulfilled the task at once:

> Nothing could be more simple, cordial and unpretending than the encouragement which he offered to all young naturalists. . . . He had a remarkable power of making the young feel completely at ease with him though we were all awe-struck with the amount of his knowledge. . . .

The Jenyns *Memoir*, to be published the following year by John Van Hoorst, Paternoster Row, made certain that the Rev. John Stevens Henslow's place in history would be secure.

It brought Charles comfort.

2.

A letter arrived from the botanist Hewett C. Watson, an admirer who was checking the third edition of the *Origin of Species* with an eye to reviewing it. In reading the new introduction, Watson logged Charles as using "I," "me," and "my" forty-three times in the first four paragraphs.

"Ah, that miserable perpendicular pronoun, 'I,'" Charles groaned as Emma and the children teased him. "Am I really such an egoist?"

"No, dear one, you're quite modest and self-effacing," Emma replied dryly, "in your belief that you are the only person on earth who knows how every species evolved."

Nettie Huxley, who had given birth to another boy, was still unhappy and unwell over the death of her first-born. Emma persuaded her to come to Down House for a fortnight with her three other children.

Hugh Falconer, who at one time had told Charles, "You will do more harm than any ten naturalists will do good," was traveling in Italy and Germany. He reported:

> . . . Everywhere have I heard your views and your admirable essay canvassed; the views of course often dissented from, according to the special bias of the speaker, but the work, its honesty of purpose, grandeur of conception, felicity of illustration, and courageous exposition, always referred to in terms of the highest admiration. . . .

Would wonders never cease! Had the *Origin* turned the corner toward unemotional respectability?

He had been wrong in his surmise that the North and South of the United States would compromise their differences. The South had fired on Fort Sumter in April. The War Between the States was mounting rapidly. Charles was not content to read the accounts in the London *Times*; he asked Parslow to pick up the *Herald* and all other available newspapers at the post office. After midday dinner as he read the news sheets, he let them fall to the floor in a semicircle around the sofa in the drawing room.

"I never knew the newspapers to be so profoundly interesting," he said. "I don't believe North America does us justice. They're afraid we're for the South because we need its cotton for our mills. I wish to God that the North would quickly proclaim a crusade against slavery."

His pleasure in writing about orchids remained as he proceeded with his study of the fertilization process. It was curious that a flower would exist which could serve to fertilize only two of its own species, seeing how abundant the pollen was. In as many varieties as he could accumulate, and in particular the Coryanthes blossom, he studied the contrivance by which British and foreign orchids were fertilized, the pollen carried from flower to flower by insects. He used lens and penknife to examine the pollen grains resting on top of the flower's bucketlike sac, into which dropped an aromatic, thickish fluid, the scent of which attracted the bees and other insects. He observed the bee burrowing in for the hallucinatory fluid, getting its fill, and in the process of backing out of the tiny basin, accumulating the pollen grains on its back. After sobering up, the bee approached the next flower, onto which it unknowingly deposited the pollen. Every species of orchid developed its own basinlike structure, large or small, deep or shallow, so that only one species of insect could get at its particular pollen.

"These orchid processes make the flowers look more ingenious than mankind," he commented.

"What happens to those orchids which cannot entice insects into their drinking trough?" William, home from Christ's College for the summer, wanted to know.

"They vanish."

In July Henrietta again felt unwell. Emma decided that six weeks at the seaside were imperative for her health. Though he welcomed the change, Charles had the task of moving sixteen souls and three quarters of a ton of luggage to Torquay, in the southwest corner of England, facing the Channel. Their rented house had a fine view of the bay's crescent. Henrietta began to improve almost immediately. It was a happy time. The boys were full of holiday enjoyment; they had frequent visitors. Erasmus came, and the Hensleigh Wedgwoods' daughter Hope, to keep Henrietta company.

When Dr. Henry Holland visited in early August, he observed Henrietta for a day or two, then remarked to his cousins:

"Etty is the family hypochondriac. Where she gets it from, I don't know."

Charles volunteered meekly:

"When I read a good review of the *Origin* in the *Zoologist* last week, I walked a good two miles out and back, which is a grand feat."

Holland said eloquently, "Huuummm."

He had long fought a suspicion that his paper on Glen Roy, which he had published twenty-two years before, was a gigantic blunder. Lyell had agreed with Agassiz that Charles was wrong to claim that the roads and shelves were former sea beaches which had been raised to their present elevation. Charles had refused to yield, stitched in by his streak of stubbornness. He now came upon a man who was willing to make the trip to Scotland to settle the controversy. The man returned with qualified proof that the shelves or roads were caused by the damming up of a lake by a glacier. Charles confided to Emma:

"I am smashed to atoms. Eheu! Eheu! That should teach me humility."

"It will, dear, for a day or two."

When he next made the trip to London he confessed his error to Lyell. They were walking along the river Thames in the late August sunshine from Waterloo Bridge at Charing Cross past the Houses of Parliament and Westminster Abbey.

"One serious blunder in all these years? My dear Darwin, you are a mere dabbler. Wait until you reach my august age and see how many blunders you will have to retract. It's an integral part of the explorer's life."

"You are a forgiving spirit. How does Antiquity of Man come along?"

"Making an antique of me."

Charles tacked.

"I believe you think with Asa Gray that I have not allowed enough for the stream of variation having been guided by a higher power."

Lyell nodded agreement, said:

"Sir John Herschel has a sentence with respect to the *Origin* that the higher law of providential arrangement should always be stated."

"Yet neither Herschel nor any other astronomer states that God directs the course of each comet, planet and falling star."

Lyell replied somewhat curtly:

"That's true enough."

Charles persisted.

"You cannot, I think, logically argue that the tail of the woodpecker was formed by variations 'providentially' ordained. Will you honestly tell me whether you believe that the shape of my nose was 'guided by an intelligent cause'?"

Lyell laughed, his good humor restored.

"No, Darwin, God did not stop in His work to design your proboscis. Or mine. I'll keep that in mind when I write my concluding chapter about you. Are you still fertilizing orchids with your penknife?"

"I'm cross-fertilizing manuscript pages with pen and ink."

He completed his paper on the orchids. Though he had foreshortened his material, leaving out a good deal of corroborative detail, he still ran to a hundred and forty pages. Too long for the Linnean Society's *Journal*, as usual! What to do?

It was a late October night, the first chill of winter seeping through their bedroom curtains. Charles banked the fire, went to bed at his usual hour, ten-thirty. Sleep would not come. He rolled over several times, not realizing that he was keeping Emma awake. At length she said:

"Charles, what you need is a hammock, not a bed."

"I'm trying to work something out."

"Won't it keep till morning?"

After breakfast he found her in the garden where she was pulling out bulbs to be stored in the cellar until spring.

"Would you join me on the Sandwalk?"

"How many pebbles around?"

"Say, five?"

Once the five flint chips had been set at the beginning of the wooded rectangle, he left her to catch on by herself.

"Why shouldn't I turn the orchids into a little book? I've already left out so much of the material, all of it valuable to my thesis. If John Murray might wish to publish I could do a respectable-sized book which would be not only innovative but definitive as well. Would it sell enough to enable Murray to recoup his costs? I am very apt to think that my geese are swans. Generally the points which interest me I find interest others. The subject of propagation is interesting to most people, even if only in flowers. At worst, it cannot entail much loss, though a large sale is out of the question. I think a little volume will do good to the *Origin*."

John Murray felt that the book would appeal to naturalists. He agreed to accept the risks, pay for the illustrations and give Charles half the profits, a generous offer. Charles said he could complete his enlarged manuscript in about two months.

Intrigued as he had been by the beauty and incredible designs of the orchid family, he found his investigations for the longer work to be by no means all beer and skittles. He wasted the work of a fortnight, including his diagrams of the butterfly orchids, because the ducts of the upper sepal ran in the wrong direction. He lamented:

"I have never seen such a case. I was a fool ever to touch orchids."

"At some point or other," Emma said consolingly, "you have said that about every book you have written."

He decided that he owed the Linnean Society a short paper, which he wrote and read himself at a Society meeting. When he had finished to restrained yet friendly applause, Joseph Hooker reached him first with congratulations.

"You produced a tremendous effect."

"By Jove, I must stop, otherwise I shall be transformed into a botanist!"

Charles was so exhausted he barely crawled home, and could not get out of bed until the following evening. He wrote Hooker:

> I by no means think that I produced a "tremendous effect" on the Linnean, but by Jove, the Linnean Society produced a tremendous effect on me. I fear I must give up trying to read any paper or speak in public. I can do nothing like other people.

He was made an honorary member of the Royal Medical Society of Edinburgh, and exclaimed to Emma:

"You remember what a brilliant student I was at the medical school at the university there? After the first few freezing 8:00 A.M. lectures by Dr. Duncan on materia medica, Dr. Monro's dull lectures on anatomy, and two operations at the hospital on children, I spent the rest of my time collecting oysters from the dredge boats of the Newhaven fisher-men, lumpfish from the black rocks at Leith, starfish, marine life from the Firth of Forth."

In November of 1861 the British mail packet *Trent*, with two South-ern commissioners on board, was stopped by the United States warship *San Jacinto*, its captain removing the commissioners under virtual ar-rest. The British Parliament and Cabinet sent a sharp note of protest to the American government. From the daily and weekly newspapers it ap-peared that Great Britain would not only recognize the Confederacy as a separate nation but might go to war against the no longer united states. Though he had never been to North America, Charles had a lik-ing for the American people, originating with the openhanded gener-osity of the American sailors he had met while on H.M.S. *Beagle*, con-tinuing with Lyell's enthusiastic reports of their young spirit, as well as his abiding friendship with Asa Gray, and gratitude to the publishers at D. Appleton in New York, who had treated him so decently.

By December he met hardly a soul who believed that the North could conquer the South, or retain the rebelling states within the Union. He poured out his unhappiness and frustration to Asa Gray.

> . . . What a thing it is that when you receive this we may be at war, and we two be bound, as good patriots, to hate each other, though I shall find this hating you very hard work. How curious it is to see two countries, just like two angry and silly men, taking so opposite a view of the same transaction! And what a wretched thing it will be if we fight on the side of slavery. . . .

The news of the war was moved off the front pages of the London newspapers by the unexpected death of Prince Albert. Charles had not known any member of the royal family, but Lyell and Prince Albert had been friends for many years. Lyell was stricken by the loss, saying that he at once felt much aged himself.

Once again it was Christmas and the New Year, and the children congregated at Down House. Charles and Emma exchanged popular novels. They had already read *East Lynne*, so they ordered out from their London bookshop the recently published *Silas Marner* by George Eliot, and *The Cloister and the Hearth*, with Henrietta reading aloud a substantial part of both books to add to the family's pleasure.

The year 1862 opened with what appeared to be a triumph. Thomas Huxley, who had been invited to lecture to the Philosophical Institute of Edinburgh, chose as his subject On Relation of Man to Lower Ani-mals. The usually mild-mannered Lyell, whose ancestral home, Kin-nordy, was in Scotland, advised against the subject.

"I prophesy that you shall be stoned and cast out of the city gate."

Charles added to Lyell's warning. Huxley, of the sharp claws, was not to be dissuaded. He told his attentive Edinburgh audience:

". . . Thoughtful men, once escaped from the blinding influence of traditional prejudices, will find in the lowly stock whence man has sprung the best evidence of the splendour of his capacities; and will discern, in his long progress through the past, a reasonable ground of faith in his attainment of a nobler future."

The two Charleses were proved wrong. The Edinburgh audiences gave Huxley sincere applause. When he rode out to Down House the following Sunday to ask Charles if he should not use the lectures as a starting point for a book, Man's Place in Nature, Charles had first to wring his hand in congratulations.

"By Jove, you have attacked bigotry in its stronghold."

"Treated like royalty, I was," Huxley replied with a huge smile engulfing his strong, dark face. "What I gave them was pure Darwinism."

Within a week the acceptance reversed itself. The Witness of January 11 lashed itself into a fury over the fact that the audience had applauded Huxley's

> . . . anti-scriptural and most debasing theory . . . standing in blasphemous contradiction to biblical narrative and doctrine, instead of expressing their resentment at the foul outrage committed upon them individually, and upon the whole species as "made in the likeness of God," by deserting the hall in a body. . . .

It had become a familiar pattern. However the vilifying attacks reached people who would not otherwise have known about the work, and who were moved by the violence of the opposition to investigate at the source.

Charles and Huxley decided it was a game to be called, "How to make adherents for modern science by abominating its advocates."

The denouncing of Thomas Huxley in the Witness was known among the naturalists of London, few of whom approved its tone. As secretary of the Geological Society, the duty of delivering the anniversary address fell to Huxley in the absence of its president, Leonard Horner. Charles did not attend the meeting in Burlington House, but Lyell brought him a report.

"I never heard an address listened to with so much interest or received with such applause, though there were many private protests against some of his bold opinions."

"His or mine?"

Charles's question was prompted by the fact that Huxley was becoming known as Darwin's bulldog.

"The heart of his argument derives from the Origin," responded Lyell, "enriched by his own thought and study. Huxley pointed out that when we go back to the vertebrata and invertebrata of remote ages, the persistency of many forms high and low throughout time, we find that we know little of the beginning of life upon the earth; often events called contemporaneous in geology may have happened ten million years apart."

The life cycle had its exigencies; there was the struggle that led to victory, at other times death was present with a razor-sharp dirk. Charles's sister Marianne had died, Susan becoming guardian aunt to the Parker children. Now Charlotte, Emma's sister, who had married the Rev. Charles Langton thirty years before, went down with an undiagnosed illness and died in January.

In February the Darwins' youngest boy, Horace, not quite eleven, became strangely ill with involuntary twitching of his arms, legs and neck. For a time they feared that there was mischief in the boy's brain, a form of palsy. The local doctors could find no cause for the disturbance, nor could Dr. Holland, summoned frantically from London. At the end of April Horace's twitchings stopped but for a year he remained an ambulatory invalid with severe indigestion.

"Clearly inherited," Charles muttered.

"Acquired," Emma contradicted.

Alfred Russel Wallace had returned to England on the first of April after eight years of travel and collecting in Malaysia, Sumatra, Java, Borneo, Celebes, the Moluccas, Timor, New Guinea. Charles considered him of heroic character to have undergone eight years in distant, primitive and frequently hostile lands. He invited Wallace to Down House. Wallace replied, thanking him, but adding:

> . . . I'm doctoring a bit now; but will come to visit as soon as I am able.

John Murray printed two thousand copies of On the Various Contrivances by Which British and Foreign Orchids Are Fertilised by Insects, in an attractive plum-colored cloth binding with a gold orchid embossed on its front cover. Charles wrote in the introduction:

> The object of the following work is to show that the contrivances by which Orchids are fertilised are as varied and almost as perfect as any of the most beautiful adaptations in the animal kingdom. . . .

He had been investigating orchids for several years, the actual writing had taken him nine months, interrupting himself only to edit the second German edition of the *Origin of Species*, and to do a paper on the remarkable sexual relations between two species of Primula: daisies and cowslips. In one way the orchid book had been the most pleasant to write because Emma and the children were equally fascinated and frequently asked Charles to read the manuscript aloud.

The book was published on May 15. Murray's price of nine shillings was an attractive one. It sold well within its field. He had expected that he would be ridiculed for his assumption of an insect with a "foot-long proboscis" and he was. Until a missionary in Madagascar would finally observe a moth with just such a proboscis enter a star orchid and emerge with the necessary pollen to fertilize other star orchids. . . .

Although the *Athenaeum* treated him with what he called "kind pity and contempt," the botanists assured him that the reviewer knew nothing about the subject. The rest of the comments were excellent, the *Parthenon* was favorable, the *London Review* superb. Even the *Literary Churchman* expressed its admiration for the volume. Asa Gray complimented him warmly from Harvard, stating that if the orchid book had appeared before the *Origin* he would have been canonized rather than anathematized by the theologians.

Charles Lyell was enthusiastic, declaring it "next to the *Origin* the most valuable of all of Darwin's work."

Most of the naturalists came down on his side so enthusiastically that Charles exclaimed:

"I am fairly astonished at the success of my book."

He wrote to Asa Gray, ignoring the Civil War issue:

. . . I had lately got to think that I had made myself a complete fool by publishing in a semi-popular form. I can now afford to damn my critics with ineffable complacency of mind.

Asa Gray reviewed the orchid book with high fervor in the *American Journal of Science and Arts*. He also twitted Charles by commenting:

I perceive that your chief interest in the orchid book has been that it was a flank movement on the enemy.

This was assuredly true, for Charles was being quoted in the British press as saying:

I have found the study of orchids eminently useful in showing me how nearly all parts of the flower are co-adapted for fertilisation by insects, and therefore the results of natural selection, even to the most trifling details of structure.

The *Fertilisation of Orchids* strongly enhanced Charles Darwin's reputation as an accurate and daring reporter on the previously hidden or neglected processes of nature. It helped take some of the poison out of the sting of the *Origin's* critics. Though he told Alfred Wallace, out of sheer habit, "My health is, and always will be, very poor; I am that miserable animal, a regular valetudinarian," he felt well enough to proceed on a wholly new venture, the movements and habits of climbing plants, still another field which was almost untouched. He had read a short paper on the subject by Asa Gray several years before.

Lyell thought that the time had come for Charles to be knighted.

"That would be the equivalent of our Prime Minister recommending to the Queen the knighting of the *Origin*," Charles replied. "Cabinets have fallen for lesser reasons."

"We shall see," Lyell responded patiently. "Hooker, too, should receive that honor. After he becomes director of Kew Gardens. Huxley? Never. He is most brilliant but too abrasive. He does not know how to oil the wheels of his cart."

"That's an interwoven part of his genius," said Charles. "He wouldn't be caught dead flattering people the way I do."

3.

The favorable reception of the orchid book relieved Charles's anxiety. His emotions eased their way back to health, without dizziness, palpitations or flatulence. Why then did his hands break out with eczema? Could it be a result of Richard Owen's renewed attacks on him? Owen, lecturing and publishing prolifically, was achieving the legerdemain of pummeling Darwinism at the same time that he was ceding almost every part of Charles's conception of natural selection. Lyell, Darwin, Hooker and Huxley, meeting for dinner at the Athenaeum, decided in their magisterial judgment, over a bottle and a bird, that Owen's performance was manic.

Or was the eczema due to one of the chemicals he was using in his experiments? He remembered developing a similar eruption about the mouth when he was a student at Christ's College. He had taken small doses of arsenic to dry up the blisters, a remedy he had read about in the *New Dispensatory* while at the Edinburgh Medical School. His father had cautioned him against using the drug, but the outbreak had vanished, even as it did now . . . without the arsenic.

Their circle got a leg up when Thomas Huxley was appointed to the prestigious Hunterian professorship at the Royal College of Surgeons. Here he could impart to his students, sometimes by osmosis, the Darwinian theory of evolution: that man had evolved from the very first organism that came to life in some distant sea. He now had a more subtle post from which to serve as Darwin's bulldog.

In Down House there was little rejoicing. Their next to youngest son, Leonard, who was scheduled to enter the school at Clapham where his brother George was in the first class and could watch over him, broke out in a rash, developed a sore throat, made the transition to a serious attack of erysipelas which developed into scarlet fever. They called in Dr. Engleheart from Down. Emma and Charles kept Leonard alive by feeding him a spoonful of port wine every three quarters of an hour, night and day. Dr. Engleheart, nicknamed Spengle, came in several times a day. After a time Leonard managed to swallow a mouthful of soft porridge.

"I think he has passed his crisis," Emma murmured, brightening up the boy's room with a big bucket of early June flowers.

That evening, to his parents' astonishment, Leonard asked, with his eyes tight shut:

"Are my stamps safe?"

"Yes," Charles answered. "Professor Gray sent you one from America. You shall see it tomorrow."

"I should awfully like to see it now."

Charles went for the stamp. Leonard opened one eyelid with great difficulty, glanced at the new stamp and then with a sigh of satisfaction said, "All right."

An hour later Charles brought a second lot of stamps newly sent from America. Leonard raised himself on one elbow, said:

"You must thank Professor Gray awfully."

By the next day Leonard was substantially mending. As Charles and Emma relaxed in the cool darkness of the garden, Charles ruminated:

"Children are one's greatest happiness, but often a greater misery. A man of science ought to have none; perhaps not a wife. For then there would be nothing in this wide world worth caring for, and he might— whether he could or not is another question—work away like a Trojan. Ah well, I hope in a few days to set my brain in order. . . ."

Emma glanced at her husband's tired relief and felt sorry for him.

As Leonard continued to improve, Charles again invited Alfred Wallace to Down House. He came during the first week of August. Charles had a strong feeling about the younger man; he believed him to be not only an equal but of crucial importance to the development of the natural sciences, and that Alfred Wallace would fit in well with their foursome.

Through his oblique mirror, Charles watched Wallace descend from the fly he had sent for him. Wallace was tall, over six feet, lean, broad-shouldered but narrow-hipped, with long sturdy legs which had carried him over vast mountain ranges. He sported a rich head of dark hair, waving over his brow; a trim mustache, side whiskers and a dark beard which he parted in the center. It was not until Parslow had ushered him into the study that Charles saw that Wallace's deep-set blue eyes were quiescent, and were barely covered by a tiny pair of rimless glasses, smaller even than Hooker's. Wallace, now thirty-nine, was dressed in a wide-lapeled gray waistcoat, a long-tailed dark coat and light-colored trousers. His black boots were not too well polished. He was living in London with a married sister who had afforded him a loft for the separation of his collections.

Charles asked Parslow to bring them a pitcher of cool lemonade. Once Wallace had quenched his thirst, Charles said:

"Wallace, you had thirty-five articles published in our natural history journals before you returned to England! I stand in awe of your clear writing style. I have the devil's own time setting down a simple declarative sentence."

Wallace flushed with pleasure, protested:

"I'd be content if I could produce two books of the quality of your *Journal of the Beagle* and the *Origin of Species* in my lifetime."

"I've been curious; how did you come upon the theory of natural selection, identified with only the two of us?"

Wallace took another long draught of the lemonade, wiped his tiny glasses with his kerchief, the better to remember.

"Mr. Darwin, it's hard to believe, but at that time, in February of 1858, I was in the Moluccas, suffering from a severe attack of malaria. One day while lying on my bed, wrapped in blankets although the thermometer was 88°, the problem again presented itself to me, and something led me to think of the 'positive checks' described by Malthus in his *Essay on the Principle of Population*, a work I had read several years before, and which had made a deep and permanent impression on my mind."

"As it had upon mine."

Wallace added shyly:

"I had a proper background. I first read your *Journal* around 1847. As the journal of a scientific traveler it is second only to Humboldt's *Narrative*; as a work of general interest, perhaps superior to it. . . ."

Charles blushed; he was genuinely touched.

Wallace was one of the few men who spoke precisely as he wrote, in a straightforward style, with well-structured sentences.

". . . These checks—war, disease, famine and the like—must, it occurred to me, act on animals as well as on man. That these causes or their equivalents are continually acting . . . and as animals usually breed much more rapidly than does mankind, the destruction every year must be enormous in order to keep down the numbers of each species. It suddenly flashed upon me that this self-acting process would necessarily *improve the race,* because in every generation the inferior would inevitably be killed off and the superior would remain—that is, the *fittest would survive.*"

It was now noon. Charles asked if Wallace would like to try the Sandwalk.

"Very much so. It's rather famous in London, you know; called 'a path to the future.'"

"Is it, indeed? Many of my best ideas emerge there."

At the dinner table Wallace got along capitally with Emma and the young, who liked the way his shy manner alternated with his hearty laugh.

"It will take me quite a while," he confided, "before I can make an ample living out of my articles and books. I have had some lonely times. I should like to have a wife and children and home."

When Leonard seemed well enough to travel the family set out for Bournemouth for their summer holiday; but by the time they reached Southampton, where their son William had established himself as a partner in a banking firm after his graduation from Christ's College, Emma came down with scarlet fever. Charles sent the well members on to Bournemouth, where he had rented a house, keeping Emma, Leonard and an older housekeeper with him in William's house at 1 Carlton Terrace in Southampton. The house was plain but large enough to hold the family.

Charles hired a nurse but spent most of the day and part of the night attending to Emma. The fearful distress over first Leonard, then Emma came near to shattering him. It was weeks now since he had been able to attend to anything but his sick ones. Happily Emma's attack proved to be light. Charles moved his wife and son to Bournemouth, but not before he had rented a second house there, one for the ill, with whom he remained, the other for the well.

After Emma recovered and the family was reunited they enjoyed the sun, sand and sea at Bournemouth. They returned to Down House at the end of September.

Charles had long yearned for a hothouse in which to work. Just before Christmas Sir John Lubbock's first-rate gardener, Horwood, came over in a cart loaded with plants and bulbs from Lubbock's greenhouse as a gift from the Lubbocks. Charles said plaintively:

"You know, Horwood, I've always wanted a little hothouse of my own."

Horwood was a clever fellow whose plants won many prizes. He was also observant.

"Only waiting for you to suggest it, Mr. Darwin. Already have Sir John's permission to help you. I'll draw your plans, if you like. We should succeed with a little patience."

Horwood came for an hour each day. They decided to build the hothouse near a well located a short distance from the house, close to the kitchen gardens, beyond the sundial by which Charles set his gold watch and the grandfather clock in the hallway. It would face fragrant Lime Avenue, the tree-lined path through the gardens to the Sandwalk, and be fifty feet long, ten feet wide, with a tin roof sloping toward the path. Horwood designed stout door beams at either end, with matching uprights to keep the structure solid. Squares of glass were inserted into the roof and front wall to provide light and warmth. There would be two rows of shelves and protected planting areas on either side of the interior walkway; the heating supplied by stoves.

Charles was happy as a schoolboy during the days of building. Horwood proved to be an excellent supervisor. When the glasshouse was completed in mid-February, Charles rode over to the Lubbocks'.

"My little hothouse is finished," he announced, "and you must permit me to thank you for allowing Horwood to superintend the work. Without his aid I should never have had the spirit to undertake it; and if I had, I should probably have made a mess of it. It will not only be an amusement to me but will enable me to try many little experiments which otherwise would have been impossible."

When next Charles saw Joseph Hooker, he told him with a rush of enthusiasm:

"The new hothouse is ready, and I long to stock it. Could you tell me what plants you can give me; and then I shall know what to buy."

"We have stove plants and mosses galore."

"Would it do to send my tax cart early in the morning, on a day that was not frosty, lining the cart with mats, and returning here before night? I have no idea whether this degree of exposure could injure stove plants; they would be about five hours on the journey home."

"We'll cover everything carefully," said Hooker, "so they'll stay warm and come to no harm."

When Charles's sister Susan learned that Hooker had become an avid collector of Wedgwood, buying as many pieces as his modest income would allow, she sent several of the older medallions and vases from The Mount. Joseph Hooker was overjoyed at the gift. Charles wrote to him:

> You cannot imagine what pleasure your plants give me. Far more than Susan's Wedgwood ware can give you. Horwood

and I go and gloat over them, but we privately confessed to each other that if they were not our own, perhaps we should not see such transcendent beauty in each leaf. . . .

Charles Lyell's book, *Geological Evidences of the Antiquity of Man,* was published in early February 1863. He had shown not a page of manuscript to Charles, nor had anyone else seen a line of it. When Charles received a copy from Lyell he turned immediately to the last chapter and was shocked to find that neither he nor his work was mentioned. There was merely a brief quotation from a review of the *Origin of Species* in *Fraser's Magazine.* The closing argument had been given to Asa Gray, who pointed out that "there is no tendency in the doctrine of Variation and Natural Selection to weaken the foundation of Natural Theology." Lyell had concluded his book by stating:

> . . . They who maintain that the origin of an individual, as well as the origin of a species or a genus, can be explained only by the direct action of the creative cause, may retain their favorite theory compatibly with the doctrine of transmutation.

Charles did not quite believe what he had read.

"In short," he said to himself, sick at heart, "there is no such thing as objective truth. One may believe what one feels like believing regardless of the facts staring him in the face."

Thoroughly upset, his mind out of focus, repeating to himself Lyell's early statement, "I'm saving my reference to you for the concluding chapter," Charles rose from his chair, laid down Lyell's book, and went out into the air. It was overcast, with a cool wind moving through the fields. He did not feel the cold, only a sense of dislocation. He turned to the most therapeutic occupation he had found over the years: pulling weeds in the garden. It got rid of a useless growth and cleared the cobwebs out of the brain. After half an hour he felt better, returned to his study and began reading at page one.

There was no question but that Lyell had accomplished a thoroughgoing overview of man as derived from *geological* evidences. There were fair reports on the work and beliefs of Hooker, Huxley, Wallace. Chapter XVI was devoted to "Mr. Darwin's Theory of the Origin of Species by Natural Selection," and it was also a fair statement of Charles's point of departure.

"It was only at the end of the book that Lyell came up short," Charles mused with a touch of bitterness. "He could not face the challenge."

Then an errant thought struck him, and he laughed aloud.

"Emma will be relieved! She's been dreading the idea that Lyell would come over to my side."

Over the next weeks Charles read several reviews of Lyell's book. It was an immediate success. He was happy about his friend's acclaim, yet remained disappointed that Lyell had not permitted him to present his case about the beginnings of man, and had limited himself to the geological base.

The Lyells came for a visit on a blustery March day, occupying the front bedroom above Charles's study. Mary Lyell chatted with Emma over tea in the drawing room. Charles and Lyell sat on hard-backed chairs at the dining-room windows, overlooking the muted garden and the grazing fields beyond. Lyell had just declined a seat in Parliament to represent the University of London.

"I believe I can be more valuable by continuing my geological researches," he explained.

"I agree. It is a decision I too made early on, when it looked as if I might have an appointment at Christ's College."

A farm cart went by on rickety wooden wheels which were groaning for axle grease. Charles waited until the horse and drowsing driver had disappeared around a curve. He knew that Lyell was awaiting his reaction to the *Antiquity of Man*, yet he was hesitant to speak for fear of offending his friend.

"I have been deeply interested in your book," he said finally, "although I have hardly any remarks worth making."

"Come now!" Lyell shook his head. "I have been watching your facial expressions for over two decades. I can tell that you have a great many remarks worth making."

Charles swallowed, hard.

"Since you grant me permission I will first get out what I hate saying, that I have been greatly disappointed that you have not given judgment and spoken out fairly what you think about the derivation of man."

Lyell sobered.

"I knew you would be disappointed that I did not go further with you. I can only say that I have spoken out to the full extent of my present convictions."

The wind had abated; though there were dark clouds overhead, the sun had found a rift to peer through.

"Would you like to stretch your legs on the Sandwalk?" Charles proffered. "Fresh air might clear our heads."

"Mine is clear," Lyell responded, "but I have been looking forward to the walk."

Charles set the pieces of flint at the corner of his enclosed woods before he spoke.

"I think the *Parthenon* reviewer was right when he said that you leave the public in a fog."

Lyell was not pleased at the allusion.

"Do you? Both you and Huxley have gone further into the domain of the unknowable . . ."

Charles interrupted.

". . . no doubt the reader may infer that, since you give more space to myself, Hooker and Wallace than to Lamarck, you think more of us. But I had always thought that your judgment would have been an epoch on the subject."

Lyell watched Charles kick aside one of the flint stones.

"As a matter of fact," he said, "I went further in my reasoning toward the processes of change in all living things than I feel. Perhaps for that reason I shall lead more people on to you and Hooker than one who, born later, like young Lubbock, has comparatively little to abandon of old and long-cherished ideas."

Charles was surprised at Lyell's admitted conservatism. But he had no desire to upset his companion. He suggested that they return to the house for dinner. Both wives were surprised that their husbands discussed no science during the meal. Neither man wanted it to be known that for the first time in their relationship they had seriously stubbed their toes on a rock of disagreement. After a sherry and hors d'oeuvres of sardines, oysters and croutons, Emma served fish quenelles, a roast leg of lamb, spinach and potatoes, pie and custard.

"Shall we knock the billiard balls about?" Charles asked.

They played in desultory fashion, even the successful clicking of the balls giving them little pleasure.

"Lyell, I quite understand," Charles said in a semi-apologetic tone. "From now on I will only think of the admirable skill with which you have selected the striking points and explained them. No praise can be too strong for your inimitable chapter on the development of language in comparison with species."

Lyell was too perceptive to be shaken off by half praise, in particular from the one naturalist he most admired. He laid down his billiard cue, spoke slowly and with precision.

"I don't care what people have been expecting as to the extent to which I may go with you, but certainly I do not wish to be inconsistent with myself. As I have only been gradually changing my opinion, I cannot insist on others going round at once. When I read again certain chapters of the *Principles*, I am always in danger of shaking some of my confidence in the new doctrine. I see too many difficulties to be in the dangerous position of new converts who outrun their teacher in faith. Hooker says that in science people do not like to be told too plainly what they must believe; though in religion they wish to have it laid down for them."

Charles was contrite at having made Lyell face the fact that his book was only a halfway house. He too laid down his cue, walked to Lyell's end of the table.

"I know you will forgive me for speaking with perfect freedom, for you must know how deeply I respect you as my honored guide."

Lyell tried to rescue the emotional scene with a flash of humor.

"Did you see that the *Saturday Review* called my book 'Lyell's Trilogy on the Antiquity of Man, Ice and Darwin'?"

Charles contributed:

"Did you read anything so wretched as the *Athenaeum* review of your book and Huxley's *Man's Place in Nature*? Your object, apparently, was to make man old; Huxley's to degrade him. The wretched writer has not a glimpse of what the discovery of scientific truth means."

Lyell smiled.

"Do you suppose that reviewers are the natural predators of book writers? Created to keep the writing population down?"

They laughed together. Lyell cast off his confession that he had stopped short of the full challenge; Charles put aside his bitterness that his friend had not been able to reach beyond the bounds of his own character. . . . Until they returned to the study.

Charles leaned forward in his chair as if physically to bridge the gap.

"I fear you might be a little huffed with me still."

Lyell's smile was affectionate.

"I could never be angry at you for more than a passing moment. I feel about you much as John Henslow did. In many ways you have become the son and inheritor I never had. Under those circumstances I could never be content with anything less than full honesty from you."

Charles took a pinch of snuff from the jar he had brought in with him from the outside hall.

"I must still think that a clear expression from you would have been potent with the public." Then he had an amusing thought, asked mockingly:

"You wouldn't let me rewrite your last chapter on the *descent* of man, would you?"

"You bloody well won't," shouted Lyell. "You'll write your own book. If you have withstood the abuse over the *Origin of Species*, and you have, you will survive the tumult and harassment over the descent of man from the apes . . . and lower. . . ."

Charles rose, started wandering around his study, touching articles on the tables and shelves: microscope, rare minerals, specimen bottles.

"It is nearly as much for your sake as for my own that I so much wish that your state of belief could have permitted you to say boldly and distinctly that human races were not separately created. Nor man himself; that he evolved, like all other living creatures."

Lyell sat with his jaw set. When he spoke he did so with clearly articulated syllables.

"It's your field, and your obligation. The day will come when you will have to face the task."

Riding back in the carriage from Beckenham station where he had deposited the Lyells, Charles rewound the spool of the weekend's confrontation. He knew that the patterns in a man's life repeated themselves. Any book he might publish on the descent of man which did not correspond to the Western world's belief would meet with the same outcry and abuse as had the *Origin of Species*; would bring down upon his house extreme censure. He also knew that there was little question but that he would write it. Was that why he had been so outspoken and angry with Lyell for not doing so?

As the horse found its own way past the church and little graveyard in Down, turned and went slowly up the slight incline of the Darwin lane, he knew that he would accept his Uncle Jos's sentiment:

"Do what you must, and let fate overtake you."

4.

He retained his position as magistrate, though he was rarely summoned to Bromley to hear a case. He still kept the account books of the Down Friendly Club. He continued to invite friends to Down House and enjoyed working in the warm, moist area of his hothouse with the intermingled fragrances of the flowers and shrubs and the plants with which he was experimenting. But because he found himself unable to do any writing at all, the year 1863 was proving to be the most difficult he had had to endure. His health broke down completely. He was used to intermittent stretches of being miserable, nauseous, with stomach discomfort, tiring and sleeping poorly. But now he was not only consistently ill but he could not even remain in his study or hold his pen to write.

In the beginning of May he and Emma went to Hartfield for a fortnight to see if he could improve, staying at the homes of the Rev. Charles Langton and then Charles's sister Caroline and Joe Wedgwood. The rest and change did him no good. Back at Down House he went to bed for a week. He abandoned the idea of going to Malvern when he learned that Dr. Gully was too ill to treat him.

Emma sometimes used the term "anxiety." But he felt none. His father and a succession of doctors from Gully onward had declared him organically sound. And he was not a hypochondriac, never had been.

Never? A crack opened in the curtain.

He knew that he went through cycles, though no one knew what caused them. He thought back to all the cures he had attempted, some of them temporarily effective: hydropathy, chalk, nitromuriatic acid, ice packs, diet, Condy's ozonised water, the brass and zinc wires moistened with vinegar he had wrapped about his waist and neck. . . .

How much better a life he would have had as a country clergyman, with a quiet parish and beetles and butterflies to collect. There would have been no H.M.S. *Beagle*, no *Journal*. Just peace and acceptance, perhaps in the exquisite chapel above Maer, with Emma as his wife, and the enchanting Maer Hall as his home. Or as a fellow of Christ's College, might life not have been far easier for him? With companionship, bottles of wine being presented in the combination room after the evening meal, bowls full of walnuts to be cracked? Could he not have avoided the wretchedness that kept draining the energy and life force out of him?

What diabolical predetermination had precipitated him into this most disputatious position in the modern world? Was the *Origin of Species* the beginning of his troubles? Not really. Nor the end. There was still his need to penetrate to startling upheavals of human belief. It was a cross he did not wish to bear. But where was the escape hatch, the small boat that could be swung out when H.M.S. *Thetis* crashed against the rocks and sank?

He displayed an untroubled face and good-natured attitude toward his wife, children, staff. On those rare occasions when the severest physical illness or depression overtook him, he picked up his copy of *Paradise Lost* and pondered over Milton's lines:

> The mind is its own place, and in itself
> Can make a Heav'n of Hell, a Hell of Heav'n.

For her part, Emma laid down a number of strictures to her children and servants.

"We have to accept all this philosophically. We must strive to be amiable to each other. It is a condition with which we must live and which we must make the best of. It is nothing we will talk about, analyze or debate, or even notice. Health is like the weather, something we can neither predict nor control. Father's attacks are not to set an example for the rest of you. I want no hypochondriacs created in Down House because you might think that imitation is flattery."

Charles did not follow his wife's dicta. He described to his friends the minutest details of his malaise. He found it therapeutic to speak openly of his ailments, giving such clinical details as the retching, bile, diarrhea, inertia. It brought him a measure of relief akin to confession. Yet he made it clear that he was an invalid, not a recluse. Was he looking for sympathy, justification for remaining embattled within the walls of his home and grounds? It was a ridiculous statement anyway, he decided, an invalid could not have created a new concept of everything that lived on the earth and in the seas. Revolutionized all human thought. No invalid could do that! Only a man of courage and strength! To be an invalid meant not to be valid. More and more of the Western world was saying that Charles Darwin was the most valid man alive!

Though he tried to keep it out of his consciousness there was the knowledge that he had to write the book about the descent of man. Prove irrefutably that man had evolved, as had the horse and all other living things, and not been "created whole in God's image." Even were it to bring upon him earthquake and fire more devastating than the one he had witnessed at Concepción in Chile. But when? And how?

In the meanwhile they did everything to make life passable for themselves. Emma and Henrietta read aloud the latest popular novel, *Sylvia's Lovers* by Elizabeth Gaskell. Emma trimmed her bushes and shrubs in the garden. They took their younger children to London to see the decorations and crowds who welcomed Princess Alexandra of Denmark, affianced to the Prince of Wales; and to admire the London City Police, who had abandoned their tall civilian hats for helmets.

Charles was nominated for the Copley Medal, the highest honor in the British scientific world. He had strong support from his friends in the Royal Society, as well as strenuous dissent from the older members. Somehow Rear Admiral Robert FitzRoy started the rumor that he had had to oblige Charles to leave H.M.S. *Beagle* because of seasickness. Erasmus was visiting Down House and reported the bit of gossip. Charles was furious.

"FitzRoy never persuaded me to give up the voyage on account of seasickness, nor did I ever think of doing so, though I suffered considerably; *but I do not believe it was the cause of my subsequent ill-health, which has lost me so many years, and therefore I should not think the seasickness was worth notice.*"

The next time Erasmus caught Charles retching, some three hours after dinner, he said with a touch of irony:

"Perhaps you had better go back to Father's remedy of raisins and biscuit. I'll buy you a hammock for your next birthday."

On land or sea, it did not matter; Charles was defeated, the Copley Medal went to someone else.

What returned him to work was still another discovery and another love: climbing plants. He had the plant *Echinocystis lobata* in his study and was surprised to find that the uppermost part of each branch was constantly and slowly twisting around, making a circle. It would sometimes go round two or three times, and then at the same rate untwist and twist in the opposite direction. It generally rested half an hour between its travels.

All of the children except William were home for the summer. They were fascinated by this activity. They asked if anyone else had noticed the phenomenon. He told them that two Germans had mentioned the activity, and also Asa Gray, but that the process was totally unexplored.

"I'm going to write a little book about it. A peaceable one, though startling."

"It's pretty, Papa. How does it work?" asked his youngest.

"It *is* pretty, Horace. Every one and a half or two hours the plant sweeps a circle of from one foot to twenty inches in diameter, and immediately the tendril touches any object its sensitiveness causes it to seize it and start climbing. The Lubbocks' gardener says that he believes the tendrils can see, for wherever he has put a plant it finds out any stick near enough. The tendrils have some sense, too, for they do not grasp each other."

In this sporadic period of energy and concentration he also moved along on his book Variation of Animals and Plants under Domestication, beginning the chapter Selection on June 16 and completing it by July 20, a chapter of soundly researched materials. However he confessed to Hooker:

"I am getting very much amused by my tendrils; it is just the sort of niggling work which suits me, and rather rests me while writing."

Emma, relieved by the relaxation he was taking in his study and in the hothouse with the climbing plants, set out to accomplish something she had long contemplated: having a humane animal trap substituted for the small steel traps in common use. The smaller animals caught in the traps suffered for eight or ten hours before they died. She wrote a long article which the Gardeners' Chronicle published, then interested the Society for the Prevention of Cruelty to Animals in putting up a prize for the most humane trap invented. She also began raising money to supply the funds for the prize.

The family was proud of her.

The surprise of the summer was that Katty and the Rev. Mr. Langton, widowed on the death of Charlotte Wedgwood, became engaged and were to be married in October. The news of the engagement startled the Darwin family. Twenty-year-old Henrietta was the first to erupt.

"It seems to me almost indecent for anyone over fifty to think of such a thing as marrying."

"That's beside the point," Charles rebuked her. "Katty has neither good health nor good spirits, and both she and Langton have strong wills. I'm doubtful as to her happiness."

"It's an anxious experiment," Emma agreed, "but surely they must have come to know each other over the years of visiting back and forth? They will give each other companionship."

"Why has Katty waited all these years, until she is fifty-three? She was popular; she must have had a dozen chances to marry well."

"We'll go to the wedding, of course," Emma decreed. "They must never suspect our misgivings."

"That leaves Susan alone at The Mount," Charles mourned.

"We'll invite her to come to Down House and live with us," said Emma.

What he called his present "hobbyhorse" was the tendrils. It was exciting to watch the Apocynaceae with shoots eighteen inches long steadily searching for something to climb, the climbing being the simple result of the plant's spontaneous circulatory movement of the upper internodes. He learned that with a mere touch of a pencil to the two branches of the tendril he could mold them into any shape he liked. He had already examined the passion flower, Virginia creeper, the common and everlasting pea, and was in frequent communication with Joseph Hooker asking if he knew of any plant which he could give or lend, or Charles could buy, with tendrils of odd or peculiar structure.

When he did not have the energy to write, he dictated to his womenfolk. His only hour of comfort came in the evening when, stretched out on the chaise by the piano, he listened to Emma play his favorite arias from the operas. He never tired of Handel's *The Harmonious Blacksmith*. There was his midday reading of the London *Times*, which often made him furious, particularly because the *Times* was defending the South in the American Civil War and, by implication, slavery.

"The *Times* is getting more detestable than ever," he told his children. "Mama wishes to give it up but I tell her that is a pitch of heroism to which only a woman is equal. To give up the 'Bloody Old Times,' as Cobbett used to call it, would be to give up meat, drink and air."

He went to Malvern for hydropathy for all of September and half of October. It did him no good. He was ill to the end of the year, and until mid-April of 1864. He asked himself, "Where do the weeks and months go? I shudder at the cruel waste when I still have so much work to complete. I suppose I shall never recover. My life is finished at the early age of fifty-five."

He awakened on April 13, after a sound night's sleep, feeling well, and went to work immediately after breakfast, writing On the Movements and Habits of Climbing Plants. He felt strong enough to concentrate steadily for four months to complete the monograph. After the light veil of gloom that had overhung Down House when he was totally incapacitated, it was a cheerful time for the family. He told Emma:

"Writing this one-hundred-and-eighteen-page article has been sheer entertainment. Eheu! Eheu! I wish all writing could be that diverting."

"It can be. Stick with your hobbyhorses."

The Linnean Society published his study in their Journal, and printed a goodly number of the monograph for commercial sale at four shillings. Charles had two hundred copies run off for mailing around the world to his circle of correspondents. The reception of Climbing Plants was as joyous as the writing had been. The naturalists were titillated and enlightened.

Now that he could write his letters himself, he resumed his correspondence with his close friends in London. Lyell's Antiquity of Man had gone into a third edition. He had been elected president of the British Association and made a baronet. While in Berlin, Lyell had met with England's Princess Royal, married to the Crown Prince of Prussia, who had told him that after Darwin's Origin of Species "the old opinions had received a shake from which they would never recover." Charles had the honesty to admit to Lyell:

"I have the true English reverence for rank."

Thomas Huxley had enjoyed a publishing success with his Evidence as to Man's Place in Nature, which quickly went into a second printing. He complained to Charles:

"In spite of working like a horse or, if you prefer it, like an ass, I find myself scandalously in arrears. I wake up in the morning with somebody saying in my ear, 'A is not done, and B is not done, and C is not done, and D is not done.' I feel like a fellow whose duns are all in the street waiting for him."

Charles enjoyed being with young Huxley again.

"Tell me all that you are doing."

"Editing lectures on the vertebrate skull and bringing them out in the Medical Times. Rewriting lectures on elementary physiology; thinking of my course of twenty-four lectures on the Mammalia at the Royal College of Surgeons for next spring. Working at a 'Manual of Comparative Anatomy,' may it be damned, which I have had in hand these seven years. Finally, I am pestered to death in public and private because I am what they call a 'Darwinian.'"

Charles chortled.

"You should be more careful about whom you choose to support."

Thomas Huxley's book, *Six Lectures to Working Men on Our Knowledge of the Causes of the Phenomena of Organic Nature,* had just been published. Charles read in the copy sent to him:

> I believe that if you strip the *Origin of Species* of its theoretical part, it still remains one of the greatest encyclopedias of biological doctrine that any one man ever brought forth; and I believe that, if you take it as the embodiment of an hypothesis, it is destined to be the guide of biological and psychological speculation for the next three or four generations.

Joseph Hooker, his dearest friend, had completed his account of the botany of Syria and Palestine for Smith's *Dictionary of the Bible.* He was doing his best to keep Kew Gardens from being despoiled by incompetent gardeners and dishonest accountants whom his aging father did not recognize as such. A tragedy had struck Joseph and Frances. They had lost their six-year-old daughter Minnie. Joseph was as crushed as Charles had been at the death of Annie. Joseph wrote to him:

> . . . I tried hard to make no difference between her and the other children, but she was my very own, the flower of my flock in everyone's eyes, the companion of my walks, the first of my children who has shown any love for music and flowers, and the sweetest tempered, affectionate little thing that ever I knew. It will be long before I cease to hear her voice in my ears, or feel her little hand stealing into mine; by the fireside and in the garden, wherever I go she is there. . . .

Charles replied:

> I understand. Annie was truly my companion among the children. Why do we somehow lose the one who is closest to us?

Alfred Wallace had fallen in love with the daughter of one of his chess-playing friends but was courting her in such a shy manner that the young woman had no idea she was being wooed. After a year he proposed by letter and was rejected. He persisted and the young woman accepted; meetings were arranged to set the wedding date . . . and at the last moment she broke off the engagement on the grounds that she had heard that Wallace had been engaged once before. Wallace was not stupid enough to believe this; nor was he dense enough not to recognize that the woman obviously had no feeling for him. He was still living with his sister, earning modest sums from the two books he had had published and from magazine articles. He had brought back enough material from his years in unknown lands to make him one of the leading naturalists of his time.

During Charles's wasted months he had decided that since he had nothing better to do he might as well grow a beard. If he had not flourished, the beard surely had. By now it had bushed out, a pure gray. He kept it trimmed in a neat oval shape under his chin. He also grew a mustache, which turned out to be lighter in color than the dark hair at the sides and back of his head. He kept the mustache austerely trimmed, even as he fastidiously shaved the rounded portion of his cheeks. His dark brown eyes seemed more deeply set under the powerful protruding brows. At table one day he asked Emma and the children proudly:

"Do I not look reverent?"

"They will be calling you the Bishop of Cambridge," Henrietta said. "Like Bishop Wilberforce of Oxford."

"But never Soapy Charles!"

He began to think of time as "intervals." Short intervals. Long intervals. Intervals of being well and productive. Intervals of inactivity. Time was a frozen ice pack at the North Pole. Time was an ice floe, breaking up, melting, running now slow, now fast and faster. While assembling and reading the material on the differing races of mankind, present and ancient, his mind made a quantum jump which startled him. He came to suspect that sexual selection had been the most powerful means of changing the races of man. He noted:

> I can show that the different races have a widely different standard of beauty. Among savages the most powerful men will have the pick of the women, and they will generally leave the most descendants.

"Here's a mischief, indeed!" he growled to himself. "Following this line of 'sexual' selection, I will infuriate the greater part of our society where the dread word is never uttered, not even in the most spurious novels. I will be compounding my felonies a hundredfold."

Shortly thereafter he received in the post a copy of Alfred Wallace's article, "The Development of Human Races under the Law of Natural Selection," published in the *Anthropological Review*. Instead of being troubled over priority as he had been when he read Wallace's first paper on natural selection, he found himself as disturbed and disappointed over Wallace's approach as he had been with Lyell's. Wallace had written:

> . . . Man is, indeed, a being apart, since he is not influenced by the great laws which irresistibly modify all other organic

beings. . . . Man has not only escaped natural selection himself, but he is actually able to take away some of that power
from nature which before his appearance she universally exer-
cised. . . .

Surely Wallace could not believe that! He was still young and adapt-
able. If he turned over to Wallace his new concept of sexual selection,
would Wallace then not have a road on which to follow man back to his
beginnings? Would he not become converted? It would be a way to get
out of the cruel burden Lyell had so grievously laid upon him. He wrote
to Wallace:

> I have collected a few notes on Man, but I do not suppose I
> shall ever use them. Would you like at some future time to
> have my references and notes? I am sure I hardly know
> whether they are of any value. . . .

By the autumn, having gone back to "Variation of Animals and
Plants under Domestication," and completing another long chapter, he
felt depleted. If it did not release his body from pain, it helped his
spirits that his children were flourishing. William, now twenty-four, was
contented with his lot as a banker. That summer he had his four
brothers, George, Francis, Leonard and Horace, down to Southampton
for a holiday. He gave them claret cup and sumptuous breakfasts, and
while Leonard was swimming filled his trousers with stones, a game they
had played when they were all younger. He took the boys to the Isle
of Wight on a clear Sunday, where they wandered about Bonchurch and
Ventnor. They returned to Down House brown and chirpy. Emma
wrote to William:

> . . . How well you succeeded in giving them a happy
> visit. . . .

Charles was immensely pleased with William, for it was his fondest
wish that his children should remain in a close and affectionate family
relationship. He was also gratified that his second son, George, now
nineteen, had passed his "little go" at Trinity College in Cambridge.
George had a turn for mathematics; he planned to try for a scholarship
at Trinity.

Francis, at sixteen, had decided he wanted to become a doctor and
follow in the footsteps of his grandfather and great-grandfather. He was
the artist among the five boys. He delighted in music, taught himself to
play the flute, oboe, bassoon. He wrote good verse when the family
played the Poetry Game; drew amusing cartoons for their Picture
Game. He was a charming chap, with an incisive sense of humor,

though he suffered occasional fits of depression. Of the five Darwin boys he was the most interested and intrigued by his father's work, asked to be taught how to use the microscope and how to cross-fertilize plants. He read his father's books and demanded explanations on materials he was too young to grasp. Leonard, the fourteen-year-old, had become excited by photography, taking such good pictures of his father that Charles sent copies to his friends. Horace, the youngest at thirteen, lived away at school, where he was flourishing.

Elizabeth, their younger daughter, was now seventeen, on the plain side and plump, a good deal Henrietta's inferior in intellect, yet more sensitive. If she was a little helpless in practical affairs—her brother George had not been able to convince her exactly what five per cent meant—her judgment of character was better than Henrietta's. She had always been skeptical about Henrietta's poor health and had the courage to show it. Henrietta had frequently put Elizabeth down, maintaining her position as the older and cleverer sister, but the family found Elizabeth to be shrewd in many matters.

Henrietta, now twenty-one, asserted her independence by reading Thomas Huxley's books and making critical assertions about them. She went alone on her visits to Erasmus and the Hensleigh Wedgwoods, and to the Langtons, who were living in Wiltshire.

The children decided that they were now too grown up to call their parents Mama and Papa. They decided to call them Mother and Father. Charles hated the idea. He declared:

"I'd rather be called Dog."

The names stuck. William had been Willy as a child; he now demanded his proper name, and kept it. Henrietta remained Etty; Elizabeth became Bessy; Francis became Frank; Leonard became Lenny. Neither George nor Horace lent himself to change.

Now that the children were largely self-reliant, Emma found more freedom. In the spring and summer she took drives in the pony carriage by herself, frequently coming home by twilight round High Elms where she saw the Lubbocks playing cricket. She extended her gardening, often being surprised to see how cheering a little exertion of that kind could be. She liked cutting and carving among the shrubs but found that her opinion of what shape they should be was opposite to that of the rest of the family. With a freshly acquired feeling of independence, she fought back, with her gardener and her family.

"You box the shrubs too rigidly for my taste," she informed them. "I'm going to set out a certain portion of the garden where I'll carve out more rounded forms."

She also took to visiting about the neighborhood by herself. For this purpose she had a new gown made which she described to her two daughters as "respectable and handsome." She visited the family of the village doctor, the one who had taken care of Leonard during his illness. Spengle was always in difficulties because of being too indulgent with his poorer patients. When she saw in what straitened circumstances he lived, she suggested to Charles that he advance the man some money against future medical services. She enjoyed visiting the Lubbocks at High Elms, where she got into debates as to whether the younger Lubbocks should beat their father at billiards. She sometimes stopped for tea at the home of the Rev. Brodie Innes and invited the vicar and his wife to Down House for dinner after the Sunday services.

It was time for the next awarding of the Copley Medal. Charles was urged to send in additional material but declined, saying, "Once through that mill is enough." Hugh Falconer took up the cudgels by writing a lengthy nominating letter to the Royal Society from Europe where he was traveling. It included the assertion:

> I am of the opinion that Mr. Darwin is not only one of the most eminent naturalists of his day, but that hereafter he will be regarded as one of the great naturalists of all countries and of all time. . . .
>
> . . . And lastly, Mr. Darwin's great essay on the *Origin of Species by Natural Selection.* This solemn and mysterious subject had been either so lightly or so grotesquely treated before, that it was hardly regarded as being within the bounds of legitimate philosophical investigation. Mr. Darwin, after twenty years of the closest study and research, published his views, and it is sufficient to say that they instantly fixed the attention of mankind throughout the civilized world. That the efforts of a single mind should have arrived at success on a subject of such vast scope, and encompassed with such difficulties, was more than could have been reasonably expected. . . .

This letter and others won Charles the medal.

He decided not to attend the award meeting because of the emotional strain, since some of the older men of the Society had opposed him for it. Lyell offered to make the after-dinner speech, which Charles gratefully accepted. The presentation caused a near scandal. Joseph Hooker brought the story to Charles.

"President Edward Sabine said in his address that in awarding you the Copley all consideration of your *Origin* was 'expressly excluded.' Huxley got up and asked how that could be. He insisted on the minutes of the council being produced and read, in which of course there was no such exclusion.

"Lyell made a fine effort to compensate for Sabine's denigration of

664 "I AM LIKE A GAMBLER, AND LOVE A WILD EXPERIMENT"

the *Origin* by making a confession of faith in the book. He declared, 'I have been forced by the *Origin* to give up my old faith without thoroughly seeing my way to a new one.' He sent you a message: 'I think you would have been satisfied with the length I went.'"

"Did Sabine promise to correct his remarks in the printed version of his address?"

"He inferred that he would."

He did not. When Charles received the printed copy of President Sabine's speech he found that Sabine included the phrase:

> Speaking generally and collectively, we have expressly omitted the *Origin of Species* from the grounds of our award.

That bit of "shuffling" took some of the shine off the medal. Emma volunteered:

"Sabine is merely trying to placate the older members who voted against you. I suppose that's one of the functions of a president, to keep peace in the family."

"At all costs?" asked Charles angrily. "To deliberately falsify the written record? That's chicanery."

When he received several notes from colleagues which, he told Emma, "have warmed my heart," he added:

"I often wonder that so old a worn-out dog as I am is not quite forgotten."

Emma was accustomed to his habit of self-deprecation.

"Old? Worn out? With the notes for half a dozen books cluttering up your study?"

Charles sighed.

"You're right, of course. I shall probably live forever."


5.


He had not expected that winning the Copley Medal would trigger a new attack by his opponents, who had lost ground through his getting the award. They unleashed a campaign of articles, sermons, even published books. It was hard for Charles to take, yet once again the Copley, plus the new bombardment, spread knowledge of the *Origin of Species* to areas it had not yet reached. The outburst might conceivably be constructive in the long run.

Henrietta had taken to reading scientific materials. She instantly fell upon the manuscripts arriving at Down House by Huxley, Hooker and Wallace, making remarks about their word usage. Huxley, in particular, was amused. After Henrietta had read his *Lectures on the Elements of Comparative Anatomy*, she told him:

"I wish you would write a book."

"I've just written a great book on the skull, Miss Etty."

"I don't call that a book. I want something that people can read. Do you not think you could write a popular treatise on zoology?"

"Miss Etty, my last book is a book. Marry come up! Does your ladyship call it a pamphlet?"

"A monograph, merely."

Charles, lounging in a nearby chair, said:

"I sometimes think popular treatises are almost as important for the progress of science as original work."

"I have just finished a set of lectures to workingmen on the various races of mankind, which would make a book in Miss Etty's sense of the word."

The year 1865 was fatal for many of Charles's colleagues. Hugh Falconer died in late January on his return from Europe, just three months after securing the Copley for Charles. His good neighbor, Sir John Lubbock, died of heart disease in June. Sir William Hooker in August. Vice Admiral Robert FitzRoy had committed suicide on April 30. It was FitzRoy's slashing of his own throat that most saddened Charles.

"From my original beau ideal of a captain to death at his own hands seems a hard road to travel," he mused aloud, Emma being within earshot. "Yet I often feared for him. His uncle, Lord Castlereagh, had killed himself at roughly the same age; that sometimes preyed on FitzRoy's mind even when he was in his twenties."

The answer emerged after the funeral. FitzRoy had run through his entire fortune. A subscription had to be raised to pay his debts. He had been overworked, ill, despondent because he had become dissatisfied with his job at the Meteorologic Office. But most dispiriting of all, he had been rejected on his most important contribution since H.M.S. *Beagle* returned in 1836. By studying all the weather maps that had been accumulating, he had come to the conclusion that the weather could be forecast. The London *Times* had ridiculed what they called "his mysterious utterances." There was severe criticism, followed by neglect. Robert FitzRoy had continued to be one of Charles's most persistent and voluble attackers.

"Poor FitzRoy, he took some of the bitter-tasting abuse he spooned out to me," said Charles. "No, I'm not pleased that I have one enemy less," he decided as though answering his own question. "My mind goes back to those wonderful years on the *Beagle* when he gave me friendship and abetted my explorations. He was a friend then, and he shall remain so in my memory."

He never knew when new concepts would be born, yet he could definitely chart their beginnings and growth. For several years he had been studying bud and seminal variation, inheritance, reversion, the idiosyncrasies of reproduction for his Variations. It had become a passion to try to connect all such facts by some sort of hypothesis. Now he coined the word *pangenesis* to explain the phenomenon of heredity: that every separate unit or cell of an organism reproduced itself by contributing its share to the germ or bud of the future offspring.

When he had written out his idea of pangenesis in thirty pages he made the trip to London to talk with Huxley and ask him to read the material.

"A very great favor from one so hard worked as you are. Pangenesis is a very rash and crude hypothesis, yet it has been a considerable relief to my mind, as I can hang on it a good many groups of facts."

When Huxley had consented, Charles cried:

"Splendid. I must say for myself that I am a hero to expose my hypothesis to the fiery ordeal of your criticism."

Huxley's reaction to the manuscript was that "It is too much reflective of Buffon and Bonnet, the French naturalists."

"I do not doubt your judgment," Charles murmured, disappointed. "I will try to persuade myself not to publish it. The whole affair is much too speculative; yet I think some such view will have to be adopted."

Huxley apologized.

"I did not at all mean by what I said to stop you from publishing your views, and I really should not like to take that responsibility. Somebody rummaging among your papers half a century hence will find pangenesis and say, 'See this wonderful anticipation of our modern theories and that stupid ass Huxley prevented his publishing them.' Publish your views, not so much in the shape of formed conclusions as of hypothetical developments of the only clue at present accessible. Don't give the Philistines more chances of blaspheming you than you can help."

Charles studied the books of Bonnet and Buffon, found that they were on different tracks. However he gave them credit for their attempts in a long footnote.

It was Emma's impression, and that of the children as well, that Charles's pre-eminent quality was his abhorrence of cruelty. Slavery of human beings had long been anathema to both the Darwin and Wedgwood families. The Darwins had rejoiced when Abraham Lincoln's Emancipation Proclamation was reproduced in the London newspapers back in 1863. They had been inestimably relieved when the American Civil War ended on April 14 of 1865 with General Lee's surrender to

General Grant at Appomattox on the ninth. However the *Times* carried such a burden of bad news that Charles at last succumbed to Emma's pleas to stop reading the newspaper:

The historic Savile House in Leicester Square burned to the ground in February. A strike of the shipwrights severely injured the shipbuilding business on the river Thames, causing widespread distress. The "Fenians," an Irish republican brotherhood, whose purpose it was to free Ireland from English rule, planned the first of two uprisings against British stationed in Ireland. The government in London got wind of the plot, seized the Fenian office and arrested the ringleaders, one of whom was sentenced to life imprisonment.

Closer to home, when Charles learned that a neighbor had allowed some sheep to die of starvation, he rode about the parish collecting evidence, presented it to a magistrate and had the man convicted of neglect.

Even without the newspaper, he learned that cattle imported from Holland had brought with them a plague known on the Continent as *rinderpest*. It spread with alarming rapidity. The Darwins kept only a couple of cows at Down House for the family's dairy products; but plenty of cattle grazed in the lush fields of Kent. Before the end of 1865, 73,559 animals had been attacked, out of which 55,422 had died or been killed. A fever of anxiety swept the country, for the loss of its herds would be a tragic blow to England. The cattlemen, working with scientists, several of whom Charles knew, found a means to stamp out the dread disease. When the scare was over, Charles said with a touch of triumph:

"Parliament has always neglected science. Perhaps a lesson has been learned about its practical value. We need supportive bills and financial grants for research, particularly in medicine and the control of diseases of men, cattle, sheep, trees, plants, all living creatures."

It was a united Darwin family that had been concerned with the succeeding crises. But late in the year 1865 there came the Jamaica uprising, which brought about one of the rare quarrels in Down House. The uprising consisted of a group of about one hundred and fifty Negroes who attempted to free a native prisoner. Twenty-eight of the ringleaders were arrested, whereupon the blacks fell upon the whites, killing and wounding a number of them, destroying property. The British governor of Jamaica, Edward Eyre, used his troops to shoot and hang the rioters. The upheaval shook England when Governor Eyre then arrested the alleged leader of the rioters, George W. Gordon, a black member of the House of Assembly, had him tried illegally before two young navy lieutenants, and summarily hanged. The execution of Gordon, who apparently had had nothing to do with the uprising, as well as Governor Eyre's subsequent vengeance on all Negroes, split England into hostile and warring factions, those in favor of Eyre's actions, those opposed. When William came home for a visit he remarked at the dinner table:

"In Southampton we have recently held a public meeting in favor of Governor Eyre. Our speaker denounced the committee that is prosecuting him. Southampton is solidly for the governor. I must say I agree."

Anger flared in Charles's eyes. He turned on William in a fury of indignation, cried:

"Then you had better go back to Southampton!"

The next morning at seven he stood by his son's bedside.

"William, I'm sorry that I have been so angry at you. I have not been able to sleep all night. Forgive me. Though I disagree with you thoroughly on the Governor Eyre matter, that does not mean that you are not entitled to your independent opinion."

Charles spent a good part of each afternoon catching up on the scientific literature in the back numbers of the periodicals, finding and annotating studies for his Variation under Domestication. He also spent an hour each day on horseback. The change of seasons was continually exciting.

Katty's marriage to the Rev. Charles Langton had proved to be a good one. However Katty was frequently ill, her suffering acute. When Susan fell ill at The Mount, Katty returned to Shrewsbury to nurse her and give her company. It helped Susan, but then Katty could no longer get out of bed, dying quietly in her sleep. Charles mourned his younger sister, who had looked so much like him. She had been his companion during his years at home.

"I shall try once again to get Susan to come and live with us," he told Emma. "She would be reassured in your company."

His study, frequently a battlefield, became a refuge. His probing mind kept him in good spirits. Following his reasoning about sexual selection, he observed that butterflies offered an excellent example of beauty always being displayed in a conspicuous part of the anatomy. The male, much more brilliantly colored than the female, habitually exhibited the gaudy underside of its wings to attract the female. Into Charles's mind flashed the male frigate bird of the Galápagos who, in the mating season, lined the beaches and marshes by the thousands, their throats of a brilliant orange or flaming red, ballooning out to attract a mate.

It was a discovery similar to the one he had made about flowers: that they became more beautiful to make themselves conspicuous to insects. He began exchanging letters with two German botany professors, one at the University of Freiburg, the other in Munich, about sage, the transition of organs, the purpose behind the evolved beauty of flowers and fruit.

He became so absorbed in tying his latest observation into his overall theory of natural selection that Emma asked:

"Wouldn't you like me to take over the household accounts? I shouldn't mind."

He had always enjoyed keeping records but was avid for the extra time. John Murray had written that a fourth edition of the *Origin* was wanted. Charles was vexed by the fact that corrections and alterations were needed. Still in all, Murray was printing another twelve hundred and fifty copies from which he stood to earn two hundred and thirty-eight pounds.

"That will look good on your account books," he told Emma.

He also corrected, revised, added new materials to the manuscript of Variation. He already had a thousand pages, but was leaving his concluding chapter until the body of the book had been sent to the printer. He made such gratifying progress and felt so well that around the middle of April he suggested to Emma that they go to London to Erasmus's house for a holiday. He had been urging them to come.

Emma was delighted. It was a long time since she had been to the theater or heard the philharmonic. They decided to take the girls with them.

Erasmus was overjoyed at how well Charles looked. Erasmus had just overcome a bout of ague but was as cordial and charming as ever. They all went to see *Hamlet* with the famous actor Fechter, who played his part beautifully. Erasmus scolded Emma when she confessed:

"It was a wonderful production but I should prefer anything to Shakespeare, I'm ashamed to say."

The following evening Emma's sister Elizabeth picked them up for the philharmonic. There was an excellent program, the Pastoral Symphony by Beethoven, even though they knew it almost too well; and a Hummel concerto.

The most important event was Charles's wanting to attend a soiree at the Royal Society. He dressed scrupulously in a new shirt, cravat and boots for which he had shopped the day before, and set out for the Society in the early evening, the first time he had gone to Burlington House in many years. He received such a cordial reception from his surprised and elated colleagues that it gave him a warm glow.

"Charles Darwin! How wonderful to see you again! . . . You're slim as a young lad. . . . We have missed you! . . . Congratulations on the Copley. No one deserved it more. . . ."

He noticed that several men were staring at him in an odd way. Lyell laughed heartily.

"They don't recognize you in the beard. Come, let us sprinkle your name among them like birdseed."

Lyell was right. When the members heard Charles's name pronounced they broke into smiles, wrung his hand, talked about his work. Edward Sabine, still president and conscious of his former dissembling, hung back, embarrassed. When the Prince of Wales arrived, Sabine made the grand gesture of seeing that Charles was the first to be presented to him. Only three members were presented.

"Sabine is trying to make it up to you," Hooker whispered, while Huxley added, "That noble gesture made you the top member of the Society."

Charles grimaced.

"The Prince looks a nice, good-natured youth, and very gentlemanlike. He said something to me that I could not hear so I made the profoundest bow I could, and went on."

He heard a voice behind him say, "There's nothing wrong with your hearing."

Charles turned to find himself facing Dr. Henry Bence Jones, his latest doctor, who had put him on a diet of small portions of meat and toast, which had slimmed him down fifteen pounds; he had also ordered him to ride his horse Tommy every day.

A hamper full of new kittens greeted them when they returned to Down House refreshed by the excitements of the city.

James Sulivan, now an admiral, came to visit with his wife. He had grown big in girth and red of face. Together they mourned the untimely death of Robert FitzRoy. Then Sulivan tacked about:

"Darwin, I've discovered an astonishingly rich accumulation of fossil bones not far from the Strait of Magellan. They should be collected and you are the right man for it. I could take you with me as my naturalist next time I sail south."

Everyone laughed. Charles enjoyed being with his old shipmate who had caused so much amusement during the *Beagle* years. He was the only one Charles still saw. The others, Dr. Benjamin Bynoe, John Wickham, Stokes, King, all had disappeared into their separate lives. Nor had he ever heard from Conrad Martens, the painter who had settled in Australia and whose water colors still hung on their walls. Augustus Earle, he had learned earlier, died in 1838, two years after Charles's return to England. Charles, immersed in his own collections, had not had a chance to see an exhibition of Earle's art.

The work went on apace, as did the summer of 1866. One day, returning from her carriage ride, Emma exclaimed:

"I had quite forgotten how pleasant it was to feel brisk all day."

"So had I. But all goes well. The chapters of Variation are shaping up. Huxley is getting his first academic honor, along with Thomas Carlyle, at the University of Edinburgh. Wallace is going to marry Annie Mitten, the eighteen-year-old daughter of a botanist friend. He is twenty-five years older than the girl but he's such a virile man that I think the marriage will work. Lyell is publishing the tenth edition of his *Principles*, a miracle for a scientific book. He is adding freshly observed material. Hooker, as director since his father's death, is busy at Kew, where he is able to expand and modernize the gardens, to run them more scientifically. He says he works out of doors six hours a day."

The boys were again home from school for the summer; Francis would be entering Trinity College in September. They were frisky as colts. Charles joined in their games. Henrietta was in the South of France. She was ecstatic about St. Jean, which she described as "a little harbour with the gorgeous lateen sails of yellow and red." Elizabeth, now nineteen, came into her own. She read aloud to her father from the popular literature of the day, Emma listening in when she was free: *Hereward the Wake* by Charles Kingsley; *Felix Holt, The Radical*, about English affairs at the time of the first Reform Bill, by George Eliot; *The Dove in the Eagle's Nest* by Charlotte Yonge.

In the autumn, when Charles was coming toward the end of the Variation manuscript, he decided that he would add a climactic chapter on the descent of man. It would be a natural ending for the book, make it complete. He felt it imperative that he fulfill the overall task which Lyell had failed to finish.

"In that way, I can complete my work on man, and not have to do a whole volume on the subject. I'll be free."

His sister Susan had never been willing to leave The Mount, ill as she was, declining invitations not only from Charles and Emma but from other members of the family as well. She died in October, at sixty-three, and was buried in Shrewsbury. Meeting with Caroline and Erasmus, Charles said:

"I think I know why Susan would never leave The Mount, even though she died there alone. She was afraid she would lose the presence of our father. He was the love of her life, the only love. That's why she never married."

"I sensed that," Caroline replied quietly.

He received the account of the auction of The Mount's contents, from which a goodly sum had been acquired. The particulars, including the furniture, the books and piano, his father's well-built blue brougham by Thorn of London, with pole and shafts, "luggage basket on top"; . . . Dr. Darwin's "strong phaeton on patent axle, painted green, lined in drab cloth"; . . . "a fashionable four-wheel dogcart, nearly new." . . . He closed his eyes and saw his father arriving home at the end of his long day.

The money from the auction was distributed among Marianne Parker's children as Susan had wanted it to be. When the house went on sale Charles suffered a severe bout of nostalgia. "Very beautiful old flower garden, terrace walk, first-class walled garden and glasshouse, in all about 5 acres." Also advertised were four stalls, coach house, harness room, blacksmith's forge, dog kennel, outside larder. Available in the vicinity were "hunting, shooting, golf."

There had been no golf when Charles lived at home but the hunting and shooting in the country around Shrewsbury he could well attest to, as the hunting had been good at nearby Woodhouse, where he had fallen in love with Fanny Owen. Since his return to England he had not heard a word about the sisters, Fanny and Sarah.

It was after Susan's death, when he had taken several days off, that he began to realize that he could not add a chapter on the descent of man to his Variation. Two reasons laid themselves out before him. The first was that the chapter on man would be the one the critics would pay attention to, particularly the theologians; the other thirty or more chapters on plant and animal breeding would be ignored.

Secondly, he knew he could not treat the evolution of man in a single chapter at the end of a thousand-page manuscript. He needed room to state his theory and his proofs, to link evidence that would build an irrefutable case. A full book would take perhaps years, but it would not be difficult; he had already accumulated much evidence pointing toward man's evolution. He would want to include ethnic studies of peoples and races from the beginning of time.

By December 21 he had completed all of his Variation corrections and was satisfied that the manuscript was the best he could do at that particular moment. John Murray was alarmed at the length of the book, and told Charles that there was too much material to be put in one volume. The print would have to be small, the leading and margins too narrow. He advised that it be done in two separate volumes of nearly equal length. That would make the venture expensive; the book would have to sell for about one pound ten. He replied to Murray:

> I cannot tell you how sorry I am to hear of the enormous size of my book. I fear it can never pay. But I cannot shorten it now; nor, indeed, if I had foreseen its length, do I see which parts ought to have been omitted. If you are afraid to publish it, say so at once, I beg you, and I will consider your note as canceled. If you think fit, get any one whose judgment you

rely on, to look over some of the more legible chapters. . . .
Pray do not publish blindly as it would vex me all my life if
I led you to heavy loss.

He spent the following days feeling vexed and annoyed waiting for
Murray's reply. His sense of drifting in space with nothing solid to put
his feet on was allayed when Murray notified him that, although forty-
three woodcuts were needed to illustrate the text, he was not concerned
about the costs. He was going to press in spite of the fact that he had
referred the manuscript to a literary friend who had brought in a somewhat adverse opinion.

He completed his final chapter for *Variation of Animals and Plants
under Domestication*, which he called Concluding Remarks. It was
brief but included the admonition:

> If an omnipotent and omniscient Creator ordains every-
> thing and foresees everything, we are brought face to face with
> a difficulty as insoluble as is that of free will and predes-
> tination.

It would take him a year to blacken the printer's sheets with revisions
and clarifications. But his sense of security now that Murray was
publishing—for who else would do it?—put him back into his writing
chair in the study, with its board of green felt, to write the first chapter
of the Descent of Man. He again reversed his thinking about the
projected length of the manuscript, deciding that he would "keep it
down to a very small volume."


6.


In February, to celebrate Charles's fifty-eighth birthday and their
twenty-eighth anniversary, they went to stay for a week with Erasmus in
London. Charles had written ahead making appointments with Wallace, Huxley, Hooker and Lyell. His first visit was to Wallace, now living at 9 St. Mark's Crescent, at Regent's Park Road, with his wife Annie
due to give birth to their first child that summer. If a boy they were
going to name him after the philosophical scientist, Herbert Spencer,
who had invented the phrase "survival of the fittest," in his *First Principles*, an expression which had attached itself to Darwinism. The two
men had a long conversation, mutually satisfying to begin with, then,
moving along the avenue of "survival of the fittest," Charles said:
"My difficulty is, why are caterpillars sometimes so beautifully and

artistically colored, seeing that so many species are colored to escape danger . . . ?"

"May I suggest that conspicuous caterpillars and other insects which are distasteful to birds are thereby easily recognized and avoided?" Wallace ventured.

Charles beamed with joy.

"Wallace, I never heard anything more ingenious!"

He turned to his present involvement.

"The reason for my being so much concerned about sexual selection is that I have almost resolved to publish a little essay on the origin of mankind. Sexual selection has been the main agent in forming the races of man."

A sudden stiffness came into Wallace's posture, a glaze across his eyes. After a moment of silence he replied:

"I doubt if we have a sufficiency of fair and accurate facts to do anything with man."

Was Wallace discouraging him? Why? Could he be planning a similar book? Was there once again a situation of prior publication? He could not believe so. Wallace would never attempt to restrain him; he was too great-hearted. Had he not insisted in one of his articles that Charles Darwin was the originator of the origin of species through natural selection? His mind cleared of the unworthy suspicion. Another took its place. In Wallace's article, "The Development of Human Races under the Law of Natural Selection," had he not set man apart as not being influenced by the laws which influenced all other organic beings? Was that the basis for his discouragement? He said:

"I had intended giving a chapter on man in *Variation under Domestication*, inasmuch as many call him, not quite truly, an eminently *domesticated* animal. But I found the subject too large for a chapter. My sole reason for taking it up is that sexual selection has always been a subject which has interested me much. I thought I would amuse myself with my new hobbyhorse. The subject is, I think, more curious and more amenable to scientific treatment than you seem willing to allow."

The following day he rode out to Kew Gardens to visit the Hookers. In the frost and heavy snows of January many of the oldest trees and almost all of the tender pines and cypresses, and more than half the shrubs, had been destroyed. He had expected to find Hooker dejected. Instead his friend was buoyant.

"I needed courage and faith to face the destruction but once the shock was over I saw that much good could come out of the evil. It is in fact an opportunity to replant to a system which will open vistas and provide a complete collection of specimen trees. The first Kew Gardens was my father's. The next will be mine." He smiled shyly at Charles, murmured, "I admit to a passion for landscape gardening."

Hooker demonstrated the seven grass avenues which would radiate from the Pagoda; the avenue which would run parallel to the river along the finest reach of the Thames above London; the newly extended areas for seasonal flowers and shrubs.

"Ah, Hooker, this is going to be a happy and creative time for you. When everything is grown, the 'Joseph' Hooker Kew Gardens will be among the most beautiful in the world."

Hooker pulled on his long and bushy eyebrows until they reached down to the circles beneath his eyes. He laughed softly at himself.

"That is my intention. I want you to be proud of me."

A couple of days later he went with Huxley to hear him lecture on the appalling privations of the East End's unemployed. It was an excoriating talk against the "haves" who allow the "have nots" to rot in hunger and filth. When they left the lecture room, Charles said:

"We are all for social justice and against abject poverty. But you do something about it! Your voice will be heard."

Next they went to a meeting of progressive schoolmasters, where Huxley attempted to get the teaching of science into the public (private) schools. Lyell was working on this at a higher level of influence. He and Emma had tea with the Lyells in Harley Street. Lyell asked Charles if he could read the proofs of *Variation*. Charles promised him the first set off the press.

Back at Down House he asked himself why, since the writing of the *Variation of Animals and Plants under Domestication* had been so satisfying, he should find the labor of correcting so prosaic. The weeks stretched into months and he was still at it.

In May Emma and the two girls went up to Cambridge to be with George and Francis and watch the boat races. The brothers met them at their inn. After dinner they walked about the city to see the magnificent stone colleges. The next morning they hired a carriage and drove three miles to a boggy meadow by the riverside. It was a fine sight, the twenty boats full of handsome, athletic young men rowing slowly by the starting point, each boatload in jerseys of a different color. After the starting gun had been fired the crowd rushed along the towing path to watch the boats shoot by. The river Cam was too narrow for more than one boat; when the hindmost bumped the one in front of it, the foremost gave way and retired to the side. After the race they had tea with George: fish, cutlets and every sort of teacake. The two following days they rushed about having breakfast at Francis's, then luncheon, claret cup and other treats, from the Trinity kitchen. On their last evening the weather turned warm and with the two boys they drove out to Ely to visit its great cathedral.

Then Emma, seeing that Charles was well and the household happy, took a rare holiday by herself to Ravensbourne, six miles northwest of Down, which she found restful partly because the summer rains good-naturedly confined themselves to the nighttime. She carried with her a book with an amusing title, *Lancashire Wedding, or Darwin Moralized*, which she read in the carriage. She wrote home to the family:

> The moral is that it is not wise to give up a pretty, poor, healthy girl you love, and marry a sickly, rich, cross one you don't care for; which does not require a conjuror to tell one. The story ought to have been giving up a pretty, sick girl you love and marrying a healthy one you don't care for. It is too dull to give to the village library.

Charles, entrenched in his study, was happy to see his womenfolk enjoying themselves. Since Kate Terry, one of the more famous actresses in England, was giving some farewell performances before her marriage, Emma and the two girls went up to London to see several of them, returning each night. They had two fast little gray horses and drove the six miles to Bromley, now the nearest station, in the open carriage. It was enchanting summer weather; the drive back in the starlit summer night was almost the most delightful part of what Henrietta described as "the nearly unheard-of dissipation which my mother was as eager about as any one of us."

As the corrected proofs of *Variation* reached him, he sent copies to Lyell, and to Asa Gray in Boston. Charles's greatest excitement in the book was his chapter on pangenesis and heredity. He wrote to Asa Gray:

> . . . Is it a mad dream, or a dream worth publishing? At the bottom of my own mind I think it contains a great truth.

Alfred Wallace, who had just published a paper on sexual selection among birds, continued his strange and uncharacteristic attempt to dissuade Charles from writing about the descent of man but, when he became reconciled that Charles was going to push ahead, told him:

"It is a glorious subject but will require delicate handling."

Charles had an almost eerie feeling about the comment. Who in the world would know better than he that such subjects required careful handling? Did he not know the full strength and durability of the opposition? But "delicate" handling of this most provocative subject of the era? There was no way of being delicate about the truth of evolving nature. One either saw the facts and told them precisely as they existed, or one fled. He knew full well that the heavens would fall on him.

Whatever doubts he may have had about the reception of *Variation of Animals and Plants under Domestication*, they were dispelled when he received a note from Lyell, who was on his way to Paris to see an exhibition for which Hooker was to judge the botany section. He wrote:

> I want to say what a privilege I feel it is to be allowed to read your sheets in advance. They go far beyond my anticipations both as to the quantity of original observation, and the materials brought together from such a variety of sources, and the bearing of which the readers of the *Origin* will now comprehend in a manner they would not have done had this book come out first.

Those few lines from Lyell cheered him inordinately. Then, in late October John Murray had his autumn sale, announcing that he would print fifteen hundred copies. At the sale the booksellers bought twelve hundred and sixty copies in advance, which was a relief to both the publisher and the author.

A third edition of the *Origin of Species* came out in German, a second in French. Honors were coming to him which he regarded as unimportant in his scheme of life except as they reflected the seriousness with which his work was being taken in foreign countries. He was made a knight of the Prussian Order Pour le Mérite, a rare privilege for an Englishman; was elected to the Imperial Academy of Science in St. Petersburg.

The book was finally released to the general public in January 1868. Interest and sale were strong from the beginning. John Murray had bound the two volumes attractively in smooth green cloth. In a matter of a week he informed Charles that he would need a second printing immediately. If Charles wished, he could send in his list of *errata* right away. Charles had had to list twelve *errata* after the sheets were printed, but now had only one correction to make.

He read all of the reviews he could lay his hands on. His friends sent him the rest. The *Pall Mall Gazette* was a good review, the *Athenaeum* dreadful as usual. The *Gardeners' Chronicle* was capital. Charles told Emma and the children, "This above all will help our sale and distribution." One of the Edinburgh papers treated him with profound contempt. The Duke of Argyll published a book which sneered at the work. However Asa Gray thought it magnificent. He quickly did a review for the *Nation*, interesting the naturalists and scientists of America in it. As Charles had predicted, the book stirred no controversy. The volumes were treated as a naturalist's report on the development of species. The only strong opposition came from Richard Owen and others who refused to believe or accept natural selection as a way of life; or of death.

Time became an umbrella protecting him from the burning sun and the pelting rain. The months during which he felt well and could extend his concentrated work stint to three and four hours, as well as penning as many as ten letters a day to specialists who provided him with information on sexual selection, gave him a sense of continuum. More than ever his spectrum had an indivisible wholeness. In his diary he noted how long it took him to complete the chapters On the Manner of Development of Man from Some Lower Form and Comparison of the Mental Powers of Man with the Lower Animals.

For Emma too, the years now flowed like a smooth river. There were night and day, Sundays when she donned her proper gown and bonnet for church. In her younger years time had appeared to be a series of mountain ranges to be climbed and crossed. Now life was an ongoing plain, with only an occasional gentle rise in the distance, and for both of them the sense of the world having settled down was heightened by the success of their boys at school. George became a second wrangler at Trinity, which meant that he came in second highest in the mathematics examination. A prize went along with it, as well as the probability of a scholarship. The telegram arrived at eleven one morning. Parslow brought up a bottle of cold champagne from the cellar and Charles and Emma drank a toast to their offspring. Charles dashed off notes to William in Southampton and Leonard and Horace at Clapham, telling them the good news. Francis helped George celebrate at Trinity.

Charles wrote to George:

> I am so pleased. I congratulate you with all my heart and soul. I always said from your early days that such energy, perseverance and talent as yours would be sure to succeed; but I never expected such brilliant success as this. Again and again I congratulate you. . . . God bless you my dear old fellow—may your life so continue.

The next day he was surprised to see in his study mirror his younger boys come running up the driveway. He went to the front door, cried: "What are you doing home?"

Horace, flushed and excited, replied:

"When your note about George arrived at school we were excused, and played indoor football, to the great danger of the windows and pictures."

Leonard continued:

"The headmaster had us all assemble in the hall where he told us what a great thing it was that a graduate of Clapham could become a second wrangler at the demanding Trinity College. Said it made Clapham that much more important in scholastic circles, and to celebrate he was giving the whole school a day off."

"We took a fly to Keston Mark," said Horace, "then walked the rest of the way. The other chaps went to the Crystal Palace but we wanted to be with you to celebrate."

Emma hugged her two boys. Charles shook their hands. Leonard said:

"I'm going to do just as well as George because I want to win admission to the Royal Military Academy at Woolwich and become a Royal Engineer."

Charles felt tears smart behind his eyes.

When he began the actual writing of his book on man on February 4, 1868, he realized that at fifty-nine years of age he was reaching for the apex of his life's work.

"Not that there aren't more books I plan to write, a good half dozen on subjects which have aroused me for years: the expression of emotions, insectivorous plants, the like. . . ."

They would be modest contributions to the growing lore of science, be a rounding out of his original two-thousand-page manuscript of the *Origin* which he had never intended to publish in the first place. In no sense would he consider these later books an anticlimax, but rather a logical extension of the observing and analyzing of the physical world which he had begun on H.M.S. *Beagle* when he rigged up a four-foot bag, attached it to a semicircular bow, dragged it behind the vessel and, finding that the catch of the net was very great, attempted to explain the manner in which so many creatures of good size lived so far from land.

He had written in his diary the following day, January 11, 1832:

I am quite tired having worked all day at the produce of my net. . . . Many of these creatures, so low in the scale of nature, are most exquisite in their forms & rich colours. It creates a feeling of wonder that so much beauty should be apparently created for such little purpose.

And he had taken his first step, without knowing it, toward becoming a "finished naturalist" as John Henslow had predicted. And spending his life searching for answers.

7.

His greatest disappointment in the reaction to *Variation of Animals and Plants under Domestication* was over the theory he had named pangenesis, which he defined as the phenomenon of heredity, with each unit or cell reproducing itself, and which the reviewers had ignored. This contribution seemed to him the most important element in the book, perhaps because it was his freshest idea, as yet untested except on Huxley, who had not liked it, but who had insisted that Charles publish it anyway. When he next went up to London for a visit with Erasmus he went to the zoo to study peacock tails, the stripes on zebras, the giraffe's elongated neck. He spent his evenings with Lyell, Hooker and Wallace asking for their reactions.

Charles Lyell, sitting across the Athenaeum table, declared, with his expansive laugh:

"I say to everyone, 'You may not believe in pangenesis, but if once you understand it, you will never get it out of your mind.'"

Out at Kew Gardens Hooker half demurred about this latest of Charles's hobbyhorses.

"I fear you will laugh at my density but I cannot see that in pangenesis you are doing aught but formulating what I have always supposed to be a fundamental idea in all development doctrines, that is, the transference to the progeny of any or every quality the parent possessed. . . . Be all this as it may, I regard your pangenesis chapter as the most wonderful in the book and intensely interesting—it is so full of thought, of genuine mind; and you do so love it yourself! I should not care a farthing were I you what people thought of it. Not one naturalist in a hundred can follow it, I am sure. I have not yet mastered it myself."

Sir Henry Holland came to dinner at Erasmus's in an affable mood. He said:

"I found the book very tough reading but I admit some view closely akin to it will have to be admitted."

It was Alfred Wallace, who seemed still to be opposing Charles's writing of the Descent, sitting across the tea table at Erasmus's, who gave him the finest accolade.

"I read the chapter on pangenesis first, for I could not wait. I can hardly tell you how much I admire it. It is a positive comfort to me to have any feasible explanation of a difficulty that has always haunted me. I shall never be able to give it up till a better one supplies its place, and that I think hardly possible."

Then the brickbats began to fly. Victor Carus, the fastidious German translator, wrote him an unfavorable verdict; the theory was too complicated. George Bentham, Hooker's collaborator on the plant encyclopedia, said he could not digest pangenesis. One English review said that the proposition was incomprehensible.

Asa Gray's article in the *Nation* gave the Americans an idea of what Charles was trying to establish as a law of nature. He gratefully wrote to Gray:

> Pangenesis is an infant cherished by few as yet, except his tender parent, but which will live a long life. There is parental presumption for you!

Five men, Charles Darwin, Sir Charles Lyell, Joseph Hooker, Thomas Huxley and, for the past six years, Alfred Wallace, had evolved into the most creative and productive group in the wide area of natural history in Great Britain. Without the others, Charles Darwin knew his life would have been narrow and restricted, minus the life-giving fluids of friendship, constructive criticism, encouragement and acceptance. In a definite sense they were the equivalent of a college professorial staff. Earlier on, in 1844, Charles had said, "I always feel as if my books came half out of Lyell's brain." Everything they thought and projected came partly from each other's brain. Their hailstorm of letters, articles, monographs and books traveling all over the world, affording insights and knowledge, educated an entire generation. Together they had turned the world around; had changed the pattern of man's thought about himself and the world he lived in, wiped out prejudice against those who were unorthodox in their religious beliefs, provided release from the rigid dogma of the Church as well as escape from the power of the clergy, not only the hierarchy's interlocking control of the schools, press, government, but the mass of people who did not have the right to determine the manner of living their daily lives. Now there was a hope for intellectual independence, the individual's freedom from the shackles of dictatorial restraint. With man's brain no longer encased in iron chains of mythical belief, what wonders would he not accomplish? Becoming his own master, man would have the freedom which creates greatness.

Though they had never intended it to be so, or made any conscious effort to achieve it, together they constituted an organization, a Society, regarded as such by other naturalists. They were thought of abroad as an Authority, studied and discussed from St. Petersburg in the north to Naples in the south. The correspondence that passed between them, the many-paged letters discussing their scientific problems, if bound together would have made half a dozen first-rate John Murray publications.

It was the height of good fortune that they had come together at the same time and in the same place. Even as Sophocles, Euripides, Socrates and Plato in Athens had created a modern world of drama, education, philosophy; as Michelangelo, Leonardo da Vinci, Lorenzo de Medici, Raphael, in the cities of Florence and Rome, had turned the sixteenth century into a high rebirth of art; between them these five in London had established a birth of interest in the earth and its beings. Had a special ambience created them? Or had they created each other? Or was the need for them so great that the very times and society itself created the base on which they could flourish?

Charles believed intensely that no one of them could have played so consistently urgent a role without the warm affection and steadfast support and devotion of the others. The intensity of their feelings could properly be called love. They had fought for each other, valiantly, sometimes when it was not merely inconvenient but dangerous. Yet never did they fight each other, indulge in jealousy, envy or spite. There was not a destructive bone in their corporate body.

The Darwin and Wedgwood family loyalties remained equally firm. Emma's sister Elizabeth, she of the crooked spine and lifetime of pain, had moved into London upon her sister Charlotte's death and the sale of the two homes in Hartfield, Sussex.

"Charles, I think Elizabeth should make her final move to Down," Emma decreed. "The beggars of London are harassing and fatiguing her and the bustle of city life is too much for her at seventy-five. There are houses for sale close by. She could bring her little dog Tony, and her devoted servants. Then I could keep watch over her."

They found Tromer Lodge, with a pretty drawing room upstairs, nice bedrooms and, best of all for Elizabeth, the talented gardener of Maer Hall, the added inducement of a greenhouse. Elizabeth became a familiar sight as she walked the path, followed by her dog Tony. Her first question always upon entering the house was, "Where is Emma?"

Emma would put up whatever she was doing in order to go to her sister, to greet her warmly. She set up a bedroom so that when Elizabeth stayed for supper she could remain overnight. Elizabeth bloomed under Emma's surveillance and devotion.

All of this brought Charles satisfaction. He was repaying a part of his debt to his Uncle Jos.

He plowed steadily ahead on his chapters, The Races of Man and Secondary Sexual Characters in the Lower Classes of the Animal Kingdom, working for a number of hours each day, riding Tommy out for rest and exercise.

Then, inexplicably, on June 23, his health broke down and he had to stop work. He was more irritated with himself than depressed.

"It's two and a half years since I had a breakdown. If I could understand the cause, I wouldn't be so troubled."

"Instead of searching for causes," Emma replied, "let's look for a good house on the Isle of Wight where we can take the family for a holiday."

In mid-July they found accommodations at Dumbola Lodge, the home of a Mrs. Cameron. After two days Charles felt well again, though the yellowish tinge of his skin, which had appeared during the weeks of his indisposition, was slow to fade. A few days later they opened their newspaper to find that Leonard had come out second best in the entrance examination for the Royal Engineers at Woolwich, which meant his automatic acceptance. Charles exclaimed:

"I shall burst with pleasure! Is it not splendid? Who would have thought that poor dear old Lenny would have got so magnificent a place?"

"I would," replied Emma.

Erasmus joined them at Freshwater, Fanny and Hensleigh Wedgwood came for a visit, bringing their oldest daughter. Dr. Henry Holland came with Saba for a few days at the Lodge. Joseph Hooker, recently elected president of the British Association for the 1868 Norwich meeting, arrived, having written beforehand:

> I shudder at the thought of bringing you my presidential address for the meeting. At the same time I cannot bear the cowardice of not doing so.

Hooker stayed for three days. He was extremely nervous about his talk, fearing it was a hodgepodge of botany and evolution. Charles made a number of suggestions as the two men walked about the Isle of Wight. After Hooker left they did a bit of socializing. Mrs. Cameron knew everyone in the vicinity; she took them to visit the poet Alfred Tennyson, in the pouring rain, so that Tennyson brought in a bottle of white wine to "correct the wet."

They returned to Down House toward the end of August, refreshed. Charles ordered the *Times, Telegraph, Spectator, Athenaeum* and a bundle of other papers to read their reports on Joseph Hooker's address. Though Hooker had nearly lost his voice because of the miserable acoustics of the hall, he received a chorus of praise. The *Spectator* however pitched into him about his lukewarm theology, and Hooker reported that there was a good deal of coolness on the following Sunday morning in his church at Kew. Charles was convinced that Hooker had immensely advanced the belief in the evolution of species. He immediately wrote to him:

> Your great success has rejoiced my heart. I have just carefully read the whole address in the *Athenaeum*; and though, as

you know, I liked it very much when you read it to me, yet, as I was trying all the time to find fault, I missed to a certain extent the effect as a whole; and this now appears to me most striking and excellent. How you must rejoice at all your bothering labour and anxiety having had so grand an end. I must say a word about myself; never has such a eulogium been passed on me, and it makes me very proud. I cannot get over my *amazement* at what you say about my botanical work. . . .

At the same meeting the issue of pangenesis was fairly well resolved when M. J. Berkeley, a fellow graduate of Christ's College, famous throughout the world for being the first to treat the pathology of plants systematically, gave a speech before Section D, the same Section D that had been presided over by John Henslow in Oxford when Hooker and Huxley routed Bishop Wilberforce over the issue of the *Origin of Species*. Berkeley said:

> . . . It would be unpardonable to finish these somewhat desultory remarks without adverting to one of the most interesting subjects of the day, the Darwinian doctrine of pangenesis. Like everything which comes from the pen of a writer whom I have no hesitation in considering as by far the greatest observer of our age, whatever may be thought of his theories when carried out to their extreme results, the subject demands a careful and impartial consideration. . . .

The address was published. Pangenesis was established, even as the *Origin of Species* had been after the Oxford meeting.

Needing specific information for a chapter for the Descent, Charles invited to Down House Alfred Wallace, who came from London for the weekend, accompanied by J. Jenner Weir, an expert on insects, and Edward Blyth, for twenty years curator of the Museum of the Asiatic Society of Bengal, distinguished for his knowledge of Indian birds and mammals. Over the years he had vouchsafed Charles an enormous amount of information otherwise difficult to find. It was a rousing weekend, with the three men giving fully of their knowledge, while Charles led the discussions on theoretical and disputed matters.

Another weekend Joseph Hooker brought Asa Gray and his wife for a visit. Charles had not seen Asa Gray since he first met the American at Kew Gardens a number of years before.

"The admiration and affection you three men feel for each other," Emma observed, "is beautiful to behold."

The day after Christmas, Boxing Day, Charles interrupted his efforts on Descent to begin revisions for the fifth edition of the *Origin of Spe-*

*cies* of which John Murray was printing another two thousand copies. The task took him five weeks since there was much to do to keep the book up to date; natural history being a living creature which grew in every direction almost every day.

"It is only about two years since the last edition of *Origin*, and I am fairly disgusted to find how much I have to modify, and how much I ought to add."

He was at the same time sitting for a sculptor who was making a bust of him, a dullish duty since he would neither read nor write while the sculptor worked.

He finished the corrections in time for Emma to give him a sixtieth birthday party. Erasmus, the Wedgwoods, with their children, Dr. Henry Holland, came down from London. His sister Caroline and Emma's brother Joe came over from Leith Hill Place. Emma also invited the young John Lubbocks, Dr. Engleheart with his wife; the Rev. Brodie Innes and his wife. Henrietta was back from touring Switzerland with friends, completely independent now. George was celebrating a fellowship at Trinity, which augured a career in Academia should he wish it. Francis was also at Trinity and Horace had entered the previous autumn so that the three brothers were in the same college at the same time, a rare occurrence in Cambridge.

In the midst of the congratulations, it was Dr. Henry Holland who declared:

"You are celebrating a sixtieth birthday. Whoever would have thought that possible? You've been expecting an imminent death for several decades!"

The cook had prepared a large yellow cherry cake covered with white icing. Across the top Parslow, using a small paper cone, had written *Happy Birthday!* Studded in a circle in the center of the cake were six flaming white candles. Dr. Holland murmured to Emma:

"A pound will bring you a pound and a half that you'll be celebrating Charles's seventieth birthday with seven candles on the cake."

He worked steadily on sexual selection of mammals and man, making slow but detailed progress; "at railway speed," he grumbled, suffering an occasional setback with whatever grace he could summon. Nice things happened along the way to buoy him:

Alfred Russel Wallace published his book of travels, *The Malay Archipelago*, which he dedicated to Charles, who thanked him for the honor, saying, "It is a thing for my children's children to be proud of."

An English translation appeared of Fritz Müller's German book about Darwin called *Facts and Arguments for Darwin*. Charles bought a number of copies of the book to send to his friends. In thanking his disciple for the honor, he observed:

> . . . A man must indeed be a bigot in favour of separate acts of creation if he is not staggered after reading your essay.

In April the routine of his days was altered when his quiet cob Tommy stumbled and fell, rolling onto him and bruising him badly. For three years now, Charles had found Tommy not only quiet and gentle but brisk and willing and with the most easy of paces. He did not ride again for some time.

He encountered a second "accident," equally bruising. In the April number of the *Quarterly Review* Alfred Wallace reviewed the tenth edition of Lyell's *Principles of Geology* and the sixth edition of *Elements of Geology*. After praising Lyell for giving up his opposition to evolution, he then added that he, Wallace, upheld the view that the brain of man, as well as the organs of speech and the hand, could not have been evolved by natural selection.

Charles marked his copy with a triple-underlined "No" and with a shower of notes of exclamation. He felt obliged to tell Wallace, "If you had not told me otherwise, I should have thought these lines had been added by someone else. As you expected, I differ grievously from you, and I am very sorry for it."

As Admiral James Sulivan had informed the Darwins at their dinner table, H.M.S. *Nassau* sailed through the Strait of Magellan and explored a fossil deposit at the Gallegos River. The fossils were turned over to Thomas Huxley. Huxley was particularly enthralled by one of the fossil jaws in which nearly all of the teeth were in place. This proved it to be a new breed of mammal, with teeth in uninterrupted series, as big as a small horse. He immediately told Darwin:

"What a wonderful assemblage of beasts there seems to have been in South America!"

By June, after four months of concentrated writing, he began to feel as he had the previous June, drained and seedy. He and Emma went to North Wales and settled at Barmouth, of which Charles had pleasant memories from his college days. Five of the children joined them, all except William and Horace, who could not get away. On the way to Barmouth they stopped at Shrewsbury to visit The Mount. The present owners showed them over the house, with its new furniture and decorations. As their carriage rattled along the North Wales road, Charles said:

"If I could have been left alone in that greenhouse for five minutes, I know I should have been able to see my father in his wheelchair as vividly as if he had been sitting there before me."

The house they rented at Barmouth, Caerdeon, was a pretty one on the north side of the estuary looking across at the range of mountains in front of Cader Idris, with a foreground of woody hills. There were three long terraces in front of the house, with flowers and roses all along them. Charles, languid, walked arm in arm with Emma up one terrace and down the other. The family's great interest was a velocipede from Paris, the first they had seen, which Charles promptly bought for the boys. There was a flat road on the nearby mountain so the boys practiced the magic of skimming along on the two wheels. Soon Leonard had a fall with the bicycle landing on his ankle, and Emma became cross with the machine.

They returned to Down House at the end of July. Charles went back to work on the Descent. North Wales had obviously done him good. Early in August he started rereading all of his completed chapters on sexual selection. He had a note from Huxley, who had spoken at the British Association meeting at Exeter, and been nominated president of the 1870 meeting which would be held in Liverpool. Huxley, with his savage sense of humor, wrote:

> As usual, your abominable heresies were the means of getting me into all sorts of hot water at the Association. Three parsons set upon you, and if you were the most malicious of men you could not have wished them to have made greater fools of themselves than they did. . . .

Without Charles's knowledge, John Murray placed a notice in the *Academy* about the upcoming Descent of Man. It brought him a flock of excited mail from friends and associates wanting to know how soon they could secure a copy.

If in every life a little rain must fall, Charles's constant rainfall came from the *Athenaeum*, where John Robertson wrote bitterly in his review of the fifth edition of the *Origin of Species:*

> Attention is not acceptance. Many editions do not mean real success.

Good news accompanied bad. The newspapers announced that Joseph Hooker had been made a Companion of the Order of the Bath in recognition of his revitalization of Kew Gardens. Charles went to London to congratulate Hooker, whose associates had been a bit nettled when he had not received knighthood. Charles said:

"I must say 'Hurrah' about your C.B., though I too wish it had been K.C.B., as it assuredly ought to have been."

Hooker replied:

"Pray do not put C.B. in your letters to me. I can't stand it. I own that C.B. gratified me in a service point of view, and it is very useful officially in Indian and Colonial correspondence, but scientifically I rather dislike it. How are you getting along with 'Man'?"

"Putting ugly sentences rather straighter. As the subject is all on sexual selection, I am weary of everlasting males and females, cocks and hens."

Hooker's eyes laughed behind the small metal-rimmed lenses.

"Victory is not necessarily to the brave, but sometimes to the persistent. Impatience is only a virtue in the young."

"Yes, but you get the world conquered a lot faster that way," replied Charles.

Summing up the year, looking at the nearly completed pile of manuscript before him, Charles decided that 1869 had been a good one for himself and for the "Association." The Swedish edition of the *Origin of Species* had been well received. Charles, along with Huxley and Hooker, had been made members of the American Philosophical Society in Philadelphia. Hooker was working on his Student's Flora of the British Islands, which had been requested by several Scottish professors as being desperately needed. The old one, written by his father, was out of date. Hooker's book stood a chance of being adopted throughout the schools of England and Scotland.

Wallace and Huxley were publishing steadily, Museums for the People and papers on dinosaurs. Alfred Wallace and his wife Annie had been trying to buy a large section of land in the country with extensive wild growth and a stream through the property. He sent Charles a copy of his book, *Natural Selection*. When Charles read the preface he found that it was almost a solid eulogy of "Darwinism." He replied to Wallace, with whom he was still amiably feuding over the origin of man:

> I wish that I fully deserved it. I hope it is a satisfaction to you to reflect—and very few things in my life have been more satisfactory to me—that we have never felt a jealousy towards each other, though in one sense rivals. I believe that I can say this of myself with truth, and I am absolutely sure that it is true of you.

The family grieved when Brodie Innes left as vicar of Down. He was replaced by the Rev. Henry Powell, of whom they knew nothing. To offset this loss of companionship, Charles acquired a dog called Bob, a black and white half-breed retriever which walked at his side during his turns around the Sandwalk. When Charles stopped to putter in the hothouse, Bob sat outside with an unhappy expression on his face. Charles made a note about this for his book on the emotions. When one of the children, or their parents for that matter, wore an impatient or sad look, one of the others would be sure to remark:

"You're wearing Bob's 'hothouse face.' Eheu! Eheu!"

Henrietta had been reading Charles's manuscript, making a suggestion here and there for clarity. When she went to visit her cousins in Cannes, in the south of France, Charles sent her the pages of his chapter, Mind. When she returned them, he adopted the greater number of her corrections and suggestions, and found several of her transpositions to be most just. Henrietta wrote a clear hand and had evolved a method of placing her corrections which saved Charles a deal of trouble. He wrote to her:

> You have done me real service; but, by Jove how hard you must have worked, and how thoroughly you have mastered my MS. I am pleased with this chapter now that it comes fresh to me.
>
> Your affectionate and admiring and obedient father.

The engravings in his books had hitherto been a great misery. Descent of Man would need a good number of woodcuts. This time he found a Mr. Ford through the Keeper of Zoology in the British Museum, who did a beautiful job, particularly on the feathers of the birds. Charles had to touch them to make sure that the page was flat. His woodcuts of the reptiles were equally fine. Charles had thought that by March he would have been on the press, but as always his subject had branched off into subbranches which had cost him infinite time. He was never idle, but told a visitor:

"Heaven knows when I shall have all of my manuscript ready."

He wrote sections on mental powers, moral sense, development of the intellectual faculties, descent from earlier forms.

> . . . We thus learn that man is descended from a hairy quadruped, furnished with a tail and pointed ears, probably arboreal in its habits, and an inhabitant of the Old World. This creature, if its whole structure had been examined by a naturalist, would have been classed among the Quadrumana, as surely as would the common and still more ancient progenitor of the Old and New World monkeys. The Quadrumana and all the higher mammals are probably derived from an ancient marsupial animal, and this through a long line of diversified forms, either from some reptile-like or some amphibian-like creature, and this again from some fish-like animal. In the dim obscurity of the past we can see that the early progenitor of all the Vertebrata must have been an aquatic animal, provided

with branchiae, with the two sexes united in the same individual, and with the most important organs of the body (such as the brain and heart) imperfectly developed. This animal seems to have been more like the larvae of the existing marine Ascidians than any other known form.

He now suspected that he would go to press in the autumn of 1870. His concentration on the manuscript was so intense that he had seen only one scientific man in several months. For relaxation he was rearing cross- and self-fertilized plants, some in his glasshouse, others on his mantelpiece where he could watch them closely. He achieved curious anomalies and interesting results. They explained why nature had taken such extraordinary pains to ensure frequent crosses between distinct individuals. Even now he stood in awe before his discoveries, and as so often in the past, murmured:

"Strange world! Wondrous world!"

8.

In late May they decided to visit their boys at Cambridge and reserved rooms at the Bull Hotel. It was thirty-three years since Charles had last been there, many years since he had elected not to return. The greensward Backs of the colleges dropping down to the river were as paradisaical as he had remembered them, the Fellows' garden with Milton's tree at Christ's College as gloriously beautiful.

On a Monday morning he saw Adam Sedgwick, who greeted him most cordially. Sedgwick was eighty-five; his brain appeared to Charles to be enfeebled. However that evening he was brilliant. He proposed taking Charles to the museum and so thoroughly covered the exhibits that he utterly prostrated his younger friend. Sedgwick commented:

"Oh, I consider you as a mere baby to me!"

Charles invited Sedgwick to dinner at the Bull Hotel. As they were parting, Sedgwick said:

"I was overflowing with joy when I saw you in the midst of a dear family party, and solaced at every turn by the loving care of a dear wife and daughters. How different from my position—that of a very old man, living in cheerless solitude!"

When they were alone, Charles turned to his wife with a pained expression on his face.

"Why did he not marry Susan? He was greatly attracted to her. She had the kind of mind that could have kept up with his. How different both their lives would have been."

Emma replied gently:

"Perhaps he did propose and she declined his offer. You have said that your father was the only love in her life. Perhaps she could not bring herself to leave The Mount."

Back in his study he tackled problems for Emotions, trying to determine whether birds erected their feathers when frightened or enraged. He had already tested fowl, swans, tropic birds, owls and cuckoos. He wrote to an ornithologist to find out whether the wild sheldrake pats or dances on the tidal sands to make the sea worms come out; he already knew that when sheldrakes came to ask for their dinner they patted the ground with what Charles called an expression of hunger and impatience.

Admiral James Sulivan was given the title of K.C.B., Knight Commander of the Order of the Bath, one degree higher than Joseph Hooker's. A short time later Lord Salisbury, on assuming the office of Chancellor of the University of Oxford, invited Charles to come to Oxford to receive the honorary degree of D.C.L., Doctor of Canon Law. He politely declined on the score of ill-health, and the *Oxford University Gazette* of June 17, 1870, published the word that Charles Darwin was an invalid. It was not true. Charles was well, but he told Emma:

"I could no more go through that elaborate and formal ceremony in Oxford than I could a ball at Buckingham Palace."

Oxford University withdrew its offer of the D.C.L.

Emma was disappointed for Charles. She wanted him to have this honor from Oxford since Cambridge had not offered one. She did not protest and, having already read several notes on the expression of emotions in man and animals, was careful not to show any sign of her feelings which Charles could read as a rebuke. Her disappointment was somewhat allayed by Francis's graduation from Trinity with a first in natural science tripos, having passed his honors examination. Francis had decided to follow in the footsteps of his grandfather and great-grandfather and become a doctor. He had been accepted by St. George's Hospital in London near Hyde Park, where he would begin his medical training in the autumn.

The Darwins went up to London for the last week in June and, since they had not seen the recent improvements, made a grand tour in Erasmus's carriage past Grosvenor Place, where Lord Westminster's row of houses looked like the Tuileries; then to the new Westminster Bridge and the Embankment, its scene lively with steamboats, then across to see St. Thomas's Hospital, like six palaces fronting the river toward Lambeth. They came back by the new Blackfriars Bridge and the Holborn Viaduct. The open space by Westminster Abbey and the Houses of Parliament was very grand.

Charles visited Joseph and Frances Hooker and their children while Emma, Elizabeth and Henrietta went shopping. Hooker had recently dined with the Duke of Argyll and had found him to be a "cleft stick."

"His chief quarrel with the *Origin* is that you do not state that the order of evolution is preordained. I told him that I did not think this was any business of yours, that you did not pretend to go into the origin of life, only into its phenomena."

Charles indulged in a long sigh.

"My theology is a simple muddle. I cannot look at the universe as the result of blind chance, yet I can see no evidence of beneficent design, or indeed of design of any kind, in the details. As for each variation that has ever occurred having been preordained for a special end, I can no more believe in it than that the spot on which each drop of rain falls has been specially ordained."

Finally during the month of August he completed his manuscript on the Descent of Man, and Selection in Relation to Sex and sent it to the printer. Almost all introductions were written after the manuscript had been completed. Charles thought it best to tell the reader the truth; he began by saying that the nature of the work would best be understood by an account of how it came to be written; the many years he had collected notes on the origin or descent of man without any intention of publishing on the subject, but rather with the determination not to publish as he thought that would only add to the prejudices against his views. . . .

. . . It seemed to me sufficient to indicate, in the first edition of my *Origin of Species*, that by this work "light would be thrown on the origin of man and his history"; and this implies that man must be included with other organic beings in any general conclusion respecting his manner of appearance on this earth. Now the case wears a wholly different aspect. . . . It is manifest that at least a large number of naturalists must admit that species are the modified descendants of other species; and this especially holds good with the younger and rising naturalists. The greater number accept the agency of natural selection. . . .

. . . I have been led to put together my notes so as to see how far the general conclusions arrived at in my former works were applicable to Man. . . .

For his last paragraph he wrote:

Man may be excused for feeling some pride at having risen, though not through his own exertions, to the very summit of the organic scale; and the fact of his having thus risen, instead of having been aboriginally placed there, may give him hope for a still higher destiny in the distant future. But we are not here concerned with hopes or fears, only with the truth as far as our reason allows us to discover it. I have given the evidence to the best of my ability; and we must acknowledge, as it seems to me, that man with all his noble qualities, with sympathy which feels for the most debased, with benevolence which extends not only to other men but to the humblest living creature, with his god-like intellect which has penetrated into the movements and constitution of the solar system— with all these exalted powers—Man still bears in his bodily frame the indelible stamp of his lowly origin.

John Murray thought they could have the book ready for Christmas. To celebrate, the Darwins went to Southampton to visit William, who did not leave for his office before nine-thirty in the morning and came home before six. William was a good host, cheerful and agreeable. Since the bruises of both Charles and the cob Tommy had long since healed, Charles had brought the horse with them and rode out each morning, for there was a great variety of lovely vistas. In the evenings they talked about little but the Franco-Prussian War. Bismarck had apparently needed such a war to consolidate the German states into a nation. The French had been ill prepared for the contest; there was danger of their collapse. Leonard commented that almost all of the young men at Woolwich were on the French side, chiefly because they longed to get into the war. Leonard himself was a staunch Prussian. Instead of getting into arguments on either side, Emma read aloud Lanfrey's *Memoirs of Napoleon I*. They found it refreshing to read a French writer who cared nothing for *la gloire* of conquest.

"It makes one ashamed of Louis Philippe for giving in to such baseness as bringing the body of Napoleon from St. Helena and making a sort of saint of him," Emma commented. "I mean to skip all the Russian retreat as it is too horrid."

Returning from Southampton, they learned that Thomas Huxley as president of the British Association would not only preside at the week of meetings in Liverpool but also give an urgent speech on the universal derivation of life from precedent life; and that Nettie Huxley could not accompany her husband because of their seven children at home, of whom the oldest was a girl of twelve. Emma insisted that all seven be brought to Down House for a fortnight. The children filled the house and grounds with their chatter, laughter, games, excited at being free from the confines of their house in London. Henrietta and Elizabeth helped to take care of them. Emma loved having the young ones around her. Charles was amused.

"It's rather like a circus, like our early days at Maer Hall and The Mount. I feel as though these young Huxleys are my nieces and nephews. Who but you, my dear Emma, would have thought of taking seven children into her home so that a friend could accompany her husband for a week in Liverpool?"

He kissed her tenderly.

"Emma, there are moments when I suspect that you may be a saint."

He did not begin receiving the proofs of the *Descent of Man* until the end of November, and could not resist grumbling.

"Good Lord, what a muddled head I have got on my wretched old shoulders."

This sentiment was quickly obliterated when he learned that John Murray had ordered twenty-five hundred copies from the printer. His concentration was interrupted only once. George, having graduated from Trinity, was chosen to join a group of scientists going to Sicily to observe the total eclipse of the sun. He was to have left from Naples for Catania in the Admiralty dispatch boat *Psyche*. The *Psyche* was wrecked off Acireale. When the family learned of the wreck they were in a frenzy of apprehension. Then word reached them that George had missed the ship and was safe, since he had followed in an ordinary steamer. He was about to make his way up Mount Etna to watch the eclipse.

By Christmas Charles had only one short chapter of proofs left to correct. He could easily do that by the turn of the year.

The *Descent of Man, and Selection in Relation to Sex* was published on February 24, 1871, in two volumes. The price was set at one pound four shillings, but in no way impeded the sale. The copies of the first issue were sold out in a matter of days, and the printer ran a second issue of two thousand copies.

The reviews and critiques beginning to arrive at Down House were primarily friendly. The *Saturday Review* said:

> He claims to have brought man himself, his origin and con-
> stitution, within that unity which he had previously sought to
> trace through all lower animal forms. The growth of opinion
> in the interval, due in chief measure to his own intermediate
> works, had placed the discussion of this problem in a position
> very much in advance of that held by it fifteen years ago. . . .

The *Spectator* ran its review in two parts, March 11 and 18, saying that Charles came nearer to the kernel of the psychological problem than many of his predecessors, and concluded with the thought that the *Descent of Man* was a "vindication of Theism more wonderful than that in Paley's *Natural Theology*."

"Paley's *Natural Theology*," Charles exclaimed. "My favorite book at Cambridge, along with Humboldt's *Personal Narrative*. Whoever would have thought I would end up as a disciple of Paley in vindicating theism?"

The *Pall Mall Gazette* ran their review in three successive issues, reporting:

> Mr. Darwin's work is one of those rare and capital achievements of intellect which effect a grave modification throughout all the highest departments of the realm of opinion. . . .

The *Athenaeum* continued its tradition of heaping coals upon his head. One letter from Wales called him an old ape with a hairy face and thick skull. The London *Times* wrote:

> . . . Even had it been rendered highly probable, which we doubt, that the animal creation has been developed into its numerous and widely different varieties by mere evolution, it would still require an independent investigation of overwhelming force and completeness to justify the presumption that man is but a term in this self-evolving series.

The review was unsigned. Charles observed that the reviewer "has no knowledge of science, and seems to me a windbag full of metaphysics and classics . . . though I suppose it will injure the sale."

It did nothing of the sort. The sale continued at a galloping pace. Joseph Hooker reported with amusement:

"I hear that ladies think it delightful reading but that it does not do to talk about it, that the only way to get it is to order it on the sly! Which no doubt promotes the sale. I dined out three days last week and at every table heard evolution talked of as an accepted fact, and the descent of man with calmness."

Sir Charles and Lady Mary Lyell were visiting at Down House when Alfred Wallace's review appeared in the *Academy*. Lyell admitted that he agreed with Wallace's stricture that man could not have descended by natural selection from a primitive organism. Charles was disconcerted; Emma's cheeks flamed with pleasure.

"I am most happy and grateful to have you on my side. To have Alfred Wallace on my side as well. And Asa Gray at Harvard. If you three authorities agree that man is a very special species, then God is still very much in our midst!"

Thomas Huxley, quite naturally, thought the *Descent of Man* a masterpiece.

In April John Murray had to order another printing, bringing the total to seven thousand copies within two months, truly a wonder in the world of scientific books. More and more he was drawing in readers from the general public, who were getting their first exposure to natural history.

A cutting review appeared in the *Quarterly Review*, unsigned. It appeared to be the last major attack against the *Descent of Man*. The religious press, which had been so combative about the *Origin of Species*, simply used the *Descent of Man* as the *Spectator* had, turning Darwinism into a testament of faith in the magic of God's creative powers. A number of naturalists disagreed with his basic premise, but for the most part quietly and in private, as did the Rev. Brodie Innes, now at Forres, Scotland, in an amiable note. Doubtless there were sermons preached against it, but if so, they were not published, as had been so many of the *Origin of Species* sermons.

Over all the years since the publication of the *Origin of Species* and the knowledge that he must one day write the *Descent of Man*, he had feared a recapitulation of that stormy, abusive scene. But there was no mention of Charles Darwin as the Devil incarnate, or the anti-Christ.

The fire had gone out from under the caldron.

"I have been anxious, worried, feeling trepidation all this time! What a waste of energy, of peace of mind! At long last I've made my heresies respectable. All in my own lifetime. I, who had never planned to publish a word about them. Eheu! Eheu!"

# BOOK THIRTEEN

*Hold Fast to the Promise*

1.

H E had won a crucial battle; he had by no means won the war. Over his enemies, or over himself. He continued to describe himself as an invalid in letters to friends but used the term as a protective cloak to safeguard him from meetings or social gatherings which he wished to avoid.

Within weeks of the publication of *Descent of Man*, St. George Mivart, a biologist of reputation, published a book called *Genesis of Species* which severely criticized natural selection and attempted to annihilate the concept. The book caught on and was widely discussed. Charles read it, made annotations in the margins, compared each section with the one in his own book. Mivart did not convince him a ha'penny's worth. Yet the publication distressed him.

"In your stomach?" asked Emma.

"No, oddly enough. In my psyche. I have reached the age where I can take even voluminous criticism without feeling ill."

"God be praised!"

Despite a series of affectionate letters which St. George Mivart wrote to Charles, he continued his attack in the press, and had apparently been the author of the unsigned malicious review of the *Descent of Man* in the *Quarterly Review*, a behavior Charles could not fathom. He observed:

"I conclude with sorrow that, though he means to be honorable, he is so bigoted that he cannot act fairly."

Chauncey Wright, an American naturalist, took Mivart apart so thoroughly in the *North American Review* that Charles asked Wright's permission to issue the article in pamphlet form for a shilling. Huxley too rushed to his defense, though Charles calmed him by saying:

"It will be a long battle, my friend, and continue after we are both dead and gone."

Nevertheless Huxley wrote a trenchant passage for the second edition of the *Descent*, comparing the brain of man with that of the ape.

Hooker also discussed Charles's antagonists, particularly Mivart and Owen, then added:

"Each of us should have one person in the world to hate. It makes for a neater emotional balance." His expression became grim. "I have one as well, Acton Ayrton, the new Commissioner of Works in Gladstone's government. The gentleman is overbearing and anti-scientific in his attitude toward Kew Gardens. He is doing everything in his power to force me to resign. Since he is my superior I try to work with him but he has the hide of a rhinoceros."

Nonetheless for Charles the decade of the seventies would prove to be the easiest since the decade of the thirties, when he had sailed on H.M.S. *Beagle,* returned to Cambridge to sort out his collections, moved to London, married Emma and begun his serious writing as a geologist and naturalist. There remained little cause for him to be sensitive. He had been elected honorary or foreign member of scientific bodies all over the world; *Descent of Man* was published in the United States and translated into a half dozen languages. He had an occasional flare-up or exhaustion from overwork at his microscope, studying the secretions of meat-eating plants; but these were passing incidents. Each day, even when the weather was cold, he took his five- to seven-pebble turn around the Sandwalk followed by his dog.

Evidence that the years were rolling by came in June, while they were spending a week with Erasmus in London. Henrietta, now nearly twenty-eight, met a man named Richard Litchfield, and in August they were married. The Darwins liked Litchfield. He was thirty-nine, under middle height but broadly made, with a massive forehead and shortsighted eyes which gave him a faraway look. He was a graduate of Trinity College, Cambridge and had become a barrister and founder of the Working Men's College, as well as its treasurer and one of its teachers. After the ceremony, Charles observed:

"We've just witnessed the start of a new cycle. Our young will be leaving the nest, one by one, to the tune of a clergyman's sermon."

"I should hope so!" exclaimed Emma. "Now that we're in our sixties, it's time to have grandchildren."

Charles gave his daughter only one piece of advice.

"Your mother is twice-refined gold. Follow her example."

Emma's face was unlined, though there were shadows under her eyes. There was gray mixed into the brown of her hair, but she still parted it in the center and combed it forward over her ears. When she went visiting she wore pert bonnets with wide ribbons tied under her chin. She had survived ten childbirths and was in robust health, always finding "scrattles," the family word from Maer Hall, to keep her busy.

She was proud of her husband; after all, he was referred to in many countries as "the first scientist of the world," and she had had a part in that, having nurtured and nursed him for well over thirty years. She had long since reconciled herself to the fact that they would never agree on the Divinity. He comforted her with the confession:

"I am definitely not an atheist. I do not deny the existence of God. I am probably an agnostic; I simply don't know for sure."

They found gratification in their children. There was not a bad apple in the barrel. William devoted much of his time to getting funds appropriated for poverty and medical relief since Southampton was the most pauperized city in England after Bristol. They visited with him often. Henrietta and Richard Litchfield settled in London but visited Down House frequently. They made editorial suggestions for Charles's manuscripts, Litchfield being particularly astute in spotting duplications. They also corrected the proof sheets of the new issues which kept arriving from John Murray, releasing Charles for his microscopic work on the sundew and its insect-eating mechanisms.

George, their second son, had decided to become a solicitor, then returned to his fellowship at Trinity College to continue his exploration in mathematics and to teach. His ambition was to become a full professor of astronomy.

Charles approved.

"I've had solicitors tell me that the law is fine if you don't mind eating sawdust without butter."

Leonard was doing extremely well in the Woolwich Royal Military Academy, as were Francis at St. George's Hospital in London and Horace at Trinity.

Elizabeth blossomed as the single daughter of the household.

During their school recess George and Francis went for a tour of the United States.

"Bring me back a report on the Americans," said Charles.

"Come with us, Father, and see the country for yourself."

He shuddered. "I'm not even going to set foot in a boat to cross the river Styx."

While visiting a friend of Horace's they enjoyed the veranda of the house where the family and friends gathered for tea, to read the daily newspapers and the new books. It was protected, cool, comfortable, and expanded the companionship of the people living there. It was the first veranda the Darwins had seen attached to a private home. Toward the end of their stay Emma asked:

"Couldn't we have one? Extending out from the drawing room?"

He called in two carpenters from Down and sketched a veranda the same length as the drawing room, and twelve feet wide. The construction was simple: a concrete base, the sloping roof starting between the ground floor and the first story of the house and made of glass. The front was entirely open, the sides partially enclosed with three-foot walls, lattice work above and built-in benches. The furniture was inexpensive wicker with red cushions.

The veranda changed the pattern of life at Down House, making it more informal. In good weather they could bask in the sun; the young people particularly liked it; they indulged in hours of talk there, reading, playing cards or backgammon. The row of fragrant lime trees to the west protected it from the hot afternoon sun, and from the veranda they could see the flower gardens and the sundial. Charles and Emma watched their offspring and their friends play croquet on the lawn.

"Isn't it strange how a simple little porch can bring a family closer together?" commented Emma.

"I should have thought of it years before," Charles agreed. "We can live out of doors more, closer to nature."

When he was able to secure the piece of the Sandwalk owned by the Lubbocks in exchange for a piece of the Darwin field exactly the same size, he felt that his world was now secure.

He had well in mind several books he wanted to write to complete his *Origin of Species* project. They were mostly in the field of botany: insectivorous plants, the different forms of flowers and plants of the same species, the effects of cross- and self-fertilization in the vegetable kingdom, the power of movement in all plants. He now had more than sufficient material to build a proper book of his monograph *Movements and Habits of Climbing Plants* which had been published by the Linnean Society in 1865.

John Murray was constantly wanting new editions of his books and Charles was too conscientious to allow him simply to reprint the earlier editions. There were always illuminating researches and additions to incorporate, many of them growing out of his own work in expanding the field of natural history. His dozens of narrow, labeled files, built when he had moved into Down House in 1842, were crammed with the fertile fruits of day-by-day observations culled over the face of the earth. He worked for over two months on the sixth edition of the *Origin of Species*, expanding the content, correcting early errors, and in January of 1872 finished the proofs for an inexpensive edition. It was printed on a poor quality of paper, with small type, but would widen the audience for the book. He also gave himself, in this new edition, the satisfaction of answering St. George Mivart in strong and documented language. His ideas penetrated distant borders, in terms of both geography and the landscape of men's minds. However his concept of pangenesis, the carry-all structure of cells, aside from his intimate circle, Lyell, Hooker, Wallace, Dr. Holland, still found little favor among his fellow naturalists. After his theory had been further criticized in a newly published book, Charles wrote to Wallace:

. . . I do not strike my colours as yet about pangenesis. . . .

After the publication of the *Descent of Man* he had felt rather seedy and could work only half a day. A few days' stay in London refreshed him. For the entire year of 1872 he had written only one despondent sentence; this was to a young German disciple, Ernst Haeckel:

. . . I am growing old and weak, and no man can tell when his intellectual powers begin to fail.

Obviously his had not. He was turning out monumental amounts of research and correspondence, including articles for *Nature* and the *Gardeners' Chronicle*. Relatives, friends, visitors from Germany, Russia, Holland, the United States came and stayed at Down House. Rather than fleeing after ten minutes or half an hour as he had done so frequently in the past, he enjoyed their company with good spirit.

Unfortunately his closest friends were in a variety of troubles.

Joseph Hooker continued to be paralyzed at Kew Gardens by the Commissioner of Works, who cut his budget for its laboratories, museum, library; getting some of his key helpers fired, spreading word that Hooker should be removed from his post. Hooker wrote to the Prime Minister, Mr. Gladstone, urging him to look into the matter. Gladstone did nothing. The Commissioner, Mr. Ayrton, had Richard Owen, long hostile to Hooker, prepare, anonymously, a paper for reading before the House of Commons which was published as an official report on Kew Gardens. Owen impugned both the dead Sir William Hooker and his son Joseph, sneered at the Hookers' herbarium, pointed out trees that had died, implied neglect and mismanagement. Charles told his friend:

"I used to be ashamed of hating Owen so much. Now I will carefully cherish my hatred and contempt for him to the last day of my life."

He joined with a group of naturalists, including Lyell, Huxley, George Bentham, to write a paper on Kew Gardens and the Hookers, which they presented to the Prime Minister. At the same time Joseph Hooker was elected president of the Royal Society, the highest post in England for a scientist.

Thomas Huxley fell ill from overwork and was unable to carry on his duties, or rest. His doctor, Andrew Clark, ordered travel but Huxley had not a pound to spare. Charles and Hooker tapped their friends and associates, raising the goodly sum of twenty-one hundred pounds.

"Now comes the difficult part," said Hooker. "He'll refuse the money on the grounds that it's charity. I don't dare write and tell him."

"I will write the letter," Charles assured him; "in such a way that he'll have to accept with his pride intact."

Huxley accepted. Hooker offered to accompany him to France and Germany. Before they left, Hooker reported:

"I am loaded with injunctions from his physician as to what Huxley is to eat, drink and avoid. How much he is to sleep and rest, how little he is to talk or walk. I'm going to be his nurse and hospital combined."

Huxley returned feeling strong and bursting with enthusiasm over projected books, articles, lectures, the restructuring of England's public education.

When the *Expression of the Emotions in Man and Animals* was published in November 1872, public interest and amusement more than the reviews made it the fastest-selling of his books, nine thousand being in print by the end of the year, topping the *Descent of Man* by a full thousand copies. He had used a number of illustrations for the book: a cat with its teeth bared against its ancient enemy, a dog; a swan driving away an intruder; youngsters crying or pouting. The book piqued the curiosity and interest of readers of all classes. It was a wholly new area of observation and invention, and was so successful Charles was obliged to pay fifty-two pounds in income tax to the Exchequer.

"That's the most they've ever taken from us," he complained to Emma. "Do you suppose the taxes will go up every year?"

"Think of it as bittersweet; the more books you sell, the more money you make, the more taxes you'll pay. Admiral Sulivan says the Royal Navy is going to conquer the world. Those ships must cost a pretty penny. Didn't H.M.S. *Beagle?*"

Charles let the discussion fall of its own weight.

When the *Athenaeum* gave him a "not unfavourable" review, he suggested to Francis, spending a week working in Charles's study:

"We have apparently eliminated an antagonist."

The *Edinburgh Review*, another old and practiced antagonist, said:

. . . Mr. Darwin has added another volume of amusing stories and grotesque illustrations to the remarkable series of works already devoted to the exposition and defence of the evolutionary hypothesis.

"They give me a fit of the wibber-jibbers," growled Charles, working at the microscope. "Now I turn out to be a humorist! It's the first time I've been called amusing since Adam Sedgwick said that parts of the *Origin* made him laugh."

Francis looked up from his leaf study, said:

"Do be a good Christian, Father, and not hate them. Come and watch what is happening to the raw meat you fed the insect-eating plants."

The plants were absorbing the raw meat, just as they had assimilated the concoction of cabbage leaves and peas he had fed them. With his eye at the microscope, Charles murmured:

"By all that's holy, I do not think that any discovery has given me more pleasure than proving a true act of digestion in Drosera."

He was equally gratified by his Indian telegraph plant, the dwarf leaflets of which moved by a series of twitches. One evening when they were ready to retire, Charles said to Emma:

"Let us see what the telegraph plant does at night."

They went into the study, found the plant asleep, all but the little ears, which were having what Charles described as "most lively games. I never saw any of this in the daytime!" he cried, delighted.

He completed a first draft of Insectivorous Plants in January of 1873 and took a week off to visit London. In early February he commenced work on a proposed book, "The Effects of Cross- and Self-Fertilisation in the Vegetable Kingdom." He had already done a great deal of experimentation on cross-fertilization, but self-fertilization was largely unobserved by both himself and the botanists. He spent hours in his hothouse as well as watching the plants on the mantel and table in his study to learn that all orchids were male and female at the same time, and while insects fertilized orchids, when there were two flowers on the same spike, A and B, all the contrivances were also on hand for A to pollinate B, and B to pollinate A. The flowers had a stigmatic surface on which the seed pod was set. When it rained, the raindrops filled the cup, causing the pollen to float . . . and fertilize the very same flower from which the pollen originated! Along with the orchids, he found buttercups to be the most frequent self-pollinizers.

For the first time they went to stay with friends in the country, the Thomas Farrers of Abinger Hall in Surrey; Farrer had married one of Hensleigh Wedgwood's daughters. Yet Charles could not shed his skin.

"We promised to stay for two weeks," Emma admonished when he prepared to leave after the first week.

"We can come back. My notes are piling up on self-fertilization. I cannot be idle. Work is life."

A large portion of the increasingly heavy amount of letters coming into Down House was from people who wanted to discuss religion. He answered all but the scabrous ones. Requests also came regularly from newspapers and journals for articles on his religious beliefs. To each he answered politely:

> I am unwilling to express myself publicly on religious subjects.

However he did express his approval when all theological tests were abolished at Oxford and Cambridge except for divinity students.

When a Dr. Conway of the American Harvard Divinity School came to Down House, Fanny and Hensleigh Wedgwood asked to meet him. Dr. Conway had preached and published a stirring sermon on Darwinism. The Wedgwoods read the sermon aloud, which seemed to please Dr. Conway. When they had all left, Emma sat back reflectively and remarked to herself:

"I sometimes feel it very odd that anyone belonging to me should be making such a noise in the world."

A siege of dying most distressed them.

Adam Sedgwick died in Cambridge at the age of eighty-seven. Charles reminisced about their trip into North Wales, and their warm reunion at the Bull Hotel less than three years before. Gone was the stinging memory of Sedgwick's castigation of the *Origin of Species*.

Mary Lyell went next, after a brief illness. Lyell, now seventy-five, looking very fatigued, was more stunned than grieved. He told his friends:

"I never imagined she would go before me. She was so much younger than I, twelve years! I always expected to go first."

Henry Holland, knighted since 1853, died on his eighty-fifth birthday. Long-time physician to Her Majesty Queen Victoria, his funeral procession was joined by members of the royal family.

"He was tactless but kind and helpful to us for many years," lamented Charles.

Their daughter Elizabeth added triumphantly, "He agreed with me about Henrietta being a hypochondriac. Since she's been married she's been as strong as a filly."

Emma waited until Charles had left the room, then said to Elizabeth in a whisper:

"Bessy, there is an old adage: 'Never mention rope in the house of a man who has been hanged.' "

In August a new kind of illness assailed him. He described it to Emma as "much loss of memory and severe shock continually passing through my brain." Alarmed, she insisted that they go into London and consult Dr. Andrew Clark, who had been so helpful to Thomas Huxley.

Dr. Clark turned out to be a genial man with soft sympathetic eyes. His face was fair, rather handsome, with a bony-ridged nose and immaculately trimmed gray-black beard. There was no sign of pretentiousness, even though he stood at the top of London's medical profession. He was genuinely interested in his patient's recital of his symptoms, and his examination of Charles was thorough. When he had finished, he said comfortingly:

"I know that I can do you some good, Mr. Darwin. There is a great deal of work in you yet." His tone took on an authoritative ring. "First of all there is diet. It must be carried out rigorously."

Charles ate nothing but what the doctor prescribed. After a week he complained:

"This diet is abominable."

"You appear to be better."

"I am. I shall continue to insult my stomach in order to keep my brain clear."

After abstemious months on the "abominable" diet, he made up for lost time by eating heartily. Breakfast of brown bread and butter with a pan-fried egg or fresh fish, or the soft part of the wing of a cold chicken; at the close of the meal a cup of cocoachina, sipped slowly. Dinner, fresh tenderly grilled meat, bread, mashed potato and either a rice pudding or boiled green vegetables. He drank an ounce of brandy in plain water. On going to bed he sometimes took half an ounce of brandy in five ounces of water.

He had no further difficulties despite his letter some months later to his cousin Fox, who had been a kind of crying post over the years, saying:

I forget myself only when I am at work.

When he received a questionnaire from a cousin, Francis Galton, who was preparing a book to be called "English Men of Science," Charles gave himself back the half inch he had lost in his hammock in the chart room of the Beagle, listing his height at six foot.

2.

He was so fascinated by what he was finding under his microscope, the results of his crossbreeding of plants, that he did not consult Dr. Clark again for four years; and then only because of spells of dizziness.

Long gone were the upset stomachs, retching, palpitations of the heart. Emma insisted that they take a holiday frequently. They returned to Abinger Hall, home of their friend and cousin Thomas Farrer, at one time staying for a month. Charles liked to explore the nearby Roman ruins, and found cut-leaved vines which seemed splendid for graft hybridism.

In Southampton they stayed with William. After one visit Charles said:

"I have not felt so rested and improved and full of enjoyment since the old Moor Park days."

In London they stayed with Erasmus or with Henrietta and her husband. Richard Litchfield asked permission to bring sixty members of his singing class at the Working Men's College to Down House for tea on the lawn. Charles and Emma welcomed them, joining in when the aging Parslow and two maids served crisp cucumber sandwiches and biscuits.

There was rarely a time when one or more of the Darwin children were not in London with Erasmus. A whole new dimension was added to the family's pleasure through Erasmus's love for his nieces and nephews, Hensleigh's and Fanny Wedgwood's children, as well as the Darwins'. He simply adopted them all. His house on Queen Anne Street became their second home. Uncle Eras, as they called him, told them they could visit any time they wanted, stay as long as they wanted, use the house, carriage, anything he had.

"Have you any idea how wonderful it is for me to have twelve children without ever having married?" he cried.

Emma was enjoying her freedom. She went about the task of establishing a lending library in the village. Charles Mudie, a London stationer and bookseller who had founded a series of circulating libraries around London, had considered Down too small a town to be included. The people around Down could secure books only by going into Bromley or London, or having the weekly courier fetch them. Mudie also censored the books he permitted to circulate. The Down church had a tiny collection of outdated theological tomes. Emma developed her reading room, selected some of the books, bought and solicited others. The subscription for borrowing books was set at thirty shillings a year for each family.

Francis, their third son, took his medical training at St. George's Hospital but had never practiced. He was twenty-five when he fell in love with Amy Ruck, a North Wales girl who had endeared herself to Charles by sending him a package of leaves from North Wales containing a number of captive insects. He went to Charles's study, closed the door behind him, sat on the green hassock.

"Father, you know that I don't want to practice medicine."

"Neither did I. What do you intend to do?"

Francis inched the hassock forward to get closer to his father.

"I've given it a lot of thought. I know what I most want to do. You need a secretary, someone to help with your enormous amount of work. My training in medicine has taught me a good deal about the natural sciences. I'm qualified."

Charles did not have to think very long about it.

"You could make my life much easier. What arrangements do you suggest?"

"I'll just start to work. When Amy and I are married, I'd like us to move into Down House and live here as part of the family."

"Have you asked Amy about this proposal?"

"Yes. She would like it as much as I would."

"Have you told your mother?"

"Not yet. I had to make sure you wanted me."

"Then let's find her. She's scrattling around somewhere."

Emma embraced the idea, for there was only Elizabeth of her seven children left in the roost. William was in Southampton, Henrietta in London, Leonard had graduated with second honors from the Royal Engineers the year before, and was so highly thought of by his supervisors that he was sent out to New Zealand with a group to observe the transit of Venus, which would provide materials to measure the distance between the sun and the earth. Horace, the youngest of the clan, had passed his "little go" at Cambridge. He would become the mechanical engineer he had always wanted to be, going wherever the job was.

Sometimes Down House rattled with its own emptiness.

Emma had met Amy Ruck and liked the slender, quiet girl, of a pleasant nature and good manners. She kissed Francis by reaching up quite a bit.

"It will be good to have a son and another daughter in our home. Tell Amy we await her with open arms."

Charles added:

"We'll give one of the big rooms with the three bow windows overlooking the garden a fresh coat of paint."

Francis and Amy were married. Amy got along splendidly with Emma and Elizabeth. She was a lovely though somewhat delicate young lady with glossy black hair coiled into a bun at the back of her head. Her face was slender, oval in shape, her dark eyes wide set, intelligent and contemplative. She and Francis were very much in love. Since Amy insisted, Emma turned over to her certain household responsibilities. Elizabeth did not mind; she was not good at practical things and avoided responsibility. The midday meal in the dining room at Down House became a lot livelier, as did their leisurely tea on the veranda.

Francis quickly demonstrated that, although he could be an excellent secretary, he hoped to be a good deal more, an assistant in fact, in the manner that university scientists had laboratory assistants. He helped to put the manuscript on insectivorous plants together. With Charles's consent and encouragement, he began setting up original programs to observe and record his findings.

One day Charles looked up from the microscope, having discovered something about the mucus lining of a leaf, and exclaimed to his son:

"Work is my sole pleasure in life!"

"Better not let Mother hear you say that!"

They did let Emma hear the news from Lyell at the British Association meeting in Belfast, with the physicist John Tyndall giving the presidential address. Lyell wrote on September 1:

> I have been intending from day to day to congratulate you on the Belfast meeting, on which occasion you and your theory of evolution may be fairly said to have had an ovation. Whatever criticisms may be made on Tyndall, it cannot be denied that it was a manly and fearless out-speaking of his opinions. . . .

The address caused a stir in Ireland, which had been hostile to his work, and was reproduced through the press of England.

In 1874 the work of Britain's naturalists on behalf of Joseph Hooker and his management of Kew Gardens finally bore fruit. Mr. Gladstone could no longer fly in the face of the British Association, as well as favorable reports on Hooker in the *Times, Daily News* and *Pall Mall Gazette*. He transferred the Commissioner from the Board of Works to the office of the Judge Advocate General. Hooker was permitted to engage an assistant director, William Thiselton-Dyer, an excellent botanist who helped Charles in his work on insectivorous plants.

Early in February of 1875 Joseph Hooker came to visit. Frances Hooker had died suddenly three months before, leaving six children behind her. Hooker was prostrated with grief.

"Why? Why Frances? She was well. She was happy. She adored her children. . . ."

Emma said softly:

"It's God's will. You must have faith and trust in Him. He will keep Frances in peace."

Charles could only put his arm about his friend's shoulder.

When Emma asked solicitously how he was getting along, Hooker replied, depressed:

"No one can have an idea, who has not experienced it, what a house of six children is without a female guide."

"Perhaps, after a proper interval, you would consider marrying again?"

Hooker shook his head, "No," with pursed lips.

In the study, he asked about Charles's progress on the book on insectivorous plants.

"I thought it was decently written but I find so much that wants rewriting, it will not be ready to go to the printers for another two months."

"What is two months in your creative life?" Hooker murmured. "During that time you'll be formulating still another book."

"I read yesterday that a man in America by the name of Remington is manufacturing something he calls a typewriter. It appears we don't have to write in pen and ink any more; just strike keys with the letter of the alphabet on them. I'd never learn how to operate one but Francis might. He is young enough for any kind of dangerous experiment."

Sir Charles Lyell did not have another two months of creative life. He died on February 22, 1875, nearly two years after the death of his wife, primarily of old age. His close friends had been expecting it. Hooker took the initiative to have him buried in Westminster Abbey, among England's famous. Consent was granted. England's greatest geologist, pioneer in the field, teacher through his books of all scientists in his century, was laid to rest with high honors. Charles and Joseph Hooker wrote the tribute to be engraved on the slab under which Lyell rested.

Charles was grief-stricken. He would desperately miss his oldest friend.

He had spent three months of what he described as "a devil of a job" concentrating on a second edition of the *Descent of Man*. Even with George home from Cambridge for a spell helping, the task had taken until the end of the year. *Insectivorous Plants* was published by Murray in July, twenty-seven hundred copies selling immediately out of the first printing of three thousand. Once again the English public was titillated by the weird and hardly believable findings of that ever strange mind of Mr. Charles Darwin. He wasted little time in celebration, plunging at once into his expansion of *Climbing Plants*, increasing the monograph by ninety pages of recent findings. Alfred Wallace told him:

"Your beautiful little volume on *Climbing Plants* forms a most interesting companion to your *Orchids* and *Insectivorous Plants*. They make a natural threesome."

Charles began drawing up an account of his ten years' experiments in the growth and fertility of plants raised from cross- and self-fertilizing flowers. He explained in a letter to Ernst Haeckel:

. . . It is really wonderful what an effect pollen from a distinct seedling plant which has been exposed to different conditions of life, has on its offspring.

There had been no disunity in the family since William had spoken out for the British Governor, Mr. Eyre in the Jamaica revolt back in 1865. Now Henrietta came out from London carrying with her a petition drawn up by a Miss Cobbe, to outlaw vivisection in England. She said:

"Miss Cobbe has persuaded a number of important people to sign. There's quite a controversy over it in London."

"I'm aware of that," Charles replied dryly. "It's in the newspapers."

"I would like you to sign it, Father."

"No, my darling daughter, I will do nothing of the kind."

"Why not?"

"Because I have long thought physiology one of the greatest of sciences. Sooner or later it will benefit mankind, and can progress only by experiments on living animals." He tapped the petition with one hand. "This proposal to limit research to only those points which we can now see as having bearings on health, I look at as puerile."

There was a hint of tears in Henrietta's eyes.

"Father, think of all the suffering inflicted on those defenseless animals."

"The animals are carefully anesthetized. Our purpose is to protect animals, and at the same time not to injure physiologists. Their discoveries can help prevent pain and death in humans."

The row over vivisection went on for a long time. Henrietta's husband brought Charles the sketch of a bill to be put before Parliament out of which a royal commission would be formed to study the question. Charles testified before the commission, on which Thomas Huxley served. So many compromises were made that the final bill was satisfactory to no one. Huxley observed:

"The law which permits a boy to troll for pike or set lines with live frog bait for idle amusement, and at the same time lays the teacher of that boy open to the penalty of fine and imprisonment if he uses the same animal for the purpose of exhibiting one of the most beautiful and instructive of physiological spectacles—the circulation in the web of the foot—makes no sense."

When their invaluable Parslow, who had been a member of the family for thirty-six years, retired to his nearby home, and to his wife and children, Emma gave him odd jobs to do, paying him enough to make sure his income remained at a comfortable level. She soon found another butler, named Jackson. He was a little man with red cheeks and loose curly wisps of side whiskers, who had the aspect of a comic. What he lacked in intelligence he made up for in good humor. While waiting at table, even when there were guests, he would follow the conversation as he picked up plates or passed platters of food. If anyone said something amusing, he burst into hilarious laughter. Emma asked Charles:

"Do you think I ought to restrain him?"

"No need. The guests enjoy his laughter. Someone last night described him as a 'cure.'"

When toward the end of the year 1875 England paid four million pounds for a half interest in the Suez Canal, Charles complained: "Now I know where my tax money goes. And to think I won't even know which half we bought."

Jackson thought that was funny, laughing aloud and almost applauding.

"I think we must call him a 'wag' rather than a 'cure,'" Francis observed.

Smith Elder, his early publisher, asked him to prepare an updated manuscript on *Coral Reefs, Volcanic Islands* and *Geological Observations on South America*, published thirty years before. Geologists and students still needed and wanted them. As always Charles resented interrupting his current work.

But he did not lose his sense of humor. He wrote to Asa Gray in America:

> . . . Pray give our very kind remembrances to Mrs. Gray. I know that she likes to hear men boasting, it refreshes them so much. Now the tally with my wife in backgammon stands thus: she, poor creature, has won only 2,490 games, whilst I have won, hurrah, hurrah, 2,795 games!

He made a special trip to London to the Royal Society to see Hooker sitting in the president's chair, and returning home told Emma:

"My outing gave me much satisfaction. I saw lots of people, and it has not done me a penny's worth of harm."

There was good news early in the new year from Amy. She was pregnant. Emma and Charles could expect to become grandparents sometime in the middle of September.

"At last we shall have a grandchild," Emma said exultantly. "It is a day I have longed for."

"You should have many," Charles assured her, "with four sons still to be married, and another daughter."

There were times when it appeared to him he was cross-fertilizing his own books. By May he was making corrections for the second edition of the *Orchid* book. In June he went over for the second time his manuscript on cross-fertilization.

In July a German editor asked him to "write for me an account of the development of your mind and character, with some sketch of your autobiography." It was an interesting idea; no one had asked for his personal story before.

"It's something you should leave for your grandchildren," Emma suggested.

"Yes, I like the idea. Particularly since it will get me away from peering through that microscope lens for a while. I'm half dead."

"Why don't we go to Surrey? Hensleigh and Fanny have offered us their summer house several times."

"Good. I'll write and puff myself up like a pouter pigeon."

He got off to a good start in Surrey, writing easily and unpretentiously in the morning, going for walks in the afternoon. He wrote the story of his childhood at The Mount, about his father, Dr. Robert Darwin, his seven years at the Shrewsbury School, three and a half years at Christ's College, the five-year *Beagle* journey. . . .

My habits are methodical, and this has been of not a little use for my particular line of work. . . . I have had ample leisure from not having to earn my own bread. Even ill-health, though it has annihilated several years of my life, has saved me from the distractions of society and amusement. . . .

. . . My success as a man of science, whatever this may have amounted to, has been determined, as far as I can judge, by complex and diversified mental qualities and conditions. Of these the most important have been—the love of science—unbounded patience in long reflecting over any subject—industry in observing and collecting facts—and a fair share of invention as well as of common sense. With such moderate abilities as I possess, it is truly surprising that thus I should have influenced to a considerable extent the beliefs of scientific men on some important points.

They returned home where Charles finished his autobiography at the beginning of August. He gave the completed script, less than a hundred pages, to Emma. She read it, sitting out on the veranda. When she had finished, she said:

"I find it interesting. Others will more so. Do the Germans plan to publish it?"

"I think I won't allow that. They can quote from it, but basically it's what you wanted: a little story of my life for my grandchildren. My children know all about me."

Joseph Hooker courted and married Hyacinth Symonds, daughter of a respected geologist and widow of an ornithologist. She was a good deal younger than Hooker and was respected among the naturalists. The Darwins were happy for him; he would now have companionship, and the children would have a female guide!

When Amy's time was approaching, she asked Francis if she could go back to North Wales for the delivery.

"I know how much your father relies on you, Francis. Why don't you stay here, and let me go alone? I'll be perfectly safe with my parents and family doctor."

Francis protested. He wanted to accompany her home. If a long waiting period was indicated, he would return to Down House knowing that she was being cared for. Amy insisted she could make the journey without difficulty. Francis was not happy about it; but he let her go.

The message, when it reached Down, left the family stunned. Amy had died in childbirth. No explanation was given. The infant, a boy, was in good health.

Racked by despair, as well as a raging sense of guilt, Francis left at once for North Wales to bring the baby home. The shock and loss of Amy affected Emma deeply; she became fearful and anxious. Francis retreated into a pained silence. But the child, named Bernard, was a great delight. Emma hired a nanny and took up the nursery cares. If they cut into her independent activities, she did not complain.

*Effects of Cross- and Self-Fertilisation in the Vegetable Kingdom* was published in November. William Thiselton-Dyer, Hooker's assistant at Kew Gardens, wrote a stirring review for *Nature*, which got the book off to a good start, fifteen hundred copies having already been sold.

Charles had a birthday on February 12, his sixty-eighth. His short gray beard had become a long white one. He was successful in persuading Emma to let the birthday pass unheralded. Not so his admirers in Germany and Holland. Each prepared a handsome album containing photographs of their own scientists, and under each picture a tribute to Charles signed by the contributor. Charles was deeply touched; the two albums had obviously been in work for a long time. To the men in the two countries he wrote:

> . . . I suppose that every worker at science occasionally feels depressed, and doubts whether what he has published has been worth the labour which it has cost him, but for the few remaining years of my life, whenever I want cheering, I will look at the portraits of my distinguished co-workers and remember their generous sympathy. When I die, the album will be a most precious bequest to my children.

When a new honor came to Charles, Francis asked:
"Father, how many of these awards have you received?"
"I don't know, Frank. I never counted them."
"Would you like me to?"
"If it would amuse you."

Francis found seventy-five honorary and foreign memberships, perhaps the largest number of international honors tendered to a single scholar-writer-scientist since Sir Isaac Newton, who had graduated from Cambridge and was a professor there from 1669 until 1701. Sir Isaac, who had represented the University of Cambridge in Parliament, was best known for his formulation of the law of gravitation, and for the law of motion. Unlike Galileo, a hundred years before him, who was tried and imprisoned by the Inquisition in Rome for stating that the earth moved around the sun, and unlike Charles Darwin, working a hundred years later, Isaac Newton had been accepted and knighted.

It was a week after his birthday that he received a notice from the Down Friendly Club, which he had served as treasurer for the past twenty-seven years, that the members had decided to disband and distribute the eleven hundred and fifty pounds in their treasury. They had two reasons: fear that the government intended to unite all the clubs throughout England into a single one, and then divide the funds. The second, that they had become so prosperous there was no further need for it. Charles gave them a severe paternal lecture.

"I can assure you that all the rumors about uniting the clubs to form a common fund are lies, spread for some evil purpose. I have consulted an actuary, who could have no motive to deceive you; he has calculated that you may divide about one hundred fifty pounds. About one thousand pounds must be retained. No reasonable man will doubt that the above sum is necessary to pay the burial fees, and to insure provision during ill-health. Therefore I hope that you will allow me to warn you all, in the most earnest manner, to deliberate for a long time before you dissolve the club, not only for the sake of your wives and children, but for your own sakes. I hope that you will admit that I can have no bad motive in expressing my deliberate judgment. . . ."

The members took his advice.

Joseph Hooker became Sir Joseph Hooker. It put him out of countenance that he, eight years younger than Charles, and in his own eyes infinitely a lesser contributor to science and knowledge, should be honored above his friend and mentor. Many of Charles's colleagues were shocked, outraged, insulted that Charles Darwin was being passed over. They mounted the best campaign possible but were not so much refused as ignored. No one apparently, in government or at court, was willing to take the responsibility for causing an uproar in the Church.

"I don't care a fig for it," Charles told his supporters, in full honesty. "My books comprise my knighthood."

Five days after Hooker's daughter Harriet was married to William Thiselton-Dyer, bringing him into the Hooker-Henslow botanic family, Sir Joseph left for the United States at the invitation of Professor

Hayden, chief of the American Topographical and Geological Survey, to join an official surveying party, including Asa Gray, working in Colorado, Utah, Nevada and California, ending in San Francisco. Sir Joseph's task was to render a botanical report, especially in regard to the character and distribution of the forest trees.

"I could almost be envious of him," said Emma. "It seems that everyone, including our boys, has been to the United States, except us."

"Find me a land bridge connecting the two continents, and I'll take you," Charles replied. "In the meanwhile we have one of the wonders of the world right here in England. Why don't we visit Stonehenge?"

They took George with them and had a fine time. George, the mathematician, showed them how the location of the stones might possibly have been used to observe the celestial beings.

To his son Horace, who had asked a leading question, he answered:

"I have been speculating what makes a man a discoverer of undiscovered things, and a most perplexing problem it is. Many men who are very clever, much cleverer than discoverers, never originate anything. As far as I can conjecture, the art consists in habitually searching for causes or meanings of everything which occurs. This implies sharp observation and requires as much knowledge as possible of the subject investigated."

When Hooker returned from the United States he told Charles:

"Crowds of people asked for you in America, so pray accept the national greetings through me."

3.

Charles's work took on an accelerated pace. His first project was a technical book on the different forms of flowers on plants of the same species. He had all his information in his notes and had only to assemble it. He and Francis made fast work of the manuscript so that it was published on July 9, 1877. Charles dedicated the book to Asa Gray, who kept articles about Charles's work in every American journal that would have them. John Murray printed only twelve hundred and fifty copies but these were snapped up by those in need of his close observation.

Charles told his friends:

"I am all on fire with the work."

This meant that he also felt well. In fact he had so much energy left that he wrote an article about infant behavior from his notes about William, which was published in *Mind*, and attracted a good deal of attention.

A project which interested him, and which he imagined would be his last, also amused him greatly, in part because others who heard about it felt either dismay or disgust. His subject was worms!

He had mused about the subject since his return from the H.M.S. *Beagle* voyage. While paying a visit to Maer Hall, his Uncle Jos had pointed out to him the quantity of soil that had been brought up on the Maer lawn by worms. A year later he had written and read before the Geological Society a paper which suggested that, given sufficient time, worms could bury everything on the surface of the earth. Nobody reacted to the article for over twenty years, at which time someone attacked his theory in the *Gardeners' Chronicle*. Charles had determined that when the right time came he would do a thorough investigation of the anatomy, habits and work of the earthworm.

That time had come.

For many months he had been keeping in his study worms in pots filled with earth. He told Francis:

"I wish to know how far they act consciously, and how much mental power they display. I am the more desirous to learn something on this head as few observations of this kind, as far as I know, have been made on animals so low in the scale of organization."

Francis replied with a shrug. "Most people think earthworms good only for baiting fishhooks."

"That's a mistake. Worms have had a share in the formation of the layer of vegetable mold which covers the whole surface of the land in every moderately humid country."

"Does this mold serve any purpose? How do worms create it?"

"Through their castings, which may be seen in extraordinary numbers on common chalk downs."

"What else do we want to know about them?" Francis's tone indicated that he was not at all sure that this was a worthy field of endeavor for Charles Darwin, M.A., F.R.S.

"Everything: their structure, senses, food and digestion, glands, habits, intelligence, how they excavate their burrows, how they undermine large stones and cause them to sink, the weight of the earth they bring up. . . ."

Francis whistled.

"Back to the microscope! Little did I think I would be dissecting worms the way you dissected barnacles!"

"Worms have played a more important part in the history of the world than you would suppose. Archeologists ought to be grateful to them as they protect and preserve for an indefinitely long period of time every object not liable to decay, by burying it beneath their castings as effectively as you or I using a shovel or spade."

Emma was not as surprised as Francis.

"Anywhere that life exists your father will go . . . in his mind, that is." She wrote to Henrietta:

> . . . Father was made very happy by finding two old stones at the bottom of the field. He has now got a man at work digging for the worms. He wants to observe the effect produced by earthworms in gradually undermining and covering up stones. I must go and take him an umbrella.

Walking over a nearby field which he had known for thirty years, he found that worms had buried every flint that had been on the surface, a quarter of an inch each year. A more difficult task was to determine precisely how much earth the worms could bring up; and he learned that on the chalk hills near Down they brought up eighteen tons of earth annually!

After all these years of being content with his study, though he sometimes had to wear a shawl around his shoulders because of the closeness of his work space to the windows, he at last felt hemmed in by his books, files, instruments, globe, maps, specimens, photographs and portraits on the walls. He decided to build himself a new, larger study behind their drawing room. He accepted the less expensive estimate, supervised the construction, including a new entranceway, front door and front porch.

He had all his possessions moved into the new study by the autumn of 1877. Now there was room for a sofa on which to lie down, a deep leather armchair, a long wide table which held manuscripts, papers, letters, writing supplies, inkwells, folders. His writing chair was, as always, in a corner near a tall window with a capacious sill for books and journals. He had a Down carpenter put rollers on its four legs so that he could whip about the room.

The move did him little good; within a matter of months the new study was as cluttered as the old. When Emma saw the volumes packed solid on one wall, she murmured:

"Nature abhors a vacuum."

When Charles went walking alone, in his long cape and soft hat, he would stand in one position in the fields so very long, immersed in his thoughts, that the Down House squirrels imagined him to be a tree, climbing up his legs and back. This drove Polly, the rough-haired fox terrier Henrietta had left behind when she moved to London, half out of her canine senses. She knew Charles was not a tree. He was a very big puppy. She bounded into his lap whenever she could.

He had become fair game for the cartoonists. The *London Sketch Book*, *Punch*, *Hornet* ran caricatures of him, amusing rather than vicious. His head, face, long white beard were accurately depicted but the rest of his body was drawn in the form of a hairy ape, with claws for feet.

Their eldest son, William, became engaged to an American girl, Sara Sedgwick.

"I'm mighty pleased about that," Charles exclaimed. "At thirty-eight, I thought he was going to remain a bachelor."

When William was thrown from his horse in Southampton, Dr. Andrew Clark put him through a series of gymnastics to prove that nothing serious had happened to his head. Horace, now twenty-six, served as William's nurse and secretary, writing his business mail. Next Leonard, who had been building forts for the British Empire, fell on the earthen tennis court, bruising his knee so badly he had to spend several days on the sofa being spoiled by Elizabeth, who had taken over his nursing. When Litchfield became ill, Henrietta nursed her husband with the skill and tenderness she had watched her mother lavish on her father. Emma approved, telling Henrietta:

"Nothing marries one so completely as sickness."

It was Emma, in the end, who suffered the worst fall. She and the Rev. Mr. Innes had worked together cordially for years on all church matters, the local school, the care of the poor; as she had with the Rev. Henry Powell who had replaced him. Now she found that she simply could not get along with the newest vicar, the Rev. George ffinden. He was a Tory, against everything the Wedgwood and Darwin families had ever stood for. She disagreed with him so consistently in their meetings about Down's affairs that she stopped attending them. Then the Rev. Mr. ffinden committed the ultimate gaucherie; he attacked Charles Darwin and his books in a Sunday morning sermon, while Emma and Elizabeth were sitting in their family pew.

The two Darwin women promptly rose and left. Emma fumed all the way up the hill to Down House. She stormed into Charles's new study, cried:

"He's an insufferable idiot! I shall never go into Down Church again as long as he serves there. Next Sunday I shall walk the two miles to Keston and join the congregation."

After hearing the details, he said:

"I'll make an official appearance with you. But what about the winters, when there's rain and mud? You don't like to make our driver work on the Lord's Day."

Emma was indignant all over again.

"If I can't walk two miles in the mud of a Sunday morning, I don't deserve to call myself a Christian!"

He took her in his arms, soothed her.

"You're not only a Christian, my dear, you're a Christian martyr. I can see you in the Colosseum in Rome, brushing the lions aside while you call the Emperor a heathen!"

Mollified, she kissed his cheek, asked:

"Why, in all of England, do we have to be apportioned a bigot?"

Charles chuckled. Here was Emma, whose theology probably was similar to the Rev. Mr. ffinden's, doing battle for her apostate husband.

Nor had Emma ever set aside her sense of injustice that Charles had not been knighted. The University of Cambridge now announced that an honorary LL.D. would be conferred upon him in the Senate House on November 17; an even forty years since Christ's College had awarded him his master's degree. It was the highest honor the university had to confer. Charles had the good grace to accept.

The family stayed at the Bull Hotel. The next day Emma, Elizabeth, Leonard and Horace slipped into the Senate House by a side door. It was a most striking sight; the gallery on each side of the Senate was crammed to overflowing, the floor jammed with undergraduates climbing on the statues and standing up on the window sills.

There was periodic cheering. When Charles entered in his red cloak the noise became deafening. He smiled and waited for the Vice-Chancellor to arrive. Soon a monkey appeared dangling from cords which had been stretched between the two galleries; it was greeted with a burst of laughter, the students happy with the prank they had played on Charles Darwin.

At last the Vice-Chancellor appeared, in scarlet and white fur; there was bowing and handshaking, and then Charles was marched down the aisle behind two authorities with silver maces. The public orator got through his tedious Latin harangue, constantly interrupted by the traditional shouts and jeers of the undergraduates. Then the procession marched to the Vice-Chancellor. Against tradition, Charles did not kneel. Then it was over and everybody came up and shook hands.

Many parties had been planned for the Darwins. Charles made a sentimental journey to his old rooms at Christ's College and took his children to see the flourishing botanic garden which John Henslow had begun, walking around town with his LL.D. in the pocket of his silk gown. That evening Thomas Huxley gave a Darwinian speech to the Cambridge Philosophical Society. It appeared to Charles that he had come full circle; it was this same society which in 1835 had published extracts from his letters to John Henslow written aboard H.M.S. *Beagle*, with observations by Adam Sedgwick.

Sir Joseph Hooker surprised everyone by fathering a son with his young wife. Thomas Huxley surprised no one by fathering an avalanche

of penetrating lectures, monographs, books, ending with the same
LL.D. from Cambridge which Charles had received.

Charles spent a month with Francis in the new study working to
prove that the sleep of plants is to lessen the injury to the leaves from
radiation. In the spring he went into London to see Dr. Andrew Clark
because of giddiness. Dr. Clark put him on a dry diet. The good doctor
would not accept a fee, even when he made the trip to Down, now
changed by officialdom to Downe. This made it difficult for Charles to
summon him.

William continued his social work in Southampton, being chiefly responsible for opening a trade school which taught such opposite subjects as art and chemistry. When he came to Down House for a visit
Charles asked:

"Would you please get Dr. Clark to accept at least a token fee? I'd
feel so much more comfortable that way."

William tried. Dr. Clark was affronted.

"Down House is Mecca for the scientists of the world. Does one get
paid for the privilege of coming to Mecca?"

Francis's son Bernard, a year old, was a frolicsome, bright-eyed boy
and added consistent joy to the family. Nevertheless Emma insisted
that Charles take frequent holidays. They visited the beautiful Lake
District in Cumbria where they walked on top of the steep rock cliffs,
Charles speaking of the scenery in glowing terms even as he complained:

"My despotic wife!"

"I consider you a national treasure," she retorted.

He wrote to Alfred Wallace:

> I keep moderately well, but always feel half-dead; yet man-
> age to work away on vegetable physiology, as I think I should
> die outright if I had nothing to do. . . .

Alfred Wallace's trouble was his need for money. His sole income, on
which to raise a growing family, was from his books and articles for the
journals, whose pay was modest. He had known, particularly after his
marriage, that he must find a permanent job. He had previously applied
for the paid position of assistant secretary to the Royal Geographical
Society. His friend and companion of past journeys, Henry Bates, was
appointed. He had subsequently tried for the directorship of the museum at Bethnal Green, and for the place of superintendent of Epping
Forest. This third failure depressed him and made him fearful for his
family's future. While in London, Charles gathered a group for dinner
at Erasmus's house.

"There's no help for it," he told Hooker and Huxley; "we simply have to secure a government pension for Wallace. He's too great a man to be abandoned."

They plotted strategy. Charles's letters were to lead the way. After twelve months of continuous pleading, they persuaded the government to grant Wallace a pension of two hundred pounds a year for life.

The seasons had begun to act crazily. June of 1878 provided a tropical thunder and hailstorm, with stones so large the family was afraid they would break through the veranda roof. Now in October a heavy snow fell prematurely, before the trees had lost their leaves. The accumulation on the branches of the Down House trees caused them to snap off.

A windfall came in the form of a note from a Mr. Anthony Rich of Heene, Worthing, saying that he and his sister were the last of their family, and that under the circumstances "those should be remembered whose abilities had been devoted for the benefit of mankind." Therefore he had bequeathed to Charles nearly all of their property, a share of houses in Cornhill which brought in rather above a thousand pounds annually.

Charles wanted to turn down the bequest. He could find no one to agree with him, not Emma, his children, Litchfield, Hooker, Huxley, Wallace. They all said, in effect:

"Accept the money! Let the thousand pounds a year be given through the Royal Society to a young naturalist who needs help. It will set a wonderful example. Other people might begin leaving part of their estates to naturalists and scientific societies. That has never been done before."

He accepted. When the Turin Society awarded him the Bressa prize, with an accompanying hundred pounds, he wrote to the Naples Zoological Station suggesting that if they wanted some piece of apparatus of about the value of a hundred pounds:

I should very much like to be allowed to pay for it.

A few weeks before his seventy-first birthday he walked into his study and saw a beautiful fur coat lying across his table. He stood looking at it, stupefied, as the children burst in. They cried in unison:

"Surprise! Surprise! Happy birthday! That's your present from all of us to you. Try it on!"

The fur coat fit him perfectly. He embraced his sons and daughter Elizabeth; Henrietta had participated from London.

"But I could never wear it!" he cried.

"Why not, Father?"

"Because it would never be cold enough."

He wore it so constantly that he soon was afraid he would wear it out.

In November of 1880 he received an account of a flood in Brazil from which his friend Fritz Müller had barely escaped with his life. He immediately wrote to Hermann Müller, inquiring whether his brother had lost books or instruments in the catastrophe, begging in that case "for the sake of science, so that science should not suffer," to be allowed to help in making good the loss.

At about the same time their youngest son, Horace, married the daughter of their friend and relative, Thomas Farrer. The Darwins liked the idea of their children marrying inside the family. Only Francis and Elizabeth remained at home, and little Bernard, the raising of whom became a nostalgic experience, taking them back to 12 Upper Gower Street when they had had their first children.

Like the unseasonal weather of a couple of years before, a purely gratuitous confrontation sent the family into conference, though Charles was only remotely involved. Samuel Butler, grandson of Charles's master at Shrewsbury, and famous for his publication *Erewhon*, "nowhere" spelled almost backward, and a graduate of St. John's College, Cambridge, wrote a book called *Evolution Old and New*, which advocated the views of Dr. Erasmus Darwin over those of his grandson. At the same time Dr. Ernst Krause, a German science editor for his periodical *Kosmos*, had written a short scientific biography about Dr. Erasmus Darwin which he was going to expand into a book. He asked Charles for a short introduction about his grandfather. Butler, in an angry letter to the *Athenaeum*, accused Krause of using passages from his book without acknowledging the source, and Charles of being a party to the deception.

"Father should defend himself!" the Darwin boys proclaimed.

Emma, Henrietta and her husband Richard were dead set against answering Butler at all.

"Don't dignify Butler's attack by taking notice of it," Litchfield counseled.

Samuel Butler published a second letter in the *St. James's Gazette* in which he inferred that Charles Darwin was a liar.

This time Huxley said with a sardonic grin:

"Allow me to quote from Goethe, whose character also had been attacked: 'Every whale has its louse.'"


4.


At the beginning of August 1881, Charles and Emma went to London to visit Erasmus. William was there on banking business. Francis was there, escorting his sister Elizabeth to the theater and exhibits. Charles told Erasmus:

"Your Queen Anne Street house seems like an extension of Down House."

"So it is. Just as Down House is an extension of The Mount."

The Darwins stayed only three days. Erasmus seemed frail; he was already seventy-seven, but in good spirits. All the more shocking then, when a telegram was delivered to Down House on August 26 telling them that Erasmus had died after a short illness, but without severe suffering.

For Charles it was as though a part of England had fallen into the sea and was gone forever.

"I'm not going to let Ras be buried in London," he told the family. "I'm going to bring him to Down and have him buried in the graveyard next to the church. That way, we'll pass his grave every day, and he'll know he's not forgotten."

Erasmus was buried where Charles wanted him to be. William spoke for the family, after the simple funeral, when he said:

"Next to coming to Down, one of my greatest pleasures was going to see dear Uncle Eras whenever I was in London. He seemed to me much more than an uncle, and from quite a little boy I can remember his steady kindness and pleasantness, always knowing how to make me feel at ease and be amused. After I grew up, year by year, it was a greater happiness for me to go and see him. To me there was a charm in his manner that I never saw in anybody else."

Charles could only add, when writing to Thomas Farrer:

. . . The death of my brother Erasmus is a very heavy loss to all of us in this family. He was so kind-hearted and affectionate. Nor have I ever known any one more pleasant. It was always a very great pleasure to talk with him on any subject whatever, and this I shall never do again. He was not, I think, a happy man, and for many years did not value life, though never complaining. I am so glad that he escaped severe suffering during his last days. I shall never see such a man again.

Erasmus left a comfortable sum for his sister Caroline. The remainder of the estate, including the home on Queen Anne Street, was left to Charles and Emma. It was a considerable inheritance. Charles told Emma:

"I doubt we'll ever touch Ras's estate. He wanted it to go to our children. We'll save it for them."

Charles had not weathered the years nearly as well as Emma. He looked older than she, though they were, within a matter of months, the same age. Perhaps it was the long bouts of illness; perhaps the concentrated periods of incredibly hard work; perhaps it was his snow-white, all-encompassing beard and hair under the soft black hat; but Charles Darwin now looked as though he were the Patriarch of the World. His eyes were sunken; he carried the look of a man who was about to say farewell; and did not mind at all. His life had been lived to the very brim or, to use one of his early expressions, to the very cone of the volcano.

He kept a pot of worms on Emma's piano in the drawing room. Emma thought it better not to suggest that the pot of worms belonged in the hothouse. Charles used whistles and other noisemakers to see how the worms would react. They took no notice. Then he started striking bass notes on the piano. The worms scurried into their burrows. Emma observed tartly:

"Charles, you've got to be the only man in the world who entertains worms with a piano recital!"

He had a big stone moved onto the lawn. Horace attached an instrument which kept an accurate measure of how long it took the worms to make the stone sink how far. Francis was fascinated by the experiment; the women of the family were curiously indifferent.

*The Formation of Vegetable Mould, through the Action of Worms, with Observations on Their Habits* manuscript was delivered to John Murray in April of 1881 and the book was published on October 10. Two thousand copies sold immediately, five thousand by the end of the year.

The life and times of earthworms became the subject of the day. Charles exclaimed:

"My book has been received with almost laughable enthusiasm!"

Joseph Hooker, one of the world's most knowledgeable botanists, confessed to Charles:

> . . . I must own I had always looked on worms as amongst the most helpless and unintelligent members of the creation; and am amazed to find that they have a domestic life and public duties! I shall now respect them, even in our garden pots; and regard them as something better than food for fishes.

Charles had little appetite for another long-time investigation. Rather he did odd jobs: "a couple of months observing the effects of carbonate of ammonia on chlorophyll and on the roots of certain plants, but the subject is too difficult for me, and I cannot understand the meaning of some strange facts which I have observed. The mere recording of new facts is but dull work."

He heartily congratulated Horace and Ida on the birth of their first son. Dried little Bernard's tears when his nanny married and left. Asked William, the experienced banker, to handle his money affairs. Demanded of his son how much his estate was worth, how much each of his children would receive. William estimated his father's holdings at £280,000 plus Emma's money. William then worked out a formula by which the two daughters would receive £34,000, each son £53,000. Exercising normal prudence, the Darwin offspring would be independent for life.

That was what Charles had aspired to.

What he did not tell Emma or William was that he had a weak pulse. Francis took him to London to see Dr. Clark. The doctor told them:

"There is some derangement of the heart, but it is not serious."

Charles knew better but kept his own counsel. A few days later, while walking to the home of a friend in London, he had a seizure. He managed to make it to the front door. His friend was out but the butler, seeing how ill he was, asked him in. Charles declined. The butler asked if he might fetch a cab. Again, Charles declined, saying:

"I would rather not give so much trouble."

He also refused to allow the butler to accompany him. He walked with difficulty in the direction in which cabs could be met but, after going some three hundred yards, staggered and had to catch hold of the park railing to keep from falling.

It was the beginning of the end. But not the end itself. A cough pulled him down and made him miserable. Emma insisted on his taking quinine, which did him much good. He still had time to contribute two hundred and fifty pounds to Hooker's *Index*, which was designed to provide an authoritative list of the names of all plants which had been identified, with the author of each and the place of publication. He also wrote a note to his executors and other children directing them to pay Hooker two hundred and fifty pounds annually until the *Index* was completed.

When George tried for the Plumian professorship of mathematics and natural philosophy at Cambridge, at eight hundred pounds a year, which he got the following year, Charles told his family:

"I believe that someday George will be a great scientific swell."

Since the British Association was to have its annual meeting for 1882 in Southampton, William felt he owed it to his father to take on the arrangements, a formidable task. Charles cautioned:

"The willing horse is always overworked."

As a last gesture of the will to live, he wrote two short papers for the Linnean Society about his studies on roots and chlorophyll bodies. He also had the satisfaction of seeing Leonard married to a young woman by the name of Elizabeth Frazer. Now four of his five sons had been married.

During the last week of February and the beginning of March he suffered attacks of pain in the region of the heart, with irregularity of pulse each afternoon. On warm days he sat in the orchard with Emma because he "liked to hear the birds singing and see the crocus flowers wide open."

On March 7 he attempted a sentimental visit to the Sandwalk, but suffered a seizure. His illness became so serious that Emma sent for Dr. Clark. Specialists were called in from St. Bartholomew's Hospital, as well as from St. Mary Cray. There was little they could do to alleviate his sensations of exhaustion and faintness. He recognized with deep depression that his working days were over.

On April 15 he was seized with giddiness at the dinner table, rose from his chair, then fainted trying to get to the chaise longue in the drawing room. Two nights later he became unconscious. It was with great difficulty that he was brought around.

He was being nursed by Emma, Francis and Elizabeth. Henrietta was notified. She arrived on the morning of the nineteenth, as Charles had had an even more serious attack at noon the day before. With Henrietta there to watch over him, Emma went downstairs for a little rest. Henrietta and Francis kept vigil from either side of the bed. Charles regained consciousness for a moment, gazed at his daughter and son, said softly:

"You are the best of dear nurses."

He was slipping away. Henrietta went to get her mother and sister. Charles opened his eyes for the last time. He managed to put his hand into Emma's, murmuring:

"I am not afraid to die."

She kissed him on the brow, whispered:

"You shouldn't be."

A few moments later he breathed his last. One of the doctors closed his eyes.

Emma and her children went downstairs to join the relatives waiting in the drawing room. To Henrietta, Emma appeared calm and natural. Tea was brought in. Emma let herself be amused by some little thing, smiled for a moment. Henrietta asked:

"What is the secret of your calmness and self-possession?"

Emma paused for only a moment, then turned her sympathetic brown eyes on her daughter.

"Perhaps Father did not believe in God. But God believed in him. He will rest in peace where he has gone."

The family decided they would have a quiet funeral, bury Charles in the ancient graveyard adjoining the church, near his brother Erasmus, and his children, Mary Eleanor and Charles Waring. John Lubbock thought otherwise. He had twenty members of the House of Commons sign a petition addressed to Dr. Bradley, Dean of Westminster. It read:

HOUSE OF COMMONS, APRIL 21, 1882.
Very Rev. Sir,—We hope you will not think we are taking a liberty if we venture to suggest that it would be acceptable to a very large number of our fellow-countrymen of all classes and opinions that our illustrious countryman, Dr. Darwin, should be buried in Westminster Abbey.

John Lubbock told the family:

I quite sympathise with your feelings and personally I should have greatly preferred that your father should have rested in Down amongst us all. . . . Still from a national point of view, it is clearly right that he should be buried in the Abbey.

The funeral took place on April 26, 1882. The pallbearers were Joseph Hooker, whom he had called "the dearest of friends." Thomas Huxley, "Darwin's bulldog." Alfred Wallace, who stated that "the origin of species belongs solely to Mr. Darwin." John Lubbock, who declared, "Darwin is my Master." James Russell Lowell, the American minister to the Court of St. James's, who wished to have his country represented. William Spottiswoode, president of the Royal Society; Canon Farrar, the Duke of Devonshire, the Earl of Derby, the Duke of Argyll.

The Abbey was filled with representatives of France, Germany, Italy, Spain, Russia, and by those of the universities and learned societies, as well as large numbers of personal friends and admirers.

He had never been knighted, had never become Sir Charles Darwin, but the Church of England and the gentry of Great Britain were doing him proud in his last public appearance. Under the "Order of the Procession" the Crown came first, the mourner canons, the canons, the Dean's verger . . . then the casket carried by the pallbearers, followed by the family; after that their servants; then the scientific bodies. . . .

As a pure act of genius, the Dean of Westminster had chosen for Charles a spot in the north side of the nave, close to the angle of the choir screen, a few feet from the grave of Sir Isaac Newton.

It was an imposing ceremony. No person had been admitted who was not in mourning; yet there was little sense of sadness. Rather the atmosphere in the Abbey was one of triumph that such a man should have lived.

Emma Darwin thought this most proper. She had never become Lady Darwin, but she was gratified for her husband of forty-three years, "who had made such a noise in the world."

On the way back to Down House, William said to Francis:

"I hope it doesn't sound irreverent, but can you imagine what delightful conversations Father and Sir Isaac Newton will have each night after the Abbey is closed, and all is quiet?"

The last simple task was to compose the inscription for Charles's gravestone. Hooker and Huxley made several attempts but found it impossible to characterize Charles Darwin's contribution in two or three sentences. Huxley proffered:

"The best thing we could put on that stone is the tremendous line from the American poet, Emerson:

*Beware when the great God lets loose a thinker on this planet.*"

They were forestalled. Charles had left a note of instruction behind. He wanted nothing on his tomb. His words had already been chiseled on stone, ineradicably.

The slab over his grave read:

CHARLES ROBERT DARWIN
Born 12 February, 1809
Died 19 April, 1882

He had turned the world around.

Though not entirely.

The day after the funeral in Westminster Abbey, a letter was sent by a firm of clockmakers in Fleet Street to Martin's Bank, London.

> Sir,
> We have this day drawn a cheque for £280-0-0 which closes our account with your firm. Our reasons for thus closing an account opened so many years ago with your house are of so exceptional a kind that we are quite prepared to find that they are deemed wholly inadequate to the result. . . .
> Our reasons are entirely the presence of Mr. R. B. Martin at Westminster Abbey yesterday, not merely giving sanction to the scene as an individual, but apparently as one of the deputation from the Society which has especially become the endorsers and sustainers of Mr. Darwin's theories. We feel that the day has come when a most avowed stand must be taken by all who are not ashamed to affirm the Truth of the Living

God in His statements as to the Creation in Genesis at Sinai, and in His Written Word throughout.

We are anxious that God at least should be a witness to our confidence in His Veracity in Every Statement He has made in His Word from Genesis to Revelation.

We are content to know that our own feeble voice will be drowned in the turmoil of an exultant anthem to the praise of a man whose wicked and ridiculous theories *we* hold to be awful Blasphemies.

Let it be so. The Day is hurrying on, which shall burn as a Fire. We shall see then who has spoken Truth, God or Mr. Darwin.

Yours respectfully,
Barraud and Lunds

# ACKNOWLEDGMENTS

A book of this nature could not have been written, at least not by me, without the wholehearted support of everyone to whom I turned for help.

In England I am indebted to Basil J. Greenhill, Director of the National Maritime Museum in Greenwich, and Margaret Deacon in the Department of Manuscripts, who did everything in their power to provide me with a reasonable facsimile of H.M.S. *Beagle*. Dr. and Mrs. J. Michael Tellwright, the present owners of Maer Hall, were more than hospitable, affording me a set of the original plans of the home, as well as documents authenticating its historic background. Mr. Douglas Campbell, District Valuer, of the Inland Revenue Service, whose offices are now housed in The Mount, gave me free run of the house with ruler and camera, as well as documents which detailed The Mount as Dr. Robert Darwin built it, around 1800.

At Christ's College, Cambridge, I am indebted to their archivist, Donald Misson, and to Rita Beaumont.

At Down House, as well as the tender loving care bestowed upon us by Sir Hedley and Lady Judy Atkins, whose guests we were for two weeks, the Custodian, Mr. Philip Titheradge, and his wife Eleanor were enormously helpful, searching out information that could be ascertained only at Down House.

I am grateful to the Director of Kew Gardens, Mr. J. Heslop-Harrison; and to the then Chief Librarian and Archivist, Mr. V. T. H. Parry, and his associates in helping me with the voluminous Joseph Hooker material in their care. To K. Twyman-Musgrave and C. J. Edwards of the Public Records Office in London for the muster book of the *Beagle*. Also to G. T. Corley Smith, Secretary-General of the Charles Darwin Foundation, for arranging for our stay at the Darwin Station in the Galápagos Islands; to Dr. Craig MacFarland, its then Director.

Warm thanks are due to Lynn Miller, Assistant Curator of the Wedgwood Museum; and to Dr. Ian Fraser of Keele University, who supplied me with valuable information from the Wedgwood archives, of which he is in charge. I also wish to thank James Barber of the Plymouth Museum and the librarians of the Plymouth Public Library. Lastly, my gratitude to David Stanbury, editor of *A Narrative of the Voyage of H.M.S. Beagle*, who not only shared with me important letters he had unearthed, but was kind enough to read the first half of the book, concerning the *Beagle* voyage, to make sure that a landsman such as myself did not fall overboard too often.

In the United States I wish to thank my friends and associates who gave so unselfishly of their services. Professors George Kennedy, who encouraged me from the very beginning and Willard Libby of U.C.L.A., who gave me valuable assistance. The always cooperative librarians at U.C.L.A., including James Mink and Brook Whiting in Special Collections. Paul H. Barrett of Michigan State University, co-author of *Darwin on Man*, editor of the two-volume *Collected Papers of Charles Darwin*.

Dr. Milton Uhley, the medical historian for this book and for several preceding ones. Dr. Milton Heifetz, also for his medical opinions about the last century. Peter Vorzimmer of Temple University in Philadelphia, author of *Charles Darwin: The Years of Controversy*, for his discussions and friendship. Dr. Ralph Colp, Jr., author of *To Be an Invalid*, which is bound to be an authority on Charles Darwin's illness.

Louis and Annette Kaufman, my ever-ready authorities on the music of the period. Dr. Franklin Murphy, who provided me with articles about Charles Darwin and evolution which I might otherwise have missed. Stanley Dashew for his advice on the building and structure of sailing vessels. Mrs. Robert Nathan, who agreed to keep me from falling into Americanisms. Robert J. Lavenberg, Curator, Section of Ichthyology, of the Natural History Museum of Los Angeles County, for clues to the understanding of barnacles.

In conclusion, I should like to thank Mr. Gerald Pollinger, my long-time English agent, for helping me to locate rare books, necessary to our purpose. And of course my loyal and affectionate friends at Doubleday and Company through my forty-year association with that publishing house.

# SELECT BIBLIOGRAPHY

BOOKS BY CHARLES DARWIN

*Narrative of the Surveying Voyages of His Majesty's Ships "Adventure" and "Beagle" between the years 1826 and 1836, describing their examination of the Southern shores of South America, and the "Beagle's" circumnavigation of the globe.* Vol. III. *Journal and Remarks, 1832–1836, 1839; Journal of Researches into the Natural History and Geology of the countries visited during the Voyage of H.M.S. "Beagle" round the world, under the command of Capt. Fitz-Roy, R.N.,* 2nd ed., corrected, with additions, Colonial and Home Library, 1845; *Zoology of the Voyage of H.M.S. "Beagle,"* edited and superintended by Charles Darwin, 1838–1843; *The Structure and Distribution of Coral Reefs,* 1842; *Geological Observations on the Volcanic Islands visited during the voyage of H.M.S. "Beagle,"* 1844; *Geological Observations on South America,* 1846; *Geological Observations on Coral Reefs, Volcanic Islands, and on South America,* 1851; *A Monograph of the Fossil Lepadidae; or, Pedunculated Cirripedes of Great Britain,* 1851; *A Monograph of the Sub-class Cirripedia, with Figures of all the Species. The Lepadidae; or, Pedunculated Cirripedes,* 1851; *A Monograph of the Fossil Balanidae and Verrucidae of Great Britain,* 1854; *The Balanidae, (or sessile cirripedes); the Verrucidae, etc.,* 1854; *On the Origin of Species by Means of Natural Selection, or the Preservation of Favoured Races in the Struggle for Life,* 1859; *On the Various Contrivances by Which Orchids Are Fertilised by Insects,* 1862; *On the Movements and Habits of Climbing Plants,* 1865 (John Murray edition, 1875); *The Variation of Animals and Plants under Domestication,* 2 vols., 1868; *The Descent of Man, and Selection in Relation to Sex,* 2 vols., 1871; *The Expression of the Emotions in Man and Animals,* 1872; *Insectivorous Plants,* 1875; *The Effects of Cross- and Self-Fertilisation in the Vegetable Kingdom,* 1876; *The Different Forms of Flowers on Plants of the Same Species,* 1877; *The Power of Movement in Plants* (assisted by Francis Darwin), 1880; *The Formation of Vegetable Mould, through the Action of Worms, with Observations on Their Habits,* 1881.

BOOKS ABOUT CHARLES DARWIN

Special notice must be given to Ralph Colp, Jr., M.D., and his book *To Be an Invalid,* University of Chicago Press, 1977. It is the only penetrating and completely researched study of Charles Darwin and his illnesses.

Mea Allen, *Darwin and His Flowers*, 1977; Philip Appleman, ed., *Darwin*, 1970; Nora Barlow, ed., *The Autobiography of Charles Darwin*, 1958; Samuel Anthony Barnett, *A Century of Darwin*, 1958; Jacques Barzun, *Darwin, Marx, Wagner*, 1941; Gamaliel Bradford, *Darwin*, 1926; John Chancellor, *Charles Darwin*, 1976; Evelyn Cheesman, *Charles Darwin and His Problems*, 1954; Francis Darwin, ed., *The Life and Letters of Charles Darwin*, 3 vols., 1887; Francis Darwin and A. C. Seward, eds., *More Letters of Charles Darwin*, 2 vols., 1903; Sir Gavin de Beer, *Charles Darwin, A Scientific Biography*, 1964; George A. Dorsey, *The Evolution of Charles Darwin*, 1928; Loren Eiseley, *Darwin's Century*, 1958; Loren Eiseley, *Darwin and the Mysterious Mr. X*, 1979; Benjamin Farrington, *What Darwin Really Said*, 1966; Michael T. Ghiselin, *The Triumph of the Darwinian Method*, 1969; Phyllis Greenacre, *The Quest for the Father*, 1963; Arthur S. Gregor, *Charles Darwin*, 1967; Howard E. Gruber and Paul H. Barrett, *Darwin on Man*, 1974; Leo J. Henkin, *Darwinism in the English Novel, 1860–1910*, 1963; Gertrude Himmelfarb, *Darwin and the Darwinian Revolution*, 1959; Charles F. Holder, *Charles Darwin*, 1892; David L. Hull, *Darwin and His Critics*, 1973; Julian Huxley and H. P. D. Kettlewell, *Charles Darwin and His World*, 1965; Stanley Edgar Hyman, *The Tangled Bank: Darwin, Marx, Frazer and Freud*, 1962; William Irvine, *Apes, Angels and Victorians*, 1955; Sir Arthur Keith, *Darwin Revalued*, 1955; Edward Manier, *The Young Darwin and His Cultural Circle*, 1978; A. J. Marshall, *Darwin and Huxley in Australia*, 1970; William E. Ritter, *Charles Darwin and the Golden Rule*, 1954; Peter J. Vorzimmer, *Charles Darwin, The Years of Controversy*, 1972; Henshaw Ward, *Charles Darwin, The Man and His Warfare*, 1927; Geoffrey West, *Charles Darwin*, 1937.

ARTICLES ON CHARLES DARWIN

Prof. S. Adler, "Darwin's Illness," *Nature*, Vol. 184, October 10, 1959; Prof. J. H. Ashworth, "Charles Darwin as a Student in Edinburgh," *Proceedings of the Royal Society of Edinburgh*, Vol. IV, 1934–35, Part II; Sir Hedley Atkins, "The Darwin Tradition," *Annals of the Royal College of Surgeons of England*, Vol. 36, January 1965; Sir Hedley Atkins, "The Attributes of Genius from Newton to Darwin," *Annals of the Royal College of Surgeons of England*, Vol. 48, April 1971; Nora Barlow, "Robert FitzRoy and Charles Darwin," *Cornhill Magazine*, Vol. 72, April 1932; Nora Barlow, ed., "A Transcription of Darwin's First Notebook on 'Transmutation of Species,'" *Bulletin of the Museum of Comparative Zoology at Harvard College*, Vol. 122, No. 6, April 1960; Paul H. Barrett, "Darwin's 'Gigantic Blunder,'" *Journal of Geological Education*, January 1973; Paul H. Barrett, "The Sedgwick-Darwin Geologic Tour of North Wales," *Proceedings of the American Philosophical Society*, Vol. 118, No. 2, April 1974; George Basalla, "The Voyage of the *Beagle* without Darwin," *Mariner's Mirror*, XLIX, 1963; Tom Bethell, "Darwin's Mistake," *Harper's Magazine*, February 1976; Harold L. Burstyn, "If Darwin Wasn't the *Beagle's* Naturalist, Why Was He on Board?" *British Journal for the History of Science*, Vol. 8, No. 28, 1975; "Charles Robert Darwin," *Christ's College Magazine*, 1909; Ralph Colp,

Jr., M.D., "Charles Darwin and the Galapagos," *New York State Journal of Medicine*, Vol. 77, No. 2, February 1977; Sir Gavin de Beer, ed., "Darwin's Journal," *Bulletin of the British Museum (Natural History) Historical Series*, Vol. 2, No. 1, 1959; Sir Gavin de Beer, ed., "Darwin's Notebooks on Transmutation of Species. Part I, First Notebook (July 1837–February 1838)," *Bulletin of the British Museum (Natural History) Historical Series*, Vol. 2, No. 2, 1960; Sir Gavin de Beer, ed., "Darwin's Notebooks on Transmutation of Species. Part II, Second Notebook (February to July 1838)," *Bulletin of the British Museum (Natural History) Historical Series*, Vol. 2, No. 3, 1960; Sir Gavin de Beer, ed., "Darwin's Notebooks on Transmutation of Species. Part III, Third Notebook (July 15th 1838–October 2nd 1838)," *Bulletin of the British Museum (Natural History) Historical Series*, Vol. 2, No. 4, 1960; Sir Gavin de Beer, ed., "Darwin's Notebooks on Transmutation of Species. Part IV, Fourth Notebook (October 1838–10 July 1839)," *Bulletin of the British Museum (Natural History) Historical Series*, Vol. 2, No. 5, 1960; Sir Gavin de Beer and M. J. Rowlands, eds., "Darwin's Notebooks on Transmutation of Species. Addenda and Corrigenda," *Bulletin of the British Museum (Natural History) Historical Series*, Vol. 2, No. 6, 1961; Sir Gavin de Beer, ed., "The Darwin Letters at Shrewsbury School," *Notes and Records of the Royal Society of London*, 1968; F. D. Fletcher, "Darwin," 1975; R. B. Freeman and P. J. Gautrey, "Darwin's Questions about the Breeding of Animals, with a Note on Queries about Expression," *Journal of the Society for the Bibliography of Natural History*, 1969; R. B. Freeman and P. J. Gautrey, "Charles Darwin's Queries about Expression," *Journal of the Society for the Bibliography of Natural History*, 1975; Sir Archibald Geikie, "Charles Darwin as Geologist," The Rede Lecture, 1909; Howard E. Gruber and Valmai Gruber, "The Eye of Reason: Darwin's Development during the *Beagle* Voyage," *Isis*, Vol. 53, Part 2, No. 172, 1962; Jacob W. Gruber, "Who Was the *Beagle*'s Naturalist?" *British Journal for the History of Science*, Vol. 4, No. 15, 1969; Sandra Herbert, "Darwin, Malthus, and Selection," *Journal of the History of Biology*, Vol. 4, No. 1, Spring 1971; Douglas Hubble, "Charles Darwin and Psychotherapy," *Lancet*, January 30, 1943; Douglas Hubble, "The Life of the Shawl," *Lancet*, December 26, 1953; Henry Festing Jones, "Charles Darwin and Samuel Butler," 1911; Bruce Mazlish, "Darwin and the Benchuca," *Horizon*, Vol. XVII, No. 3, 1975; Prof. L. C. Miall, "The Life and Work of Charles Darwin," Lecture delivered to the Leeds Philosophical and Literary Society, 1883; C. F. A. Pantin, "Darwin's Theory and the Causes of Its Acceptance," *School Science Review*, No. 116 (October 1950), No. 117 (March 1951), No. 118 (June 1951); E. A. Parkyn, "Darwin, His Work and Influence," Lecture delivered in the Hall of Christ's College, Cambridge, 1894; A. C. Seward, ed., "Catalogue of the Darwin Library," 1908; Arthur F. Shipley, "Charles Darwin," privately printed, 1909; Sydney Smith, "The Origin of the 'Origin,'" *Impulse*, November 1959; Robert M. Stecher, "The Darwin-Innes Letters," *Annals of Science*, Vol. 17, No. 4, December 1961; Phillip V. Tobias, "Darwin, 'Descent' and Disease," *Transactions of the Royal Society of South Africa*, Vol. 40, Part 4, December 1972; University of Cambridge,

"Handlist of Darwin Papers at the University of Cambridge," 1960; Alan Villiers, "In the Wake of Darwin's *Beagle*," *National Geographic*, October 1969; Peter J. Vorzimmer, "An Early Darwin Manuscript: The 'Outline and Draft of 1839,' " *Journal of the History of Biology*, Vol. 8, No. 2, Fall 1975; John H. Winslow, "Darwin's Victorian Malady," *Memoirs of the American Philosophical Society*, Vol. 88, 1971; Edward Woodall, "Charles Darwin," *Transactions of the Shropshire Archaeological and Natural History Society*, 1884; A. W. Woodruff, "Darwin's Health in Relation to His Voyage to South America," *British Medical Journal*, March 20, 1965.

WRITINGS BY AND ABOUT CHARLES DARWIN'S CONTEMPORARIES

GENERAL. Sir Archibald Geikie, *The Founders of Geology*, 1905; Bentley Glass, Owsei Temkin, William L. Straus, Jr., eds., *Forerunners of Darwin*, 1959; R. C. Olby, *Early Nineteenth Century European Scientists*, 1967; Henry Fairfield Osborn, *Impressions of Great Naturalists*, 1924; Donald C. Peattie, *Green Laurels*, 1936; Robert A. Rosenbaum, *Earnest Victorians*, 1961; Robert E. Schofield, *The Lunar Society of Birmingham*, 1963.

FRANCIS BEAUFORT. Alfred Friendly, *Beaufort of the Admiralty*, 1977.

LEONARD BLOMEFIELD (JENYNS). Rev. Leonard Jenyns, *Memoir of the Rev. John Stevens Henslow*, 1862; Rev. Leonard Blomefield (Jenyns), *Chapters in My Life*, 1889.

THOMAS CARLYLE. Louis François Cazamian, *Thomas Carlyle*, 1932; John Stewart Collis, *The Carlyles*, 1971.

ROBERT CHAMBERS. Robert Chambers, *Vestiges of the Natural History of Creation*, 1844.

SYMS COVINGTON. J. Ferguson, ed., *Syms Covington of Pambula*, 1971.

DARWIN AND WEDGWOOD FAMILIES. Sir Hedley Atkins, *Down House. The Home of the Darwins*, 1974; Bernard Darwin, *The World That Fred Made*, 1955; Dr. Erasmus Darwin, *Zoonomia*, 2 vols., 1794–96; L. Jewitt, *The Wedgwoods*, 1865; Desmond King-Hele, *Erasmus Darwin*, 1963; Desmond King-Hele, ed., *The Essential Writings of Erasmus Darwin*, 1968; Desmond King-Hele, *Doctor of Revolution: The Life and Genius of Erasmus Darwin*, 1977; Ernst Krause, *Erasmus Darwin*, translated by W. S. Dallas, with a preliminary notice by Charles Darwin, 1879; Henrietta Litchfield, ed., *Emma Darwin: A Century of Family Letters*, 2 vols., 1904; Carol Macht, *Classical Wedgwood Designs*, 1957; Eliza Meteyard, *A Group of Englishmen*, 1871; Eliza Meteyard, *Life of Josiah Wedgwood*, 1865–1866; Gwen Raverat, *Period Piece*, 1952; Anna Seward, *Life of Dr. Erasmus Darwin*, 1804.

AUGUSTUS EARLE. Augustus Earle, *A Narrative of a Nine Months' Residence in New Zealand in 1827: Together with a Journal of a Residence in Tristan da Cunha*, 1832.

ROBERT FITZROY. H. E. L. Mellersh, *FitzRoy of the Beagle*, 1968.

ASA GRAY. Asa Gray, *Darwiniana*, 1876; A. Hunter Dupree, *Asa Gray*, 1959.

JAMES GULLY. James M. Gully, *The Water Cure in Chronic Disease*, 1846.

JOHN HENSLOW. Rev. Leonard Jenyns, *Memoir of the Rev. John Stevens Henslow*, 1862; Nora Barlow, ed., *Darwin and Henslow, The Growth of an Idea*, 1967.

JOHN HERSCHEL. John Herschel, *Preliminary Discourse on the Study of Natural Philosophy*, 1830.

HENRY HOLLAND. Sir Henry Holland, *Medical Notes and Reflections*, 1855; Sir Henry Holland, *Recollections of Past Life*, 1872.

JOSEPH DALTON HOOKER. Mea Allen, *The Hookers of Kew*, 1967; Joseph Dalton Hooker, *A Sketch of the Life and Labours of Sir William Jackson Hooker, K.H.*, 1903; Leonard Huxley, *Life and Letters of Sir Joseph Dalton Hooker*, 2 vols., 1918; W. B. Turrill, *Joseph Dalton Hooker*, 1963.

ALEXANDER VON HUMBOLDT. Douglas Botting, *Humboldt*, 1973; Alexander von Humboldt, *Personal Narrative of Travels to the Equinoctial Regions of the New Continent during the Years 1799 to 1804*, translated by Helen M. Williams, 7 vols., 1818.

THOMAS HENRY HUXLEY. Cyril Bibby, *T. H. Huxley: Scientist, Humanist and Educator*, 1959; Cyril Bibby, *Scientist Extraordinary*, 1972; Leonard Huxley, *Life and Letters of Thomas Henry Huxley*, 2 vols., 1900; Thomas H. Huxley, *Critiques and Addresses*, 1890; Thomas H. Huxley, *Man's Place in Nature and other Anthropological Essays*, 1915; Thomas H. Huxley, *Collected Essays*, Vol. II, 1915.

CHARLES LYELL. Sir Edward Bailey, *Charles Lyell*, 1963; Mrs. Lyell, ed., *Life, Letters and Journals of Sir Charles Lyell*, 2 vols., 1881; Charles Lyell, *Principles of Geology*, 3 vols., 1830–1833; Charles Lyell, *Geological Evidences of the Antiquity of Man*, 1863; Leonard G. Wilson, *Charles Lyell. The Years to 1841*, 1972.

THOMAS MALTHUS. Thomas Malthus, *An Essay on the Principle of Population*, 7th ed., 1872.

CONRAD MARTENS. Lionel Lindsay, *Conrad Martens. The Man and His Art*, 1920.

HARRIET MARTINEAU. R. K. Webb, *Harriet Martineau*, 1960.

ROBERT MCCORMICK. Robert McCormick, *Voyages of Discovery in Arctic and Antarctic Seas*, 2 vols., 1884.

ST. GEORGE MIVART. St. George Mivart, *On the Genesis of Species*, 1871.

JOHN MURRAY. George Patson (pseud. for E. M. Symonds), *At John Murray's*, 1932.

RICHARD OWEN. Rev. Richard Owen, *The Life of Richard Owen*, 2 vols., 1894.

GEORGE JOHN ROMANES. George John Romanes, *Mental Evolution in Animals*, 1884.

ADAM SEDGWICK. John Willis Clark and Thomas McKenny Hughes, *The Life and Letters of the Reverend Adam Sedgwick*, 2 vols., 1890.

SYDNEY SMITH. Gerald Bullett, *Sydney Smith*, 1951.

JAMES SULIVAN. Henry Norton Sulivan, ed., *Life and Letters of the Late Admiral Sir Bartholomew James Sulivan*, 1896.

ALFRED RUSSEL WALLACE. Arnold C. Brackman, *A Delicate Arrangement, The Strange Case of Charles Darwin and Alfred Wallace*, 1980; James Marchant, *Alfred Russel Wallace: Letters and Reminiscences*, 2 vols., 1916; H. Lewis McKinney, *Wallace and Natural Selection*, 1972; Alfred Russel Wallace, *Darwinism: An Exposition of the Theory of Natural Selection*, 1891; Alfred Russel Wallace, *Natural Selection and Tropical Nature*, 1891; Alfred Russel Wallace, *My Life*, 2 vols., 1905; Amabel Williams-Ellis, *Darwin's Moon*, 1966.


GENERAL REFERENCES

Paul H. Barrett, ed., *The Collected Papers of Charles Darwin*, 2 vols., 1977; P. Thomas Carroll, ed., *An Annotated Calendar of the Letters of Charles Darwin in the Library of the American Philosophical Society*, 1976; Francis Darwin, ed., *The Foundations of the Origin of Species*, 1909; Robley Dunglison, *A Dictionary of Medical Science*, 1874; R. B. Freeman, *The Works of Charles Darwin: An Annotated Bibliographical Handlist*, 1965; A. T. Gage, *A History of the Linnean Society of London*, 1938; Charles Coulston Gillispie, *Genesis and Geology*, 1951; William T. Keeton, *Elements of Biological Science*, 1967; David M. Knight, *Natural Science Books in English*, 1972; Thomas S. Kuhn, *The Structure of Scientific Revolutions*, 1962; Sidney Lee, ed., *The Dictionary of National Biography*, 1937; John Marshall, ed., *Royal Naval Biography*, 1832; John Milton (Christopher Ricks, ed.), *Paradise Lost and Paradise Regained*, 1968; Everett C. Olson and Jane Robinson, *Concepts of Evolution*, 1975; Commander Crawford Pasco, *A Roving Commission. Naval Reminiscences*, 1879; Morse Peckham, ed., *The Origin of Species by Charles Darwin: A Variorum Text*, 1959; George Sarton, *A History of Science*, 2 vols., 1952; R. C. Stauffer, ed., *Charles Darwin's Natural Selection*, 1975; Tracy I. Storer, Robert L. Usinger, James W. Nybakken, *Elements of Zoology*, 1968; Horace G. Woodward, *The History of the Geological Society of London*, 1908; *The Shorter Prayer Book*; *The Book of Common Prayer*.

THE VOYAGE OF THE *Beagle*

Nora Barlow, ed., *Charles Darwin's Diary of the Voyage of H.M.S. Beagle*, 1933; Nora Barlow, ed., *Charles Darwin and the Voyage of the Beagle*, 1946; Henry Baynham, *From the Lower Deck*, 1969; Richard H. Dana, *Seaman's Manual*, 1844; William Falconer, *Marine Dictionary*, 1780; Captain Robert FitzRoy and P. Parker King, *Voyages of the Adventure and Beagle*, 2 vols., 1839; Prof. Richard Keynes, *The Beagle Record*, 1979; Michael Lewis, *The Navy in Transition*, 1965; Christopher Lloyd, *The British Seaman*, 1968; Paul Andrew Love, *Seaman's Eyes*, 1968; Alan Moorehead, *Darwin and the Beagle*, 1969; Charles Robinson, *British Tar in Fact and Fiction*, 1909; Sierra Club, ed., *Galapagos, The Flow of Wildness*, 2 vols.; David Stanbury, ed., *A Narrative of the Voyage of H.M.S. Beagle*, 1977; Ian Thornton, *Darwin's Islands*, 1971; Alan White and Bruce Epler, photographed by Charles Gilbert, *Galapagos Guide*, 1972.


LIFE IN NINETEENTH-CENTURY ENGLAND

David Elliston Allen, *The Naturalist in Britain*, 1976; Richard D. Altick, *Victorian People and Ideas*, 1973; Mrs. *Beeton's Cookery Book*; Nancy Bradfield, *Historical Costumes of England*, 1958; Michael Brander, *The Victorian Gentleman*, 1975; Anne Buck, *Victorian Costume and Costume Accessories*, 1961; William Cullen, *First Lines of the Practice of Physic*, 1816; Phillis Cunnington and Catherine Lucas, *Occupational Costume in England*, 1967; John Eberle, *A Treatise on the Practice of Medicine*, 1830; Elison Hawks, *Romance of Travel*, 1931; Louis James, ed., *English Popular Literature, 1819–1851*, 1976; Sydney R. Jones, *English Village Homes*, 1937; James Joyce, *The Story of Passenger Transport*, 1967; James Laver, *Victorian Vista*, 1954; Arthur Loesser, *Men, Women and Pianos*, 1954; A. M. Low, *England's Past Presented*, 1953; Stanley C. Ramsey, *Small Houses of the Late Georgian Period*, 1919; Lionel Stevenson, *The English Novel*, 1960; Sir Henry Thompson, *Food and Feeding*, 1884; F. Alan Walbank, ed., *England: Yesterday and Today*, 1949; Horatio C. Wood and Reginald H. Fitz, *Practice of Medicine*, 1897; W. V. Wood, *The Railway Industry of Great Britain*, 1929; Doreen Yarwood, *The English Home*, 1956.


LONDON

K. Baedeker, *London and Its Environs*, 1879; Felix Barker and Peter Jackson, *London, 2000 Years of a City and Its People*, 1974; Sir Walter Besant, *London in the Nineteenth Century*, 1909; James Elmes, *Elmes' Topographical Dictionary of London*, 1831; L. Gomme, *London, 1837–1897*, 1898; Francis Sheppard, *London 1808–1870: The Infernal Wen*, 1971.

CAMBRIDGE

B. W. Downs, *Cambridge. Past and Present*, 1926; Arthur Gray, *Cambridge University, an Episodical History*, 1912; Arthur Gray, *The Town of Cambridge*, 1925; Bryan Little, *Portrait of Cambridge*, 1955; Bryan Little, *The Colleges of Cambridge*, 1973; M. D. Lobel, maps compiled by W. H. Johns, *Historic Towns: Cambridge*, 1974; J. E. Marr and A. E. Shipley, eds., *Handbook to the Natural History of Cambridgeshire*, 1904; Enid Porter, *Cambridgeshire Customs and Folklore*, 1969; Sir Arthur E. Shipley, *Cambridge Cameos*, 1925; C. P. Snow, *The Master*, 1951; Louis T. Stanley, *Life in Cambridge*, 1953; D. A. Winstanley, *Early Victorian Cambridge*, 1955; *Mems and Gems of Old Cambridge Lore*, 1902(?).


ENGLAND MISCELLANEOUS

C. W. Bracken, *A History of Plymouth*, 1970; George Alexander Cooke, *Cooke's Topographical Guide to Great Britain*, 182–?; Rev. J. Nightingale, *Beauties of England and North Wales*, 1801–1816; *A Guide Through the Town of Shrewsbury*, 1845.


GENERAL HISTORY

Emily Allyn, *Lords Versus Commons*, 1931; Arthur Lyon Cross, *A Shorter History of England and Great Britain*, 1920; Elie Halevy, *A History of the English People: 1830–1841*, 1949; Elie Halevy, *A History of the English People: The Age of Peel and Cobden*, 1949; Elie Halevy, *A History of the English People in the 19th Century*, 1951; Edwin Hodder, *Life of a Century*, 1901.


MISCELLANEOUS ARTICLES, PAMPHLETS AND MONOGRAPHS

F. J. Bingley and S. M. Walters, "Wicken Sedge Fen," 1966; P. M. S. Blackett, D. C. Martin, Sir John Summerson, Lord Holford, "The Royal Society at Carlton House Terrace," 1967; J. H. Bullock, "Bridge Street, Cambridge"; "Milton and His College," *Christ's College Magazine*; Lois Darling, "The 'Beagle'–a Search for a Lost Ship," *Natural History*, Vol. 69, 1960; Lois Darling, "H.M.S. *Beagle*: Further Research or Twenty Years a-Beagling," *Log of the Mystic Seaport*, Vol. 29, No. 1, April 1977; Warren R. Dawson, ed., "The Huxley Papers," 1946; H. P. Douglas, "FitzRoy's Hydrographic Surveys," *Nature*, February 6, 1932; John C. Hartnett, "The Care and Use of Medicinal Leeches in 19th Century Pharmacy and Therapeutics," *Pharmacy in History*, Vol. 14, No. 4, 1972; Rev. J. S. Henslow, "Address to the Members of the University of Cambridge on the Expediency of Improving and on the Funds Required for Remodelling and Supporting, the Botanic Garden," 1846; William Irvine, "Thomas Henry